VALERIOS

ROAD TO MASTERY 3

aethonbooks.com

ROAD TO MASTERY 3

Aethon Books
www.aethonbooks.com

Print and eBook design and formatting by Josh Hayes. Artwork provided by Kaion Luong.

Published by Aethon Books LLC.

ALSO IN SERIES

Road to Mastery

Road to Mastery 2

Road to Mastery 3

Road to Mastery 4

Check out the entire series here! (Tap and scan)

CHAPTER ONE
NEW CONSTELLATION, NEW ME

A STARSHIP FLEW THROUGH SPACE. STARS FLICKERED RESTLESSLY ON ALL SIDES, yet the silence was deafening and the wind non-existent, giving the impression that the ship was standing still. In reality, it was moving at multiple miles per second.

A green planet was slowly growing in the distance.

"That's the way, Brock," Jack said, reclining in his seat. His dark hair tumbled over his shoulders, contrasting the perfectly white chair, while his eyes seemed to contain a universe of their own. If a pre-System person looked into them right now, they would probably shit their pants and bow in worship. "Keep her steady. We're in perfect trajectory for... what was the planet's name again?"

Brock shrugged. "No idea."

"*Noidea* it is. Great name."

The first time they'd flown a starship, it had taken both of them to be even barely functional. However, that time had been under pressure, and with "race mode" accidentally activated.

The starship they were currently flying was much more convenient. It had four rooms—a cabin, a bathroom, a helm room, and an exit room—as well as controls that didn't jitter like a ticklish baby. It was certainly an upgrade.

As a result, both Jack and Brock could easily drive it. They took turns.

They had also named the starship, *Bromobile.*

"We're almost there!" Jack shouted excitedly, the planet growing so large it dominated their view. He could clearly make out the continents and seas, as well as a large mountain ridge. The sight was nostalgic enough to almost bring tears to his eyes. It reminded him of Earth. Of home. It had only been three months since he left, but with everything that happened, it left like an eternity.

He had grown so much since then. In three short months, he had risen through the entire E-Grade and broken through to become an immortal. He had also inherited the Life Drop—a drop of blood from Enas, the Old God of Life who was trapped in a black hole—and achieved a King Class called Cosmic Fist—which he looked forward to exploring.

Jack still struggled to comprehend how strong he'd become. He was an immortal now, with a lifespan of a thousand years. He possessed the power to level mountains. And he was, what, twenty-eight?

Time was weird like that. The four months since the Integration had felt like a century. For some reason, even the two hours it had been since he teleported out of Trial Planet, killed the three Hounds, and declared war on the Animal Kingdom—though they didn't know that yet—felt like months.

Unfortunately, even though those Hounds were fifty levels above him, they had only given him enough experience to level-up six times, reaching Level 131. Leveling would become harder from now on.

I really should complete my PhD at some point, he thought, absent-mindedly watching the planet approach through the starship's windshield.

"*Bromobile* down," Brock said. He pulled on a lever to reduce their speed, then tilted the steering wheel upward to make them glide in parallel with the planet's surface instead of hurtling straight at it. They descended through the atmosphere smoothly, unfettered by gravity. Clouds filled their vision. When they cleared, an entire world stretched beneath their feet, with valleys and mountains and forests.

"Wait," Jack said. "This place isn't empty, is it?" After all, they needed to find a teleporter and head towards the Exploding Sun.

Fortunately, it only took him a moment to discover a large dirt road wrapping around a mountain in the distance. Since they were still in the Animal Kingdom constellation, which was part of the System-Integrated space, civilization meant cultivators—and, most importantly, teleporters.

Brock brought the starship to a halt and approached the windshield. A moment later, he pointed down. Jack followed with his gaze, noticing a man riding a horse through a field below.

"Let's go ask him," he said.

Brock grabbed the controls again. They descended like a comet next to the horse rider, who froze in terror and went pale as a sheet. He was a thin man with a long black mustache, whose hard face looked out of place twisted in such terror. He was also surprisingly young—maybe twenty years of age?

"Angh," he tried to say.

"Hello. Do you not speak our language?" Jack asked, having used Space Walk to teleport outside the starship.

Human (Galipede), Level 32 (F-Grade)
Faction: -

The man jumped back in fright. His horse frothed at the mouth and started bucking, throwing the rider, and running away.

Jack was having none of that. He flew after the horse, grabbed it from the back, and lifted it over his head so that its legs kicked harmlessly at the air. He then deposited the horse gently before its rider, leaving both shell-shocked. If they could, they would have probably hugged each other.

"Sorry," Jack said. "We didn't mean to scare you. We're just looking for directions."

The man managed to utter a few words, "Directions to what?"

"The nearest teleporter that can take us off-planet."

"I, uh... It's that way, venerable immortal," the man said, pointing to the far-off mountain. He had regained his composure somewhat. "A city in the middle of a lake. It's called Califrede. You can't miss it."

"I see. Thank you. Is there any way I can repay the favor?"

The man's eyes went wide. Once again, he mustered his courage to say, "I, uh, I was heading in the same direction, venerable immortal. I need medicine for my daughter. If you could carry me along, even in the trash compartment of your starship, I would be beyond grateful. Extremely grateful."

"No problem. Can you open the door, Brock?"

A door at the side of the starship slid open. There was no ramp, so Jack simply carried both horse and man inside, fitting them in the helm room—which was suddenly a bit cramped.

Needless to say, the man was simultaneously scared, relieved, and unable to believe his good luck. The horse was frozen in fear.

"Brock," Jack said, "can you inform this horse that good bros don't defecate in each other's starships? It looks scared, so you never know."

Brock nodded and mimed the instruction. To everyone's surprise—including itself—the horse nodded.

"No need to be scared, man," Jack said, smiling at the pale horse rider. "I may be an immortal, but I'm a pretty friendly guy. I won't harm you. What's your name?"

"Lionel, venerable immortal."

"Well, Lionel, enjoy your flight. Can you point us in the direction of this lake city within the mountain range you mentioned?"

The horse rider—Lionel—numbly pointed in a direction. Brock grabbed the helm and smoothly led the starship over the grassland then the mountain. With their speed, it only took ten minutes to reach the city—a horse rider could have easily taken half a week.

"Looks like you hit the jackpot, Lionel," Jack said. "Completely pun intended."

Lionel nodded numbly. "You have my eternal gratitude, venerable immortal. I can never repay the help you have given me."

"It's no big deal. No need to get all formal."

"Thanks to you, my daughter may survive," Lionel continued, tears glistening in his eyes. "I was going to ride day and night to arrive in time. Thank you. Thank you!"

"Oh... Well, glad we could help."

The lake city was, indeed, a city built on a lake. Jack couldn't tell if there was an island under it or not, but he could see random spots of water everywhere, so he suspected not.

It was an architectural wonder. Floating platforms and small boats made up most of the city, which was inhabited by human and amphibian-looking humanoids alike. They seemed to be getting along just fine.

It also smelled a bit, but Jack had been through worse. When undergraduates fucked up in his laboratory, the stench was often putrid enough to burn his nose.

"Do you have enough money to buy that medicine, Lionel?" Jack asked.

"I do, venerable immortal. You have already provided me with enough fortune to last me ten lifetimes!"

This Lionel fellow had a particular way with words, but he seemed like a good man overall—even likable. Jack and Brock deposited him at a pharmacy—or apothecary shop, as the sign indicated—and Jack joined along to buy some stuff of his own. They then insisted on giving Lionel a lift back home, so he could treat his ailing daughter. They could spare a half-hour round trip to save this guy days of ceaseless riding.

Lionel accepted with superfluous words of gratitude. His horse wasn't relieved by any means, mostly due to not understanding, but it should have been, because Lionel's plan of ceaseless riding included the horse dying of exhaustion mid-way.

To punish him for that, they dropped him off a few minutes away from his village. Though it was more of a prank. Unless the horse learned how to speak, nobody would ever believe him.

"Thank you for choosing the Jack and Brock Airline," Jack said as they dropped Lionel off. "Enjoy your stay!"

After once again accepting Lionel's superfluous and oddly-worded gratitude, they flew back to the lake city and landed near a furnace-shaped building that served as the teleporter. Jack willed the starship to shrink to the size of a needle—a very handy function—then stored it in his pocket.

He took another look at the surrounding people. They were dressed in thigh-long, airy robes, kept their hair long, and walked around on wooden shoes. The amphibian humanoids didn't have hair, but fins that stuck out from the top of their head, as well as gills on both sides of their throat, and webbing between their fingers. Besides those, they resembled humans.

"Huh," Jack said, scanning a random amphibian person, "would you look at that."

Fishfolk (Galipede), Level 14 (F-Grade)
Faction: -

His biologist instincts insisted he stay for a while and study them. Unfortunately, he had a job to do—and little time to admire the galaxy's wonders. The Exploding Sun awaited.

There was a long line before the teleporter. Just as Jack braced himself for a wait, someone scanned him and exclaimed. The surprise spread like a wave, with everyone moving aside and bowing. Murmurs of "venerable immortal" spread through the crowd, making Jack feel slightly awkward.

"It's all right," he said, lifting his hands. "At ease."

They were not at ease. Apparently, the immortals of this planet enjoyed extremely high status. Jack thought back to the stories of Vlossana, the passenger of the *Trampling Ram*—her continent only had a single D-Grade cultivator. If this planet was similar, it was no wonder people reacted like that.

He felt like a celebrity.

Therefore, Jack and Brock skipped the line and arrived before the door of the teleporter building. They escaped the outside noise and found themselves in front of a peak E-Grade guard who was busy scribbling something down on a piece of paper.

"Wait outside the door," the guard barked, not raising her gaze from the paper.

"Are you sure?" Jack replied.

The guard looked up. A moment later, her face went pale. "Venerable immortal! My deepest apologies! If I knew who you were, I would never—"

"Yeah, yeah," Jack cut her off. "Apology accepted. Can you help me teleport to the Exploding Sun constellation?"

"I—Certainly, venerable immortal," the guard replied, straightening her back in a military salute. "Do you have a specific destination in mind?"

"I am headed to the Exploding Sun headquarters, so the closer to it, the better."

"Of course, sir. May I recommend Earth-309?"

"Sure."

"Also, pardon me for daring to ask, but could I have your name and affiliation, please? It is for record-keeping."

"You cannot."

The guard froze. "I cannot?"

"You cannot."

After all, Jack was currently wanted by the Animal Kingdom. When news of him escaping Trial Planet reached the Hand of God, they would probably join the hunt, too. He had to travel incognito as much as possible.

The Bare Fist Brotherhood was usually visible when people scanned him, giving away his identity, but Jack had thought ahead. When they stopped by the apothecary shop earlier, he'd bought a Disguise Potion—the same kind he'd used at the start of the Integration Tournament. When he drank it on the starship, it changed his facial structure and hid his faction from System scans. As for titles, he'd already removed them all from showing. Only his Level remained unchanged, but that didn't matter much.

Jack currently looked like a chubby, middle-aged man with a short but fluffy mustache.

Now, only two hints gave away his identity. One was Brock, but there was nothing he could do about that. He could only hope there were more brorillas in the galaxy. As for his species, which was registered as Human (Earth-387)... Well, nothing he could do about that, either.

The guard remained troubled. "Venerable immortal, that's..."

"I understand this is a problem for you," Jack said, "but if you keep insisting, you'll have a bigger one. Just let me teleport."

The guard hesitated. Jack considered using his Dao Domain to intimidate her, but that might give away his Dao, so he stared into her eyes instead. A moment later, she relented.

"Please step onto the teleporter," she said weakly. "I wish you safe travels."

Jack smiled brightly. "Thank you. Have a great rest of your day."

Being extremely powerful sure was nice.

Jack and Brock stepped onto the teleporter. A blue screen with several destinations appeared before their eyes. Jack chose Earth-309, as the guard had suggested, and felt a burst of speed as the space around him was drawn backward.

The Exploding Sun was still far away... but they'd finally left the Animal Kingdom constellation! And, this time, they were traveling completely on their own power!

CHAPTER TWO
DERION, THE POISON PLANET

Not every teleporter was as easy to access as the first one.

In Jack and Brock's journey to the Exploding Sun, they passed through many planets. Some resembled Earth. Some had inhospitable environments and transparent domes protecting the cities. Humans were even more prevalent in this constellation than in the Animal Kingdom's, being by far the most common species, but there was more than just them.

Jack saw animal people, plant people, rock people. Apparently, anything sentient—and sometimes, not even that—could develop intelligence and evolve into their planet's dominant species. Everything he thought he knew about biology was torn asunder, and new, more expansive knowledge took its place.

Throughout their journey, they were introduced to many things.

Golems made of the elements. People of glass. A race of sapient moles with entire cities underground, steeped in darkness, with only the torchlight of visitors flickering through the city like uneasy fireflies.

It was an eye-opening experience.

Of course, most places only gave Jack a glimpse, since he was in a hurry to reach the Exploding Sun. At every teleporter, people parted to let him pass. By now, Jack had no idea where he was, nor how far away from Earth. He only knew that he was lost in the endless wonders of space, a sea so colorful and enormous that even a thousand lifetimes wouldn't be enough to explore it fully.

But it didn't matter. They were a man and a brorilla touring the stars. It was amazing.

As one planet led to another, however, and Jack and Brock approached the Exploding Sun headquarters, the ambience changed. The medieval civilizations that filled the constellation's fringes gave way to high-tech wonders similar to what they'd seen in Pearl Bay, where they'd boarded the *Trampling Ram*. Bustling metropolises replaced the countryside cities, filled with skyscrapers and starship docks.

Not all planets were like that, of course. Most were at rather low levels of technology, but the closer one came to the center of the constellation, the more advanced civilizations became.

This advancement included cultivation. Out on the fringes, there were only a handful of D-Grades per planet. Deeper in, every metropolis was ruled by one, and there were even C-Grades helming entire planets. The teleporter guards remained at the peak of the E-Grade, but Jack got more respectful. He no longer dared to just throw his weight around and demand to pass without a proper inspection.

Therefore, he forged a new identity for himself. He was now Lionel Horseman, a human cultivator of Earth-387, as he couldn't change how the System displayed his species. This was the best he could do. By now, he didn't need to be too careful, either. The Animal Kingdom and Exploding Sun were adversaries, if not enemies, so the bounties of one faction probably wouldn't reach this deep into the other.

On the eleventh planet, Jack and Brock emerged into a bustling hub similar to the one on Belarian Outpost, from where they'd teleported to Trial Planet. They were surrounded by a hexagon of teleporters, with three of them on each side for a total of eighteen. Long lines stretched before every teleporter, filled with people of all species and levels. There was more than one immortal waiting in line.

The moment they exited the teleporter, they were ushered away by a peak E-Grade guard, making room for the next batch of people to appear. A steady stream of cultivators carried Jack and Brock to the exit and then outside the hub, where they saw—

A desert?

Well, not really. It was just endless brown, barren wilderness, covered in dusty rock and with barely any visible plants. There were no animals, either.

"What is this place?" Jack wondered. "Where is the city? The metropolises? The people?"

The place they were in resembled more a town of the Wild West than an interplanetary trade center. A few houses stood at the side of the main street, framing the wilderness. Outside the town, several square miles were occupied by camps, starships, and all sorts of mobile accommodation.

Moreover, gray clouds stretched everywhere overhead, and the sky visible through their gaps was a sickly green instead of blue.

"First time in Derion?" a man's voice came from behind Jack, who turned to see who would speak so informally to an immortal. Unsurprisingly, the other man was an immortal himself—heavily-built and filled with muscle, he was a humanoid made of wood. Flowers sprang from gaps in his bare skull, while his bark-like body was only covered by a pair of green shorts. Naturally, there was no hair on his face.

Treant, Level 197
Faction: Triple Helix (C-Grade)

"Yeah," Jack responded. "What is this place?"

"A handy teleportation point," the man replied, laughing. His voice was deep and gritty. "Derion is an inhospitable planet at a key location. The air is toxic—F-Grade cultivators get poisoned after a few days here, and E-Grades after around a month. Instead of trying to terraform it, the Exploding Sun turned it into a planet-sized storage and teleportation checkpoint. A good part of the constellation's traffic goes through here, relieving the nearby planets, and some of the teleporters have long enough range to reach other constellations."

"Huh. Smart," Jack said, stretching out a hand. "I'm Jack, and this is Brock."

"Torm," the treant replied, returning the handshake. His skin really was bark—rough and hard. "Where are you headed?"

"To the Exploding Sun headquarters."

"I see. Trying to get recruited?" Torm gave Jack a suspicious side glance.

"...Yeah? Why the long face?"

"Forgive me. It's really none of my business, just the rarity of seeing a disguised immortal."

Jack grimaced. The Disguise Potion only worked on mortals—anyone at the D-Grade or above could see right through it if they tried to inspect him.

"I have my reasons," he replied defensively, ready to walk away.

Torm laughed. "Relax. As long as you are not my enemy, I couldn't care less."

"I certainly hope so." Jack smiled. "So... Any idea how I get to the headquarters from here?"

"Simple. You go to the registration desk, declare your destination, and take a buzzer. Then, you can camp around and relax. When you are within a thousand people of getting teleported, your buzzer will buzz and glow, notifying you to come here and join the line."

Jack looked around. Several people were holding a glowing circular thing and rushing to the teleporter hub. Torm had a similar buzzer strapped to his belt, though it didn't shine—he had just received it.

"I see," Jack replied. "And how long does that take, usually?"

"Two, maybe three days. Depends on the traffic."

"Alright. Then, I better go take my ticket. Thanks, Torm."

"No problem," the treant replied, slightly disappointed. "If you're looking for drinking company, come find me anytime. I'll be staying at the tree-shaped tent."

"You got it."

Both men waved and headed in opposite directions.

Torm looked like a nice, friendly guy seeking company to pass the time. However, he was far too quick to trust a disguised immortal. Maybe he just believed in his judgment of character, but Jack was in no state to take unnecessary risks. That someone knew of his real identity—or at least his faction—was unnerving enough. He'd just take his buzzer and camp somewhere far away, only to return when it was time to leave.

Could there be more disguised people? he wondered.

As he entered the teleporter hub through another entrance—the one he'd exited from was strictly an exit—he tried scanning everyone around. Most people were at the E-Grade and decidedly not disguised—or, at least, he didn't see anything suspicious. The few immortals he chanced upon were also not disguised. Thankfully, none of them looked back.

Am I the only one? Jack wondered. If so, that could be dangerous.

He reached one of the registration desks, where the line was pleasantly short and fast-moving. For good reason, too—how long did it take people to declare a destination and receive a buzzer?

The Exploding Sun wasn't big on bureaucracy.

Manning the desk was a peak E-Grade human who didn't spare Jack a second glance. "Destination?"

"Exploding Sun headquarters."

Aren't they at all worried about disguised criminals? Jack wondered, receiving his buzzer—a plain dark blue disk. Maybe the real check happens before teleportation, like airport security. That would explain why it takes so long.

Looking around, he did spot D-Grade guards around each of the teleporters, staring at every person who passed.

Right. So, I should drop the disguise before leaving. Got it. I hope that won't be a problem...

He remained there for a moment, lost in thought. His mind went over all possibilities as his eyes idly scanned the crowd. Amidst all the inspection, he almost didn't notice the one screen that was out of place.

Feshkur, Level 134
Faction: Animal Kingdom (B-Grade)

Animal Kingdom? What is he doing here? They're supposed to be enemies with the Exploding Sun. Even if they aren't at war, it's weird for someone of the Animal Kingdom to just be walking around this deep in enemy territory, right?

Jack blended into the crowd, watching the feshkur. He had the gray skin, slim physique, and tall stature that characterized his species, along with a hard glare that bore holes through anyone in his way. Many E-Grades sensed it and rushed to give him space.

Typical Animal Kingdom behavior, Jack thought.

The feshkur approached the registration desk and waited. When his turn came, he declared, "Belarian Outpost. Large cargo." He received his ticket and went on his way, not passing remotely close to Jack.

Large cargo? Jack thought, the gears of his mind spinning. What could the Animal Kingdom be sending through the Exploding Sun constellation, guarded by an immortal?

It wasn't just curiosity. The Animal Kingdom were his enemies. Anything he could do to harm them, he would.

"I guess we won't be bored after all, Brock," Jack said, shadowing the feshkur from several dozen feet behind. In the dense crowd, he was unnoticeable.

Brock smiled predatorily. "Yeah."

The feshkur escaped the crowd and immediately took to the air. With a glance behind him, which didn't seem to locate Jack, he flew away at moderate speed, heading toward the distant mountains.

Brock climbed on Jack's back, who waited a few moments before flying, too. He headed in a different direction from the feshkur to avoid raising suspicions. A few moments later, when the feshkur was just a dot in the distance, he adjusted his path upward and dove into the clouds. He then turned sharply and accelerated in the feshkur's direction.

The clouds resembled Earth's in color, but there was something wrong about them. They smelled awful, almost putrid, like a carcass left to rot in the burning sun. As soon as Jack emerged above them, the sun's heat intensified so abruptly that he could sense Brock fidgeting.

This must be why the air is toxic, he realized, but tracking the feshkur was more important than analyzing the planet's environment. Thankfully, Brock was at the E-Grade—even if they flew through the clouds for an hour, he would be fine.

After flying ahead at full speed for a minute, Jack dove back into the clouds and peeked his head out from the bottom. He was over the mountains now, and the feshkur was nowhere to be seen.

Before he got disappointed, however, he spotted a fast-moving dot in the distance. The feshkur had turned slightly, too, but Jack had found him just in time.

He smiled. “Got you,” he muttered, then flew back above the clouds and sped forth. At the end of the day, both of them were low D-Grades, but Jack was far, far stronger than his level would indicate. He could easily run down a random immortal.

This went on for a while, with Jack regularly peeking from the clouds to make sure the feshkur was still in sight, but not daring to get too close. Twenty minutes later, the feshkur suddenly began to lose speed and altitude. He entered a canyon in the wasteland.

“We’re here,” Jack said. He waited half an hour, just in case the immortal was looking out for people tracking him, then flew directly above the canyon and looked down. “The hell?”

CHAPTER THREE
TESTING ONE'S POWER

Several people were walking or standing on the bare rock. There were feshkurs, animal people, humans... Jack inspected a few, finding them all to be part of the Animal Kingdom.

Of course, not everyone was an immortal. Everyone parted as the D-Grade feshkur that Jack had followed entered a large red tent. The only other immortal Jack saw was a clean-shaven human man at Level 136.

The most notable sight, however, was a large cage in the middle of the encampment. Jack couldn't see inside it, as he was looking from above and the cage had a metal roof, but he could barely make out a few shackled hands sticking out of the bars.

Prisoners? he wondered. Or... slaves?

The feshkur had mentioned they were carrying "large cargo." There were no crates or anything of the sort here, so he had to be referring to the cage.

However, slavery was forbidden by the Star Pact, the galactic law signed by every B-Grade faction. Even if the Animal Kingdom was engaging in such practices, which they really shouldn't, they couldn't be doing it so openly.

In other words, these weren't slaves. So, what were they?

"What do you think, Brock?" Jack asked. "Should we take a look?"

Brock—who was still on Jack's back—considered it, then nodded.

"You're right," Jack said. "The enemy of my enemy is my friend. Whoever these people are, we might share common interests... Oh. Unless they're criminals. That would be complicated."

Brock nodded again.

"Thanks for the confirmation, bro," Jack said.

"No problem."

"In any case, we have a few days here, according to that Torm. Sabotaging the Animal Kingdom is a fine way to pass our time, right?"

"Yes."

"Hmm. What if things go wrong? They have at least two low D-Grades. Think I could take them?"

"Yes."

Jack turned his head a bit to glance at Brock. "You sure believe in me, bro."

"You are strong."

Jack chuckled. "Guess I am. How does this sound? We discreetly collect information on these guys, then decide if it's worth risking our lives to go against them. We also observe them for a while to see if they have anyone stronger than a low D-Grade."

"Okay."

Observing them came first, since they were already here. Jack found a distant mountain peak and landed there, getting them out of the miasmic clouds. Hidden behind the rocks of this peak, they could observe the camp below without being noticed.

"Let's take turns," Jack suggested. "Two hours each, then we swap. After eight hours total, we leave and go collect information. Okay?"

"Okay."

Jack took first-shift. When it was Brock's turn, he watched the camp almost without blinking. Just before Brock's shift was over, he nudged Jack, who was lounging on a rock. "Bro."

"Hmm? Yes?"

Brock pointed ahead. Jack peeked from behind the rock, catching sight of the enemy camp and a golden-haired woman who was galloping through its midst—literally galloping, as she had four legs. Everybody had their heads bowed, not even daring to look at her, while even the other two immortals—the feshkur and the human—showed subservience.

Centaur, Level 210
Faction: Animal Kingdom (B-Grade)
Title: Fourth Ring Conqueror

"Shit," Jack said. It wasn't even about her level, her horse-like lower body, or her status as a late D-Grade—though barely, since the D-Grade reached up to Level 250. The real problem was that, even from this distance, he could sense the brutality she emitted, like waves of terror that washed over everyone present. Some guards were shaking, while the prisoners had all withdrawn to the center of their cage—at least, Jack assumed, seeing as he could no longer see outstretched limbs between the bars.

The woman reached the cage and exchanged a few words with the prisoners. Soon after, she retreated to her abode—the same red tent that the feshkur immortal had entered previously.

Jack wiped the sweat off his brow. "That must be the leader," he deduced. "What do you think, Brock? Is the risk still worth it?"

Brock considered it. He then shook his head.

"Yeah. I may be able to beat her, but I may not, and she has two more immortals, plus all the complications this would create. At this point, only idiots would risk their lives like this for a small "fuck you" to the Animal Kingdom. Reaching the Exploding Sun is more important."

Brock gave a thumbs-up. Jack exhaled loudly, then sat back against the rock. "But you know," he said, "I can't help but wonder. How do I stack up against a late D-Grade?"

The brorilla gave him a weighting look.

Jack continued. "I mean, I matched an immortal while at the peak of the E-Grade. Even without the Life Drop, I was pretty much as strong as someone could be at my level, and I beat the three Hounds who were at the middle D-Grade—though I surprised them. Could I jump seventy-nine levels to fight that centaur? That's... seven hundred and ninety stat points. More than double what I have." He grimaced. "It's a lot, isn't it?"

Brock shrugged. "Maybe," he said. "But you strong."

"Right. Me strong... What's with all the mythical creatures, anyway? Centaurs, minotaurs, cyclopses... If the ancient Greeks were right, I'll eat my hat."

Brock mimed that Jack had no hat.

"I'll find one, then eat it."

"Okay."

They stayed quiet for a while, each sunk into their own thoughts. Jack kept tackling the issue of his current strength. Truth was, it bugged him. Breaking through to the D-Grade had been a massive metamorphosis, except he hadn't fought anything since then. The Hounds were only a couple short exchanges due to the element of surprise, not a real fight.

Simply put, he had no idea how strong he was.

"You know what?" he said, jumping to his feet. "We have time. Since we're leaving these guys alone, I think I'll do some testing. Sound good?" Brock smiled brightly and Jack laughed. "How are we always talking the same language, bro?"

"Because we awesome."

"Damn right!"

They high-fived. Then, Brock jumped on Jack's back, and they flew off. They followed the mountain ridge for a few miles, reaching far enough from the camp that they couldn't be spotted, then kept going for another quarter of an hour. Since this planet was mostly uninhabited, and Jack was flying at almost the speed of sound, they were now hundreds of miles away from any other intelligent lifeform.

"Here should be good," he said, diving to the ground. Another canyon welcomed them—a deep, jagged crevice dug into the flat wasteland, possibly the result of a powerful earthquake.

This time, however, the canyon was completely empty. Just a several miles long, thirty-foot-wide corridor carved a hundred feet into the earth, surrounded by jagged rock cliffs and littered with stones of all sizes.

The perfect site for testing Jack's new powers.

He was giddy. As Brock dismounted and stepped far back, eager to watch Jack's demonstration, the man himself was looking around and wondering where to start from. He brought up his status screen.

Name: Jack Rust
Species: Human, Earth-387
Faction: Bare Fist Brotherhood (D)
Grade: D
Class: Cosmic Fist (King)
Level: 131

Strength: 710
Dexterity: 665
Constitution: 685
Mental: 120
Will: 190

Dao Skills: Meteor Punch III, Iron Fist Style II, Neutron Star Body II, Brutalizing Aura II, Space Walk I
Daos: Dao Tree of the Fist, Dao Root of Indomitable Will (fused), Dao Root of Life (fused), Dao Root of Power (fused), Dao Root of Weakness (fused)
Titles: Planetary Frontrunner (10), Planetary Torchbearer (1), Ninth Ring Conqueror, Planetary Overlord (1)

"Let's start from my stats, shall we?" he asked the poor canyon.

He currently had over six hundred points in all Physical sub-stats. The average pre-System human had five—that made him at least a hundred and twenty times faster, stronger, and more durable. When combined, the results of those stats grew exponentially.

Moreover, his titles increased the efficacy of all his stats. Planetary Frontrunner (10) gave him a ten percent efficacy increase. Planetary Torchbearer (1) gave fifteen, Ninth Ring Conqueror gave a whopping fifty, and Planetary Overlord gave another fifteen. Added up, the total came to a ninety percent extra efficacy.

Jack had almost a thousand Physical all said and done. That made him...

Very, very strong.

He grinned. There were several boulders littering the floor of the canyon. He picked out a truck-sized one and lifted it easily—he barely felt the strain, even if the sight was almost comical. He put it down and went looking for a greater challenge.

The largest stone present was absolutely enormous—the size of a house. Jack stared up at it. *Can I... Nah. There's no way, right?*

But what if I can?

Most of the time, his feats of power were a result of his Dao, not just his physical body. In the E-Grade, he wouldn't even be able to budge this thing.

Jack faced off against the boulder. He grabbed it from a corner, squatted, braced himself... and lifted.

He felt it this time. His muscles tightened. His veins popped out. And yet, even as he struggled, the boulder rose from the ground, revealing a surface under it so massive that Jack gaped at his own strength. When he let it drop, the entire canyon shook. Stones tumbled from the cliffs, and the dust that rose was enough to make Brock cough a couple of times.

As an immortal, Jack didn't even need to breathe, and shielding his orifices with his Dao was easy. Dust clouds could no longer touch him.

"Sorry," he told Brock, who waved the concern away. Jack gazed back at the massive boulder. "Take that, mountain."

He then looked around and scratched the back of his head. This was only the start of what he was hoping to test. Problem was, this canyon was unexpectedly fragile. If he so much as touched a wall with his knuckles, it would collapse.

"We need a better place," he decided. "Follow me."

Grabbing Brock, they flew another couple miles, arriving at a massive mountain. It reached at least a mile into the air, was surrounded by uneven, rocky terrain, and its sides were bare like the teeth of a snarling wolf.

Standing at the mountain foot, Jack felt tiny.

"Now we're talking," he said, looking up. "Immortals are supposed to be Mountain Breakers, right? Let's see."

Stat-wise, there wasn't much else to test. Dexterity was about finesse and reflexes, not speed, and he wasn't about to ram the mountain head-first to test his Constitution.

That left only his skills.

"Oh!" he exclaimed. "Actually... Take a few steps back, please."

Brock obliged. As soon as he had enough space, Jack focused inward. He saw his Dao Tree—a mighty fist, each finger painted a different color corresponding to his Dao Seed and Dao Roots. It hovered in the middle of his soul space, concealing such powerful energy that a shiver of anticipation rushed through Jack.

In the F-Grade, cultivators first touched on the power of the Dao and used it in elementary ways.

In the E-Grade, they used the Dao to augment their body. Even projectiles or extra limbs—like Vivi's fire wings—were only projections of Dao workings that occurred inside the body. The ambient Dao was too stable to influence directly.

In the D-Grade, however...

Jack closed his eyes and focused. He reached for the power in his Dao Tree, reveled in its majesty, and drew it out. He let it seep outside his body—pitting his own will against that of the universe and winning. His Dao stretched, occupying more space around him. The infinite colored particles that made up the world's Dao retreated, leaving behind only those compatible with Jack's. He felt his existence stretch outside his body, assuming control of the surrounding space and imposing his will—his Dao—on it.

When his eyes reopened, he found himself surrounded by a dome of purple. Spectral flames danced at the edges of his vision like the fingers of a large fist, while the very air was compressed by Jack's will. He could sense the control he had over this space. Gazing at a few stones, he willed them to break in two—and they did.

This power was wondrous.

Against any mortal, Jack only had to open his Dao Domain to incapacitate them. Even against immortals like himself, his domain would greatly constrain them, unless they had a similarly powerful domain themselves—which, according to Old Man Spirit, most low D-Grades didn't.

And this domain didn't just weaken anything incompatible with Jack's Dao. It made him stronger, too. The very world was helping him. He was like a fish in water.

"How the hell did I beat Old Man Spirit in his domain?" he

wondered aloud, impressed at the power he could now wield. The D-Grade was as powerful as advertised.

Unfortunately, he had no one to test it on—Brock was still only E-Grade—but the Exploding Sun could certainly offer a plethora of strong opponents. He could wait a bit.

Which meant that, right now, there was only one thing left to test.

His Dao Skills.

CHAPTER FOUR
CULTIVATING IN THE D-GRADE

WHEN IT CAME TO DAO SKILLS, JACK ONLY HAD A FEW HE COULD CURRENTLY test. He opted to start from the weakest.

Space Walk was the upgraded version of Ghost Step. It let Jack teleport anywhere within a mile from himself, which was a simple yet extremely overpowered ability. Sure, it was exhausting to use, but it was *teleportation*. And for an entire mile.

In hindsight, calling it the weakest skill was misleading, but oh well.

Jack looked up at the mountain peak and stepped through the folds of space. Something resisted—like he was trying to walk through a wall of extremely thick gel. A large quantity of Dao left his soul and assaulted the gel, forcing it to yield.

Jack managed to take a step. The world spun, and he caught a glimpse of darkness. Next thing he knew, the air was rushing away from him, and he was halfway up the mountain. He looked back down, where Brock was waving at him—nothing more than a dot in the distance.

"Heh," Jack chuckled, glancing at the mountain peak. He used Space Walk again. Instantly, he was standing at the very peak of the mountain. The clouds were closer now, and their smell reached here, reminding Jack of a rotting carcass—a smell he'd grown familiar with in the Forest of the Strong.

He was exhausted from the two Space Walks, too, but he had no mind for that.

The view was breathtaking. As far as he could see, he was the tallest thing in all directions. The crisp air of this planet showed off a brown wasteland stretching to the curved horizon, dotted with hills and cracks. He caught a glimpse of vegetation in the distance, but it was tiny—who knew what plant could survive here.

The gray clouds were cracked in parts, revealing hints of the green sky beyond.

Jack took a deep breath, uncaring about the toxicity and acrid smell. He closed his eyes and enjoyed the moment. He couldn't stop the ends of his lips from rising.

This is it. Why I left Earth. What cultivation offers me. This poisonous beauty and this distant world... only thanks to my power could I ever see it. Thank you, world, for trying to kill me.

He opened his eyes, letting them shine with stars. His Dao—the Fist—burst out from inside him and filled his entire being. Even after he left this mountain, this kind of scene, this wondrous feeling wouldn't disappear. It would stay with him forever. This would be his life from now on—every day until he died.

He loved it. Power filled him, coupled with exhilaration.

"Watch me, Brock!" he roared, jumping up and taking to the sky. He turned back down to stare at the mountain peak beneath his feet, a dead titan of brown rock. He clenched his fist. The sky was torn asunder, and the clouds dispersed as the entire world was sucked into Jack's fist.

Of his remaining Dao Skills, he couldn't test Iron Fist Style, Brutalizing Aura, or Neutron Star Body without a sparring partner. Which left one.

Light and sound disappeared. Only a large purple meteor remained, hovering in the sky above the mountain peak, silent in its lethality. Jack grinned wildly. He swung down. With all sound gone, only his roar remained, a herald of destruction: "METEOR PUNCH!"

The meteor was nailed into the mountain peak. A purple shockwave spread faster than Jack could react, tossing him several hundred feet into the sky. A terrible crashing sound hit him like the rumble of a giant, threatening to burst his eardrums, and the sounds of demolition filled the air. The wind was strong enough that he spun several times before righting himself. The dust cloud was so oceanically massive that he felt lost in another world.

Shit! he thought before calming himself. Well, nevermind. Brock won't die to some flying rocks.

He waited, floating in midair. The dust cleared, and when it did, he was left stunned.

There was no mountain peak anymore. The top one-third of the mountain had been shattered, sent flying in all directions as rocks and dust. The mountain now ended in a bowl-shaped crater, like God had reached down from the sky and scooped up its peak.

Jack expected something similar, but not nearly at this scale. This was almost cataclysmic. The crater had a radius of at least a hundred feet, and a depth of fifty. He could fit an entire building block in there.

If it ever rained on this planet, this mountain would be topped by an actual lake.

"Holy shit," he eloquently expressed his shock.

But shock was better shared. Jack glanced at the foot of the mountain, where Brock stood in a patch of empty ground surrounded by rubble. His Staff of Stone was in his hands, as he'd probably used it to deflect the flying rocks.

Besides everything else, Brock's monkey face was stretched in an expression of utter stun. His eyes were wide, his jaw almost touching the ground, and his mouth gaping so widely that he must have swallowed at least some of the dust still flying around.

Jack admired his scene of destruction for another moment before flying to Brock's side.

"Bro..." the brorilla said, unable to form words.

"Hehe. Cool, huh?" Jack replied smugly. "And I didn't even use my Dao Domain."

Brock's eyes went from shock, to glee, to anticipation. He set his jaw and nodded to himself—probably affirming his decision to become an immortal, too.

"Of course you can," Jack said. "I suspect you're even more talented than me."

Brock shook his head, then gave a thumbs-up. "Bro awesome."

"I am, Brock. But so are you."

"Yes."

Jack laughed. "Anyway, I think that's enough testing. We should run. This impact was larger than I anticipated, and people might come to check what's going on."

"Mm, yes."

"Perfect. Hop on."

They flew away at top speed, in the direction opposite the Animal Kingdom camp, snickering all the while.

The rest of the day went by quickly. Jack and Brock camped at yet another canyon, far away from both the teleporter town and the Animal Kingdom camp. As they could just place their starship on the ground and live inside it, they were fairly comfortable.

They didn't have much to do, so they spent the day with Jack teaching Brock new words.

When night came, Brock retreated to the cabin, and Jack stayed in the helm room. Both were cultivating.

Jack sat in the middle of the helm room, legs crossed, and eyes closed. His chest rose and fell rhythmically, and the Dao came and went around him like it was breathing, too.

The nature of cultivation changed when one reached the D-Grade.

Before, killing things had been Jack's sole way to progress. The System awarded him levels and enhanced his body, mind, and soul, while also discreetly helping with the Dao.

Starting from the D-Grade, however, killing was no longer necessary. Jack now possessed the ability to engage directly with the ambient Dao, absorbing it into his soul to become stronger. At regular intervals, the System acknowledged his efforts, awarded him with a level-up, and helped him utilize this Dao he'd absorbed to enhance himself as he pleased—through the use of stat points.

Old Man Spirit had explained this before Jack left Trial Planet, and it brought all sorts of questions into the fore.

Was this how things always worked? Had the System been saturating Jack's body with the Dao since Level 1? Was that where all stat points came from? And, if so, what specific Dao did it use back then?

Maybe it was a combination of all Daos, or any Dao that was readily available. Then, how did the System use it to create his Skills? How did they work? What was the connection?

And, if not for the System, would that process happen by itself? Would the excess power of the Dao naturally spread across the cultivator's body, mind, and soul, enhancing them in the same way that stat points did? That would explain why Brock, despite not having access to the System, didn't seem disadvantaged compared to other cultivators. But then, why did the System go through such trouble to achieve what could be done by itself?

The more things Jack learned, the less he took for granted, and the more questions he had to answer. Everything had a reason for being the way it was—he just had to find it.

Thankfully, he had plenty of time.

Right now, he could focus on absorbing enough power from the world to become stronger.

The multicolored motes of Dao surrounded him in all directions. He could see them; particles that moved in currents and obscure patterns. There were truths in their circulation that he couldn't currently comprehend, but that was fine. His job was simple.

Relaxing, he spread his perception outside his body. It brushed against the particles, which got excited at his mental touch. He carefully shifted through them to discover the Daos most compatible to his, then projected his own Dao like a sieve to separate these particles from all the other Daos. When they were pure, or as pure as he could make them, he slowly drew them in, attracting them to his Dao Tree like moths to a flame—or like baby ducklings to their mother.

The particles swooped in and joined his Dao Tree, merging with it and making it stronger.

A Dao Tree—just like a Dao Seed or a Dao Root—was a storage of power, among other things. It could hold a finite amount of Dao particles inside it. Currently, Jack was drawing in more than his core could take, maintaining a concentration of energy that was slightly uncomfortable. As he did that, the Dao pushed against the walls of his Dao

Tree from the inside, increasing its size and storage space in a painfully slow manner.

But it did work.

Level-up! You have reached Level 132.

Still with his eyes closed, he smiled.

Of course, not everyone advanced at the same speed. The better one's foundations, and the stronger their Dao, the faster they would advance, since they could draw in the Dao more efficiently and compress it harder without harming their core.

Jack had a perfect foundation. Naturally, his cultivation speed blew most other cultivators out of the water, which was how he got one level in just a few days. Most people would spend weeks to achieve the same increase.

Unfortunately, his leveling speed would decrease the further he advanced. Even at his speed, reaching the C-Grade at Level 250 would take years. And, if he wanted to defeat the Planetary Overseer in time, he only had eight months.

There were other ways to save Earth, which was why he was heading to the Exploding Sun, but not meeting his goal left a bitter taste in his mouth.

Well, whatever, he thought, opening his eyes. I'll try my best, and whatever happens, happens. Maybe I'll find a way.

The sun blinded him.

What the fuck?

It had been night when he started cultivating, and it only felt like a few minutes ago. Yet, reality was hard to challenge The sun hung in the middle of the sky, bright and burning. Even the clouds had disappeared.

"Brock," Jack said, looking around. Brock, who was lounging on a chair with his hands behind his head and his feet resting on a stool, jumped.

"Bro."

"How long was I cultivating for?"

Brock raised ten fingers, then another five.

"Fifteen hours? Are you kidding me?"

"No."

"Wow. It felt like fifteen minutes." Brock shrugged, while Jack sighed. "I should keep an eye out for this… Oh! The teleportation!"

He hurriedly fished the buzzer from his pocket. Thankfully, it wasn't glowing. Torm had mentioned the wait was usually two to three days. Who knew what happened if you missed your turn.

"We should move closer," Jack said. "If the buzzer activates while we're far away, we may not be able to return in time."

Brock agreed and headed to the helm—to which he'd taken a liking. Their ship gently rose out of the canyon and into the sky. They could have also flown on Jack's back, but there was no need. The ship burned the infinite Dao as fuel.

They cruised through the sky at a comfortable pace—almost at mach speed. They passed by the mountain where Jack had tested his Meteor Punch, finding a few Exploding Sun officials scratching their heads at the new crater.

They laughed as they passed far overhead.

Next, they flew close to the Animal Kingdom encampment. They kept their distance, of course, and they were also shielded from inspection inside their starship. Nobody would realize who they were.

However, the prison camp was slightly different from when they'd left it. The prisoners were no longer in their cage. Instead, they were now out of the canyon, using pickaxes to break up rocks in the vicinity. Dark iron shackles were wrapped around their wrists, and nobody was using the Dao.

The sight birthed fury inside Jack. There was absolutely no reason for the prisoners to be breaking rocks—the guards were making them do it just for fun, under this planet's burning sun and in the toxic air. Meanwhile, they, the slave drivers, were resting in the shade and laughing.

However, before Jack's rage could unravel fully, it was suddenly overwhelmed by surprise.

Because he recognized someone down there.

CHAPTER FIVE
JACK-STYLE BREAK-OUT

"VANDERDECKEN!"

Of all the people Jack expected to see as a prisoner in this Animal Kingdom encampment, Vanderdecken was not one of them.

The man had changed quite a bit. Last time Jack saw him, was back in Earth's Integration Tournament, when he used his magical electric guitar and Dao of Metal to fight against the Animal Kingdom forces. Back then, he'd been a spirited young man with long hair, chains hanging from his leather jacket, and permanently raised pinkies and index fingers.

Now, he looked like a defeated version of his previous self. His long hair hung soullessly down his shoulders, dirty like he hadn't bathed in a month. All the chains had been torn away from his clothes, dark shackles bound his wrists, and his guitar was nowhere to be seen. He now wielded a rusty pickaxe, repeatedly smashing it into random rocks under this planet's scorching sun.

In short, he looked terrible.

"Terrible," Brock muttered from the side.

"That's what I thought!" Jack replied. "What is he even doing here? He's not supposed to be out of Earth, let alone out of the Animal Kingdom constellation. And why is he captured?"

A quick scan confirmed that this was, indeed, Vanderdecken. His planet of origin was pretty conclusive. At least he'd broken through to the E-Grade.

Human (Earth-387), Level 52 (E-Grade)
Faction: -

There was no title visible, even though Jack knew Vanderdecken had at least acquired a Planetary Frontrunner variant. Probably a Planetary Torchbearer, too. He must have chosen not to display them, like Jack had.

Unfortunately, it hadn't helped him.

"Bro," Brock said. "Help?"

"Absolutely. We've fought shoulder-to-shoulder with that guy. We can't just let him be a prisoner of the enemy."

Brock chuckled and bumped his fists together. "Brock smash."

"Right. Brock smash. The question is, how?"

Jack had previously decided not to bother with this Animal Kingdom encampment, as it was not worth the risk. The moment he saw Vanderdecken, however, that decision was instantly reversed.

Now, they just had to find the best way to go about it.

"Charging them wouldn't work," Jack contemplated aloud. "The E-Grade guards are negligible, but they have a late D-Grade and two low ones, plus anyone else that we haven't spotted. We'll have to find a way to sneak in?"

Brock nodded.

"And then what?" Jack resumed his train of thought. "Say we break them out. All the guards will be on us instantly, so we'll have to fight them anyway. We can't exactly run away while carrying a bunch of prisoners."

A quick inspection revealed that, of the prisoners, none were at the D-Grade. They couldn't help Jack against the D-Grade guards. They couldn't escape fast enough either, even if Jack found a way to remove their shackles.

"I guess we have to fight the wardens after all," he concluded. "Time to see if I can match a late D-Grade. I probably should... right? I defeated the three middle D-Grade Hounds. Why not one late D-Grade?"

Brock nodded. "Yes. But." He tried to find the right word, then pointed up at the sun and mimed it arcing all the way to below the horizon.

"Night?" Jack tried.

"Yes."

"Sure. Even if it all comes down to combat anyway, we can try to sneak in at night. The element of surprise is a dependable ally."

"Good bro."

"Exactly." Jack reached into his pocket and retrieved the buzzer they'd received from the teleportation hub. "Now, we just have to hope this doesn't—" The buzzer began to glow and echo with a low buzz. "You have got to be fucking kidding me."

This buzzer was supposed to activate when there were a thousand people in line to teleport, and it meant they should rush over. It had only been one day, not three!

"Fuck my life," Jack said, sighing. "Well, no choice. Guess we have to miss our flight."

Brock nodded like it was a natural decision.

Which it was. What kind of person would abandon their brother in arms when they could just go get a new buzzer at anytime? Waiting another day, or couple of days, was nothing.

Jack tried to deactivate the buzzer. When he was unable to, and so was Brock, they flew away and left it on top of a distant mountain, where it could buzz alone for as long as it liked.

Then, it was strategizing time.

The first thing they did was fly to the teleporter hub and get a new buzzer. The process went without a hitch—all they had to do was declare their destination to the register. Jack's disguise had been broken when he used Meteor Punch before, so he didn't need to worry about it being spotted by the guards.

In return, he had to worry about people recognizing his faction and deducing his identity, but it shouldn't be a problem this deep into the Exploding Sun constellation—Animal Kingdom presence or not.

After getting their new buzzer and leaving town again, they landed on the same mountain peak they'd previously used to spy on the Animal Kingdom encampment. Hidden behind boulders and cliffs, they set to watching the wardens while waiting for night to fall.

The sun moved fast. Jack didn't know much about Derion—the planet they were currently on—but its day and night cycle was noticeably faster than Earth's. After about four hours, the sun had descended from its peak to the horizon, where it slowly disappeared after painting the sky dark red for a while.

The night was dark on Derion. The heavy miasmic clouds hid away the stars, and Jack failed to spot any moon. In combination with the planet's empty wastelands, it was like someone had draped a black blanket over the land. The only source of light in sight was the pale torchlight coming from the Animal Kingdom encampment.

In fact, this night was so dark that Jack couldn't even make out the ground from where he stood on the mountaintop. It felt like he was trapped in a lightless, empty sphere, like the dark part of Trial Planet's Space Ring.

It was terrifying. At the same time, it made their job easier.

Hardening their hearts, a man and a brorilla descended from their peak, one flying and the other riding on the first's shoulders. They flew low under the cover of the night, until they were at the lip of the canyon where the Animal Kingdom had set up camp.

They peeked down.

Not many things were visible in the little light. The large red tent stood in the middle, only licked by the torchlight when the wind made it sway. Four more tents were spread around it, gray in color. The cage stood ten feet away from the red tent, its steel bars doing little to shield the prisoners from the cold night wind, while three guards patrolled the perimeter inside the canyon. There were another three outside the canyon, but given its size and the night's darkness, Jack had easily remained unseen.

Overall, the canyon stretched for miles in either direction, had a width of several hundred feet, and a depth of at least fifty. The encampment took up one of its broader parts, leaving heavy darkness on either side.

Jack took all of this in with one glance. The three immortals stayed in the red tent, so he had to remain as far away from it as possible. Thankfully, it didn't look like they expected an attack, or there would have been an immortal standing guard as well.

"Let's go," he whispered to Brock.

He let himself fall into the canyon, gliding smoothly next to the wall to remain shrouded in darkness. Despite that, he tried to avoid the guards' gazes as best as possible—maybe they had darkvision.

When his feet touched the canyon floor, he crouched and waited, ears tense to pick up any sign of activity.

Nothing. The guards stayed on their patrol routes, and the red tent remained undisturbed. It looked like they weren't noticed. *Good*, Jack thought. Brock dismounted from his back, and the two of them crept together to the nearest tent.

Jack had flashbacks of his infiltration into the goblin village in the Forest of the Strong. He couldn't help the grin on his lips.

They reached the tent and stayed still. Brock held his breath, while Jack just deactivated his, which was more of an instinct than a necessity at this point. When no suspicious sounds came—besides discreet snoring from inside the tent—they circled around it to come face-to-face with the cage. They crouched by the side of the tent, where the darkness was densest.

Fifteen feet still separated them from the iron bars, but they didn't actually need to approach it. The D-Grade came with all sorts of nifty abilities. Flying was one of them. Transmitting your thoughts into another person's head with the Dao as your conduit was another.

Jack glimpsed Vanderdecken's angular face, tucked into a ball between other prisoners. His eyelids were flickering, and his body was shaking from the cold.

"*Vanderdecken,*" Jack thought, focusing. No response. "*Vanderdecken!*"

The man's eyes shot open, and he looked around in confusion and fear.

"Don't make a sound!" Jack said telepathically. "I'm an immortal here to rescue you. I am currently speaking inside your mind. You can reply the same way. Pretend there is nothing wrong, or the guards might be on to us."

Vanderdecken closed his eyes and pretended to fall back asleep.

Silence reigned for a while. As Jack was beginning to believe the man really had returned to his sleep, a tired voice rang inside his mind, transmitted back from the same Dao strand that Jack was using as a conduit.

"How do you know my name?" Vanderdecken asked.

"Because I'm Jack Rust."

Silence fell again. Jack could almost hear Vanderdecken's disbelief.

"Jack Rust?" he finally asked.

"Yes. It's a long story, but let's just say this is a huge coincidence. It doesn't matter. All that matters is, I'm here to rescue you."

Vanderdecken sounded hesitant when he asked, "Who did you shag during the Integration Tournament?"

"...This is highly inappropriate."

"It's something a fake wouldn't know. Answer me."

Jack ground his teeth from he hid in the shadows.

"Come on. It wasn't a secret, anyway."

"Vivi."

"Dude! Holy shit, it really is you!" Vanderdecken's mental voice did a sudden one-eighty, and back was the hopeful young bard. *"It's been so long! How the hell have you been?"*

"Pretty good. I explored a bit, kicked some ass, became an immortal. You know, typical Monday stuff."

"Duuude, that's awesome. Can you, like, fly now?"

"I can."

"Will you take me for a ride?"

"You do understand that you're still a prisoner, right?"

"Please?"

"...Yeah, I will. But focus. Chitchatting can wait until later. Right now, we have to rescue you."

"How did you become an immortal so fast!"

"Vanderdecken. Focus."

Jack was also looking forward to talking, but there needed to be priorities.

"Sorry. I'm focusing. Okay. Rescuing me. Dude, I'm so glad you came. These guys are massive dicks."

"I can imagine. I saw you breaking rocks."

"Yeah. For no reason at all. They just want us tired so we don't think of escaping."

"Speaking of. Where is the key to the cage? Also, can you use your Dao?"

When watching the camp before, Jack had seen no prisoner utilize even the tiniest bit of Dao. It was to the point where he suspected something was up.

"These shackles are System items. They lock down our access to the System, which includes our skills."

That was interesting information. Jack's training with Copy Jack had taught him just how much he relied on the System to execute his skills, but it had also taught him that, with proper practice, he could learn to use them himself. If somebody put these shackles on E-Grade Jack, they wouldn't have worked as well.

"As for the keys," Vanderdecken continued, "the Warden has them. But be careful; she's a late D-Grade. You can't fight her."

"Oh, I will, but I'd rather rescue you first. Is there any other way to let you out?"

"Uh... None that I can think of? Even if you did, another warden has the keys to our shackles. I... I don't know how you could do it."

Jack nodded somberly. He could sense the despair creep back in Vanderdecken's voice. As a rule of thumb, the fewer "dudes" he used, the more lost he was.

"Don't worry. We are brothers in arms—I will rescue you no matter what. It will be fine. I just need you to calm down, okay?"

"Okay."

"Good. Now, I have a plan. Can you do me a favor and go stick to the steel bars farthest away from the red tent?"

"*...Okay?*" Vanderdecken stood up, grabbed his waist as if it hurt from sleeping in the same position, and went to lie down near the steel bars where Jack had indicated. "*Now what?*"

"Now, just watch."

If Jack used even the tiniest bit of his strength, the immortals in the tent would pick it up and rush him. Thankfully, Jack and Brock had already discussed what they would do in this situation.

"Plan A, bro. One of the low D-Grades has the shackle keys," Jack said. Brock nodded. They fist-bumped, then Jack walked out of the darkness and into the light, reaching a corner of the cage in an instant. He was now right between the cage and the red tent. The torchlight flickered sharply at the edge of his vision—some guard had spotted him, but it didn't matter.

"Intru—"

The guard's shout was overshadowed by Jack's fist smashing right through the steel bars, eliciting a terrible shriek from the metal. The roof of the cage dented inward as the bars pulled at it, and the entire cage slid a few feet to the side, but even the metal's innate resistance wasn't enough to resist Jack's strength. A hole was instantly made in the corner of the cage, where two bars were shorn off enough for a grown man to crouch through.

Before anyone could scream, Jack unleashed a full-power Meteor Punch at the red tent, which was in the opposite direction from the cage.

"Good fucking morning!"

CHAPTER SIX
BROS TO THE RESCUE

JACK'S METEOR PUNCH TURNED NIGHT INTO DAY. A PURPLE SUN BLAZED INTO existence, disintegrating the red tent and scattering any materials that survived. The strike kept going, annihilating another tent before crashing into the far wall of the canyon, and causing a part of it to collapse.

At the same time, the shockwave of the attack was unleashed at a wider range, blowing a tent clean off its base and sending multiple guards flying. As for the cage behind Jack, though it had been struck by a mighty wind, it remained unmoved.

In the blink of an eye, half the camp had been destroyed. Such was the power of an immortal.

"Good fucking morning!" Jack shouted. "Come out to meet your daddy!"

A hostile aura burst out of the red tent's remnants. It was a black sphere arced with lightning, and two large, red eyes hovered in its middle, staring down at Jack.

"Who dares attack me?" an imposing female voice rang across the canyon, snuffing out the cries of the injured.

"Come here and find out!" Jack roared back.

The black aura parted, revealing a female centaur in its midst. Blood ran down the side of her face, while one of her four legs was broken. She didn't seem to care. Her eyes burned with rage, scanning Jack like she was about to tear him apart.

She was a weird person to look at. Her face was soft and circular, with beautiful features. Blonde hair cascaded down her back, creating an image of purity which was instantly shattered by the sheer cruelty visible in her eyes, a gaze made to terrorize whoever met it.

Jack scanned her again.

Centaur, Level 210
Faction: Animal Kingdom (B-Grade)
Title: Fourth Ring Conqueror

Two hundred and ten. Seventy-eight levels over him—seven hundred and eighty stat points, along with a greater storage of Dao energy.

A powerful adversary.

But she stood alone.

The two early D-Grades lay in the rubble behind her—the human was dead, his chest caved in, while the feshkur was still bleeding out. Jack's attack had cracked his skull, broken several limbs, and burned his entire back.

Even though these two immortals were of a slightly higher level than Jack, they couldn't handle his surprise attack.

The centaur did not spare them a single look. Neither did she glance at the many dead or injured guards who were running away. Her eyes remained glued on Jack's, and the terror they brewed only intensified.

The Dao of Terror? Jack wondered. Of cruelty? Or pain? Something like that.

His heart almost cowered before the gaze of this centaur, but he quickly recovered. He was Jack Rust. The embodiment of the fist. The conqueror of Trial Planet. He could not be intimidated by a single gaze.

He grinned at the centaur, weathering her heart assault without blinking. Her eyes narrowed at that.

"A low D-Grade who can stand against my aura..." she muttered. Her gaze ran over him and his status screen again. With intelligence befitting an immortal, she put two and two together. "So, you are the infamous Jack Rust. I hadn't heard you became an immortal."

"What can I say? I'm fast where it matters."

The centaur remained silent, her eyes narrowing a hair more. "I sense no others. Did you really come alone?"

"Almost. I have a monkey."

There was no point in trying to hide Brock. As they spoke, the brorilla was busy rushing the prisoners through the hole Jack had made in the cage. The centaur could easily sense him and deduce the connection between them—but Jack didn't plan on letting her do anything about it.

"You cannot possibly think you can match me," she said.

"And what if I do?"

"Then you're a fool." Her aura rose, becoming a dome of darkness deeper than the night. It covered the entire canyon. Screams rang inside it—auditory illusions made to break one's spirit. "A fool who landed right into my arms."

Surrounded by darkness, Jack chuckled. "That remains to be seen."

His own Dao Domain burst forth. A purple dome unraveled from the deepest parts of his being, vying with the woman's for supremacy. The two domains ground against each other, one on the inside and one on the outside. Jack's was smaller, but it was also far more compact—though he could only cover a radius of a hundred feet compared to the centaur's half-mile, the control he wielded was far superior.

The Warden frowned and pushed harder. Her domain crashed inward, growing smaller and stronger. The screams rang louder—and, though Brock and the prisoners were safe inside Jack's domain, he suspected that many of the Animal Kingdom guards outside of it were screaming.

She didn't care about them at all.

Neither did Jack, to be honest. His hands were full with resisting her domain. Where black and purple met, Dao particles of fist smashed into those of pain. Their understandings warred, seeking gaps to compromise the other's integrity. After a while, no domain emerged as the victor—the two had formed an unsteady balance, with the constant pressure neutralizing each other's forces.

If two immortals had a great disparity in power, the stronger one could just rip through the other's domain and dominate them. If they were closer in power, however, neutralizing another immortal's domain was difficult.

"How can your domain stand against mine?" The centaur's voice was filled with incomprehension. "You're just an early immortal!"

"An early immortal who's about to kick your ass," Jack corrected her, his gaze stormy. "Let's take this to the sky."

In the wider galaxy, it was customary for immortals to fight in the sky. This was because, with their powers, fighting on the ground could ruin entire cities and genocide populations.

In this case, however, the centaur couldn't care less about her guards, while Jack had to protect Brock and the prisoners.

She opened her mouth and laughed with malice. "I don't think—"

Jack was upon her instantly. His domain contracted around his body, pressurized to form a tiny patch of the world completely under his control. He appeared in front of her, ducked down, and sprang upward into an uppercut.

Dao Domains were used for posturing or suppressing weaker opponents. In a battle between equals, there was no reason to constantly keep it up.

The centaur raised her body and crossed her front legs to block. The punch hit them straight. With the crack of a bone, the Warden's entire body was sent flying upward like a missile, ascending hundreds of feet in the blink of an eye. She screamed.

Jack Space Walked right before her. Now that they were high enough, he had no reason to hold back. "Meteor Punch!" he roared, drilling at her chest.

A black spear appeared between her hands. She twirled it and brought it down on his fist. "Pain and Misery!"

Spear and fist collided in an explosion of color. Purple and black were unleashed into the sky, each spreading into a hemisphere behind their wielder, but the purple area was larger and richer. Jack pushed his fist forward to break the stalemate, and the centaur flew back while spitting bright red blood.

Jack had won the exchange, but he still gripped his wrist tightly. "Ouch," he muttered breathlessly. The centaur's attack wasn't just physical. The moment they collided, he felt a tremendously strong pain drill through his bones, like his entire forearm was liquified and compressed.

That hadn't really happened. He was fine, but the pain he'd just experienced was quite extreme.

However, Jack wasn't unfamiliar with pain. This was nothing compared to the torture he'd endured when assimilating the Life Drop, or even the all-penetrative lightning of his breakthrough's heavenly tribulation.

Dao of Pain my ass, he thought, gritting his teeth as he raised his eyes to meet hers. He was angry now. He didn't just want to fight her—he wanted to destroy her.

Apprehension entered the centaur's gaze. "Why are you not screaming?" she shouted from a distance. "How can you overpower me? What the hell is wrong with you!"

"Because I'm Jack fucking Rust," he growled, then charged forth.

The centaur unleashed something between a roar and a scream, raising her spear to meet him. They clashed again—and the sky was torn apart by colors.

Brock watched his big bro punch the horse-woman to the sky. He nodded in acknowledgement—that was a good strike.

He didn't need to keep watching the battle. He knew Big Bro would win. He just focused on extracting Guitar Bro from the cage, along with the other cage bros. When enough of them were out that they could help the others—even in their shocked confusion—Brock left them and sprinted for the ruined red tent.

There were two bodies there—one was the dead human, and the other the half-dead feshkur. One of them held the keys to the shackles of the cage bros. Brock had to find them, rescue the bros, and help them fight off the remaining guards.

He went for the human first. Rummaging through his pockets, he found nothing but a green credit card and a small bag—both of which he kept. He then rushed to the feshkur. He spotted the ring of keys hanging from a leather ring embedded in his belt. The only problem was, how to get it out?

Brock narrowed his eyes at the keyring. He had never faced such a mechanism before. The keys were hanging from a large iron ring, which in turn hung from another ring fused into the feshkur's belt. How could he remove one ring from the other, since they were clearly interlocked?

Why did smart bros have to make things so complicated?

Just as Brock was considering the issue, a weak groan came from the feshkur's mouth. His eyelids fluttered as if he was about to wake up. "Help—" he started saying.

Brock smashed his Staff of Stone into the man's face, repeatedly. When he stopped moving, Brock nodded. "Bad bro, stay sleep," he said, returning to the ring problem. He then realized he'd spent his entire short life working out for a reason. He grabbed the leather belt and pulled it out, making the feshkur's body spin in the process, then grabbed the keys and ran to the prisoners.

"Bro!" he shouted at Guitar Bro, who was currently helping his bros out of the hole in the cage. Guitar Bro noticed the keys, and his entire face shone with relief—and a little bit of surprise.

"Thanks!" he shouted, pushing his wrists forward with the lock at the top, so Brock could unlock it. "But why did you take the entire belt?"

Brock did not respond. If Guitar Bro wanted to make snarky comments, then Guitar Bro could go fetch his own keys. Or at least tell his human bros to stop making silly stuff.

Who even needed belts?

The shackles fell off, and Guitar Bro's face lit up like a Godrilla lantern. He raised his hands and looked at them in wonder. "Alright!" he shouted, Dao overflowing from him. Brock felt his blood boil and a need to shake his head up and down like a maniac. "It's show time, baby!"

Guitar Bro jumped up, ready to unleash his powers, but Brock grabbed his wrist firmly and gave him the keys. He pointed to the other cage bros. "You," he said.

"Me?"

"Yes. You. I fight."

The remaining guards were already regrouping and preparing to assault them, and Brock didn't plan on letting some random bro have all the fun. He wanted to fight, too. The Staff of Stone appeared in his hands—retrieved from the makeshift strap on his back—and he flexed at the approaching enemies, showcasing his ultra bro-like physique.

The guards were a bit confused, but also appropriately intimidated. After all, Brock could sense that only a few of them could match him in combat. The rest were just punching-bag bros.

"Brock Smash!" he shouted, jumping staff-first into the fray while Guitar Bro struggled to unshackle the rest of his bros.

Jack piled into the centaur. The sky spun around them as they exchanged a kaleidoscope of strikes, each attack pushing the centaur back a bit. Her body was bruised and battered now. Her dark robe had been torn in places, and her once-savage face was contorted into equal parts humiliation, anger, and fear.

As for Jack, he was fine, though the constant spikes of pain were taking their toll on his mind. They were also making him more determined to kill her. His strikes came faster and faster, ignoring the pain. The centaur was slowly growing weaker.

It wasn't an easy battle, but Jack held a comfortable advantage.

"Why don't you fall?" she screamed.

"Because I don't want to!" Jack retorted, punching her even deeper into the sky. Finally, she made a mistake. Her spear went too wide. Jack angled his punch straight into it, pushing it away, then pivoted midair and prepared to plant a massive fist into her gut.

Got you.

Suddenly, a feeling of wrongness assaulted him. He abandoned his attack and teleported away just in time to see a large green column fall through his previous position. If he hadn't dodged, he would have been smashed by it.

No. It's not a column!

He turned his gaze to the sky. What had originally seemed like a column was now clearly a thick vine stretching down from the clouds above. Jack remained frozen until he realized what was going on.

"Who's there?" he roared. "Show yourself!"

At least the centaur woman looked equally confused.

A man slowly descended through the clouds. His heavy-set body was made of bark, he only wore a pair of brown shorts, and one of his arms had transformed into the long, thick vine that had almost speared Jack.

Treant, Level 197
Faction: Triple Helix (C-Grade)

Jack stared at the man, trying to remember where he knew him from. "Torm?" This was the easy-going guy who'd spotted Jack's disguise and explained some things about this planet.

"Jack Rust," the treant replied with a satisfied grin. "And here I thought I'd lost you. You were smart to skip town, and even smarter to miss your appointed teleportation. I almost got you at that cratered mountain, too. Thank the System you took the initiative to start fighting again."

"Who the hell are you?" Jack asked, still confused.

Torm laughed. "I knew it! Only a recently Integrated fool could travel the galaxy without knowing about the premier bounty hunting faction: the Triple Helix." His grin settled into a professional stare. "It's the end of the line for you, Jack. Please surrender quietly. Your bounty is higher if captured alive."

CHAPTER SEVEN
FIGHTING LATE IMMORTALS

Brock danced with the Animal Kingdom guards. The Staff of Stone glided around him, its weight perfectly balanced as it tore into calves and elbows, heads and knees.

He wasn't too experienced in battle, but he possessed more than enough strength to make up for it. His body was covered in well-toned muscles. Every time he swung, people went flying. Their weapons couldn't reach him, and if they did, he would just clench his skin muscles to avoid any serious injuries.

"Brock Smash!" he shouted, bringing his staff down on a guard's helmet. He fell asleep.

"Get the monkey!" two other guards shouted, rushing for him.

Brock didn't even look their way. A bald, muscular woman and a lithe man appeared to block them—she wore iron gauntlets, while he wielded a polished saber.

"Leave our bro alone!" they shouted—Brock and Guitar Bro had already educated them on the proper terminology.

The two former prisoners clashed with the guards. All four of them were strong—at least as strong as Brock. He watched as they exchanged strikes but did not worry; they were his cage bros. Of course they would win.

After the cage bros had found a chest with their weapons, the camp had collapsed into a terrible battle. Brock was leading the charge, strong enough to defeat any weaklings and hold his ground against the stronger guards. Only a couple of them were decisively stronger than him, but there were similarly strong cage bros who had his back, allowing Brock to go bananas on the other guards.

Thanks to the cage bros' resentment and berserk fighting, they were slowly but surely winning. A harsh melody came from the back, where Guitar Bro was going nuts on his guitar, and a phantasmal gate to hell had appeared over his head, spewing black mist. There was even a large red hand emerging.

As for Brock, this was the first time in his life that he got into a proper large-scale battle—he found it very fun.

Jack observed his two opponents. One was the female centaur Warden of the Animal Kingdom, who was in bad shape from his previous beating but could still fight. The other was Torm, the treant bounty hunter who was still fresh as a daisy.

One was Level 210, the other Level 197. Jack was 132.

The centaur started laughing. "You played yourself, Jack Rust! Join me, bounty hunter, and you can get the entire bounty. I just want my superiors to know I helped."

The treant smiled. "Deal."

Jack's hopes of these two infighting were dashed. He couldn't retreat either, as Brock and Vanderdecken were still down there. All he could do was fight and hope for the best.

If worse came to worst, he could just use his Life Drop and hope nothing bad happened... though that would open an entirely new can of worms.

Jack readied himself. His purple aura flared to life, shrouding him in spectral flames formed of sheer willpower. His eyes narrowed. "Come!" he commanded, and the two immortals charged him.

The treant's limbs morphed into vines. The hand of bark that Jack had once shaken was now a gigantic vine, growing through the air to spear him. Two more awaited at the treant's legs, ready to assault him at the first opening.

The centaur charged ahead of the treant. She knew Jack couldn't destroy her in one blow, so she aimed to disorient him by flooding him with pain. A sadistic smile adorned her blood-covered face, and all four of her legs galloped through the air to reach him faster.

Jack considered his two opponents coldly. Since he was on the weaker end, he had to fight wildly. He clenched his fists.

"SUFFER!" the centaur screamed, thrusting her spear forward. A black aura shone on its tip. A vine came from behind her and above, seeking to impale Jack's torso. The treant was clearly experienced—if he'd gone for the head, Jack could have dodged the attack, but now he was forced to block.

Or take it.

Unfortunately, the attacks came in sync, and he couldn't deal with both of them at the same time. His punch struck the spear tip, sending it and its wielder flying away as the vine struck his chest, shallowly piercing into the skin. The Neutron Star Body, Jack's defensive skill, was strained to its limit.

He caught a flicker of surprise on the treant's face when the vine failed to reach his organs, but that was all he had time to see. The vine hadn't stopped growing. It accelerated, pushing Jack along as it sought to nail him into the ground. If that happened, he would be cleanly skewered.

He was falling at extreme speed. With no time to think, he grabbed the vine and pushed himself away from it, then flew sideways to barely escape its trajectory. The vine kept going. A fraction of a second later, it crashed into the ground, embedding itself deep inside the rock.

The power of that vine was no joke.

The centaur was on him again. With a wailing sound that upset his heart and shook his mind, she threw her spear at him. It fell like a dark comet. Jack twirled, barely dodging the attack, but even being in the vicinity of that spear tip made him feel like he was burned alive. He howled in pain.

"Suffer!" the centaur cried out again, licking the blood from her lips. "Oh, I'll enjoy this!"

Jack's fury began to rise. This woman wasn't causing him any fear—only an urge to fight back. Two vines were crashing down from the sky, one coming from the left and one from the right—he ignored them.

"You think you're scary?" he asked the centaur. "Let me show you real terror."

He stepped through space to appear behind her. The vines tore through empty air where he used to stand, and it took the centaur a moment to realize what happened.

"Teleportation!" the treant's shocked voice came from higher up in the sky, but Jack was completely focused on his soon-to-be victim. He didn't strike out right away. Rather, he invested all of his focus into activating Brutalizing Aura, the skill of terror he inherited from his previous Class, Fiend of the Iron Fist.

The air around him was dyed the color of blood. Jack's hair fluttered in the wind as his form was covered in darkness, leaving only his eyes shining red. Tendrils of shadow reached down to lay on the centaur, who tried to fight them off, except they were incorporeal.

Jack channeled his twin understanding of Power and Weakness. With the power gap between them, he was in absolute control of her fate. But he wouldn't just kill her—he would brutalize her. She would die in gore and iron.

And there was nothing she could do about it.

The centaur's Dao of Pain rose to shield her soul. Unfortunately, not only was it weaker than Jack's Dao, it was the completely wrong Dao to defend against this kind of attack. Its resistances melted under the pressure of Jack's Brutalizing Aura, and all it achieved was to enhance the pain of her eventual defeat.

The centaur's Dao Domain had been activated at some point. So had Jack's. It crushed down on her, and as her resolve wavered, her domain shattered, crushed under the iron grip of the Fist. The centaur was left holding her head in her hands and wailing for mercy.

Jack wasn't an idiot to let an enemy go—much less an enemy with such a twisted Dao.

He punched her in the face and nailed her into the ground far below, cracking the rocks and forming a crater. Without the protection of her

Dao, her defenses had fallen—her head now lay broken in the center of the crater, dead beyond the shadow of a doubt.

Level-up! You have reached Level 133.
Level-up! You have reached Level 134.
Level-up! You have reached Level 135.
Level-up! You have reached Level 136.

Jack turned to regard the treant, panting but wrathful. “So, you want my head,” he said darkly. “Come take it, if you dare.”

The treant didn’t dare, his gaze filled with apprehension, scanning the area widely in search of something he could use. Unfortunately, there was nothing—and, given the teleportation skill that Jack just exhibited, he couldn’t escape either.

“Let’s forget about this,” he tried. “I only scratched your skin. Let bygones be bygones, and I can offer you—”

Jack’s laughter interrupted him. “When you thought I was weak, you didn’t hesitate to attack me and even glower about it. Now that you can no longer bully me, you want to just leave like nothing happened? As if! No, Torm, you started this fight. You will finish it.”

Torm gritted his teeth. Escape was not an option, as he clearly didn’t specialize in speed, and neither was negotiation. All he could do was fight.

“Don’t force my hand!” he roared, pulling out a glowing green vial from his pocket. One of his vines had turned back into an arm at some point. “I don’t want to use this here, but you will die if I do! This is your last chance! Let the matter drop!”

“Fuck you! If I don’t kill you today, I am no man!”

Torm was a decisive individual. Seeing that Jack wasn’t budging, he popped off the vial’s cork with his thumb and gulped it down. Instantly, he doubled over in pain. Green veins appeared under his bark-skin, pulsing like flames.

In the next moment, a green aura that almost seemed alive erupted from his body. It stretched for miles around. The miasmic clouds were dispersed, revealing a dark sky interspersed with stars. Torm hovered in the middle of it, staring down Jack with the might of a God. Green flames slithered out from under his skin, like his innards were on fire, but the intense power he radiated was an entire tier higher than it used to be.

"You made me do this!" he shouted. "Now, die!"

The air exploded in rings as Torm dove, reaching Jack in an instant. His domain shrouded them both. Jack's domain rose to resist, but it was suppressed to a five-foot radius around his body, like someone trying to punch a forest wildfire and having to retreat.

Torm's charge carried a desperate air about it. He was like a cornered animal—he had nothing to lose. His newly-gained power was quickly evaporating; by the time he reached Jack, only ninety percent remained. It was clear that whatever he used was really burning his body from the inside.

That didn't make his attack any less terrifying. In the instant before Torm arrived, Jack realized that maybe he should have activated his Life Drop already, but it was too late. There was no way he could dodge in time. He tried using Space Walk, but even space was locked down by the other man's domain, making his skill useless.

The treant was upon him. Both arms stretched into vines, which crashed down like columns from the sky. Torm howled.

Jack set his jaw. If there was no way out, he could only go forward. A purple aura flared in the green. It couldn't absorb the sounds and colors, but Jack poured all his remaining power into it, birthing a purple sun that could momentarily rival the real one in brightness. This punch was so strong that Jack could barely control it—the most powerful strike he'd ever unleashed.

He shot it forth. His punch reaching tremendous speeds, meeting the vines at the very apex of its trajectory. A purple tail blossomed behind it, showering the world with stars.

"VINE DESCENT!" Torm shouted.

"METEOR PUNCH!"

The point of impact exploded. Green and purple flames spread across the sky, filling it for miles in all directions. Jack's face and chest were burned from the shockwave. All bones in his arm cracked. His fist was completely mangled. The vines broke and burned away, revealing a stunned Torm who was launched away from the explosion and into the sky, spitting out a long line of green blood.

A booming sound followed, spreading across the sky as a visible shockwave, tearing into the rock below and carving it like a scythe. Jack remained anchored in the center of the explosion, crossing his arms before his head to protect himself. The pain was tremendous, both from his ruined arm, as well as his burnt face and chest.

But he remained, while Torm was gone. He'd won the exchange. The battle, too. With the rate of burning in Torm's body, there was no way he was up for another round, even if he wasn't dead already—which he probably was.

Level-up! You have reached Level 137.
Level-up! You have reached Level 138.
Level-up! You have reached Level 139.

Scratch that—he was definitely dead.

Jack had fought two high-level immortals and won. The power he exhibited, the victory he achieved... He raised his other fist into the air and roared in triumph.

Gone were the days of his weakness. Now, he was strong enough to take on the world and win. He was strong enough to go to war.

He was a true immortal.

Let the hearts of his enemies swim in fear, because he was coming for them, and there was nothing they could do about it.

CHAPTER EIGHT
TYING UP LOOSE ENDS

THE ROUND-UP WAS EASY.

After the three wardens were defeated, including the late D-Grade centaur, the remaining guards surrendered. Their numbers had already been halved by Brock and the prisoners, anyway.

Brock's greatest injury from the fight was a deep purple bruise on his shoulder, caused by a guard's mace. That guard survived the battle, only to receive a long, hard glare from Jack, which probably convinced him to start a more peaceful life in another part of the galaxy, if he made it out of here alive.

There was also a group of low D-Grade officials from the Exploding Sun who came to see what was going on. Seeing that the battle was already over, they left.

That left Jack, Brock, the prisoners, and the guards.

"I have many questions," Jack said after rounding everyone up, "and I hope you will all answer them."

"Yes, sir!" the guards and prisoners replied, each struggling to seem more helpful than the previous person.

"First of all, what are you doing here?"

A cacophony of voices rammed into his ears as everyone started speaking together.

"Silence!" Jack ordered. Everyone shut up. "You, with the red sword. Step forward and explain what is going on."

"Yes, siiir."

The person he'd pointed to was the only surviving peak E-Grade guard of the Animal Kingdom. He resembled a bipedal goat and spoke with a slight bleating.

Goatee, Level 124 (E-Grade)
Faction: Animal Kingdom (B-Grade)

"The Animal Kingdom has a looot of enemies. We were tasked with traveling to the far side of the Exploding Sun constellation to pick up a captured group of criminals, then deliver them to Hell. We were currently on our way back."

"And what have these criminals done?"

The goat-man hesitated. "They were space pirates in our constellation, sir."

"Bullshit!" shouted one of the former prisoners, a heavily muscled woman with iron gauntlets. "With all due respect, sir, we are not pirates. We're revolutionaries. We only attacked ships of the Animal Kingdom. Down with their tyranny! Down with their oppression! We are the Iron Bodies, and we will die saving the constellation!"

The rest of the former prisoners, with the exception of Vanderdecken, cheered.

Jack massaged the ridge of his nose. "Are you also part of their crew, Vanderdecken?"

"Uh, no," the man replied. "The Animal Kingdom just randomly found me in this constellation, and they picked me up after seeing my planet of origin."

"Then, what were you doing here?"

Vanderdecken smiled widely. "I joined a talent show on planet Elzin!" he replied proudly, then raised three fingers. "I even got third place, dude!"

Jack closed his eyes, took a deep breath, then reopened them. "That's great. I'm happy for you."

"I know, right? I'm gonna be a rockstar!"

“But... the Dao of Metal...”

“It’s a figure of speech, dude.” He raised both his pinkies and index fingers. “I will have my concerts, but I remain loyal to THE DEVIL!” He also struck a chord on his guitar to emphasize his words.

The space revolutionaries looked at him oddly. “You can join us if you want,” said their leader.

“I appreciate the offer, but no thanks. I am loyal to THE—”

“We get it, we get it, Vanderdecken,” Jack interrupted him before this turned into an impromptu concert. He turned back to the goatee guard—who happened to also sport the appropriate facial hair. “Is what they’re saying true? Did they only attack Animal Kingdom starships?”

“We don’t have all the data, sir...” the guard said. After receiving Jack’s glare, he quickly added, “but it is possible.”

“Okay. Then, here’s what we’re going to do.”

Jack paused there to make sure he was making the right call. On one hand, the Animal Kingdom was his enemy. On the other, these guards were his prisoners of war now. He couldn’t just kill them off—be it in accordance with the Star Pact or the Geneva Convention.

“Space revolutionaries,” he said. “I am also an enemy of the Animal Kingdom. I respect your actions. You can take your stuff and go be free, or revolutionaries again, or whatever you prefer.”

“Thank you, sir.” Their leader, the iron-gauntleted woman, stepped forward and placed both hands over her heart. “You saved our lives. We will engrave this kindness in our hearts and use it to hit the space tyrants even harder.”

“It was just in passing. Don’t worry about it.”

The woman nodded respectfully and stepped back in line.

“Guards,” Jack continued, “you are my prisoners of war, so I cannot just kill you off. At the same time, you seriously mistreated your prisoners before, so I consider you to have committed war crimes. You will wear the System-limiting manacles and be in the custody of the revolutionaries, who will decide your punishment in accordance with morality and galactic law.”

The guards went a shade paler, while the revolutionaries wore devious smiles. “However.” Jack stared strictly at the revolutionaries. “I expect you to treat these people with respect and humanity—or whatever the multi-species equivalent is called. You may imprison or execute them if you deem it proper, but I don't want any torture, inhumane conditions, or injustice because of your deeply-rooted hatred against their faction. You will not commit the same crimes they did. You will be just. Am I clear?"

"Yes, sir," the woman replied, looking down.

"I need your word, leader of the revolutionaries," Jack told her seriously. "Promise me, on your honor, that you will allow no mistreatment of these people."

She raised her eyes to him. "On my honor, I will not allow any mistreatment of these people. I will treat and punish them fairly. That, I swear."

Jack held her stare for a moment before she looked away. "Good," he said. The guards were extremely relieved at this exchange, while the revolutionaries didn't seem to care overly much. "That concludes my business here. I will also loot the bodies of the four D-Grades I killed, as well as their tent and storage spaces. Everything else is yours."

"Yes, sir," the iron-gauntleted woman replied, her gaze filled with admiration. Apparently, she approved of Jack's handling of the situation, and was even impressed by it.

"Good," Jack said again, giving everyone a final look to make sure he wasn't forgetting anything.

"What about me, Ja—sir?" Vanderdecken asked.

"You're coming with me. We still have some things to talk about."

"Oh, score!"

The entire time, Brock had stood by Jack's side, nodding in approval and emphasizing his big bro's decisions with appropriately hard stares.

Unfortunately, the three wardens and the bounty hunter weren't carrying anything particularly valuable. Jack only found a shrunken starship—many of them possessed this feature, apparently—which he gifted to Vanderdecken. He also found three emerald credit cards. With Brock donating the fourth—he'd pocketed it at some point during the battle—Jack now had a wealth totaling to 80,560,011 credits, sixty million of which came from Torm the bounty hunter.

Their generous donation brought him very close to the hundred million mark, which he needed to buy the telepathy function for his faction. That would allow him to communicate with the professor and find out what was going on in his absence, as well as coordinate his efforts with theirs.

In the meantime, he had Vanderdecken.

The two of them sat in Jack's starship, while Brock flew them across the wasteland towards the teleportation town.

"Dude... What the hell have you been up to?" Vanderdecken asked, looking around the starship in wonder. "You're an immortal now, and you have your own starship... It is so much faster than the ones on Earth, too!"

Jack smiled. "It's a long story, my friend."

"I have time."

Jack laughed. "Fine." He then proceeded to summarily narrate his adventures, leaving out all sensitive subjects. By the end of it, the bard's eyes were full of stars.

"You conquered Trial Planet!" he asked, mouth gaping. "That's... sensational!"

"It is, so use that knowledge wisely. Tell it to the professor and let her distribute it as she sees fit."

"You got it, dude."

"Now, tell me about Earth," Jack asked, leaning forward, suddenly full of worry. "What is going on back there?"

And Vanderdecken spoke. He told Jack about the cold world war that ensued after the tournament, where the Bare Fist Brotherhood and Flame River allied against the Ice Peak. About the battles for dungeons, the conflicts and subterfuge, the ambushes, the infiltrations, the war of misinformation conducted by both sides. How the planet was divided, only waiting for a spark before erupting into all-out war.

Jack's face was growing darker by the minute.

"So, Alexander didn't sit still..." he said. "I'm glad that the professor and Vivi are okay, but this cannot go on. Maybe I should head back and squash the Ice Peak."

"No!" Vanderdecken raised his hand. "You can't do that! If you do, the Planetary Overseer will intervene and kill us all!"

"Why? I'm a native. I can do whatever I like on the planet."

"You're an immortal now, dude! If you show up on Earth and start attacking people, the Animal Kingdom will definitely twist that into an excuse to ignore the grace period and fight back. They've been trying to do that for a while now—actually, the alliance is constantly trying to avoid actions that can be interpreted as "threatening the planet's population," which would let the overseer intervene."

Jack frowned. "So what? I can't return to my own planet?"

"Not unless you're ready to fight the Kingdom. Come on, dude. I know this is hard, but you seem to be doing fine out here. Let us fight our own battle."

Jack snorted. "Hmph. I wouldn't put you guys at risk, you know that. It's just frustrating."

"Yeah, I understand."

"Then again... it doesn't change much, does it? My plan remains as is. Grow as strong as possible, then return to fight the overseer before the grace period is up. Even if my presence on the planet lets them break the rules, we'll destroy all the teleporters beforehand so she has no backup, and then I'll kick her ass."

"Kick her ass? The overseer's ass? But that's impossible!"

"I can fight a late D-Grade now, and there's eight months remaining. Maybe it's possible."

"I... I guess so, dude. I mean, the difference between a late D-Grade and a middle C-Grade can't be that large, right?"

Jack thought back to the large gap in power between the E and D-Grades, he didn't comment.

By now, they'd reached the teleporter town, where Vanderdecken could get his buzzer to start the trip back. Jack also transferred him a hundred thousand credits; enough to cover all teleportation fees from here to Earth ten times over.

"This is where our paths diverge, Vanderdecken. I'll be out of town for a bit, but you should be fine here. There are plenty of E-Grades around," Jack said after they exited the teleportation building. "Send my greetings to everyone on Earth, okay? And let them know to hang on. I *will* be back before the grace period is up, and I *will* conquer Earth for us. Even if not with my own strength, I'll definitely find a way. Okay?"

The man's eyes shimmered with unformed tears. "You got it, dude!" he said, rushing in for a hug. "Go become great!"

"I will, Vanderdecken," Jack replied, holding the other's back. "I will."

As he watched the bard walk away, the weight of Jack's entire planet had never been heavier on his shoulders. Only now did he truly feel the responsibility he bore, as well as how far away from home he was.

He was lost in space, all alone.

Brock grabbed his shoulder. Jack smiled at the sight of the short brorilla, who barely reached Jack's chest. "Right," he said. "I'm not alone. I never will be, because I have my brother."

Brock nodded, smiling. "Bro."

"Bro."

They settled down in a distant mountain range, where Jack could cultivate and test his powers as needed. Every time he did, they changed locations, just in case there were more bounty hunters on the loose.

He also allocated his new status points. He had leveled up seven times after defeating the centaur Warden and Torm. Since every level in the D-Grade gave ten stat points—compared to two in the F-Grade and five in the E-Grade—this amounted to seventy points, plus the ten from the level he'd received cultivating—eighty points in all.

Once upon a time, it would have been an extraordinary amount. Now, it was just an everyday occurrence.

Still maintaining the 8-1-1 distribution that Master Shol had suggested, Jack put all the points into Physical. He then admired his status.

Name: Jack Rust
Species: Human, Earth-387
Faction: Bare Fist Brotherhood (D)
Grade: D
Class: Cosmic Fist (King)
Level: 139

Strength: 790
Dexterity: 745

Constitution: 765
Mental: 120
Will: 190

Killing things is still much faster than cultivating, huh...

One battle had saved him weeks, if not months of effort. He needed that to reach his goal. All he feared was the path it signified...

War, he thought, gaze hardening. To save my planet... the Animal Kingdom must suffer. And so they will.

But first, he had to visit the Exploding Sun. As much as he wanted to defeat the Planetary Overseer with his own power, he wasn't selfish enough to ignore more reliable ways of saving Earth.

Plus, he looked forward to meeting Master Shol again.

I wonder if he still qualifies to be my master, Jack thought, smirking. We're in the same Grade now. How will he react when he sees that? Hehe.

After cultivating for a day and gaining no more levels, the buzzer finally began to glow and hum. Jack and Brock returned to the teleportation town and waited in line. An hour later, it was their turn to stand before the teleporter.

"Name, faction, and destination," the guard said, while a low D-Grade stared at Jack discreetly from the side.

"Jack Rust. Bare Fist Brotherhood. Exploding Sun headquarters."

The guard and the D-Grade exchanged a subtle look. Both nodded. "The teleportation fee is ten thousand credits per person, please." The guard extended a credit card.

Jack raised a brow at the sizeable fee. He touched his card to the guard's, willed the twenty thousand transfer, and stepped in the teleporter with Brock.

Due to some function of the teleporter, only a single destination appeared before Jack's eyes: Field Nebula.

What a name, he thought, grinning, and chose it. Space lurched under his feet—and, a few moments later, he finally arrived at the Exploding Sun.

CHAPTER NINE

FIELD NEBULA

The teleportation was punctuated by solar gasses, colors, comets, and shimmering stars... And when it was over, nothing changed.

Jack and Brock stepped out of the teleporter and looked around.

There was no sky. As one looked up, their gaze met a sight that looked like a dream. Instead of the darkness of space, purple and orange gasses filled the distance, glittering with stars. These gasses were present in all directions, surrounding the planet from an incalculable distance away.

It was like being wrapped in a gassy, colorful bubble.

Jack looked down. They were standing on a large rock—a comet, maybe? A moon? A dome stretched around them, transparent if not for the shimmering of air, creating a habitable environment only a mile in diameter. Inside it was the teleporter, where they currently stood, as well as what resembled a small town made of slick, modern houses.

Three planets were also visible. They surrounded this place equidistantly, slowly revolving around it like it was their sun, and they weren't too distant—maybe as far away as the moon was from Earth. Two of them were covered by lush greenery and dark blue seas—Jack could even see starships flying to and from each planet, swarming them like bees to honey. As for the third planet, it was devoid of starships and surrounded by clouds, which prevented Jack from inspecting it properly.

"What is this place?" he wondered, looking around with mouth agape.

"Welcome to Field Nebula," a woman's voice came from behind them. She wore long, yellow robes bearing an image of an exploding sun, her skin was tanned, her hair dark and long, and her eyes piercing in their brownness.

Human (Earth-44), Level 130
Faction: Exploding Sun (B-Grade)

"Field Nebula," Jack repeated the name, tasting it. His eyes flashed. "Wait! Do you mean we're inside an actual nebula?"

The woman smiled with amusement. "Indeed. Surrounding us is the Bow Nebula, the birthplace of stars. And the place under your feet is the Center Moon, part of the capital of the Exploding Sun faction."

"You guys live inside a nebula!"

"We do."

Jack knew what nebulas were—the basics, at least. If he remembered correctly, when stars died, they formed titanic gas clouds. These clouds gravitated toward each other and formed even larger gas clouds called nebulas. Inside these nebulas, the most condensed gas clouds combined due to gravity, forming large gas spheres that, due to nuclear fusion reactions, began to burn and unleash tremendous amounts of energy.

These spheres were called stars. Therefore, nebulas were the birthplace of stars, formed and maintained by the death of older stars, like a phoenix rising from its ashes.

Jack knew those from Earth science classes. However, he had never heard of planets existing inside nebulas, let alone inhabitable environments.

"Sorry," he said to excuse his surprise, "I just didn't expect this at all."

"Why not?" the woman replied, laughing. "Nebulas are made of gasses, but they also contain all sorts of space rocks. Some of them are planets, formerly belonging to a solar system long gone. If such a planet is stable, terraforming it is not too difficult."

"Are there more places like this?"

"No." Her face shone with pride. "Field Nebula is the only widely-inhabited, intra-nebulaic space in the galaxy. Its history is quite intriguing... but, if you don't mind, perhaps it could wait until after we settle the details of your arrival?"

Jack coughed in his hand. In his excitement, he'd completely forgotten that he'd just teleported to the capital of a B-Grade faction. Obviously, there was a procedure to be followed.

"My apologies. I am Jack Rust, here to visit my master, Shol. He is a deacon of the Exploding Sun."

"I am Brock," said Brock.

"I also have this." Jack reached inside his pocket and removed the plaque that Lady Priya had given him back in Trial Planet—it was a bronze disk with the Exploding Sun insignia carved on it, and it was supposed to act as a guarantee of his identity here.

The woman's eyes widened when she saw the disk. "May I?" she asked. Jack handed it over, and she stared at it, ascertaining its authenticity. "It's an honor to assist you, sir," she said, her attitude instantly turning deferential. She handed him back the plaque. "I will contact Deacon Shol immediately. Would you mind waiting in our guest lounge for now?"

"Of course. It would be our pleasure."

The woman led them to a building next to the teleporter. Inside was a luxurious garden complete with a refreshing fountain, short trees, birds, and even a small river with a wooden bridge crossing over it. There were comfy chairs placed throughout the carefully trimmed garden paths, so any guest could sit wherever they preferred to enjoy this place.

"I'll be with you shortly, sirs," the woman said. "Please wait inside the garden."

"Of course."

She took off, leaving Jack and Brock alone. She'd called this a guest lounge, but there was nobody else here—maybe it was only for important guests?

"Did we just fly business class, Brock?" Jack asked.

Brock didn't get the joke, obviously, but he was too busy admiring the garden anyway. This place reminded Jack of something he would only find in a five-star hotel on Earth.

"Gardens like this, terraformed planets inside a nebula, and D-Grades as attendants..." He sighed. "Why do I get the feeling we just dove in the deep, Brock?"

"Yes."

"Yes, indeed."

Time passed. Jack spent it watching the sky—or rather, the space above. Starships and immortals were constantly flying overhead, shooting from one planet to the other, while the nebula shone in the background. Even though there was no sun illuminating this place, the nebula's brightness created a similar effect.

Brock spent his time admiring some fish in the river.

An hour later the door to the garden opened again. Jack glanced over, expecting to see the D-Grade attendant.

Instead, there was a bald man in monk robes and a yellow cape. His eyes were glittering like the nebula above, while his smile stretched from ear to ear. "Jack!" he exclaimed.

Jack's face mirrored that wide smile—his first genuine one in a while. "Master Shol!"

Old Man Spirit had teleported Jack all the way from Trial Planet to the fringes of the Animal Kingdom constellation, from where he'd made his way to Field Nebula.

Others, however, had it easier.

Swoosh.

With a warp of space, Nauja appeared on a rock. The very first thing she did was look up, and her face beamed with excitement.

"I'm here!" she shouted. "I'm out of Trial Planet! I can see space! The stars, the sun! Look, Salin, it's—Salin?"

She looked around. She stood alone on a rock, in a small bubble of air on the ruined surface of Trial Planet. Her excitement was doused. She struggled to form words. "But..."

With another warp of space, Salin appeared at her side. "Hey," he said.

"Salin! What happened?"

"Sorry, I got lost."

"Wh—In the teleportation?"

"Yeah." She looked him dead in the eye. He grinned. "Happens to the best of us."

"You know that doesn't make sense, right? We touched the pedestal at the same time. We should have teleported together. And you can't get lost mid-teleportation."

"Sheesh. And here I was looking forward to your first time in space."

"Oh!" Her eyes widened. "Right! I'm in space, Salin, look! There's the stars! And the twin satellites! And that over there is a sun! Oh, Salin, this is so beautiful! So large, too!" She made a circle around herself, admiring the endless expanse of space. "How can anything be so big!"

He opened his mouth to make another joke, but at the last moment, he held it in. His gaze mellowed. "It really is your first time outside..."

"Of course it is. Why, did you think I was lying?"

"No. It's just..." He shook his head. "Nevermind. I'm glad you like it."

"Like it? I love it!"

Nauja felt like a child. She was so full of wonder, and excitement, and yearning to see the world. She could adventure now. She could grow strong, and meet new people, new civilizations, witness all sorts of magnificent sights. She'd heard stories of spinning stars and holes darker than black, of white planets and space monsters patrolling the depths of space.

She would see it all. Her chest was already tingling. Thinking to that point, she looked down. "I'm not dressed weirdly, am I?" she asked. Her fur clothing was fine in her ring, but maybe the people of the galaxy dressed otherwise?

"I think you're lovely," Salin replied, bringing back her smile.

"Great! I think so too. Oh, what's that? That star which looks like it's flying our way?"

"It *is* flying our way, but it isn't a star. It's a starship."

Her mouth widened. The needle-shaped metal contraption grew in her sight until, only seconds later, it landed right before her. It was soundless.

Salin pulled her arm and leaned close to her ear. “They’re from the Hand of God,” he whispered as the starship doors slid open. “Remember; after waiting for a month, we saw no sign of Jack and decided to leave. Brock is still in Garden Ring. Okay?”

“Hmph. I remember, of course,” she replied.

“Good.” Salin straightened his hair. His sharp canines glittered in the light, slightly longer than a human’s would be. “Then, it’s time to turn traitor.”

“Really?”

“I told you, didn’t I? I’m a free man now. Fuck the Animal Kingdom. Let’s go to the Exploding Sun, where that knight said Jack would meet us.”

“Right.”

They’d been planning to visit Earth, too, but it could wait. Not only was it dangerous, Nauja technically couldn’t go, as she was not a local.

Two women descended from the starship. Each had white hair and skin pale as a sheet, but they were both immortals. Nauja simply accepted that fact, while Salin raised a brow.

“Names and affiliations, please,” they ordered. “And display your ring conqueror titles, if you would.”

They did, both showing off their Seventh Ring Conqueror achievement.

“Nauja,” she said. “Unaffiliated.”

“Gan Salin. Also unaffiliated.”

They raised a brow at Salin. “Your System inspection says you are part of the Animal Kingdom?”

“Oh, whoops. I knew I’d forgotten something.” He laughed. “System, get me out of the Animal Kingdom faction, please.” A moment later, he added, “Yes, I’m sure.”

Nauja scanned him.

Canine (Earth-387), Level 79

Faction: -

Title: Seventh Ring Conqueror

The two women raised their brows at Salin but did not comment. So did Nauja.

There was great significance in leaving one's faction. Salin had already betrayed the Animal Kingdom multiple times, but they wouldn't really care about that, so long as he was strong enough. Now that he left the faction, however... Rejoining would be a major issue.

"I know what you're thinking," he said with a smile, making her look away, "but it will be fine. I will never go back."

"If you say so... I'm glad to hear that."

They smiled at each other. One of the two women coughed in her hand, then asked, "We will now transfer you to the satellite, where you will be deep-scanned and questioned in accordance with Hand of God policy. After that, you will be free to use our major teleporters to reach any constellation of your liking. Could you please inform us of your next teleportation destination?"

Salin nodded. "Field Nebula. We have an appointment."

CHAPTER TEN
THE EXPLODING SUN FACTION

JACK LOOKED OUT OF THE WINDOW. A PLANET DOMINATED HIS VIEW, COVERED IN stripes of green and blue, while purple-orange gasses hung in the background, shimmering with a thousand newborn stars.

"This place is amazing," he said.

"Of course it is," Master Shol replied proudly. "It's my faction!"

The man was reclining on a sleek, white chair that did not at all match his monk-like attire. A yellow cape was draped over his shoulders, simple leather shoes covered his feet, and the smile refused to leave his face. His entire body, however, was covered in dense muscles that no clothes could ever hide.

Brock, meanwhile, was snoring on another chair. He couldn't sleep well on Derion and was making up for it now.

"I have to admit, master," Jack said, "you look much more intimidating when you are not a ghost."

"Who wouldn't? And I told you to stop calling me that. Master this and master that. Bah. We're of the same Grade now—just call me big brother."

Jack couldn't keep the wry smile off his lips. He had never felt more accomplished. "Alright, brother Shol."

"Big brother."

"That's what I said."

"Hmm... I guess you did."

Both laughed. Jack inspected mas—Shol, again, unable to believe he'd finally caught up. It was this sort of thing that put all his adventures into context.

Human (Earth-44), Level 249
Faction: Exploding Sun (B-Grade)
Title: Fifth Ring Conqueror

Well, "caught up" was a bit of an exaggeration. Shol remained over a hundred levels ahead and a great deal stronger, but at least they were of the same Grade!

"It's incredible," Shol said. "The kid I mentored three months ago became an immortal already... If someone told me that before I saw it, I would have beaten them up for mocking me. And yet... Somehow, you did it." He shook his head, strong eyes glued on Jack. "Well done, kid. Well done."

"Please. You don't need to call me kid anymore—just Jack will suffice."

Shol kept his smile down, but how could he hide it from Jack? "I suppose so. I look forward to hearing about your adventures, Jack, but let's wait until we meet my master. No sense in having you repeat everything."

"Can you tell me about this place in the meantime?" Jack asked, turning back to the window. "It's unreal."

Shol laughed. "What do you want to know?"

"Everything. How does the Exploding Sun work? Why are you here? Why do you have three planets?"

"Let me give you a basic rundown of our faction." Shol stood, walking to the window beside Jack. He pointed to the nearest planet. "Field Nebula is the capital of the Exploding Sun constellation and faction. It is made up of three planets. The one we're heading toward is the inner planet; it's where the elders, enforcers, deacons, and inner faction disciples reside."

"Inner disciples?"

"Right." Seeing the confusion on Jack's face, Shol explained further. "Most factions divide their disciples into inner and outer ones, with the inner disciples being superior in status. In the Exploding Sun, like all B-Grade factions, outer disciples are those who are in either the F or E-Grade. D-Grade cultivators are inner disciples. Technically, I am one too, though I also possess the title of deacon, which holds higher seniority."

"Which means this planet is inhabited exclusively by immortals?"

"Pretty much."

Jack gazed back at the window, at the entire planet they were heading toward. Even from this distance, he could make out towns and structures.

"Just how many immortals do you have?" he couldn't help but wonder. All around the galaxy, D-Grades were considered apex existences. Every one of them Jack had met so far was revered and respected. Only one out of every hundred thousand cultivators became an immortal. On the fringe planets of the constellation, they could command an entire continent, even an entire planet.

Here, they were merely disciples. Even the attendant who'd welcomed them before was a D-Grade.

Shol laughed—a deep, pleasant, honest sound. "I see your surprise. But you must understand that the B-Grade factions are completely different existences from the outside world. D-Grade immortals are nothing here—the inner planet alone holds twenty thousand of them, with even more spread around the constellation."

"Twenty thousand immortals!"

"Well, roughly. Could be nineteen."

Jack struggled to wrap his head around this. It felt like he'd just surfaced into a much vaster world than the one he knew.

It had to be said that, by pre-System Earth standards, even the weakest immortal could be called a God. And this inner planet had twenty thousand of them...

"Cheer up, Jack." Shol clapped his shoulder, laughing. "You're one of us now. Having more immortals is a good thing! It means you have plenty of competition to help you grow."

"But... Twenty thousand immortals?"

"We have hundreds of C-Grades, as well."

"Hundreds of—" Jack stammered, feeling the need to sit down. His entire planet was hounded by a single C-Grade, who towered over him like an impossible mountain. Everything Jack did was to have even the slimmest hope against her.

Yet the Exploding Sun housed hundreds of C-Grades. Tens of thousands of D-Grades. And at least a few B-Grades, who were in an entirely different realm...

"Brother Shol," he said, "I think I'm slightly out of my depth here."

It wasn't a statement Jack would make lightly, but when faced with armies of gods, there was a limit to the grandeur one man could withstand.

"Oh, don't be a wuss. You'll get used to it," Shol gleefully chided him. "If all goes well, you will soon become an inner disciple here, too. You'll get the chance to meet and practice against the most capable cultivators this constellation has to offer—and, most importantly, you'll get one of these nice yellow capes."

Jack scowled. "It is a nice cape. But you have hundreds of C-Grades, and you were so stingy that you couldn't help me beat one of them to save Earth?"

"The Animal Kingdom is similarly powerful to us, if significantly uglier. It's not about one C-Grade—it's about the relationship between two colossal factions."

"Yes, of course, I understand..." Jack replied weakly, taking a seat on Shol's chair. "So. Infinite immortals. Got it. What else?"

Shol gestured to the window. "As I was saying, that's the inner planet. It holds our inner disciples, the deacons, and the elders, as well as all the C-Grades who are not elders, whom we call enforcers."

"Right."

"Now, if you look at the right-hand window"—he gestured to where another window showcased a planet that was basically one large landmass and one large ocean—"you can see the outer planet, where the outer disciples reside. Obviously, we can only accept a limited number of outer disciples, so the mortals there are the most talented and promising recruits of our constellation. Each of them is approximately as talented as the weaker Integration Tournament finalists of your planet."

Jack nodded numbly. The scale no longer shocked him. Maybe he would never again be surprised in his life.

"Finally," Shol's expression turned reverent as he pointed at the final planet, the one covered in gray clouds, "we have the core planet. Only three people live there—the Faction Leader and the two ancestors. Our three B-Grades."

At this, Jack couldn't help but raise a brow. Giving an entire planet to just three people sounded excessive.

"I know what you're thinking," Shol said, "but I assure you, our B-Grades are more than worth it. Each of them is an indispensable pillar of our faction. Without them, the nebula would collapse around us, and we would be conquered within a year."

"Conquered within a year? What about all those C-Grades?"

"If you think a C-Grade can hold a candle to a B-Grade, you are sorely mistaken," Shol said, smiling sadly. "Let alone us weaklings at the D-Grade. Now, that's enough chatting. We have arrived."

They had been continuously approaching the inner planet. By now, it was so large that it completely filled the window, and Jack could easily make out the mountain ridges and lakes on its surface.

The starship descended through the sky, unbothered by the friction and heat of the air, to approach a tall mountain that stood alone in the middle of a valley. A sprawling estate covered its peak. Hanging gardens, tall buildings, snaking corridors, and all sorts of people running around.

Most importantly, people were flying, as were animals. Magic was everywhere, and the Dao was so thick that Jack could almost smell it.

"Wow," he said. "Is this where the inner disciples live?"

"Of course not!" Shol laughed. "This is just my master's house."

"This entire thing?"

"That's right."

Jack did a double take. No matter how he looked at it, this was a town on top of a mountain. Maybe not a big town, but definitely not one person's house, either.

"Everyone you see is either a servant, a disciple, or someone else's family," Shol explained. "This entire estate belongs to my master."

Jack struggled to believe this. "Your faction is a bit extravagant."

"We only have twenty-one elders," Shol replied proudly. "They get the best we can offer. One mountaintop is nothing—amongst elders, my master is considered quite modest."

"...If this is all one massive joke, I will not laugh."

"You would. But is not a joke. This is the real world, Jack; your world. You're a big boy now." Shol smiled. "And you'll get used to it."

Jack shook his head. When faced with such grandeur and extravagance, what could he even say? That his legs were jelly? That his entire worldview was challenged?

The starship landed gently on a plaza designed expressly for this purpose, and a score of servants ran over to welcome them. Jack expected them to be overly subservient, and himself to tell them to take it easy.

Shol threw the door open. "Hello, my friends!" he shouted, laughing. "I'm back! Haha!"

"Welcome, deacon!" the servants replied, bowing lightly. Despite being servants, they didn't seem mistreated as Jack had feared—if anything, they were smiling at Shol like he was their friend.

Jack nodded with approval.

"This is Jack," Shol said, grabbing Jack by the shoulder and pulling him closer. "My brilliant disciple, who managed to become an immortal at only four months since being Integrated! He will be your big brother from now on, so treat him with respect."

"Uh... Hello, everyone," Jack greeted them. Brock poked his head out of the starship, inspected everyone, then smiled warmly.

"I am Brock," he said. "Brock big bro, too."

The servants looked at Jack like they'd seen a ghost—for multiple reasons. Hurriedly, a few of them nodded. "Welcome, brother Jack," they said, and Jack returned their greetings.

Leaving the starship to the servants, the three of them took off, following a stone-paved path to the manor at the very top of the mountain.

"What exactly is the deal with servants?" Jack asked carefully when they were alone. "It sounds a bit..."

Shol stopped to give him a good look. "That is a bit of a touchy subject. Servants are workers—they get paid a salary, given resources to cultivate, and are generally well taken care of. In return, they help keep the estate running and in good condition. However, not everyone treats them as nicely—even in our faction." His face darkened for a second. "In any case, I expect you to treat everyone in this estate with kindness, no matter their status. That is how my master behaves, that is how I behave, and that is how you will behave as well."

Jack raised his palms. "Of course. That's how I would act even if you didn't tell me."

"I know you would. I just had to make sure." Shol's face brightened again. He was about to say something, but his eyes were suddenly lost in the void. A moment later, he glowed. "Really? Of course, master! We'll be on our way!" He then turned to Jack. "Great news! An appointment was canceled, so my master has some free time right now. I will take you to meet her immediately."

"Weren't we already going to do that?"

Shol scowled. "Of course not. What do you think, that a kid like you can see an elder whenever you want? I was going to situate you in a room, where you would wait until she could spare a few minutes. It could have been days."

"Oh," Jack said weakly. "Then yeah, that is great news."

"Prepare yourself, Jack! You are about to meet one of the greatest people in the entire galaxy!"

Jack nodded somberly. Brock raised his hands and said, "Yay!"

CHAPTER ELEVEN
MASTER HUALI

As opulent as the mountain estate was, the manor itself was not. Sturdy yet simple wooden walls, a floor made of tanned planks, and red columns to break the monotony. There weren't many servants here, either. Jack spotted two playing checkers in a side garden, along with one reading a book while telekinetically controlling a broom.

Shol greeted them all—a greeting they smilingly returned. They were all immortals—ranging from level 140 to 230.

"The mansion is inhabited by master's students," Shol explained. "Not all of them, of course; just the ones worthy and willing."

"Are you worthy and willing?"

"Worthy, yes. Willing, not so much. I prefer privacy. I live in a small cottage on the outskirts of the estate."

"So, amongst your master's students, you are the hermit genius type."

Shol smiled. "Not a hermit; just genius."

"Are you really?"

"What do you think? That anyone is invited to participate in the Integrations of other constellations? I'm the top disciple here."

"For real? Wow."

Master Shol had always been a towering figure in Jack's mind. When he finally became an immortal, he thought they would be on similar footing—but they remained leagues apart.

The mansion may have been empty, but it possessed a different kind of beauty—a view. As it was built at the top of the mountain, there was nothing to block it. Every window gazed at a different spectacle—be it the hanging gardens of the estate, the lush valley at the base of the mountain, or the distant mountain ridge, where large birds flocked the sky.

Behind everything, the nebula's purple and orange gasses swam across the sky, glittering with the light of a million tiny stars.

"We're here," Shol said as they arrived before a double wooden door. "Prepare yourself. And make sure you're presentable."

Jack looked over his clothes. He still wore the loose purple robes that Old Man Spirit had gifted him. Below that, he was barefoot—most shoes would disintegrate under the immense strain of his movements.

"Um," he said, pointing down, "is that a problem?"

Shol glanced over, frowning. "Obviously. If you want to be eccentric, you have to earn it first. Come."

He led Jack through a corridor and into a storage room, where he quickly dug out a pair of form-fitting leather shoes from a closet full of them. Jack tried them on; they were two sizes too large.

"It's okay, just wear them," Shol urged him, practically pushing him back into the corridor. "We can't leave the master waiting."

"Why do I have to dress up, but Brock can come in with just his red shorts?"

"Because I am handsome," Brock said, lifting his chin.

Jack frowned. "I didn't teach you that word."

"Brock knows."

"Enough talking, let's go." Shol urged them back through the corridor and before the door, where they waited. As they did, Jack snuck a side glance at Shol, seeing him nervous for the first time. Not due to fear—it was more like the anxiety of introducing one's spouse to your parents.

Finally, after fifteen minutes of waiting, a calm voice resounded in their minds. "Come in."

Shol sprang forward, quickly yet calmly pushing the double door open. Beyond it was a room that resembled a mountain cottage. A fireplace occupied one corner, while two of the walls were made of glass, revealing an exquisite view. There was no sky on this planet—not really. Purple and orange gasses danced in the distant space, wrapping around each other and dying the world in their colors. It was like the entire planet had been built inside a colossal kaleidoscope.

And yet, there were people, animals, plants that lived a completely normal life. For most of them, this fantastic space was all they'd ever known. They had no concept of a sky, just like Nauja's tribe, but where the latter had stone ceilings, these ones had the canvas of the cosmos.

Jack only admired the beauty for a moment before turning to Shol's master. A heavy wooden desk sat at the back of the room, empty besides two orderly stacks of paper. A large, soft chair was behind it.

Shol's master was not by her desk.

She sat on an orange pillow in another corner of the room. Besides her pillow and herself, it was empty—but it was located right in the corner between the two glass walls, where the view was at its most magnificent. Cultivating there while gazing outside must have felt dreamy.

"Master," Shol said, bowing deeply.

"Master," Jack repeated, bowing too. He wasn't sure if that was the proper thing to call her, but he had no better ideas. As for Brock, he simply bowed—he knew how to say "handsome," but "master" was something he had yet to learn. Jack was just glad he hadn't called her "very big girl bro."

"Shol," the master said, smiling gently. Shol had revealed her name to Jack in the starship—it was Huali. "I hope you've been well. Is this young cultivator your only disciple? The one for whose sake you disobeyed my direct orders?"

Jack felt nervous. Back in the Integration Tournament, Shol's master had received an order from her faction's Grand Elder to stay away from Jack Rust. She had communicated that order to Shol, who promptly stashed it where the sun didn't shine.

Admittedly, this wasn't the first thing Jack expected to hear.

"He is, master," Shol replied calmly. He then smiled widely. "Impressive, isn't he?"

His master turned her gaze on Jack—and its olive intensity was such that he felt his soul pierced and his body unraveled. A small smile tugged at the corner of her lips. "He is. As expected from the top disciple of my top disciple."

Shol's master looked like an old yoga instructor. Orange robes covered her body, along with a blue cape over her shoulders. She was bronze-skinned and tanned, with laughter wrinkles on her face and olive green eyes that seemed to hold the world behind them. Her hair was white and straight, reaching just under her shoulders, while her body was slim and energetic. Even as she sat there cross-legged, releasing none of her Dao whatsoever, her presence resembled a mountain that anchored this entire planet to reality.

Human (Earth-44), Level ??? (C-Grade)
Faction: Exploding Sun (B-Grade)

"My name is Jack Rust, and this is Brock, my spiritual companion," Jack said, bowing again. "It is an honor to meet you, master."

She nodded slightly. "I have heard great things about you, Jack. That you show great promise; that you follow the path of one of our faction's founders; and that your character is as striking as your fists."

"I wouldn't dare accept that praise, but I am flattered."

"Don't be. Becoming an immortal within four months of Integration is a remarkable achievement, even in the entire galaxy—especially with a foundation as robust as yours."

"Hehe. I told you," Shol piped in. "Integrations can create monsters. Well, here's one."

"That they can."

Master Huali's gaze lingered on Jack, who felt almost naked before her eyes. It was like being stared at by a god—similar to when the Planetary Overseer had invaded his mind, or to that vision of Enas in the black hole, which he'd seen after getting the Life Drop.

Can she detect the Life Drop? he wondered, before realizing that she probably couldn't. The Ancient voice had said so.

"I hope you will allow me to cut directly to the main issue, Jack, as I am busy these days," Master Huali began, her voice growing a hint more serious. "Shol tells me that you seek asylum for your faction. Is that still true?"

"It is, master," Jack replied, still unsure on how to address her. "Not just my faction; my entire planet."

She raised a brow. Shol jumped in to add, "Jack misspoke. Anything we can offer will please him greatly."

"I do not believe I did," Jack retorted calmly. With his head still lowered, he said, "I have been recently informed that my planet is in the midst of war. My faction and their allies, which include many other factions and countries, are risking their lives to fight against oppression. Even if it was possible to rescue my faction and a few other people, we would not be willing, as abandoning the war would mean the doom of anyone left behind. They would have to pay for our retreat. We are not willing to do that. We will fight, and live or die as one—like a fist."

Neither Shol nor Huali replied. Jack, despite meaning everything he said, found himself sweating.

"I mean absolutely no disrespect," he added. "I have the utmost gratitude for even your consideration of my circumstances. I am simply explaining the situation as accurately as I can."

When they still didn't reply, Jack kept his head low. His words were already risky. The least he could do was remain bowed.

"You can raise your head," Master Huali said in the same amused tone as before. "I do not fancy talking to your hair."

Jack obliged, feeling awkward. He found Master Huali staring at him with a calculated gaze, while Shol's was made of stone.

"You understand that planet poaching is a completely different issue than simply recruiting your faction," she said. "It would rub the Animal Kingdom in all the wrong ways."

"I understand that your two factions are enemies," Jack replied calmly. "My current strength might be inconsequential to the Exploding Sun, but my potential is not. I am perfectly willing to join your faction in body and soul, as long as you can help save my planet."

"Your potential is not?" Master Huali replied—now, her voice and expression were unreadable. "Those are grand words, Jack Rust. What makes you think you are worthy of us provoking the Animal Kingdom?"

"A constellation has tens of thousands of inhabitable planets, but only hundreds of C-Grades. If I have high chances of becoming one in the future, is a single planet not a worthy trade?"

"It is not about a planet. It's about the relationship between two factions."

"I still believe myself worthy of your investment. I will strive to reach the C-Grade as quickly as possible, and do everything in my power to make myself useful to the Exploding Sun."

"Reach the C-Grade as fast as possible? Do you really have the face to stand before a true C-Grade and claim to be able to reach this realm? Do you even understand how difficult this is?"

Despite her cutting words, she was not angry—if she was, Jack couldn't see it. She was discussing as calmly as she would about the weather. Maybe it was a test. Therefore, Jack decided that pushing was the best course of action.

"It is true that I do not understand everything. However, I know that some D-Grades become C-Grades. Maybe it is one in a hundred. Maybe one in a thousand. And, potential-wise, I am confident in being in the top one-thousandth of D-Grades. In fact, I am confident in being at the very top."

At this, Master Huali seemed genuinely surprised. "According to what Shol has told me, you are not an idiot... What makes you say such bold words? Just winning this year's Garden Assault is not enough. Do you know how many Garden Assault winners get stuck at the D-Grade, forever unable to progress? Even if that wasn't the case, strength isn't the only factor. There is also a great deal of luck involved in reaching the C-Grade, and that is something we cannot predict."

Under her criticism, Jack felt his confidence slipping away. However, he had already chosen to ride the tiger—he couldn't get off. All he could do now was persist.

It wasn't like he was out of cards to play. The fact that he'd conquered Trial Planet was still a secret. If he revealed it, he felt pretty certain they would let him in and give him anything he wanted. However, he remained hesitant. He would tell her if he had to, but he first wanted to see if they would accept his offer without it.

After all, he didn't feel that he was lacking in potential. They should accept him regardless of his Trial Planet conquest. If not, he would be selling himself a bit short.

"It is as you say, master," he finally replied. "I am not very familiar with the galaxy, with the Grades, or how cultivation works at the higher stages, but I know with confidence that my potential is great. I reached the D-Grade within four months, with a perfect foundation, a King Class, and four Dao Roots. I was the winner of Trial Planet's Garden Assault. Just before coming here, I defeated two late D-Grades simultaneously. If even those are not enough... then all I can do is promise to work as hard as I possibly can. I am in dire need of help, and all I have to offer is my allegiance."

CHAPTER TWELVE
THE COWARD

AFTER FINISHING HIS PASSIONATE SPEECH OF WHY HE WAS WORTHY, JACK CAUGHT Shol and Master Huali exchange a glance, but he couldn't read its meaning.

"And what if I decline?" Master Huali asked.

"Then I will still cultivate as hard as possible," he replied. "I will sneak into the Animal Kingdom and fight them wherever I can. According to what I know, that should be the fastest way to cultivate. In the process, I will also look for more powerful allies to help me reclaim my planet. If I don't find any, then I will visit the planet at the end of the grace period, destroy all teleporters, and challenge the C-Grade Planetary Overseer. Win or lose... that will be my fate."

She gazed at him deeply. "You are determined."

"I am a fist. Forward is the only path I know."

She cracked a smile. Jack spotted it. She saw him spot it.

"What do you think, Shol?" she asked.

"I think Jack is a horse to bet on," Shol replied confidently. "He is a brilliant cultivator blessed with unstoppable drive, desperate circumstances, and the luck to get great titles. If he doesn't perish mid-way, I believe he has good chances of reaching the C-Grade in his lifetime."

"And what if he does perish?" Master Huali retorted. "He is

desperate and reckless. He just described assaulting the Animal Kingdom as an early D-Grade. If he survives, maybe he will reach far... but will he survive? Or will he risk his life time and time again until something goes wrong?"

"Cultivators can only bloom on the knife's edge, master. You know that. With our faction backing him, he will have great chances of surviving and prospering. It is the correct investment to make. If the unfortunate still happens... Well, we can only blame our luck."

Master Huali fell quiet, contemplating. Jack held his breath. Finally, she said, "Okay. Let's do that. Jack Rust, starting today, you will join our faction as an inner disciple and enjoy all the benefits that correspond to your position. Your brorilla will also join as an outer disciple. Furthermore, you will be my personal disciple, like Shol, and enjoy all the benefits of that position as well. As for your planet..."

Jack's breath caught in his throat, but he needn't have worried.

"While I had received orders from the Grand Elder to stay uninvolved, your strength and potential are simply incomparable to back then. Additionally, the Grand Elder passed away a month ago. Therefore, I see no problem with overruling that order. When the grace period is over, the Exploding Sun will send people to oversee the planet poaching of Earth-387, and if the Animal Kingdom has an issue with that, they can take it up with me. However, there are three conditions: One, you will survive until then. Two, you will not cripple yourself and ruin your future prospects. Three... While I absolutely intend to save your planet, I will not harm my faction for it. I reserve the right to take back this promise in case of extraordinary circumstances. Are you in agreement?"

Jack didn't think twice. This was a dream come true. "Of course I am!" he replied, bowing his head deeply, as he had when Shol accepted him as a disciple. "Thank you, master."

Master Huali, finally true to her title, nodded. "If there is nothing else..."

"Actually, master," Jack said, looking forward to what was coming, "there is one thing I forgot to mention."

Her gaze sharpened. Jack felt like he was trapped in the heart of a burning sun, doomed to melt away in eternity. Sweat formed on his brow, and he hurried to speak before they misunderstood completely. "It's a good thing, I promise!"

The pressure disappeared. "Then, speak," Master Huali ordered.

"About Trial Planet... I didn't actually stop at Garden Ring. I conquered the Final Ring as well."

Silence. Both Shol and Master Huali looked at him like he'd said he was a cat. Huali was the first to open her mouth. "What?"

"It's true."

"That is impossible," Master Huali said.

"Jack!" Shol cried out. "There is no need to lie to the master, let alone such a blatant lie! Master, I apologize, I don't know what—"

"Scan me," was all Jack said. *System, display my Ninth Ring Conqueror title.* He'd hidden all his titles before—anyone could do it.

Their gazes bore into him and the screen that appeared as they scanned him. In the next moment, their eyes went wide.

"But... That's..." Shol was lost for words. "Is that true!"

"Absolutely, brother Shol," Jack replied with a grin. Seeing their shocked expressions, even of the high and mighty Master Huali, he couldn't help feeling smug. Next to him, Brock was standing with his chest puffed out, chin raised, and a triumphant glint in his eyes.

"By the System..." Master Huali muttered, barely maintaining her composure. "How?"

"By defeating the Final Guardian."

Her gaze burned him. "I know that, Jack. I'm asking, how did you *achieve* it?

"I reached the apex of strength as an E-Grade, then got lucky."

He wasn't going to tell them about the Life Drop. That was a secret far more dangerous than his conquest of Trial Planet.

Master Huali narrowed her eyes, considering him fully for the first time. Everything up to now had been a regular day at the office for her. Now, things had gotten serious.

"Master!" Shol exclaimed. "He conquered Trial Planet! My disciple *conquered Trial Planet*!"

"I thought I was your brother now," Jack joked.

"Hush! You were still an E-Grade when you did it, so you were still my disciple. You cannot take that honor away from me!"

Jack laughed freely. Though he still revered Master Huali, he felt more comfortable after impressing her like that.

"This is terrific news," she said, nodding deeply at Jack. "You were wise not to spread that information. I can take care of that. But... Again, this is terrific news! If I didn't see the System title, I would never believe you... I've spent seven thousand years hearing how impossible the Final Guardian is. I faced him myself, once upon a time, and lost decisively." She shook her head. "It appears you weren't lying. Your potential truly is impressive."

By his side, Brock puffed his chest out as much as he physically could. "My bro," he said, as if that explained everything.

"I want to hear it," Master Huali said. She was still reeling, but gradually pulling her composure back under control. Her eyes were filled with genuine curiosity and wonder. "Your experiences in Trial Planet, what led you to the apex of strength, and how you defeated the Final Guardian. I had another appointment five minutes ago, but it can wait. Tell me everything."

And so, Jack did. He told them about his fourth Dao Root in the cave, his fight against the Final Guardian, and his breakthrough inside the Final Ring. The only things he hid were the Life Drop and the tribulation—as he felt that the two were connected.

Master Huali's eyes narrowed. "You are hiding something."

"I am not, master."

"There have been people with four Dao Roots. None of them defeated the Final Guardian."

"It was a terrible battle... and I only won through a trick. The Final Guardian fell for a very desperate feint, and I was able to strike him with a full-power blow in the face. That is the only reason why I won."

"And his Dao Domain? Did he not use it?"

"He did, but only at the very end. I countered it by expelling my Dao wildly for a few moments."

She stared at him with narrowed eyes. Once again, Jack felt naked before her sight but comforted himself with the fact that it was only an illusion. She couldn't read his thoughts—if she did, he could hide nothing, anyway.

"Very well," she finally replied. Whether or not she believed him, she chose not to press the issue, for which Jack was very glad. Perhaps her excitement from recruiting the first conqueror of Trial Planet played a part. "Taking you as a disciple is my pleasure, Jack. I look forward to seeing the heights you will reach. Now, if you would please return to your accommodations. I have many meetings to hold and only limited time—and keep your achievement private for now, please. It can be used strategically to the benefit of all of us."

"Of course, Master."

"And rest well, Jack; your training starts tomorrow. Shol will see to it."

"Yes, Master," Shol replied.

"Goodbye," Brock said, waving at Master Huali. Being silent for so long had taken its toll on him. She nodded slightly in return.

As Jack was leaving the room, he didn't forget to hide his titles again. A moment later, a blue screen appeared before his face.

You have been invited to join the Exploding Sun (B-Grade). Do you accept?
Yes/No

Yes, he thought, still unable to believe he was finally here. Had he just saved Earth? Could it really be that simple?

Or, as always, would there be a catch? Master Huali had mentioned extraordinary circumstances, and with Jack's luck, he felt half-certain they would somehow occur.

I will cultivate as hard as I possibly can, he thought, reaffirming his resolve. No matter what happens, I will be strong enough to handle it... And now, I will have the resources of a B-Grade faction on my back. Even if she goes back on her word, I will still profit until then. He smiled. Woohoo!

Back on Earth-387, the professor was eating lunch when a blue screen suddenly appeared before her face.

Congratulations! Your Faction Leader has joined the Exploding Sun

(B-Grade.) The Bare Fist Brotherhood is now a subordinate faction of the Exploding Sun (B-Grade.)

Her spoon stilled halfway inside her mouth. *What?*

"Is everything alright, Professor?" her assistant asked.

"Yes, yes. It's just..." Her eyes glowed with moisture. "My son is such a great man..."

Vivi paced up and down her throne room, getting a debriefing. As everyone on Earth leveled up, the remaining F-Grade dungeons were falling faster. The war had accelerated—and, along with speed, it had also become much more brutal.

"We estimate there are only six hundred F-Grade dungeons left," Shemarke, a former lieutenant general and her main advisor, reported. "At this point, we have to consider the pros and cons of sending E-Grades to conquer the dungeons. We lose out on the rewards, but we can claim resources faster and get ahead of the Ice Peak."

Vivi considered it. It had only been two days since she broke through—pushed to the brink by Edgar and Alexander's duel. After hearing news of her enemy's victory and E-Grade status, the pressure had been enough to light the spark inside her. Now, she was the second E-Grade of their alliance.

"Sending E-Grades will only lower Earth's power in the long run," she said. "We shouldn't ruin our future if we can help it. Send a message to Alexander. Tell him we should sign a treaty that E-Grades are not allowed inside F-Grade dungeons. He will agree."

"Commander!" Shemarke exclaimed. "This is the best time to push. We have two E-Grades to their one. We hold a temporary advantage."

"We do not have two E-Grades," Vivi replied calmly. "Edgar will not fight. Plus, his assault on the Ice Peak headquarters impacted their F-Grade forces. We can take them now. That is where our advantage lies, Shemarke, not the E-Grade. Not yet, anyway."

"I understand, Commander, but if the Coward can be convinced, our alliance can—"

"You will not insult my brother in arms," she cut him off, glaring into his eyes. Shemarke held it for a moment, then looked aside.

"It is not just me, Commander. Everyone calls him that after the duel. It is his new moniker."

"I don't care. You will not mention that in my presence. You will not mention it to any of our soldiers, either, and you will ensure that anyone who calls him that is punished. That will be your first task after leaving this room. Understood?"

"...Yes, Commander."

Vivi sighed. "You don't understand, Shemarke. You are not at the E-Grade yet, so how could you? Edgar is not choosing to stay cooped up in his forest. He is forced to. In fact, he's in the worst position of us all..." Her eyes went hazy for a moment before refocusing. "But, let's return to the matter at hand. The professor has made me responsible for the dungeons, and I will not fail her."

CHAPTER THIRTEEN
FIRST DAY AT THE SECT

Jack awoke to a brorilla jumping up and down on his chest. "Oof!" he exclaimed. "Brock! What are you—Oh! Right!"

A smile instantly blossomed on his face. He ripped off the covers and Brock with them, then jumped up and got dressed in a heartbeat. Only then did he greet the brorilla.

"Morning, brother! Did you sleep well?"

"Yes."

Brock's reply was curt, but he was equally excited. His face was morphed into a permanent monkey grin, and he was hopping from one leg to the other like he was itchy. Jack understood the feeling. He had it too. Today was their first day in the Exploding Sun faction!

"Let's go!" he exclaimed, grabbing Brock and pushing the door open.

The space he'd been given was a spacious courtyard close to the estate's wall. He had his own little house and garden, with the caveat that he had no servants yet, so he had to take care of everything. But that wasn't an issue. When he lived alone in Valville, he did everything by himself, too.

His house was made up of a living room, a kitchen, a cellar, a bedroom, and a bathroom. It was small yet cozy, made of warm wood with red trimming. It also had many windows, which Jack enjoyed. As for his bedroom, the only room he'd used so far, it contained a double bed, two bed stands, and a wardrobe.

The houses in Master Huali's estate were neither opulent nor spartan—something in-between.

Jack didn't mind or care. He didn't plan to stay at home much. He had one job here, and that was to cultivate!

With Brock hopping onto his back, Jack dashed out through the open window and took to the sky, drawing a deep breath of clean, fresh air. He saw the estate under him—a sprawling collection of houses, gardens, courtyards, and snaking paths. Vegetation was aplenty, including many beautiful flowers carefully tended to by gardeners. A few immortals were flying, like him, but most went about their lives on the ground.

Jack spotted servants laughing as they worked, taking walks, chatting, or drinking what looked and smelled like tea. Nobody was in a rush. A pleasant atmosphere enveloped the entire estate, and under the light of the solar gasses that surrounded this place, it looked like a slice of heaven.

Master Huali's manor dominated the very top of the mountain, while a forest stretched around its base, extending in all directions like the mountain was a thumb rising from a plain.

There couldn't be too many people here; a few thousand, maybe, the vast majority of which were servants. Which, as Jack was realizing, was an inaccurate name. The estate was like a small town, and these people were its citizens, going about their lives joyfully and respectfully. Their only job was to take care of the city they lived in, as well as assist the immortals when possible.

It looked like a happy life.

Jack did wonder how food was produced here, or how it was distributed, but he temporarily found the image too beautiful to ruin with mundane issues. This was a place of gods. Food should be the smallest of its concerns.

"Jack!" a voice boomed through the sky as Shol flew up to meet him. He was smiling, but also looked slightly annoyed. "What are you doing up here? I was waiting at your garden."

"Oh. I didn't know."

"Hello, bro," Brock said, waving from Jack's back.

"Hi, Brock. You *should* have known. We agreed to meet."

"I didn't understand you'd be waiting in *my* garden."

"It went without saying. Bah! Forget about it. Maybe I'll just go be a hermit somewhere."

"No, brother, don't do that!" Jack replied, laughing. "Sorry, sorry. Good morning."

"Good morning to you, too. To both of you. Now, there's a lot to go over today. We should get started."

He broke off like a sprouting rainbow, forcing Jack to follow. "Where are we going?" he yelled through the wind.

"You'll see!" Shol responded.

They crossed the air like arrows, drawing many eyes from the servants below. They waved. Smiling, Jack waved back.

Their flight ended a few moments later, when Shol landed before a round building with a domed roof. It was brown and made of wood, with few windows, and the entire thing exuded an earthly aura. "We're here," Shol said as Jack landed. "This is the artificing laboratory. Every personal disciple of Master Huali is allocated a Dao Magnet, and we are here to get yours."

"Does master have many disciples?" Jack asked.

"Only a few dozen—but not for lack of volunteers. She's just very selective."

"Why so? So this estate doesn't run out of space?"

Shol snorted. "Expanding the estate is easy. However, as I think I've explained to you before, immortals do not take disciples lightly. This applies to D-Grades taking mortal disciples, as well as C-Grades taking D-Grade disciples. If the disciple does not reach the same Grade as the master, their lifespan will be far shorter. A master can watch many generations of disciples wither away and die, which takes a great toll on a person's soul. I admire my master for taking on so many disciples."

"I see. Is that why you have none?"

"I have one. You. And you're a handful, anyway, so you count for ten."

He opened the door. The chime of a bell welcomed them from above, as well as the sight of a wide open space surrounded by shelves along the circular walls. A staircase stood at the far back, leading both down and up, while a large square table took up the center of the building, covered in all sorts of tools and materials. Jack also saw some metal contraptions there, whose function was a mystery.

What he did not see was the person who ran this place.

"She'll come," Shol said. "Give her a minute."

"Sure. You said that C-Grades have longer lifespans than D-Grades?"

"Oh, yes. From the D-Grade onward, every major breakthrough increases your lifespan by ten times. D-Grades, like us, live for around a thousand years. C-Grades live for ten thousand years, and B-Grades for a hundred thousand."

"A hundred thousand years... Wow."

Jack couldn't wrap his mind around that length of time. It was beyond the scope of his experience. To him, even a thousand years was tremendous—enough time to witness mortal empires rise and fall, and see civilizations evolve from medieval to spacefaring.

What would someone even do for a hundred thousand years? Watch the tectonic plates move?

"Very big," Brock agreed, nodding alongside Jack's thoughts.

Jack looked over in surprise. "How did you—"

"I am smart."

Their train of thought was interrupted by a green girl emerging from the stairs. She was blonde and small, barely reaching up to Jack's chest, but carried herself with such frantic energy that it almost made him dizzy. But that was no girl. She was a goblin!

Goblin, Level 67 (Elite)

Goblins are weak, primal humanoids who move in large groups. They are barely intelligent enough to cook their food, and they often derive pleasure from torturing their victims. Cultivators are advised to kill them on sight.

This particular goblin has discovered the Dao and began cultivating. As such, it has ascended beyond the norm for its kind—though its inner nature remains to be seen.

• • •

"Sup," the goblin said, zooming through the room to arrive before the large table. She only spared them a single glance before her eyes surveyed the tools before her, then she picked up a screwdriver and started tightening the screws on... something.

"Good morning, Goblinete," Shol said. "We would like a Dao Magnet for master's new personal disciple."

"This guy here?" she asked, glancing up at Jack. "Or the monkey?"

"The human."

"Sure."

She reached under the table to retrieve a device from a drawer. To Jack, it looked like a large battery—but it felt wobbly in his Dao sense, like something wasn't quite right.

"What are you looking at, newbie?" she asked him, still buzzing with energy. "I don't have all day. Stuff your Dao inside this already."

"Stuff my Dao?"

At his question, she had to force herself to slow down and take a deep, irritated breath. Jack felt like he was slow—which shouldn't be the case. He was an immortal! And she was a goblin! Who the hell gave her the right to call him a newbie?

Brock, however, seemed to be enjoying this very much.

"Touch the port at the top and push your Dao inside the magnet," she explained, still speaking faster than most people. "Got it?"

"I think so."

He approached and did as she said. As soon as he touched the metal at the top, he felt its insides empty of Dao. He knew this feeling. This was a Dao vacuum!

With a triumphant smile, he willed his Dao of the Fist inside and filled it to the brim.

"Oh, good," the goblin said, a hint of surprise in her eyes. "At least he got this part."

"He can be quite slow sometimes," Shol agreed with sorrow.

Jack raised a brow. "Hey."

"*Very* slow," Brock corrected, receiving Jack's stunned stare.

"What the fuck, bro? You are literally a monkey. How do you even know these words?"

"Because I am smart."

Jack ran his hand over his face. He turned to the goblin. "I thought you were in a hurry."

"I am. But this magnet needs time to adjust, and I can do two things at the same time—big shocker, I know."

Indeed, she hadn't stopped tinkering with her tools all the while. By now, she had tightened the screws on all of the table's contraptions and was moving on to the table legs.

"You're just tightening screws," Jack said.

"Don't underestimate good labor. Do you even know how many people die every year because their machines had a slightly loose screw? Many. But none from *my* machines. Since they go loose from use, I always screw when I have the chance."

"That's... not even funny."

She didn't seem like she'd said that on purpose. Once again, Jack wondered about the System's universal translation. How well did puns like that carry over from the goblin language to English?

A purple light appeared in the middle of the Dao Magnet.

"Ready," Goblinete said, basically throwing the magnet at Jack's lap. "If that's all, you can go."

"That's all," Shol said. "Thank you, Goblinete."

She looked back and smiled. "No problem, Shol. Take care. And, newbie, brorilla... Welcome to Master Huali's estate."

Jack was surprised by that. "Thank you."

"Now go. I really am busy."

She dove back down the stairs before they even left her shop.

"What the hell was that?" Jack asked.

"That was Goblinete," Shol explained calmly. "The most competent artificer around. She may not seem like much, but she's very important to us disciples."

"She's a goblin," Jack said, shivering at the memory of the first goblin he ever killed. "And she called me a newbie."

"So what if she's a goblin?"

"Goblins are supposed to be enemies."

"And brorillas are supposed to live in jungles, but look at Brock. He's doing just fine."

Jack opened his mouth to speak and closed it again. "I guess... Anyway, what is this Dao Magnet?"

"An extremely useful contraption. Most immortals never get one in their lifetime, but Master Huali is kind to us. Treat it very carefully—if it breaks, you don't get a second."

"What does it do?"

"It enhances your cultivation chamber," Shol explained. "You have cultivated at least once since reaching the D-Grade, yes? Did you feel that the environment contained all sorts of Daos, and you had to filter it for the ones compatible with you before absorbing them?"

"Yes."

"The Dao Magnet does that for you. After it attunes to your Dao, you can just place it somewhere, and it will draw in compatible Daos while repelling incompatible ones. When cultivating beside it, things will go much faster."

Jack's eyes widened in surprise. When he'd cultivated on Derion, the teleporter hub, he had to pass the environment's Dao particles through a mental sieve before absorbing them. Naturally, that took significant time and effort. If this little Dao Magnet could get rid of that procedure, then over the course of his entire D-Grade, it would save him an incalculable amount of time.

"I see," he said. "Thank you, brother Shol."

"Don't thank me. Thank our master, who is generous enough to provide these to each of her disciples." Shol turned to Jack and looked at him seriously. "You may not understand the weight of your position, but let me tell you: it is highly coveted. If Master Huali expressed the desire to take a disciple, there would be thousands of immortals lining up before her gates for a chance to impress her."

"Is she that impressive?"

"Of course! Not only is she an elder of the faction, of which there are only twenty, but she is special even amongst them. When the next Grand Elder is selected in a few months, she is one of the main candidates for the position."

"That does sound impressive."

"It is."

"Do you think she'll get it?"

Shol's face hardened. "Let's not talk about that now. Let's stop by your house so you can leave the Dao Magnet in your cultivation chamber. After that, I have more things to show you."

Jack did a double take. "I have a cultivation chamber?"

"Of course. Did you not see the trapdoor in your kitchen?"

"I assumed it led to the cellar."

"You do not need a cellar. It's a cultivation chamber. Let's go."

They took to the skies, but Jack remained morose. "Oh, man. I liked my cellar."

CHAPTER FOURTEEN
THE LIBRARY

"For the last time," Shol said, pulling open the trapdoor in the corner of Jack's kitchen, "you do not have a cellar."

"Well, I want one. I've always dreamt of having my own cellar."

"Have it elsewhere."

"You know what? I think I'll just turn my cultivation chamber into one. Fist Wine. Fist Beer. I'll call it... Fistables."

"You're out of your goddamn mind. Just put the Dao Magnet inside so we can get going."

"Fine."

Jack hurried down the stairs to the empty cultivation chamber and placed the magnet at the very center. Its effect wasn't pronounced at first—but, when Jack focused on his Dao perception, he noticed a subtle flow of Fist Dao toward this place. "Impressive. It works."

"Of course it does." Shol crossed his arms with pride. "The Dao Magnet is an artificing wonder, a highly sought-after resource that factions can only afford for their best disciples. In fact, it was invented so recently that it isn't even Inspectable yet."

"Really?"

"It's more complicated than it sounds. Now. The most efficient way to use this thing is to let it gather the Dao for around triple the time you spend cultivating. In other words, you should only cultivate for one hour every three hours for maximum efficiency. The Dao concentration that a magnet produces peaks at around sixteen hours in, so most people just cultivate for eight hours a day and spend the rest of their time doing other things."

"Hmm. I can spend the day training and the night cultivating, right? Immortals don't need to sleep."

Shol threw him an odd stare. "You can. But, as you'll come to realize, training and cultivating are both exhausting."

"No problem. I have a planet to save; the least I can do is tolerate some exhaustion."

Shol's eyes twinkled. "We'll see about that. Now that we've settled the issue of your cultivation chamber, we can proceed. Follow me."

They flew away again, Brock riding Jack's back as usual. Their next destination was a pyramid of white stone set on the back of the mountain, surrounded by a silent, calm garden that reminded Jack of the Center Moon's guest lounge. People sat on benches throughout this garden, relaxing, and many reading books. A few greeted Shol as they flew past.

"This is the library," Shol explained as he landed in front of the pyramid. "It contains all sorts of skills, visions, and knowledge that the master has unearthed throughout her life, as well as books on history, the System, the B-Grade factions of our galaxy, and other important stuff."

"Other important stuff?" Jack raised a brow. "You don't sound well-versed."

"I am not. While history is important, I will have time to immerse myself in it after reaching the C-Grade. For now, strength is my most important goal."

"Not a family?"

"Don't go there, Jack."

The change in mood was sudden and abrupt. Jack realized he'd misspoken. Something told him he'd accidentally hit a painful point—and he resolved to be more careful from now on. Five hundred years could give anyone a lot of wounds.

"Sorry," he said.

"The library is a place you will frequent," Shol continued like nothing had happened. "Each personal disciple is allowed to borrow three items every year—and I say items, because there is more to this library than books. Since this year will be extremely important for you, given your planet's situation, I would suggest waiting a bit longer before making your selection. However, you can still peruse the library and see what it has to offer."

"Can Brock borrow books, too?"

Shol turned to the brorilla, who gave him his best wide smile—not because he could read, but because he wanted to help Jack.

"He is not a personal disciple, so no," Shol shot them down. Seeing their disappointed expressions, he added, "But don't get ahead of yourselves. The master set the three item rule not to limit you, but to help you. A novice in a thousand skills is no match for a master in one."

"Hmm, that was wise," Jack said. "Could you use the same wisdom to help me pick the best... items? Whatever those are?"

"I can, and I will." Finally, Shol cracked a smile. On his middle-aged face, it looked almost mischievous. "How about you tell me more about your Dao and Class as we explore the library?"

"Sure thing."

There were no guards in front of the pyramid, so they entered freely. They were welcomed by a forty-foot-tall open space whose slanted walls were covered in five levels of books. There were no platforms to stand on, however; anyone wanting to access a book higher than the first level would have to fly.

"The higher up you go, the higher the level of the items," Shol explained, hovering an inch over the ground. "The first level is meant for mortals. The other three are meant for early, middle, and late immortals respectively. Nobody will stop you if you try to access a level above yours, but it is usually ill-advised."

"I see." Jack looked around. The pyramid was made of white stone, both on the inside and outside, and had no openings besides the entrance. There was no furniture except for the bookshelves and a lonely chair by a corner, and it was also completely devoid of people. "But, if there are no guards here, who is to stop me from taking more than three items?"

"Your dignity," Shol replied. "Stationing guards here would imply that any of the disciples our master hand-picked could be vile at heart —which would be an insult to the master's insight."

"I see. Pardon me for asking," Jack said humbly.

Shol's hard face mellowed. "Although, accidents happen. We may not have guards, but we do have a librarian."

A man appeared right in front of Jack. He did not walk there, teleport, or anything like that; he simply popped into existence. There had also been no indication of him beforehand—no smell, no sound, no breeze of breath or an errant glance from Shol. Even Jack's Dao perception, which came as natural as breathing, hadn't picked up the slightest sign that there was an invisible man standing right before him.

Most people in Jack's situation would have jumped back or frozen at the surprise. Not Jack. Before his brain had even registered what was happening, his fist was already hurtling forward, seeking to punch a hole through this man's chest.

Shit, he realized at the last fraction of a second, but it was too late. Everything had happened instantly. He had no time to stop it.

A hand wrapped gently around his fist. And, just like that, it stopped. There had been no impact. Its momentum was simply extinguished without resistance. It was like a tremendous force suppressed Jack's body and Dao, wiping away all hints of the attack.

Now Jack stood frozen, fist outstretched and still in the other man's grasp.

This was a thin, stick-like old man. A white mustache extended from either side of his mouth, while his lips were drawn into a kind smile. Long white hair hung to his shoulders, and he wore an orange gown that looked extremely comfortable. When he spoke, his voice was smooth and pleasant to the ears.

"I apologize," the old man said, laughing lightly. "I admit, I expected a calmer approach, but this remains my fault for surprising you. Please accept my apology."

He let go of the fist, which Jack retrieved slowly. He gazed at the man before him in shock.

Human (Earth-44), Level 249

Faction: Exploding Sun (B-Grade)

Only now did Brock recover from the shock. "Bro!" he exclaimed, pointing at the old man. "Not cool."

"I should not have tried to show off," the old man replied, still smiling. "I am sorry, little brorilla."

Brock mimed that the only thing little around here was the old man's genitalia. Thankfully, the man didn't seem to get it.

"Okmer!" Shol exclaimed, laughing. "I should have warned you. Jack has been through a lot; his battle instincts are well-honed."

"No harm, no problem." The old man laughed too, wrapping Shol in a hug. With his stick-like body, he looked like a child compared to the hard-faced, strong-looking Shol. "How have you been, my friend?"

"Excellent. More than excellent, in fact. The master just accepted my only disciple as her disciple!"

"Oh!" The old man's eyes flashed. "Is it this young warrior? It is an honor to make your acquaintance, my friend."

"This is Okmer," Shol introduced the old man, throwing an arm around his shoulder. "A deacon like me, and the librarian of our estate. He is also a personal disciple of the master, like most immortals around here."

"I'm Jack, and this is Brock." Jack reached out for a handshake, which the old man readily accepted—as gentle as his grip was, Jack did not forget the ease with which his strike had been neutralized. "Sorry for punching you. I was just surprised."

"No problem at all."

"Jack here was going to peruse the library a bit, see what he could find," Shol said. "How about he tells us about his Dao and Class, and we see if we can help him out? Are you okay with that, Jack? Okmer here is a trustworthy, knowledgeable individual."

Jack considered it. As Shol had explained shortly before, withholding his personal information from this old man would mean insulting his master's insight—therefore, he couldn't refuse. Not that he really wanted to, either. If this guy wanted to harm him, a little secrecy wouldn't save him.

"I cultivate the Dao of the Fist. My current Class is called Cosmic Fist, and I believe it is space-themed, though it gave me no Dao Visions. It's also a King Class. My signature skill is Meteor Punch, which does exactly what it says."

Okmer whistled. "A King Class! We don't see those often, do we, Shol?"

"Not really, no," Shol replied.

"Well then, we should find you skills of the appropriate rarity! Before that, however, let me reciprocate your trust. I cultivate the Dao of Suppression—that is how I was able to suppress your attack so effectively, and also how I was suppressing my presence before."

Jack's eyes brightened; he appreciated this. "I see. Thank you for trusting me with this information."

"No problem. Now, items." Okmer got into excited librarian mode. "If I may be so blunt, do you feel that your current skillset is missing anything important? The library has a lot of things, ranging from Dao Visions that can help you develop additional Daos, to D-Grade elixirs that can greatly augment your attributes, to Ancient artifacts and weapons, to Dao Skills. Books, too, as you can see."

Jack had enough attacking power from Meteor Punch. Space Walk gave him mobility, while defense was probably his greatest asset. Additionally, he also had an aura skill that could help both against strong enemies and groups of weaker ones. As for the technical parts of his fighting, those were handled by Iron Fist Style, his constant sparring against Copy Jack, and his many life-or-death battles so far.

He really wasn't missing much, as he always tried to work on his weaknesses.

"I guess... some sort of cheap mobility?" he finally decided. "I already have a mobility skill, but it's exhausting, so I can't use it freely in battle."

"Mhm. Any other specifications?"

"Make it space-oriented or fist-oriented, if possible."

"I was just telling Jack that it's better to wait a bit before making his selection," Shol quickly jumped in. "When I mentioned helping him, I meant ideas, not just handing him the best thing."

"Waiting is one thing, and delaying is another," Okmer replied, his eyes shimmering. "Let's take a look at what we have here, and if anything catches your eye, you can take it. What do you say, Jack?"

"That sounds good."

"Excellent! Wait here."

Okmer floated into the air and started rushing from shelf to shelf, gathering an assortment of items. Only a few seconds later, he landed and presented Jack with three items—one of which was a book.

"This is a manual on all things space," Okmer explained, raising a thick, leather bound tome. Its cover was black with white letters, boasting an image of a galaxy—its title: *A Scientific Introduction to the Universe.*

Jack nodded.

"This," Okmer raised a brown statuette of a woman in a running pose, "is an imprint of a movement-based Dao Skill. It is similar to what you described—it simply allows the user to dash in one direction. It has a short range and doesn't involve teleportation or anything complex, but it gets the job done, even for low immortals."

"Hmm," Jack hummed, cupping his chin. "You keep mentioning Dao Skills, but I thought they couldn't be taught? That everyone had to form their own Dao Skills that correspond to their Dao?"

"Correct," Shol explained. "They cannot be taught, but we can record someone demonstrating a skill. By watching it many times and meditating on it, you may be able to develop a skill that operates on similar principles, just based on your Dao. Consider it a form of Dao Vision."

"Oh!" Jack exclaimed. He'd actually gotten a Dao Vision like this when he broke into the E-Grade. Back then, he'd seen a man with scars on his chest release a mental aura that decimated an entire city. After meditating on it, he'd eventually developed Brutalizing Aura, his own version of that skill.

The skill that Okmer had described sounded useful, just... a bit basic.

"What about the last item?" he asked.

"This is the one I thought of first," Okmer said. It looked like a snow globe, except pitch-black inside and filled with glittering stars. "It's a Dao Vision related to the Dao of Space. By meditating on it, you can achieve that Dao or something similar, which would synergize well with your Class."

Jack's eyes widened in excitement. This sounded intriguing. However, he maintained some doubts.

"I thought my Dao was cemented when I formed my Dao Tree," he said. "That I could no longer get new Dao Roots."

Old Man Spirit had said so, and Old Man Spirit was an unimaginably powerful and ancient being. He couldn't be wrong.

"Correct," Okmer said. "However, a Dao Tree doesn't make you blind to everything else in existence. You may be unable to form new Dao Roots, but you can still comprehend Daos and use them to create new Dao Skills or improve your existing ones. Plus, the more points of view one conquers, the wiser they become—and the faster they will advance in their Dao."

"So, I can understand a new Dao and use it with my skills, just not add it to my Dao Tree?"

"Precisely. It will never be a core pillar of your power, not unless you reach the C-Grade and let your Dao branch off, but it can make you stronger and wiser. Plus, it lets you expand your Class to its full potential—which, given its rarity grade, should be tremendous."

"Hmm." Jack hummed again, though he'd already made his choice. Now, he was just running it through his mind to make sure he had no lingering objections. "Okay. I'm convinced. I will get this space Dao Vision."

"Excellent!" Okmer smiled.

"Have you thought this through, Jack?" Shol asked. "Once you've decided, you cannot change your mind until next year."

"I have," Jack replied. "Getting even a bit of insight on the Dao of Space can help me unlock the potential of my Class. Plus, many of my skills are already space-themed: Meteor Punch, Space Walk… I get the feeling this is the direction I must go in."

Shol nodded. "Very well. If you are certain, then go ahead. You have two more items to pick, anyway."

"Great!"

Jack received the ball and put it in his pocket—these new robes had some, unlike his previous attire.

"You will have more time to peruse items later," Shol said. "For now, there is one more place I have to show you. See you, Okmer."

"Take care, Shol! And it was nice meeting you, Jack and Brock."

"Likewise." Jack smiled.

"Goodbye, bro," Brock said.

They exited the pyramid, once again taking to the air. They hadn't flown ten feet, however, when another group of flying immortals approached them.

"Brother Shol!" their leader shouted. She was a tall, short-haired ginger in wide clothes. Appearance-wise, Jack would estimate her to be around forty—though her real age was probably in the hundreds.

"Melia," Shol replied, smiling. "How are you doing?"

"Pretty fine! Auburn and I were just going for a little spar in the cloud field."

"What a coincidence! So were we."

Jack nodded at this Auburn, who nodded back. She seemed like a kind, energetic individual, with orange-ish robes and hair, small nose, and wide eyes. She was also young—looking less than thirty, though her actual age could be anything.

Jack scanned them both.

Human (Earth-44), Level 201
Faction: Exploding Sun (B-Grade)

Human (Earth-44), Level 178
Faction: Exploding Sun (B-Grade)

"These are Jack and Brock," Shol introduced them. "My former disciple who just got accepted by Master Huali, and his extraordinary spiritual companion."

"A pleasure to meet you," Jack said.

"The pleasure is all ours—though I suspect you already know our names," Melia replied, beaming at him. She glanced at Shol, and the two of them exchanged a look that Jack didn't quite decipher. "I don't know if brother Shol told you already, Jack, but it's customary for new personal disciples of our master to spar against a more experienced disciple when they first visit the cloud field. Brother Shol himself is far too strong for a spar to have any meaning, as am I, but you and Auburn are relatively close in level. What do you say? Wanna give it a go?"

CHAPTER FIFTEEN
FIGHTING AUBURN

Jack raised a brow at the challenge. Brock grinned sardonically.

Shol, however, scratched the back of his head and smiled awkwardly. "Um, how do I say this... It's customary for new disciples to fight someone much stronger, but... Jack is quite strong himself, so—"

"Strong enough to match another personal disciple forty levels ahead?" Auburn said. Her voice came reserved, somewhat contrary to what her appearance indicated, but her words were appropriately sharp. Immortals could be reserved, but they could not be weak.

"Auburn is right, brother Shol," Melia said. "Only the most talented immortals get chosen as master's disciples. Jumping a tier to fight is doable against random people, but not here."

"Besides," Auburn added, looking straight at Jack, "I never was fond of this traditional beating. If brother Jack can actually spar against me, that's even better."

Shol shook his head. "It's... Well, I'll let him decide. What do you think, Jack?"

Jack's brow was permanently raised now. These guys had a tradition of pitting every new disciple against someone much stronger... so he could get beaten up?

They weren't even discreet about it!

"Sure," he replied. "Why not?"

As stupid as that tradition was, he didn't mind getting beaten up. He looked forward to fighting against someone stronger, to really find out how strong the elites of the galaxy were.

Plus, he believed he could win. From the way everyone talked, this Auburn didn't seem particularly impressive. How strong could she be?

Jack locked eyes with Auburn. Saw the hint of challenge in her green gaze.

"Perfect!" Melia exclaimed, clapping her hands. "Let's go, then. I'm looking forward to it!"

Jack, with Brock still on his back, followed the other three immortals... to the sky!

"Where are we going?" he asked as the mountaintop estate grew smaller and smaller under their feet.

"Immortals cannot fight near the estate, as we could accidentally destroy everything," Shol explained. "As a matter of fact, creating any sort of battle arena on the planet's surface would be dangerous. The strongest immortals have enough power to cause earthquakes and destroy the land for many miles around them. Therefore, one of our faction's B-Grades, Ancestor Bolaui, created battle arenas and training fields for immortals high in the sky."

"As in, flying arenas?"

"You'll see."

Angling themselves diagonally, they moved over a barren part of the plains as they ascended. They entered a layer of clouds, and when they exited, Jack was surprised to see a large platform situated on top of the clouds.

It was a square a mile across, constructed entirely out of light blue stone. There was no railing on its edge, leading to a steep drop many miles down, but that wasn't a problem, as whoever wanted to reach this place needed the ability to fly—or, on second thought, a starship.

The blue platform was almost empty. The only furniture was a weapon rack in a corner, filled with all sorts of threatening objects, along with three D-Grade robots waiting patiently around the field. There were people, too. An immortal was meditating, clad in loose blue robes, with long dark hair that swayed in the wind, as well as another immortal performing the same turtle-like movement again and again, like she was practicing a new skill.

All those, however, paled in comparison to the sheer beauty of this place: a light blue platform floating on the white clouds like a ship at sea, framed by the purple and orange gasses that made up the nebula around them.

Really, everything in Master Huali's estate was constructed with special attention to aesthetics.

"Wow," Jack muttered breathlessly.

"Bro!" Brock exclaimed, eyes wide in wonder.

Shol smiled. "I present you, the training field of immortals. The cloud field!"

The four of them—five with Brock—approached the field, where the woman who was practicing nodded at them from afar. She almost went back to her skill, then caught sight of Jack and approached.

"A new disciple?" she asked. If not for her almost divine powers, she would look like your average next-door girl, with smiling brown eyes, freckles, and loose dark hair. "It's a pleasure to meet you. My name is Hemira."

"I'm Jack. Likewise." He smiled back at her, always ready to reciprocate kindness.

"Come, Hemira," Shol said. "Let's watch Jack and Auburn spar."

"Yes, brother Shol. Good luck to both of you." She flew away with Melia and Shol, who had also taken Brock along. They went to the meditating man in the corner and alerted him to the fact that there was going to be sparring. Nodding absent-mindedly, but with eyes as bright and smiling as the blue sky that this planet lacked, the man sat next to the others and watched.

Jack thought it was weird they interrupted a meditating cultivator, but then again, this place wasn't meant for meditation, but for battle training.

The three robots had also retreated to the edge of the platform, leaving Jack and Auburn alone in the very middle.

"Good luck, bro!" Brock shouted from the edge, making Jack smile.

"That's a spirited spiritual companion," Auburn said, smiling slightly. She looked quite likable.

"He's been with me since my Integration," Jack replied honestly. "He is my brother."

"Integration? I see..." Auburn's gaze became filled with something between pity and realization, which quickly disappeared. "I suppose he was accepted as an outer disciple?"

"Correct."

"Then, you may want to drop him off at the outer planet for the duration of your stay here. Maybe leave him with some friends? It would be much better for his growth, as this place is not meant for E-Grade spiritual beasts. He would have more fun, too—though, of course, there is always danger."

That was a slightly invasive comment, but Jack felt no ill will coming from this girl, just a genuine desire to help.

A deep unease still infiltrated his psyche at the mention of sending Brock somewhere else, even if only temporarily. They were brothers. They had been together since the Forest of the Strong. Since then, Jack's life had been wild and unpredictable—everything changed all the time. His only constant was Brock, the brother he never had before.

What would it feel like to be alone?

A mental weight crashed down on Jack, a heavy slab of loneliness and desolation. He could face the world; he could go against everyone and fight for what was right, laughing uproariously in the process; but he didn't want to do it alone.

Without realizing it, Brock had become his source of power and stability in an ever-changing world. He was the cornerstone of Jack's mental power.

"I didn't mean to upset you," Auburn said, sounding a bit worried. "Sorry if I said something wrong; I just wanted to help."

Jack snapped out of his thoughts, realizing he'd been contemplating silently for some time now. At that thought, the Fist reared its head inside him, snapping him back to the present and infusing him with the will to fight. Jack became one with his Dao. His heart caught on fire.

"Don't worry about it, Auburn. My thoughts just ran wild for a bit. I'll consider what you said seriously. Thank you for bringing it to my attention. Now... Shall we?"

Auburn smiled—a hard smile on a soft face. No immortal reached this level without a fair amount of bloodshed, so all of them were accustomed to battle.

"We shall."

Auburn jumped back, stretching her hands wide. The sky behind her turned the color of her namesake. Leaves swayed in the breeze, each following its own, unique trajectory and filled with the melancholy of autumn.

This was a wizard immortal. He hadn't faced a skilled wizard in a while.

Whichever stat Auburn used, either Mental or Will, the foundations of such a battle hadn't changed since the F-Grade. Each of them would fight using their own strength, trying to overwhelm the opponent with their Dao.

Jack didn't let the leaves dance freely. He charged. He reared back a punch and threw it, shaking the sky and moving the earth. A tremendous shockwave tore into the storm of leaves, tearing many of them into pieces or sending them off their trajectories. Many remained unaffected, however. They turned into a torrent that flew toward Jack, seeking to smother him with softness.

Jack threw out a barrage of punches to meet them. Dozens of fists flew out, intercepting the leaves and stopping them in their tracks. However, he observed that the more leaves he tossed away, the more came to attack him. It felt futile—like trying to repress a feeling, only for it to reappear stronger every time you pushed it under the rug.

In just a moment, his vision was filled with swirling leaves, a wall of autumn sliding toward him, swallowing the robots and platform on its way.

Jack didn't want to end this too quickly. He wanted to enjoy the spar and get to experience an immortal wizard's powers. Except if he kept tearing into the leaves, he would just be playing the other person's game—not to mention the magical melancholy with which the leaves tried to invade his heart with, a melancholy that somehow felt stronger than it should have been.

Jack's mind flashed with realization. His lips curved into a wry smile. When Auburn made that comment about Brock earlier, it wasn't out of a desire to help; she had been trying to influence Jack's emotions. The battle had already begun at the time.

He didn't begrudge Auburn for this trick. There was nothing wrong with it. If anything, he was grateful. Nobody would show him mercy in a real battle, and she had just taught him a very important lesson.

Even if he felt stupid for being outplayed like that.

"You little shit," he muttered.

"What was that?" Auburn shouted back.

"I said, eat this!"

Space Walk!

Jack stepped through the void. A colossal resistance sought to entrap him, but he tore it apart with sheer physicality. In the next moment, he was right behind Auburn, shooting out a punch. It wasn't a Meteor Punch—this was just a spar, and he didn't want to risk injuring this friendly co-disciple.

Auburn turned around with a surprised look on her face. Jack's fist tore through it. As it did, her surprise morphed into a sad smile, and her entire body dissipated like dust in the wind, like the memory of a long-lost loved one.

Only leaves remained where Auburn used to stand. There were leaves everywhere, actually. Auburn had expected Jack to reach this place, and she'd surrounded herself with leaves at a wide radius. It was a trap.

Though she hadn't expected Jack to arrive so quickly. The leaves here were far fewer than the ones he had been facing before.

Jack lost track of Auburn. His Dao perception was blocked by all these leaves, each of which radiated its own, melancholic Dao, and his eyes were similarly blocked. He could teleport outside and reconsider his approach—in a real battle, that is probably what he would have done.

Again though, this was a spar. Jack wasn't just aiming for victory. He wanted to use this experience to understand his powers better and test their limit against the talented immortals of the Exploding Sun.

The leaves wrapped around him, trapping him in an ever-shrinking sphere. If he didn't do something, he would be neutralized soon. As the sphere closed, hiding Jack from sight, leaves flew out in random spots, like someone was punching the sphere from the inside. Unfortunately, every time leaves were punched away, more spawned out of thin air to replace them.

Feelings didn't go away by punching them.

"Ai..." Melia sighed from where they watched the battle. "I guess this is the end. He fought well, though. If Auburn didn't have a decoy set up, she might have lost."

"Hmph." A sneer from the side drew her attention. Turning, she saw Brock gaze at her with mockery.

"What?" she asked. "Do you still think your brother can win? This is a lock in space; he can't even teleport out."

"Well, let's wait and see," Shol said, watching the spar with an almost imperceptible smile.

The ball of leaves shrunk down until it was the size of a single room, then barely large enough for a man to stand inside. Just as the leaves were about to stick to Jack's body and immobilize him, a violent presence burst forth with enough intensity to shake the air.

Suddenly, there was not a man trapped inside the leaves, but a harbinger of death. The leaves shook and stopped. As the violent aura radiated from the inside, the melancholy of the leaves melted away, as did the leaves themselves, revealing a Jack whose hair and robes swayed in the wind, whose mouth was twisted into a snarl, and whose eyes flashed with cold cruelty.

Brutalizing Aura!

The ball disintegrated around him, leaving him dominant in the sky, a promise of a torturous, brutal, and merciless death.

It was nice to use this skill so effectively.

Jack's eyes sought Auburn, but she was nowhere to be found. A wall of leaves still swirled in the near distance, hiding everything behind it from sight as it slid toward Jack like old age—slow but unstoppable.

Jack could not detect Auburn, but he had an idea of where she could be hiding. He reared his fist back. Spectral flames sprang around it, burning like a purple sun, and the vibrancy of the sky itself was sucked into the punch. The world went quiet. The wind died down. The clouds turned gray, the distant nebula darkened, and even the leaves lost their spirit as they turned from brown to ash.

Only the light blue platform under their feet remained unaffected.

"Meteor Punch!" Jack shouted, the only sound in existence, as he drove his punch forward. In the next moment, the sky exploded. Strong winds carried the shockwave into the densest part of the wall of leaves, completely blowing them away. Millions of them went flying in all directions, revealing a shocked Auburn in their thickest part. The shockwave pulled at her hair and robes and sent her flying back a few feet, forcing her to cross her arms to defend.

That was her real body.

Jack teleported behind her. Auburn's eyes went wide as she felt the source of Brutalizing Aura within arm's reach, but a punch was already flying at her. With a shout, an auburn sphere appeared around her body. Leaves filled the air again, forcibly resummoned to strike back.

An intense feeling of regret hit Jack as he was about to punch the wizard's shield. Almost like he was striking his mother in the face—like he had to stop right this instant, no matter what.

However, Jack had not reached this level by being frail of heart. He possessed the Dao Root of Indomitable Will. His heart broke the illusion, and his fist continued forth, if slowed down a bit.

Jack's second Meteor Punch crashed into the compacted auburn sphere, cracking it and sending Auburn flying away like an arrow. She bled wildly from the nose in her efforts to keep the protective sphere from shattering. Her eyes went hazy. At the same time, leaves surrounded Jack, flying into him before he could recover from his attack. There was no pain, only warmth; and yet, blood streamed from shallow cuts all over his body.

Jack crossed his arms and focused on his Brutalizing Aura to defend.

The truth was, the instant when Jack chose to defend, he could have ignored the attacks. His body was sturdy enough to take it. Instead of defending, he could have teleported to Auburn a third time and smashed out another Meteor Punch. There was no way the shield could take it; it would shatter like glass, Jack's fist would reach her, and he would be the winner of this sparring match.

Jack chose not to do that.

He was the new guy here, and everyone he'd met so far had been friendly. He didn't want to humiliate Auburn by making her lose publicly to someone forty levels weaker than herself.

Plus, Auburn herself was pretty strong. Significantly stronger than the treant and centaur Jack had fought before, even though they were of a higher level than her. Jack could respect that.

Apparently, it was true that not all immortals were the same—and random riffraff could never compare to a B-Grade faction's elites.

Jack also didn't want to just lose on purpose. Plus, if the battle continued while he went easy on his opponent, he might lose for real—their powers weren't too far apart.

Just as he was considering how to best handle this situation, Shol appeared in the middle of the blue platform, between Jack and the far-off Auburn.

"That's enough!" he declared with a smile, raising both hands. "Sparring usually goes to first blood. Since both fighters were injured at the same time, let this be a draw. Congratulations to both of you; it was a battle well fought!"

Jack took a moment to digest this, then retrieved his aura. The leaves around him disappeared at the same time. "Thank you," he told Shol, hoping the man understood his hidden meaning, then turned to Auburn. "It was a great battle! I learned a lot. Thanks for going easy on me."

The witch smiled with slight bitterness. Then, she shook her head, and the bitterness was gone. "I could say the same," she said. "Drawing someone forty levels over you is quite an achievement—and I am not weak myself. Congratulations, Jack. I'm sure your future will be as bright as a sun."

"As will be yours." Jack smiled back.

From the side, everyone clapped, even the robots. Brock winked at Melia, who rolled her eyes and looked away.

CHAPTER SIXTEEN
PURE DAO CULTIVATION

THE ATMOSPHERE AROUND THE CLOUD FIELD GREW WEIRD AFTER THE SPAR. Auburn exchanged a few words with Melia before taking off—she'd mentioned they'd come here to spar, but Auburn's mood was too sour after failing to defeat Jack, who was forty levels weaker than herself.

Which was a normal response, actually. Auburn was a young D-Grade immortal who had been taken in as a personal disciple of Master Huali. Her talent was undeniably superb. This had to be one of the hardest losses she'd ever taken.

It was just her bad luck for running into Jack.

Melia, however, approached Jack and started socializing. Her eyes no longer sparked with arrogance, but with respect. The meditating cultivator with long dark hair and flowing blue robes, whose name was Fang Long, also approached Jack, as did the woman who was practicing some sort of turtle skill. Both overflowed with energy and wit. Jack found himself chatting and laughing alongside them, enjoying a camaraderie that he hadn't felt in a while. Most strangers tried to kill him lately.

This really brought into focus how important strength was for cultivators. Before proving himself against Auburn, Jack would have been greeted with much less enthusiasm. Now, everyone was rushing to meet him.

That didn't make them bad people or opportunists. When meeting someone with great potential, you would naturally be more friendly to them compared to the same person with less potential. If you were busy with something else, you would put it aside for a moment to make a useful connection. It was just how the world worked.

Some time later, Jack extracted himself from their company and paced over to Master Shol, who sat cross-legged on the platform's edge, gazing at the nebulous sky. Brock was beside him—his monkey eyes filled with wonder, his breaths deep. He seemed to enjoy this very much.

As Jack approached, Shol gave him a smiling glance. "What do you think, Jack?"

"Of what?" Jack replied, taking a seat beside them. Unlike everyone else, he did not sit cross-legged, he let his legs dangle over the edge, an Earth-like posture that cultivators didn't adopt often.

"Of my faction," Shol replied. "You have seen our facilities. You have met a few cultivators. You even spoke to my master. So; what do you think?"

Jack chuckled. "Does it matter? I already agreed to join."

"Of course it matters. You used to be my disciple; now, you are my brother. Your opinion is important to me."

Jack stared long and hard at Shol, who was back to staring in the distance.

Time and time again, Shol had helped him. Back on Earth, he'd guided Jack regardless of their disagreements. He had asked his own master—Huali—to protect Jack from the Animal Kingdom. When she declined, Shol hadn't hesitated to go against her orders to help Jack further, and it was only because of his assistance that he survived. Now, once again, Shol brought Jack to his faction, where he would be safe, and took time out of his day to introduce Jack to the important locations of this estate.

The world of cultivators was a harsh one. With survival at stake, people worshiped power above all. They backstabbed each other. Everyone had hidden thoughts and hidden interests.

In Jack's experience so far, few people in this world were genuine... but Shol was undoubtedly one of them.

"Thank you," Jack said, not specifying why. Shol didn't ask. "I like it here. The people seem nice, and everything in the estate is pleasing to the eye. It's almost too good. I expected the entire world to be cutthroat and tyrannical, but your faction has surprised me pleasantly."

"Not my faction; just my master's estate. As you will come to realize, we are a small island of virtuousness in a sea of filth."

"Then, it seems I've come to the right place."

This time, it was Shol's turn to chuckle. He glanced back; the rest of the cultivators had returned to practicing, each in their own way. Nobody could hear their thoughts.

"I am glad to hear that, Jack," he said honestly. "This really is a nice place. It is a part of your journey that is necessary, as well as a safe port for when trouble knocks on your door. You will grow much more powerful here." He then paused, considering his next words. Jack let him—he turned to enjoy the breeze, the sky, and the simple fact that he was alive and free.

"However," Shol finally continued, "I want you to remember that a faction is just a safe port. It is home, but nobody should stay cooped up forever. Ships are not built to stay in the harbor. If you really want to grow strong, I would suggest stabilizing yourself here, increasing your strength in safety as much as possible, then going out to adventure. That is how young cultivators should act."

Brock looked on with interest. Jack raised both brows. "Why do you say this?"

"Because I know you. I know your path. Safety is insidious. It has a way of making you relax and decay, losing sight of your goals. Before you know it, you are a turtle in its shell, your edge dulls, and you are afraid of stepping out into the world again. You rest on your laurels, letting time flow by, and suddenly, all your momentum is gone, as is your bravery and youth, leaving you an aimless, risk-averse husk."

Jack frowned. "Thank you, brother, but I wouldn't do that. I have goals."

"Everyone does. Do you know how many young cultivators I have seen stepping into the faction with fire in their eyes, only to end up comfortable and content? I know you wouldn't want to let this happen, but you wouldn't see it coming. It is a slow and sly process. Comfort seeps into your bones. Now that Master has agreed to save your planet, you have no intense despair pulling you forward, and to keep pushing yourself may be your greatest trial yet."

Jack did not pretend to understand everything. He took his time considering Shol's words. "I know this aimless husk you speak of. It is me; used to be me, before the System arrived on my world. And I understand that resisting comfort is much more difficult than it sounds... but your reminder certainly helps. Thank you, brother. I will do my best to keep my Dao sharp, to keep myself thirsting for more power without losing my virtue, to rush ahead unstoppably, because one moment of pause can easily turn into eternity. I will not relax just because I can."

Shol nodded. "That's what I expect from my brother."

"Me too," Brock said, his eyes spouting kind flames. "I am strong."

"Brock, you are the strongest person I know," Jack said. "Even if the world collapsed, even if I turned weak, I know that your heart would never stop burning. You are, from head to toe, a true bro."

"And you are a fist," Shol pointed out, smiling wryly. "Don't sell yourself short. Not many people can boast a perfect Dao Seed."

"Now you're just flattering me."

"It's the truth! And don't forget, you achieved that while I was your master. I deserve the accolade."

Jack laughed, as did the other two. A few moments later, Shol said, "Well, that concludes your tour of the estate. There are other things on this planet, of course, but they can wait. Familiarize yourself with the estate first. In the meantime, is there anything you want to ask?"

Jack considered it. There was something, actually; a thought that Auburn, perhaps accidentally, had brought to the fore.

"Do you know anything about spiritual beasts?" he asked.

Brock's ears perked up. Shol nodded. "I do."

"Then, can you explain how Brock's cultivation works? He doesn't have access to the System, but he seems to be growing just fine so far."

Shol adopted a sagely look. It reminded Jack of his basement during the Integration Tournament, where Shol and Sparman would beat him up mercilessly, each in their own way. Those were fun times. "The

System doesn't make you stronger," Shol explained. "It just makes progression easier. Brock is cultivating as the pre-System people did; by simply focusing on his Dao."

"But what about stats? And skills?"

"Skills are nothing but applications of the Dao. The System facilitates them, but it is not necessary. If anything, using your Dao without the System gives you a better and wider understanding. As for stats... Well, that is not a problem. Have you noticed how, in the D-Grade, you can absorb the Dao to enhance yourself?"

"I have."

"The same thing happens in the earlier Grades, just slower and unconsciously. As Brock contemplates his Dao, its power naturally enters his body, merging with the parts that fit it best. The same happens to everyone. All the System does is quantify some attributes and let you distribute that power, instead of letting it settle in naturally, as well as grant you additional power upon defeating enemies."

"Then Brock has no disadvantage for lacking the System?"

"Not yet," Shol pointed out. "The System is meant to help mediocre cultivators rise in power faster. As long as Brock remains active and truthful to his Dao, he will not have a problem. If he starts taking it easy, that's when the System's absence will become noticeable, and his progress will slow to a crawl."

"I see. So, Brock has to keep pushing himself, just like you told me to do."

"Exactly. No wonder the two of you are brothers."

"Hear that, Brock? You really should—"

Jack's words were interrupted by Brock's laughter. He sounded happy and carefree as a daisy. "No worry," he said. "I am strong."

Jack wanted to say more things. He wanted to remind Brock to never give up and to always strive for more power. To warn him against letting his edge dull.

However, he kept his mouth shut. Brock knew all those things—and to remind him of them would be almost insulting.

"Okay," was all he said. "Go get them, bro."

"Yes."

Shol chuckled. "Attaboys. Any other questions?"

"Oh! I have two friends who were coming to the Exploding Sun: Gan Salin and Nauja," Jack said. "Both gifted E-Grades. Could you help me check if they've arrived?"

"They have. I was told they said my name upon entering the sect, but I didn't go to meet them. I believe they joined as outer disciples and are currently situated in the outer planet." His brows creased. "However... Wasn't that Gan Salin one of the Animal Kingdom scions on your planet?"

"He was, but don't worry about it. He's a good guy now."

"If you say so..."

"I think we should go visit them soon. Right, Brock?" Jack asked, giving his brorilla a meaningful glance. Brock nodded. Some things went unsaid between them, but both understood. As spiritual companions, they were on the same wavelength.

"Right then, before I forget; take these."

Shol reached into his pocket and removed two perfectly folded squares. As he unrolled them, they revealed themselves to be two capes: one medium-sized yellow, and one small red. Both had the insignia of the Exploding Sun—an exploding sun—woven into the fabric.

"Woah," Jack said, receiving the yellow cape. It felt soft and smooth to the touch—he had no doubt it was the best fabric he had ever touched. "We get our own capes?"

"I told you." Shol winked. "These capes are a symbol of your identity in the faction, as well as a symbol of status in the outside world. Don't lose them."

"We won't!"

"Then, welcome to the Exploding Sun!"

Both donned their capes, latching them closed under the neck, and let them flutter freely in the wind. They fit perfectly. "Thank you, brother," Jack said earnestly, while Brock gave Shol a grateful handshake.

"No problem. I didn't make these. Delivering them is just my duty," Shol said, then turned towards the sky.

"Before we go," Jack said, "I have a final question. As a deacon of the Exploding Sun, you probably have access to some information networks. Could you do me a favor and ask about a starship called the *Trampling Ram*? They helped me escape the Animal Kingdom, but they were attacked afterward, and their fate is unknown. They are good people."

"I can do that. Can you give me more details?"

"It's a small vessel; maybe it can fit ten people? The captain is a D-Grade cyclops called Dordok, and they were carrying an ambassador of the Fair Way Continent to the capital of the Animal Kingdom three months ago. Three Hounds intercepted them outside Earth-321, which is where I was separated from them."

"Okay. I will see what I can find out and get back to you."

"Thank you, brother. I really hope they're okay."

"Since they helped you, I hope so too." Shol stood, dusting off his robes. "Now then. Since my business here is done, I will be going. I have other responsibilities, too. If either of you has a problem, you can come find me whenever."

"Will do, brother. Thanks," Jack said. Brock gave him a thumbs-up. Shol returned the gesture.

"What will you do now?" he asked.

Jack exchanged another glance with Brock. "I want to cultivate. I want to experience the Dao Vision I got in the library and make myself as strong as possible as quickly as possible. Before that... I think we should visit Salin and Nauja in the outer planet. I hope they don't have any problems—though they're probably the ones *creating* problems."

CHAPTER SEVENTEEN

THE WAR FOR EARTH IS BREWING

HARAMBE CHEWED ON A BANANARM AS HE WATCHED THE OTHERS SPEAK. THE fruit juices ran over his chiseled jaw, dripped to his muscular chest, then collapsed to the ground between his trunk-like legs. He finished the bananarm and reached up the tree to get another.

"Are you paying attention, Harambe?" the human woman with glasses asked him. Harambe nodded. "Good. How do you propose we go about this?"

He stared at her emptily. Though he'd recently developed the Very Big Thought of Muscles, his speaking muscles remained weak.

"Harambe... wants..." he started saying, then gave up. He shrugged. Beating his chest lightly, he pointed at himself.

"Are you saying you'll handle it?" the woman asked.

He nodded.

"There are many points of entrance to this forest, Harambe. Even with our energy walls, one person is not enough. If it was, we could just rely on Sparman."

Leaning against a tree opposite her, Sparman gave a thumbs-up. "Thank you for your trust. As much as I would love to run around this forest all day every day to prevent random weaklings from setting it on fire, I unfortunately lack the speed."

"See what you did?" the woman pointed to the robot while looking at Harambe. "Now you got him talking."

"Oh, so I can run myself dry to protect you, but I cannot complain about it. Okay. I guess my iron bones will rattle in my grave, which I will make sure is dug directly under your bed."

"You have no bones. I checked."

"Just because I sound full when you knock on me, doesn't mean I actually am full. Wait—I am. Full of your *shi*—"

"Language, Sparman. Please."

Harambe was always baffled by this. How could this woman talk back to Sparman the robot, who was so much stronger than herself? Did she not fear he would accept her challenge?

Which he never did. The disrespect he could stand was stunning. Then again, it was always like that with humans, even metal ones. They made little sense.

Maybe they broken, he thought, a sun appearing over his head. Hmm. Yes. Head muscles go strong.

"So, since none of you have meaningful suggestions, let me propose a plan," the woman said. "We will split the forest into four sections. Harambe, you and your brorillas will defend the northeastern part, since your home is here. The forces of the Bare Fist Brotherhood will handle the northwestern area, while Sparman will take the entire southern half. I know it is a bit much, but at least it's better than defending the full length of the perimeter, as you have been doing so far."

Sparman raised a brow. "I can handle more than that."

"I know you can, but you've already been helping so much. Everyone needs some rest once in a while. Even D-Grade robots."

He stared at her suspiciously, then laughed. "Thanks, Professor. I appreciate it."

"No problem."

Harambe also didn't have a problem with this arrangement. He'd always claimed that his pack could protect themselves. However, he did have a question; one he couldn't properly articulate, but he didn't need to. He looked at the professor and asked, "Edgar?"

The magic man was strong. He had fought the ice-man in the sky over the forest, wielding powers that even Harambe himself had not possessed at the time. He was the strongest human present. Therefore, he should stand at the front to defend his pack.

"Edgar won't fight," the woman said, shaking her head. "I know you don't understand this, but trust me when I say there is no other choice. He has already done his best."

Harambe frowned deeply. Perhaps he should visit the magic man and make sure his head was in the right place.

"Hey, hoh, keep it in your pants," Sparman chimed in. "We've been through this before. Don't get violent with our allies."

"Yes," Harambe replied. The robot was undeniably stronger than himself; he had to obey. In fact, this robot was the strongest creature Harambe had ever seen.

But... brother Jack? he wondered, thinking back to the man to whom he'd entrusted his only son. By now, perhaps he would be strong enough to fight the robot.

Or not.

Harambe found his heart muscles clenching. He wished for Jack to be safe, because that would mean Brock, his son, was also safe. It would also mean they were weak. Strength did not come from safety, it came from danger and battle, surviving predators and hunting prey.

Harambe had realized this recently, when lifting weights no longer made him stronger. He yearned for battle, to work out by lifting his life up and down the line of death.

That would make his muscles really shine. It was also why he was excited about his new assignment.

"Enough?" he asked.

"If nobody has an objection, then yes," the woman replied. "This meeting is dismissed."

Harambe didn't need to be told twice. He walked on his knuckles to reach the clearing where his brorillas waited for the news. After that, he would rush to the border of the forest and wait for the poor invaders.

No matter who came, he was going to beat them up.

"Jack joined the Exploding Sun!" Vanderdecken exclaimed, sipping from his mug. "That's superb! I knew he had it in him."

"It's a double-edged blade," the professor replied with a sigh, sitting opposite him in the Bare Fist Brotherhood headquarters. She looked like she'd just returned from a walk in the forest. "He will now get much stronger... but our enmity with the Animal Kingdom is cemented. Any chance of reconciliation or mercy is gone. The moment the grace period ends, they will attack and annihilate us."

"Oh, dud—ma'am. That sounds terrible! And you want me to join?"

"You will have to pick a side anyway," she replied. "There aren't many E-Grades on the planet, and you are the most famous of them, with the exception of Jack. Even the planet's greatest rock star is nothing but a pawn to the Animal Kingdom's games."

Vanderdecken shuffled in his seat. "And if I don't?"

"We will have nothing to say about it, naturally. But the Ice Peak will. Anyone not their ally is their enemy, so don't be surprised if Alexander himself shows up at your next concert."

"I'll sing the hell out of him."

"You can try. However, if even Edgar couldn't defeat him, what makes you think you can?"

"Oh, don't worry about me. I'm pretty strong."

The professor sighed. "I made you misunderstand. It doesn't matter if you're stronger than Alexander, because he won't come fairly. You saw what happened to Brother Tao's monastery. He will scout you out and bring the appropriate number of troops so you have no chance."

"He came fairly for Edgar."

"It was a calculated risk because he knew he could win."

"Fair enough." Vanderdecken leaned back, passing a hand through his long dark hair. "Dude... I hate this. Why do I have to get involved in a war? I just want to sing."

"You can always hide away. Find a remote island and sing to the waves for a year. Nobody will bother you then."

"The waves can't appreciate my music. Without my fans, I would die of boredom."

"I understand. Which is why I insist you have to pick a side. And, between us and a tyrant, who will you go for?"

Vanderdecken narrowed his eyes. "You sound like you're trying a bit too hard."

"You know my allegiance. Obviously, I am not impartial, but facts don't lie. Look at the situation of our territories. In our half of the world, we are ushering in a new era, with System-oriented development and timely support for the areas that were impacted the most. Meanwhile, the Ice Peak territory is deeply sunken into poverty. People are exploited and forced to level-up like madmen. They die in scores. Families are torn apart, children starve to death, the elderly are abandoned, and those who cannot fight are decimated by diseases and uncontrolled beast hordes. All while their ruined cities dig out their own flesh to offer soldiers for Alexander's armies."

Vanderdecken flinched. "You're painting a vivid image."

"He does. I just say things as they are."

"Why don't they rebel?" the metal bard asked. "If the situation in those areas is so terrible compared to your territories, why don't the people just rise up for themselves?"

"Because all power is under the Ice Peak's complete control. Plus, they have no idea—information is so strictly regulated in that half of the world that they think *everyone* is suffering like they are. They don't like Petrovic, but they think we are even worse."

"Can't you just... let them know? Airdrop leaflets or something?"

The professor smiled sadly. "We're trying, but it's not that easy. The spread of information is a battlefield just like any other. Our forces contain entire organizations focused on cultural and ideological warfare."

"Just like the Ice Peak, I suppose."

"Yes. It is an undesirable but unavoidable aspect of war."

"And I suppose you also plant your own propaganda?"

"We do. There is no need to lie about it—not to you." The professor shook her head. "It is just a part of war. Whether you want to call it informational warfare or propaganda, everyone does it. Even the good side."

"So you're not the good guys here. You're just one side of the conflict."

"We are better than the Ice Peak and the Animal Kingdom. Are we saints? No. But are we as virtuous as we can be? Yes. We just cannot afford to pull punches."

Vanderdecken shook his head. His eyes were conflicted. "I don't know, dude... I'll need to think about this. It's all so ugly. I'm not sure I wanna get involved."

"You can make your own choice," the professor said, standing up to dismiss him. Her gray hair and white glasses caught a glint of sunlight from the window, illuminating her deeply sunken eyes. If Vanderdecken wasn't already feeling defensive, he would have felt pity for her—an old lady forced to take the world on her shoulders. "In the meantime, you are free to stay here or leave. Nobody will stop you. I just pray that, if the Ice Peak comes knocking, you will not make the wrong choice."

"I will not ally with them," he assured her. "I know they suck ass—and sorry for the language. I'm just not sure if I want to dirty my soul by getting involved in a war that, in the end, will matter very little. We're all going to die, anyway."

"Jack *will* return before the grace period is over, Vanderdecken," the professor said, her voice taking on a hard edge. "He is out there trying to save the world. He has already gone above and beyond anything we ever thought possible. He will find a way, I know it. And when he does, the groundwork we've set with blood and tears will let us save millions, if not billions of lives. A new world will dawn, free of oppression; but not if we give up without a fight."

"I sure hope you're right, Professor," Vanderdecken replied, standing himself. He picked up his electric guitar and slung it over his shoulder, then extended a hand. He hadn't felt so tired in... a long time. "In any case, thank you for your time. I will think deeply about what you said."

"I hope so, Vanderdecken. Fare well."

CHAPTER EIGHTEEN
BROS HELP EACH OTHER SHINE

THE OUTER PLANET CONSISTED OF ONE LARGE LAND MASS AND ONE MASSIVE ocean. Its colors resembled Earth's, reminding Jack of Pangea, the massive supercontinent that existed on Earth hundreds of millions of years ago.

As their starship dived through the atmosphere, Jack and Brock could observe the supercontinent with increasing clarity. Most of its surface was taken up by forests, deserts, savannas, icy tundras, and all sorts of natural biomes. Civilization was mostly gathered in large hubs, with sprawling megacities housing millions taking up entire mountain ranges.

The technological level didn't look too advanced. As the starship approached the ground, they spotted dirt trails and medieval cities. The air was clean, too. There were no factories, cars, planes, or other means of pollution. As for ships, this planet's sole supercontinent had little need for them.

All in all, this planet had a wild feeling to it. With pockets of civilization surviving in the wilderness, surrounded by dangerous environments and strong monsters in every direction.

It looked like the perfect place to train your E-Grades.

Jack's modern sensitivities protested that thought, but his System experiences agreed with the sight. This was a training planet. It was supposed to be rough.

The starship slowly touched down at the edge of one of the smaller cities—though still humongous. The moment Jack stepped out, with his yellow cape swaying and D-Grade status visible for all to see, the nearby people bowed slightly in deference. Many of them wore red capes with the Exploding Sun's insignia.

"Inner disciple..." Whispers began to spread as everyone arced their necks to take a better look. Jack felt like a celebrity.

A hint of his Dao seeped outside his body, manifesting as a breeze that struck the onlookers. "At ease," he commanded, and everyone scampered away.

Disembarking the starship, Brock took in the sights. He saw the clear sky, the clean, oxygen-filled air, the lack of technology, and the fighting spirit in everyone's eyes as they spotted his red cape. He grinned.

After shrinking and pocketing the starship, they walked a bit inside the city.

Unlike the general medieval look, every street and house here was numbered. The Exploding Sun kept precise records of where everyone lived, just in case they needed to be contacted. It didn't assign random quarters to each outer disciple, preferring to let them settle where their Dao could shine best. They were required to declare their place of residence every year.

Prior to coming here, Jack and Brock had visited the record-keeping department of the faction and gotten the address of Salin and Nauja. They lived together—though Jack yearned to find out how Nauja handled Salin's insanity.

Reaching a nice little house with the words "Sunrise Street 2A, 603" painted on its entrance, they knocked on the door. While they waited, they admired the house itself—a white, one-story building with a narrow garden surrounding it, situated at the edge of the city, where the noise wasn't too bad. It was a far cry from the accommodation offered to an inner disciple, but it was decent. Jack even felt a pang of nostalgia at the sight of something so simple, yet so inviting.

The door opened, and Salin stood there, clad in full leather armor and with a suspicious gaze. He froze when he recognized them. "Jack! Brock!" he exclaimed, drawing them both into a hug. "It's been so long!"

"Bro!" Brock shouted emotionally. Jack laughed.

"Barely a week, Salin. I didn't think you'd miss us so much."

"Are you kidding? Last I heard, you were trapped in—" He cut himself off mid-sentence, looking around the street. The few people around were all staring at them. "Come on in," he urged them. "Nauja is here, too."

They stepped in, admiring the simple yet clean architecture. There was a main room that served as both a living room and a kitchen, as well as a bathroom and a bedroom behind a closed door. That was it. Clay bowls and mugs sat neatly on shelves around the main room, while a table with four chairs stood in the very middle.

"Coffee?" Salin asked.

"Yes, please," Jack replied, while Brock shook his head.

"Oh, um, I don't actually have any. I was hoping you'd say no."

"Ha! Well then, some water would be fine."

"I'll bring you some tea, too."

Jack and Brock took a seat each, while Salin headed to a large water bucket and filled a few mugs, then took a teapot and started messing with it. The bedroom door slammed open, revealing Nauja in clean barbarian furrings, her eyes open wide. "Jack! Brock!" she exclaimed, completely mirroring Salin's reaction as she pulled them into a hug.

"Copycat," Salin muttered from the bucket.

"You made it out!" Nauja exclaimed. "How?"

"It's a long story," Jack replied. "We'll tell you all about it over tea."

"Great! Make some tea, Salin."

"I didn't hear the magic word."

"...Please?"

"There you go! I already made it, actually."

Salin joined the trio with four cups of water and four of tea. Brock smelled his cup suspiciously before trying a sip. His eyes brightened, and he downed the whole thing in a single gulp before getting disappointed that it was over already.

Jack passed him his own cup.

"Are you guys settled well here?" he asked.

"It's great!" Nauja replied, gesturing around the house. "Look at how many things we have! And it's all for free! Back in my tribe, all I had was an empty hut, but now I have my own... What did you call that, Salin?"

"A bathroom."

"I have a walled-off bathroom! For myself!" she shouted excitedly. "Now, no dinosaur can get me while I'm vulnerable!"

Jack smiled warmly. When one comes from grass roots, they are satisfied with impressively little. "Salin, did your house look like this when you were living in the Animal Kingdom?"

"Oh, no. I had a mansion for myself, with servants and all sorts of, uh, pleasant people."

Nauja narrowed her eyes at him.

Jack caught that and smirked, leaning forward on the table. "So. Are you guys together now?"

"No!" Nauja said.

"Not yet!" Salin replied at the same time.

Nauja glared at Salin.

"What?" he defended himself. "We're living together. It's bound to happen at some point."

"I don't even like you like that."

"Neither do I—*yet*. That's the key word. Give it a couple months and you'll see."

She rolled her eyes. "I'd rather be eaten by a hadrosaur—and they have a lot of teeth."

"Sorry for asking," Jack said.

"Not a problem," she replied. "We're living together because it's much better than living alone. We know nobody here. We need someone to have our back, plus it's nice to be living with friends."

"So, like, roommates."

"Housemates," she replied, looking at him like he was an idiot. "There is more than one room."

"Yeah, that's not what I—Well, whatever." He quickly scanned them, too.

Human (Trial Planet), Level 110 (E-Grade)

Faction: Exploding Sun (B-Grade)

Canine (Earth-387), Level 81 (E-Grade)
Faction: Exploding Sun (B-Grade)

Huh. They leveled up, too.

They must have scanned him back, because their eyes widened a tiny bit—though not as much as he expected.

"So, you really did become an immortal," Nauja said.

"I did. And I admit, you are less surprised than I expected."

"The knight in Trial Planet told us you were about to break through. Plus, you have the yellow cape of inner disciples flying behind your back."

"I guess." He laughed. I'm laughing a lot today, aren't I? Well, it can't be helped. These guys put me in a great mood.

"How did you escape?" Salin asked, unable to hold in his curiosity any longer.

Jack first scanned the surroundings with his Dao perception. Finding nothing suspicious, he narrated everything that happened from the moment he beat the Final Guardian to being accepted as a personal disciple of Master Huali.

"Huali? The elder?" Salin's eyes went wide. "Man, you really hit it big. I hear she's going to become the next Grand Elder!"

"I've heard something like that, too," Jack replied. "That she's one of the candidates... I didn't know she was the favorite."

"Well, there are only two candidates. It's only her and Elder Monsoon, so I hear it's quite the competition. Here in the outer planet, there are entire betting rings about this."

"Really?"

"Yeah, man! The Grand Elder is the highest authority after the Faction Leader and the B-Grade ancestors, who never leave their planet anyway. Whoever holds that position basically runs the entire constellation."

"Really!" Jack said, his eyes widening. He hadn't realized that Master Huali was *that* important. It would also explain why she was so busy the day he met her—running for Prime Minister of the constellation was bound to be time-consuming.

"And how is the position decided?" he asked.

"I can't believe you don't know this," Nauja said.

"The Council of Elders will convene nine months after the death of the previous Grand Elder—so in seven months from today—to elect the next Grand Elder," Salin said. "Three months after that, the Faction Leader will officially appoint them in a grand ceremony. Technically, the Faction Leader can veto the Council's decision and choose someone else, but that has almost never happened before."

"Huh. So they don't just battle each other for the position?"

"Of course not. They're elders, not animals."

"Oh yeah, wrong faction."

"Well, that's how it works. But it's just gossip for us outer disciples. The truth is, we don't care. We just stay here, train as hard as we can, and hope to one day become inner disciples like you."

"You will succeed," Jack said confidently. "I'm sure."

"Only one in a thousand E-Grades becomes an immortal. Well, a bit over that for outer disciples, but the chances are still abysmal."

"It doesn't matter. Both of you are experienced people in line with your Dao. As a D-Grade myself, I can promise you that you will both eventually succeed, unless you give up or grow soft along the way."

Gan Salin and Nauja glanced at each other. "Thank you," Salin said. "But it's not just us; I see that Brock here is doing even better."

Jack turned to Brock, who had a smug look on his face. Come to think of it, I haven't scanned him in a long time, have I?

Brorilla, Level 99 (King)

A gorilla variant from planet Green. Brorillas usually live with Gymonkeys and train them in the ways of working out. It is due to the Brorillas' unmatched pecks that Gymonkeys use poop to fight—they consider themselves too weak for anything else.

Brorillas are usually calm, measured animals. However, if anyone harms their little cousins or invades their territory, they go bananas.

This particular brorilla is a variant that visually resembles a gymonkey.

Though not weaker than other brorillas, the members of this variant are often shunned due to their lack of bulging muscles.

That is not the case for this specimen. Through intense determination, it has achieved much greater strength than its species' norm, as well as a perfect Dao Seed. Due to this specimen's potential, taming or slaying it are advised.

"Level 99!" he cried out. "And King? Brock, you didn't tell me you grew so much!"

"Maybe it's because he can't speak," Salin said, while Brock just wore a proud smile on his face.

"I can," he said.

"Oh, you can?" Salin challenged him, tapping at the table. "What is the word for this thing here?"

Brock frowned. "Bad bro need smack?"

"I was just kidding, my big brother. Of course you know how to speak."

Brock nodded.

"That is actually one of the reasons we came," Jack said, his voice betraying seriousness. "The truth is, the inner planet is not the best place for an E-Grade to train. There are few monsters, and everything is designed for immortals. I... It's great for me, but it is holding Brock back. I intend to leave him here, with you, so you can all advance together."

Salin and Nauja were shocked, and most of all Brock. No; he wasn't shocked, because he expected this. Just conflicted.

"Bro..." he muttered.

"I know, Brock. It feels weird to me, too. But you shouldn't delay your cultivation just because I'm on the inner planet." Jack forced back a choke he didn't expect, then pressed on. "Besides, it's not like we'll separate forever. Just for a bit. I'll come to visit often, too, and when you break through, you'll join me at the inner planet or wherever we go next."

Brock looked straight into Jack's eyes, his expression unreadable. Jack's heightened senses caught the brorilla's bottom lip quivering. It made his heart ache. Sometimes he forgot that, for all of Brock's strength and determination, he remained a child. He was just four months old.

However, this had to be done. Good brothers didn't hold each other back. The outer planet was where Brock could shine, not cooped up in a planet for immortals and made to follow Jack around like a mascot. Here, he could adventure with Salin and Nauja, he could fight monsters, hone his strength, make new bros. At the same time, Jack could also focus on his own cultivation.

And it really would be just a short separation. As soon as the time came to adventure, they would go together again. They were a team. They were bros. And, despite Brock's currently lacking strength, he had the talent required to follow Jack to the ends of the world.

Both of them understood these things. Though their Daos confirmed the decision, it remained hard. Besides Jack's month of closed-door cultivation in Garden Ring, they had not been separated since Harambe entrusted Brock to Jack, back when one of them was a baby and the other was only Level 34.

Now, it was finally time for Brock to grow on his own. This period of time would be critical—and, when they adventured together again, they really would be partners who fought back-to-back.

Hopefully.

"Okay," Brock said, and this simple word carried all the weight in the world.

Jack slapped the table, forcing himself to smile. "Well, I'm not going yet. Since I'm here already, let's spend some time catching up."

Salin excused himself and left the house. A few minutes later, he returned with a large jug of wine, which he placed on the table.

"Fuck tea," he said. "This is wine time. Drink up!"

Everyone laughed.

There was no night in Field Nebula. The gasses always shone in the sky, surrounding the three planets and the central moon. Despite that, Jack and Brock stayed in Salin and Nauja's house for several hours, drinking to their heart's content. Due to their cultivation, alcohol didn't make them drunk, just gave them a gentle buzz.

Jack did wonder if drunk driving applied to starships before realizing he could just expel the alcohol from his blood anytime he wanted to. Being an immortal had many perks.

In these hours, the four of them really bonded. They exchanged stories of their childhood, coming from four very distinct backgrounds. They spoke about their fears and worries. About their hopes and dreams.

Brock said he wanted to become the biggest bro there was. Jack wanted to reach the apex of power and be truly free. Salin wanted to enjoy himself and be happy, while Nauja wanted to see the world.

They poured their hearts out for each other, and for those few hours, that little house on a far-off planet in the middle of a nebula was the closest thing to home they'd ever felt.

As time passed, they laughed, too. Brock juggled clay mugs while dancing to Salin's terrible singing of the Animal Kingdom anthem—he was changing a word here and there to make it sound ridiculous.

They drank and cried. It was a night to remember.

At some point, Jack stood to leave. "I will not forget you, bro," he told Brock, clapping both his shoulders. "As soon as we're out of this place, let's adventure together again. The time will come before you know it. Okay?"

Brock nodded bravely. "Okay, bro."

Jack walked away, alone into the night, waving goodbye to his three best friends in the world—with the possible exception of Edgar.

For a little bit, he would be without Brock, alone. The thought made him sad—but he consoled himself with the knowledge that this would really help Brock shine. Here, on the outer planet, he would become a beast, and that was the only way for them to continue adventuring together in the future.

And, who knows? By the time they left this place, maybe Brock would have become bros with this entire planet. The sky was the limit.

CHAPTER NINETEEN
BEING A BIG BRO

Brock raised the Staff of Stone and smashed it down. Boulders went flying. The grass bent by the wind. The wolf that was facing him was instantly obliterated, its head caved in, while the rest of the pack jumped on Brock from all sides.

He twirled. His staff followed an uneven trajectory, mowing through bodies even as the wolves attempted to pile on him, more than he could deflect. A set of jaws wrapped around his leg. Another aimed for the throat.

An arrow came out of nowhere, zipping into the wolf about to behead Brock and nailing it to a tree. Gan Salin jumped out of the shadows, sinking his fingertips into a wolf's back. "Five Star Grasp!" he shouted. The wolf fell to the ground bleeding from the five deep wounds.

Brock had still suffered a wound to the leg, but it was far from enough to stop him. He released a monkey cry and swung his staff around, augmenting it with the full power of his muscles. His biceps bloated like bananarms. One wolf was sent flying, and another had its head dug into the ground.

The three remaining wolves retreated.

"That's right!" Salin shouted, waving his fist at them. "Run with your tail between your legs! That's what you get for attacking the Salin Squad."

"For the last time, we are not called that," Nauja replied, stepping out of the shadows. "If anything, we are the bros."

"You are a sis."

"I don't think "bro" is gender-specific. Is it, Brock?"

"No." Frowning at the wound on his leg, Brock looked around. Shortly afterward, a squirrel dived down from a tree, carrying a few strange leaves in its mouth. Brock smiled brightly. "Thanks, bro."

The squirrel gave Brock a tiny high-five and scampered away, completely uncaring about the five dead wolves sprawled across the forest floor.

"Can I get some—" Salin started saying, but the squirrel was already gone. "Bummer."

Brock shook his head. He then mimed that good bros did not seek to use, but to help each other. The squirrel would know if Gan Salin was being genuine.

Of course, nobody understood his miming.

"I'll get you an encyclopedia," Nauja promised. "Then, we'll be able to talk normally."

Brock shrugged.

"Isn't it weird that he can understand us but can't speak?" Salin asked.

"A bit," she admitted. "But can we talk about it later? We're still swimming in dead wolves."

"Oh. Right."

They walked on, leaving their little battlefield behind. The forest scavengers would take care of it.

They were in a place called the Endless Forest. A wooded area close to the city they lived in, infested with all sorts of predatory animals. They were strong, too—at least at the E-Grade, boasting either extraordinary attributes or a connection to the Dao. Here, any F-Grade animals were at the very bottom of the food chain.

This was an area the nearby E-Grade disciples visited often. It lent itself to adventure and battle, making for the perfect training grounds.

Of course, it was also dangerous; many disciples entered this forest to never return, turned from predator into prey.

Unlike what its name indicated, this forest wasn't actually endless. Its physical dimensions were well set. However, its deeper parts were infested with extremely strong monsters, including King peak E-Grades and even the rare D-Grade. People couldn't cross from one end to the other, which led to them naming it Endless Forest.

Brock, Gan Salin, and Nauja were three of the many disciples adventuring through the forest today, as they often did. Thanks to their high levels and Brock's addition to their party, they decided to venture deeper than before, aiming for an area with known ogre sightings. In the meantime, they didn't shy away from the forest's natural predators.

"Did you level-up in the last fight, Nauja?" Salin asked. "I got one level."

"No. The wolves were only around Level 90. It takes more than that to level me."

"Hmm."

"What kind of forest hides its strongest predators, anyway?" she wondered aloud. "Where I come from, tyrannosauruses roam everywhere, not just the deep end of the jungle."

"There is no deep end here. It is endless."

"Right."

"We're pretty far in, actually," Salin said. "We should enter the ogre area anyti—"

Brock raised a hand, and Salin promptly shut up. A moment later, Salin whispered, "What's the matter, big bro?"

"Trouble," Brock replied, his brows low. His grip tightened around the Staff of Stone as his nose and ears twitched.

He didn't actually sense anything. He picked up no suspicious sound, sight, or scent. However, he felt a sudden lack of bros in this area. The various insects and small animals he befriended along the way had disappeared or gone silent. Like the forest was holding its breath.

Brock looked around, still seeing nothing. Glancing back, he caught Nauja looking up. Her eyes widened. She struggled to react in time, her legs bending ever so slightly, her center of balance tilting backward. The glint in her eyes indicated she might not make it in time. Brock had no such concerns. His muscles were well-honed, able to react faster than thought. He jumped back, ramming into Salin and Nauja and taking them along as he tumbled into the grass, barely dodging the large shape that smashed down from the branches above.

Brock turned around to find an ugly stone club heading for his face. He swung his Staff of Stone to meet it. Stone crashed into stone, and fragments flew everywhere as Brock lost the exchange, the club pushing the staff into his ribs and sending him flying into a tree.

"Brock!" Nauja shouted, already on her feet with an arrow nocked. Salin was rushing to make some distance as Brock dislodged himself from the bark he'd been buried in and turned to regard their assailant.

A colossal form towered over them. A tall humanoid wrapped in multiple layers of fat, bursting with thick muscles underneath. It only wore a loincloth around its privates, leaving its pale skin visible for all to see. Its eyes were filled with mindless fury, and two short tusks jutted out of its mouth, dripping thick saliva.

"An ogre!" Nauja exclaimed, her eyes widening. "Wait; it's an elite!"

"And Level 124, too," Salin replied. "I think this is a whoops moment. Should we run?"

The ogre was at least twice as tall as Brock and three times as wide. It was a mountain of muscles.

Brock slowly rose from the ground. He stood against the ogre, tiny as he seemed in comparison, and cracked his neck. Blood was escaping from scrapes on his arms, while his ribs felt numb. He looked right into the ogre's fury-filled eyes, then said, "Come."

The ogre was not used to being challenged by something so tiny. That infuriated it even further. It opened its mouth to release a mighty war cry that reverberated across the forest for multiple miles, showering Brock in saliva.

Brock was not one to take this lying down. He was the leader of his pack. He couldn't lose a war of roars.

Still holding the Staff of Stone, he beat hard at his chest. The thuds came like sledgehammers on stone, his gorilla roars rising to meet the ogre's. The two of them matched roars, then stopped at the same time as they prepared to fight.

"Assist!" Brock called out. His muscles bulged. His chest was filled with the urge to fight. He drew his staff back and charged for the ogre, which charged right back.

"Shit," Salin and Nauja said at the same time, both jumping into the fray.

Brock feinted jumping at the ogre. The club came down with little finesse other than an excess of force, pushing the air so hard it ricocheted off the ground. It missed Brock and smashed into a tree trunk with enough force to shatter it.

The tree titled and began to fall. The canopy was ripped apart. Leaves and splinters flew everywhere as branches were pulled in different directions, unraveling the complex designs they'd spent decades weaving. The tree landed on another, stabilized for now, but it was just momentary. This place was not a clearing. There was no space to fight. The ogre would demolish this entire area of the forest.

Brock's eyes narrowed as he considered his opponent. It was too strong. His ribs still hurt from the previous exchange, and it had even been a hasty strike. He couldn't take this creature head-on.

"Bring it," he said, jumping into battle. The club fell around him like lightning, crashing through everything and anything in its path. Trees fell. Trunks shattered. Bushes were uprooted and sent flying, while entire strips of ground were torn away. Brock danced between the strikes, channeling all of his muscles to move fast and sharply enough. His concentration was razor-sharp—he had to predict the ogre's every move if he wanted to dodge.

At the first opening, he struck. His Staff of Stone went sharply for the ogre's knee, hitting it from the front in an attempt to bend it the wrong way. The ogre groaned and stumbled, but its bone held. Brock tsked. He let the club sail under him as he jumped up, thrusting the staff upward to ram into the ogre's jaw. Its head went flying back—but again, the layers of fat and muscle were enough to protect the bone.

With a roar, the ogre smashed its staff upward, and Brock had to step against the ogre's chest to dodge.

An arrow flew over his shoulder and into the ogre's exposed throat. The power of the Dao trailed it—more power gathering the farther it flew. It wasn't much at this distance, but it was enough. It pierced cleanly into the ogre's throat, the tip poking out the other side. At the same time, Salin came from behind, swiping his claws over the ogre's ankle to sever its tendons.

With a groan, it stumbled. Its tendons held, somewhat, but they were injured. It turned to Salin and swung, but he'd already retreated. "Too slow!" he taunted. "Maybe cause you're dumb."

Despite the arrow lodged in its throat, the ogre was still alive. It didn't even seem to register its impending death. Blood spurted out of the wound and dyed the forest red as it charged for Salin, who yelled, "Oh shit!" and ran away.

However, the level difference between them was just too much. Salin was Level 82; the ogre was 124, and an elite. It would catch up in three steps.

Brock appeared over the ogre's head, smashing down with his club. Its head jiggled from the hit, further aggravating the throat wound. "Me," he demanded, staring at the back of the ogre's head.

It ignored him. Somewhere in its tiny brain, it understood that turning to attack Brock was a bad idea. Its gaze remained glued on Salin, pursuing him as fast as its wounded leg could handle. Salin paled. He ducked between trees, dove into bushes, jumped on branches. The ogre's club was a menace. It tore through the forest to reach him, destroying everything in its path. Entire trees tumbled and were smacked around like pinatas. At the speed they fought, even gravity seemed slow to react.

Roars echoed through the forest as the ogre pursued. Arrows showered it, embedding themselves deeply into its limbs and torso, but it didn't care in the slightest. It seemed to hold infinite blood, and there had to be some type of magic helping it, or it would have collapsed from the throat wound by now.

Durable Dao, Brock realized, his brows falling. He was still pursuing the ogre, trying to stop it without getting too close. He knew that, as mindless as it was, it remained an animal—the moment he made a mistake, it would turn around and pounce. His staff fell on knees and elbows, joints and fingers, but the ogre's durability was simply off the charts. It shrugged everything off.

A second arrow found the ogre's throat. That finally made it stumble. It looked around, trying to locate the hidden attacker. It succeeded

—but Nauja was too far away, and she could use her mastery of wind to escape easily, should it pursue.

The ogre must have finally sensed its death approaching. It turned to Salin and started attacking even more frantically, desperately trying to take him along to the grave. No matter how Brock and Nauja attacked, it ignored them.

However, in doing so, it gave Brock the opening he needed. Not a physical one, but one of the Dao. Because, in choosing to attack the weakest member of their party in a final act of bitterness, it had acted un-bro-like.

And Brock's Dao refused to let that stand.

Facing an unworthy bro, Brock felt his heart beat harder. Blood pumped everywhere fast. His muscles stretched and grew as the spirit of the bro lent him its righteous strength, letting him act like the big bro he really was.

This time, he was no longer afraid of the ogre. He flashed before it, right between it and Salin, protecting his little brother. This gave him even more power. He could feel himself overflowing with righteousness, as well as the belief that, as long as he was in the right, he could not lose.

The Dao of the Bro would not permit that.

The ogre bellowed and brought its club down. Brock roared and swung back. The two weapons met. But the ogre had received many wounds, and its power was drained. And Brock was now enhanced by his perfect Very Big Thought of Brohood.

As the two weapons clashed, the air cracked around the point of impact. A strong gust was unleashed in all directions, framed by falling trees in the background. Brock pushed forward, investing everything into this strike for brohood. The ogre's club gave an inch—and instantly, it flew back, out of its wielder's grip. Brock's attack carried on and smashed into the side of the ogre's neck, bending it out of shape along with the two arrows still embedded in it.

Multiple cracks resounded. The ogre fell to the ground, its eyes perpetually open in bitterness, and it never moved again.

They had won.

"Oh man, that was dangerous," Salin said, approaching. "Good job, guys. I got three levels! But how the hell did you overpower this thing, Brock?"

Brock turned and regarded him, the spirit of brohood still playing in his eyes. This battle had given him some insights. He ought to ponder them soon.

"Because I am big bro. And good bros never lose."

CHAPTER TWENTY

THE STRUGGLE FOR GRAND ELDER

AS TIME PASSED, JACK FELL INTO A SCHEDULE.

During the morning, he meditated on his Dao. He sought to explore the essence of the fist, what it really meant, and how it coexisted with the world. How all his different Dao Roots interacted with each other to form one complete whole, and how he could push forward the mastery of his Dao Skills.

In the afternoon, he practiced combat. He became a regular of the cloud field, sparring with any willing immortal. These battles really widened his experience, letting him see a dozen different Daos. Sparring against people with completely different fighting styles forced him to constantly adapt, exploring the limits and applications of his skills. It also trained his mind to think outside the box, be ready for anything, and improvise effectively when outside familiar waters. It was far more efficient than training against Copy Jack, whom he hadn't visited much lately.

Through these sparring sessions, Jack became known in Huali's estate. Everyone wanted to see the young immortal who was on the cloud field every afternoon, ready to demonstrate his might against any willing opponent. Before long, people lined up to fight him, awed by his strength. Even here, where his opponents were some of the brightest immortals in the constellation, no other low D-Grade was a match for Jack. Of the middle D-Grades, those between levels 170 and 210, Jack could only beat around half.

Of course, his opponents weren't constrained at those levels. He fought many late D-Grades as well, though he won against none of them. Their strength was incomparable to the centaur and treant he'd fought on Derion.

Over time, Jack accumulated a lot of battle experience against diverse opponents, as well as fame that resounded even outside the estate.

That was his every afternoon.

At night, he did not rest—cooped up inside his cultivation cellar, as he had come to call it, Jack reaped the Dao that the Dao Magnet had collected during the day. He cultivated in place of sleep, exactly eight hours per day, then jumped right into his morning routine.

However, even while cultivating like that, he wasn't nearly as fast as he imagined.

The people who reached the D-Grade were the best of the best—one in a hundred thousand cultivators, roughly. Despite that, they spent decades and centuries to reach the peak of this Grade, if they ever could. Jack had aspired to reach the C-Grade within a year, but as it turned out, he'd greatly underestimated the difficulty of that goal. The D-Grade was a massive stretch—it contained as many levels as the F and E-Grades combined.

Even in the estate of Master Huali, assisted by a Dao Magnet, and with no problems to distract him from cultivation, his progress was far from fast enough. When he dropped off Brock at the outer planet, Jack had been Level 139. After cultivating for two weeks, he'd only reached Level 144, and these were supposed to be the fast levels. In the late D-Grade, his progress would slow by dozens of times.

That painted a very clear picture in Jack's mind. If he stayed in this place, no matter how hard he overworked himself, he would never become strong enough. He had to leave and adventure as Shol advised. That decision was further punctuated by how, on his way to Field Nebula, he'd defeated one late D-Grade and one almost-late, and he'd gotten eight levels in a day. It was incredible just how much faster battle was compared to peaceful cultivation.

Of course, it hid the risk of death, as well as the reduction of the overall power in the galaxy. In that way, cultivation remained balanced—to get one level through combat, Jack might have to kill an immortal with a hundred and fifty on his back. It made sense why it wasn't as encouraged as slowly cultivating in the faction. Most immortals had time.

Jack didn't.

Even though Master Huali had agreed to save Earth, he did not believe his enmity with the Animal Kingdom would just disappear. Sooner or later, problems and enemies would arrive at his doorstep, and unless he was strong enough to protect everyone he cared about, things would go very wrong very quickly. He had to work hard now so he could deal with the problems that had yet to appear.

On the bright side, even though he lacked time, what he did not lack was enemies. The Animal Kingdom had very kindly volunteered its immortals as fodder for Jack's cultivation, and he was determined to go pick them up at some point.

He set himself a time limit of one month in the faction. After that, he would head to the Animal Kingdom and wreak havoc.

He could have gone right away, but, as always, cultivation consisted of two stages—expansion and consolidation. Jack's strength had risen meteorically in Trial Planet, which meant he needed to spend some time stabilizing his foundation. He had to get familiar with his current level of power, his new Class, his new Dao and domain, his Dao Skills, his attributes... The consolidation of his power was his current goal, along with gathering battle experience against different kinds of immortals. That was also why he hadn't yet explored the space-related Dao Vision he'd gotten from the library.

Half a month into his cultivation, he wasn't particularly stronger than before, but he was far more aware of his limits, as well as more conscious of the best ways to use his different powers. He was setting the foundation that would later allow him to slaughter Animal Kingdom immortals instead of getting slaughtered himself.

However, this period of intense cultivation did not come without problems.

Immortals didn't need to sleep, but that didn't make them machines. After two weeks of working nonstop, Jack was mentally and physically drained. His eyes had dark circles underneath. His mind was drowsy instead of sparking from one idea to the next. His movements in battle became rigid and mechanical, especially against opponents he'd faced before, resulting in several preventable losses. When meditating, Jack often found himself distracted, his mind wandering into unrelated subjects.

Only cultivation itself—drawing in the Dao of the environment to strengthen himself—remained efficient, as it wasn't a particularly mind-intensive task, but it was not the focus of his current training.

As a result, on a day when meditation felt simply impossible, Jack decided that he needed to take a break.

"Slow and steady wins the race," he consoled himself, rising to his feet. "A day's break now can save me several days of turtle-paced progress later on. Right, Bro—"

He paused. Even now, he still sometimes forgot that Brock was on a different planet, undoubtedly going through his own training. His absence was a gap in Jack's soul, like something was just not right.

Spiritual companions were more than a figure of speech.

"But what do I do today?" he asked himself, speaking aloud to alleviate the loneliness. "I could visit the others at the outer planet. Or maybe Shol wants to hang out. Or both. Why not both?"

During his two weeks here, Jack had realized that not many trained as hard as he did. The other immortals in the estate were consistent and diligent, but they only practiced for about eight hours a day, splitting that time between cultivation, sparring, and meditating. Jack practiced for about twenty-four hours a day.

As a result, they had free time. Many people had invited Jack for coffee, tea, or food, but he always declined, too busy training.

"Let's go check on Shol," he decided. He flew out of his cultivation cellar and out of his house, rising to the sky. Immediately, he spotted Auburn flying nearby. The other immortal spotted him as well and came over for a greeting.

They'd sparred multiple times and became almost friends. Auburn had even apologized for the dirty tactic she used in their first spar—though Jack didn't consider it as such.

"Good morning, Jack," Auburn said. Her orange hair floated behind her, accentuating her auburn robes while framing her small nose and wide eyes. "What happened? You're not cultivating."

"Yeah. I decided to take a break."

"You? A break?" She looked around. "Did hell freeze over?"

"I just got tired," Jack replied, laughing. "Even I cannot go on forever."

"Says the guy who doesn't sleep."

"I close my eyes sometimes."

"Sure. Next time you blink, I hope you wake up well-rested."

He smiled. "Are you doing anything today, Auburn? We could hang out."

"I was planning to visit the city, actually. I have some shopping to do. You can join me if you want."

"The city?"

"Yeah. Stripe City. It's half an hour of flight away."

"Oh. Sure, count me in." Jack had yet to leave the estate and explore the inner planet. Going with Auburn was a great opportunity to do that. Plus, he wondered what a city of immortals would look like. "When are we going?"

"How about right now? I was on my way."

"Alright. It's not like I have anything to do. Should we invite Shol, too? I was planning to hang out with him later."

She bit her bottom lip. "That's... not a good idea. Brother Shol can't leave the estate for now."

"Why?"

"It's about the Grand Elder struggle. Master Huali and Elder Monsoon are fighting for reputation right now, so their disciples are looking for any chance to humiliate each other. Elder Monsoon's head disciple is the strongest D-Grade in the entire faction, so if he hears about Shol being anywhere outside the estate, he will rush over and find an excuse to challenge him. That's why he cannot leave. As the head disciple of our master, he cannot afford to lose right now."

"I see... This Grand Elder struggle is more complex than I expected."

"Of course it is. The Grand Elder is appointed for life, and the previous holder of the position kept it for three thousand years. We don't discuss it much here in the estate, but outside, it's all anyone ever talks about."

"Huh."

"Just huh? We're talking about *once-in-a-lifetime* events here! If Master becomes the Grand Elder, the status of all of us will be elevated as well!"

"Well... I hope our master wins, obviously, but I've only been here for two weeks. I don't see these things the same way you do. Speaking of, if Shol can't leave because he may be challenged, is it alright for us to go shopping?"

"We'll be fine. Shol is more involved because he is our master's head disciple. Even if a disciple of Monsoon runs into us and wants to create trouble, nobody will really care. Unless we do something stupid, of course."

"Oh, don't worry. I never do stupid things."

She stared at him. "You don't sound very convincing."

"Trust me. Smart is my middle name."

"And yet, you strike me like the kind of guy who punches first and asks questions later."

"I'll have you know I was a scientist before my planet got Integrated. The ripped muscles and good looks are just the newest addition to my kit."

"Right..." She looked him up and down with disapproval, then shook her head. "Whatever you say."

Jack laughed. "So, wanna go?"

"Yep. Follow me!"

Auburn darted into the sky, and Jack followed her. They rose over the sparse clouds, admiring the green terrain below, and spent their time making idle conversation—telepathically, as the wind was not very helpful for their actual voices.

Soon after, short, colorful buildings appeared on the horizon: Stripe City.

CHAPTER TWENTY-ONE
THE ART OF COURTING DEATH

STRIPE CITY LOOKED JUST AS ITS NAME INDICATED. A THIN STRIPE OF architecture shoved in between two mountains, extending for at least five miles and maybe one in width. It was nowhere near the size of the bustling metropolises of the outer planet, but it remained a respectably sized city.

"Wow," Jack said, gazing at it from afar. "Transportation must be hell there."

"It's alright. There are great lanes for E-Grades to run on, letting them reach anywhere they want pretty quickly."

Jack did a double take. Indeed, the city was filled with streets just like the ones on Earth, except there were no cars. People just ran from one place to the other, their speeds varying between that of a normal human at full sprint and a motorcycle. There were many cultivators flying, too; both E-Grades with flying abilities and immortals.

"I guess..." he replied, still shocked. "It will never cease to surprise me."

"It?"

"The things cultivators do. Where I come from, we ride mechanical, uh, chariots from place to place. Running would just exhaust us and make us smell bad."

"That sounds terribly inconvenient. What if someone steals your chariot?"

"It happens. Then, you have to use the public chariots."

"It must be fascinating to be so weak."

"That's not the word I would use, but it's certainly different."

They glided through the clouds, approaching the entrance of Stripe City. Both mountains that surrounded it were lush with greenery, while the buildings were short and colorful, painted in all colors of the rainbow. It was a strong enough sight to almost be disorienting, but Jack didn't mind. He couldn't ask for everything in the universe to adapt to his aesthetical sensibilities.

Perhaps this multicolorism was inspired by the solar gasses filling the sky, shining like a full starry night.

"By the way," Auburn said as they landed, "I'm glad to hear you sent your brorilla to the outer planet. He will have a more fruitful time there."

"I sure hope so. Your suggestion helped me do it."

"Do you miss him?"

"Very." A wave of nostalgia rose in Jack's chest. "Wait. Are you trying to get under my skin again?"

She chuckled. "We aren't going to fight this time. I'm just curious."

"Hmm."

The city gates were large arches of blue stone. A thin crowd surrounded them on all sides, filled with people at the E and D-Grades. Jack did not expect to make much of an impression.

The moment they landed, however, whispers began to spread.

"Isn't that Auburn? The disciple of Elder Huali?"

"What is she doing here?"

"Will there be a fight?"

"Is that a new disciple?"

Jack raised a brow as his ears caught some of the whispers. "What is all this about?" he asked Auburn.

"I told you, the Grand Elder succession is all everyone talks about nowadays. It's even reached the point where people memorize the faces of each elder's disciples, hoping to not miss any gossip. If you ask me, they would be better off investing that effort in their cultivation."

"I thought you said we would be fine."

"We should be. Even if there is some trouble, it's not like it will matter much. Besides, what else are we going to do? Stay in the estate like scared mice?"

"I guess not." Jack met a few eyes, making them turn away. "Whatever. Let them stare."

"That's the spirit. Now, let's go, the earlier we start, the earlier we'll finish, and we can grab some food after."

As they were on the move into the city, whispers still rose around them, but much sparser—by the time more people noticed their presence, Jack and Auburn were already gone.

They walked down a central avenue, then turned into another. Colorful buildings and shops of all kinds surrounded them, but Auburn was focused on something specific. En route, they did not rush; they strolled along casually, talking about this and that. Auburn explained some things about the planet to Jack, while he shared some of his adventures—minus the sensitive parts.

"It's incredible that you won the Garden Assault," Auburn admitted, sighing. "I participated five years ago as the Lady of the Exploding Sun, but I lost to a man from Dragon Valley. Well, joke's on him—I think he's still a E-Grade."

"You were a Lady? Do you also have three Dao Roots?"

"Of course. What did you think, that I was some weakling? Most personal disciples of our master have three roots. That is why your strength is so impressive—we are elites, but you can jump an entire tier to fight us."

"What can I say? My fist is just too strong."

"Whatever, smart guy. Here we are, the apothecary."

A large building shaped as a cauldron stood before them. It was multiple stories high and covered an entire block. Jack had to crane his neck backward to see its top.

"I didn't know you practiced medicine," he told her.

"We call it alchemy; but yes, I do dabble a bit. It's a nice pastime. I brew wine, too."

"Really? I have a cellar."

"That's great. When we get back, I'll gift you a barrel—I'm making them faster than I can drink them."

Jack wondered how a barrel of wine would interact with his Dao Magnet but didn't voice his question. They entered the shop and spent over two hours there—it housed a thousand different kinds of herbs, along with medicine, manuals, equipment, pills, experience balls, and anything apothecary-related Jack could and couldn't imagine. It was so large that it housed many smaller shops inside it, like a mini shopping mall devoted solely to apothecary.

Jack got a Disguise Potion, just in case.

Auburn toured everything. She was overflowing with enthusiasm, not staying silent for a moment as she explained the properties of many different plants to Jack, who was more absent-minded than listening to her. The exhaustion of the past two weeks was getting to him.

Maybe I should have stayed home and slept... he considered but did his best to remain pleasant. Two hours later, they exited the Cauldron Mall—as it was aptly named—with Jack carrying four large bags full of herbs. Auburn pranced ahead of him.

"Thank you for keeping me company," she said, smiling widely. She'd loosened up quite a bit during their shopping tour. "Let's go get food now. My treat."

"Are you sure?"

"Of course! It's my thanks for coming all the way out here—plus, you can consider it an initiation gift from your big sister."

"There is nothing big about you. Since I'm stronger than you, I'm the senior here."

"Dream on, Jack. Let's go!"

This time, they didn't walk. Jack had had enough, so they simply flew to the terrace of the tallest building in town, which housed a restaurant. They sat at a table by the edge, Stripe City stretching under them. Auburn ordered a bunch of stuff Jack had never heard before, along with some wine—and, from the careful questions she asked the waiter, she really did sound like a sommelier.

Soon after they were done ordering, two people arrived and sat at the table next to them. One was a bare-chested, muscular mountain of a man. The other was a lithe woman with long dark hair and a sharp nose. Both looked to be in their forties—though, since they were immortals, their actual age was probably far greater.

Auburn did not react visibly to their appearance. However, the moment they sat down, her voice rang in Jack's mind.

"Be careful! These people are disciples of Elder Monsoon. Since they sat next to us, they'll probably look for an excuse to cause trouble. We should eat fast and leave."

Jack snuck another glance, inspecting them.

Human (Earth-44), Level 181
Faction: Exploding Sun (B-Grade)
Title: Eighth Ring Conqueror

Human (Earth-44), Level 165
Faction: Exploding Sun (B-Grade)
Title: Seventh Ring Conqueror

The man held the highest level between the two. Still, Jack estimated that he and this man were on roughly the same level of power, even if he had the Eighth Ring Conqueror title that not many people boasted.

Even the fact they displayed these titles spoke volumes about them. It was bragging. Most people chose to hide theirs.

Jack snorted. "Why should we eat fast and leave?" he replied mentally. "If they want to cause trouble, let them."

"That is not a good idea."

"Yeah, for them."

Auburn didn't reply. They kept on chatting about irrelevant things. Jack caught the bare-chested man sneak glances their way but pretended to see nothing.

Their food arrived—a set of large platters containing everything from cheese to meat to salad. It was made from materials suitable for immortals—even a whiff of its fragrance made Jack salivate. He couldn't wait to eat.

Except the bare-chested man from the other table started laughing loudly. Jack couldn't stop himself from looking over—the man was staring at them, as if mocking them.

"Is there a problem?" he asked.

"A problem? Of course not," the man replied. His voice was deep and aggressive, and his smile was predatory. "I was just wondering why great immortals such as yourselves would order something so cheap."

There were dozens of people in this restaurant, all of them D-Grades. As the man spoke, everyone went silent and turned to look. Jack felt their gazes. He couldn't care less; all he cared about was the other man's challenge.

"We can eat whatever we want," he replied. "We don't have to flaunt our wealth like you flaunt your titles."

"Oh? Do you mean my Eighth Ring Conqueror?" the man shot back, laughing rowdily. "I am proud of it, so I display it. What's the issue? If you aren't embarrassed, how about you display yours, too? As a disciple of the renowned Elder Huali, you will not have something worse than me, right?"

This guy wasn't even bothering to hide his intentions at all. Jack even got the urge to display his Ninth Ring Conqueror title and make this guy eat his words, but that was a secret—he wouldn't reveal it over some childish taunt.

However, since he couldn't display that title, he had no good way of refuting the insult.

"What am I, a circus animal?" he replied with a snort. "You think I will do something just because you told me to?"

"I thought you would protect your honor. Then again, your cheap meal makes it clear that you don't care about appearances—unless, of course, you are just not willing to spend a lot for the average-looking woman sitting beside you."

The man pushed as far he could go. Since Jack didn't display his title, the muscular man naturally assumed it was inferior to his, which gave him the high ground. He felt certain he would succeed in humiliating Jack, which was undoubtedly his entire reason for coming.

He'd pulled all stops and deeply insulted both of them. He was just itching for a fight, at this point—and Jack was inclined to give him one.

After all, if he backed down from suffering such heavy insults, people would say that the disciples of Huali were cowards.

"Auburn," he asked mentally, "will something bad happen if I escalate?"

"Only if you lose," she replied. "But be careful. He's strong."

"Don't worry. So am I."

"You're going too far," he said, glaring dismissively. "How about you shut the fuck up before bad things happen to you?"

"Oho. What bold words, my fellow cultivator. I was just pointing out some truths; how come you got angry?"

"Truths? All you were doing was pointing out your own flaws. You just told everyone that not only do you have terrible taste in women, but you are also vain enough to flaunt your wealth, as you have no other way to impress those around you, and cheap enough to try and save money when dining with someone you don't like too much. These things make it pretty clear that you're a loser; and the woman beside you, a prostitute."

The entire restaurant had gone so silent you could hear a pin drop. People stared with their jaws hanging; a couple broke into snickering. The muscular man had gone pale as a sheet, while the sharp-nosed woman next to him was glaring at Jack so intensely, if he weren't an immortal, he would have gotten a headache.

Then, the man finally registered the extent of Jack's insults, and his entire face turned red with anger. He seemed ready to jump and come to blows.

"You said too much, kid," he growled.

"Oho. What bold words, my fellow cultivator. I was just pointing out some truths; how come you got angry?"

Jack shot the man's previous quip back at him. More people snickered around the restaurant. This man had come here to create trouble, but he was the one getting demolished instead, while Jack just sat there with an innocent expression.

The surrounding snickers were the final straw to break the camel's back. A brutal aura radiated from the muscular man, filled with explosive anger. Every snicker disappeared instantly.

The man stared deeply into Jack's eyes. Then, emphasizing every word with his barely contained anger, he said, "You are courting *death*."

CHAPTER TWENTY-TWO

BETTING THE NAME OF ONE'S MASTER

THE TENSION IN THE RESTAURANT ROSE, EVERY PATRON HOLDING THEIR BREATH. Jack met the man's hard eyes and replied, "So what if I am?"

The other man may have been infuriated, but at the end of the day, he remained an immortal. He wasn't an idiot.

They were thirty-seven levels apart. In his eyes, that was an insurmountable difference. Therefore, Jack must have had some trick up his sleeve.

But what could it be? Jack had just insulted him so hard that now they *had* to fight. For the muscular man, it was the perfect scenario. He could restore his honor *and* publicly humiliate a disciple of Elder Huali in one go.

No matter what trump cards Jack was hiding, there was no way he could overcome such a level difference against a true elite—or so the muscular man thought.

"Very well," he said, his aura radiating in waves. Actually killing other disciples was forbidden in the Exploding Sun, but everything else was fair play. "When I break your limbs, don't say I wasn't justified. I will show you the power of my Dao of the Fist."

Now it was Jack's turn to be shocked. "*Your* Dao of the Fist?"

"That's right. I cultivate the Dao of the Fist, and I will use it to brutally crush you."

Jack was untouched by the other man's bravado. He was too busy being impressed. Could there be such a coincidence in the world? Do we really cultivate the same Dao?

He was excited. In all his travels, this was only the second person with the Dao of the Fist he met. The first had been a woman Rufus Emberheart killed in the Integration Tournament.

"What a coincidence," he said. "I also cultivate the Dao of the Fist."

The man's anger became colored with surprise. "Really?"

"Really."

The man laughed aloud. Jack had just presented him with the perfect opportunity to up the stakes and connect this conflict to the standing of their masters. "Excellent! Truly excellent! You really dug your own grave, kid! Let me witness the Dao of the Fist that Elder Huali teaches and see if it is better or worse than what Master Monsoon taught me. Let's compare our masters' ability in teaching!"

He was in a great mood now, as if he couldn't believe his luck. He was overflowing with confidence. His anger had grown so intense that it now manifested as joy; as raucous, explosive laughter laced with expectation of the pain he was going to cause to Jack.

"In fact," the man continued, "I propose something else. If I defeated you in a battle, people would say I was just bullying you. Victory would obviously go to me. However, since we share the same Dao, how about we compete in that instead?"

Jack narrowed his eyes. "I'm listening."

"We'll rise to the sky, and I will let you punch me. Your pure offensive power against my defenses. Then, I punch you, and we keep going until one of us becomes unable to continue. That way, my higher attributes won't play that much of a role, and you have a chance of winning. I'll even give you the first strike, since you're young and stupid. What do you say?"

His smile was crooked. He had to be absolutely certain of himself, or he wouldn't suggest such a thing.

The problem was, Jack possessed four Dao Roots and a perfect foundation. There was no way this guy's understanding of the Dao was superior. He wouldn't know what hit him.

Jack opened his mouth and laughed uproariously, floating out of his chair to stand in the air. "Very well! Let's do that, but don't complain when you lose. As for the first strike... I don't want it. You should have it. That way, when I knock you unconscious in a single punch, my victory will be much more impressive."

The muscular guy sneered. He did not doubt his victory in the slightest, so he probably assumed Jack was just trying to seem brave so his defeat didn't impact his master's reputation too hard.

"Don't spout bullshit," he replied. "You get the first strike."

"No, you go first. In fact, let me add another rule: as long as you go first, you can use your entire strength to hit me without worrying about anything at all. Even if I die, I declare in front of all these witnesses that you will not be held accountable. It will just be the result of my own weakness."

The muscular guy was about to retort, but he couldn't believe his luck. In his eyes, Jack was committing suicide at this point. If he could kill a disciple of Elder Huali here, especially when said disciple was being completely stupid and reckless, the incident would spread across the planet. Huali's reputation would take a hard hit. This was so much better that it didn't matter if he struck first. He just had to accept this offer.

It was almost too good to be true. Yet... no matter how he racked his brain, he found no way for him to lose.

"Very well, kid," he replied. His own chair flew back as he took to the air, staring Jack down with all his might. "But remember, you are the one who insisted on this. I cannot be held accountable for anything."

"Don't worry. You are too weak to harm me."

Black lines ran over the muscular man's forehead. In his eyes, Jack just didn't know when to stop. "Come, if you dare." He took to the sky, flying upward so fast that the air split and shrieked behind him.

Jack looked at Auburn and winked at her.

"You are an idiot," she whispered, eyes tinkering with a smile, "but a brave one. Go get him. Don't you dare lose."

"Don't worry; I won't. See you in a bit."

He took to the sky as well, rising like a reverse comet. The muscular man was waiting two miles over the city, at a distance where they were barely visible.

Jack and the muscular man stood a hundred feet away from each other, their robes fluttering and their auras already wrestling for supremacy. "I never got your name," said the muscular man.

"My name is Jack Rust. Engrave it deeply into your soul, for I am the man who will destroy your confidence and cut short your path of cultivation."

"Heh. Bold words for someone about to die. I am Dan Bolon, the man who is going to kill you."

"You can certainly try," Jack replied with a smile.

The raging auras of immortals weren't exactly discreet. By now, many people in the city had noticed their stand-off in the sky, and even more were realizing it by the second. A few people had even flown closer to observe the battle, keeping a respectful distance from Jack and Dan Bolon. Auburn was one of them, as was the woman accompanying Dan.

"Fellow cultivators of Stripe City!" Dan Bolon said, using his Dao to spread his voice over the entire city. "I am Dan Bolon, a disciple of Elder Monsoon, and the man across from me is Jack Rust, a disciple of Elder Huali. Today, we have decided to fight for our honor. As we both follow the Dao of the Fist, we will compete by punching each other until one becomes unable to fight. We have also agreed to use our full strength; even if one of us dies, they can only blame their own weakness. Are my words true, Jack Rust?"

The entire city quieted as they awaited Jack's response.

Jack couldn't help the grin on his face. This battle, this setup... Dan Bolon was trying to corner him, but he was cornering himself at the same time. He was cutting off all avenues of escape for both of them.

The truth was, Jack wasn't completely certain he could win. He was confident, of course, but something could always go wrong. Maybe the other man was an ultimate prodigy. Even in a punching duel, the forty-level difference still played a part.

This uncertainty emphasized the fear of death inside Jack and made the stakes seem real—and it was exactly this feeling that roused his battle spirit from its slumber, letting him smother all other emotions and fully dive into the battle, risking everything just because he could.

It had been a while since he'd felt like that. He missed it.

"Your words are true, Dan Bolon," Jack replied, also using his Dao to make his voice reverberate across the city. "However, why are you holding back? Say things as they are. We argued, we insulted each other's honor, and now we will fight to resolve our differences. As we share the same Dao, this battle involves more than just us—it reflects our masters' ability in selecting disciples and teaching them a Dao."

Gasps came from everywhere. Jack had openly bet his master's name on this battle—if he lost, it would be terrible. On the other hand, if he won, it would be great.

Dan Bolon laughed, unable to believe his luck. This was exactly what he wanted. He couldn't say everything out loud or people would say he was a bully, but Jack was playing right into his game.

"Precisely!" he exclaimed. "Very well. Let us begin. On Jack Rust's insistence, I will go first."

Many surrounding immortals frowned or spoke in protest. Since Jack's level was far lower than his opponent's, it was proper that he went first, not Dan Bolon; but Bolon was beyond caring. This little improperness was nothing before the massive stakes of this fight.

"Come," Jack said, opening the upper part of his robes and letting it hang from his waist. He revealed a bare chest as if chiseled in marble, and muscles so compact they triggered a sense of harmony.

Dan Bolon floated before him. At only three feet away, the intensity of his aura was staggering. Jack remained unfazed. This was the first sign in Dan Bolon's mind that something was wrong, but there was no use thinking about it now. All he could do was duel.

He clenched his hand, channeling his entire strength into it. His fist caught fire. Yellow and orange flames blossomed around it, making it look like a sun in his palm. The heat was such that Jack began to sweat—if he were a normal person, he would have been immolated already. Only the supreme quality fabric prevented his robes from suffering the same fate.

Jack stared into his opponent's eyes and saw pure, unadulterated strength. It felt like facing a wild animal—or a gun's open barrel. His every instinct screamed at him to fight back or get away, but he used his iron will to push them down. He had agreed to take this attack. Even if it killed him, he would not back down.

For cultivators, defending against a full-force strike was difficult, but not *too* difficult. Jack focused on defense—he had Neutron Star Body, the Life Drop, and the Dao Root of Indomitable Will. He was confident in surviving even an all-out strike from himself, let alone this man, who hopefully had a shallower Dao understanding.

He hardened his eyes, glued them right onto the other man's, and waited with his chest exposed.

"I told you, you were courting death," Dan Bolon said in a normal voice. His fist shook from the accumulated power, and his eyes betrayed the intense desire to kill Jack. "You were asking for it. Now... die. Solar Punch!"

His fist shot forward at blinding speed. Jack did not move in the slightest. The punch impacted his chest, and instantly, it was like a sun had been born. Jack felt his ribcage cave in. His skin turned to ash, the hot winds rode along his body and burned his face and back. That single strike may as well have placed him inside an industrial oven.

He did not scream.

At the same time, the impact itself was strong enough to send him flying. The air boomed as his body broke the sound barrier, flying back and down until he crashed into one of the two mountains flanking Stripe City, creating a crater the size of a house.

Every eye in the city looked at the crater, waiting to see if Jack would emerge or not. Smoke and dust flew everywhere, obstructing the view.

CHAPTER TWENTY-THREE
BREAKING DAN

A CLOUD OF DUST COVERED THE CRATER, AND THAT WAS A GOOD THING, BECAUSE Jack's body was mostly broken. Dan Bolon's attack had been stronger than he expected. His ribcage was bent, multiple organs had been punctured, and he was unable to breathe. The world swam before his eyes, and even maintaining his consciousness was a tough task.

Then again, that wasn't too bad. Strong immortals had the power to demolish entire mountains. Jack had only survived the impact because of the extreme defense offered by Neutron Star Body, his defensive Dao Skill. It was the evolution of Iron Fist Body, and it gave him some properties of neutron stars, making his body extremely compact and resilient, as well as resistant to the elements.

At the same time, the skill had been enhanced by the Life Drop, offering him extreme regenerative powers. Jack could already feel his body knitting itself back to health. His flesh was pulsing with the powers of life, moving bones around, sucking off the rampant blood from internal injuries, and repairing the punctured organs.

Within ten seconds, Jack could breathe again. Within a minute, he could walk. His hearing came back then, catching Dan Bolon's passionate speech about how one should respect their superiors and not be a reckless idiot.

Jack did not pay too much attention. As the dust was clearing and people were gathering to see his corpse, he shocked them all by walking out of the crater. He looked like shit, and the regeneration had made him completely exhausted, but he was certainly still able to fight.

The moment Dan Bolon caught sight of him, he froze mid-speech. His eyes widened, and he paled like he'd seen a ghost. "How?" he asked. "How are you still alive!"

"Alive?" Jack replied, his voice hoarse. "Did you think that little love tap was enough to kill me?"

He slowly rose to the sky, enjoying everyone's respectful and shocked gazes. So what if the front of his torso remained blackened from the burns? So what if his hair was messy, he was covered in dust, and blood was visible on several parts of his body?

He was alive, and his fist looked good enough.

Slowly, Jack arrived before Dan Bolon, who remained shocked. "I have received your strike, Bolon. It was... decent. Now, I believe it is my turn."

Only now, seeing Jack survive his full-force attack, did Dan Bolon realize that he had made a mistake. Only now did he understand why Jack had dared challenge him—because he really might win.

Bolon focused on offense. His defense wasn't too strong. He had been confident in taking a strike before, but with the strength Jack just revealed, he suddenly didn't like his chances.

This really might kill him. He had half a mind to resign.

"Do you dare receive my strike, Bolon?" Jack asked, seeing through his thoughts. "Or are you a coward who will soil his master's name?"

Dan Bolon's heart was filled with bitterness. He had already used his strongest strike. Now, he was forced to defend against the attack of someone at his level of power?

Hell! He couldn't do that!

But after what Jack said, he couldn't quit either. If he did, Head Disciple Qian would come and kill him himself.

Fine, he thought, gritting his teeth. He crossed his arms before his chest, which wasn't really allowed, and waited for Jack's strike. He galvanized his Dao as intensely as he could and even revealed his Dao Domain, hoping to pressure Jack and lower his strength.

He did not expect Jack to completely ignore his domain, revealing his own which perfectly countered it. In fact, Jack's was even a bit stronger.

Dan Bolon was beginning to see death, but he couldn't back down. He just had to hope he could take the strike.

"Give me your worst, Jack Rust!" he shouted to hype himself up.

Jack laughed loudly. "Those are big words for someone who's crossing his arms to defend. I didn't do that. I let you hit me freely."

Dan Bolon's brows fluttered. Everyone could see that Jack was right, but if he dropped his arms, he really might die! "We agreed not to fight back," he retorted with a snort. "Defending is obviously allowed."

"I guess you are a coward, then. I really expected a disciple of Elder Monsoon to have some balls, but well, it looks like I was wrong."

The agreeing murmurs from other immortals only emphasized Dan Bolon's ugly position. He gritted his teeth so hard they almost broke.

If I really let him attack me, will I die? No. He must focus hard on defense. That's why he could survive my attack. His offense must be much weaker! His eyes shone. Yes, that's it! I can do this. I can survive! It's all or nothing!

He uncrossed his arms, stating bravely, "Very well. If you can take an attack without defending, then I, Dan Bolon, can do the same. Let no one say that I am a coward!"

Jack's ridiculing smile did not comfort Dan Bolon at all. "Who's courting death now?" he replied. "I respect your resolve. Very well. May you die a brave man rather than live as a coward."

Dan Bolon did not speak. He waited, chest completely vulnerable, to receive Jack's attack.

Suddenly, the world lost its colors. Sound was gone, too. Dan Bolon's Dao Domain was torn apart as a single purple meteor dominated the sky, glowing around Jack's fist like it was about to fall from deep space. Just the ripples of power were enough to send shivers down Dan Bolon's spine. It took every iota of his resolve to keep his arms from rising to defend.

I can take this, he kept telling himself. I have to.

He already regretted his decision to come here and cause trouble. He could have just stayed at home and relaxed, but he'd chosen to kick the iron wall that was called Jack Rust.

Unfortunately, there was no medicine for regret.

Dan Bolon's thoughts disappeared as he devoted his entire being to defense.

"Meteor Punch!" Jack's voice rang across the sky, the only sound in existence, a divine decree of destruction. The meteor hurtled forward. Before it even reached Dan Bolon's body, he could feel his skin caving in by its ripples of power.

Dan Bolon's Solar Punch contained a heavy element of fire. That was painful and disorienting for enemies, but it wasn't all that deadly. If anything, the power that went into creating the flames was removed from the punch's physical power.

Jack's Meteor Punch, on the other hand, was different. Any explosion was just an afterthought. The sound and light effects were just a result of the ambient Dao bowing to the punch's superiority. The entire power of the strike was focused on punching as hard as possible.

Shit, Dan Bolon realized, but it was too late. He no longer had time to defend. The meteor exploded on his chest. Dan Bolon sensed his ribcage bend and shatter into a million tiny bone fragments. His back burst open from the impact, and that was the last thing he ever felt.

As light and sound exploded back into existence, Jack watched Dan Bolon's broken body fly to the other mountain and crash into it like a meteor, forming a crater slightly larger than Jack's. Of course, he would never stand up again, because he was dead before he even hit the ground.

Level-up! You have reached Level 145.
Level-up! You have reached Level 146.

All the free points went to the Physical sub-stats, obviously.

Unlike Bolon, Jack did not give a long speech of condolences to make himself appear virtuous. He didn't need to. Seeing the level difference between the two of them, as well as Dan Bolon's previous conduct, everyone could tell who started this fight.

As all the immortals of Stripe City stared at him in shock, all he said was, "Huh. I guess the disciples of Elder Monsoon are not that strong after all."

The city burst into an uproar, but Jack didn't pay them any mind. He returned to his table at the terrace restaurant, still bloody and dusted—nobody dared tell him anything. The woman accompanying Dan Bolon screamed like a banshee and flew away at top speed.

As soon as Jack landed under everyone's incredulous gazes, Auburn looked him in the eyes and said, "Wow."

Jack shrugged. "He got what he was looking for. After all... he was courting death, wasn't he?"

She burst into laughter, the tension melting off them both. "I guess he did," she replied.

Their food was still there, and the two of them ate in peace. Nobody else bothered them. Bellies full, they left the city, flying all the way to Elder Huali's estate.

"Thanks for the tour, Auburn," Jack told her as he dropped the bags of herbs—which he'd volunteered to carry—at her door. "It was fun."

"I don't know if fun is the right word for what happened, but... Yeah. I did have fun." She smiled at him. "What will you do now?"

"Take a shower, obviously. After that, I think I'll go see brother Shol, and then, we'll see. Maybe visit my friends on outer planet. In any case, starting tomorrow, I'll be cultivating."

"Don't lose yourself in it again," she said with a caring look. "You are good company. There is more to life than cultivation."

"Not when I have a planet to save. In any case, we'll both be around—I may be able to take some time off my busy schedule."

She stuck her tongue out. "Damn you, Jack Rust. Is this how you treat all girls?"

He laughed as he took to the sky. "See you around, Auburn. Next time, let's have some tea at a place without troublemakers."

"Sure!"

And Jack flew away.

At the same time, in a far-off estate that looked quite different than Huali's, a man with long, blond hair sat cross-legged in the middle of a small pond. The water was perfectly still beneath him, supporting his weight as easily as it would support a leaf.

A knock on the courtyard's door shook him out of his meditation. "Yes?" he replied.

"A thousand apologies!" a man cried from outside. "Can I come in? This is urgent."

Head Disciple Qian frowned gently. "You may."

A short man dressed in purple entered the courtyard, his head lowered in respect. "A thousand apologies for interrupting your cultivation, Head Disciple, I only—"

"Just speak," Qian said coldly. "And be quick about it."

"Yes. Brother Dan Bolon went to Stripe City today to cause some trouble for two weak disciples of Elder Huali... but things got out of control. It turned into a huge spectacle, where brother Dan and one of Huali's disciples bet their honor and master's name on a duel. Brother Dan lost, and he even died in the process, but both fighters had already announced to the entire city that death was an acceptable result."

Qian frowned. The water under him rippled gently, but even that was enough to instill fear in the messenger's eyes. "Was Dan a brainless fool?" Qian said calmly. "Why did he pick a fight with someone he couldn't beat? And he even had to drag our master into it... Now everyone will ridicule us. If Dan wasn't dead already, I would kill him myself."

"Head Disciple, if I may speak, brother Dan was an absolute idiot, but his opponent was surprisingly strong. Nobody expected him to win. He was forty levels weaker than Dan."

That gave Qian pause. "Someone surpassed a forty-level difference to beat Dan?"

"Yes, sir. A new disciple of Elder Huali. A man named Jack Rust."

Qian's brows fell. A thousand calculations occurred inside his brain in the blink of an eye. "I see. Tell me everything you know about this... Jack Rust."

CHAPTER TWENTY-FOUR

THE FATE OF THE THOSE LEFT BEHIND

As Jack flew over the estate, news of his victory over Dan Bolon had already begun to spread. Servants pointed up at him with reverence, like he was a famous footballer, while many immortals nodded deeply at him as he passed.

"Would you look at that," Jack said to himself midair, "I'm famous again already."

In the time it had taken him to shower and get dressed, he managed to become a celebrity. His burnt skin was already recovered, too.

As he approached Shol's residence at the edge of the estate, his big brother was already there. "Jack! What the hell happened?"

"Nothing too special," Jack replied as he landed. "I just took care of an idiot."

"Dan Bolon hardly qualifies as an idiot. He was one of Elder Monsoon's most promising disciples." Shol looked around, making sure they weren't watched. His face split into a wide grin. "Good job," he whispered, clapping Jack's shoulder. "That was very well done."

"Thank you," Jack replied modestly. "I appreciate Master Huali's assistance. This is the least I could do to repay her."

"Don't be fake modest with me, Jack. Come inside and tell me everything."

Shol's house was smaller than Jack's. It was just a single cabin surrounded by a small vegetable garden near the wooden walls of the estate—which, given the immortals' ability to fly, were purely ornamental.

The inside of the cabin was as spartan as its exterior. Going through the door, Jack stepped into a living room that could barely fit a table, chairs, and a kitchen. Two closed doors led to what he assumed was the bathroom and bedroom, while a trapdoor under a half-raised carpet led to Shol's cultivation chamber.

"I see you also have a cellar," Jack said, nodding in approval. "Very nice. I already arranged to get some wine for mine."

"For the last time, it's not a cellar."

"It is a cultivation cellar, yes."

"Of course." Shol sighed. "Come, take a seat, and tell me all about your duel against Dan Bolon."

"Haven't you heard the details? Everyone else seems to know already."

"I have, but I want to hear your first-hand accounting. Would you like some tea?"

"Yes, please."

Jack sat on one of the simple wooden chairs and began retelling what happened at Stripe City. He briefly mentioned the Cauldron Mall, then talked about the restaurant and the insults he and Dan Bolon hurled at each other. Finally, he described the setup of their battle with great detail, as well as the end result.

When he was done, Shol shook his head. "You have a penchant for infamy, Jack. Even back when you were a tiny F-Grade, I remember you caused one scene after another."

"It wasn't always my fault."

"Didn't your spiritual companion hurl shit at Rufus Emberheart once?"

"He started it."

"Didn't you masquerade as someone using the Dao of Spanking, then proceeded to tear all those talented people new assholes?"

Jack laughed. "Oh, yeah. Fun times."

Shol was trying to be serious, but he couldn't help smirking.

"Making the world turn around you is a good thing. It means that challenges and power will rain your way. Of course, it can kill you. But if it doesn't, you'll grow strong fast. You're stealing the momentum of the world to enhance your cultivation."

"Those are grand words, brother. All I did was stand up for myself."

"You did far more than that. Disciple disputes happen all the time, but very rarely do they escalate to such lengths—and so publicly. As I understand it, you both went ahead and staked your masters' name on that battle. It would have been a disaster had you lost; since you won, it's actually a great fortune. Word of your duel has already spread far and wide. Everyone has heard of Jack Rust, the young disciple of Elder Huali who publicly defeated and even killed a disciple of Elder Monsoon forty levels above himself."

"Oh, good. I was worried my actions would have somehow embarrassed our master."

"Nonsense. We aren't made of porcelain, we're cultivators. We fight and die as needed." Shol leaned back into his chair, weaving his fingers together before his chest with a content smile. "No, Jack; that victory of yours helped our master greatly. One of Monsoon's greatest advantages is that his disciples are stronger than our master's. Which isn't exactly true, but it's difficult to contest when his head disciple is stronger than me. Thanks to you, we have now reminded the inner planet that each elder has more disciples than just the head ones, and that Monsoon's head disciple superiority doesn't necessarily carry over. If anything, we are better; defeating an elite forty levels your senior is a great achievement."

"Is Elder Monsoon's head disciple really that strong?" Jack asked. "I heard you couldn't leave the estate to avoid him challenging you, but..."

Shol's gaze darkened. "Yes, he is strong. His name is Qian Monsoon, a direct descendant of Elder Monsoon. While we are both at the peak of the D-Grade, his strength is significantly greater than mine—if we fought ten times, he would win nine of them."

"Ouch. That's a lot. But people already know he's the strongest D-Grade of the faction, right? If you fight him and lose, it's no big deal. If you win, it changes everything."

"It doesn't work like that. If the head disciples of the two elders dueled publicly, it would be perceived as the deciding duel for the Grand Elder position. If I lost, people would understand that Huali lost to Monsoon. That cannot be allowed."

"I see..." Jack sipped from his mug, finding this tea much to his liking. He had been more of a coffee person on Earth, but when meditation became a core part of his life, he found the calmness of tea much more helpful than coffee's energy boost.

"Your victory over Dan Bolon, while unexpected, was an important event in the battle between the two elders," Shol said, appearing somewhat conflicted. "However, for that reason, I have to ask you not to leave the estate for a while. I hope you understand. Your situation now is similar to mine. Your standing is connected to our master's."

"How is that similar? If they send anyone near my level, I will defeat them. If they send a late or peak D-Grade, sure, I'll lose, but nobody will accept it as a fair battle."

"And yet, that's exactly what they're going to do. They will send their late D-Grades to bully you, and so what if it's not a fair battle? Our late D-Grades will not be able to protect you, because if they try, the disciples of Monsoon will just escalate the situation until I am forced to duel Qian."

Jack's frown persisted. A few moments of thought later, it eased. "I see. Fine. I'll stay inside the estate for now. However, I had been planning to leave the faction in a few weeks to adventure in the Animal Kingdom. If you need me to not do that, I'm afraid it will be difficult."

"Hmmm... Ideally, you shouldn't... But I will not constrain you overly much. I understand your need to get stronger quickly, and indeed, adventuring is what you should do. All I ask is that you be careful."

"Of course."

"Good. With that out of the way, I have another matter to discuss with you."

"Go ahead, brother."

"Remember how you asked me to find out what happened to the *Trampling Ram*? The starship that helped you escape the Animal Kingdom?"

Jack put down his cup and listened attentively. The crew of the

Trampling Ram had helped him tremendously, and he had implicated them in his own troubles; he really hoped they were okay.

"Unfortunately, the news I got is not too good. When the *Trampling Ram* was attacked near Earth-321, the three Hounds teamed up with the dryad immortal of that planet to defeat them. The *Trampling Ram* itself managed to warp away with most of its crew, but the captain was captured. Soon after, he was transported to Hell, where he will remain imprisoned in perpetuity."

Jack's heart clenched. The captain aside, he remembered what a sorry state they were in when the Hounds attacked. They had just gotten away from a space monster horde; Vashter was heavily injured, and the rest weren't exactly at peak form, either. They had been going to Earth-321 to seek medical aid. If they were forced to warp away like that...

Jack shook his head to clear it. "You said the captain was taken to Hell. What is that?"

"One of the core planets of the Animal Kingdom. It's where they keep their most dangerous criminals. At the same time, it serves a function similar to our inner planet—it's where their most talented D-Grades go to cultivate. I have heard that prisoners are often slaughtered by the inner disciples to give them levels, or they are used as sparring partners against their will. Oftentimes, they are partially crippled and released into the wild, where disciples hunt and kill them as part of their training."

Jack's gaze darkened dangerously. "Can't the Animal Kingdom be decent even once?"

"They don't want to. They chase after power at all costs and care about little else."

"Those fuckers."

Jack was livid. He stewed in his seat, barely containing his aura from leaking out. Captain Dordok was going to be hunted for sport, and it was his fault.

"Is there a way to save someone from Hell?" he asked.

"The only way is to make a deal with the Animal Kingdom... For you, I guess that's impossible. And even more for us, since we're enemies." Shol shook his head. "I'm sorry, Jack."

Jack held his breath. Then, he drew the air in deep and let it wash his brain clean. It didn't rid him of the sadness or guilt, but it did let him think clearly again.

Just one more reason to get stronger, he thought grimly. "What about the rest of the crew? After they warped away, did you have any more news of them?"

"None. They could be dead or in hiding. They're wanted criminals now. Even the ambassador of Fair Way Continent who was on the ship is wanted for treason, and his entire court and family was wiped from Fair Way to set an example."

"When you say wiped, do you mean..."

"Yes."

Jack's heart clenched further. Vlossana and her father were good people. He still remembered her Dao of Joy, how she always jumped from subject to subject, full of energy and wit.

Now, her entire family had been slaughtered just like that. All because the Animal Kingdom wanted to set an example.

And because Jack had drawn them into his conflict.

"I need some time," he said, standing up abruptly. His cup was still half-full. "Thank you for the hospitality and information, brother Shol, but I have a lot in my head. I will return another day to chat more pleasantly."

"Of course. It's no problem at all," Shol replied, gazing at Jack with warmth. "Try not to take it too hard. On the path of cultivation, these things are common. People are roped into each other's conflicts all the time."

"Thank you," Jack replied politely, but he didn't agree. Yes, being strong made the world revolve around you, but it wasn't the case this time. He had just lied to some people to save his own life, which resulted in those people suffering greatly. The Animal Kingdom was certainly in the wrong, especially considering the Fair Way situation, but so was he.

When he left the cabin and flew home, his head remained muddled. He was grieving. Only when he landed in his courtyard did he regain himself enough to consider the situation.

Cultivation gave the mind clarity. In addition, Jack followed the Dao of the Fist. He wouldn't let himself be overtaken by grief or guilt.

He'd fucked up. But losing himself wouldn't help. All he could do now was work hard to fix his wrongdoings as much as possible. He would do his best to save Captain Dordok, if possible, and he would try to locate and help the remaining crew of the *Trampling Ram*, along with Vlossana and Count Plomer. If they were dead, he would take revenge.

It wasn't enough, but it was the best he could do. That, and trying his best to never fuck up like that again.

Jack made his way to his cultivation cellar and sat cross-legged. He had planned to take the entire day off, and it was still afternoon. Plus, the Dao Magnet hadn't reached its peak concentration, so cultivating now would be inefficient.

But those mattered little. Jack could not afford to take it easy. If not for his people on Earth, then for the crew of the *Trampling Ram*. The ones he'd let down, and whom he still didn't have the strength to compensate.

I need to become stronger, he thought. The fire inside him was reignited. He thirsted to advance.

Reaching into his robes, Jack removed the dark crystal ball he'd taken from the library, the one that contained a Dao Vision. He sank his mind inside it, dove deep into its pitch-black essence... and suddenly, he was in space.

CHAPTER TWENTY-FIVE
DAO VISION OF SPACE

JACK FLOATED IN SPACE. HE WAS AN INCORPOREAL GHOST, A FIGMENT OF imagination that may or may not be real.

Endless darkness surrounded him on all sides. Stars shimmered, so far away that even an immortal's lifetime wouldn't be enough to approach them. The silence was almost deafening.

In this endless void, one figure stood alone. It was a woman with eyes the color of sunset and dark robes that floated soullessly in the absence of air. Her skin was pale, her features slim, and her long hair as dark as her robes as it fell over them.

Her gaze, however, was intense.

Jack inspected her.

Vampire, Level ??? (C-Grade)
Faction: Dead Lands (A-Grade)

It was the first time he read about an A-Grade faction, but that wasn't the most shocking part.

All three of Jack's Dao Visions so far had contained C-Grades. The bald man who'd easily annihilated a skyscraper-sized monster with a single punch, the bare-chested man who'd faced an entire city of cultivators, and now this woman.

However, there was something different about this one.

Maybe it was because Jack had begun to approach this level of power, or maybe her level was just higher than the others. Whatever the case, as he laid eyes on her, he felt a power of such volume it was incomparable to the two C-Grade men in the other visions. Her mere presence enriched the surrounding Dao. The world was bowing before her might, spontaneously manifesting Daos more compatible to hers in the emptiness of space.

Or, rather, it was exactly this emptiness that radiated in waves from the woman, coloring the world around her like the golden touch of Midas.

Facing her, Jack felt like he was back at the Integration Tournament, where he received the Planetary Overseer's pressure as a mere F-Grade. She was a creature far above and beyond anything he'd ever experienced before—a God.

The only possible exception was Elder Huali, who had never let her aura show in front of Jack. Old Man Spirit, too. Though Jack had seen him struck down by the heavenly tribulation, that was hardly a normal occurrence. His power remained an enigma.

Then, the woman moved. She reached out to the void with both hands. An expression of deep concentration was plastered on her face.

Jack erased all other thoughts and watched with rapt attention.

The woman's hands moved slowly, yet steadily. Like she was confirming her progress with every inch forward. At some point, she closed her fingers around nothing and twisted.

The world danced around Jack. Instantly, he was lost. The woman was simultaneously right in front of him and far away. He could see her from different angles, like he had eyes everywhere. Even he, himself, was warped, his limbs stretching and contorting without him feeling anything wrong.

He remained uninjured, but he couldn't tell if that was part of the woman's magic or a result of being an ethereal body in a Dao Vision.

However, he knew what she was doing; he could sense it clearly, a calling that emerged from the depths of his soul.

She was manipulating space.

Jack had a relevant Dao Skill, Space Walk, but he didn't understand how it worked. He knew nothing about space. It was the System that guided him to use it. Jack simply willed it to happen, and then he'd break through space to teleport up to a mile away.

This woman's manipulation was far more elaborate. If space was clay, all Jack could do was punch it, while this woman shaped it freely into anything she wished.

He struggled to maintain his concentration while his body was warped beyond his control. The woman remained deeply focused. She moved her hands as if molding that clay, making tiny movements that somehow destabilized the entire area. The rise of a finger could make her invisible, shrink her, or enlarge her. It could turn Jack into spaghetti or a donut.

Jack kept his Dao perception activated for as long as he could, but it was flooded. He was assaulted by tremendous waves of Dao. Not because the woman emanated anything, but because her every tiny movement created tsunamis in the ambient Dao, like it was such a delicate force that it responded to her prods with great exaggeration.

When Jack used the ambient Dao, it was like pushing an oar through sand. Every inch was an achievement. When this woman did it, her control was so precise that a gentle flick could upturn entire sand dunes, achieving the same results as Jack with a hundred times less effort. The Dao was bending over backward to accommodate her.

Due to all these Dao waves, as well as the rampant space manipulation around him, Jack could understand very little. His Dao perception was useless. He was lost underwater without a sense of direction. His only source of information was the curvature of light, which he could glimpse through the changes he witnessed in the woman's form. Light always traveled in a straight line through space—so, if he saw it curved, that was because space itself was curved.

However, Jack had a feeling that, despite everything around him being warped, the woman herself was not. Through the multiple angles she showed him, he never saw her body change shape. She rested in an oasis of calmness amidst a storm that extended who knows how far.

Jack dared to look backward. All the stars danced as space rippled like a pond. His Dao perception was locked around himself, so he had no way of knowing how far the woman's influence stretched, but something told him it was a large, large area.

Nauja had once called C-Grades Continent Crushers. Jack had never really believed that. Only now, sensing the power of what was undoubtedly a top C-Grade, did he really comprehend how long the road of cultivation was. And he was blown away by awe.

A gentle sigh echoed through the dancing darkness. "Still not enough."

Suddenly, space was drawn back to its natural form like a spring uncoiling. Jack was warped in reverse so hard he lost his train of thought. He caught a glimpse of the woman's dark brows creased into a frown. She was staring right at him—through him. It didn't feel like she could really see him, but more like she was inspecting something occupying the same space as him.

Jack felt her attention clamp down around him like a steel vise. He lost his breath.

The woman's eyes shone like she'd figured something out, and her frown deepened. "My Dao belongs to me," she declared, her voice a divine decree. "Begone."

She waved a hand and space collapsed around Jack. For the first time, he was afraid for himself in a Dao Vision. He felt himself shatter.

In the next moment, he was alone in his cultivation chamber, sweating buckets, his heart racing. "What the hell?" was all he managed to say. Nevermind that woman's extreme control over space and the Dao—how had she noticed him? He was in a Dao Vision. What the hell?

He didn't even know that was possible.

Then again, what is a Dao Vision? he wondered.

It wasn't fake images. Shol had confirmed that the bald man in his first Dao Vision was one of the Exploding Sun's founders. Then, could the System be watching and recording interesting applications of the Dao to hand out later as Dao Visions? Was it watching him, too? Would someone see a Dao Vision of Jack Rust in the future?

And, if it was recording him, what else was it doing with those recordings? What else could it do? Could it steal his Dao?

The ramifications of the woman's final words rained down on Jack, rendering him vulnerable. Was the System watching his every move, recording him, and using those recordings for its own benefit? Was he just a mouse in its cage?

No, he quickly calmed himself, thinking back to what he already knew. *It can't be watching everything. When we were in the Ancient ruins, the System didn't know about it until we scanned something. It didn't see me in the Ancient Trial. When I later used the Life Drop to fight that chameleon, or against Old Man Spirit, the System couldn't have seen me, because if it had, it would have set out a bounty for me like it did for the ruins.*

So, it's not watching at all times. But it can watch. The space woman showed me that. Come to think of it, she caught the System watching, so there has to be some kind of hint. Like a Dao camera... or something. Maybe it's monitoring high-level cultivators when it thinks they're about to showcase something interesting?

Then, it looks like I'm not that strong yet... at least, I wasn't while in the E-Grade. Now... How could I know?

Jack spread out his Dao perception, scanning every cubic inch of air with his full awareness, finding nothing.

It can't be watching all the time, he decided. *But maybe, when I'm about to showcase my powers, it will. I have to be careful with the Life Drop. Even when there is no one around, I cannot use it. Not unless I absolutely need to.*

Jack finally raised his gaze. He remembered the words of Nauja's father, the tribe chief: "Don't trust the System."

He must have known.

This thought then led him to the Black Hole Church. They were against the System. Against the Immortals who created it. What more did they know? How did they stay outside the System's surveillance?

And, in the end, what should he reply to their standing offer? The Sage had invited Jack to join them. Should he?

The more he learned about the System, the more he leaned towards yes. And yet he still knew so very little. Could he discover more without aligning himself with a major force?

Then again, he'd already done that. He was a member of the Exploding Sun.

I have to ask Shol about the System and all these things, Jack resolved himself. The thought of anyone being able to watch and record him without his permission—even his Dao—was more unnerving than he'd like to admit. *I suppose it is a fair trade for what the System offers me, but I must know the truth.*

First, comes training. If I am to somehow escape the System's surveillance, I will need the ability to use my full strength without it. Specifically, my Dao Skills. I should rely on the System as little as possible. I know it's doable.

Between cultivating, sparring, and meditating to expand his Dao, Jack had almost forgotten about this part. He'd actually discovered it back on Trial Planet—the System helped him with his Skills and Dao Skills, making them far easier to use than they were supposed to be. In return, his mastery over these skills became incomplete.

The System accelerated his growth greatly to a point, with the price being that he cut corners.

The way Jack had found to combat this was to use his skills inside his soul world. The System didn't have access—it was simply him, Copy Jack, and the Dao. Practicing there would teach him how to use his skills by himself, without the System's assistance. He could gradually cut out the middle-man. It would also raise his mastery over his Dao Skills, and, by extension, their tier and power.

And the first one he would work on was Space Walk. It was a skill granted to him directly by his Class, but he didn't have the first idea of how it worked. Thankfully, he now had a Dao Vision that could teach him about space—the first step to mastering his skill.

And who knows what other benefits it would bring him.

Therefore, Jack closed his eyes, focused on the dark crystal sphere, and re-entered the Dao Vision. Space was an extremely useful Dao. He needed to understand it. And he would explore this vision until he did.

CHAPTER TWENTY-SIX

SOLVING THE VISION

The Dao of Space was slippery and abstract. It was obtuse, mystical, and complex. Far more difficult to comprehend than the simpler Daos of the Fist, of Indomitable Will, Power, or Weakness.

Those were concepts based on emotions. They had equivalents in everyday life, making them easy to relate to.

But how could one understand space?

Jack dove into the concept with zeal. He relived the Dao Vision time and time again, until the vampire woman's face became familiar and her moves predictable. He could replay everything with his eyes closed if he wanted to. Thanks to his enhanced mind, he could recall every fluctuation of space, every glimmer of light coming from odd directions. Or, at least, he could try.

Jack was, first and foremost, a scientist. A researcher.

He went at the Dao Vision with a sledgehammer. He divided it into several parts, focusing on each of them separately before proceeding to the whole. First, he paid close attention to the woman's hand gestures, memorizing the precise movement of her every slender finger. When he tried those movements himself... nothing happened.

But he wasn't discouraged. This was just the start.

He then attempted to memorize the patterns of light and his own body warping. These were the only hints he could use to decipher the spatial manipulation enforced by the vampire woman.

Finally, he spent dozens, maybe even hundreds of iterations of the Dao Vision focused solely on his Dao perception. This was the most difficult part. The warping of space completely ruined his spatial awareness, meaning his Dao perception became inaccurate. He attempted to sense how the woman manipulated the Dao around her, but the curvature of space distracted him, making him unable to understand what went where. It was like observing the movement of her Dao through a hundred small screens arranged in a ten-by-ten grid, except that each screen wasn't steady, and constantly flew around randomly.

Naturally, precisely observing her Dao like this was impossible.

That wasn't enough to stop Jack. He was a fist. When a problem seemed unsolvable, he just brute-forced it.

If a dozen iterations weren't enough, he would try a hundred. If a hundred weren't enough, he would try a thousand!

Time lost all meaning as Jack entered a trance. He replayed the Dao Vision over and over until being lost in space was second nature, until the real world, with its smooth and orderly curvature of space, seemed jarring. Every time he opened his eyes, he half-expected the walls to start dancing.

Maybe it's my imagination... but how fragile does space seem. This stability could be broken at any minute. It is smoke and mirrors—merely an illusion.

Closing his eyes, he dived into the vision again.

The System was unhelpful during this cultivation session. Space was not a part of his Dao Tree, so the System saw no reason to assist him. Jack was alone against a task of impossible complexity. All he had was his System-enhanced mind.

However, he also had the gift of hard work.

As impossible as this task was, he set to it with fierce resolve. Iteration after iteration, he began to memorize every small movement of space. The hundred angles through which he observed the woman slowly came to fit into his mind. He observed how each of them changed and swam throughout the Dao Vision, forming a tapestry of viewpoints that was completely random and extremely complex, yet always the same.

Thousands of iterations later, his brain was so trained to these patterns that it began to adapt. It was similar to how, if you watched the world upside-down for a while, your eyes would adjust and you would be able to see normally. To enhance this process, Jack did not open his eyes when exiting the Dao Vision—he simply dived into it again, over and over, until it became his entire world.

His brain gradually adapted. It no longer expected to see a stable world. It expected a world that was dancing and turning and warping in the precise way the Dao Vision did. It learned to automatically slot in the right viewpoint in the right section of Jack's vision, forming a complete image yet again.

As complete as it could be at any rate. Even a System-enhanced human brain had limits. Jack now looked through the swimming space and saw an image of the woman that was blurry, fuzzy, hazy, and almost made sense.

It wasn't optimal, but it was enough.

Only now could he truly begin to comprehend the movements of her Dao.

His Dao perception adapted in the same way his eyes did. Repeatedly diving into the vision, he now focused on the world around the woman's hands, observing it as clearly as he could through his sliding kaleidoscope. Multicolored particles of the Dao floated everywhere, dominated by what felt empty but was actually not.

Space itself was made of Dao.

The countless tiny particles that comprised existence were not everything. There were more of them. He just couldn't see them before, as they were colorless and formless, a part of the world so natural that it served as the background.

Only when the woman grabbed those particles and wielded them did Jack comprehend their existence. All at once, it was like his eyes had been opened for the first time—he perceived something in emptiness, a force he always missed before. Now, it was so obvious. He felt like a deep sea fish that discovered the existence of water.

Finally, Jack realized the importance of this Dao Vision, and he felt eternally grateful. If he didn't see the woman manipulating space so clearly, it wouldn't matter if people sat him down and explained exactly how it worked. How many years, how many decades would it have taken him to comprehend this concept otherwise?

How valuable was the Dao Vision he'd so casually received?

B-Grade factions really have amazing resources... he thought, still shocked at the weight of this insight. He refocused on the woman again. This was no time to daydream. It was time to learn.

He observed her movements as clearly as he could, iteration after iteration. At first, he understood nothing. Space bent oddly, following the movements of her fingers and spreading like a wave, but he had no idea how she'd achieved that.

Eventually, his vision sharpened further, and he began to see anew.

When she waved her hands, that was only a symbolic movement. It probably just helped her focus. The real driving force was the Dao particles she controlled at an extremely fine level.

To Jack, the Dao was like water. It was formed of many tiny droplets, but when he wielded it, he moved those droplets in the millions. When this woman focused, she could control a single line of droplets, a force so thin Jack more imagined than perceived it. She drove that line between the folds of space, slicing it open as one would a curtain, then easily moved the piece of cut-off curtain as she pleased.

Of course, her application was more advanced than this. She wielded these ultra-thin lines of particles freely, slicing space open in various places and then dancing around with the loose fabric, twirling and twisting it to her will.

Jack now pictured space as a giant curtain, of which he could only see a tiny part in the middle. There was no end to pull, and the entire curtain was too heavy to move. If he had a razor to slice it open, he could then manipulate a part of the curtain.

He could bend space to his will.

If he could achieve that, he could do whatever he liked. Teleportation? All he had to do was slice the curtain open and move through its folds. He would no longer be constrained by the distance. It was just a manifestation of space. He could simply ignore it and appear wherever he wanted.

Despite his growing understanding, this concept was hard to grasp. Jack felt like he was squeezing his mind into a hole where it wasn't supposed to fit. It was jarring and disorienting. The only reason he could even touch upon this concept was that he saw the woman tearing the curtain open, and the implications registered in an area of his brain he wasn't entirely sure he understood.

On one side of the curtain, the one everyone stood on, distance was a thing. But there was no floor under the curtain. It was draped over a sphere of zero radius and infinite surface. On the inside, all points in space coincided, effectively allowing him to reach anywhere he wanted instantly—with the added bonus that he didn't pass through all the space in between.

Of course, that had to be extremely taxing. Jack didn't quite get why, but he knew that was obviously the case or everyone would teleport all the time.

However, he finally felt that he understood a bit of how space worked. Although, understood was an overstatement—he had an inkling of an inkling, the barest idea of how things worked and how he could alter them to his liking.

And, maybe, it would be enough.

He kept watching the woman manipulating space, letting several iterations of the vision flow by, gradually growing more and more familiar with the way her every movement affected the world. He watched her Dao razors sink into the tiny gaps between the infinitely clustered particles of space, slice them open, then use the flat part of the blade to push the fabric of space in a direction of her choosing.

Though Jack had focused on the concept of teleportation, which interested him most due to Space Walk, this woman was purely manipulating space, moving it from side to side and wrapping it around itself. She had no goal that Jack could discern—merely practicing.

He was so engrossed in understanding that he almost didn't notice when he hit a wall. Suddenly, delving any deeper into the woman's secrets was impossible, like the Dao he perceived through the curtain grew blurred—and not by lack of ability.

Tsk. That was it, huh?

Dao Visions, as he'd come to understand, contained a single insight, either large or small. Everything else was blurred out so he couldn't get it. This was the reason why he had never revisited the Dao Vision of the bald man from so long ago. Besides the basic essence of the Dao of the Fist, he could glean nothing of importance.

Fair, I guess. Can't look a gift horse in the mouth.

He glanced at the woman, who was manipulating space in front of him for the umpteenth time. For the first time in who knows how long, he did not focus on perceiving, but simply enjoying what was happening. It was like the first time, except he understood a tiny bit more.

"Still not enough," the woman said with a sigh, then noticed the System spying on her. "This is my Dao," she declared. "Begone."

Jack felt himself collapse and shatter, and he was back in the real world. He opened his eyes, finding the task more difficult than he remembered.

He fell to the floor. His brain tried to perceive the real world through the space dance enforced by the woman. Everything swam and nothing made sense. Jack couldn't even stand.

"Ohh," he groaned. He used his Dao to stop himself from puking, then simply waited, enduring the nausea until the world stabilized again. His brain finally realized they were back to normal—though the process felt like hours.

"Oh, man. What a ride." Jack sat up, noticing that his entire body was stiff. "How long did that take?"

Surely, not too long. It was a single meditation session.

Come to think of it, hadn't he seen several thousand iterations of the Dao Vision? If each of them took a couple of minutes, then...

Jack paled. "Shit."

Then again, it wasn't like he had anything to do. So what if he'd spent several days meditating? He was an immortal now. He could do whatever he wanted.

Somehow, his mind felt fresh, not at all exhausted like he anticipated.

He itched to go out and make sure everything was alright, but there was something he wanted to do even more: practice the Dao of Space.

Reaching inside himself, he retrieved an amount of the Dao of the Fist as small as he could make it. It still contained thousands of purple particles, clustered together like the stitches of a carpet. Tenderly, he reached inside it and tried to minimize the amount of Dao, removing the particles by batches.

Some time later, he was down to around a few hundred, and he discovered that going any lower was impossible. It was like trying to untie a knot with extra thick fingers.

He formed that Dao into a line as thin as he could make it and attempted to wedge it between space itself.

He sensed it bump against something. The slit was there, just a bit thinner than what he could manage. He kept trying for a bit, not managing to slice space open even in the slightest.

But it was progress. He'd come somewhat close. That gave him hope. And, since he still felt fresh...

He knew a place where the Dao was more accepting of him than in the real world: his soul world.

CHAPTER TWENTY-SEVEN

SLICING SPACE

JACK SANK INTO HIS SOUL WORLD.

The scenery here had changed since he reached the D-Grade. This used to be a field under a blue sky, stretching as far as the eye could see and with a light breeze constantly caressing the grass. Jack found it soothing.

Now, the field, grass, and breeze remained, but there was no sky. He could see straight into space, a black dome interspersed with a thousand tiny stars. Their light was ample, and their illumination gentle. Instead of making the field hard to see, it only made things clearer, showering the world in a warm light that highlighted the details and made the terrain seem almost romantic.

There were four moons, too: one silver, one dark blue, one green, and one black. They were small and discreet, though noticeably larger than the stars, with their multicolored lighting not ruining the view in the slightest.

Copy Jack lay on a hammock between two trees; the only two trees in this expanse. Jack had no idea how Copy Jack knew what a hammock was, or how he'd learned to grow trees.

The moment he saw the real Jack appearing, Copy Jack waved lazily from his hammock.

"Hey," Jack said with a smirk. "Sorry to interrupt your beauty sleep. I'm just here to try out some things. You don't mind, do you?"

Copy Jack waved for him to go ahead, then lay back down and closed his eyes.

Jack had a moment of realization. Relaxing on a comfy hammock under the starry sky, swayed gently by the cool breeze... That must have felt nice. Torturously nice. If only he didn't have a planet to save. If only he wasn't pushing himself every waking hour.

A pang of yearning crossed Jack's heart, but he suppressed it. Maybe after everything was over.

Turning away from Copy Jack, he sat cross-legged and closed his eyes. His Dao perception spread as a wave, taking in everything in the near vicinity.

This wasn't the real world. It was a terrain inside Jack's soul. The ambient Dao wasn't made up of every concept, but simply of the Dao of the Fist. No matter how far Jack spread his perception, all he saw was purple particles swimming in the air, sparser than in the real world and lacking the innate stability which came with variety.

Here, manipulating the Dao was very easy, because all he had to do was manipulate the thing he knew best: the Fist.

Jack inhaled deeply, then exhaled. The infinite particles followed his movement, swirling like purple wind. He did not start experimenting yet; he only pushed his perception deeper, trying to observe the surrounding space as clearly as possible.

A question had been born in his mind: If everything here was made of Fist, how did space exist?

In the Dao Vision, he'd seen clearly that space existed due to the Dao of Space, which in turn was comprised of infinite colorless particles bound together. But that was clearly not the case here, as there were no other particles besides his purple ones.

Let alone space. How did even air exist? How was there grass, and stars, and light?

Jack was surprised that he'd never considered this before. He observed his surroundings, seeking the source of this wondrous enigma, and found it quickly.

They were all made of Fist.

Particles of Fist swirled around like wind and rooted in place like the earth. He saw them clustering in bright packs—the stars—and even connecting to form life—the trees between which hung Copy Jack's hammock. Surprisingly, even Copy Jack was made of the Dao of Fist, though his structure was far more complicated.

Even Jack himself lacked any other Dao inside his current body, besides the Fist and his Dao Roots.

Be it this world or the real one, everything was a manifestation of the ever-present Dao. However, Jack now understood that a manifestation wasn't determined solely by the nature of its Dao. The structure of that Dao also played a part, as did the way with which it pulsed.

Of course, in the end, Fist could hardly become grass.

This entire world was an illusion. The Dao of the Fist masqueraded as everything else, guided by natural laws that Jack couldn't even dream of grasping. It was just another of the soul's mysterious innate properties—like the fact it was inviolable, even to the System. Maybe it was a result of the Dao Soul he'd once ingested.

Jack put these wondrous questions aside and focused on the task at hand. He scoured the air until he pushed everything else away, revealing the pure background—space.

He found endless purple particles bound together, forming a space-like fabric that served as the foil of this entire world. It embodied concepts Jack couldn't yet grasp and gave meaning to distance. Otherwise, his entire soul world would be a single point, which wouldn't be very conducive to training.

That space here was a manifestation of the Fist had both positive and negative effects. On one hand, manipulating it was easier; on the other, the insights that Jack could glean wouldn't be perfect. At the end of the day, this was just the Fist masquerading as space. There were bound to be differences between a copy and the real thing.

For now, he thought it would suffice. His level of understanding was so elementary that any differences would probably not come into play.

Copy Jack had left his hammock at some point. He was now squatting on the ground next to Jack, gazing at him with curiosity. Jack kept his eyes closed. He ignored Copy Jack, letting him watch freely, then pushed away the world as he entered deep meditation.

A line of Dao particles emerged from his chest. It was several particles wide, not as thin as it should be, but much better than it had been in the real world. He carefully guided it to sink deeper into space, touching upon its many particles, which were more thinly clustered here than real space.

Without realizing it, Jack pushed his hands outward, moving them in the same gestures he'd memorized from the vampire woman.

His line of particles formed into a razor blade, which slowly sank into the gap of space. He felt when it happened. It was a unique sensation, like he was feeling the inside of his mouth for the first time. Like he was touching something he had no business touching.

But wasn't that the point of cultivation?

Jack ignored the sensation of wrongness and slowly slid his blade backward, along the gap, tearing it open. He suddenly realized that he had no idea if the backside of space existed here; what if he was just cutting his own soul open, effectively suiciding?

Thankfully, that wasn't the case. Sliding his perception through the gap while still holding the blade in place, Jack felt the same counterintuitive lack of distance. He grabbed a few particles, as few as he could grasp, and pushed them into the gap, attempting to teleport them.

For the first time, Jack experienced the workings of teleportation.

It wasn't easy. Changing the world in any way, including altering your location, always required energy. The concept of distance made that intuitive—if you wanted to change locations, you had to expend energy to physically move from one point to another. Simple and easy.

Only now, Jack was a big boy cultivator, and he had to work with the real world, not the user interface.

Teleportation similarly required energy, but without the medium of distance. Jack experienced this demand for energy as an innate resistance on the other side of the fabric. Every possible point in space was just a thought away regardless of distance, and the natural laws demanded he pay a price in energy to move, and that energy was exponentially greater than the energy he would have to use to move there physically, over the fabric of space.

In essence, teleportation saved time at the expense of energy.

Finally, Jack realized why Space Walk was so exhausting; moving a mile like this was like moving a thousand miles the normal way.

He pushed the ball of particles into space and teleported it ten feet to the side. The resistance he faced was minimal, as appropriate for such a tiny task.

To his surprise, he succeeded! He'd discovered teleportation!

His eyes snapped open with a full grin on his face, meeting Copy Jack's equally joyful expression.

"Do you even know why we're happy?" he asked, but the copy just laughed. Jack shook his head. "Fine. Watch me, Copy Jack. I'm about to teleport!"

Copy Jack kept his eyes on Jack, slightly narrowed, watching as he'd been instructed. Jack stood and prepared himself. He visualized his Dao razor again, sinking it into space and slowly dragging it around himself, cutting out his three-dimensional outline. Suddenly, he existed within a loose part of the fabric, only separated from the spaceless void by a thought.

His razor sank slightly deeper into the fabric, then pushed out its end. It was made of Dao. Jack used his will to grab and move it, revealing an invisible opening into the void, which he quickly stepped into. He pictured himself arriving a mile in the distance, like Space Walk did.

He appeared only a hundred feet away, wheezing and gasping for energy. He was exhausted. Out of breath. Starving. It felt like every ounce of energy not necessary for his survival had been sucked out of him.

Thankfully, the green moon shone brightly above, and a little bit of energy re-entered his body.

"Fuck me," he muttered, still panting heavily. "That's so difficult."

The energy expenditure didn't just scale with distance, but also with the cultivator's proficiency. A master of space could cross the same distance as Jack with only a fraction of the energy. As proof of that, the System could teleport him one mile away for only around a fourth of his total stamina.

Jack himself moved a hundred feet at the cost of every scrap of energy he possessed.

Plus, the entire process had taken him around ten minutes. The System could do it for him instantly.

It really was a very useful tool.

And a tool it remained. The more aware Jack was of the process, the less he needed the System.

Congratulations! Space Walk I → Space Walk II

Space Walk II: Space is a constraint you have learned to escape. By spending a large amount of energy, take a step through the fabric of space to reappear anywhere within a *three-mile* radius.

"Hell yeah!" Jack shouted, pumping his fist. The description remained the same, but the one-mile limitation had been increased to three miles.

On second thought, Jack remembered that, from his experience, the energy requirement of Space Walk didn't change much depending on the distance traveled. Even if he teleported just a few feet, he always spent the energy needed to teleport three miles away. In other words, this upgrade hadn't made the skill easier to use, just increased its range.

"Well, whatever," he said. "I earned much more than just a skill upgrade—I now understand the basics of the Dao of Space! Maybe the energy adjustment will come at a later tier—and, in any case, I won't even need the skill once I grow proficient enough. I will be able to teleport without the System's assistance, simply by manipulating space. Isn't that awesome, Copy Ja—"

He paused mid-sentence, noticing that Copy Jack's eyes were closed. He had an expression of utter concentration as his hands reached out, moving in similar patterns to the vampire woman's—something he'd copied from Jack himself.

"Hey, are you trying to teleport?" Jack asked him from a hundred feet away. "I applaud the effort, but it's—"

With a pop, Copy Jack stepped into space, disappeared, and reappeared wheezing ten feet behind Jack. He'd traveled a hundred and ten feet.

Jack blinked. "Fuck you."

Copy Jack raised a hand to ask for space, then laughed as energy returned to him.

"No fair!" Jack complained. "I spent who knows how long to learn that. Just because you're Fist and space here is Fist, and you benefit from the insights inside my soul, that doesn't make you smarter than me!"

Copy Jack just kept laughing and tapping his temple.

Jack rolled his eyes, but he wasn't really mad. He liked Copy Jack; it was part of his soul. If he could easily teleport inside the soul world, that could only benefit Jack—somehow.

"Anyway," Jack said, "I got to go now. I think I've spent too long meditating this time, and people will be looking for me. Plus, I could use some rest."

His piled-up exhaustion was finally showing, and it was so intense it made him dizzy. He'd been meditating nonstop for... days? Weeks?

"See you, Copy Jack," he said. The copy waved, and Jack reappeared in the real world, where he promptly fell asleep on his cellar floor, snoring soundly.

CHAPTER TWENTY-EIGHT
THE NEW BRO SQUAD

Gan Salin ducked under an arrow, letting it whistle over his head until it smashed into a tree far behind. He coiled himself and sprang forward, his momentum carrying him over a fallen branch and into a roll, dodging a second arrow. The third found him in the shin, ricocheting off his ogre-leather armor and pushing him back.

"Ouch!" he exclaimed. "Take this! Kage Bunshin no Jutsu!"

He split into three clones and attacked.

He didn't really split into three. He just imagined he did—and, thanks to his Dao Seed of Insanity, so did Nauja.

Arrows of wind were loosed from her bow. The string twang continuously. Her arms blurred. Each of Salin's clones was darting to the left and right, bobbing, weaving, and generally doing their best to dodge. They hid behind trees and bushes, crawled on the ground, climbed the canopy. The forest was riddled with arrows. The trees became sieves.

The first clone fell on Nauja from above while another sprang at her from below. She jumped backward, letting the air carry her as she let loose two arrows, piercing the clones and making them dissipate into thin air.

This success came at a cost. A third clone jumped on her from behind—the real one, ready to dig his open fingers into her back. "Five Star Grasp!" he shouted triumphantly.

Suddenly, his face fell. A tremendous gust of wind erupted under his feet, so strong that it couldn't possibly have been just created. It had been lying there in wait for a while.

He flew up, spinning wildly.

"You're predictable, Gan!" Nauja shouted, turning around in midair and releasing another hail of arrows. Each aimed at one of his limbs, arranged in such a way that he could not dodge.

"Impossible! I'm the very definition of the opposite!" he cried out in protest. He tucked his head and limbs in his chest, becoming a ball that dodged most of the arrows, though some grazed him.

That was the trick with Nauja's arrows. Just dodging them wasn't enough. You had to dodge them widely, or she could use her wind to redirect them mid-flight.

One of the grazing arrows drew blood.

"Ha!" Nauja shouted. "I wi—"

Salin crashed into the canopy feet-first. He pushed against it to launch himself back towards Nauja, who did not react in time, thinking she had won. But Salin's wound was nowhere to be seen. The blood already dissipated.

Salin hadn't really been hit. He just thought he had. Because he was insane.

He reached the forest floor in a blink, mid-flight swiping at the face of Nauja, who barely dodged in time. He landed in a crouch and kicked her legs from under her, then predicted the angle at which she would dodge, grabbed her throat, turned, and smashed the back of her head against the dirt. He then remained over her, panting, his claw-like fingernails poised to strike.

Nauja lay on the ground, shocked. The crowd, nine men and women, cheered.

"You cheated," she said.

"How can I cheat in a spar?"

"You never used that skill before. You saved it for the public match."

"Oh, I must have forgotten about it. Because, you know, I'm insane."

She rolled her eyes, then threw his hand from her throat and sat up.

Salin, who was already standing, reached out with a smile. She smiled back as she grabbed his hand and used it to stand.

"Nice fight," she said.

"You did pretty well yourself."

The crowd cheered again, shouting, "Gan Sa-lin! Gan Sa-lin!" over and over again, while he smiled and waved.

"For the record," Nauja said between the cheers, "his score against me is one win, nine losses."

"But I got the last one!" he replied, beaming. "If we had been really fighting, you would be dead."

"No, because you would have already died nine times."

"I'm a canine. I have ten lives."

"That's... so wrong I can't even begin to explain it." Nauja gave up, sighing. "You did win. Enjoy it while it lasts; next time, you're going down."

"I'm looking forward to it!"

The two of them weren't too far apart in strength. Thanks to this forest expedition, their levels had already risen to 92 and 110 for Salin and Nauja respectively. Both had the Seventh Ring Conqueror title, but Nauja's Direct Descendant title only gave her an extra 15% efficacy in stats, while Salin's combined titles of Planetary Frontrunner (10) and Planetary Torchbearer (10) gave him a 20% increase total.

As a result, Nauja remained stronger stat-wise, but Salin made up for it by having an extra Dao Root. He possessed the Dao Seed of Insanity, fused with the Dao Root of Resolve and not-yet-fused with the Dao Root of Loyalty. Nauja had the Dao Seed of Wind fused with the Dao Root of Archery, and she was actively looking for a second Dao Root to develop. She refused to be overtaken by Gan Salin!

"Fat luck, sweetheart," he told her, reading her thoughts as they left the stage. "I've been through a lot of shit. I've got a Dao Root more, whether you like it or not."

"We'll see about that," she challenged him. "This expedition is pushing me, too. Plus, if I could use my Sun Piercing Arrow, you would never win a spar."

"It would have to hit me first."

"Oh, it would."

Nauja's strongest skill, Sun Piercing Arrow, was too dangerous to use in mock battles.

"Speaking of, I'm going to practice," she said. "The sun won't pierce itself."

"Alright. I'm going to find Brock and tell him all about my victory. See you!"

She rolled her eyes and walked away. Salin, meanwhile, went in another direction with a big grin on his face. He was in such a great mood that his posture was goofy; his torso was leaning backward, he took long steps, and had his hands clasped behind his head.

People nodded at him as he passed, offering him thumbs-up or handshakes.

"Good job, bro!" one man said.

"You finally did it! Nice trick!" a girl shouted at him.

"Thanks, guys! I couldn't have done it without you!" He could have certainly done it without them, but a winner needs to be gracious!

Tents and treehouses were at his sides as he paced through the camp area, heading for where their big bro was resting.

Once upon a time, it had been just the three of them touring the forest in search of ogres or easier prey. But Brock wasn't playing around. He guided them deeper and deeper into the forest, challenging anything they could defeat and escaping from anything they couldn't. They were risking their lives far more than Salin and Nauja expected, but they were onboard; this was why they had come here. To become stronger.

Of course, they weren't the only ones around. The ogre territory was expansive, and many had the same idea as them, but nobody went at it with the same fervor as Brock. Nobody had a reason to risk their lives.

When their group ran into two people chased by an ogre, they helped them defeat the beast. Then, somehow, Brock exhibited great charisma and convinced the two strangers to join his group so they could go after larger prey. A few fist-bumps and handshakes later, they started calling him "big bro."

And he really was. Through it all, Brock turned out to be a brilliant team leader. He coordinated the five of them perfectly, arranging them in such a way that even a couple ogres at once was little trouble. Where their formation had deficiencies, Brock was always there to plug in the gap with his great personal strength—and he always knew the right thing to say to keep the morale sky-high.

They delved even deeper. Their levels kept rising. In the process, they ran into and assimilated two more groups, increasing their total strength to such a degree that the ogres no longer stood a chance, and Brock led them to scour the forest until they almost decimated the native ogre population. The weakest of them had gotten over a dozen levels, and the strongest, around three or four. And that was after only two days. This speed was unprecedented.

Plus, this wasn't how the cultivation world was supposed to work. The outer disciples were always looking for a chance to backstab each other in this forest for a few easy levels. And yet Brock seemed to gravitate to the perfect people, who joined them easily and were quickly bonded by brotherhood. Even Nauja, who was biased against cultivators from her barbarian days, had formed friendly relations with the others.

Salin was confident that, if something happened, every single member of their group would gladly lay down their lives to let their bros escape.

It was impressive, really. Much more difficult than it sounded—otherwise, everyone would be doing this. It required extreme charisma, leadership, and strength.

And all that had been achieved by a five-month-old brorilla.

Sometimes, Salin suspected that Brock was a prodigy even greater than Jack. It made him feel inferior—and, even worse, his Dao of Loyalty was beginning to acclimate to Brock's leadership. That wasn't good. He could yield to Jack, but not to a monkey!

Oh well. If he's worth it, he's worth it.

"Hey, big bro!" he shouted, approaching Brock. The brorilla was lounging on a horizontal branch, letting three of his limbs hang down while his remaining hand held on to a banana he'd gotten from god-knows-where.

Hearing Salin's approach, Brock perked up. "Bro."

"I just came to let you know I defeated Nauja in a spar!"

"Yes?"

"For sure, dude! I totally kicked her ass!"

Brock smiled proudly. He put his banana down to give Salin a thumbs-up. "Good job."

A surge of pride swept through him at Brock's approval. *Man, the Bro Dao is dangerous.*

"What about you? Are you training?" he asked, jumping to the branch and taking a seat next to Brock. "Or resting for our next hunting trip?"

"Training," Brock replied. "No time. Big Bro need me."

"Don't overwork yourself, man. Jack prefers you being alive than strong."

"Yes. But alive without strong is nothing."

Salin took a moment to digest that. "I guess you're right. So, any progress? A new Dao Root, perhaps?"

Brock shook his head. "No. Difficult. But close."

"Of course it's difficult! Only Lords have three roots, and they've been cultivating for years, if not decades. Two is more than plenty."

Brock, again, disagreed. "No. Two is few. Three is okay. Four is good. Big Bro perfect. I must perfect too, or I stay behind."

There was no self-pity in these words, no worry. When Brock claimed he would achieve four Dao Roots, he was simply stating a fact. Salin couldn't help but admire that.

"Which ones do you have already?" he asked. "I was a scion once. I know stuff. Maybe I can help."

"Bro. Very big. Then, work out. And..." he paused, trying to remember the word, "tightness."

"That's not even a real word, big bro. You're just shitting with me."

Brock winked.

"Alright, well... Maybe you could meditate on hard work? Or the Dao Root of the Staff, since you use a staff? Or stone? Or something to do with gorillas, trees, or bananas?"

Brock shook his head. "I no need help. I got this. I only say because you curious."

Salin had indeed been curious, which was why he'd asked... but how did Brock know that!

"Man, big bro, how can you be so cool?"

Brock pointed at his heart, then gave Salin a wide monkey grin. "Heart!"

The canine laughed. So did the brorilla. Then, Brock placed a hand steadily on Salin's shoulder, looked him in the eyes with a confident smile, and said, "Now, go. It is time. We hunt."

"Yes, big bro!" Salin jumped down and rushed to gather the others. He hoped everyone was well-rested. They were about to get even more levels! All of them!

And they called me mad... Hihihi. Peak of the E-Grade, here we come!

CHAPTER TWENTY-NINE
ELDER MONSOON

When Jack awoke, he was lying face-first on his cellar floor. The air around him thrummed with the Dao of the Fist, while the Dao Magnet stood silent beside him.

He stood slowly, grabbing his head. "Ugh... Not my best morning."

A splitting headache was tormenting him. It felt like Brock had taken a sledgehammer and went to town on the inside of Jack's skull. Moreover, there was a persistent, piercing pain above his right eye, where it always hurt if he thought hard.

"That was the most intense meditation session I've ever had," he said, forcing himself to stand. "I lost track of time completely... It must have been days. I wonder if there are painkillers for immortals."

Thanks to his control over his body, as well as his high pain tolerance, this splitting headache was more an annoyance than anything else, but it remained an annoyance. He could do without it.

Jack dusted himself off, then realized he was short of breath. Immortals didn't *need* to breathe, but they still did it. Right now, after being locked in a cellar for who knows how long, the air was stuffy and heavy, his lungs struggling to process it. He floated to the trapdoor on the ceiling and pushed it open, taking a deep breath as he flew out of the cellar, out of the still-open window of his kitchen, and into the sky.

"Ah..." He sighed in contentment. The air was so clean it felt like medicine.

As Jack gazed at the surrounding estate and the valley beneath, he felt an urge to use his new understanding of Space and teleport. It took him a second to remember that he couldn't—space in the real world was more difficult to pierce than in his soul world.

But he could try Space Walk. It could now teleport him up to a distance of three miles—how far away was Shol's cabin? Huali's estate was grand, but three miles in a straight line was a lot.

Jack's eyes pierced the world below to land on a small cabin, barely visible even from this height. He then took a step through space and disappeared. With the whooshing of air, he found himself before a humble wooden door. He was slightly short of breath, as was always the case when he teleported.

To test his earlier theory, he teleported three feet to the side. When he reappeared, the energy expenditure was practically identical to when he teleported three miles.

Inconvenient... but I guess, if I could teleport constantly for next to no cost, I would be unstoppable in battle. Maybe I'll get to that point later.

Jack hadn't come here just to try out his teleportation. He wanted to tell Shol about his achievements in the Dao of Space and ask for advice on how to proceed. He also wanted to thank him. If Shol hadn't taken him to the library in person, maybe the librarian wouldn't have given Jack this Dao Vision. It was undoubtedly very precious.

However, as he raised his hand to knock on the door, he hesitated. What if Shol was cultivating? Jack couldn't just show up unannounced at his house, could he?

A moment later, he decided to just knock very discreetly. If Shol was meditating in his chamber, he wouldn't hear the sound—and, if he wasn't, he would.

A gentle rap of the knuckles was all Jack did. A barely discernible sound that a pre-System human wouldn't even register.

"Come in," Shol's voice came from the inside, and Jack opened the door.

He found himself in a world of paper. The once cozy cabin was now decorated with orderly stacks of white paper, most of which rested on a heavy wooden desk, behind which Shol sat and read.

"Jack!" he exclaimed. "You're out of meditation! And you came to rescue me! Thank you, little brother. Take a seat—tea? And close the door behind you."

"Yes, please," Jack replied, slightly confused. "What's going on?"

"I'm neck deep in work, that's what. The struggle for the Grand Elder position has escalated since you killed Dan Bolon, to the point where we're actively campaigning for the other elders' support. There are conflicts all over the inner planet, mostly between our disciples and Monsoon's, while every outing is now a strategic move. I'm trying to piece together all these reports and deduce the next moves of Monsoon's disciples, so we can send the right disciples at the right spots and win most of the conflicts. I can't even begin to explain how much I dislike this."

"Can't you just... organize a public battle to settle this? Have ten pairs of disciples duel each other to get rid of all the complexity?"

From where he was preparing tea, Shol raised his head to glare at Jack as if insulted. "This complexity is nothing before our devotion to Master. It is the best way forward—I would rather endure this a hundred times over than risk our master's chances by organizing a series of duels that would probably not end in our favor."

"I see. I didn't mean to imply that."

"I'm just stressed, that's all." Shol sighed as he placed two teacups on the table and plopped down opposite Jack. "It's a good thing you came. Even immortals need breaks. My head feels like it's about to burst."

"Yeah, mine too."

"Yours? Why yours?"

Jack laughed, then explained his process of understanding the Dao Vision and the benefits he'd reaped.

Shol's eyes grew wider. "You mean that, not only did you comprehend the vision in one go, but you even achieved enough progress to advance one of your Dao Skills?"

"Yep."

"Jack! That's great! Most disciples who get this vision spend months on it, if not years, and even then, comprehending it in its entirety is very rare. You did it in two weeks!"

Now, it was Jack's turn to be surprised. "I was meditating for two weeks straight?"

"Oh, don't give me that face. Two weeks to comprehend one of the fundamental building blocks of the universe? Please. Others would kill for that."

Jack smiled proudly. "How long did it take you, brother Shol?"

"Well, that's irrelevant, isn't it? What I'm thinking is, your method of brute-forcing it in one go might be the most effective one. After all, it worked."

"It wasn't easy." Jack thought back to the thousands of times he'd repeated the vision until his brain had adjusted to its every chaotic second. "If I stopped mid-way through, I would probably need to start all over again the next time."

"That's why we don't recommend what you did. The chances of success are small, and the price is that you lose all your progress if you fail. But, well, it worked for you. We usually tell disciples to go at it for a couple hours every day, deepening their understanding gradually as they get used to the fluctuations of space."

"Then, why didn't you tell me that beforehand?"

"I had a feeling you'd find your way." Shol smiled widely. "Plus, you wouldn't have listened to me. You're in a hurry."

Jack didn't even need to think before responding, "Yeah, I wouldn't listen. Good call."

Both laughed as they sipped from their tea.

"So, how's it going?" Jack asked. "The struggle for Grand Elder, I mean."

"Decently," Shol replied. "The situation is fairly balanced. Both Monsoon and Master Huali have been visiting the other elders, but neither has made much progress. Most elders are staying on the side-lines for now."

"I see."

"As far as public opinion goes..." Shol's face darkened. "We aren't doing too well there. Your victory over Bolon helped, but these things are all too easily forgotten. Now, the eyes of the people are focused on the many conflicts happening around the planet, and Monsoon's disciples win most of them. It's unavoidable. They're stronger overall."

"Hmm. And that is pressuring the elders?"

"Well, a bit. Public opinion doesn't matter too much because the elders are the only ones voting, but word gets around. If an elder hears their disciples gossip that Monsoon's people are stronger than Huali's, that affects their opinion on the matter. Thankfully, our master has an excellent reputation, enough to outweigh the disciple insufficiency—for now." He tightened his grip around the teacup ever so slightly. "But it sucks for us. Our master's strength and reputation are both stellar. The only thing holding her back is us."

Jack nodded, considering the issue. "So, Monsoon's reputation is inferior."

"Oh, yes. Monsoon is an outstanding cultivator, but he is known as a cutthroat, power-hungry individual. That doesn't mesh well with the Exploding Sun's principles. The other elders fear him, while they respect our master."

"Wait. Are you saying there are cultivators who actually care about being good people?"

Shol threw him a weird look. "Of course. We're the minority, but we live and prosper. Power, by itself, does not bring corruption. Not everyone is like the Animal Kingdom."

"Huh. I thought... Nevermind. But if the Exploding Sun doesn't like Monsoon, why consider him?"

"It's not so simple. There needs to be a balance between righteousness and power, or we wouldn't exist. Monsoon might push the faction in a direction most of us would be uncomfortable with, but he will bring prosperity, too. It is a sad reality of life."

"But, and excuse my French, you just said he's an asshole."

"What is *French*?"

"An expression."

"Well, please mind your language. I wouldn't call any elder of my faction that."

"French?"

"Asshole."

"Right." Jack nodded. "I don't know. I guess I just don't understand politics. I always found the subject unsavory."

"It always is, until you start to understand it. Then, it's just the nature of ruling... which can challenge one's perception on morality."

"I guess."

"Don't guess. Start getting used to it." Shol gave Jack a serious look. "You are important now. You wield great personal power and basically rule an entire planet, at least for now. You cannot afford to hide behind your finger. Uncomfortable realities are something you must learn to face."

"Right... Yes, you're right. I'm sorry. I almost made the weak choice of not thinking."

"No problem. You are still young; there is much to learn."

"By the way, since I spent two weeks cultivating—"

An unexpected sound interrupted them. Booming laughter filled the sky and shook the mountain under them as an overwhelming presence washed over Jack and Shol, making their eyes widen and their bodies sweat.

"Huali!" a male voice dominated every other sound. "I came for tea! I hope I am welcome?"

Jack paled. This presence was far superior to the Planetary Overseer's, the only other C-Grade aura he'd experienced. "Who's that?"

Shol, however, did not reply immediately. His eyes were glued on the cabin roof, and his mind was running over a thousand calculations every second. Finally, he replied, "Elder Monsoon."

"Monsoon? What is he doing here?"

"I don't know... but it can't be good. Come!"

Shol launched himself out of the open window and into the sky. Jack followed a beat later, leaving the rest of the tea to grow cold—was he doomed to never finish a cup in Shol's house?

They weren't the only immortals flying to see what was going on. Dozens of them, all Huali's personal disciples, were looking up and whispering to each other. They stayed right above the buildings, not daring to rise higher.

In the center of the sky stood a man with a blue cape fluttering behind him. He was of average height and solidly built, with sleek muscles outlined under his purple robes. His sleeves were long, as was his dark hair, while his angular face carried a wide jaw and a smile too bright to be true. His eyes, however... Jack felt uncomfortable just glancing at them from afar. Though they were glued on the manor at the mountain peak, Jack felt their pressure deep in his soul.

This was Elder Monsoon. One of the two strongest elders of the Exploding Sun, alongside Elder Huali, and one of the competitors for the Grand Elder position. Excluding the reclusive B-Grades, this man was in the top two people in the entire constellation.

As for his aura, it was so wide and heavy that it stifled Jack's breath. It was only slightly weaker than the vampire woman's in the vision, though that may have been because she had been actively using her powers, while he was simply standing in the sky with his arms crossed behind his back.

Human (Earth-44), Level ??? (C-Grade)
Faction: Exploding Sun (B-Grade)

So impressive was the elder's presence that Jack almost didn't notice the second man, standing slightly behind and below the elder. He wore blue robes, a yellow cape, and had blond hair, emanating a presence like that of a rippling pond. His expression was calm.

Human (Earth-44), Level 249
Faction: Exploding Sun (B-Grade)
Title: Eighth Ring Conqueror

As Jack was done ogling, the doors of the manor opened, and two figures slowly floated out. One was Elder Huali—Jack's current master, who reminded him of an old yoga instructor. The other person was a C-Grade, scholarly-looking man whose robes were half-white and half-black. He stood right beside Huali—another elder?

The third elder was giving out no aura at all, but Huali was, completely canceling out Monsoon's and letting her disciples breathe again.

The moment she took to the sky, Shol flew over, taking a respectful position right behind and below her, mirroring the man behind Monsoon.

"Monsoon," Elder Huali said, her smile purely for show. "Of course you are welcome. To what do I owe the pleasure?"

CHAPTER THIRTY
MONSOON'S PROVOCATION

"The pleasure is all mine, Huali," Monsoon replied, standing in the skies above her estate. "I just heard you've gotten a new batch of million-leaf tea. I couldn't stop myself from coming to get a taste!"

"Of course, a pot of million-leaf tea is nothing before such a distinguished guest," she replied diplomatically, pointedly not inviting him to her manor. "However, I am not used to Elder Monsoon visiting me for such a trivial matter. Is there something else?"

Monsoon smirked. He raised both open palms and said, "Ah, you got me. There is another reason, of course, but nothing too important."

He was a charismatic man, Monsoon. He displayed confidence and assertion, joking around with Huali like they were alone instead of watched by hundreds of eyes. He seemed almost perfect—if not for the clear malice hidden in his sudden arrival. After all, Monsoon and Huali were opponents for the Grand Elder position; there had to be a reason for this sketch.

"And what could that be, Monsoon?" Huali asked, clearly not willing to play the other elder's game. "For it to coincide with Elder Mahadaji's visit, it can't be anything *too* small."

"Oh, just a coincidence. If I knew Elder Mahadaji would be present, I would have brought that gift I owe him."

The scholarly man dressed in white and black nodded. While he was positioned next to Huali, as a guest should, he didn't seem inclined to participate in this discussion.

"Jack!" a voice came from the side. Turning, Jack found Auburn flying beside him, her auburn robes and hair fluttering in the wind. "Shit! This is bad!"

"How so?" he asked, eager to know more.

"Well, that's Elder Monsoon, and that man over there is his head disciple, Qian. If they came here together, they probably want to cause trouble and force a duel between Qian and brother Shol..." She bit her lip.

Jack, however, wasn't convinced. "If forcing a duel was so easy, why haven't they done it already?"

"I don't know, but there has to be a reason. Maybe Monsoon has a new card up his sleeve."

"Hmm. What about that other man? Elder Mahadaji?"

"He's one of the neutral elders, but he has some clout. Huali and Monsoon have both been trying to swing him over. Since Monsoon chose to arrive while Mahadaji was here, he probably plans to use him to put extra pressure on our master. After all, refusing a duel in front of Mahadaji will certainly make him see Master Huali as the least favorable candidate to support."

"I see." Jack's eyes narrowed as he looked at the sky. "In any case, there is nothing we can do. Let's just wait and see."

"Yes."

Up there, Monsoon smiled as he spread both hands apart. "I heard some wonderful news the other day, Huali. You took in a brilliant disciple—someone who can jump a tier to defeat other personal disciples."

Every immortal at low altitude turned to look at Jack. He wanted to curse. His words just now, that there was nothing he could do, had been tossed back at his face.

"Indeed," Huali responded, showing a rare smile. "Jack is a talented young cultivator. If nothing goes wrong, I trust he will be a great asset to our faction in a few centuries."

"Talented youth is always nice to have," Monsoon agreed. "I only hope the price was worth it."

Whispers spread amongst the immortals. Even Elder Mahadaji glanced at Jack from up high, discovering him in an instant.

Huali's face remained relaxed. "The price?"

"The price," Monsoon confirmed. "I heard that you made a promise to this disciple when recruiting him. That you would use the Exploding Sun's resources to poach his recently Integrated planet from under the Animal Kingdom's nose."

More whispers. Elder Mahadaji raised his brows. "Is that true, Huali?"

Jack bit back another curse. This was supposed to be a secret—after all, planet poaching relied on the enemy not expecting it. Monsoon, however, not only knew about this, he also chose to publicize it.

Of the many thoughts that raced inside Jack's head, one rose above the others: *Shit.*

"It is true," Huali replied without the slightest hesitation. "May I ask how you heard about this, Monsoon? Such matters are supposed to be secret. Making them public is unexpectedly unwise of you."

"I am simply looking out for my faction's interests, Huali. In fact, that's why I came directly to you; if I told the other elders of your willingness to risk the delicate balance between our faction and the Animal Kingdom, just to recruit a promising disciple for yourself before the Elder Assembly, they wouldn't take it too well, would they?"

"You accuse me of risking the faction to help myself," Huali said sharply, dropping the pretense of cordiality. "Is that right, Monsoon?"

"Yes," he replied simply, staring at her in challenge.

"You know I would never do that. Jack is not a boon to me—his recruitment was to the benefit of our entire faction, an investment in our future. Compared to his talent, which you already admitted yourself, one more conflict against the Kingdom is nothing."

"Those are strong words, but of little essence. Does our faction not have enough disciples? Do we not possess young talent? What about all the immortals floating below us, your treasured personal disciples? Do you not believe in them? Is our faction's talent so low that we need to recruit high-cost outsiders?"

Monsoon's words were now striking deep. Huali did not bend, replying with grace and ease.

"You can exaggerate, Monsoon, but you cannot change the truth. Is it not common for our faction to recruit outsiders? To pad our forces with the talented youth of this and other constellations? We do not lack in talent, but only a fool would miss the opportunity to make themselves even stronger."

"We may not lack talent, but what about resources? The more disciples you accept, the less you can assist each of them. Every Dao treasure he consumes is one that your other disciples will not."

"What are you trying to say? That I should limit my number of disciples?"

"That would be wise, too, but it is not my point. I am simply saying that one disciple, no matter how talented, is not worth the price you promised. Inter-faction relations are far more important than someone who will probably never reach the C-Grade. By recruiting this man for your own benefit, you want to waste years of the Elder Assembly's efforts."

"Hmph!" Huali's snort echoed across the sky, accompanied by the subtle release of her aura. Jack felt a wave of heat pass over his body, making him sweat, along with a colossal presence pressing down on his head. Huali's aura wasn't the slightest bit lacking compared to Monsoon's. Neither was her temper.

"Is your young brain filled with rot?" she asked. "Or are you really that naive? Do you think anyone here will fall for strongly-worded fallacies? I have served the faction for seven millennia, never betraying it in the slightest, and I do not intend to start now. Since I recruited Jack, I naturally believe the benefits outweigh the costs. How can you come here, possessing far less information than me, and claim that my decision was wrong? How dare you insinuate that I would harm the faction for my personal benefit!"

The air was billowing and heated, like everyone was placed inside an oven. Monsoon raised his hands, and an invisible Dao bubble was formed around himself and his head disciple, protecting them from Huali's wrath.

"Pace yourself, Huali," he said without the slightest crease in his brows. His smile remained friendly. "I am not here to accuse you, only to ask you whether the things I heard were true."

"Hmph." With a second snort, her aura disappeared like it had never been there. She'd made her point. "Spare me the acting, Monsoon. Just get to the point."

"Very well. As I said, I am here to take a good look at this disciple of yours, so I can ascertain whether his talent is as great as you make it to be. Could he rise so we can all see him?"

Jack did not move. He glanced at Huali, who met his eyes and nodded. "Fly higher, Jack Rust," she commanded, and he obliged.

As he rose, he met Auburn's worried eyes, as well as the eyes of all surrounding immortals, some of whom he'd never met before. Many held accusation in their gazes—others, curiosity, and a few more, amusement.

When he finally reached an altitude close to that of the two elders, he flew behind and below Shol, who was behind and below Huali. He had no idea if this was the right etiquette, but it felt appropriate. He also positioned himself low enough that Elder Monsoon had a clear view.

"Say nothing about the ninth ring," Shol's voice rang in Jack's mind. "I will explain the reason later. For now, just stay quiet."

Jack did not reply, remembering how the Planetary Overseer had demonstrated the ability to spy on his telepathic conversations. If she could do it, so could Elder Monsoon.

The eyes of both Elder Monsoon and Elder Mahadaji landed on him, inspecting him thoroughly. He felt naked and vulnerable. It took all of his concentration to keep his face calm, pretending to feel nothing.

"Interesting," Monsoon said. "A perfect foundation... You don't see that often. What ring of Trial Planet did you reach?"

Jack tried to reply. "Honored Elder, I reached the eighth—"

"Silence, disciple!" Qian, the head disciple of Monsoon, who'd remained quiet up to now, berated him. "You will not speak before the elders."

Jack held his tongue. He'd just been asked a direct question. What was he supposed to do, ignore Monsoon?

Asshole.

In any case, he understood that this was not his field. He looked to Shol and Huali for guidance.

"He reached the eighth ring," Huali replied in Jack's stead.

"Decent. However, a good foundation doesn't guarantee success. I believe a direct demonstration would be more convincing—how about we let Jack prove his prowess by sparring against my disciple, Qian?"

And there it was.

The other shoe had finally dropped, and Jack could see the core of Monsoon's ploy. If he and this peak D-Grade guy sparred, it wouldn't even be a demonstration. Jack would lose instantly, which was obviously the expected result, one that would give Monsoon the grounds to keep pressing the issue. Most importantly, it would be humiliating for Elder Huali to submit her own disciple to a beating just because Monsoon asked her to.

On the other hand, if she declined this duel, he would have grounds to ask for other things. Somehow, he would reach the point of Qian challenging Shol, and that would be the end of things.

Not to mention that Elder Mahadaji, an important person, was present.

CHAPTER THIRTY-ONE
MAKING A BET

EVERYONE ELSE MUST HAVE UNDERSTOOD THE SAME THING, BUT HUALI SIMPLY frowned and replied, "Your disciple is a hundred levels over Jack. It would be like a human slapping a mosquito."

"It's not about victory. It's about seeing how far Jack can push my disciple before losing. Plus... considering what happened to my other disciple, Dan Bolon, this Jack of yours seems to enjoy battling."

Obviously, Huali wasn't considering whether to accept or decline this duel, as accepting it would just humiliate her. But she couldn't just decline, either.

"How about you bring someone closer to Jack's level?" she suggested. "I will not submit my disciple to a beating simply because you ask."

"I have no other disciples available, and such important matters need to be settled quickly. We should strike when the iron is hot. If you have nothing to hide, what's the problem with letting Jack spar against Qian? Cultivators spar against stronger opponents all the time. It is not a big deal."

Huali hesitated again. No matter how anyone saw it, she had the weaker position here, if only because Monsoon had revealed information she'd tried to keep secret. The problem was, she was currently trapped between a river and a cliff.

Monsoon knew this, and he stepped on the gas. "How about this: If you are concerned about Jack getting injured by my disciple, there is another way. At its core, this issue is about whether your judgment in prospective disciples is insightful enough. I believe this recruitment was not worth the price, while you believe the opposite. We could solve this by having Qian spar against your head disciple, Shol. The master of the winner will obviously have the better judgment when it comes to disciples, and there is no mismatch between them, be it in level or status. What do you think, Huali?"

This was even more undesirable. If Shol and Qian dueled publicly, Shol would most probably be defeated, and Huali would lose a lot of face. Given Monsoon's foxlike maneuvers, he could probably exaggerate this issue to win him the Grand Elder position. Plus, if Shol lost now, Monsoon's accusations would increase in credibility.

It looked like the only option was to have Jack spar against Qian, choosing to endure the lesser humiliation instead of the greater one. However, now that the other suggestion had been made, having Jack duel instead of Shol would mean recognizing that Shol was weaker than Qian. Elder Mahadaji was present—this implication wouldn't be lost on him.

In fact, his eyes were trained on Huali, waiting to hear her answer.

Jack, meanwhile, was feeling terrible. Not because he was challenged, or even because he might receive a beating.

This was happening partly because of him. Master Huali had offered to help him, and because the matter had been leaked, she was now placed in such a tight spot. And, okay, that wasn't really his fault. However, since the plan had been leaked, was it even feasible anymore? What would happen to Huali's promise of saving Earth?

If anything, Jack's current position was even worse than Huali's. She was just going to lose some face, while he was in danger of losing his entire planet!

His mind spun with calculations, and he concluded that, no matter what happened, things would turn out terrible for him. If he wanted the best chance of still receiving Huali's assistance, he had to bail her out of this impossible situation.

But, perhaps, there was another way.

A plan slowly formed inside Jack's mind. A plan that could help Master Huali, but which would also corner her and make her unable to go back on her word, like she'd done last time during the Integration Tournament.

Jack had had enough of asking people to help him. This time, he would demand it—and try to get all birds with the same stone.

"Could I speak, master?" he asked, bowing in Huali's direction. His eyes were earnest, and his chest puffed, showing clearly that he had a plan.

Qian's face warped as he almost berated Jack again, but since he had asked the question directly to Elder Huali, Qian had no authority to speak. Shol did, but after glaring fiercely at Jack, he chose not to—since he also couldn't find a way out of this, all he could do was hope for the impossible.

Maybe Elder Huali thought the same thing. Maybe she expected Jack to humiliate himself to get her out of this.

"You may," she replied.

"I am young and eager to prove myself," Jack began. "There is nothing I would love more than to showcase my talent before the elders. However, I believe that this is not the best opportunity. I am still too weak to meaningfully compare myself to someone like fellow disciple Qian. Therefore, I propose this: how about we agree on a public spar, so I can showcase my talent, in six months' time? I don't hope to win, but that would give me enough time to at least be able to fight Qian."

Silence fell as everyone tried to digest his words. Huali gazed at him deeply, pondering the ramifications of his suggestion, but it was Qian who beat her to the punch.

"Such arrogance!" he exclaimed. "Do you really think you can reach my level in only six months? That's absurd. It took even me a century to reach the peak of the D-Grade."

"I don't just think so; I am confident it can be done," Jack replied fast enough so no one could stop him. "In fact, how about we make a bet, Qian? When we fight in six months, I will be able to exchange three strikes with you without losing. If I can't, I will publicly acknowledge that my talent is insufficient and leave the Exploding Sun faction, not demanding that Master Huali help me with my planet's situation anymore. However, if I do manage to exchange three strikes with you, you will have to publicly admit that my talent is greater than yours, that my master was correct in her judgment, and that yours was not."

Another bout of silence. Even the air had stopped blowing to better hear Jack's brazen words.

Jack himself was feeling the pressure. He believed in winning the bet he proposed, but there were more layers under it. He was escalating the situation. If his proposal was accepted, that bet would become a huge deal. It would probably be the deciding factor for the position of Grand Elder. In other words, Huali would have to pour all her resources into him until then, accepting him as her champion. If he won, he would secure enough status to guarantee the Exploding Sun's assistance in the war for Earth—hopefully.

If he was defeated, on the other hand, he would lose his honor and momentum. He would be forced to publicly humiliate himself by apologizing, the Dao of the Fist would drown in doubts, and he would have proven himself an arrogant dog which barked but could not bite. On top of that, Huali herself would pay for his defeat; losing the position of Grand Elder. The two of them were bound together now.

Most importantly, the date he'd set was six months away, which was only a month before the end of Earth's grace period. His plan was to have the power to fight a middle C-Grade by then—if he couldn't even take three strikes of a peak D-Grade, he would have already failed.

It was a daunting goal, and one he believed he could reach if things went his way. With Huali's full assistance and some hellish training, he was confident.

He didn't dare look back at his master. His gaze was glued on Qian, who was frowning slightly as he considered Jack's words. Monsoon, however, laughed out loud.

"He has a quick mind, at least!" he exclaimed. "Very well. Unless you disagree with your disciple's suggestion, Huali, we accept the challenge."

Only now did Jack dare glance to his master, where Huali's wisdom-filled eyes were inspecting him carefully. Shol was staring at Huali with his eyes half-closed, no doubt conversing mentally.

Whatever they said, it somehow went to Jack's favor.

"Very well," she replied. "Let it be so. In six months, one day before the Elder Assembly, Jack will duel against Qian. If he can last more than three strikes, it will be his victory, and this matter will go to me, with you publicly apologizing for your false accusations. If he fails, I will accept that my faith was misplaced, and Jack will have to leave the faction and my tutelage."

Monsoon only laughed again. He obviously didn't mind the stakes—he was convinced that, no matter what happened, Jack couldn't even come close to Qian's level.

"Alright, Huali. We have a bet! Let me just add that, if Jack somehow perishes before the duel, victory goes to me."

"Naturally," she agreed.

"And I shall be the witness," Elder Mahadaji said. His voice carried great power but remained somehow restrained, as if he were the introverted type.

"Elder Mahadaji's words honor us," Monsoon replied, bowing slightly. He seemed in a great mood. "In that case, there is nothing more to say. The truth behind this matter will be revealed in six months' time. I wish you a pleasant wait, Huali."

She did not reply. Monsoon and Qian flew away, with the latter not forgetting to shoot Jack one last, mocking glare. The two of them soon disappeared into the clouds.

"I will be leaving too," Elder Mahadaji said. "Given what happened, my visit here lost its meaning."

"Indeed. Thank you for visiting, Mahadaji, and I wish you a pleasant return trip," Huali replied politely, smiling at him with confidence.

"Mm." Mahadaji nodded, he, too, shooting Jack an inquisitive glance before disappearing into the clouds.

"Shol," Huali said, turning to her mansion, "you can handle this matter for now. I have a task that takes no delay."

"Yes, Master."

Huali flew away, back into her mansion. All C-Grades had left, leaving only a flock of confused immortals hovering in the sky. The moment they were left alone, Shol glared at Jack so hard that his eyelids almost froze open.

Jack scratched his head, then gave Shol his best smile. “You know, all things considered, I’d say this went pretty well.”

Shol’s glare did not abate in the slightest. “My hut. Now. Everyone else, disperse.”

In the end, even the immortals flew away, leaving that patch of sky completely empty. However, the effects of this argument were not so easy to disperse; they would echo throughout the entire faction and beyond for a long time, until everyone knew that Jack, a low D-Grade, had challenged Qian, the faction’s strongest disciple, and that the next Grand Elder would be decided by the outcome of their duel.

CHAPTER THIRTY-TWO
HELLISH TRAINING

"Your gamble was devious," Shol said as he and Jack entered the cabin. His mood was impossible to read; he could have been furious, relieved, or both.

"I didn't see much choice," Jack replied calmly.

"So you took things upon yourself and bet the master's success on your strength."

"I have confidence in winning."

"Of course you have. Especially with all the support you will now undoubtedly get."

Jack gave him a straight look; not challenging, not yielding, either. "Yes."

Shol sighed. "You really turned things on its head, Jack. I have no idea what Master is thinking right now."

"What about you?"

"What about me?"

"What are you thinking?"

"That you're an arrogant, thoughtless individual who took advantage of the situation for his own benefit."

"Am I really? What was the alternative? You fighting Qian in front of

Elder Mahadaji, or me getting a beating from Qian and throwing away Master Huali's face?"

"The alternative was to let the people who have lived a hundred times longer than you figure it out."

"I didn't see them coming up with anything. I didn't see *you* suggesting something better."

Shol glared at him. "Master Huali is infinitely smarter than you, Jack. If there was such a simple solution, she would have found it in a split-second."

"Would she? She may be extremely smart and experienced, but she does not understand my strength and potential as much as I do. I believe the solution I proposed works, and that is only because I am confident in my chances. She could have been considering the same thing. And don't forget; I asked for permission before I spoke. If she wasn't out of options, she wouldn't have let me."

"You are hasty and selfish."

"I'm just not a fool. I found a solution that benefits me and lets Master Huali escape the corner she'd been pushed into. What else did you expect me to do? Wait on the sidelines until she was eventually forced to go back on her promise *again*?"

Shol's eyes reddened. "You will not insult my master."

"I am not insulting anyone, just stating the facts. Would you have acted differently in my shoes? If the future of the Exploding Sun was at stake, would you leave it up to fate, or would you find a win-win solution that also helps your benefactor?"

Despite Shol's anger, he hadn't lost himself, taking his time to answer. Jack, meanwhile, remained calm and confident.

In the end, Shol could only sigh. "What's done is done. Master Huali will handle this issue as she sees fit. For now, all we can do is prepare for the battle in six months as best as we can. There is no time to lose. If we want you to have even the slightest chance of victory, we must start preparing immediately."

"Is Qian really that strong?" Jack asked. "I just have to survive for three strikes, right? How difficult could that be?"

Shol's eyes widened a fraction. "You know that he is stronger than me, right?"

"I do."

"Good. Watch."

Without warning, a terrifying aura spread from Shol's body. His monk robes fluttered in the resulting wind, the cabin's furniture was tossed to the walls, and all the stacks of paper were scattered. Booms filled the air.

Jack was suffocating. Shol had become a mountain of a man, an unsurpassable existence, a sun about to implode. His form was made of dancing flames, and his eyes shone red like burning iron. Everything else—the cabin, the chairs, the world outside—vanished from Jack's perception.

When Shol clenched his fist, it felt like a star's death rattle, the final clenching before its core exploded in a massive supernova. Jack was nothing more than a normal man tied to train tracks, watching his rapidly approaching death. Surviving this cataclysmic force was impossible. He was completely powerless. Even the Life Drop could not save him.

In the next moment, the sensation was gone. Jack was left sweating with his eyes wide, gazing upon the form of a hardened, battle-ready monk with a tight smile. "Do you see now?" Shol asked.

Jack gulped. "I do... And you say Qian is even stronger?"

"He is. Do you understand now what a hundred levels mean?"

"Yeah..."

Jack may have been impressed, but he wasn't overwhelmed. He already knew his current strength was nowhere near enough. Though with six months—and, five months ago, he had only been a biologist working on his PhD—there was a chance.

That was plenty of time to work miracles.

"I can get the levels," he said. "My plan had always been to reach the C-Grade in a year. Technically, I'm still on schedule. Even if things go badly, I should be able to take three hits from a peak D-Grade, right?"

"There was never a schedule, Jack. I have said it before, and I will say it again, you cannot reach the C-Grade in a year. It is impossible. Even reaching the late D-Grade is a stretch... and Qian is not your average peak D-Grade, either. His strength is already approaching the C-Grade."

"Really! He's that talented? But, still, I was the only E-Grade to ever beat a D-Grade, right?"

"The chasm between the E and D-Grades is especially wide, yes. It is a qualitative transformation. Between the D and C-Grades, the difference is slightly easier to bridge... Still, it's quite impossible. Even Qian is only approaching the strength of the C-Grade—not reaching it."

"I see." Jack fell into deep thought. He sipped from his previous cup of tea, which had gone cold by now but remained fragrant. A moment later, he spoke up again. "So, what do we do?"

"What do we do? Obviously, we level you up, that's what we do!"

"I have a plan for that, actually. Remember how I told you that I was planning to adventure in the Animal Kingdom?"

Shol narrowed his eyes. "Yes."

"Well, I still do, because that's the only way to level-up quickly enough. However, I have an even better idea: I will go to Hell."

"Hell!" Shol shouted. "To rescue that starship captain, right? Impossible. You'll die there."

"Maybe I won't. Think about it. It's an entire planet, right? If somebody comes after me, I can certainly find somewhere to hide. Plus, you mentioned that the Animal Kingdom's inner disciples also live there. Where else would I find so many immortals? I need them to level-up. It's the perfect training ground for me."

"You're spouting bullshit. How could it be so easy? Even if you somehow manage to sneak into Hell, it's not like their immortals will stretch their necks for you. The moment you start acting up, they'll find you and send peak D-Grades after you."

"I can handle peak D-Grades."

"No, you can't."

"Right now, I can't. But they won't send out their big guns right away. I will hide and sneak around, nabbing a few immortals here and there, leveling up in the process. By the time they catch up, I will have gotten a ton of levels. Even if I can't fight a peak D-Grade, I should be able to escape."

Shol grumbled. "It's not that simple... Are you even sure you *want* to do this? You're basically suggesting a massacre."

Jack snorted. "The Animal Kingdom is my enemy, and those inner disciples are its soldiers. They are hunting prisoners for sport. I have no qualms hunting them back."

"Assuming you can succeed," Shol said, considering the issue very seriously, "that will be an extremely fast way to level-up indeed... Perhaps the only way to reach the level you need in time. Sneaking into Hell is possible. We can make it happen. And, even if they realize what you're doing in there, they won't send C-Grades after you. Their pride won't let them, as that would be implying that their D-Grades are incapable of handling you.

"However, there are two problems. One, they have D-Grades on the level of me and Qian. If things escalate to that level, they will easily annihilate you. And two... Hell is a prison planet. Getting in is easy, but getting out is hard. How will you escape afterward?"

"I... I don't know. I don't think I can plan for that beforehand. However, I'm confident that I will find a way when the time comes. It is a risk I must take."

"Normally, I would advise against this... but you need to reach my level in six months. It should take you centuries. I don't think there is any other way—and, since you had the audacity to bet our master's name on your success, it's appropriate to bet your life, too."

Jack smiled. "Well said, brother Shol."

Shol was now fully onboard with the idea. "We must plan carefully. Maximizing your chances is essential. The Exploding Sun will provide you with all sorts of treasures, though you will have to leave the faction to not implicate us. Besides that, we have some spies in the Animal Kingdom—maybe they could be of help."

"Right!" Jack's eyes shone. "Those would all be very helpful."

"But the issue remains that their peak D-Grades will eventually slaughter you. Unless..." Shol mumbled something. "Fine. There is no other choice. I'll join you."

"You'll *what*!"

"Are you deaf? I said I'll join you."

"But—"

"No buts. You already made my job redundant by betting this entire reputation war on your duel. To help our master, the best I can do is protect you. I will not steal your levels; I will just be there to advise you and help you deal with trouble if too much of it appears at once."

"Wait... Are you certain?"

"Absolutely. Do I look like a coward to you?"

"No, but—"

"Then, it's decided. Your plan is approved. We will sneak into Hell, where we will power level you by having you hunt the Animal Kingdom inner disciples. With some luck, we will survive long enough for you to reach at least the late D-Grade, at which point we will try to escape. With our combined powers, I believe we will find a way. We will both leave the Exploding Sun, too, so they cannot accuse the faction of anything. We will act as rogue cultivators."

Jack was touched. What he suggested was almost a suicide mission, and he'd only done so because he was desperate to get stronger quickly. And now, Shol was willing to risk himself and tag along? True, he was doing it for his master, not for Jack, but still...

"Thank you, brother Shol," Jack replied, but Shol waved the gratitude away.

"No need to thank me. I'm not doing this for you. If you have time to be grateful, spend it preparing yourself. The day is still young. I will go talk with Master and prepare some things. You also go deal with any loose ends you have here. We depart tomorrow."

Jack couldn't believe this was already happening. Things were unraveling so fast—he liked that. "Will do!" he replied, puffing his chest out. "I'll visit Brock as well. I need to see how he's doing, and whether he can join us or not."

"Probably not," Shol replied, "but yes, do pay a visit. He's your spiritual companion. You two are as close as can be."

"Of course."

"If you have nothing else to do, I suggest also visiting the library to choose the other two items you can borrow, then spend the rest of the time meditating. Your strength is about to explode—consolidation is crucial."

"Yes, brother."

"Then, let's—"

Jack did not hear the rest of the sentence. A voice suddenly rang inside his head—Master Huali's.

"Jack," she said, her voice not betraying any emotion, "come to my manor at once. I need to show you something."

CHAPTER THIRTY-THREE
SUPERNOVA

As Jack was discussing with Shol, Master's Huali voice rang in his mind.

"Wait," he told Shol, "Master just summoned me."

"She did?" The monk's eyes widened. "That's unusual. Get to it, then. It wouldn't do to leave our master waiting."

"Alright. Should we meet here in, say, six hours?"

"Yes. See you then."

"See you. And, Shol?"

"Yes?"

"Thanks. For accommodating my selfish needs."

Shol smiled. "Nothing selfish about wanting to protect your people, Jack. Besides, it works out for everyone. Now go. The clock is ticking."

"Yes, brother!"

He rushed out of the window, thinking, once again, he didn't finish his cup of tea. Perhaps that was a cursed cabin.

Jack crossed the sky, flying over the estate to land in the courtyard of Elder Huali's manor; a building as imposing as it was simple, dominating the very peak of the mountain. Two guards stood before the gate, eyeing him strangely; they'd seen the results of Monsoon's visit, so his arrival wasn't too unexpected.

"Are you here to see Master?" one of the guards asked, and Jack nodded. Before he could reply, however, Master Huali's voice rang in his mind once again:

"Just teleport inside."

She also released a soft wave of energy to indicate her precise location. Jack didn't dare tally. He gave the guards a helpless shrug, then stepped through space and reappeared in the same room he'd seen Huali the previous time. Large glass windows showcased the estate and the lands beneath it, while the horizon was tinged with soft clouds and a colorful sky.

"Good. You came quickly," Huali said before Jack could speak. She rose to her feet. "Come. We don't have much time."

"Greetings, Master. Much time for what?"

"You'll see."

She took three steps to reach him, then placed a hand on his shoulder. Jack noticed she was taller than him. In the next moment, space warped around them, much harder and faster than when Jack teleported. When it stabilized again, they were in the sky, illuminated by the nebula's solar gasses and surrounded by white clouds.

There was also a starship. It floated in the sky before them, completely still, as if anchored in space itself. No Dao energy emanated from it, and yet, there must have been some, or how could it fly?

"Master?" Jack asked.

"This is my personal vessel, the *Ray*. Step inside."

Things were happening a bit too fast for Jack's taste. He trusted Huali, but still...

"What is going on?" he asked.

"I'll explain on the way. Just get in."

Jack steeled his heart. If she wanted to harm him, she could do it easily. As a door on the side of the starship silently slid open, he stepped through, finding himself in a simple, sharp interior. It could fit three people comfortably, maybe four. Windows surrounded them on all sides—even though he was sure there were none on the outside—giving him a clear view of everything.

"One-way metal. Very handy," Huali explained, entering the starship herself and shutting the door. She crossed to the front of the starship and placed her hands on a sun-shaped helm, infusing it with energy.

"Well, I'm here. Could you explain what is going on, Master?" Jack asked cautiously.

She smiled at him. "Do you not trust me, Jack?"

"I do. I'm just curious."

"Then, you can wait a little bit. Some things are best served as surprises."

Jack grumbled. Not that he had a say, anyway. This tall, slim woman who looked like an old yoga instructor held the power to level entire continents. Plus, she was his master. If she wanted to make something a surprise, it would be a surprise.

The helm under Huali's hands reached saturation. The energy of the Dao of Space—Jack could recognize it now—surrounded the entire ship, and suddenly, they lurched through it, traveling at unprecedented speed.

Jack had experienced starship teleportation aboard the *Trampling Ram*. Back then, it was a process which took a long time to set up, and a long time to execute. They also traveled dozens of light years per teleportation.

In this case, the lurching of space stopped almost immediately. They were now surrounded by solar gasses in all directions, flickering predominantly with purple and orange, but also various other colors.

He thought it was time to say something. "Where are—"

His voice was cut off as they teleported once again. With another jump, they traveled an unknown distance. The terrain changed—solar gasses still stretched in the distance, but only behind the starship. Its front side pointed outside the nebula, where a single, giant red star dominated the vast expanse of space.

"We're here," Huali said with relief, "and just in time, too. Brace yourself. We're going out."

"That's—How far did we just travel?"

"A hundred and twenty light years."

He whistled. Huali pressed a button to open the side door, and both of them flew into space. They didn't teleport, Huali just wanted them out of the starship. A cloud of gasses stretched behind them, while the vast empty space ahead was only illuminated by a large red star.

And illuminated it was, because the star was *burning*. It was a gas giant exuding so much heat that even Jack struggled to withstand it. It looked bloated, too, as if it was drawing in a large breath to achieve... something.

"What am I watching?" Jack asked.

"One of the most violent events in the universe," Huali replied, almost reverently. The last few words were whispered. "A supernova."

Jack drew in a cold breath—or at least, he tried, before the vacuum of space decided to disagree.

"Are you serious?" he asked. "That thing will blow us away!"

"Why are you afraid? You are with me." She looked calm and certain. "I am a peak C-Grade, an Elder of the Exploding Sun, a candidate for the next Grand Elder. And this event is exactly where our faction got its name."

Jack raised his brows. "Really?"

"Of course. Don't tell me you never made the connection."

"I did, but..."

She smirked. On her wizened face, it was almost scary. "There were two founders of our faction. One was a warrior following the Dao of the Fist, of whom you've seen a Dao Vision, as Shol informed me. But the greatest founder, and the original leader, was an exceptional human woman named Elandra."

Jack loved stories like this, but the sight of the nearby star worried him. Even now, from an incalculable number of miles away, he could see it expanding with a speed visible to the naked eye. He could almost picture its imminent collapse.

Was this really the best time for storytelling?

"Elandra's signature skill," Master Huali continued unfazed, "was called Supernova. A tremendous explosion inspired by the collapse of a large, dying star. Of course, even a B-Grade cultivator cannot imitate the power of a real supernova, but there are records of her using one explosion to annihilate a planet."

"An entire planet!"

"That's right. You are familiar with the power scale of the Grades, correct? F-Grades can break people, E-Grades can break hills, D-Grades can break mountains, C-Grades can break continents, and B-Grades can break planets."

"I've... heard of it."

Nauja had described this back in Trial Planet. Of course, he never really believed people could destroy planets, but if Master Huali said so as well...

Huali nodded and continued. "Elandra and her husband roamed the galaxy freely. They were among the strongest B-Grades of their time, and they even formed a new B-Grade faction in a time when the political terrain was considered stable. And all that was possible because of one thing, that even the strongest cultivators of the galaxy feared: Supernova."

"Supernova..." Jack repeated, tasting the words. "Then, I assume this is to help me get that skill as well?"

"Exactly. The Dao Vision we possess of this skill is currently unavailable, but some people over the years have managed to comprehend it through watching a live supernova eruption. It is unlikely, but given your talent, I hope you may be able to do it. After all, not many can brag about conquering Trial Planet."

Jack laughed. "Speaking of that... How come you didn't use my achievement against Monsoon? My Ninth Ring Conqueror title would have made him shut up on the spot."

"Because it is a weapon too strong to be used for a mere Monsoon. And also because—Wait. It's starting."

Jack whipped his head at the star, finding that its expansion had ceased. Its "skin" was stretched to the extreme, colored a deep red and struggling to expand, only for another force—gravity—to hold it down. It had run out of steam.

In the next moment, the star shed its red skin, which harmlessly flew away as hot gasses. What remained started shrinking. Fast. Too fast.

A transparent orange shield materialized before Jack. He could still see the shrinking star, as he could see Huali, who stood beside him with her hands glowing orange.

"Listen carefully," she commanded. "I will limit the heat to a point you can withstand. You will be safe. However, I need you to give it your all. Stare at the explosion until your eyes melt. Spread your senses and Dao awareness to perceive as much of the mysteries as you can. *Feel* the supernova—only then will you be able to master it."

Jack steeled himself, but he couldn't stop the gnawing terror. The implosion before his eyes was the strongest thing he'd ever seen. Even from millions of miles away, he knew its strength was enough to annihilate entire solar systems in the blink of an eye, enough to destroy each and every B-Grade faction with ease.

B-Grade cultivators could break planets? So what! Before the true ancestral forces of the universe, even the strongest cultivators were nothing. Before Jack's very eyes, the universe was reclaiming its rightful throne!

Jack watched with rapt attention. He tried to calm himself. All around, he could sense terror in the Dao itself as the star compressed ever more. Particles swam with agitation as if the entire galaxy was holding its breath in fear of what was about to happen. The orange shield seemed soft, like glass—would it hold?

And then, the shrinking was over. As the star contracted to a size so small Jack could barely see it, a titanic explosion covered the void. The Dao erupted. Space sank and shattered. A shockwave spread like God's angry roar, and the universe itself was instantly colored with infinite destruction. It was a display of power above and beyond anything else possible.

For Jack, time slowed down. He focused his entire attention on the explosion, scouring it with his eyes and trying his best to feel the ripples of power through his Dao perception.

Light appeared, and its intensity kept rising, never stopping. Jack went blind. Master Huali had told him not to look away, but he didn't even have the chance to. Everything happened too quickly.

At the same time, tremendous heat assaulted his body, as if plunged into a boiling cauldron. His strengthened body, with 835 Constitution and 90% increased efficacy, melted away like snow. His natural regeneration worked hard to stave off the collapse, but it could do nothing for the waves of searing pain that blared over his senses, not letting him perceive a thing.

The heat reduced slightly, and Huali's voice rang in Jack's brain: "*Focus! Endure! Observe the waves!*"

Jack didn't want to do that. He wanted to run away, to escape. Yet something inside him forced him into focus. Some part of himself grabbed the panic and suppressed it with iron will. Steel swam in his veins; his soul was steady like an anchor.

The pain remained, but he was in control. Still screaming, he tried to perceive through the pain, and what he saw was the Dao burning and vibrating with an intensity that shocked him.

His brain, trained by the Dao Vision of Space, caught on to a pattern. Then another. The heat of the supernova spread and affected the world in particular ways, ones that he could not comprehend now, but that he could remember for later.

His body kept melting. The pain was still shooting up. And yet, the more intense the pain, the sharper Jack focused. He'd ascended beyond his body, as if he were a god, as if pain was inconsequential and felt by someone else, not him. He was made not of flesh and blood, but of iron will and sharp focus, as well as the resolve to never, ever stop.

In one moment of epiphany, he saw it. Though he had no eyes, the supernova's Dao reactions became clear, just like a blueprint burned into his brain.

Suddenly, the heat disappeared. Jack felt his body pulled—though it was hard to feel anything—and then the miraculous state was gone, and the pain he'd been ignoring so far returned fiercer than ever.

Unfortunately, it was not enough to rob him of consciousness. It tried, but the Dao Root of Indomitable Will held strong, and the Dao of the Fist prevented Jack from giving up. No, scratch that; he didn't *want* to give up. He would persist. If not, then his name was not Jack Rust!

The moments passed in agony. His regeneration worked hard to repair his body, but it wasn't for free. Under the pain, he grew exhausted. At the very least, he couldn't see himself, as he remained blind.

An indeterminate amount of time later, Jack was healed—his eyes came last, mercifully. He remained whole and mostly uninjured, with his miraculously pristine robes covering any remaining burns.

Master Huali caught on to that, too.

"Those aren't normal robes, are they?" she asked, eyeing them with some confusion. "Where did you get them?"

"Trial Planet," Jack answered truthfully. His voice came hoarse, but a voice nonetheless. "In the last ring."

"You should hold on to them. Not many materials can survive that kind of heat."

Jack was so exhausted and traumatized that he had to force himself to pay attention. These robes had been given to him by Old Man Spirit when he broke into the D-Grade. Now, Jack was very glad for that gift, as his clothes getting destroyed in battle had become all too common lately.

"I will," he replied simply. He caught Huali's eyes, and in them, he saw pity. Or was that regret?

"I'm sorry you had to go through this," she said, "but it was a worthy risk. On the path of cultivation, pain is nothing. Do you feel that you gained anything?"

Jack forced himself to chuckle. "I saw some things... but only time will tell whether they help me or not."

"I certainly hope they do." Huali gave him a last, approving look before placing her hands on the helm, which immediately started glowing. "Let's head back. There is already a hot meal waiting for you—you're going to need it."

Jack smiled, still splayed on the floor. "Yes. And, master?"

"Yes, Jack?"

"Thank you. For the experience."

She smiled at him—and, if any of her smiles were honest, it was this one. "No problem."

CHAPTER THIRTY-FOUR
RIPPING OFF THE LIBRARY

THE RETURN TRIP WAS QUICK. WITHIN A MINUTE OF RECOVERING, JACK FOUND himself in the mountaintop mansion, where a large meal was already prepared for him. There were sparkling steaks, rich salads, pies, and fruit, and cheese of all kinds.

Jack gaped. "This is all for me?"

"Of course it is," Huali replied. "You used up a lot of energy just now. These are all products of D-Grade beasts. A single of these steaks would be enough to sustain an army of F-Grades for a week. For you... Well, I hope this table will suffice. We can prepare more if needed."

"I... It's plenty!" Jack exclaimed quickly. "Thank you, master. This is great."

"I hope so. Unfortunately, I have other business to attend to, so I cannot keep you company. I wish you happy adventuring, Jack. Return safe and strong."

"I will try my best."

"I expect nothing less." With a smile, she cracked the door open and walked out. "Enjoy your meal."

Jack was currently in a room adjacent to the kitchens, though the soundproofed walls could hide that fact. There was nothing besides himself, the food-stuffed table, and a few wooden chairs—this must be where the cooks ate. With one last, respectful nod at the closed door, Jack picked a chair at random and sat down to eat. He really was exhausted.

It was the best food he'd ever had. Meat that melted on the tongue, rich with flavor and juices; fruits and vegetables which infused his entire body with vitality; even the cheese was heavenly, with each bite activating his taste buds in different ways.

By the end of the meal, Jack was swimming in ecstasy, and he'd only eaten three-quarters of the food—he simply couldn't have another bite.

"Man," he sighed, leaning back in his chair with hands folded over his belly, "what a meal..."

As he relaxed, the insights he'd gotten from watching the supernova tried to come to the fore. They wanted to be inspected, investigated, understood. Yet, Jack pushed them back; there would be time to meditate later. For now, he had more things to do.

Allowing himself five minutes of relaxation, he then pushed off the chair with a grunt. He scanned the remaining food regretfully; it really pained him to let it go to waste.

On the bright side, he didn't need to.

Mustering his courage, Jack walked to the nearby kitchen and asked to take the remainder with him. The cook threw him a funny look but didn't decline. She even gave him a yellow metal box that would preserve the taste. Jack left the mansion whistling and with the food of gods in his lunchbox.

The next stop was the library.

He took to the air, crossing the estate under the complicated gazes of the servants to arrive at the pyramidic building that housed the estate's wealth of knowledge. This time, the librarian met him at the door.

"Jack," he said with a slight smile. His white robes flowed in the soft breeze, as did his long, silver beard. "Shol told me you were a talented young man, but I have to admit, I still underestimated you. Making enemies of an elder? Brave."

"Isn't that the duty of a disciple, brother Okmer? To make enemies of his master's enemies?" Jack replied smiling.

"It is indeed. Have you come to choose your remaining two items?"

"Right."

"Then, come on in."

The inside of the library was as empty as last time. Spiraling bookcases climbed the walls, hiding enough knowledge to blind any mortal sage. There were books upon books, mystical texts, Dao Visions, weapons, armors, and all sorts of mysterious items.

Jack was a man of science. He would have loved to spend months here, reading about the mysteries of the universe and the discoveries of a million-year-old galactic civilization. Unfortunately, fate hadn't given him time, only enemies.

Later, he promised himself, steeling his mind.

He'd had a long time to consider what kind of items he wanted. In the few weeks he'd been here, this had been one of his primary concerns, and he had settled on three options, of which he could only choose two: an escape treasure, a treasure that could increase his meditation speed, and a new Dao Vision. Thankfully, the supernova he'd just witnessed took the place of a Dao Vision, so Jack's mind was set.

Of course, he still needed to see what specific items the library had to offer.

"First of all, I would like a treasure that can increase my speed of understanding the Dao," he said. "Is that something you can offer?"

Since he would be leveling with extreme speed in the following months, he needed the Dao insight to match. Even if he did find one such treasure, and if he combined it with the Dao Soul he already possessed, matching his Dao understanding with his cultivation speed would be a struggle.

"It is..." the librarian replied. "I do have one item like that... though it is usually reserved for deacons."

Jack sensed the opening. "Come on, big brother. I can play a crucial part in the contest for the next Grand Elder. I'm sure Master Huali would approve of a little courtesy."

"That's true." Okmer nodded. "Fine. Here."

He raised his hand, and an item floated down from the highest level of the library. It was a twelve-sided glass box, within which flickered a phantasmal crimson flame tongue. Jack tried to inspect it but came up with nothing.

"This is a Flame of Understanding," Okmer explained as the box floated into his open palm. "At the end of their life, a C-Grade may choose to condense all their Dao Fruits into a flame such as this. By ingesting it, a D-Grade cultivator can accelerate their cultivation speed by approximately three times for a limited time period. It is an extremely valuable treasure... and, obviously, extremely rare."

"Hmm. When you say ingest, do you mean this is a one-time use item?"

"Precisely."

"I see." Jack's eyes narrowed, and he hastily nodded at the librarian. It was clear this was the best he could get. "Thank you. This means a lot to me."

"Don't worry." Okmer waved a hand. "We have more of them. Investing one in such a talented cultivator is no waste at all."

"Then, I'll take it. Thank you very much."

"The box itself is also a minor treasure," Okmer said as he handed over the item, "but no need to worry about returning it. You can keep it to store any volatile items you harvest in your... excursions."

"That's great." Jack pocketed the box—it barely fit, being the size of his fist. "Can I ask you one more thing? How come I couldn't inspect this? I thought that every high-rank item could be inspected. I could even do it on some E and F-Grades treasures on my home planet."

Okmer smirked. "The question isn't whether an item *can* be inspected, but whether *you* can inspect it. What is your Intelligence, if you don't mind me asking?"

"Um... I don't really have that. All I have is Mental, which is at around two hundred, including the added title efficiencies."

"Ah. Pretty good for a Physical cultivator. However, two hundred is just too low to inspect any high-level items."

"I see." Now, it made sense why he couldn't inspect the Dao Sprouting Pill at Trial Planet, or basically anything in the Final Ring, including Old Man Spirit. He'd always found that weird. "Thank you for the information."

"No problem. By the way, have you made any progress with the Dao Vision of Space you got last time? I have a few tips to share."

"I've already comprehended it, actually. Here, you can have it back."

Jack fished the globe from his robes and handed it to the librarian, who couldn't help but raise a brow.

"You comprehended it?"

"I did."

"In two weeks?"

"Right."

"Well, that's impressive. In my four-hundred-year career of being the librarian here, you are the first person to do that." Okmer could barely contain his surprise. "Are you certain you comprehended it fully? Did you piece together the image and decode the vampire immortal's finger movements? Did you perceive the dance of space particles?"

"Yes, yes, and yes. I struggled a lot, if it makes you feel any better," Jack replied with a wry smile. "Took me several days of nonstop meditation."

"Admirable!" Okmer exclaimed. "Experiencing the space shambling again and again while your memories deteriorate is the hardest part of this Dao Vision... Though it seems you managed to skip that by going all in. A risky prospect, as failure could have set you back to the very beginning, but an interesting one. Your willpower is admirable."

"It was just in line with my Dao."

"Don't underestimate yourself, my young friend. D-Grades are the best of the best, but nobody could do what you did. I cannot help but wonder what you've been through to develop such mental fortitude."

Jack's smile darkened a hint. "I just never had a choice."

"Of course. Forgive me for asking. Perhaps, when things calm down, we could exchange stories over a bottle of Star Dew?"

Jack didn't know what that was, but it sounded alcoholic. "It would be my pleasure, Okmer."

"Great! Then, I shouldn't keep you too long; have you decided on your third item?"

"I have... kind of. Back in the F-Grade, I once fought a guy who used a magical device to teleport away after he lost a fight. Is there something similar for D-Grades?"

"An escape talisman," Okmer said. "Smart choice. A D-Grade version does exist, but it's a highly valuable item, so I can only give you one."

"One is plenty."

"Then, here."

A wooden plaque appeared out of thin air between them, almost causing Jack to jump—he'd forgotten about Okmer's ability to suppress the presence of things. The wooden plaque was rectangular in shape, three inches tall, and completely smooth, save for the word "ESCAPE" written vertically on its surface in thick black ink.

Even just by looking at it, Jack could feel the Dao of Space thickly condensed inside the wood.

"This is an escape talisman meant for use by peak D-Grades," Okmer explained proudly. "If you break it, you will instantly teleport one thousand miles in the direction of your choosing—way farther than the perception range of any D-Grade. Moreover, the spatial turbulence left behind will be so chaotic as to be untraceable. Just make sure to keep running, as a peak D-Grade can cross a thousand miles fairly quickly."

"That's exactly what I was looking for!" Jack replied, excitedly pocketing the talisman. "Thanks, Okmer. You're the best."

"I try." Okmer's smile was wide, though slightly complex. Jack couldn't tell why, so he simply let it pass.

"That's all from me," Jack said. "If there's nothing else..."

Okmer reached out for a handshake. As Jack shook the hand, however, the librarian's voice rang telepathically in his mind.

"There is one more thing," he said. "Master Huali contacted me some minutes ago. She asked that, when you show up, I was to give you this."

Before Jack could reply, he felt something appear between his hand and the librarian's. It was an object that felt small, round, smooth, and cool to the touch—like a bead of ice.

"A high-level storage bead. Break it, and you will unleash power equivalent to the full-power attack of an early C-Grade. It only works once, so make it count."

"Wow. Thanks, Okmer."

"Thank our master. These things are vanishingly rare."

Thanks to the mental powers of immortals, this telepathic conversation took place in only a fraction of a second. On the outside, their handshake had been completely normal.

"Always a pleasure, Okmer," Jack said like nothing had happened.

He retracted his hand, gently wrapped around his new treasure, then used his Dao to move it inside his sleeve. From there, it flew into an inner pocket of his robes. "See you soon!"

"Good luck, Jack. May luck be on your side!"

Armed with a Dao treasure, an escape talisman, a C-Grade's full-power attack in pocket edition, and significantly higher chances of survival, Jack waved goodbye to the elderly librarian and flew away. He couldn't help the smile on his face.

Why the secrecy, though? he wondered. Could people be watching us even here, inside Master Huali's estate? Or is Okmer just being paranoid?

Well, whatever. I'll just be careful too. Next stop... his smile widened, Brock!

CHAPTER THIRTY-FIVE
SEEING ONE'S FRIENDS

THE *BROMOBILE* LANDED ON AN EMPTY PATCH OF GROUND NEAR THE TOWN gates. The door slid open in a puff of steam; a man walked out, then raised his hand, and the entire starship shrank and flew into his sleeve.

"The outer planet," Jack said to himself, inspecting the walls and gates that any immortal could just fly over. "Almost nostalgic."

He had met with his master and watched a supernova erupt. He had visited the library and equipped himself for the perilous adventure ahead. Now, only one thing remained: Brock.

There was a line for the town gates, but everyone had already spotted him and moved away; his fluttering yellow cape, signifying him as an inner disciple, commanded their respect. Only the guard on duty hadn't noticed Jack yet, busy rummaging through some paperwork.

"Next!" he shouted. Jack stepped forth, and only now did the guard raise his eyes. "Hey, bro, what can I help you—Oh *shit*, you're a big bro!"

Jack raised an amused brow. This was a large, slim, dark-skinned man that seemed full of energy. The guard reached out for a fist-bump, which Jack bemusedly returned. "I'm just here to see a friend," he replied.

"Of course, no problem! Inner disciples get a free pass. Go right in."

Jack nodded and walked past, still smirking. Of course, he could have flown over the walls or just landed in Brock's backyard, but there was no need to get disrespectful.

As he crossed the empty streets, he watched the town calmly. The situation here seemed better than last time. There was less fear in the air, less of an unkempt vibe. In fact, he regularly spotted people working on the town's well-being, gathering garbage or removing tasteless graffiti while leaving the good ones alone. They smiled and worked with zeal, humming tunes that Jack didn't recognize.

What a transformation, he told himself. I wonder what caused it.

A few feet away from Jack, a pedestrian wasn't paying attention and almost ran into a worker tending to the street-side plants. Appearance-wise, both seemed like gangsters. "Woah," the first guy said, hurriedly jumping aside. "My bad, bro."

"It's okay, bro. Enjoy the rest of your day."

"You too."

They fist-bumped and went about their separate lives.

Jack frowned over the exchange. Nah, he thought. Must be my imagination. Come to think of it, the entrance guard was a bit weird too, wasn't he?

The longer he walked, the odder the town got. Everyone was going about their jobs with purpose. Safety and joviality had taken over the town, like everyone was cooperating instead of competing.

They didn't even recoil at the sight of Jack's yellow cape, as they had the first time. He received respect, but not fear. Not complete and utter subservience. In fact, he had the suspicion that if he tried to bully anyone, the entire town would rise up against him.

Since the last time he was here, their quality of life had increased tenfold!

What the fuck? Jack couldn't help wondering about the mysteries he witnessed. *Is this... No. It can't be.*

Salin, Nauja, and Brock's home was close to the town gates, thankfully, so Jack could solve this enigma faster. He reached their door and knocked. A moment later, he began to wonder if they weren't home. Not that finding them would be particularly difficult, but it would be a pain.

The door opened wide. "Sup," Salin said, greeting Jack with a stern, imposing presence that he *definitely* didn't possess a while ago. In the next moment, his chest deflated, his jaw softened, and he returned to being the Gan Salin that everyone knew and loved. "Jack! You're here!" he exclaimed, turning to the inside of the house. "Guys, it's Jack!"

Happy monkey noises came from inside as Brock rushed over, ducking under Salin's outstretched arm and giving Jack a manly hug. To his surprise, Brock now reached his chest in height—he just kept growing.

"Big bro!" the brorilla said with a wide smile, which Jack returned.

"Brock! How are you doing, buddy?"

"Great."

"Oh hey, it's big bro!" a guy shouted off the street. As Jack turned around, elated to finally be recognized, he noticed that everyone was looking not at him, but at Brock. Every single passing pedestrian nodded to the brorilla, gave a thumbs-up, or found some other way to convey their respect before moving on. Brock gave everyone a slight nod.

Jack was left speechless. "This is... No. How?"

"Brock magic," Salin explained with a laugh, stepping aside to let Nauja pass. The barbarian girl was the only one looking exactly as Jack had left her. *Thank God.*

"Been a while, Jack," she said, wrapping him into a hug. "How have you been? We heard some rumors that you killed a guy."

"Oh, yeah. He was being a dick."

"I understand."

"Wait till you hear what else I did. But first... Brock, what the fuck?"

The brorilla smiled so brightly Jack thought he'd go blind again. The supernova would look at those teeth with jealousy. "Bro Code," was all he said, as if it was self-explanatory.

"Do you mean that you taught these people the Bro Code? How to be proper bros?"

"Yes."

"To an entire town."

"Not yet."

"Brock here is the most talented team captain I have ever seen," Salin stepped in. "You should have seen him, Jack. I don't know if it's magic or sheer charisma, but he's pulling everyone in. We're talking genuine gangsters seeing the light. Enemies becoming brothers in a single week. I swear to the System, give this guy ten minutes with literally anyone on the planet and he'll convince them to call him big bro."

Jack turned an incredulous gaze to Brock. "How the hell did you do that?"

Brock shrugged. "It easy because it true."

"Of course it's true," Nauja added. "It's how we always lived in Barbarian Ring. Took you cultivators long enough."

"But..." Jack was struggling to wrap his mind around this. "But what about competing for resources? Resolving disputes? Arrogant young masters?"

"I don't know what that last part means, but for resources, like hunting grounds or experience balls, we compete over them fair and square, no hard feelings," Salin explained. "As for disputes, resolving them is very easy when all parties have good intentions."

"Wow."

Jack was impressed. More than that, he was elated. His little bro was doing great!

"To be fair, it's mostly the Dao at work," Nauja explained, "but also that Brock is a seriously charismatic guy."

"Despite only being able to say, like, three words." Salin laughed.

"But isn't that mind control?" Jack wondered.

"It's instilling a healthy mindset. But hey, you can call it whatever you want. It works."

"Yeah, I guess it does."

On his way here, most people had a spring to their step, fire in their eyes, and happy smiles. Whatever Brock was doing, it was clearly good for everyone, so Jack dropped the issue.

"I want to hear everything," he said. "Can I come in?"

Brock nodded. "Yes."

Once again, Jack sat down for a cup of tea, but this time, he finished it. Nobody disturbed them. He stayed with Brock, Nauja, and Salin for three hours, listening to them detail their adventures in the nearby forest. His jaw dropped.

They'd fought beasts and ogres, then recruited everyone they met to push even deeper into the more dangerous areas. They went the high-risk high-reward route, and thanks to Brock's excellent leadership, it paid off in spades.

Brorilla, Level 115 (King)

A gorilla variant from planet Green. Brorillas usually live with Gymonkeys and train them in the ways of working out. It is due to the Brorillas' unmatched pecks that Gymonkeys use poop to fight—they consider themselves too weak for anything else.

Brorillas are usually calm, measured animals. However, if anyone harms their little cousins or invades their territory, they go bananas.

This particular brorilla is a variant that visually resembles a gymonkey. Though not weaker than other brorillas, the members of this variant are often shunned due to their lack of bulging muscles.

That is not the case for this specimen. Through intense determination, it has achieved greater strength than its species' norm, as well as a Dao Root. Despite that, it remains an adolescent. Due to this specimen's potential, taming or slaying it are advised.

Canine (Earth-387), Level 103 (E-Grade)
Faction: Exploding Sun (B-Grade)
Title: Seventh Ring Conqueror

Human (Trial Planet), Level 123 (E-Grade)
Faction: Exploding Sun (B-Grade)
Title: Seventh Ring Conqueror

Everyone who followed them benefited greatly, too, and their casualties were minimal. That excursion was repeated twice more, with their numbers increasing each time until Brock had to set his foot down and limit their followers to forty-seven. Including the three of them, they were fifty strong, and the brorilla felt that was the maximum number of people he could coordinate effectively.

Jack had known Brock was strong, so he wasn't surprised to hear about his performance in battle. However, since communication had always been difficult, he'd never realized that his little bro was so intelligent, too! Let alone a gifted leader.

"I am so proud of you, Brock," he said, making the brorilla's chest inflate like a balloon. "And I'm so glad you remained here, where your talents can shine."

"But not forever," Brock replied with a toothy grin.

"Not forever. We are bros. We go together. This is just a training break so we can truly fight side-by-side later on."

"Good."

"On that note..." Jack said, "I, uh, may have done something risky."

And so, he went on to tell them about the events following his duel with the late Dan Bolon: Monsoon's arrival, the heated exchange over the estate, and his agreed-upon duel against Head Disciple Qian in six months.

"You're going to fight the head inner disciple!" Salin asked, gaping. "Are you insane, too? But *I'm* supposed to be the insane one. Don't steal what makes me special."

"What will you do?" Nauja asked. "You're still so many levels away. There is no way you can become strong enough in time. Do you have a plan?"

"*I* have a plan!" Salin exclaimed. "First, you become the world's best thief. Then, you sneak up to that guy, steal a couple dozen levels, and boom! You win."

Jack laughed. "There is a plan, it's just a bit risky." In hushed tones, and spreading his perception to make sure nobody was eavesdropping, he explained his coming excursion into Hell.

"Okay, I take it back; you can be the crazy one." Salin shook his head. "You know that's suicide, right?"

"Sounds good to me," Nauja disagreed. "What's the point of living if you're a coward?"

"Living."

She threw him an empty look. "But... You confuse me so much, Salin."

"Exactly. I'm a big mystery—but a good one! Now, Jack, I have to say that despite my token misgivings, I also approve of your plan very much. You know why? Because it's insane."

"Thanks, Salin," he replied. "Way to encourage me."

"Anytime."

"It good," Brock replied, having considered the issue thoroughly while the others joked around. "Two bananarms with one hand. Kill the enemy and get levels. Danger, yes, but possibility of survival, and for strong big bro, possibility of survival mean survival. I approve."

Jack stared. "Your vocabulary is really growing, Brock. You can speak now."

"Always could speak," Brock replied, "just not with mouth."

"But how are you getting better this fast!"

"Because words are my bros."

"Yeah, I could have guessed that." Jack laughed. He liked his friends. He laughed a lot here—in the estate, not too often. He grabbed his cup and brought it to his mouth, finding it empty.

"I could refill that," Salin offered, but Jack shook his head.

"It's fine. I really should get going, anyway. Shol will chew me out if I'm late."

The other three exchanged a look and nodded, following Jack as he stood. "It was great seeing you, man," Salin said. "Really. We may live on different planets currently, but we haven't forgotten about you. You do the same, alright?"

"It goes without saying. Bros once, bros for life."

Jack reached out to shake Salin's hand, then pulled him into a hug. "Oof!" the canine explained. "Control... your... strength!"

"Oh, sorry." He hurriedly let him go. "Still, really good to see you."

"Jack!" Nauja exclaimed, also diving into his arms. "We miss you, alright? Especially Brock. If you let anything happen to you, I'll shoot an arrow all the way from here to your eye."

"I'll keep that in mind." Once again, he laughed carefreely. Only here, with his friends, could he truly relax.

Nauja pulled away, leaving only Brock, who approached Jack and gave him a thin, confident smile. "You will be okay," he said. "I believe in you."

"And I believe in you, Brock. Keep making me proud. When I return, let's go to Earth together and kick some ass."

"Yes."

"Oh, by the way, I brought you lunch." He retrieved the lunch box in which he'd placed the remains of the D-Grade meal he had in Huali's estate. "I ate some, and it should be of help to you, Brock. It contains a lot of energy."

Brock received the lunch box tenderly. One sniff was enough to raise all his fur on end. "Thanks, bro."

"You're welcome."

The two had a big, long hug, then pulled away at the same time and fist-bumped. Only now, exchanging goodbyes with Brock as complete equals, did Jack realize that his little bro had grown up. He was a man now.

It was touching.

"See you around, little bro. You too, guys," Jack said, walking away. The other three accompanied him to the door.

"Take care, Jack!"

"Remember to take a coat!"

"See you, bro."

Jack waved, and flew away. His surging pride over Brock's progress didn't abate for many minutes. Finally, once he was in the *Bromobile* and halfway to the inner planet, he managed to turn his mind to other matters.

All his loose ends had been tied. He was ready to go to Hell.

CHAPTER THIRTY-SIX

A CULTIVATOR'S GUIDE TO THE GALAXY

THE SKY FLICKERED WITH RED AND PURPLE GASSES IN THE FAR DISTANCE, AS IF the clouds had retreated deep into space. Under that sky, Huali's estate was serene. Creeks pulsed with water, plinking as it fell from stone to stone, while small animals darted left and right, coexisting with the many servants and cultivators wandering the premises.

Jack took a deep breath. This would be the last time he saw this place in a long while—if ever. He hadn't even managed to fill his cellar... but that was the cultivator life. Always traveling. Always fighting. Always pushing forward.

Putting his sentimentalism aside, Jack crossed the last mile to reach Shol's cabin, where he found the monk waiting with arms crossed before his door.

"Jack," Shol greeted him.

"Shol," Jack replied, landing smoothly. "Thanks for waiting."

"No problem. I also had some things to do." He looked over Jack, who carried nothing but the robes on his body and whatever his pockets could fit. "Are you ready?"

"I was born ready."

"Excellent, because so was I."

"How are we getting to Hell?"

"My contact responded already," Shol explained. "We have to reach the Belarian Outpost in the Animal Kingdom constellation. From there, we will travel to the Eternal Gate, a smaller outpost connected to Hell. It is there that we will meet my contact."

"We have to get that close to Hell by ourselves? What if we're spotted?"

"Don't worry. We'll get a Disguise Pill for you, and even if an immortal recognizes you through the disguise, they will not dare act with me present. Neither the Belarian Outpost nor the Eternal Gate are considered private territories, so there won't be many checks."

"I see."

"The only problem is that we need to get a starship. We may not find one later, and mine is in for repairs, so come and we'll ask Okmer to—"

"I have a starship, actually."

"You do?" Shol raised a brow. "A real one?"

"What do you mean?"

"Can it teleport?"

"Yes."

Jack had never used his starship's teleportation function, but Old Man Spirit had mentioned its existence.

"Then, great. Nice thinking, getting one ahead of time. As expected of my former student."

Jack laughed. He waved his sleeve, and a small, needle-shaped object flew out, enlarging to the size of a proper starship. "We call it the *Bromobile*," he said proudly.

"Hmm." Shol inspected it with curiosity; from its cyan walls, to the flat behind, to the windshield, which he rapped with his knuckles. "Solid construction. Where did you get this?"

"Trial Planet."

"Ah." He didn't press the issue. "And I suppose you call it *Bromobile* because you and Brock are bros, and because this starship is a mobile object."

"Kind of. Ever heard of Batman?"

"Who?"

"Nevermind."

Shol gave the starship a final, appraising look, then nodded. "Very well. I approve. If you're ready, we can be off."

"Alright! Shol—to the *Bromobile*!"

"I... am already here?"

Ignoring Shol's questioning gaze, Jack laughed and opened the sliding door. Inside the starship, the two had just enough space to be comfortable—a far cry from the spacious *Trampling Ram*.

Thinking to that point, Jack couldn't help wondering what happened to the *Ram* and the rest of its crew. The last he knew of them was that they'd run away, heavily injured after Captain Dordok was captured by the Hounds.

Did they survive? he wondered. Or...

"I like your furniture," Shol said, finding a slim seat and reclining into it. The back bent slightly to accommodate him. "Oh... This is nice."

"Glad you like it, Shol, because from this point onward, you are officially promoted to my sidekick."

"What? I am your venerable senior. If anything, *you* are *my* sidekick."

"Oh yeah? Where's your starship? Your sholmobile?"

Shol grumbled. "I would never give it such a dumb name."

"And that's why you are the sidekick. You lack imagination and grumble a lot, with a witty line here and there. You're perfect."

"I have received better compliments. Now, if you're done spouting nonsense, take us to the Center Moon. We can teleport to Derion, and from there, directly to the Belarian Outpost."

"You know what? I just had an idea. I think I will take us to the Center Moon, from where we can teleport to Derion and then the Belarian Outpost."

Shol closed his eyes and sighed. "Is it too late to change my mind?"

"Yep. Off we go!" Jack placed his hand on the helm, and it shone cyan, the starship smoothly rising off the ground and catapulting into the sky. Thanks to its Dao enhancements, the acceleration hit them muffled, letting furniture and cultivators remain in their spot.

Once again, Shol nodded in approval.

"What did Master want with you, by the way?" he asked.

"She showed me a supernova."

"She did!" Shol's eyes widened for a moment before narrowing. "I suppose that's to be expected. Her reputation is riding on your success as well. However, to witness a supernova up-close... Did you develop the Supernova Dao Skill?"

"Not yet. But I got some insights. In time, I think I'll manage it."

"That's excellent!" Shol's voice was colored with excitement. "It's a supreme skill. If you really can master it, it will help a lot. The reason Qian is stronger than me is precisely because of this skill."

"Really? I assumed he was a swordsman."

"He is, but so what? He has a slashing variant."

"Oh."

"A few centuries ago, Master also took me to watch an explosion..." Shol said in a low voice, then shook his head. "But even now, there is always something missing. A final insight to tie everything together. Perhaps this adventure will be the turning point I need to figure it out."

"I believe you can do it. Do you often go out to adventure, Shol? Or do you cultivate in the sect?"

"In the sect, mostly. Not because I want to, but because my responsibilities as a deacon hold me back... Plus, there aren't many places in the galaxy for someone of my strength. Inter-faction tournaments and sparring against my fellow disciples is the best I can get."

"Hmm. I understand the difficulty of finding a place to train, but as for those responsibilities... If it's holding you back, why do you remain a deacon? Why not resign and go explore the galaxy?"

"What bullshit are you spouting now?" Shol snorted. "I have my honor. The faction helped me become who I am—without them, I would be nothing. When the Exploding Sun and Master Huali invested in me, it came with the unspoken agreement that I would pay back that investment by working for the sect. I can't just take what they gave me and walk away. What sort of person does that?"

Jack gazed deeply at Shol, taking in his orange robes, the goatee, the hard lines around his eyes and mouth. He thought back to when Shol was teaching him. This was a harsh man, both to others and himself. A man who would rather break than bend.

Jack could respect that. The Fist stirred inside him, pulsing with approval.

"Come to think of it," he asked, "I've never seen you fight, Shol. What's your Dao?"

Shol stared aggressively, then relaxed. "Explosion."

"Ah. It suits you."

"Idiot disciple. Of course it does," the monk responded harshly, but cracked a smile. "And you are quite a fistful yourself."

"Thanks!"

They lapsed into silence, each lost in their own thoughts. The solar gasses flowed beyond the windows, an ever-changing kaleidoscope. Before long, they landed on the Center Moon.

"Don't forget about this," Shol said, handing Jack a familiar pill. Jack ingested it immediately. In moments, his hair grew longer, his body got shorter, and his muscles lost some volume. Moreover, his facial structure warped and clicked into a different configuration, making him seem like a totally different person.

"Man," Jack said in a slightly altered, natural-sounding voice, "no matter how strong I get, Disguise Pills remain creepy."

"A necessary evil, not-Jack. You look great. Let's go."

They disembarked, and Jack pocketed his starship as they approached the teleporter.

The minute they spotted Shol, every guard and attendant stood at attention. "Deacon Shol! We pay our respects, sir!"

"At ease," Shol replied easily. "Teleport us to Derion."

"Yes, sir!"

As he stepped into the teleporter, Jack mentally bade farewell to the Exploding Sun. It had been a pleasant and fruitful month. Who knew if he'd ever make it back?

No, I certainly will, he thought, eyes hardening. Because Brock is here. And I would never leave him behind.

Space swam around them, and in the next moment, they were hurtling through the stars. Gasses and meteors and solar systems passed them by as the endless galaxy shrunk to accommodate their trip. No matter how many times Jack witnessed this, it remained extraordinarily beautiful—as well as humbling.

When space stabilized, they were in one of the many teleporters of Derion, the poison planet.

Jack expected a multi-day wait here, as had happened the last time he passed by. However, the moment the guards caught sight of Shol, they stood at attention just like the ones on Center Moon.

"Deacon Shol!" everyone called out, and the busy teleportation hub skidded to a halt.

"At ease," Shol growled. Everything continued like nothing had happened, except for the reverent gazes they received and the peak E-Grade guard who rushed to assist them. "We're going to the Belarian Outpost," Shol informed him.

"Of course, sir. Please, come this way."

Jack was speechless. No buzzers, no waiting in line, no fees, no questions. This was the luxury of the powerful!

"Hey," he whispered, sneaking up to Shol's side, "are you going to receive this kind of attention everywhere?"

If so, that would be troublesome. They were trying to be low-key.

"No," Shol replied simply. "Few people will recognize me outside the Exploding Sun territory."

"That's good."

Following the guard, they cut through a long line—to everyone else's frustration—and entered the largest teleporter around, a behemoth with a radius of several dozen feet. They were surrounded by large crates stacked almost to the fifteen-foot-high ceiling, as well as people of all species and levels. Jack inspected them—none belonged to the Animal Kingdom faction.

"Merchants," Shol explained, waving one of them away when she tried to introduce herself.

Once again, space warped around them, and they launched through the galaxy at even greater speeds than before, zooming past stars and every other kind of stellar object. They crossed an entire constellation in moments, appearing at the Belarian Outpost, near the very core of the Animal Kingdom constellation.

Jack could scarcely believe they'd traveled so far in such little time. In his mind, he was still at the Center Moon.

This was his second time at the Outpost. The first had been when he went to Trial Planet with Gan Salin. Unlike that time, however, he now had time to look around.

Unlike Derion, the Belarian Outpost was efficient and neatly organized. The Animal Kingdom's tyrannical administration had its benefits; people crowded in rapidly-moving lines, the bureaucracy kept to a minimum to facilitate speed. Feshkurs ran left and right, using their powerful, boney gray bodies to unload crates off teleporters and load them with new ones.

However, despite the seeming efficiency of this teleportation hub, Jack noticed one teleporter with a massive, slow-moving line in front of it. A quick scan revealed that everyone on that line was E-Grade, and they didn't look particularly rich, either. In typical Animal Kingdom fashion, the Belarian Outpost had just thrown everyone unimportant in one line to make things easy for everybody else.

"We can get through here in moments," Shol leaned in to explain, "but if you're poor and weak, it could take you a month. The Animal Kingdom is no place for losers."

Jack nodded. There was no point in thinking about this further; he already didn't like the Kingdom, so their blatant elitism changed nothing.

Shol led him to a teleporter with slightly more guards stationed around it, all of them D-Grades. Before Jack had time to panic, they were stopped by a towering feshkur with a sledgehammer strapped to his hip. "You have a disguised immortal with you," the feshkur said. "We must see his real face and status first."

"I am a deacon of the Exploding Sun, here on official business," Shol retorted. "My companion would like to remain anonymous."

The feshkur scanned them both, then turned to his fellow guards and exchanged a few glances. "Okay," he said, stepping aside, "but be warned that your companion will need to drop his disguise before accessing any Animal Kingdom core territory."

"Noted."

Jack held back the sigh of relief that almost escaped his mouth as he followed Shol into the teleporter. "*That was close,*" he said mentally, not daring to whisper.

"*There was no need to worry. Our factions exchange anonymous representatives all the time,*" *Shol replied.* "*You wouldn't imagine the kinds of business some C-Grades are up to.*"

"Do I want to know?"

"No."

"Good."

Space warped around them. Jack sensed it through his newfound awareness of the Dao of Space, a methodical tearing of the veil behind which hid nothingness.

Wait a moment, he realized. If this teleportation works the same way as mine, why isn't it instant? How can I see the stars and space in between as I travel?

Before he could consider the issue further, space was torn asunder, and he was once again launched through the stars. Next stop, the Eternal Gate. And shortly afterward... Hell!

CHAPTER THIRTY-SEVEN
ENTERING HELL

THÉ ETERNAL GATE WAS AS DEAD AS DERION, THE POISON PLANET, EXCEPT IN A different way.

As soon as Jack arrived, he noticed the absence of wind. The air was thin here, making breathing difficult, and there was no sound to be heard. No squawking of animals, no birds flying overhead, no activity across the barren, flat landscape. There were few plants, mostly colored a grayish green that made them seem half-dead.

This blanket of silence fell heavy over the planet, influencing the people who stayed here. Nobody spoke much. There was only a village of teleporters surrounded by silent camps of waiting people. Again, it reminded him of Derion, though this place appeared less like the Wild West and more like a graveyard without tombstones.

"Is there a reason why teleportation hubs are placed on dead planets?" he inquired, leaning closer to Shol to whisper.

"They tend to upset the local economy. Plus, the existence of so many high-Grade cultivators is unsafe for the population. Placing these hubs on dead planets makes them much easier to manage, and it also makes use of otherwise useless space."

"I see."

The presence of the Animal Kingdom was strong here. Guards

were everywhere, all sorts of half-animal half-people hybrids with hard glares and steel weapons. There were even several D-Grades present, including a half-cat woman at the late D-Grade. Undoubtedly, there were even peak D-Grades and even C-Grades, so close to the epicenter of the Animal Kingdom's influence, though they remained hidden.

All those immortals threw Jack dirty glares, taking note of his disguise, but Shol's presence was enough of a guarantee to let him slide.

"State your business," a middle D-Grade guard ordered, singling them out from the crowd.

"A business meeting," Shol replied. The guard stared, waiting for Shol to elaborate. He did not. Eventually, the guard grunted and stepped aside, letting them pass.

"Your details have been taken," the guard informed them. "You have permission to remain here for three days. If you require more—"

"That's plenty," Shol cut him off, walking away under the guard's glare. Jack followed quickly.

"Is it really?" he asked.

"You'll see."

Jack rolled his eyes. "You take after Master. She said the same cryptic shit too."

"If you must know, we will only be here for a few minutes," Shol retorted calmly. "However, you should speak about your master with a little more respect."

"Oh no, I like surprises. I'm just saying."

"Then you should perhaps say less and think more."

"And you should take it a little easier. We're far from home now. A little joke here and there helps us stay sharp."

Shol grunted non-committedly. Jack followed him into the camp next to the teleportation hub, where entire crowds of cultivators awaited their turn. Some stayed in tents, others in their starships, and some, the most confident ones, simply sat cross-legged and meditated.

Very few of those present belonged to the Animal Kingdom, and Jack could easily imagine why. The Kingdom's cultivators took priority in teleportation. As did D-Grades, as evidenced by the fact that everyone here was at the E-Grade. Jack and Shol themselves had received no buzzer or ticket to indicate their turn in line. They could teleport whenever they wanted to.

"I understand the concept," Jack commented, "but I have to admit that this blatant favoritism kinda rubs me the wrong way."

"It's efficient," Shol responded.

"Then why don't you use it?"

"Because it rubs us the wrong way. But it remains efficient."

Jack laughed. "Do you follow the Dao of the Contrarian?"

"I'm just speaking the truth," Shol replied, then sighed. "Sorry. Being here has put me on edge."

Jack narrowed his eyes. "Hmm. Do you think we'll be discovered?"

"...No."

"Shol?"

"I don't think so. There is a chance. But I don't think so."

"Alright. I trust you."

"As you should. I didn't come here to be doubted by some kid that's still wet behind the ears."

"That kid has really hard knuckles, too. Wanna see?"

At this, Shol finally cracked a smile. "Save your bravado for fifty levels later. Right now, you're one explosive slap away from becoming paste."

"And *you* are very outspoken for a sidekick."

Shol chuckled. Both were men of action; such light-hearted jousts made their blood boil, lifting their spirits.

"We're here," Shol finally said, approaching a starship parked between a red and a green tent. It was needle-shaped, as were most, but it was large, easily three times the size of the *Trampling Ram*. In fact, this ship towered so high over its surroundings that Jack had spotted it the moment they arrived on this planet.

A crew of feshkurs were frantically unloading large crates and stacking them in front of the ship, while a woman wearing a tattered brown cape oversaw them. Jack scanned her.

Feshkur, Level 156

Faction: Animal Kingdom (B-Grade)

Title: Fourth Ring Conqueror

The rest of the feshkurs also belonged to the Animal Kingdom, though they were at the E-Grade.

Unexpectedly, Shol walked right past the starship and its working feshkurs without a second glance. Jack didn't halt his steps, following his former master until they were several tents away.

"You didn't mean that ship?" he asked.

"We must be discreet," Shol said. "Just wait."

They kept walking to the very end of the camp, several miles away. There, Shol removed a cube from somewhere in his robes and threw it on the ground, where it formed into a red tent. "In," he said, and both entered.

On the inside, the tent was completely empty, leaving enough free space for two people to be comfortable.

Which, in the end, didn't really matter.

As soon as the flap closed behind them, Shol took a deep, tired breath. Jack felt his exhaustion. "From this moment on," said the monk, "we're operating illegally. If we are captured, we cannot implicate the Exploding Sun. Therefore..." Another breath, trembling and even deeper. "System, I would like to leave the Exploding Sun faction. Yes, I am sure."

Jack's eyes widened. He knew this was coming, but Shol had been a deacon of the faction for centuries. It was his home. His origin. He had status and history there. To see him leave the faction so decisively and risk his life just to help Jack...

It was touching.

"Thank you," he said. "I really appreciate what you are doing for me. I will not forget it."

If Shol was hurt, he did not show it. "Just leave the faction as well so we can be on our way."

Jack nodded. "System, I would like to leave the Exploding Sun faction."

Leaving the Exploding Sun Faction. This action cannot be reverted without a Faction representative's approval. Are you sure?

"Yes, I am sure."

And just like that, he was out of the Exploding Sun. He still remained part of the Bare Fist Brotherhood—he was its leader, so he couldn't leave even if he wanted to—but it felt like an oddly final decision.

Right as he was done, he spotted Shol clenching his yellow cape and burning it until there was only ash. This time, his eyes were misty. His hand remained steady, and he showed no weakness. "Give me yours as well. These capes signify our allegiance. We no longer have a right to wear them."

Jack handed over his cape, letting Shol burn it to ashes.

"Are you okay?" Jack asked.

"I am always okay."

Shol then grabbed Jack's shoulder, split the curtain of space, and stepped through it. Jack did not resist. Next thing he knew, they were in a cramped office surrounded by jet black walls and a window overlooking the camp. Opposite them sat the feshkur woman from before, her arms crossed before her chest.

"Took you long enough," she said with a frown.

"Come on, Vegna," Shol replied, letting go of Jack and opening his arms wide. The moisture in his eyes was gone. "Is that any way to greet an old friend?"

Her frown morphed into a smile as she stood and closed the distance between her and Shol, wrapping him in a tight hug. She was taller than him, if significantly slimmer. "I missed you, Shol. How have you been?"

"Tired... but now, thanks to my star disciple here, I'm about to liven up my old bones again." He pulled away, smile strained, and pointed at Jack. "This is Jack."

"Jack Rust," she said, eyeing him up and down. She reached out for a handshake. "I've seen your wanted poster. You have some illustrious achievements, don't you?"

"Some idiots keep challenging me," Jack replied, shaking her hand. "Can't help but beat them up."

"Spoken like a true feshkur. Your species should be proud." She grinned. "If you're going to punch a hole into the Animal Kingdom's side, I'd be glad to play a part."

"But aren't you part of the Kingdom?"

"So what? I work for them, but it doesn't change the fact that they're assholes. And I'm allergic to assholes."

Shol coughed in his hand.

Jack didn't comment, and instead asked, "So, what's the plan?"

"You'll hide in one of these boxes," Vegna explained. "They contain food to be shipped to Hell—mostly meat. They'll be scanned, of course, but we've warded them to shield you from the guards' Dao perception. Adding on the fact that you're practically made of meat yourself, and you'll be fine."

"I'm not just meat. I also have an active core of condensed Dao inside me."

"Didn't you hear me mention wards?"

"Alright. I trust you."

"Vegna is an old friend of mine, and very trustworthy," Shol stepped in. "Also, I've financed these wards myself. I can assure you they're the best money can buy."

"Then, I trust you twice."

"Since you're here, there is no reason to delay," Vegna said. "The longer we stay, the greater the chances something will go wrong."

"Right. Let's go," Shol approved.

The fehskur captain led them to the hold, where a few crew members saluted them. "I trust my crew with my life," she assured them. "Your secret is safe with them."

Jack didn't mind. Trust was transferable. He trusted Shol, who trusted Vegna, who trusted her crew. Therefore, he also trusted her crew—albeit slightly less.

The food crates were as tall as Jack and equally wide. Spreading his perception, he sensed all sorts of materials inside, from salted meat to compressed vegetables. Shol was the first to climb into one. The moment he did, his presence vanished. The food was still there, completely undisturbed, but Shol wasn't.

"Wow," Jack exclaimed, turning to Vegna. "How does this work?"

"The crates are warded to emit the Dao footprint of meat and vegetables. Those aren't their actual contents—though, in this case, they happen to be. No matter who is inside, their presence is blocked at the crate walls."

"Huh. Neat," Jack replied, while considering all the uses people could have for wards like these. "But if these wards exist, aren't there checks against them?"

"Of course, but they're cumbersome, so they aren't used all the time. People want to sneak *out* of Hell, not in. For you, there are just random checks every once in a while, but if you happen to fall in that case, we can just blame our bad luck."

"What if someone opens the crate?"

"Please. Do you think these guards have nothing better to do than open crates when sweeping their perception once is enough? Not to mention I'm a trusted provider."

Jack took a second glance at her. "Thank you," he said honestly. "For staking your reputation to help us."

"No need for thanks. Just punch them hard. That should be enough." She gave him a wide, toothy smile. "Plus, if things go well, nobody will even know I was involved. You can destroy the wards as you exit the crates."

"I will certainly do that."

"Great. Jump in."

Jack chose the crate next to Shol's and climbed inside. To his horror, the moment he opened the lid, he saw it was filled with fish—though from the outside, it still felt like meat and vegetables.

Taking a deep breath, Jack slipped in and closed the lid behind him. It didn't smell *too* bad.

He could still spread his perception outside the crate, which was useful. Unfortunately, since he couldn't sense Shol, he couldn't speak to him telepathically.

Left with nothing else to do, Jack simply watched through his Dao perception as his crate was eventually unloaded. The crew placed it on the ground, where another batch of feshkurs grabbed the crates and moved them all the way to the teleporter hub, stacking them onto one of the largest teleporters.

Jack saw the guards glance at the crates, but nothing weird showed on their faces. To them, this was routine. As soon as the feshkurs had unloaded the last crate of this batch—Shol's—one of the guards pressed a button, and Jack was once again launched through space.

The teleportation was extremely smooth. The usual spatial pressure, which was the reason why F-Grades couldn't use inter-planet teleporters, was completely absent. It made sense. If a Level 49 strongman couldn't take the pressure, no crate could.

Soon after, Jack landed in Hell.

Wow, he thought. That was so uneventful.

And, of course, things went awry almost immediately.

CHAPTER THIRTY-EIGHT
SETTING HELL AFLAME

HELL LOOKED PRETTY NICE, ACTUALLY.

As Jack and his trusty crate were spat out of teleportation, his Dao perception caught glimpses of tall, lush trees, chirping birds, and grass all over. *To be fair, I don't know what I was expecting. Flaming cauldrons?*

Almost immediately, however, his attention homed in on the people around him. A steady workforce of cultivators was moving crates from the teleporter to a starship parked just to the side. Jack's crate, too, was picked up by a man who looked like he was half-bear. He lifted the crate like it weighed nothing.

Jack couldn't inspect these people, as he didn't have visual contact, but he hoped they were E-Grade. What kind of immortal did chores?

Thankfully, nobody seemed to notice that two of the crates were warded. Jack's crate was loaded into the waiting starship, as was Shol's. When all of them were on, the ramp connecting the starship to the ground slid closed, sealing off the hold, and the starship took off.

Observing the world solely through Dao perception was a dizzying experience. Jack had an idea of his surroundings, but it was like watching through really bad glasses. He could make out no details. Everything was fuzzy and bleeding into each other, while static was everywhere.

Regardless, he focused on the present. They'd gone unnoticed up to now, but they were bound to get discovered eventually. This starship was probably taking them to some population center. It was moving quickly, too, so they were probably flying over wilderness.

If they reached their destination, only bad things could happen. Therefore, this had to be the prime time to escape.

Jack could not contact Shol through the latter's ward, but he was confident in his deduction. With fast and smooth movements, he pushed all the fish aside and slipped out of his crate. Shol followed only seconds later. "You stink," he commented.

"Yeah, because your friend put me in a crate of fucking *fish*."

"The friend who staked her life and reputation to help us?"

"I'm kidding. I appreciate it. If we get out of here alive, I'm buying her dinner."

"Oh, she'd love that."

Shol turned to his crate and placed an open palm on it. Soon after, a Dao ripple passed over the crate walls, and Jack felt his perception shift slightly as the magical warding was dissolved.

"How did you do that?" he asked.

"A Dao burst. You can do it, too. Just send a sharp ripple of Dao into the crate."

"Wouldn't the people in the starship notice that?"

"They haven't even noticed us, so don't worry. They're probably E-Grades. Their perception is far too coarse for anything not in their immediate surroundings."

Jack turned and gave this Dao burst thing a shot. His first attempt was slightly too weak, only stirring the warding without dissolving it. He succeeded on the second try.

"Good," Shol said. "Now, let's just telep—"

A wave of Dao passed over them like an ocean current. It crashed and broke against his body, part of it reflected back to where it came from—the front part of the starship.

"Shit," he said. At the same time, the starship ground to a halt and an imposing voice washed over them.

"SHOW YOURSELVES!"

Jack and Shol exchanged a glance. "Do we run?" Jack asked.

Shol's eyes were hard. There was no hint of humor in them; only sadness and expectation. "We cannot be discovered yet," was all he said. Jack understood. His stomach fell. Dark feelings flooded his brain, but he embraced them and came out stronger.

"I understand," he replied, setting his jaw.

"Can you handle it?"

"Yes."

This was it. His reason for coming here. It was starting. And he hated it as much as he knew it was necessary.

A menacing aura spread out of Jack's body as he prepared for battle. Ripples of Dao shook the starship. The air drummed with power. The Fist descended, hard and resolute.

Jack stepped through space to reappear above the starship. Shol also teleported, though far to the side, indicating that he wouldn't be involved. Somehow, he also went invisible.

Jack looked down. An endless forest stretched below them. Large trees spread in all directions, some peeking over the canopy and almost completely covered in birds. The starship was a mile into the air, so Jack couldn't make out the fine details, but he could understand they were above a vast wilderness teeming with life.

But not intelligent life. As far as cultivators went, there were no witnesses.

The door of the starship slid open and two figures darted out, flying to either side of Jack. One was a half-bear, half-human man, tall and imposing, wielding nothing but his bare claws; the other was a man with goat horns and a suspiciously sturdy-looking goatee, wielding a massive, red-bladed halberd.

Jack inspected them.

Bearfolk, Level 133
Faction: Animal Kingdom (B-Grade)

Goatee, Level 128
Faction: Animal Kingdom (B-Grade)
Title: Fourth Ring Conqueror

Their levels were even lower than his—146. He could take them easily. Since there were two of them, they probably thought the same as they inspected him, not knowing he was much stronger than his level would indicate. He had no title displayed—and, even if he had, he remained under the effects of the Disguise Pill.

Of course, they could see he was disguised, but there was no way to change one's level, so they weren't worried.

"Your ally was wise to run," rumbled the bear-man. "Surrender now, and maybe the Warden will torture you less."

"Or don't," added the goatee, wearing an ugly smirk, "so I can enjoy this."

Jack took them both in coldly. He ignored their words; his attention was turned inwards, toward his own heart, where the real battle was happening.

He did not know these people. They were enemies, but at the end of the day, he was the one who invaded their territory. Maybe they had families—friends, parents, wives, children.

Yet, he was here to murder them.

What was right, and what was wrong? Jack's moral sensibilities from his time on Earth protested, but he shut them down. He had to save himself, his people, and his planet. To do that, he needed power, and these people were soldiers of the enemy.

This was war.

"What's wrong, coward? The cat got your tongue?" the goatee man mocked him.

"He's not surrendering. Let's capture him," the bear-man decided. His Dao Domain spread out, a sphere of animalistic brutality. It reminded Jack of the merciless war for survival. The goat-man also revealed his domain, and it was red and thick as blood, tasting of copper.

The two domains engulfed him, pressuring him from either side. Jack's Dao protested, a machine revving up to match the oppression. The Fist refused to be suppressed, for it was unstoppable. He closed his eyes, breathing in the double domain of his enemies.

The bearfolk and goatee both charged him.

And then, Jack's eyes snapped open. The Fist roared. A cold wind shattered the other two domains, an overwhelming avatar of pure, unadulterated power. The Fist appeared in all its glory, completely dwarfing his opponents as even the animals in the forest below went deathly silent, and the wind itself didn't dare blow before Jack's majesty.

Jack clenched his fist. The two attacking cultivators felt slow to him. Their eyes betrayed their shock as they sensed their domains get completely shattered in the blink of an eye, but it was too late to turn back. The sky lost its color. The world went dark and silent. A purple meteor descended, and before it, these two cultivators were so terribly small.

At the end of the day, they were still immortals. Knowing they could not dodge, they shot out their strongest attacks.

"CORNER DESPAIR!" the bear-man roared, clawing forward.

"LAVISH FAMINE!" screamed the goatee, slashing out a blood-colored streak of Dao.

The three strikes collided. For a moment, they remained locked with each other. The blood-colored streak broke first, shattering like glass, and the bear's claws cracked as they were pushed back. The fist broke through, having lost half its power but retaining more than enough to crush these people.

A meteor descended, and nothing could stop it. The goatee and bear-man were struck head-on. The force of the impact warped their faces and cracked their bones, sweeping them along as it headed downward. The meteor kept going, grinding the two cultivators into the roof of their starship and launching it into a violent, majestic trajectory toward the forest below.

The meteor crashed into the foliage, easily breaking through. Trees bent and were blown away. Branches flew. The birds hurried to escape, barely dodging the explosion that shook the ground like an earthquake and released a shockwave that upset the entire forest.

Where there once stood a thicket of massive trees, now only a deep crater remained. The starship was completely broken. The two cultivators were mangled beyond recognition and dead beyond the shadow of a doubt.

Level-up! You have reached Level 147.

The System notification was unsuitably cheerful. Jack shook his head. He was sad.

“You acted with determination,” Shol said, appearing by his side. “Good job.”

Jack couldn’t bring himself to smile. “We couldn’t leave any evidence behind.”

“That’s exactly correct, though one could call a massive crater evidence. How do you feel?”

“Hollow. But it’s okay. These aren’t the first people I’ve killed, nor will they will be the last. I will do what I have to.”

“Good. Now, let’s go. We’re still not far from civilization, so people might come to investigate.”

“Lead the way.”

With a wave of his sleeve, a strong breeze blew over the crater and extinguished the flames. Then, Jack willed the free points from his level-up into Physical, as he usually did, and took a brief look at this status screen. From now on, it would change rapidly. He wanted to have an idea of where it started.

Name: Jack Rust
Species: Human, Earth-387
Faction: Bare Fist Brotherhood (D)
Grade: D
Class: Cosmic Fist (King)
Level: 147

Strength: 870
Dexterity: 825
Constitution: 845
Mental: 120
Will: 190

Dao Skills: Meteor Punch III, Iron Fist Style II, Neutron Star Body II, Brutalizing Aura II, Space Walk II

Daos: Dao Tree of the Fist, Dao Root of Indomitable Will (fused), Dao Root of Life (fused), Dao Root of Power (fused), Dao Root of Weakness (fused)
Titles: Planetary Frontrunner (10), Planetary Torchbearer (1), Ninth Ring Conqueror, Planetary Overlord (1)

It was impressive. A source of pride. He remembered the times when just five attribute points had made all the difference in the world. How long ago that seemed... And yet it was only a few short months.

"Take us away, Shol," he said tiredly, but the monk only shook his head.

"I can't teleport us that far. We'll have to fly. Follow me."

An orange streak cut through the air, soon followed by a purple one. They flew away faster than sound, until the smoking crater disappeared behind them. As far as the eye could see, there was only forest.

Soon, there would be war.

CHAPTER THIRTY-NINE

THE BALL STARTS ROLLING

Juliet drove her hoe into the ground, plowing it easily. The whole process felt fake. Even five months after the Integration, she still struggled to adjust to her new powers, as did most people.

"Done already, Juliet?" another woman called out.

"Almost! Just one more line!" Juliet shouted back, her voice effortlessly carrying to the next field over. She took a moment to catch her breath before continuing. The cold winds of February broke helplessly against her bare arms, not even stinging. The frozen soil, which should have been impregnable, was molded with ease under her tools. Even the crops, which shouldn't be able to survive this cold, had been mutated by a Plantmancer in the city. They would now bloom richly regardless of the season.

What a world... she thought, wiping a single bead of sweat from her brow before diving back into her job.

Of course, everything had a price. Power never came freely. When the goblins broke out of the nearby dungeon a month after the Integration, her town had been one of the first to be overrun. Flames towered to the sky. Humans were grilled and eaten in the streets. Green-skinned hobgoblins toured the town with human body parts strung up as necklaces, their shamans launched fire across the defending armies, and their ogres felled people by the dozen with broad swipes of their clubs.

The humans had defended their homes with zeal. The goblins paid in blood for every inch of land they got, but get it they did. Thousands died. Many thousands. Juliet had lost her only brother in battle, and her elderly parents in one of the fires. She'd also participated in the defense, killing goblins until she reached Level 21. She'd bitten back her grief and thrown everything into the fight.

It was only then that the Ice Peak could spare a group of elite fighters who pushed the goblins back. Life adjusted to the new state of being. Houses were rebuilt, new fields were plowed. The property of the dead was split amongst the remaining townspeople, giving everyone a way to survive. Juliet had been devastated. She forced herself to push through the grief and got her life in order. For her husband. For her children.

Soon after the Integration, there were no soft people on Earth. They were either dead or hardened.

But trouble never ended. Even a semblance of normalcy would take a long, long time to return. The troops of the Ice Peak had pushed back the goblins but didn't have the time to destroy them once and for all; they had other people to save, they said.

The town sent its strongest fighters to continue the war, inside the dungeon this time, until the threat of the goblins was forever neutralized. Even now, that battle was ongoing.

Juliet's husband was one of those warriors, and she was left tending to the fields. She would have loved to be by her children as well, but the taxes demanded by the Ice Peak were exorbitant. Even with all the advantages of the new world, she struggled to make ends meet. In that way, her life hadn't changed.

What she truly feared was that, after her husband returned victorious and strong, he would simply be dragged to another war, this time for the Ice Peak. They would never be together again, not really. Because Juliet was weak. And, in this era of upheaval, there was nothing for the weak to do besides grit their teeth and endure; suffer backbreaking taxes and monster attacks while their strong warriors were forcibly recruited; be wrung dry of every drop of blood and hay they could manage; and hope that, eventually, the sun would rise again, and somehow, things would be okay.

Juliet didn't hold much hope. Even the Flame River, the counterpart of the Ice Peak in the south, was not much better—or so everyone said. She lived in a dark world now. She endured for her children and grew constantly stronger only for the world to push her down even harder.

But everyone needed a strand of hope. In the mouths of the common folk, a single name resounded again and again, more than the Gods and Saints who had obviously abandoned them. People prayed for the hero of Earth, the man who had shut down the Animal Kingdom, achieved impossible power, and through his actions, promised freedom.

When all seemed lost and in vain, the people of Earth only had one person to believe in: Jack Rust.

Elder Huali meditated in her manor, watching the people of her estate go about their lives under the nebulous sky. Her chest rose and fell in a steady beat, and the Dao shivered around her with every breath. However, her steady, rhythmic motions only served as a threat of breaking the pattern and erupting with explosive strength.

Without warning, a person appeared in the middle of the room. Huali hadn't seen them coming. As the veil of space parted to let them in, breaking her own spatial lock, it was clear that this person's teleportation had originated from somewhere beyond Huali's perception range.

No C-Grade in the galaxy could do that.

Slowly, Huali turned and bowed her head, catching a glimpse of pure white robes, white hair, and a stern, austere face. "Head Enforcer," she said respectfully. "To what do I owe the honor?"

Eva Solvig, the Head Enforcer of this galaxy's Hand of God branch, nodded back. "Some weeks ago, Ancient ruins were discovered in Trial Planet," she said, not bothering with greetings and preludes. "I was dispatched to investigate. After searching the entire planet, we finally located the ruins in a pocket of space between the third and fourth rings. These ruins had been tampered with. Someone had been there.

And yet, after deep-scanning every individual who left Trial Planet from the moment of our arrival onwards, we found nothing."

"That is unfortunate," Huali replied carefully. She could sense where this was going.

"Very. The Hand of God will take no chances on any Ancient inheritance surviving the Purge. Whoever that person is, they must be eliminated."

Huali nodded.

"Even though we found nothing, we have a lead," the Head Enforcer continued. "A man named Jack Rust. He was in Trial Planet at the time, and presumed dead in Garden Ring after exhibiting oddly extreme power. Shortly afterward, a tribulation descended on Trial Planet, for still unknown reasons. The System had to actively stop it."

Huali still did not reply. She was aware of the tribulation. It wasn't exactly a discreet event.

"We never saw Jack Rust exit Trial Planet. He remained presumed dead. You can imagine my surprise, then, when I received word that not only was he alive and well, but he had escaped Trial Planet while evading *my* perception, reached the D-Grade, and been recruited into the Exploding Sun as your personal disciple." By now, Eva Solvig's voice was intense. "I expect an explanation, Huali."

Huali raised her head. Though Eva's words were disrespectful, there was nothing she could say about it. Yes, the Hand of God was a B-Grade faction just like her Exploding Sun, but they were too far apart in strength. The Exploding Sun's elders were at the late C-Grade. The Hand of God's were at the B-Grade. Huali and Eva were technically of the same status, but they couldn't be further apart.

"I have heard of the tribulation and the Hand of God's mobilization on Trial Planet," Huali replied calmly. "However, I was not aware of Jack's exact circumstances. I assumed he had been deep-scanned like everyone else. Since I already had a relationship to him from his time on Earth-387, I accepted him as a personal student on the basis of his potential. I am not aware of any Ancient inheritance on his person."

"Did you deep-scan him?"

"I did not."

"Shouldn't you have? Isn't that customary for personal disciples?"

"Jack came with the guarantee of my head disciple, so I didn't want to insult them both by performing a deep-scan."

Eva Solvig gave Huali a long, hard gaze. "The Hand of God will investigate your conduct. Now, take me to Jack Rust. Let me inspect him for myself."

"Unfortunately..." Huali began, causing Eva's brows to rise, "Jack Rust left my tutelage and the faction a week ago. He is now a rogue cultivator. I am not aware of his current location, nor do I have any way to contact him."

Eva's posture turned as rigid as stone, and she lashed out, saying, "Not only did you take in a suspected criminal as a personal disciple without any deep-scanning, but you let said disciple betray you less than a month after his recruitment. Your conduct is not only suspicious, it is also shameful."

"I understand. It was my fault."

Huali waited respectfully while Eva Solvig considered her next course of action. Unfortunately, even a B-Grade didn't have the power to locate people in the galaxy. She had to resort to following the leads.

"I will speak with your head disciple, who guaranteed for Jack Rust," she said.

"Unfortunately, he also went rogue."

"Huali!" Eva's eyes widened. "What are you doing? Are you trying to betray the Hand of God!"

"I assure you that I am not. I understand how this looks, and it is my fault. I am willing to take full responsibility for the actions of my disciples—but only those committed *after* I accepted them as disciples."

Huali's voice was calm and apologetic. To all outward inspection, she was regretful. After so many millennia of life, not even a B-Grade could tell that she was actually lying. She knew exactly where Jack was. She just didn't want to reveal it because, as loyal as she was to the Hand of God, she had an obligation to protect her disciple. It was as simple as that.

She hadn't deep-scanned him on purpose. She'd suspected something was up, of course, but deep-scans went in records, and she wanted to avoid that. Plus, even if she gave Jack away, she couldn't betray Shol after his centuries-long, exemplary loyalty.

In the end, even if Jack was captured by his own failure, she couldn't be easily implicated. Her position was too high—though that would depend on how deep Jack's secrets ran.

Regardless, some risks were worth taking.

"I cannot believe this," Eva raged. "Fine. I will have my lieutenants follow their trail through the teleportation portals and unleash a full-on investigation. They will receive a bounty from the Hand of God. Are you satisfied with that, Huali?"

"I don't have a say in the matter."

"That's right; you don't." Eva regained her bearings, closing her eyes and taking a deep breath. Just like that, her purity of mind returned. "Is there anything else you can tell me about Jack?"

"He has an arranged duel against our faction's head disciple in six months. I believe he will be back for that."

"Your faction's head disciple? Qian?"

"That's right."

Eva shook her head. "Fine. Tell me about that event."

Huali did, describing the events that led to Monsoon's visit and the visit itself, ending with Jack and Qian's promise to duel.

"That is not much help. In six months, we will have already caught him, wherever he is. Are there any other clues he gave you, either about an Ancient heritage or his current location? Anything abnormal he demonstrated? Any sort of power which looked even remotely suspicious?"

"If there was anything like that, I would have investigated myself," Huali replied. Her mind raced. She would avoid revealing the existence of Jack's spiritual companion and friends, if possible, as that would undoubtedly end up with them mind-read or tortured by the Hand of God.

However, she had to give *something*.

"There is one thing," she said. "Jack Rust conquered the Final Ring."

Eva froze. "Are you sure?"

"I saw his title myself."

"And you didn't think to mention this until now?"

"I was certainly going to mention it. I just didn't want to interrupt you."

"By the Immortals, Huali... What did you get yourself involved in?" Eva's gaze grew complicated. "We've known each other for millennia. We've visited the Plasma Springs together. If I have to put you down for treason, it will be a pity."

"You insult me. My loyalty to the Immortals is unwavering. I would rather renounce my Dao than betray them."

"For your sake, I really hope that's the case." Eva sighed deeply. "I expect my agents to have free rein to investigate."

"Of course. Just, if possible, please try to keep things discreet. The selection of our next Grand Elder will happen soon, and I am one of the main candidates."

Eva threw Huali a last, long glance. Then, she parted the folds of space and stepped into them, disappearing somewhere beyond Huali's perception.

Huali did not allow herself an errant expression, or even a thought, because she knew that she was still under scrutiny—and would be for a long time. She only hoped this was worth it.

Therefore, she pushed the issue out of her mind and sat back down to meditate, spreading her perception over the estate to facilitate and observe the Hand of God agents.

CHAPTER FORTY
HELL'S TERRAIN

JACK AND SHOL SAT ON TWO BRANCHES OF A HIGH TREE LIKE BIRDS WHO'D grown tired of having wings. Their mood was somber.

"Hell is a large planet," Shol explained. "Several times larger than your Earth. It is only used as a prison and an elite training ground, which results in it being very sparsely inhabited. Ninety-nine percent of the surface is untamed wilderness."

"Meaning we have room to play," Jack replied, nodding. "Any idea how to find Dordok?"

"That's the captain of the *Trampling Ram,* correct?"

"Yes."

"I suggest we don't prioritize him. If he's at the late D-Grade, as you said, then he'll either be inside the prison itself or at a high-level hunting zone. If it's the former, you can forget about rescuing him. If it's the latter, it will still be very difficult, but doable after you level-up significantly."

Jack didn't like the sound of that, but Shol had never steered him wrong. "Can you explain?"

"There is a large facility on this planet; a true prison. It's where most of the D-Grade criminals of the constellation go. However, it is headed by the Warden, a late C-Grade overseer of this planet. Breaking out is impossible, and invading it is even more impossible. If your captain is still there, we'll have to wait."

"Wait for what? Where else could he be?"

Shol revealed a hard smile. "Remember how I told you that Hell functions as training grounds for the Animal Kingdom's inner disciples? The way this works is that there are several zones on the planet used as low, mid, and high-level hunting zones. There is also one peak-level zone. These zones contain D-Grade prisoners of suitable levels, who are forbidden from leaving the zone borders or working with each other. The inner disciples enter the hunting zones as teams of three to five people, and they hunt down any prisoners they can find. The prisoners can fight back, but since they are not allowed to work together, the damage they can inflict on teams of similarly-leveled cultivators is limited."

"So, they release prisoners, then have the inner disciples hunt them down?"

"Yes. It gives them both levels and fighting experience."

"That's brutal. It's also odd. They just release prisoners into the wild? What if they find a way to leave the planet, or escape their determined zones? What if they decide to work together despite the rules, and suddenly the Animal Kingdom has a D-Grade revolution on their hands? Not saying they would succeed, but they could take many inner disciples with them."

"It's not that simple." Shol shook his head. "The things I just described are more than simple rules. I don't know the details, but the Warden possesses some sort of controlling Dao. When he gets his hands on the prisoners, going against his orders is impossible."

Jack's frown deepened. "These prisoners are just thrown into the wild and chased like animals?"

"Unfortunately."

"And you're saying that the captain might be there as well."

"Either that, or he's still trapped in the prison. They don't release everyone at once, only to replenish the numbers when a previous prisoner is killed."

"Then people could be hunting him as we speak. He might die at any moment."

"Yes."

"Shol, that's horrible. We must hurry up and find him."

"Don't get hasty." Shol threw Jack a warning glance. "What exactly are you going to do? Rush into a high-level hunting zone? It will contain teams of late D-Grade Animal Kingdom cultivators, and you cannot even handle one of them. Even if I handle them for you, there is no guarantee I can beat them, and *even* if I do, I cannot necessarily stop them all from escaping. We'll be discovered; and the second that happens, peak D-Grade deacons will be sent after us. No. Trying to rescue Dordok now is rushing head-first into disaster."

"Then, what do you suggest? I stay here and level-up while he's running for his life?"

"What do *you* suggest?" Shol gave him a hard look. "That's our only option, Jack. If you care about this guy so much, then level-up as fast as possible and pray that he survives until then."

"He saved my life."

"Then save him back—but killing yourself will help nobody. Listen, I will be honest; what we're doing is already the height of risk. I would never condone it if Master's reputation wasn't on the line. We cannot afford to make things any harder on ourselves. Saving Dordok will be great if it's possible, but let's not stick our necks out just to fail anyway."

Shol's words came rapidly and rigidly. He wasn't angry, just intense—and Jack reminded himself that this man had dropped everything, left the faction and master he was deeply loyal to, burned his cape, and was here risking his life to help him.

Jack took a deep breath. "You're right. Let's do our best, prioritizing our survival... but if the chance appears, please forgive me for taking a small extra risk to save Dordok."

Shol's gaze was iron. "I guess I can do that."

"Good. So, what's the plan?"

"The plan, right."

Shol first calmed himself. The nearby birds that had flown away earlier—eagle-like, as large as human children, brown-feathered, and with blue beaks—returned to the tree, sensing that this monumental human's anger was dissipating.

"When inner disciples enter the hunting zones, casualties occur. It's not too rare for entire teams to be wiped out by prisoners who played their cards right. Therefore, if you enter a hunting zone and annihilate a team or two, nobody will bat an eye. Let a decent amount of time pass between raids, and you can even get away with more."

"Hunting the hunters."

"Exactly."

"I like that. And what will you be doing in the meantime?"

"Protecting you from the shadows. You saw me turn invisible before; I have a concealing skill taught to me by Okmer, the librarian back in the estate. It was tough to master, but it lets me completely erase my presence so long as nobody gets too close. I can use that to watch you from afar and intervene if anything goes wrong."

"Hmm."

Jack was hesitating. On paper, this sounded great. However, his experiences so far had taught him that the fear of death was an essential factor if he wanted to rapidly progress. With Shol watching over him, would he really be forced to go all out?

Plus, his Dao Tree of the Fist was protesting. What, was he to need constant protection, like a coward?

"I think it's better if I go alone," he finally said. "I get the sense that my progress will be way more rapid if there's nobody waiting to save me... Plus, my Dao would protest otherwise, which would make meditation difficult. Perhaps it's best if you use this time to find out Dordok's whereabouts."

"If you die... that will be terrible."

"I'll be careful—as careful as I can, anyway. But I should be fine for now. You saw how I handled those two at the starship. If I start from low-level hunting zones, I am confident that I can deal with entire teams, especially if I get the jump on them."

Shol did nothing to hide his dislike of this amendment to the plan. "As much as I hate to admit it, you make sense. Fine. Let's do that. However, you must make sure that nobody escapes to report on you."

"Of course. However, what if they report me while we're fighting? There is a faction telepathy function, correct?"

"Only for a limited number of people per faction. As long as you're not going after deacons, you'll be fine."

"Alright, and this Warden you mentioned... What if he comes after us? If he spreads his perception over a hunting zone, finding me will be trivial, and there is no way I can escape a late C-Grade—or any C-Grade, for that matter."

"You don't need to worry about that," Shol replied with confidence. "The Warden has better things to do than scan random hunting zones, even if a couple groups go missing. Plus, if he does try, it won't be too easy—these hunting zones are the size of small continents, so even a late C-Grade would need to fly over to scan it accurately. As for hunting us down... That just won't happen. It would be dishonorable for the Animal Kingdom to send a C-Grade after D-Grades. If they find us, they'll send deacons who will kill us nonetheless, but at least we'll be able to resist a bit."

"Are you sure about that? When I was at the E-Grade, the Kingdom sent three D-Grade Hounds after me."

"That was different. You were running throughout the galaxy, and they needed to find you. Here, in the epicenter of the Animal Kingdom's influence, the available D-Grades should be more than enough to handle us." Seeing Jack's doubtful look, Shol continued. "Trust me, Jack. You may not believe it, but the B-Grade factions care a lot about their reputation. Aside from throwing ourselves at the Warden by invading his prison or doing something equally stupid, he won't act personally."

"Alright. I trust you."

"As you should."

"So, I find a low-level hunting zone and hunt the inner disciples, making sure to let no one escape."

"You should also avoid prisoners. We don't know the extent of the Warden's control over them."

"Alright. And as I do that, you'll be scouring the planet and trying to find out anything you can about Dordok."

"Exactly."

"But really, don't try to protect me. Let me go alone. I promise it will be fine."

"If I said that I won't, then I won't. I swear it on Master's name."

Jack was taken aback. Truth be told, he expected Shol to tail him in secret anyway... but he wouldn't take such an oath in vain, would he?

"Why the surprise?" Shol said with a smirk. "My concealment skill isn't *that* effective. I can hide during battle, but to trail you in secret for weeks would be impossible."

"Oh," Jack replied. "I guess that's good."

"Heh. Getting cold feet?"

"Never. I'm just worried about you now—if your skill is weak, you may be discovered before me."

"I'll manage. As will you."

"It goes without saying."

The two men exchanged a battle-ready smile. Shol whipped out a parchment from his robes, unfurling it before Jack. "This is a map of the entire planet," he said.

There were dozens of continents, along with dozens of oceans. Jack couldn't quite grasp the scale, but if these continents were similar in size to the Earth ones, this planet was *huge*.

"It's big," was all he said.

"Not at all. It's just a piece of paper." Shol pointed at a seemingly random spot. "We are here."

"How do you know?"

"Because I did my research. What, did you think we stepped through a random teleporter that could lead anywhere?"

"...Yes?"

Shol looked at the blue sky. "Oh System, give me strength."

"Then why did you let *me* decide when to escape our crates?"

"I didn't. You just went out. I was waiting for us to arrive at the optimal spot, which luckily wasn't too far from where you decided to make your move. Why would you take initiative when I clearly know what I'm doing?"

"I honestly didn't expect you to think that far ahead."

"Well, I did. This is where we appeared after teleportation—" he jammed a finger into a tiny blue dot right next to their current location, then at a larger circle in the next continent over "—and this is where we were headed. A city of inner disciples."

"Sorry," Jack replied with some embarrassment. "Will they find it suspicious when the starship never reaches its destination?"

"They'll just assume a prisoner did it. This entire continent is a low-level hunting zone. Prisoners don't usually attack for no reason... but they could."

"Hmm. Well, I'm glad it all worked out."

"It won't always. You must be more careful. Think twice about your every move. This place is not a game, Jack; it's absolutely hostile territory and teeming with enemies stronger than you."

"I'll be careful," Jack said. "Thanks for the reminder."

"Anytime." Shol wrapped the scroll up. "You can keep the map. I have it committed to memory."

"Thanks," Jack replied as he pocketed it. "Since this is a low-level hunting zone, I can just start here, right?"

"Correct. But you'll have to search a bit—there are usually a dozen teams active at the same time, so there's a lot of ground to cover. On the bright side, they'll be flying, so you can spot them easily."

"Okay. And how will we find each other afterward?"

"I'll find you. Don't worry; I have my ways."

"Okay." Jack surveyed the wild lands that would be his house for the next few months. It reminded him of the Forest of the Strong. He really looked forward to it.

"And stop grinning," Shol said, sporting a smile himself. "Good luck, Jack. Please survive."

"You too, my brother."

The two clasped hands, looking deeply into each other's eyes and finding only resolve. Then, Shol streaked upward, lost above the clouds, where he began his journey to... somewhere.

Jack was left alone. On a tree. In the middle of nowhere. With enemies to hunt and a very significant chance of dying in the process.

Despite himself, he couldn't stop grinning.

CHAPTER FORTY-ONE

ANIMALS HUNTING

JACK HID IN THE FOLIAGE. HE'D SMUDGED DIRT ON HIS FACE AND BARE CHEST, trying to make himself both stealthy and inconspicuous. If people thought him a prisoner at first glance, it would save him a few seconds of suspicion.

To that end, he'd also hidden away his purple robes, leaving himself with just a pair of boots and a short, brown set of pants—his undergarments, basically.

Pretending to be an inner disciple would also work, as he could then launch a sneak attack on the disciples from up-close. Unfortunately, Jack followed the Dao of the Fist, which disdained underhanded tactics in most situations.

Therefore, dirty and barely clothed, Jack stalked through the foliage, waiting for a team of inner disciples to fly overhead.

It didn't take them long. Only a few hours after Jack got into position, he spotted four dots approaching. He clicked his tongue—four was perhaps a larger team than he'd like to start with, but he was confident enough. He couldn't afford to take it slow.

As the four dots approached, they revealed themselves as cultivators dressed in elegant yet simple attire. One was a human wearing long, green robes. Another was a turtle-human—a turtler—wearing only pants. The third person was a bearfolk in leather armor, and the fourth was a sharken, much like Shard Presht of the Integration Tournament, wearing simple leather.

All ranged between levels 130 and 160.

The four of them flew far overhead, zooming into the distance. Jack was quick to follow. He couldn't take to the air and risk being discovered, so he did his best to navigate the forest below, flying over and under branches, around tree trunks, and generally trying his hardest not to ram his head into anything at multiple hundred miles per hour.

The inner disciples who came here to hunt had a device which gave them a general indication of each prisoner's location, so they didn't have to spend weeks combing through the wilderness. Right now, they were probably following that device to the location of a nearby prisoner. All Jack had to do was not fall too far behind.

Fifteen minutes later, the cultivators slowed, then stopped midair. They hovered a mile above ground, at the edge of Jack's perception, and seemed to be talking with each other. He assumed they were formulating a plan. That meant a prisoner was nearby, and since Jack didn't want to appear yet, he made sure to remain a respectable distance away.

Since the prisoners could not hide, most opted to find a suitable location and turn it into a stronghold. They peppered it with traps and treacherous terrain, optimizing it to give them the best fighting chance against their hunters. Of course, not many traps would work against immortals, but it was better than nothing.

And, if all else failed, they could resort to running.

Jack settled in to wait. He felt for the poor prisoner who was about to be murdered, but he couldn't appear just yet. The extent of the Warden's control over the prisoners was unknown. For all Jack knew, if they saw him, so did the Warden. Therefore, he had to wait until the inner disciples and the prisoner were done fighting, and then swoop in to finish the job.

He could not give this prisoner salvation, so he would settle for revenge.

The four cultivators came to a consensus. The green-robed human spread his arms and shouted something. Suddenly, the forest around

Jack came alive. The ground shook. Trunks moaned. Roots speared out of the earth, tearing into the nearby trees and each other.

Jack didn't wait to see what else would happen. He bolted away, sprinting until he exited the spell's area of effect, and only then did he turn around to witness the destruction.

And destruction it was. An entire three-mile-radius area of the forest had collapsed, filled with fallen logs and sharp roots. Various animal carcasses lined the ground, and where the soil was visible, it was upturned and violently dug out. It was like a giant had grabbed this part of the forest and put it in the blender.

One thing remained—a woman with dark hair so short her scalp was visible, wearing nothing but dirty undergarments. Her gaze was defiant.

Human (Earth-103), Level 159
Faction: -

No faction, no visible title. Her status was as bare as her body.

From the sky, three cultivators dove down, leaving only the robed man afloat. The woman didn't back down in the slightest. She gritted her teeth and pushed her hands out at them, shouting, "DIE, TYRANTS!"

The air turned chaotic. The Dao stirred and span until spectral swords filled the air, flying at the three incoming cultivators. Each could cut through iron.

Jack whistled. That woman was strong.

Unfortunately, so were the Animal Kingdom's inner disciples. The turtler rushed ahead of his teammates, crossing his arms, and flew head-first at the swords. A solid green aura manifested around him. Clashing against it, the swords were deflected, sent spinning away. Any that remained were swiped away by the bearfolk, while the sharken swam between them, dodging everything. She cultivated the same Dao as Shard Presht, the Dao of Momentum, though at a far higher degree of proficiency.

The prisoner wasn't discouraged. She clapped her hands and forced all swords to still midair, then dive back toward her at almost double the speed they'd shown before. Clearly, she'd been holding back. At the same time, a blade of pure Dao materialized in her hand, so solid that Jack thought it was an actual sword at first. She charged.

The three inner disciples had broken through the previous wave of swords, and now as they converged on the woman, the swords came at the cultivators from behind, while the prisoner herself rushed them from the front.

Again, Jack couldn't help but admire her battle prowess. Who knows how many low immortals she'd cut down with this combo. Perhaps individually, none of her four opponents could match her.

But they were four.

Without a word, two of the inner disciples—the turtler and the bearfolk—turned to meet the hail of blades. One tucked into his shell and the other unleashed a storm of claw attacks, stopping anything from approaching the sharken woman, who met the prisoner's charge.

The sharken wore fin-blades on her forearms—large, triangular blades shaped like a shark's fins. It was the same weapon Shard Presht had used. As she clashed against the prisoner, both her body and the fin-blades accelerated and decelerated instantly, making them almost impossible to predict. At the same time, the prisoner's attacks suffered some sort of slowing effect, making her lose her rhythm.

The sharken seized the upper hand.

The prisoner could barely fight back. The flying swords were a large part of her strength, but they were stopped by the other two inner disciples. The blades that made it through were few in number, and her control wasn't good enough to control them accurately in battle—all she could do was fling them out and pull them back.

As a result, she was pushed until she almost reached the ground. Her gaze remained defiant, but there was also a hint of dread. Jack caught her glancing around, looking for avenues of escape.

The inner disciples weren't going to let her.

The sharken did not let up in the slightest, pressuring the woman even harder so she didn't have time to retaliate. Cuts began appearing on her body. At the same time, the other two were done with the hail of blades and rushed over. The prisoner was surrounded and attacked from three sides at once. She tried to summon a few more blades, clearly overdrawing her powers, but no matter what she did, her defenses were swiftly crumbling. It was a matter of seconds.

Suddenly, roots speared out of the ground and wrapped around her limbs. Her ankles and wrists were restrained, leaving her defenseless. The inner disciples weren't showing a hint of mercy; even when the woman's defeat was practically certain, they'd employed a sneak attack by their fourth member to guarantee their success.

The woman was suspended by roots, unable to move, surrounded by three armed inner disciples. "Fuck you," she spat out.

What followed was butchery. Fin-blades, claws, and spiked knuckles rained on her body, chopping her up into a thousand pieces. She died in a shower of blood.

Within seconds, almost nothing was left of this proud woman who fought to her last breath.

"Alright," the sharken said, shaking her fin-blades to clear them of blood. "Do we have time to get a couple more?"

The bearfolk shrugged. "If they're this easy, sure. But we have an appointment at sunset."

"Oh, I remember. Hey, Anker, where's the closest prisoner now?"

Jack gritted his teeth. After chopping up the woman, they simply let the remains of her body fall to the ground and... ignored it. They never even spared their butchery a glance. Not the slightest hint of honor for this brave warrior they hunted down and mercilessly executed in unfair combat.

He wished he could have helped. She did not deserve to die. Not like this. No matter what she'd done to end up a prisoner, he refused to believe that someone with such strong spirit was an evil-doer. In his mind, she was a victim of the Animal Kingdom's tyranny.

And who knows how many others died such deaths every day. Good people shouldn't have to suffer.

The thought of Earth becoming a territory of the Animal Kingdom disgusted Jack even more. He pictured his friends and family running away and being brutally cut down by these monsters. He wouldn't let that happen. Rage boiled inside him, bubbling and seething, and he let it rise freely. It wouldn't consume his reason or hamper his fighting—in fact, it would make it so damn satisfying.

The man with root magic was descending toward his friends. "Let's see," he said, looking at a device on his wrist. "Ah, not too far. Only a thousand miles to the—"

Space fluctuated behind him, and suddenly, a person was there.

"Think you're hot shit?" an angry voice reached his ears.

This inner disciple was a hardened veteran. When someone appeared behind him, he didn't even turn to look, just dashed forward at full speed. "HEL—" he tried to shout, but neither his voice nor his retreat were fast enough.

A punch connected with the back of his skull. The man was flung downward head-first and was nailed into the ground hundreds of feet below, buried in his own roots. His friends alternated their gaze between the root-man and the strange prisoner who'd appeared midair.

Jack growled at them. "I hope you haven't prepared any coffins, because you won't be needing them. You'll be left to rot on the soil, as you would have done to this woman."

The three inner disciples glanced between each other, considering whether to run or stay. They inspected Jack, finding him to only be Level 147.

"Two for the price of one," the sharken growled in response, grinding her blades against each other. "You should have used your invisibility to escape, prisoner. You took Anker; I'll make sure your death is agonizing."

"Try me."

"Don't let him run!" the sharken shouted, charging at Jack. The other two disciples followed her only a beat later. All three of their domains manifested, pushing down on Jack, who stood there and endured the strain.

He was stronger than them, or so he hoped. However, the point wasn't just to beat them; he had to make sure nobody escaped, and for that, he needed them close. That was why he'd used his trump card, Space Walk, to assassinate their wizard, and why he hadn't utilized Meteor Punch when doing so. He didn't want to scare them.

In truth, they could have realized he wasn't a prisoner, as the wizard had mentioned the closest prisoner was a thousand miles away before dying. If they'd ever seen his wanted poster, they could have also recognized the Bare Fist Brotherhood in his inspection screen. However, in their minds, the only people here were inner disciples and prisoners. He looked like a prisoner. What else could he be?

In that few seconds of time, clouded by rage, they hadn't made the connection. They charged.

And now... Now, they had approached him.

Jack grinned with violence. "Bring it on, Animal Kingdom!"

CHAPTER FORTY-TWO
HUNTING THE ANIMALS

JACK FACED DOWN THE THREE REMAINING INNER DISCIPLES.

A turtler predictably focusing on defense. A bearfolk who looked like an all-around physical fighter. Finally, a sharken specializing in speed.

The Animal Kingdom traditionally focused on Physical cultivators. By taking care of the mage early on, Jack had assured that all remaining enemies were the Physical kind, which meant they needed to get up-close and personal. That way, not only did they fight him where he excelled, but he could also capture them more easily if they decided to run.

The sharken was upon him in a flash. Her fin-blades reflected the sunlight as she slashed out, first slow and then fast, her speed oscillating between the extremes. Jack had faced such blades before. He was unarmed; blocking was unwise. He made some distance, dodging as he inspected the sharken's moves, then was forced to fight back when she pressed on.

His hands moved faster than she could manage. He slapped both blades away, then looked to drive a punch into her gut, only to be forced back into defense as the bearfolk arrived. Claws rained down, slow and heavy. Jack could handle each fighter alone, but not together.

The claws and fin-blades formed a mighty combination. Each struck where the other did not, a net of death that sought to constrict and bury Jack. His hands became blurs, parrying and deflecting all strikes, but a couple went through. Narrow blood lines appeared on his arms and torso.

His opponents frowned as their strikes, which should have severed his limbs, only created shallow wounds. How could they know his defense was his strongest point?

"Who are you?" the bearfolk roared, not ceasing his attacks.

"None of your fucking business!"

The turtler, who had been lying in wait, finally joined in the attack. He started spinning and flew at Jack from behind like a hard-shelled cannonball. All three enemies were now in range.

Suddenly, Jack unleashed more of his power. A Dao Domain erupted violently from his body, pushing away the combined force of the three enemy domains. At the same time, frigid wind filled the inner disciples' hearts. They saw their deaths. The person they were facing was no man, but a force of nature, a demon. He would destroy them methodically and mercilessly, and there was nothing they could do about it.

Jack hadn't used Brutalizing Aura in a long time, but the fear it carved on the enemy's faces was always a refreshing feeling.

However, none of the three enemies buckled. They instantly saw through his skill and calmed themselves, retaining most—but not all—of their energy. Sensing the combined might of their three Dao Domains cave under Jack's, they simply understood the extent of his strength. Instantly, their gazes went dark and serious. They were out for blood.

There were some things that all cultivators understood. When facing an overwhelmingly stronger opponent, it was better to scatter and hope that at least some of you survived. When facing an opponent only slightly stronger than you, escaping would only give them an opening to pick you off one by one; the best choice was to stay and fight with everything you had.

Of course, Jack understood this as well. He saw the thoughts race behind their eyes as the three of them exchanged glances and resolute nods. He nodded, too. Despite everything he could say about the Animal Kingdom, they were not cowards.

In truth, he looked forward to this battle. He could *probably* win, but facing three elite opponents of the same level as him would be an uphill struggle. His spars in the Exploding Sun had proven that.

"Come!" he roared, smashing his fists together. They reverberated like gongs, sending flocks of birds into the air all the way to the horizon. Just one of his Meteor Punches could cause a crater—there was no telling how far and how deeply an all-out battle would impact the land.

The three enemies charged as one. The bearfolk and sharken spread to the sides, leaving the turtler alone at the front. It was a sensible choice; he specialized in defense, so he should be able to take a few hits.

Jack let them come. His Iron Fist Style, his signature fighting skill, filled his mind with ice and his heart with fire. He danced between the strikes. Claws and blades flew left and right, but he dodged by a hair's breadth, refusing to be hit. When he struck back, his fists were iron, like a tyrant's. They were unstoppable.

Jack's fighting style also contained hints of mental warfare. As he blended into his Dao Domain, all around him becoming Fist, his opponents experienced the terror of the Iron Fist. Everything they did was countered. Their strikes were dodged, blocked, or ignored. Their defenses were pierced. The more they failed, the weaker they grew, the heavier Jack's Dao ground against them.

The Iron Fist was a fighting style meant to overwhelm the opponent and defeat them without giving up a single inch. It served a superior fighter perfectly. However, if they did force Jack to become defensive again, it would be hard for him to recover.

A fist relied on momentum. The moment it was stopped, most of its power dissipated.

Jack danced and punched. He sought opportunities to unleash a Meteor Punch, but it needed time to charge, if ever so little. Using it mid-battle was difficult; he needed an opening. In the meantime, he tried his hardest to fight off his opponents, but it was proving challenging.

The more they grew accustomed to his moves, the more they were able to use their own.

A claw flew at Jack's face. He leaned back to avoid it, but with a furious growl, the bearfolk turned his claw strike without wasting its momentum. It was the desperate power that came from a cornered animal, demonstrated and amplified to the extreme by the bearfolk's Dao. The claw raked down Jack's chest, drawing a line as deep as a fingernail's width.

Jack displayed no weakness. Compared to the torturous pain he'd endured throughout his life, this was nothing. Most importantly, his Iron Fist Style relied on dominating his opponents—he couldn't let them see that they'd harmed him.

He took the strike and returned his own. An uppercut flew into the bearfolk's jaw as Jack leaned backward, flinging his head back and throwing him a hundred feet into the sky. The turtler's punch smashed into Jack's back, bent as he was, but he simply ignored the hit. The turtler focused hard on defense. In offense, he was weak.

It still made Jack's back creak and ruined his balance, letting the sharken take the upper hand. Her fin-blades came down with extreme speed. A pre-System human wouldn't even register their movement. Jack, despite being unbalanced, reached out for them. The blades met his palms, cutting deep but not through. They came to a stop. His fingers wrapped around the blades, holding them in place, and his gaze hardened. With the bearfolk flung away and the turtler having just struck, he had a window to attack.

Jack pulled both fin-blades aside, revealing the sharken's wide open chest. He then flung out one blade and clenched his fist, shooting it forward. He'd once used this maneuver on Shard Presht with great success.

Unfortunately, this woman's mastery over the Dao of Momentum was worlds apart from Presht's. She didn't have time to bring her hand back to defend, but the moment Jack's punch impacted her chest, she stole part of its momentum to throw herself backward at a similar speed, nullifying most of the impact.

She still went flying and spat out blood, but she was fine. Almost immediately, she willed her momentum to reverse, shooting herself back at Jack.

He gritted his teeth; she was skilled. As expected of a cultivator from the five noble families.

In the instant before she returned, Jack caught the turtler from the collar of his shell and flung him out at her. She caught him and pushed him aside, continuing her charge with only a moment's delay.

In that moment, Jack charged at the bearfolk, who was only now returning from where he'd been sent flying. His jaw was dislocated, but his eyes were filled with fire. Seeing Jack charge at him, he unleashed his strongest attack.

"CORNERED DESPAIR!" he somehow shouted through his broken jaw, slashing out before him. The claws kept going. They formed a spectral outline that carried the power of a cornered animal's desperate final strike. Jack felt its weight and the life-or-death significance.

Unfortunately for the bearfolk, he'd been through a lot. He was accustomed to this life-or-death despair. The mental component of the bearfolk's attack left him unaffected, and as for the physical one...

Jack clenched his fist. Sound and light were sucked inside. The world went mute. Even the bear's claws shivered, their cornered despair countered by the helplessness of a natural disaster.

"METEOR PUNCH!" Jack shouted, his voice echoing through the sky like a god's decree, and a purple, fist-shaped meteor shot out. The claws were eradicated like they weren't even there. The bearfolk barely had time to cross his arms before the meteor exploded in his face, striking him with both intense momentum and a violent shockwave. His arms were flung backward and ripped from the shoulder. His fur evaporated. His ribcage shattered, and his entire body shot upward with enough speed that it might just reach orbit and never land again.

The shockwave spread through the sky, an exploding star that blinded the birds and deafened the forest animals. A ring of wind spread outward, upsetting the Dao in a multiple-mile radius. It was apocalypse in a fist.

It was also very risky.

Of the two remaining opponents, the sharken was too hardened to be stunned. Taking advantage of Jack's big attack, which required some time to prepare and recover from, she appeared beside him and slashed out. Her blades danced over his bare upper body. Red lines were carved under his ribs, and his chest became mangled.

Finally, Jack revealed an expression of pain.

He crossed gazes with the sharken. He was ready to keep fighting. His wounds were visibly regenerating already, and he could see the realization settling into his opponent's eyes. They could barely match him when they were three. Now, they were two, and though he was hurt, he wasn't weakened.

She turned and ran. So did the turtler, who Jack ignored, for he was too slow. It was the sharken he kept his eyes on.

In her retreat, she dashed with incredible speed. Her entire mastery of momentum was poured into her body, accelerating her almost instantly to her maximum speed. She crossed a mile in the blink of an eye. Multiple booms indicated her breaking the sound barrier.

Space parted before her, and Jack appeared. He hadn't used teleportation before in this fight, except to assassinate the root wizard, and even then, they hadn't seen it clearly and assumed it was invisibility. The sharken's eyes widened. She was stunned, but only for a moment. She redirected her entire momentum to the side, falling away in a most unnatural way. She dodged the meteor.

However, in the fraction of a second it took her to adapt, Jack had already shot out another meteor, aiming at her new location.

She reacted in time, if barely. She didn't try to defend, only evade. Her momentum reversed. She managed to dodge Jack's meteor, but not the explosion. A new shockwave appeared, a new sun was born, and the sharken was sent tumbling head-over-heels through the sky, even her control over momentum slipped momentarily.

Jack was there again. Space parted, and his fist came down. It struck her cleanly. A meteor sprang to life as the entire world was sucked into his fist.

The sharken had speed, not durability. Taking a Meteor Punch head-on, she exploded violently, raining burnt blood and flesh in a wide radius. Jack did not wait a single moment. Turning around, he teleported again, and again, then dashed the rest of the way to the escaping turtler.

This cultivator was the slowest of the bunch. He couldn't even break the sound barrier. Jack reached him and smashed a Meteor Punch against his shell, cracking it in a large explosion and nailing the turtler into the ground below, collapsing a small section of the forest in the process. Thanks to the turtler's durability, it was like a true meteor had fallen.

Surprisingly, he survived. The turtler got up and could clearly keep running, but he realized there was no point. He raised both hands and said, "Mercy, please! I beg you!"

Jack appeared before him, an avatar of violence and cold death. "I'm sorry, but I cannot."

His fist met the turtler's face and smashed him into the ground. The earth rumbled for miles in every direction. When everything ceased moving, the turtler lay dead, his skull shattered.

Jack only shook his head once to push away the darkness. It felt wrong to execute someone who surrendered and pleaded for mercy, but what choice did he have? He couldn't imprison the turtler. If he showed mercy, not only would this enemy eventually reach civilization and report Jack's presence, in the future, he might even find his way to Earth and kill everyone to get revenge for his friends.

In the cultivator world, showing mercy to the enemy was often the same as being cruel to yourself.

Level-up! You have reached Level 148.
Level-up! You have reached Level 149.

Jack quickly split all attributes points evenly between the Physical sub-stats, then sighed and shook his head again. His entire body was still in pain from the many injuries he'd sustained, but his regeneration could handle them. For now, he was just tired—and hungry.

But food could wait a moment.

Without giving himself time to rest, Jack buried what remained of the swordswoman the inner disciples previously killed, leaving her a simple, empty tombstone as a token of dignity. He then darted through the forest, trying to open as much distance as possible between himself and the four dead cultivators.

Battles between immortals were earth-shaking events. It must have been detectable hundreds of miles away. Others might run over to investigate, and no matter how thinly spread they were in this place, Jack didn't want to take any chances.

Although, he realized, *when I'm strong enough to move to the next tier of hunting zones, I could use this as a final move. Kill a team of cultivators here, then wait until more people arrive to investigate and kill them too. It's risky... but it could work. Hmm.*

CHAPTER FORTY-THREE
ANOTHER!?

Artus Emberheart opened his eyes when someone knocked on his door. Of course, he'd sensed them coming; his Dao perception stretched for a hundred miles around.

"Come in," he commanded, and the door opened soundlessly.

"Warden." The leonine who entered saluted him humbly. "I have a report on the missing teams."

"Speak."

"More of them disappeared. We've tracked down the numbers of missing people over the last month, and they are unusually high in seven low-level zones. The latest casualties were reported a few minutes ago in zone sixteen. We suspect there is someone out there hunting us."

"Hmm." The Warden's eyes narrowed slightly. His mane fluttered in the gentle breeze generated by the mere act of him thinking. "It is not a prisoner, as they would not be able to traverse multiple zones. Someone snuck in from the outside. Investigate every teleporter connected to Hell for immortals at the middle D-Grade and above, and recruit nine low immortals and a healer to scour zone sixteen. The intruders could still be there. If you don't find them, be prepared to move to the next zone where disciples go missing."

"Yes, Warden," the leonine replied. He hesitated for a split-second, then, in a voice as steady as before, added, "What if the enemy is too strong?"

Artus gazed over this leonine. He was one of his young and promising personal disciples at Level 180. It would be a pity if he died.

"It's a low-level zone," he replied. "When you find them, the deacon shadowing you will eliminate anyone over Level 165. You should be able to deal with the remaining ones. If you fail, nobody will interfere."

The leonine nodded sharply. "Of course, Warden."

"You may leave."

"Yes, Warden."

Jack shot out of the foliage, approaching four people in a small crater. They were bruised and bloody—one of their members had already fallen to his punches.

"Formation!" an eagler—a half-eagle half-human similar to Fesh Wui from the Integration Tournament—shouted. Four immortal Dao Domains sprang out, completing each other to form a whole greater than its parts. Four grand Daos boiled under it.

Jack fell on them like a missile. His Dao Domain unfolded, a purple dome of violence. Now that he'd leveled up a few times, glittering stars were visible in the purple, each a miniature fist waiting to strike. Simply watching his Dao gave one a sense of unavoidable, impending doom.

Jack's Dao Domain ground against the combined domain of the other four, slowly but surely pushing them back. At the same time, Brutalizing Aura erupted from his body, filling his opponents with visions of their deaths and weakening them. They struggled to hold on, but it only took one of them succumbing to the pressure for the formation to collapse.

The weakest of the four was only Level 130—how could they resist Jack?

Their combined Dao Domain deteriorated. It crumbled under Jack's pressure and the purple dome pushing on it from above. The four inner disciples were sweating.

"Why are you doing this? Stop!" the strongest of them, an eagler at Level 161, shouted. He was the only one above Level 140.

"Sorry," Jack replied coldly, "but you are my enemies."

The eagler cawed, stirring the very wind. Seeing that their domain was about to crumble, he let it go completely and mustered everything for a full-power strike. "WINDS OF HELL!"

Jack had been waiting for exactly that. As his domain overpowered theirs and reached the ground, pushing down everyone but the eagler, he clenched his fist and shot it out.

"METEOR PUNCH!"

The purple stars in his domain fused into the meteor, further augmenting it. When it clashed against the eagler's tornado, it didn't even stop, simply pushing through effortlessly, dominating the air and smashing hard into the earth, right where his four enemies lay suppressed.

A tremendous impact shook the ground. Jack narrowed his eyes to protect them from the explosion, letting the shockwave ruffle his pants and hair. For a moment, the world was chaos—then, everything calmed, and Jack was left alone in the wilderness with five mangled corpses.

Level-up! You have reached Level 163.

It was lucky he received a level. They'd been getting scarcer and scarcer lately. In the month he'd spent terrorizing the low-level hunting zones, his level had grown dramatically, but so had the difficulty of achieving each successive level-up. At least the System acknowledged the difficulty of finding D-Grade opponents and didn't make things *too* slow, but still… Jack estimated he must have killed at least a hundred inner disciples so far over five hunting zones, creating a tiny but noticeable gap in the Animal Kingdom's forces.

Not a single inner disciple had escaped him so far, but they were bound to have noticed something was wrong.

Perhaps I should hide out for a while, he thought calmly, *now used to the sight of immortal corpses. Or I could just move directly to the mid-level zones.*

He was a bit leery of doing that. When he first entered the low-level zones, he had been Level 146, while his opponents ranged from 130 to 165. Those first battles hadn't been easy.

If he tried to assault a team of mid D-Grade disciples while only being a low D-Grade himself, things might get too risky. Even if he could beat them, he had no confidence in preventing everyone from escaping—unless he used his Life Drop, but that was something he would really rather avoid.

However, he also didn't have time to waste. Even hunting furiously, he'd gotten sixteen levels in a month. At this rate, he wouldn't get anywhere near the peak of the D-Grade in the five months he had left.

What a dilemma, he thought again, clicking his tongue. Where are you, Shol... I need you to pick up the slack.

Done ruminating, Jack zoomed off. The more inner disciples he killed, the higher the chances of people looking for him. He flew low, crossing the jungle until he reached a distant mountain, where he darted into an obscured cave.

This place had become his house for the past few days. It contained nothing, but he was an immortal; he *needed* nothing.

Well, besides a hiding place, which the cave gladly offered.

Jack released a long sigh. He tossed his credit card and treasures on a leaf pillow he had lying by the side, then sat down cross-legged in the middle of the cave. It wasn't large—ten feet from end to end and rectangular-ish in shape.

At least it had a view, whenever he chose to remove the boulder sealing the cave mouth.

Jack reached for some of the food he had lying around—cooked bird meat, mostly—and started eating. He didn't need to do that anymore, but it helped him focus. He also spared a few glances at his credit card.

He had secured ninety million from the bounty hunter and prison guards on Derion, the poison planet. That was a massive sum.

Still, for an immortal, he was considered dirt poor. He really looked forward to reaching a hundred million and purchasing the telepathy function for his faction, but he'd discovered that the inner disciples hunting here did not carry their credit cards with them.

Misers.

At least, when he did manage to gather some money, he would be able to contact the professor and find out what was happening on Earth.

I hope everyone is okay... Man, I wish Shol had agreed to lend me some. He must be a billionaire—with a capitol B!

Hunting the Animal Kingdom disciples was a risky endeavor. Therefore, Jack couldn't slack off on safety measures. After every successful hunt, he would lay low for at least eight hours, sometimes more. When the number of immortals in a hunting zone decreased noticeably, he would change zones.

In those eight hours, he would meditate. He had no time to waste, so this was the best way to keep himself busy. He'd brought the Dao Battery from his cellar in the estate as well. It waited right next to him in the small cave, making it a Fist Cave.

This time, like every other, Jack finished his meal, then made himself comfortable and closed his eyes. He dived into his soul world, the bare rock replaced with starry terrain and a Dao Tree.

He'd been looking forward to this. Because, as he leveled up, his Dao Tree had begun to evolve.

CHAPTER FORTY-FOUR
THE TREE AND THE LIFE DROP

CULTIVATORS FORMED DAO TREES AS THEY ENTERED THE D-GRADE. HOWEVER, at first, their Dao Trees didn't resemble trees at all. Jack's inner world used to contain four Dao Roots wrapped around the Dao Seed, connected to it through a network of thin lines. All together, they formed the image of a fist, where each finger was a different color—five of them, each corresponding to one of Jack's Daos.

As he leveled up, however, things began to change.

Jack hovered in his inner world, observing the changes. His Dao Tree, once nothing but a multicolored fist, now had an actual sapling growing out of it. It was a young tree, frail yet full of potential. The Fist—both Seed and Roots—was its entire root system, and the tree itself grew out of the back of the fist shape, where the wrist was supposed to be. The tree grew upward, while the fist pointed downward.

Jack muttered a breathless wow. This was *his* Dao. His inner world.

"How beautiful..." he said in admiration. With a shake of his head, he summoned Copy Jack, wanting company to enjoy the sight. "What do you think, Copy Jack? Do you like it?"

The copy formed his lips into an "O" and nodded excitedly. Jack liked this guy. He was simple and joyful, and never seemed to grow tired of being trapped in here. What better companion to have as a Dao Soul?

"Come with me, Copy Jack. Let's take a look at this tree."

They flew through the void of the soul world. Jack could always transform this place into the field where he often trained with Copy Jack, but chose not to—this felt more familiar.

Every inner world was different. Jack's looked like an endless void surrounded by sparkling, star-like dots. It was an imitation of space, basically, with his Dao Tree hovering in the very center of existence, supporting this entire world.

In contrast to actual space, Jack could faintly smell a pure, earthly scent, like packed dirt. He could hear the distant stars echoing with the sound of fist hitting metal, and occasionally, a meteor would cross the canvas, going from nowhere into nowhere with the threat of violence.

As he approached the Dao Tree, the smell only became more intense. Jack reached the tree to find out that each finger carried its own signature sensations. The purple thumb of the Fist, thrummed with violence and dignity—an unstoppable rush. The silver index finger was made of tightly-bound steel wire, representing his Indomitable Will. The middle finger was dark blue and carried an uplifting, dominating aura, making Jack feel like the king of the world—it was his Dao Root of Power. From the other side, the pinky was black and scrawny, almost shriveled. It was the Dao of Weakness.

As for the ring finger, that was the most complex of them all. It wasn't just the Dao Root of Life; it represented the Life Drop, a drop of blood from Enas, the King of Gods, the First of the Old Ones. It currently functioned as a Dao Root for Jack, but that was just a speck of its true power. Even now, Jack could not gaze into the drop freely. Behind its thin veil hid a large reservoir of life, an ocean of unplumbed depths stretching so far inward that Jack couldn't help but admire the mastery over space that made it possible.

He couldn't reach the depths of that ocean. He could absorb part of its power to reveal his four-armed form, but he couldn't really control the Life Drop. There could be monsters hiding in there. Treasure, mysteries, and wonders. To have a mysterious object so intimately close to your soul was unnerving, but also exciting.

Jack couldn't help himself. He felt little fear and a lot of intrigue.

One day, when he plumbed those depths and conquered the Life Drop to make it truly his, just how much power would he earn?

And if the King of Gods wanted to harm him, well... He wouldn't need to go to such trouble.

Jack focused on this ring finger. It exuded an aura of life so pure that it felt like his nostrils had been unplugged for the first time since he was born, and he could finally breathe freely. Each inhalation sent his body into ecstasy, awoke the animal inside him, and made him feel like home.

But there was also danger in life; an endless race of survival, countless creatures laying down their lives only for their descendants to carry on their legacy. There was pain and sorrow, failure and death. Yet, within the depths of this war for survival hid light, for that survival was the very purpose of life, and to pursue one's purpose was the true source of happiness.

The Fist fit right in there as well. It meshed perfectly with the ideals of Life, two paths well-suited for each other.

This was the only Dao Root Jack hadn't comprehended by himself—it had been granted to him when he passed the Ancient Trial in Trial Planet—in hindsight, it synergized perfectly with his own path. So perfectly, in fact, that he couldn't help suspecting that the suitability of his Dao was a hidden requirement of the Ancient Trial.

Giving this green ring finger a final glance, Jack looked upward, at the tree that had recently bloomed from inside his Fist.

It was healthy and lively. A small tree for now, only reaching up to his waist, but a tree nonetheless. It had even begun to form bark. As it grew, some of its cells died and were pushed outward, where they compressed into the hard material that would protect the tree from harsh weather, pests, or other threats.

Of course, none of those were present in Jack's inner world, but he appreciated the tree's decency to follow the biological pattern. It let him flex his knowledge to Copy Jack, who silently and with an unwavering smile endured a ten-minute lecture.

"And that, my timid student," Jack finished, "is how trees grow."

Copy Jack made sounds of excited understanding. He then pointed at where the tree connected to the Fist—the beginning of its root system. Jack took a better look. There was a green glow there, but nothing else.

"Yes?" he asked. "Those are the roots. What are you trying to say?"

Copy Jack pointed again. Seeing that Jack did not understand, he pointed at the ring finger which signified the Dao Root of Life, then at the tree's base again.

"Are you saying that the roots are life?" Jack tried. Copy Jack only shook his head. He pointed at the ring finger again, then made a questioning gesture with his hand.

"What are you—" Jack was about to ask again when he figured it out. "Oh! Wait a moment. You're right. Where is the Life Drop!"

The ring finger was a vibrant green, full of life. Jack had habitually connected that with the Life Drop, but on second thought, he couldn't actually *see* the Life Drop inside the finger. Where did it go?

He looked around, inspecting the starlit void which surrounded his Dao Tree, but there was no divine green drop floating there. He then observed his Dao Tree again. With a figurative light bulb popping up over his head, he focused on the base of the tree, where Copy Jack had been pointing before.

Indeed, the green glow he'd written off as "magic" was not so simple. As he took a closer look, he realized that this green glow was merely the top of the Life Drop, which was embedded in the back of the Fist, right under the base of the tree.

Yet, he was certain that when he broke through to the D-Grade and formed his Dao Tree, the Life Drop had been inside the ring finger.

"Odd," he muttered. "What is going on here, Copy Jack? Is the Life Drop affecting my Dao Tree, somehow?"

Of course it did. Jack felt like an idiot. He had literally just said that the Dao Root of Life was only a tiny portion of the Life Drop's power. Why would it obediently stay inside a single finger of his Dao Fist when it could adopt a more active role?

Which instantly birthed a thousand questions in Jack's mind. Did the Life Drop possess sentience? If it could freely move around his inner world, what else could it do? Could it harm him? Could it withdraw its power and make his Dao Tree collapse? Could it turn his Dao in a direction of its choosing, pulling it away from the Fist and toward Life?

Jack still felt that if a God wanted to harm him, they wouldn't need to be discreet about it, but the Life Drop's activities were upsetting.

"Do you think I should be worried, Copy Jack?" he asked his friend, who remained fixated on the Life Drop. Jack shrugged. "You're right. Since there's nothing I can do about it anyway, I'll just hope for the best. It's only brought me benefits so far. I have no reason to distrust it."

Copy Jack still did not reply, his eyes glued on the Life Drop like he was trying to see through its mysteries.

That didn't stop Jack from performing his own inspections. He observed the Dao Tree carefully, from top to bottom, looking for signs of anything odd. "I don't know why I'm worried," he muttered mid-inspection. "It's not like anything bad *should* happen. There is infinite life under my Dao Tree. If anything, this is great."

He still kept going, out of caution. His eyes ran over the entire tree and found nothing odd. Right as he was about to turn away, however, he glanced over the growing bark again. "Wait a moment," he said, squinting. "Are those shapes?"

Generally speaking, bark formed all over the tree at once, but there could be short periods of time where some parts of the bark were more well-formed than others. Jack's tree seemed to be in exactly such a period, with some parts of his tree forming the beginning of bark while others remained a hard green. That by itself wasn't suspicious.

When he took a more careful look at the arrangement of bark...

Jack took a step back. He traced the lines of bark with his eyes. If he looked at those patterns carefully, and if he imagined them extending to meet each other, they weren't random at all.

In fact, the more he observed them, the more certain he grew that they were...

A door.

Now, *that* was suspicious. Not bad, necessarily, but suspicious.

"Copy Jack," Jack said carefully, "I think we may have a problem. Hey, Copy Jack, are you listening to me?"

For the past few minutes, Copy Jack had been kneeling by the base of the tree, thoroughly inspecting it. He hadn't even acknowledged Jack's words. It had been so long that Jack began to think something was wrong.

"Is everything okay?" he asked, approaching Copy Jack.

"Touch," Copy Jack replied.

Jack was so shocked it took him a moment to regain his bearings. "You can talk!" he asked. "And what do you mean by touch?"

"Touch," Copy Jack said again. His gaze remained glued on the Life Drop under the base of the tree, and he raised one finger as if to jam it in there.

"Wait. Don't touch that, Copy Jack," Jack said, growing worried.

"Touch."

"Don't touch."

"TOUCH!"

Before Jack could stop him, Copy Jack pierced his finger into the Life Drop. An explosion of life occurred. Jack's inner world was colored green. Copy Jack was tossed back like a ragdoll, spinning through space before eventually coming to a stop, holding his heart.

The Life Drop closed again, but the deed was done.

Jack felt himself hyperventilating. He was *too* full of life. He sensed his body in the real world suddenly grow in height and sprout two extra arms, entering his strongest form.

"Fuck," he swore, doing his best to contain the energy. Failing, he then opted to expend it as fast as possible, letting an aura of life radiate from his body. The life energy in his body slowly dwindled, but he was undoubtedly shining like a beacon in the spiritual perception of every immortal within a dozen miles.

"FUCK!" he swore again. There was a reason he never used the four-armed form. The voice in the Ancient Trial had warned him that, if he was ever spotted using it, all major powers of the galaxy would come after him with tremendous zeal. He absolutely couldn't afford that—and in Hell, a planet which housed at least one late C-Grade, he didn't want to risk it.

"Are you okay, Copy Jack?" he asked hurriedly, appearing by the side of his clone in an instant.

Copy Jack was still grabbing his heart with a pained gaze, but he met Jack's gaze and nodded. He seemed more apologetic than hurt—even his simple mind realized he'd fucked up big time.

"Never touch that again. Ever. You understand me?" Jack chided him, in a hurry to return to the real world.

Copy Jack nodded earnestly, and Jack tsked.

"Don't think this is over. For now, keep your fucking hands to yourself. Don't be a child."

Copy Jack nodded again, and Jack had no choice but to trust him because he really couldn't afford to stay here any longer. He returned to the real world, where he was blinded by green light.

"Fuck," he repeated. It was so bright that even he, with his highly-enhanced body, was blinded.

It was even worse than he thought. He hadn't realized there would be physical light. There must have been some shockwave released from his body as well, because his Dao Battery and other things were scattered randomly across the cave, and the boulder he'd used to block the entrance had rolled away.

Thanks to that, a bright green beacon streamed out of the cave, piercing the cloudy sky and visible from who knows how far away. Jack couldn't make it disappear, because he had to expel all the extra energy and get the fuck out of there.

Within seconds, the life energy ran out. The beacon disappeared and his body returned to normal. By then, he'd put on his purple robes and waved his sleeve, gathering all items inside his pockets. He dashed out of the cave at full speed and instantly felt despair.

The green beacon was gone, but it had done its job. Dots had appeared in the sky, surrounding him from three directions. They were cultivators—a bunch of them.

CHAPTER FORTY-FIVE
ONE AGAINST ELEVEN

Jack raised his gaze to the cloudy sky. Thick droplets of rain started falling before the enemy cultivators even arrived—first one and then many, drenching Jack's hair and robes.

He ignored the rain, taking in a greedy breath of air to fill his lungs. Water was the least of his problems right now.

The cultivators were here.

Eleven forms rose over Jack, looking down at him from a greater height. The rain didn't bother them; their long hair and fur were matted to their backs, and the distant flashes of lightning only enhanced their dark visage.

"I don't suppose we can postpone this due to weather conditions," Jack said, punctuated by a precise thunderclap.

"Save your mirth, human," one of the enemies replied. He had a lion's mane and a thick, wide chest, reminding Jack of Rufus Emberheart. The arrogant glint in his eye was similar, too. "Speak; why did you reveal yourself? You clearly cannot escape."

Jack chuckled darkly. "Even if I told you, you wouldn't believe me."

The enemies watched him with narrowed eyes. They seemed hesitant. Of course they would be; since Jack had practically summoned them here, they expected him to have allies hidden somewhere.

While they considered the situation, Jack inspected them all. There was a leonine, a sharken, two eaglers, three bearfolk, one elef, and three goatees. All ranged from level 140 to 165. The only exception was their leader, the leonine who'd spoken first. He was Level 180.

Eleven enemies, all similar to him in level. Eleven inner disciples who enjoyed the full resources of the Animal Kingdom. Jack could sense his death looming, but he stared at them defiantly.

"Well?" he asked. "Aren't you going to attack me?"

A faint aura seeped out of his body, a barely visible purple light. The rain curved away as if dodging him in fear, while the Dao around him aligned to the Fist.

The leading leonine saw his demonstration of power and snorted. A blanket of supremacy erupted from his body, not a domain, but an actualization of his Dao. The rain was pushed back for a hundred feet, cowering before him, while his body was draped in a golden radiance that made him seem like a king among men.

Jack laughed.

"Wait!" an eagler said, her eyes widening. "I recognize this man! I've seen his wanted poster. He is Jack Rust!"

Murmurs of realization spread through the gathered cultivators.

"So what if I am?" Jack replied.

"Fool!" the leading leonine shouted, laughing. "The killer of Rufus delivered himself to us on a silver platter! What idiocy!"

"What's your name, kitty?" Jack replied. "I'm about to become your killer, too."

The leonine's eyes hardened. He made up his mind. "If you have allies, human, they had best stay hidden. My master, the Warden of Hell, is watching; and I promise you, any of your allies that appear will be killed immediately. The Animal Kingdom does not forgive underhanded tactics."

"Unless it's you doing them."

"Your insults fall on deaf ears. Nothing but a pest's death rattle."

"And what if I kill you, kitty? Will your master intervene then?"

The leonine laughed. "If you can kill me and my soldiers, I will eat my mane."

"How about facing me in single combat, then?" Jack tried. "Since you're so supreme, why bring eleven people to deal with one?"

The leonine shook his head in mockery. "You have shown yourself to be adept in trickery. When you snuck into our territory and killed our inner disciples, did you do so with honor? When you chose to farm our people and resources for your personal benefit, did you care about the losses you were incurring us? No, human. Vermin like you do not deserve a duel. They deserve extermination."

Jack narrowed his eyes. This guy was just spouting bullshit now—clearly, he understood Jack's strength and was afraid to fight him one-on-one.

Which was a wise choice, admittedly, but frustrating.

"How can your Dao survive your cowardice?" Jack asked, but the leonine only laughed.

He then turned to his squad. "If he has allies, they will not dare intervene," he told them. "And if he doesn't, then he's easy prey. Slaughter him."

"Yes, sir!" The shouts of ten immortals shook the air.

And then, they fell on him.

Jack didn't have time to curse his luck, Copy Jack, or the Life Drop for this predicament. He needed to survive. A plan was already forming in his mind; kill the fastest of these guys, then escape. There was no way he could take eleven of them at once.

Yet the Fist protested. The injustice gnawed at him. These guys had shown up and challenged him unfairly. They were individually weaker than him, even their leader. Why should he have to run?

Jack was stuck between a rock and a hard place, but he pushed down the questions because he simply didn't have time to ponder them. The sky erupted with colors. Nine Dao Domains fell on him, constricting him in many different ways at once.

Sharp winds sliced at his skin and blew against his movement. His body felt trapped in a mire, robbed of all momentum. The despair of cornered animals enhanced his enemies and weakened Jack, while the scent and taste of copper filled his mind, sinking him into a bloody sea.

The only cultivators who hadn't released their domains and charged at Jack were the leading leonine, who'd stayed behind and coldly observed the battle, and the elef, who was their healer, taking up position at the back line.

Jack spread his arms wide, welcoming his would-be killers. He clenched his fists and grinned. “Try me,” he whispered to the winds, his voice lost the moment it left his mouth.

His Dao Domain erupted. A purple, starry haze unfolded, engulfing the enemy domains and fighting them in a tug of war. At the same time, he unleashed the full might of Brutalizing Aura, weakening his enemies; the larger the power disparity between Jack and the skill’s targets, the more effective it was.

The approaching cultivators saw death. They had poked the bear and were going to pay for it. Jack would maul them methodically and coldly, and there was nothing they could do about it.

Their experienced minds staved off the mental attack, and their numbers gave them confidence, but they still staggered.

Though nine worked together against Jack, he was much stronger than any one of them. His domain rumbled like a force of nature. The wind was punched away, momentum was seized back, despair became his to wield, and the sea of blood belonged to his enemies.

For a moment, just as Jack revealed his full power, they came to a standstill, one against nine.

Right afterward, he was pushed back. No matter how strong he was, he couldn’t contest nine immortals in raw power. Even stopping them momentarily was a feat of legend.

And it was enough to make them doubt their chances.

Jack grinned. As his domain folded backward, the purple receding to let the enemy in, he knew that his first punch had been blocked, but he’d proven he could throw it. Most importantly, he still had control over his immediate surroundings.

He laughed at his enemies. Then, he stepped through space and disappeared. An onslaught of attacks passed by where he was an instant ago, raining onto the forest below and flattening it. The giant trees were cut down, the soil was upturned, craters formed, and the grass was scorched. In an instant, several miles in diameter had been completely destroyed.

And Jack was nowhere to be seen.

"Come at me!" he shouted, appearing behind the cultivators and falling on them. "METEOR PUNCH!"

The sky shattered. His skill wrestled against their domains for control, sucking some of the sound and light, then exploded in their faces. Cultivators flew everywhere. Their defenses blocked most of the power, but enough remained to scatter them. Jack pursued the eaglers —the fastest of the noble families, wielding Daos of wind.

He caught up in an instant. A female eagler barely managed to stop her flight, only for her terrified eyes to meet his hardened ones. He showed her not the slightest hint of mercy. "Meteor Punch!" he shouted again. Her horror mounted as what had originally looked like an all-out attack was a skill he could use freely.

Her allies didn't have time to intervene. Jack blasted a Meteor Punch right in the eagler's chest, shattering her body and sending what remained flying in all directions.

One down, ten to go.

Jack turned to his enemies and roared, "If you don't come at me, then I will!"

He pressed on. The battle fever took him over completely, turning him from a man into a well-oiled killing machine. His fists became unstoppable. His spirit, unbreakable. The Iron Fist Style filled his body, guiding him into a dance of violence as the eight opponents tried and failed to suppress him.

Jack was a force of nature. He punched a bearfolk in the face, blocked the sharken's fin-blades with his bare forearms, then grabbed her by the neck and tossed her into the approaching eagler. He leaned back and flew down, narrowly dodging two claw swipes and receiving one on the leg, which he ignored. The last eagler appeared below him, ready to unleash a sharp jet of wind at his back, but Jack expected it. He rotated midair and smashed down a Meteor Punch, obliterating an entire section of the forest along with the eagler's right wing.

Green magic flared. The wing was restored, but the eagler's fright was not. If not for his extreme speed, he would have been instantly killed just now.

Jack did not stop, nor did he slow. Facing eight opponents at once, his best hope was to keep them disorganized. If they managed to sync up, he would be in trouble.

Punches flew everywhere, extending beyond his physical reach to pursue his opponents. He blocked, dodged, and parried their strikes. Any injuries he sustained were repaired with speed visible to the naked eye, and his onslaught of attacks came without pause or pattern, forcing the eight people facing him on the defensive. Occasionally, he blasted out a Meteor Punch, injuring someone, but the healer was always there.

The leading leonine still hadn't joined the fight, hovering in the sky with his arms crossed and a stormy gaze. Jack was beginning to entertain a wild thought—one that bordered on hubris.

Can I take them?

He had only killed one person, and that was due to surprise, but he could face eight of them. Even if the leader joined, how much could he turn the tide? As long as he took care of the healer, who made sure all the injuries he caused were meaningless, maybe he had a chance.

He wanted to try.

Jack navigated a complex terrain of attacks, dodging two and using the force of his domain to repel another. At the same time, he charged up for a Meteor Punch, but it was a feint; as his opponents escaped, he disappeared through space.

His immediate surroundings were under his sole control. They could not stop his teleportation.

The healer was at the very back of the battle, keeping her allies between herself and Jack. Teleportation made that useless. Jack appeared behind her with his fist already clenched, but what he saw was not the back of an elef, but the front of a leonine. The leader stared at him mockingly from nine feet away.

"You think too highly of yourself," he declared as he unleashed a punch at Jack. Their knuckles clashed. Jack was stronger, but he was unprepared; the impact knocked him backward, sending him spinning head-over-heels into a trio of enemies who'd come to flank him.

The remaining eagler and two bearfolk unleashed their attacks. A sharp, invisible jet of wind and two sets of claws came hurtling at Jack, who ought to dodge. He did not. He let the claws rend his chest, only angling himself to avoid most of the wind as he passed right through their attacks. Since they were piercing ones, they did not push him back much. His momentum remained, sending him right into the midst of those three enemies, who no longer had time to dodge.

A Meteor Punch rang out. Air itself ran away from the point of impact as one bearfolk exploded on the spot, and even the eagler was only fast enough to avoid the epicenter of the explosion but was caught by the shockwave, losing his balance. Jack finished the job with a jab to the back, penetrating right through the frail body and light bones.

His fist stuck out of the eagler's chest. Jack couldn't see his face, but it had to be a mask of terror. Immediately afterward, he used a burst of Dao to completely destroy the eagler's organs from within. He was deader than dead.

Level-up! You have reached Level 164.

Jack recovered his fist, letting the eagler topple to the ground, and quickly allocated his new stats to Physical.

Six enemies to go. Eight, including the leader and the healer.

Unfortunately, it seemed that the leader's idea of mercy was over. The battle came to a halt as the remaining cultivators gazed at the strongest leonine, who stared right at Jack.

"You're strong," he said, his voice booming from deep inside his chest, "but not enough. Prepare to die."

He raised a hand to the cloudy sky. Jack felt his hair rise, and a lightning bolt descended from the heavens, striking the leader's raised arm.

The lightning didn't disperse. It remained within the leonine's body, filling it with power. His fur rose and sparks crackled across his mane. His entire body screamed of violence.

Jack had seen this before. Rufus Emberheart had used a similar battle form in their final battle, except this one was far more advanced and infinitely stronger. Not to mention it was augmented by actual lightning, which was a very unlucky coincidence.

As if Jack didn't have enough on his plate already.

Sometimes, it felt like even the universe wanted him dead. But he wouldn't do it the favor. If the world wanted him dead, it had to come and try; and it better be prepared to pay the price.

Jack's Dao Domain erupted in a veil of violence fueled by the genuine desire to fight. Despite himself, Jack was grinning.

"Come!" he shouted.

CHAPTER FORTY-SIX
BATTLING A LEONINE

THUNDER BOOMED IN THE DISTANT CLOUDS. LIGHTNING CRACKLED, illuminating the profiles of the eight cultivators after Jack. Six of them gazed at him warily; the elf healer stood at the very back, while the leading leonine's body was wrapped in lightning, his fur standing and his muscles ready to explode with power.

The leonine dashed.

The air shivered in his wake. The winds parted. Sonic booms carved the forest underneath as the leonine instantly appeared before Jack, who raised his arms to block. It was fruitless. The force of the impact launched him backward, but the leonine was already there, weaving his fingers together and smashing both hands into Jack's abdomen.

All air left his body. He hurtled downward at extreme speed, crashing into the ground like the meteors he often threw. A crater was formed, and the earth shook for hundreds of feet.

The leonine stood proudly in the air, looking down on Jack. It didn't seem like his lightning-based combat form had a time limit.

"Did you think you could just waltz into our territory and start killing people without repercussions?" he asked. "What naivete. Have you had enough, or should I keep humiliating you?"

Jack forced himself to stand. The regenerative properties of Neutron

Star Body were already knitting his cracked bones together and repairing his bruised organs. Before long, he was in top form again—though his exhaustion crept upward at a frightening pace.

The enemy cultivators raised their brows at his recovery. Even the leonine appeared confused.

"Had enough?" Jack replied, spitting out a mouthful of blood. He grinned. The blood around his mouth only made him seem crazed. "Even if I die, it still won't be enough."

"Very well. Let's test that."

The leonine dove. Lightning sparked around his body, amplified by the electrical presence of the clouds above. His punch came at Jack's face in an instant.

Jack had already realized he could not match this guy in speed. Which had never been his strong suit. Right as he glimpsed the punch coming for his face, he fired back. All sound was sucked into his fist, and the world lost its luster.

"Meteor Punch!"

An upward meteor met a thunderbolt. The impact shattered everything in a mile radius. The ground under Jack's feet sank, but he remained steady, channeling the entirety of his considerable strength upward.

He crashed through the enemy. The leonine was flung backward, his hand shaking as the meteor exploded on him. Jack didn't go after the injured leonine, for this enemy wouldn't go down easily.

Instead, he set his sights on the remaining cultivators.

With a step through space, he appeared behind the healer. His eyes were red and spitting fire. His fist was bloody and hard. Before the elef could turn around, he smashed a punch into the small of her back, breaking her spine and bending her body at an odd angle. He followed up with a second punch from the side, breaking her neck as well.

Before anyone could respond, he teleported again. He appeared in the very middle of the enemy cultivators and started blasting. Meteors flew. Explosions filled the air. Jack had become a beast, an animal of violence, and his Brutalizing Aura made that painfully clear in the enemies' minds.

They defended with all their might. Domains sprang up,

momentum turned and twisted, blood flooded the air, and the despair of cornered animals filled them all with power.

Jack was indomitable. He broke through everything, smashing back the combined might of his enemies. One goatee was dragged into an explosion and incinerated. Another had his face caved in. The third raised her halberd to defend, but Jack's fist broke her wrists before penetrating her chest.

Without their healer, with reduced numbers, and caught off guard, these cultivators were nothing but lambs to the slaughter.

Lightning whipped through the air. The meteors' explosions were overshadowed by sonic booms, and the leading leonine appeared before Jack, his eyes wild and furious. He snapped out a kick on Jack's side, sending him flying far away from the weaker cultivators.

"Support me from a distance!" the leonine commanded. "Let's teach this human his rightful place!"

He became a streak of lightning crossing the sky. Jack tried to defend; he swiped his fist upward but only met air. A foot met his head from behind, violently rocking his neck, and a punch dug deep into his chest. He shot down like a missile, only to land on the leonine's raised knee and get launched back upward.

Jack spat blood. His ribcage was breaking faster than it could be repaired. He forced himself through the pain and into a teleport, narrowly dodging the leonine's claw which swiped right where his neck would have been.

When he reappeared three miles away, he was reeling, almost puking. He couldn't straighten his body. Several of his organs were pierced, and he simply lacked the intact musculature to stand up straight.

But the enemies wouldn't give him time to recover.

Thick claws flew at him, courtesy of the two surviving bearfolk. Despair locked him down, and the sharken appeared below him, fin-blades swiping upward and looking to sever his legs.

Jack's instincts kicked in. His life-or-death battles came to the forefront, as did his many afternoons sparring against the immortals of Huali's estate. His pain disappeared. He registered everything clearly through bloodshot eyes. Stubbornness filled his mind.

He refused to fall.

Coldly, he calculated that he could not dodge all the attacks. He let the claws rake his back to smash a fist at the sharken. His own blood spurted—but the sharken tumbled down, crashing hard into the ground.

The leonine reached him then, flying elbow-first. Jack threw a Meteor Punch. The leonine dodged with the barest of movements, reaching under Jack and punching out. Jack's mind worked in overdrive; he met the punch with his own, knuckles meeting knuckles. The leonine was pushed back, but he used that momentum to wrap around Jack and smash an elbow into his back.

Jack took the hit and held his ground, using his own Dao to keep his body still. He let his domain erupt at full force, suppressing the leonine's speed. Brutalizing Aura filled the air, fueled by Jack's intent to absolutely massacre this opponent. All thoughts of fleeing had left his mind—he would win or die trying.

Supremacy erupted from the leonine's body. He was a god, and Jack was but a man. The Dao Domain of the Fist was pushed back, held at bay by the combined forces of the leonine and the two bearfolk, who were now the only other cultivators remaining.

Jack turned to the leonine and started pummeling. A storm of punches filled the air. His knuckles were hard as steel and fast as vipers. The leonine matched him in kind, retaliating with kicks, elbows, and punches of his own. Space ruptured as they exchanged a hundred blows in the blink of an eye.

This man was nothing like Rufus Emberheart. Rufus had been a sheltered man, faltering at the first sign of danger. This man only got fiercer in the face of death, his strikes sharper, his eyes narrower. He was a trained, experienced warrior, and he was strong.

Far stronger than his level would indicate.

The two bearfolk flanked Jack. Their claws swiped at his back. In despair, he took an elbow to the face to unleash a Meteor Punch right in front of his body, pushing both himself and the leonine away. He teleported yet again, enduring the hellish strain to appear behind one of the bearfolk.

There was not a hint of mercy left inside him. His fist rammed into the bearfolk's skull and shattered it before teleporting near the other bearfolk. Claws came at him. Jack slapped the first strike away, dodged the second, and threw the third himself. His punch carried the essence of Brutalizing Aura; a strike of certain death.

Before his strike could land, the leonine flew at Jack elbow-first. He was lightning-fast. Jack had to pull back or get hit hard.

With a crazed glint in his eye, he carried through with his attack. His fist dug into the bearfolk's chest, obliterating his ribcage and sending him flying into the distance. Before Jack could feel any satisfaction, an elbow smashed into his cheek. Half his teeth flew out. His head shook so hard it almost broke his neck, and he was launched away so fast he broke the sound barrier before smashing through an entire thicket of trees and into the ground.

Instinctively, Jack teleported away the same instant he landed.

The leonine smashed after him almost immediately, nailing his foot into the ground and piercing deep. Cracks spread across the earth. Trees collapsed just by being in the general vicinity.

The leonine looked up, meeting Jack's steady, exhausted gaze. He slowly flew to the same altitude. "You are persistent," he acknowledged. He raised his proud head, mane fluttering in the wind and emitting lightning sparks. "My name is Conrad Lightning. Though you are an inferior species, you have earned the right to fight me. Be proud."

Jack raised his head to the sky and laughed. He was ugly; half his teeth were missing, and his face was covered in blood. His body bent oddly where bones were broken. Due to his many injuries and several back-to-back teleportations, his regeneration had slowed significantly.

Yet, iron flowed in his veins, and his fury was encased in steel.

"What big words!" he exclaimed, shouting at the sky. "I defeated all your soldiers, and *now* you are willing to duel me? Now that I'm exhausted and heavily injured? What a joke you are, leonine! I spit at your entire bloodline! Fight me if you dare, and I will prove that no matter what kind of blood runs through your veins, a coward like you will never be anything more than a coward!"

The leonine's gaze was dark and stormy. With a roar that shook the heavens, he attacked. More lightning descended to augment him.

The two warriors met in midair. Jack sank fully into the battle. His injuries and exhaustion played second fiddle. The opponent became his entire world. Punches flew out, lightning cracked, explosions rumbled. Time slowed to a crawl as they exchanged ten strikes, a hundred, a thousand. Jack became the Iron Fist Style. Knuckles met elbows and forearms, and sank into soft flesh. The leonine's rapid strikes slipped past Jack's defenses, pummeling his already strained body.

The two were equally matched. As the fight dragged on, lightning discharged in the air and explosions filled the sky. They did not move, only ceaselessly exchanged strikes. The forest under them, already a wounded patchwork from the previous bouts, was now completely demolished.

The more they fought, the graver their injuries became. Jack didn't care; he was an avalanche of power, a well of violence. Destroying his opponent came first, and everything else could wait.

But the leonine, as hardened a warrior as he was, did not want to exchange his life for Jack's.

Under the shockwave of an explosion, he pulled back, panting and bleeding. The lightning around him had grown weaker though remained potent. "Take this!" he shouted, pouring all of his remaining energy into his Dao Domain. His eyes had a wicked glint. "With those injuries, I refuse to believe you can command your Dao!"

A curtain of lightning spread out. Supremacy was infused into every spark, every crackle, every air particle. The domain flew at Jack and surrounded him, trying to suffocate him in his weakness.

However, Jack only laughed. "How pathetic you are! A true cultivator does not command their Dao—he embodies it!"

His own domain erupted—and as it did, the supremacy was completely drowned, the lightning was extinguished. The leonine's domain could barely resist Jack's, cracking and shattering in a few instants until the entire world bowed to the Fist. The proud leonine spat out blood as his Dao Tree suffered. He was completely engulfed by Jack's domain, and he was also unable to comprehend this.

"How!" he roared in desperate disbelief. "How can your domain defeat mine? How can you even muster it in this state?"

Jack kept laughing. Each peal of laughter boomed like thunder, echoing across the entirety of his domain. Suddenly, the supremacy in the leonine's heart was gone, and all that remained in its place was fear.

"I told you, leonine," Jack replied, raising a fist. All color and sound disappeared, leaving only his voice. "A coward like you could never be a warrior."

"No!" the leonine screamed. He looked around, scrambling to escape, but everything was darkness. "NO!"

"Stop!" another voice boomed out. Its mere sound shook Jack's domain. Raising his gaze, Jack saw a beam of light shoot out of a distant part of the forest and head toward him at breakneck speed. He inspected it.

Turtler, Level 249
Faction: Animal Kingdom (B-Grade)

"Stay your hand!" the distant figure shouted, still approaching but not actually close enough to stop Jack.

Jack laughed with bitterness. "Time and time again, your Kingdom disappoints me," he shouted back. "Could you be any more shameless? Do you not have a shred of honor!"

An aura of anger reached him from the rapidly approaching figure. "I am a deacon of the Animal Kingdom!" the turtler shouted. "And I command you to stay your hand! Do not dare strike!"

"Command me? Who the hell do you think you are? I will do whatever the fuck I want!"

"STOP!" the deacon shouted.

"WAIT!" the leonine screamed, still trapped in Jack's domain.

"Watch me break this coward!" Jack shouted back, smashing out a full-power Meteor Punch. The world went purple and exploded. The shockwave blew his robes and hair back.

The leonine crossed his arms to defend. Both were broken under the weight of Jack's attack. The power of the meteor carried on and dived into his chest, where it exploded. Strands of golden hair filled the air. Bits and pieces of the leonine flew everywhere. Where he used to stand, there was now only a misshapen mass of flesh and bones.

The approaching deacon saw red. "How dare you!" he shouted, the mere sound of his voice enough to dissipate the clouds.

"Why wouldn't I dare?" Jack shouted back. "He tried to kill me, so I killed him back. Where exactly am I wrong, deacon?"

"When I tell you to do something, you will fucking do it!"

The turtler was upon him by now. He shot out a palm strike, seeming to fill the sky. Jack saw death. He smashed out a Meteor Punch.

His domain cracked and collapsed under the pressure. His Meteor Punch barely managed to delay the palm attack, evaporating the instant it made contact. Jack barely had time to teleport three miles away, further straining his already pushed-to-the-limits body, and the shockwave of the attack alone was enough to make him spit blood and reopen all of his wounds.

Even if he was in top shape, he could never, ever hope to defeat this person. And he wasn't in top shape. He was close to death.

There were several treasures on his body that he could use to escape. However, he wanted to save them for as long as possible. This deacon was strong, but he was a turtler, which meant he was slow. Jack might be able to outpace him.

Therefore, he borrowed the remaining force of the shockwave and ran.

CHAPTER FORTY-SEVEN
A MAD ESCAPE

THE STORM WAS STILL ONGOING. IF ANYTHING, IT HAD GOTTEN EVEN STRONGER.

"Come back here!" the turtler deacon roared, shooting sideways through the sky like a confused comet. His presence was a bright beacon at the edges of Jack's Dao perception.

Jack didn't reply. His full attention was devoted to running faster, to bending the air before him through the Dao of the Fist and achieving just that little bit of extra speed. His entire body felt devoid of energy, his Dao Tree was dry, but he still had to run.

The two of them crossed the sky, disturbing the clouds through mere speed. Jack didn't know how fast he was going, but he'd created two sonic booms, so probably a little faster than twice the speed of sound. This was not his top speed, but he was injured and exhausted. His heart beat in his throat, blood drummed against his temples. He wanted to puke.

The turtler deacon kept pace. Though traditionally a slower species, his superior cultivation more than closed the gap, as the deacon himself was doing to Jack. The distance between them was shortening. Soon, the deacon would be within attack range.

Jack considered using his escape talisman, the one he'd gotten from the library of Huali's estate. He would have to do it sooner or later, as there was no way to outrun this guy. However, he wanted to delay as much as possible. There could be more deacons approaching, and he needed them all to converge on him for his escape to be successful.

"Brat! Hold it right there!" the deacon shouted, growing more enraged by the second.

"If I was going to stop, I would have done it already!" Jack shouted back.

Apparently, that was not the correct response. The deacon raised his hand and slapped it down, unleashing a palm strike. It didn't reach Jack, exploding hundreds of feet behind him, but the ensuing shock-wave ruined his balance and made him slightly slower. Before he could recover, the deacon had closed in.

"I told you to stop!" he shouted, unleashing another strike.

Jack had no choice but to defend. He turned and smashed out the strongest Meteor Punch he could muster, but it wasn't enough. The turtler's palm strike broke through the meteor and crashed on Jack, if weakened by his resistance. He was sent flying into the ground at an angle, carving a line a hundred feet wide and destroying an entire section of the forest.

Jack jumped up and kept flying away. He needed to delay. His Neutron Star Body had helped him survive the strike, but one of his arms hung broken, his current regeneration too slow to help.

At least, the turtler didn't expect such a fast recovery, so he was a second too late to pursue, letting Jack open the gap again.

"BRAT!" he roared, growing angrier every time he failed to stop Jack. "You're courting death!"

Jack ran for his life. The pain and exhaustion were overwhelming him, sinking him into despair. His body was heavy and slow, his limbs refused to obey, the Dao around him felt sluggish. Yet, he persisted. He pushed through it all, his eyes gleaming with a madness so intense it would make Gan Salin proud.

The rain was growing stronger. He must have been flying toward its epicenter. By now, Jack was whipped by winds and droplets far fiercer than what could be found in Earth storms. These wouldn't normally affect him, but he was so badly hurt that even the rain bothered him as it struck his bloodied face. His teeth still hadn't regrown, nor would they if he couldn't find a moment to rest, and his once-beautiful purple robes were now wet with his own blood.

He kept running. A mountain rose before him, its peak covered in snow, and Jack maneuvered around it. Since he was more agile than the turtler, this might give him a chance to open a larger gap.

As soon as he was on the other side of the mountain, the entire thing exploded. The turtler passed right through, having shattered the mountain peak with a single palm, and debris rained toward Jack. It wouldn't reach him, but the sight was enough to make him raise both brows.

This guy destroyed a mountain without breaking pace! Just what kind of monsters did I offend?

"Hold it right there, brat!" the deacon shouted. "The more you make me chase, the more you will pay later!"

Of course, Jack had no intention of stopping. He devoted even more of his being into fleeing. By now, even the pain and exhaustion had faded, replaced by a comforting numbness. All he could do was run. If he stopped, he might not be able to start again.

No matter what he did, slowly but surely, the deacon was gaining ground.

Jack gritted his teeth. His eyes roved around in despair, looking for any avenue of escape. Seeing the stormy, lightning-packed clouds ahead, he turned upward and dove into them. Perhaps they could give him some respite.

"BRAT!" the turtler shouted. "Where do you think you're going?"

Jack had lost sight of the man. He entered the cloud and rushed ahead in a straight line, hoping to escape in the chaos. Instantly, he was beset by the mother of all storms. The humidity was suffocating. Lightning bolts crackled everywhere, and a few even struck him, making his already frayed nerves convulse painfully.

He hoped that, in here, the turtler would lose sight of him.

The clouds exploded. A tremendous impact hit the area just behind Jack, dispersing the storm for several miles. The air sparked with a hundred lightning bolts at once, and the face of the turtler deacon was closer than ever, gazing at him as angrily as before.

"I cannot be stopped by mere clouds, human!" he roared. "Fall already. Shell Sundering Sky!"

Jack didn't see the attack, but he felt the danger. His hair rose. If he was struck this time, he really might die. He mustered every iota of strength he had remaining to teleport away once more, appearing three miles away.

The sky erupted behind him. All Jack saw was the shape of a turtle shell descending from the high heavens, large as a mountain, before a shockwave of titanic proportions hit him in the face. His nose broke. His ribs cracked. One of his legs was bent in an odd direction, and even the Neutron Star Body bent at the power of this peak D-Grade's skill.

Jack was flung away so fast he broke the sound barrier again. He lost consciousness. *No!* he roared inwardly. *I cannot stop here!*

A split-second later, he awoke, still flying. It couldn't have been more than a second, but he'd already crossed a tremendous distance. Luckily, his last-minute teleportation had made the shockwave hit him horizontally instead of smashing him into the ground as it otherwise would have.

Jack turned, borrowed the force of the shockwave, and forced himself to keep going. At the same moment, he reached into his pocket with his remaining hand and fished out the escape talisman—a wooden sign with the word ESCAPE written vertically on it in black ink. He couldn't delay any longer.

The turtler had once again failed to immediately give chase. Seeing Jack wake up and keep running, his eyes widened, and he shouted out, "What the hell are you made of!"

Jack gripped the talisman and prepared to break it. However, he was above the clouds now, and though his vision was foggy, he caught sight of two dots closing in from the distance. *Shit,* he thought with resignation. At the same time, he felt relief. He'd been right to delay. If he had used the talisman at the start, it was likely he would have stumbled upon one of the other enemies.

"Fine!" he shouted to earn some time and let the two new arrivals approach. "Say I surrender. Can you guarantee my life?"

"I guarantee nothing, brat!" the turtler shouted, approaching slowly. His gaze was stormy. A long green robe fluttered over his shell, while the front of his torso was open and covered in a softer exoskeleton. He walked on two legs. "Surrender if you want or keep running. You cannot escape!"

"Oh yeah?" Jack replied. Through his pain, he smirked. The talisman was held tightly in his hand. "Watch me."

The other two people arrived. Jack glimpsed them. Both were peak D-Grades—one a canine, the other a sharken. Of course, they were significantly faster than the turtler, crossing the remaining distance in the blink of an eye.

"What's the matter, turtle?" the sharken glowered, laughing. "Can't you even catch a low D-Grade yourself?"

"Shut up! You know I specialize in defense!" the turtler defended himself.

"So, this is Jack Rust," the canine said, eyeing him almost hungrily. His eyes sparkled with madness. "You killed three of my underlings. I will make sure you—Hmm? Wait. You idiots! That's an escape—"

Jack cracked the escape talisman. Space around him ruptured, and he was sucked inside with much more force than his own teleportations could achieve. He was spat back out a hundred miles away, so far he couldn't even see his previous location. All he spotted of the storm was a smattering of dark clouds on the horizon.

Even a deacon's Dao perception couldn't stretch this far—but that didn't mean Jack was safe. Deacons were fast, and he was gravely injured. Moreover, he had no good way to mask his presence. They would surely search the wider area, and if they chanced upon him...

I must run, he decided with urgency. He flew away. The wind rapped against his broken arm and leg, sending jolts of pain with every movement. Jack had no choice but to grit his teeth and endure. He had no more escape talismans. He needed to open even more distance and find a way to hide himself—maybe dig a hole deep enough that the soil would block the Dao perception of his pursuers.

He even dived into the forest to make himself less visible from afar.

The moment right before he did, he spotted a bedraggled, pained face watching him from afar—a prisoner clad in nothing but a simple gray robe, who ran away the second he caught sight of Jack.

Shit, he cursed. *If the Warden really can see through their eyes, I'm doomed.*

He changed directions and kept going. He maneuvered around trees, grimacing every time a branch struck his body. The miles evaporated under him. A minute later, he felt safe enough to poke his head through the foliage and gaze behind him—where he spotted two lines of light crossing the sky far faster than he could manage, with a third one trailing far behind.

NO! he screamed in his mind. Fuck! No! This is unfair!

There was no chance they'd flown in this direction randomly. They knew exactly where he was. And they were coming straight for him.

Jack flew out of the forest and kept going. He was much faster above the trees than through them, but it didn't change the fact that his pursuers were even faster. The distance was diminishing. Before long, he could make out the sharken and canine's face if he looked back, along with their predatory grins.

"What luck you have, brat!" the canine deacon shouted from afar. "To appear right next to a prisoner of our master! You might have escaped otherwise, you know!"

Next to him, the sharken laughed. "Even the Dao wants you dead, kid. Just surrender already! The more you make us chase you, the more painful your death will be!"

Jack was drowned in injustice. He refused that explanation. How could he possibly be so unlucky as to appear next to a prisoner, of which there were only around a dozen per continent?

Yet, reality was hard to argue with.

Does the universe really want me dead? he wondered. What did I do wrong?

No. It's not my fault. It's the world that is wrong. Fuck luck. Fuck chances. Fuck the world. I will survive this, no matter what.

He still had the storage bead gifted to him by Master Huali. It was capable of releasing a strike with the full force of an early C-Grade. It was his only remaining life-saving measure, and he had to use it now.

He could sense the bead inside his clothes. He could activate it with a thought. The only problem was, he wasn't sure how it worked. All he could assume was that the strike would affect everything in a certain direction, so he should wait for all the deacons to be as clustered together as possible. If a single one of them survived, Jack was dead.

Even the Life Drop didn't matter anymore—using it wouldn't change a thing.

Since there was no point in running, he stopped. He turned to face his pursuers. With an arm and a leg broken, half his teeth missing, his face bloodied, and his body in tatters, he really made for a sorry sight. But he couldn't care less. The Fist wasn't about beauty. It was about power. Survival.

He stared down the three approaching deacons with fire in his gaze, mustering every bit of willpower he possessed. If they attacked with any sort of mind invasion, he had to defend himself long enough to use the storage bead.

The only problem was, the sharken and canine were flying far ahead of the turtler, who was the slowest of the three. Jack would only get one opportunity to bring them down. Could he hold on until the turtler arrived?

There was only one way to find out.

CHAPTER FORTY-EIGHT

IRON WILL, MIND OF STEEL

JACK STOOD IN THE SKY, BLOODY AND VERY HEAVILY INJURED, BUT HIS EYES SPAT fire. Two of the enemy cultivators approached, with the third following far behind. He needed to hold on until they were all together, then use the storage bead to—hopefully—destroy them.

"Oh? The cub is looking for a fight?" the canine asked, his lips curving to reveal two rows of sharp teeth. Foam dripped off them, falling into the forest below. He laughed. "Fine! Let's see what you got!"

He and the sharken broke off to flank Jack. Panic spiked through him. This was terrible. He needed them clustered together.

"Wait!" he shouted, but they ignored him. The canine flew at him from the side. None of them unleashed a domain or suppressive skill; they didn't need to.

With less than a second to think, Jack braced himself. All he could do was wait and hope for an opportunity.

The canine appeared at his side and slapped him. Jack did his best to defend. He held his remaining hand before his face, but he might as well have been sitting still. The deacon's power was overwhelming. Jack was flung away with the sound of cracking bones, and that was only because the canine held back.

He wasn't trying to kill Jack, simply toying with him.

Before Jack could recover, the flat of a fin-blade struck the back of his head. His world went white. His rotation was reversed, sending him flying back at the canine, who brought the heel of his foot down on Jack's chest, nailing him into the ground hundreds of feet below.

Jack didn't feel the rocks breaking under his back. He was on the verge of passing out, yet he persisted. As bitter as being toyed with made him feel, it was a good thing. The more he delayed, the higher his chances of finding an opportunity.

He planned to lay down there and make them approach him, but a foreign power surrounded his body and made it fly up against his will, emerging into the sky again. It was the sharken's mastery over momentum.

"What's wrong, kid?" the canine asked, his eyes flashing with satisfaction. "I thought you were hot shit."

"I—"

Before Jack could reply, another slap came at him out of nowhere. The powers of momentum released him, sending him spinning through the air. His world was white pain.

"Did you really think you just could enter this place and kill our disciples, kid?" the canine said, flashing before Jack and kicking his broken leg. "Did you think we would stand by and watch? That you were smart and we're useless? Is that what you thought?"

He flashed ahead of Jack again, slapping him so hard that a few more teeth went flying. Jack did his best not to scream.

"Don't kill him, senior brother," the sharken said. "The master wants him alive."

"Oh, he'll be alive alright, but does the master need all of his limbs as well?"

Before Jack could react, the canine flashed over him and delivered a bone-breaking stomp into his good leg. The knee bent backward. Jack screamed.

"There," the canine said, "now he can't run. This is good, right?"

The sharken looked on coldly, while Jack experienced the world through a prism of pain.

However, even now, the canine wasn't done. "And is this the arm that killed our little inner disciples?" he asked with a wicked laugh. "Guess he won't be needing it anymore."

Jack's mind was still present, clouded with pain, bitterness, and anger. He really pondered detonating the orb in his robes right now, shattering these enemies along with his own body. The temptation was immense. In fact, he almost did it.

At the last moment, he remembered who he was. He was Jack Rust. He walked the path of the Fist. He was power, iron will, and perseverance. He was triumph in the face of adversity, an unstoppable fist careening ever forward.

Jack Rust could break, but he would never bend.

The enemy could have his arm. He didn't need it. It would regenerate if he survived, and he could move and activate the bead with just the force of his Dao.

He watched coldly as the canine slashed his claws at Jack's shoulder, ripping off the flesh and reaching to the bone. "Shit, kid," he exclaimed, brows raised in surprise, "what are you made of, sheer stubbornness?" A second swipe later, Jack's arm went flying. A stump under the shoulder was all that remained.

And Jack? He did not scream. His expression didn't change in the slightest. His eyes were ice as he stared at the hateful canine.

"What the hell is wrong with you?" he asked, Jack's gaze having hit a nerve, making him uncomfortable. "I just took your arm. Why don't you scream a bit, make me feel like I accomplished something? You don't have to be rude about it."

Jack did not reply. His focus was razor-sharp and aimed at the canine's death. Nothing else mattered.

"Sir," the sharken said again, referring to the canine with deference, "please hold back. The master wants him alive."

A shadow passed through the canine's eyes. For a moment, Jack thought he was about to die, and his awareness closed over the bead—if he was going to die, he was taking all these fuckers with him.

Eventually, the shadow disappeared, and the canine only tsked.

"Fine," he replied, looking away. "This guy is no fun anyway. He doesn't scream. Take him away."

The Dao of Momentum holding Jack in place moved, transporting him far to the side of the two cultivators. The turtler had just arrived then, panting a bit as he approached. "My apologies, sir," he told the canine. "I—"

He did not manage to finish his sentence. A bead was flying between them and Jack. A bead carrying the full power of an early C-Grade cultivator. It unraveled.

Jack's gaze remained icy, but his lips curved upward. *So long, fuckers.*

The three deacons felt the disturbance in the Dao at the same time. Their eyes widened, and to their credit, they reacted appropriately. Three powerful Dao Domains erupted, shielding them all. Their arms blurred as they tried to unleash their strongest skills.

Unfortunately for them, the orb's activation was pretty instant too.

Jack wasn't clear on what exactly happened next. It felt like the sky itself exploded, every cloud and air particle. The world was covered in a blinding white which robbed him of both sight and hearing. All he managed to see was the three domains collapsing. The canine reacted the fastest of the three, rushing behind his two companions while they still tried to muster their skills.

The sharken practically evaporated. The turtler lasted an instant longer, his shell glowing with arcane runes which absorbed part of the energy before he, too, was completely obliterated. The canine was struck last, and reality warped around him again and again. His body was continuously broken down and restored as he flew backward at many times the speed of sound.

When he left Jack's range, he was still whole, though screaming at the top of his lungs. The forest in a large cone had evaporated.

Jack himself was unharmed. The bead had released the entirety of its energy in the direction of his choosing, so that right after the explosion, half the sky was white and the other half undisturbed. There wasn't even any recoil on Jack's side.

In the next moment, however, the heat and light spilled into his side of the sky, robbing him of both sight and hearing. His skin boiled and reddened. Air became fire. Everything was fire, actually, and this was just a limited aftermath of the explosion. He couldn't imagine the power that assaulted the deacons.

Jack's world turned completely white with a hint of green emanating from his body. Under the combined weight of all his injuries, as well as the present explosion, he was finally unable to hold on to that final shred of consciousness.

He fainted.

CHAPTER FORTY-NINE

OPPORTUNITY NEVER CEASES

BROCK STOOD WITH HIS ARMS CROSSED ATOP A SMALL HILL. BELOW HIM, A hundred people were arrayed in lines, split into two groups of fifty. Dog Bro and Girl Bro each stood at the forefront of their armies, both shaking with excitement.

Brock looked over everything coldly. "Begin!" he shouted, and with a loud roar, the two teams of E-Grade cultivators crashed into each other. Magic and projectiles went flying, while the sound of Physical cultivators clashing overshadowed everything but the explosions.

Dog Bro and Girl Bro were at the center of the conflict, circling each other. Before long, illusions and arrows were flying, the two creating a wide area around them where nobody dared trespass.

Brock itched to fight as well, but he kept himself focused. He analyzed the movements of all his bros, looking for weaknesses he could point out later. In the process, he tried to understand them more deeply, see into their individual souls so he could guide them properly as their big bro.

In the process of his training, he'd realized that levels were easy to come by as long as he remained ahead of the power curve, which he certainly was. He was the strongest person around.

The difficult part was the Big Thoughts. Even now, certain thoughts eluded him, which frustrated him to no end. How was he, Brock the Big Bro, unable to comprehend some words inside his head?

Thankfully, he knew the trick. Where words and thoughts were not enough, he had to use actions. That's why he recruited the people of Broville—as the nearby town had been recently renamed—to fight before him, helping him help them get stronger. By exercising the qualities of a bro, and by helping his little bros exercise those qualities as well, his comprehension was becoming more stable—and, as the Bro Code often mentioned, a strong foundation was necessary to plant a strong bananarm tree.

Brock would build the strongest foundation possible. Both for his little bros, himself, and his own big bro, who was undoubtedly training as hard as he possibly could right now while Brock was forced to remain in relative safety.

Father had once abandoned him because of his weakness. He would never give his big bro a reason to do the same. Never. Brock would become strong, because strength and courage were the only ways to lead a happy life.

"Enough!" he roared, bringing both little armies to an instant standstill. Dog Bro and Girl Bro were at a deadlock, one's claws intertwined with the other's bow, but they obeyed their big bro's command and stopped fighting. They would get another chance soon, anyway.

As the hundred people who had just been fighting flocked to Brock to hear his advice, the next hundred prepared themselves. Dog Bro and Girl Bro rushed to the fronts of each army—due to bro seniority, they could fight as many times as they wanted to. And those would be a lot.

Because after these hundred people would come another hundred, and then another. The lines of armies reached all the way from the base of Brock's hill to the gates of Broville.

Brock couldn't count that high... but there were *a lot* of little bros here. It made him proud.

Hopefully, it would satisfy his big bro as well.

When Eva Solvig cultivated, the surroundings in a hundred-mile radius were spontaneously purified. Dirt and other impurities disappeared from rivers, the air turned clean, and the seas became crystal clear.

Some insects and small animals died and disappeared, too.

Perhaps her cultivation was the reason why her starship was spotlessly clean. Or maybe it was her crew, the least of which was at the D-Grade. She used to have an entire fleet, too, but she'd already sent it back. It wouldn't be needed for this mission.

Suddenly, someone knocked on her door. The holy aura permeating the starship and the surrounding space vanished, replaced by the mundane and crooked. Eva's eyes opened slowly, revealing the last hints of a vanishing world of purity.

"Enter," she said.

A man entered the room, respectful without being too subservient. He was Erdran Vostil, her strongest follower. Already at the peak of C-Grade within a millennium of life, he was very promising. He'd followed her for five hundred of those thousand years.

"Commander," he said, bowing lightly. "We still have no news of Jack Rust. His trail vanishes at the Eternal Gate. We believe that he and the Exploding Sun's second deacon snuck out through their own space-warping starship."

"Have you carefully scanned the planet? He could be hiding somewhere in there, right under our noses."

"We have, Commander."

"And did you check the teleportation records? Perhaps they left disguised under someone else's guarantee."

"We checked, Commander. Besides their arrival, where Jack Rust was disguised, there were no other records of disguises being used—and, after inspecting the security myself, I do not believe it would have gone unnoticed. The Animal Kingdom can be meticulous when it wants to."

"Hmm. What if they used wards to hide inside some merchant's cargo? There are many of them."

She gazed out of the window, at the gigantic brown orb that floated a few hundred miles away—the planet called Eternal Gate.

"While that is possible, Commander, we find the use of their own starship more plausible." Due to his seniority and strength, he'd earned the standing to converse with Eva. "Only trustworthy merchants go through this planet."

"When you've lived for as long as I have, Erdran, you learn that trust is an ephemeral notion." Her lips curved into a grin. "Do you have a list of everyone present on the planet within a week of Jack Rust's arrival?"

"I do."

"Recruit some local agents to go through it extensively. Find anyone connected to Jack Rust or Shol Pesna, or anyone with even the slightest reason to act against the Animal Kingdom. Interrogate them, starting from most to least suspicious, and we may find the answer we seek. After all, if they intended to just disappear in space, why do it here, of all places?"

Her follower bowed. "As you wish, Commander."

"Oh, don't give me that tone. I know it's a lot of work, but that's precisely why you exist. Dismissed."

Still bowing, Erdran left, letting Eva Solvig return to her meditation. Since she would be stuck here for a while, she might as well use the time.

While Jack was fighting for his life, and Brock was doing his best to grow stronger, on a very distant planet, a man was sitting in his office and quietly wallowed in despair.

Edgar wanted to help, too. He just couldn't. Not as a mage of awe. Not as a cripple.

He stood up to pace around, noticing his messy desk, his dirty floor. Once upon a time, cleaning them would take but a thought, but not anymore. Now, it would take work, and he just couldn't bring himself to care.

Why am I this useless? he thought, itching from his own unkempt beard. I am a waste of my titles.

A coward.

One of his legs stepped on a sheet of paper lying on the floor, inscribed with runes and sigils. The other almost stepped *through* the floor before he stopped it.

A coward for many reasons, Edgar thought, smiling bitterly at the sight of his own leg; a reminder of everything he'd lost. Not only can I not fight, but when I lost a duel to the death, I did not die... I couldn't even do that properly.

Starry orange dust made up his right leg. Alexander had cleaved it off during their duel, making blood and flesh rain down on the Forest of the Strong.

By all accounts, Edgar should have won that duel. His opponent had just broken through, not yet stabilized. Yet, his Dao wasn't as suited for battle as Alexander's, and neither was his mind. Additionally, he hadn't had time to grow familiar with his new powers, and his fighting style required careful planning and preparation.

He'd lost decisively.

With the whole world watching, Alexander took Edgar's leg and honor. Right as he was about to strike the killing blow, the wizard's falling body reached the top of the tree line, technically entering the forest. Sparman shot up like a missile, protecting Edgar and saving him from certain death. Alexander flew away laughing.

It hadn't been their proudest moment. Harambe chided Sparman and suggested that Edgar should end himself, but he lacked the courage. He was not a warrior; a warrior's pride was wasted on him. Shamefully, he lived on.

And the entire world called him a coward. Even he said that word to the mirror many times. That was his life now. He had to get used to it.

I hate myself, he thought, raising his gaze from the leg he'd lost. *I hate my Dao.*

And in return, his Dao hated him. It was broken. An alien heap that still existed inside him but barely responded. Once, he'd demolished an entire section of the Ice Peak palace. Now, he couldn't even summon the wind to clean his room.

Everyone is dying around me, he repeated for what felt like the millionth time. Everyone is fighting for freedom. And what am I doing? I sit in this room and cry over a broken path.

Maybe I'm the broken one. And rightfully so.

He made it to the window and opened it, the clean breeze reminding him that his office harbored a persistent odor. He ought to let the cleaners in, but even the thought of seeing another person scared him. He hadn't opened the door in a week.

The professor will be worried, he reminded himself, then shook his head. The professor was a purpose-oriented individual, and she had more important things to worry about than the useless fool living in her attic.

Once useless, always useless, he thought, feeling a new wave of bitterness wash over him. Perhaps Mom and Dad were right to ignore me. I didn't deserve their attention. Even when I was given power, all I achieved was to turn it pacifistic amidst a war I have every responsibility to assist in. Everyone believed in me, and yet... I only exist to disappoint.

There were times, like now, when Edgar doubted his Dao. It was the path of his heart—but what use was a heart when all your friends were dead?

What I wouldn't give to change my path, he thought, tightening his lips. To help out, even if it meant severing my own heart... But I know it's impossible.

"Is it, really?"

The voice came abruptly. So abruptly that Edgar jumped and screamed, sticking his back to the wall next to the window.

His door sure as hell hadn't opened, but someone stood before it, at the very entrance of the room. It wasn't human—it was a humanoid creature with gray skin, bat wings, red horns, spikes on its spine, and long, sharp ears. Its hands ended in short, sharp claws.

"Who are you?" Edgar shouted before thinking to inspect the creature.

Echidna Devil, Level ??? (D-Grade)

A creature manifested from an extremity of the Dao of Law. It is compelled to always keep its word, but it also gains extreme power against anyone who breaks their word to it. Therefore, it enjoys luring cultivators into craftily-worded contracts and deals that end up with it having the upper hand.

"You're an immortal!" Edgar shouted again, pointing a shaky finger at the devil. "That's— You shouldn't be here. The Star Pact forbids it."

"The Star Pact is written on my left ass cheek," the devil replied in a raspy, oddly cheerful voice. "More importantly, you should stop shouting. If I hadn't isolated this room already, people would be rushing over."

"Isolated this room? How did you do that?"

"That's the first thing you ask?" The devil laughed. "I swear, you wizards are all the same."

Edgar shriveled up on the wall, his heart still swelling with fear. This was a D-Grade creature. It could end him at a thought. "Who are you?" he asked in a trembling voice.

"Finally, you got the right question!" the devil exclaimed, clapping its clawed hands. "Though the real question here is... Who are *you*?"

"I'm Edgar. Edgar Allano."

"No, you stupid boy," the devil replied, laughing again, "who *really* are you? Are you a coward who can only tremble in an office stinking of sweat while his friends and family are dying? Or, perhaps, are you someone who would sacrifice a lot of things to help?"

Edgar's mind was finally coming up to speed. Using his high Intelligence, he connected the dots. "You want to offer me a contract," he said.

"I prefer to call it an opportunity," the devil corrected him, summoning a parchment between his fingers. It was long and red-tinted—and full of tiny letters. "What do you think?" he asked with a conspiratorial grin. "Are you interested?"

Edgar gulped.

CHAPTER FIFTY
THE REWARD OF SUFFERING

Jack awoke to the low crackling of fire. He tried to jump up straight, only for blazing pain to assault every corner of his body. His limbs refused to obey his commands. His brain spun into battle mode.

"Easy, Jack," a voice came from the side, deep yet soothing. "It's all good. You're safe."

"Shol?" Jack spoke through gritted teeth. "What's happening?"

"You're injured." The monk came into Jack's field of vision, leaning over him and hiding the ceiling. "But safe. You destroyed the people after you. With a little bit of time, your broken limbs will heal as well."

At this, Jack remembered. His battle against the eleven inner disciples, his desperate escape from the three deacons, and his final ditch effort to survive. His memories cut off when the world turned white.

"How did you find me?" he asked.

"I was already rushing over. News of your appearance had begun to spread, so it wasn't difficult to realize what was about to happen." His gaze darkened. "But I was too late. I'm sorry, Jack. If not for my tardiness, you wouldn't have had to go through this."

Jack chuckled, then grimaced as his ribs scratched the inside of his skin. "It's fine," he said. "This was my fault and my battle."

"Protecting you was my job."

"I was the one who told you to go away. Don't beat yourself up."

"Still... Anyway. I just followed the world-ending light to find you. When I did, you were unconscious on top of a burning tree, with fifty miles of forest ahead of you wiped from the face of Hell."

"Really?"

"Really." At this, he finally revealed a hint of mirth. "I don't know what you did to those guys, or what kind of treasure you used, but you sure made a scene. Early C-Grade?"

Jack nodded. "Master Huali gave it to me through Okmer. A bead that could unleash the power of an early C-Grade—but only once. I'm out of protective treasures, Shol. My escape talisman was wasted, and the bead is gone. All I have left is myself."

"And me," Shol pointed out proudly. "Since you've been discovered, free time is over. We're sticking together like ass and underwear."

"Ew. Don't say it like that."

"I will speak however I want. Now. As I said, you've been discovered. I haven't, so we still have some time, but we should hurry up and get the hell out of here. Our hunting so far should be enough."

"Leave? But Shol—"

"Silence. No matter how desperate you are, there is a line between bravery and foolishness, and you're already past it."

"That's not what I was going to say." Jack coughed. "We should obviously leave Hell. However, what about Dordok? Did you discover his location?"

Shol remained silent. His small eyes hounded Jack's, blankly snooping for his intentions.

"I did," he finally admitted. "He's in one of the late D-Grade hunting zones. Zone 17, to be precise."

"Then, since we're leaving anyway, we might as well rescue him."

"You have no idea what you're talking about. It's a late D-Grade zone. Even if there were no deacons hunting us, we would need to face teams of late immortals. What makes you think we can handle them?"

"You're a peak D-Grade, and stronger than most, too. I think we would win. Maybe someone would escape, but we don't care too much about that anymore."

"Oh, we don't? So when the Warden catches wind of our location and sends a dozen deacons after us, you will be the one to handle them, yes?"

"They would need some time to arrive. I'm sure we can grab Dordok and escape before that."

"And where does that certainty stem from? Your big head, which is the only part of your body currently working? Or deep knowledge of our escape route, which you do not yet have?" Shol shook his head with disapproval. "I promised you that we'd save Dordok if possible, and I intend to honor that, but I will not risk my life and the honor of our master for a stranger."

"I will. He's no stranger to me."

"You infuriate me." Shol swiped his sleeves, walking away. Jack could now only see a rock ceiling. "Take some time and heal up. It's weird talking to someone who can't move. In the meantime, consider our situation, and so will I."

"You got it."

Jack didn't begrudge Shol. He understood. If he was in Shol's shoes, he would harbor the exact same doubts. However, he also understood himself. Dordok had saved Jack's life and been very kind to him. His imprisonment was all due to Jack tricking him.

The problem is, how do I convince Shol... Jack thought, attempting to shake his head and instantly regretting it. Pain still flared across his body with every movement. He could feel power trickling into him as his Dao Tree absorbed and converted the surrounding Dao, but he was so wrung out that regeneration would take hours—not to mention that broken limbs took a hell of a lot of energy to heal.

Which meant he had time.

Finally, Jack turned to the blinking exclamation mark in the corner of his vision, willing it open. It was time to review his System notifications from the battle.

Level-up! You have reached Level 165.
Level-up! You have reached Level 166.

...

Level-up! You have reached Level 179.

There were more screens, but he stopped there due to sheer surprise.

179! That's fifteen levels!

Jack struggled to believe that. He opened his status screen, inspecting it with eyes wide open.

Name: Jack Rust
Species: Human, Earth-387
Faction: Bare Fist Brotherhood (D)
Grade: D
Class: Cosmic Fist (King)
Level: 179

Strength: 1040 (+)
Dexterity: 995 (+)
Constitution: 1015 (+)
Mental: 120 (+)
Will: 190 (+)
Free Points: 150

Dao Skills: Meteor Punch III, Iron Fist Style III, Neutron Star Body II, Brutalizing Aura II, Space Walk II
Daos: Dao Tree of the Fist, Dao Root of Indomitable Will (fused), Dao Root of Life (fused), Dao Root of Power (fused), Dao Root of Weakness (fused)
Titles: Planetary Frontrunner (10), Planetary Torchbearer (1), Ninth Ring Conqueror, Planetary Overlord (1)

It was true. 179! That was almost at the middle of the D-Grade!

Jack wanted to jump and cheer but could do neither. He settled for a strained smile. Looks like the System awarded me levels for the three deacons I killed... Or was it two? I didn't see the canine dying.

A flash of hatred. Jack felt the intense desire to harm that man but pushed it down. The time would come—if he wasn't dead.

He carried on to his last notification.

Congratulations! Iron Fist Style II → Iron Fist Style III
Iron Fist Style III: You have surpassed the limitations of mortal forms of combat. Your body is infused with the Dao of the Fist. Reality bends before the Dao.

The Iron Fist Style is the spine of its user. It allows you to combine all your skills, weapons, and resources, integrating them seamlessly into one fighting style.

There wasn't any difference in the skill description. Honestly, Jack hadn't even noticed a particular difference when the skill evolved either, to the point where he couldn't pinpoint the exact moment in the fight when it happened.

Well, I've had this skill since the start of the E-Grade. At this point, I feel like it's just being dragged along by everything else. Maybe it will upgrade to a different skill soon. Not that it's holding me back, but it's long overdue.

There was also plenty of recovery time ahead. His free attribute points could wait; he was still following the 8-1-1 scheme, but maybe Shol would have some new advice on the subject.

Therefore, Jack decided to relax and meditate. He closed his eyes, easily sinking into his soul world, a process that had now become as comfortable as breathing.

The moment he appeared in there, he was suffocating. The density of the Dao had fallen precipitously, and the Dao Tree was siphoning everything in. Copy Jack stood on the index finger, next to the tree, looking upset. He was cupping his hands and using them as an oar to try and push the Dao into the tree faster.

It was completely useless, of course.

"There you are," Jack said, flying over and landing next to Copy Jack. "Don't think that being adorable is going to save you. I almost died out there. *We* almost died. I had all my limbs broken and was beaten to within an inch of my life. I had to spend all my protective treasures." He crossed his arms, glaring at Copy Jack. "What do you have to say for yourself?"

Copy Jack stopped oaring. He looked down sheepishly, sneaking glances at Jack like a guilty child.

"Don't just look at me," Jack said. "I know you can speak."

"Sorry..." Copy Jack finally said. His voice came oddly, like he was still getting used to it.

"Don't just be sorry. Be better," Jack scolded him. "You're important, Copy Jack. There is far more to you than just being a training partner. You are my friend and companion. We co-inhabit this soul. We share a Dao Tree. I know you are still very young, but you cannot afford to play around like a child. The least I need from you is to act seriously. No more touching without knowing or any other bullshit. Do you understand me?"

Copy Jack stared at the ground and nodded. Jack really tried to remain angry, but he just couldn't. His glare mellowed.

"Alright. I'll hold you to your word," he said, sighing. "Now, did anything else happen when you touched the Life Drop? In you, I mean. You were grabbing your heart before. Are you okay?"

Copy Jack nodded. "Okay..." he said, drawing out the word a bit.

Jack only half-believed him, but that was good enough for now. If Copy Jack had suffered internal injuries and didn't want to admit it, so be it.

"Be careful," was all he said. He then walked past him to the tree and inspected it.

Something had clearly gone wrong before, and it wasn't only Copy Jack's fault. The Life Drop had attracted him. Influenced him. And Jack intended to get to the bottom of that right now.

He laid a hand on the tree, touching it gently. The beginnings of bark were still there, forming the broken outline of a door. They were even more complete than before. When more bark formed and the door was complete, could he open it?

Or would that be too magical?

What kind of thing is a door on my Dao Tree, anyway? Jack asked himself. Is that normal? Does everyone get it? Is it because of my perfect foundation, or something to do with the Life Drop? Or is it just a big coincidence, and what I see as a door are just random patterns?

In a moment of genius, he knocked against the "door," but nothing happened.

Worth a try.

Since there seemed to be no answers there, he turned his attention to the Life Drop buried just under the tree. He bent down and stared at it intently.

No alien influence tried to take over his mind. There was no odd draw or engrossment. For all intents and purposes, it was just glowing dirt, hiding inside it an ocean of untapped life energy.

"Why did you seduce my buddy?" Jack mumbled at the drop, almost touching his face to the soil to inspect it better. The Life Drop did not respond.

He tried to slip his perception inside it and succeeded without difficulty. The veil was parted, he snuck in, and came face-to-face with the unlimited ocean of energy that had always been there. He tried to dive deeper, and all sense of direction was lost, and he was swimming in an infinite pool. There was no resistance, but also no sense of progress.

Furthermore, the deeper he pushed with his perception—or, at least, in the direction which felt "deeper"—the fainter his connection to it became. Once he pushed too far, his sliver of perception disappeared, hidden behind a dense ocean of life. Jack was once again left at the shores, capable of nothing but watching the Life Drop.

Maybe if I find a safe place, I can try to exhaust its energy, he considered before immediately realizing that was too much of a scorched-earth idea. Is there really something down there? Or is it just life energy to the core? Could it be that Copy Jack was just fascinated by the Life Drop because he's a child?

Frustrated, Jack shook his head. He had questions, but no way to get answers. At the very least, he resolved to ask Shol about the strange bark patterns later.

He stood and turned to Copy Jack.

"I will go meditate now," he said. "If you feel the Life Drop attempting to influence your mind again, let me know immediately. Somehow. And no matter what happens... Please, try not to mess up again. I cannot survive another hunt like the previous one."

Copy Jack nodded sheepishly, and Jack, after throwing the Life Drop a last, warning glance, left the soul world. He opened his eyes briefly in reality to find out his limbs were nowhere close to healing, then closed them again and sank deep into meditation.

The battle and hunt before had been hellish, but struggle was the breeding ground of insight. He had a lot of things to consider. Dao things.

CHAPTER FIFTY-ONE
SQUEEZING WATER OUT OF A ROCK BOTTOM

What was the Dao?

Jack reiterated his understanding of the world, getting himself in the mood with the already cemented knowledge.

The Dao is the world itself. It is the essence of reality and the totality of existence. It is everything.

The Fist is one of the infinite manifestations of the Dao. It is about shooting ever forward, laughing as you advance, never stopping or slowing until the end, never bending. Staying loyal to yourself and being free.

Aligning his perspective with that of the Fist, Jack went over the previous battle. When the eleven inner disciples appeared, he stood tall and faced them. He took them down methodically, dismantling their team, and emerged victorious from unfavorable circumstances.

What really resonated with the Fist, was Jack's mental state during that battle. The resolve he'd felt, along with the cold intent to battle and kill. Deep inside, he was proud—he'd represented the Fist well. In the vacuum of battle, everything else fled his mind, leaving only the essence of the Fist, bare and clear. Battle was the time he was closest to his Dao, as well as the best opportunity to accrue insights.

Facing the eleven disciples, Jack had been an incarnation of the Dao system he'd established as his Dao Tree. He embodied both the Dao of the Fist and his various Dao Roots. That had been a step in the right direction. It strengthened his grasp of the Fist—his Fist—paving the way for more insights later on.

Facing the three deacons, however, the sensation was different. He was the weaker party. So much weaker that fighting was hopeless, and the best course of action was fleeing.

On a superficial level, retreat was not a part of the Fist. However, Jack was past the superficial level. It wasn't about actions anymore. It was about intent. The Fist was a state he could put himself in, and when he did, the decisions he made were naturally aligned with the essence of his Dao.

In this case, retreating had been the right choice, because the intent behind it was a fighting one. He was fleeing from suicide, and would return when the time was right.

He turned his mind to the pursuit of the three deacons.

While escaping from the turtler, he felt helpless. He was too weak to face the other man in battle, and he was too slow to run away. Everything he tried was in vain.

When he used the talisman to escape and a twisted coincidence prevented him, despair and bitterness filled him. It was unfair. A situation he could do nothing about, because he was weak.

The greatest insights came later—when he was forced to endure the canine's sadism. He was captured and surrounded by enemies, unable to escape, unable to retaliate. He was at their mercy. When they crippled him, all he could do was grit his teeth and endure. When they mocked him, he had nothing to say, because he was weak.

It had been terrible.

Weakness.

That was the main feeling, and it had come even more intensely than ever before. In all the previous instances of weakness he'd experienced, none had been as direct. The Planetary Overseer had suppressed him, but it was an indirect thing. Rufus Emberheart and Lord Longsword had pressured him, but never physically, at least not to that extent.

When he was tortured by the canine deacon, it was the weakest he'd ever felt. It was a feeling so deep that it threatened to upturn his psyche and shake his unwavering resolve. Even now, Jack could sense the influence of that weakness, a little imp gnawing away at the roots of his character. It was a feeling so intense it wouldn't go away for some time.

Of course, Jack had resisted it and still was, but in hindsight, even he had given in to the weakness for a moment. When the canine first started abusing him, he had really considered detonating the bead still inside his robes, destroying both himself and the enemy.

That had been a weak thought, borne of despair and bitterness. It was the opposite of his previous escape, actually—it resembled the way of the Fist, but only superficially. He'd let his emotions get the better of him. A real warrior—a real fist—would never entertain that thought. They would endure everything stoically until it was the best time to act. Only when death was certain would they unhesitatingly detonate the bead, taking the enemy along in the other world.

Jack was shaken by the realization of his momentary weakness. At the same time, he was relieved. It proved he was not yet a perfect cultivator of the Fist, and it showed him a flaw he could fix. A crack in his heart.

Part of his meditation session would be devoted to patching that up, reliving that moment again and again until he was fully in control of himself. However, every crack he experienced in his soul was a human weakness he understood intimately. He could weaponize it. What greater path to power than turning one's weakness into strength?

Before patching that crack, Jack dove into it. He let himself experience it fully. In the safety of his own mind, he relived his moment of torture and gave in to the weakness, letting it encompass him.

He saw himself screaming; saw his mind go blank, unable to endure the pain. He detonated the bead and felt the sweet release, along with the bitter hatred he inflicted on his tormentors.

When the moment was over, he experienced it again. And again. And again. He wanted to understand that feeling of weakness as intimately as he possibly could, uncaring about the pain it caused to his real mind. His soul was undermined, but he was confident it would not harm him long-term. Understanding was important. He might not get this opportunity again.

Little by little, he grew more familiar with the feeling. He let it worm inside him, let it imprint its brand upon him. When it was finally complete, he took it all in, understanding it fully—and then burned it off the surface of his heart forever.

Jack's eyes snapped open, filled with new light. His Dao of Weakness had taken a step forward.

Congratulations! Brutalizing Aura II → Brutalizing Aura III

Brutalizing Aura III: The fear of death is a primal instinct of all living creatures. By deeply understanding helplessness, you can use your aura to imprint your opponents with intense fear and a deep understanding of their own weakness, an effect which will persist in time.

Significantly weaker enemies will be paralyzed or have their wills broken. Enemies of comparable strength to you will be severely weakened, and their Dao may be temporarily suppressed. Significantly stronger enemies will be unaffected. Additionally, the fear of your enemies feeds into your own power, enhancing you as you affect more and stronger enemies with Brutalizing Aura.

This skill should be exercised with caution, as it has a wide range and can traumatize cultivators for life.

That was a long-ass description. There were no italics either, as it had been completely rewritten from the skill's previous version. Jack reread it a few times, making sure he understood.

It sounded strong. Very strong. Especially the warning at the end and the mention of persisting effects.

Am I a weapon of mass destruction? Jack asked himself. *I should be careful with that thing. The warning has merit.*

He also focused on the skill's practical aspects.

Paralyzing weaker opponents and severely weakening those of similar strength to me... That sounds awfully convenient. If I face someone on my level but they don't have a similar aura skill, I could beat them with far more ease. And the section about absorbing the fear of others to strengthen myself... That's badass.

Wait. I've had this thought before. Was that a part of the skill already?

Checking the previous version's description, he found that enhancing himself with the fear of others had already been there. He'd just forgotten about it.

That explains how I beat those eleven inner disciples. I thought I'd stand no chance, but I won. And with this new upgrade... Brutalizing Aura is now a force to be reckoned with.

I wonder, is it my most powerful skill after Meteor Punch?

The more he considered the question, the more he realized that all his skills were powerful. He only had a few of them, but each helped him greatly.

The effectiveness of Meteor Punch went without saying—it was his bread and butter. Neutron Star Body gave him tremendous endurance and durability, as well as extreme regeneration. Without it, he would have died five times over in the previous battle. Iron Fist Style let him utilize his powers effectively, essentially multiplying the power he could exhibit, and Space Walk gave him the much-needed utility to turn the tables in almost every scenario. As for Brutalizing Aura, it had proven its worth in this battle. It basically guaranteed he couldn't be bullied by numbers.

Oh wow, I'm actually pretty strong!

The understanding of how overpowered he was helped burn away the last of the weakness he'd let into himself, raising him back to his old self. The emotional residue of his recently torturous experience had been completely turned into power. Stepping off of that, Jack spent another hour reviewing his previous moment of weakness with new eyes, making sure to train himself off that reflexive despair.

If he wanted to be a true warrior, he needed full control over himself no matter what happened.

When he finally opened his eyes, he felt like a new, stronger, more mature man. Even his limbs were somewhat repaired, if still in pain, and his Dao Tree had managed to refill itself a bit. Torchlight flickered on the walls as Jack stood, inspecting the place he was in.

It was a cave little more than a hole in the rock. Ten feet away, a passage was angled upward into the rock, heading who knows where. Jack could feel no breeze coming from it.

Spreading his spiritual perception, all he saw was rock for a hundred feet in every direction. Penetrating it was hard. Eventually, he reached the air, finding to his amazement that he was deep inside...

"A mountain," Shol said, opening his eyes from where he sat cross-legged in another corner of the cave. "I dug a hole into the mountain core and blocked the tunnel with boulders. It's not the world's best hiding place, but it should do."

"Smart," Jack commented, filing away this idea for later.

"Are you healed already?" Shol asked.

"Not fully, but I'm serviceable. I also have a bunch of attribute points to distribute; should I keep going with the 8-1-1 scheme you suggested when I was F-Grade, or should I try something new?"

"8-1-1 is fine. You're a well-rounded Physical fighter, so any more specialization is unnecessary. Unless you feel the opposite, in which case, have at it."

Jack didn't need to think too much. "Balance is fine. It's worked out well for me so far."

Quickly opening his status screen again, he allocated the hundred and fifty free points in such a way that the values of his Physical, Mental, and Will attributes followed a roughly 8-1-1 distribution.

All in all, he allocated thirty points in Mental, bringing it up to 150, then put the rest into the Physical sub-stats, trying to balance them out.

Strength: 1135
Dexterity: 1140
Constitution: 1135
Mental: 150
Will: 190

He was missing five subpoints from complete balance, but he'd be damned if he let that ruin his mood—or if, god forbid, he allocated his stats to non-round numbers, like 1118.

Ew.

The familiar surge of strength lightened his mood. His mind gained clarity, his muscles compacting, his skin growing tougher, his control over his body refined.

"So," Jack said when he was done tooting his own horn, "have you come up with a way to save Dordok?"

Shol gave him an intense gaze, fully understanding Jack's meaning—he was insisting on the rescue mission.

"I contacted Vegna," he said. "She's our getaway route. We will use your starship—the *Bromobile,* yes?—to teleport a few planets away, where her starship is lying in wait. She will then utilize a large Dao Battery to teleport several times in a row, hopefully losing all pursuers."

"Very nice of her. But wouldn't that reveal her true colors to the Animal Kingdom?"

"She's been planning to cut ties with them for a while. It's okay; the Exploding Sun will protect her and her crew afterward... but yes. It *is* very nice of her."

"Hmm. Are all starship captains that kind?"

"Absolutely not. I only know of two; Vegna and your friend, Dordok, allegedly."

"Not allegedly. I know it."

"I'll believe it when I see it." Shol cracked a strained smile. "She will be in position in roughly two days, and she can remain there for at least a week, provided she's not discovered by any patrols. When she's ready, since you're so stubbornly insistent on it, we can give rescuing your friend a shot and teleport immediately afterward."

Jack beamed a large smile. "Thanks, Shol!"

"You are very, very welcome." He sighed. "But know it will be difficult. I have a way to free him from the Warden's influence, but it takes time. The entire planet will know our location the moment we approach Dordok. We may need to defend for a little bit."

"No problem. I can take on one entire late D-Grade immortal."

Shol deadpanned at Jack. "Okay."

A moment passed.

"So, uh, what do we do now?" Jack asked.

"Go cultivate in your corner, Jack. Get yourself in fighting shape. In two days, we're going after your friend."

CHAPTER FIFTY-TWO

FIGHTING A LATE IMMORTAL

JACK AND SHOL PROWLED THROUGH A DENSE JUNGLE.

Although, *prowled* was an understatement. They shuttled through at hundreds of miles per hour, dodging trees and animals as if everything else moved in slow motion. A lion tried to jump out of the way, only for Jack to circle around it regardless.

"I wonder how it feels to live on the same planet as your ancestors," Shol said. "I see lions here. The leonines originate from them."

"It's not that weird," Jack replied. "We come from monkeys, and my Earth is full of them—kind of. We just never give it a second thought."

"Hmm. I guess."

Shol glanced at his wrist, where he wore a clock-like device whose surface resembled a scanner. A blinking dot was slowly but surely approaching the center. "We're getting close," he said. "On your guard. This could get messy."

"You got it."

They fell silent, only the sound of splitting air accompanying them. Thanks to their speed, even the animal roars sounded odd. The terrain around them had transitioned from a forest to a thick jungle, making its navigation difficult and time-consuming.

Before long, sounds of explosions came from up ahead.

"Careful," Shol instructed telepathically. "I think someone is after him."

"What careful? We have to hurry!" Jack responded, accelerating ahead and taking charge. Gritting his teeth, Shol followed.

The explosions kept growing stronger. A shockwave crashed down, flattening an entire area of the jungle around them and heavily shaking the ground under their feet.

With the surrounding trees demolished, they had a clear view of the sky. Jack drew a sharp breath. Captain Dordok was there. His steel club was held high, emanating a formless, intimidating aura, and his once kind face was warped into an angry scowl.

He swiped once. The very air was pushed away from his club, creating a vacuum. A wide shockwave spread out, impacting the distant jungle and flattening another part of it.

Four cultivators stood against Dordok. One was a goatee—a goat person—wielding a large, golden halberd. The second was a bearfolk with patches of gray on his fur and scars all over. The third was a human, surprisingly, wearing long black robes, and the fourth was a one-eyed ogre just like Dordok, wielding a greatsword that emanated an aura of brutality.

Jack inspected them all.

Goatee, Level 236
Bearfolk, Level 221
Human (Parniol), Level 240
Cyclops, Level 230

All of them were in the late D-Grade, and all shared the same title: Eighth Ring Conqueror. Each of these four individuals had once been a dominant Lord in Trial Planet.

Jack also inspected Dordok, whose level was finally visible.

Cyclops, Level 245
Faction: -
Title: Far Traveler

"Traitor!" Dordok roared, bringing his club down. The ensuing shockwave cracked the air as it traveled, except it was off the mark. It simply passed by the opposing cultivators, ruffling their robes before digging a deep crater into the earth.

"You are out of your mind," the other cyclops replied calmly, hefting his greatsword. "Only an idiot fights for a lost cause."

"A powerful idiot. ORAAA!" He swung down again, also missing.

"What's wrong with him?" Jack asked, narrowing his eyes.

Shol pointed at the human man wearing black robes. "It's that guy. I can sense he's up to something. Humans in the Animal Kingdom are generally Mental or Will cultivators."

"We should help."

"Absolutely. Let's go."

Due to the distance, the other cultivators hadn't noticed them yet. That was about to change. Jack and Shol pushed powerfully off the ground, shooting up like missiles—one left a purple trail, the other an orange one. The moment they rose above the tree line, eight eyes—three pairs from the enemy cultivators and two eyes from Dordok and the other ogre put together—fell on them.

"Who's there!" the human shouted, turning an open palm toward them. Jack's world turned dark. He was trapped in an endless night where his eyes were useless, and even his Dao perception was baffled by bodiless impressions. He was lost and alone. "State your identity!" the human roared again, the sound clear despite Jack's blindness.

An explosion of power came from his side. The night shivered and cracked, rays of light slipping through the darkness. Jack followed Shol's lead, unleashing his Dao as powerfully as possible. The outline of a fist appeared around him, purple and almost corporeal, and with a shout, he shattered the other man's domain.

The sky returned to normal, revealing a man with a line of blood flowing down his nose. He gritted his teeth as he noticed the fist outline around Jack. "You are..."

"Jack Rust!" Dordok interrupted him. His one eye was widened to the extreme, and his mouth was hanging open. Apparently, the night around him had also shattered. "Level 179? How!"

"It's a long story, Captain!" Jack replied with a big smile. "I'll tell you later. For now, I'm here to rescue you!"

Dordok stared incredulously before his jaw hardened, and he raised his club again. "Lies. You're an illusion. *How dare you intrude my mind!*"

"No wait, Captain, I really am—"

Before Jack could finish speaking, Dordok swung at them. The wind around them disappeared. An infinitely powerful strike came crashing at his head, filling the entire world. He crossed his arms to defend.

Shol appeared before him. He unleashed a palm strike. Palm met club, and the ensuing explosion was enough to make Jack's head ring and obliterate a large swathe of forest under them. The club was stopped in its tracks, but Shol slid back in the air a few feet.

"Your captain is no weakling, Jack," he said with a hint of joy. "Why didn't you tell me?"

"How was I supposed to know!" Jack replied, still awestruck by the collision before him. Either of those strikes would have sent him flying for miles.

"You're strong," Dordok declared, narrowing his eyes at Shol. "Too strong for an illusion. Who are you?"

"Shol Pesna, former second deacon of the Exploding Sun. And you?"

"Dordok. Captain Dordok for you. What are you doing with my crew member?"

"Probably committing suicide, but we'll see. He dragged me here to save you."

Dordok still looked at Jack with intense disbelief. It was understandable. Only a few months ago, Jack had been a greenhorn barely into the E-Grade. And now he was in the mid D-Grade? If he told this to anyone, people would laugh at him!

Without a word, Dordok turned and struck at the four opposing cultivators. With the wizard's influence gone, his club fell true, heading for the cyclops that stood in the middle of the enemy group.

A greatsword swung upward. The other cyclops roared, and the two weapons clashed in a terrifying display of strength. The air itself fractured and whistled as it dashed around wildly, and the shockwave blew Jack's robes and hair back.

However, of the two cyclopses, one emerged superior. Dordok completed his swing, and the other cyclops screamed as his sword was pushed out of the way and the steel club met his chest. The sound of thick bones breaking echoed through the sky. The cyclops flew backward and crashed hard into the ground, creating fissures that spread for miles.

"Don't let them run!" Shol growled, launching forward. He became a shining sun as he flew straight for the night wizard. He shot out a palm. "Bright Sky!"

The wizard laughed, pushing his hands forward to unleash a beam of darkness. "I've heard about you, Shol Pesna! I've long yearned to face you. Endless Night!"

The two strikes met. They did not erupt in a shockwave but rather wrapped around each other, fighting for supremacy. Shol's palm shone with all the colors of dawn, turning into high noon, while the wizard's darkness was impenetrable by even the sharpest of Dao perceptions. It reminded Jack of the first few nights in the Forest of the Strong, where the trees and shadows hid unknown dangers.

He snapped out of the memory and charged. There were three opponents still alive; one for each of them. Jack, being the weakest of his group, decided to handle the Level 221 bearfolk.

"You will pay!" Dordok roared from above, flying club-first into the halberd-wielding goatee. Their weapons clashed repeatedly. The goatee was faster, but Dordok was so much stronger that each of his attacks sent the opponent flying. Victory was only a matter of time.

Jack focused on his own opponent.

The bearfolk, seeing her friends occupied in battle, had a very clear plan: kill Jack as fast as possible and assist them. In her mind, Jack wasn't a worthy opponent. They were forty levels apart, and the bearfolk herself was a proud genius, the star of her generation.

"Get out of my way!" she roared, charging straight at Jack, swiping her claws. A green domain flared out, tinged with redness, only for Jack's purple starry sky to erupt and hold it at bay.

"Meteor Punch!"

All colors and sounds in a narrow radius were sucked into his fist. They exploded against the incoming claws, painting the sky purple and unleashing a massive shockwave in the bearfolk's way. She flew back in astonishment. Her strike had been blocked!

"How?" she roared, but Jack was already there. It was his first time fighting a late immortal for real, so he did not intend to go easy. With a step through space, he appeared behind the bearfolk and smashed a fist at the top of her head. Skull creaked under his knuckles as the bearfolk flew downward, only to catch herself midair and turn to face him. Blood dripped down her face, yet her surprise overwhelmed her pain.

"You can even teleport!" she shouted again. "Who the hell are you?"

"I'm Jack Rust."

Brutalizing Aura—the new version—erupted out of him. Jack felt primal satisfaction well up in his chest. A formless cloud unfolded, ignoring the bearfolk's domain and engulfing her. Instantly, her face went pale; her eyes still held some fight, but the power of her domain dropped sharply, letting Jack's slowly conquer it.

A smile formed on his face. From the side, both Shol and Dordok shot him questioning glances, but none seemed particularly affected by his aura.

"Who are you?" the bearfolk asked again, full of terror.

Instead of answering, he charged. With escape no longer an option, his opponent roared and dove back into battle. Punches and claws flew wildly. This time, she didn't dare underestimate him, so getting the upper hand was harder despite her weakened state. His knuckles met her claws directly, the skin not even cracking, as the two slowly became engrossed in a dance of death.

Jack leaned back to avoid a swipe, then ducked below another to unleash a straight punch into the bearfolk's torso. The impact was enough to shatter mountains. The bearfolk grimaced taking the hit, then matched it with her own. A set of sharp claws raked down Jack's arm, drawing thick red lines, but contrary to her expectations, he did not even try to dodge. He didn't need to; his Neutron Star Body could protect him.

Jack leaned into a hard uppercut, rocking her head back then following his own momentum to rise above her and slam a second punch into her face. The bearfolk, still dazed, could not respond. She reached the ground in an instant and was nailed into it. Jack shot a Meteor Punch after her, unwilling to hold back, detonating the earth around her in a wide radius. The jungle circling that spot was already ruined, but rocks and dirt flew everywhere, and a tall cloud of dust rose for miles.

Not seeing a level-up notification, he shot another Meteor Punch. Again, an apocalypse bloomed, and the System finally acknowledged his efforts.

Congratulations! You have reached Level 180.
Congratulations! You have reached Level 181.

The higher the level of opponents he fought, the faster he leveled up. As counter-intuitive as that seemed, Jack was very thankful, as even finding late immortals to kill was a tough task. Maybe the System calculated that scarcity into the level reward.

He looked around. Dordok was standing alone in the sky over a smoking crater a hundred feet deep. Impressive, given that he was captured by three mid D-Grades—then again, he had been heavily injured when fighting them.

Shol was still wrapped in battle, but not for long. The light of day extinguished the darkness, and Shol's palm strike penetrated the night. The wizard created a black shield to defend himself, barely weakening the impact enough to survive.

As he was sent flying back, he leaned into the momentum and tried to escape, shooting away at a speed far faster than Jack could accomplish.

Unfortunately, no matter how fast he was, teleportation was always faster. Shol appeared over his head and brought his heel down on it, releasing a very audible crack. The wizard was dead before he even hit the ground.

"Well done," Shol said, eyeing the four craters across the ruined jungle. "Now let's hurry the hell up."

Not just me—all immortals are environmental hazards, Jack thought, inspecting those very same craters. Each battle destroyed a large section of the terrain. His heart ached when he thought of the many innocent creatures dragged into the aftermath of his strikes, but it was something he'd already accepted. As sad as it was, there was just nothing he could do about it.

Well, he could fight at higher altitudes, but that wasn't easy if no one else cared about the casualties.

"Dordok, I need you to stay very still," Shol said, approaching the cyclops, who eyed him warily.

"Why?"

"The Warden's mark is still inside you. I can burn it out, but you'll need to bear with me."

Dordok glanced between Jack and Shol. His one eye hid a thousand questions.

"Okay," he said, sticking out his chest. Shol placed a palm over the cyclops's heart.

"Do not resist."

Blazing light erupted where the two made contact. Dordok's eye widened, and he gritted his teeth, keeping himself from screaming. Smoke wafted upward, and the stench of burning flesh filled the air. Jack watched calmly.

Half a minute later, Shol pulled back his hand, revealing a patch of coal-like flesh underneath. The sight was so revolting that Jack wanted to puke.

"Done," he said.

"What did you do?" Dordok asked, panting and grunting. "It felt like you seared my very soul."

"Close. The mark was attached to the outer walls of your soul, so I had to burn that entire section. The physical heat was only a small part of it." He threw Dordok an acknowledging gaze. "You endured it well."

"Naturally. Did you expect me to scream like a little girl?"

"I expected you to scream like a cyclops."

"Can we get the hell out of here?" Jack intervened. "The Warden must have felt that. Every deacon in Hell could be on their way over."

"Right," Shol said. "Vegna is already in position. Jack, take out the *Bromobile* and let's go. We cannot stay on this planet any longer."

"The what?" Dordok asked.

Jack reached inside his robes. Before he could finish the motion, a heavy aura blanketed him. His hand went rigid. His Dao grew weak. A leonine now stood before them, only a mile away, and his eyes shone like suns, and his body exuded an aura of majesty that Jack could only barely resist.

Leonine, Level 249
Faction: Animal Kingdom (B-Grade)
Title: Grade Defier

"Shit," Shol said.

The leonine smiled confidently. "Got you."

CHAPTER FIFTY-THREE

FIGHTING AT THE PEAK

A LONE LEONINE STOOD IN THE SKY OVER A SHATTERED LAND AND A RUINED jungle. The breeze was cool and dry, and his mane fluttered, each hair a proud piece of art. His face was carved of majesty, while his body, its top half bare, seemed sculpted of marble. There was not one muscle on this leonine's body that wasn't well-formed.

The moment he appeared, an air of supremacy covered the land. Every surviving animal within a dozen miles bowed their heads low, disregarding their injuries. Even Jack felt inside him the urge to respect and obey this man, who had appeared in the heavens like a wild but dignified barbarian king.

"Thank the System I made it," the leonine said calmly. "If we let you escape, the other factions would mock our Animal Kingdom."

"Maximus Lonihor," Shol replied, narrowing his eyes. Though this leonine was one person and they were three, the experienced monk seemed wary. "They had you chase us personally?"

"There was little choice after what you did to Sapasun. You have killed two hundred of my Kingdom's immortals, some of them at the late and peak D-Grade. The damage you have caused us is far too great to ignore. You will die here, and the Exploding Sun will answer for your actions."

"We no longer belong to the Exploding Sun," Shol declared proudly. "Inspect us for yourself. Jack and I have left the faction. We only answer to ourselves now."

"Of course, and Hell is made of candy." Maximus laughed, a deep, booming sound. "If you think it's that easy to trick the factions, Shol, then you're even dumber than you look."

"Should I take out the starship?" Jack asked telepathically.

"Only if you want it broken," the monk replied. "Let me handle this and prepare to run."

"Who is this arrogant kitty?" Dordok asked. "His manner of speaking irritates me. Perhaps we should knock out a few of his teeth."

"You sure are feisty today, Captain," Jack said.

"Look, kid, I've been a prisoner here for months. If I don't beat up a deacon or two on my way out, I'll eat my own club."

The leonine laughed again, not at all fazed by Dordok's bravado. "Very well. Let's see if you can match your words, ogre."

"Care—" Shol tried to warn him, but it was too late. The leonine winked through space to appear before Dordok, throwing a simple punch. Dordok hurried to raise his club and defend.

The impact was deafening. A crack appeared on the steel weapon, which was undoubtedly hardened by magic, and Dordok himself was blown backward with such speed that he became a dot in the horizon.

"Looks like you can't," the leonine said. "Prepare yourse—"

Shol was already there. A miniature sun blossomed above the leonine as a heavy palm headed for the top of Maximus' head. The leonine blinked away, appearing behind Shol. Expecting it, the monk copied his teleportation mid-strike, still aiming for his opponent's head. The leonine crossed his arms to defend, and the strike pushed him down a hundred feet.

When he raised his body to its full height again, the only visible injury was a handful of burnt hairs.

"You've gotten faster," he noticed with a smile. "Good for you."

"Jack, run," Shol said, then charged. The leonine disappeared. Jack felt space warp behind him, and he barely teleported away in time to dodge a fiery fist heading for his back. Shol appeared in his spot, catching the fist and returning a backhand which slapped the leonine's chest, pushing him away.

Shol did not relent. He stayed on his opponent, pummeling him with a storm of kicks, punches, and palm strikes. Shol's orange robes fluttered wildly as he unleashed everything he had.

"Not bad!" The leonine laughed. His limbs moved as blurs, but he still found time to speak. "You can use teleportation already. That's an excellent achievement. If you agree to receive the Warden's mark and join our Kingdom, I might let you live."

"RUN!" Shol roared again, doing his best to pressure the leonine so he couldn't teleport after Jack.

"Run my ass!" Jack shouted. "There's no way in hell I'm running. We got this."

"NO!"

"Hell yeah!"

Dordok was rushing over. Besides his slightly cracked club, he seemed fine. Jack himself was confident in enduring at least a couple of the leonine's strikes.

He already suspected that Maximus was the Animal Kingdom's head disciple—the equivalent of Li Qian in the Exploding Sun. But Shol wasn't too far from that. There were three of them—they could win!

Most importantly, he would be damned if he let a friend sacrifice himself while he ran. Not again. Not when the last person to sacrifice himself for that very reason was *right here*.

The leonine laughed. "You have balls!" Crossing his arms, he threw them open, shoving Shol off-stance. His Dao Domain sprang out unbidden, a torrent of heaven-descended supremacy. The domains of Jack, Shol, and Dordok rushed out to meet it, clashing in the sky and forming a four-way war.

The supremacy bore down, heavy like the sky itself, while the three of them pushed up. Jack was shouldering only a fraction of the leonine's domain, and already his own domain struggled, teetering on the edge of collapse. Shol's domain was bright orange like the rising sun, while Dordok's was a formless domain of inexhaustible strength, roaring with the might of a thousand elephants.

As the domains clashed, they reached a standstill—no! Slowly but surely, they were pushing the leonine back! Jack was filled with hope.

"Descending Valor!" Maximus shouted, bringing down both his arms, and the sky turned holy. Winged knights in golden armor emerged from the clouds and flew around the leonine like specters around their king. At his gesture, they were unleashed at his three opponents, each knight cradling a heavenly sword and flying down tip-first.

They broke out of his domain and into theirs, their power deteriorating by the second. Jack was assaulted by a dozen knights. Each possessed the strength of a weak, early immortal—their swords whistled in the sky, and their auras carved the clouds. Though these warriors were nothing but conjured phantoms, the strength of their combined assault was equivalent to twelve Old Man Spirits charging Jack at once.

Of course, he was much stronger than he used to be. Brutalizing Aura blasted out of him, tinging the already purple sky an even deeper color and weakening the knights. He felt a trickle of power roll from their bodies into his—a small current that may or may not become significant over time.

The knights were still coming, so Jack roared and raised his fists to defend. The sky was sucked into them, then blasted out in an explosion. A torrent of power swept over the warriors and destroyed three, rendering them to nothing but golden smoke. The rest fell on him. Jack struggled to fight back. He danced in the Iron Fist Style, dominating his opponents and striking back when he could, but they cared about neither injuries nor exhaustion. Their unending assault weighed on Jack. It distracted him from the Dao battle overhead, making his domain lose its luster. The leonine pressed slightly harder.

In the corner of his eyes, Jack saw Dordok swinging his club wildly, destroying multiple soldiers with each swing, while Shol was engulfed in a tremendous, glowing orange ball that disintegrated them before they could even approach. The monk's entire body was burning, covered in flame and sunlight, and his entire attention was focused on pressing his domain against his enemy's.

But where was the leonine?

The second Jack had that thought, a cold, uneasy feeling grabbed his heart. He unhesitatingly teleported away. Without any warning, a palm emerged from space to cleave the spot where he'd been standing. The rest of the leonine's body followed soon after.

"Coward!" Shol yelled from inside his sun. "You dare attack the weakest first!"

"This is war, Shol!" the leonine laughed. "If you want a duel, let me kill your friends first."

"Over my dead body!"

Shol hurtled downward, using the entire sun around him as a shell to attack the leonine. As he passed by, Jack felt a surge of tremendous heat assault him. The very air was burning. Yet, the leonine only laughed, charging straight into the sun.

The very edges of his fur singed—and that was it.

"Such weak flames are useless against me, Shol!" the leonine shouted, laughing, while he pressured the monk. Shol's attention was split between maintaining his sun and fighting hand-to-hand, so he was less effective than before. The spectral winged knights were still assaulting his sun, but it seemed like the leonine didn't need much of his focus to keep them coming.

They devolved into a melee, but this time, Shol was pressured heavily. He kept falling back, conceding small strikes to keep himself in combat. Dordok finally took care of the knights assaulting him and jumped into the fray, heedless of Shol's sun. However, he was not as resistant as the leonine—the moment he came in contact with the orange flames, Jack saw his visage twist into a grimace and his skin turn red, but he still pressed on.

Shol dissolved his sun, welcoming Dordok's addition to the battle, but even the two of them struggled to match the leonine. Knights fell on them from all directions, disrupting their coordination and forcing them to face Maximus one at a time, greatly weakening them.

Jack also had winged knights after him, and while he fended them off, he took some time to study the leonine.

He wasn't as strong as he appeared. Truthfully, their combined domains were stronger than his, and he didn't seem able to fight Shol and Dordok at the same time, let alone the three of them.

However, he was a master of combat, completely the opposite of what Rufus Emberheart had been. Rufus had raw power. This man excelled in technique. The odds were stacked against him, but he manipulated the battlefield in such a way that he was the one applying pressure on his opponents. Shol and Dordok were constantly one step behind. Everything they tried was countered perfectly. The leonine was in complete control of the battle.

He had come here not with extra-large muscles, but with mastery and confidence.

I need to disrupt him, Jack thought. He ducked under a knight's swing, planted a fist in his armored torso, and the armor and knight both dissipated into motes of light. He then twisted his body to dodge two swords, grabbing one knight's wrist to smash him into the other before throwing a Meteor Punch and destroying both of them.

As another knight flew at him, he disappeared.

He reappeared behind the leonine right as Shol assaulted him from the front. The monk drove a sunny palm into the other's abdomen. "Bright Sky!" he shouted, birthing a sun in his palm.

"Meteor Punch!" Jack shouted, summoning his strongest strike against the leonine, who no longer had time to teleport away.

"Unbreakable Bulwark!" the leonine shouted, turning sideways and stretching out both palms. One met Shol's strike, burned by the sunlight and forced to buckle at the elbow. The other met Jack's meteor, enduring the explosion with only a slight bending. The momentum of the two attacks canceled each other out, and the leonine's hand closed around Jack's fist. His fingers were strong and hard like steel pliers.

Shit, Jack thought.

He was pulled in faster than he could react. An elbow dug hard into his chest, shattering his ribcage and launching him high into the sky. Shol managed to sneak in a kick during this opening, cracking the leonine's knee, but it was damage he could endure.

"Jack!" he shouted.

Jack was flying. His world alternated between black and white, and his ears screamed with the wind. When he regained himself, hellish pain filled his torso. He couldn't breathe. Thankfully, he didn't need to, but he was suffering heavy internal bleeding. He needed some time to—

"*Lean back,*" a voice reached him. It was neither Shol's nor Dordok's, but it was familiar, though he struggled to place it. Without the slightest hesitation, he ignored the burning pain and leaned backward. The heel of a foot crashed through the space he'd just been occupying, sending Jack flying by the mere shockwave. His wounds were agitated, but it was much better than having his skull shattered.

"How did you dodge that?" the leonine's voice came surprised as he stepped out of thin air. "And you survived my direct strike, too... If you keep going like this, I may not be able to kill you before reinforcements arrive."

Shol flashed before the leonine, leaning into a storm of strikes. Dordok flew in as well, shooting at the leonine like a missile and keeping him occupied. "Jack," he screamed in rage, "fucking run already!"

Both fighters fell on the leonine at once, pressuring him and forcing him on the back foot. More winged knights streamed from the sky, dogpiling on Shol and Dordok. The sun came back on. Dordok screamed, but the knights evaporated. The two of them kept pressing the leonine, unleashing their strongest strikes one after the other, and all he could do was defend.

This was their chance. If they could take him down now, they would—

An explosion of golden light erupted around the leonine. Jack caught a glimpse of white wings, golden armor, and a proud helmet. In the next moment, the illusion dissipated, as did all of the winged knights, but Shol and Dordok had been pushed back.

Their opportunity was gone. The leonine grinned at them. "Is that all you got?"

Jack was still flying away, gritting his teeth while Neutron Star Body worked in overdrive to patch him back together. His ribs were repaired, his punctured organs were healed, and the lost blood was replaced.

But even after he fully healed, it wouldn't help much against this beast that called itself Maximus Lonihor.

Suddenly, space cracked next to Jack. A person slipped through, meeting Jack's astonished gaze with a smile. "Hey, Jack. Missed me?"

"What the hell are you doing here?" Jack replied.

The Sage grinned. "Just hanging around."

CHAPTER FIFTY-FOUR
RETURN OF THE SAGE

Jack couldn't believe his eyes. Before him stood a man as eccentric as he was eye-catching—a worn-out jacket, crooked yellow teeth, wild hair, a mad glint in his gaze. He didn't smell, at least, but he seemed completely out of place surrounded by flying, robed cultivators.

Human (Earth-387), Level 170
Faction: -

"Sage!" Jack asked. "What the—"

"Who's that guy?" Dordok shouted, panting as he rushed into battle again. "Is he with us?"

Shol barely had time for a glance, making him furrow his brows. Immortals had excellent memory. "Is that..."

"Introductions can wait," the Sage said with a confident, if yellow, grin. "I'm here to rescue you."

"Someone came to save my saviors!" Dordok laughed. "Isn't that a treat?"

"Quite."

"Sage, what the hell," Jack said. "Aren't you supposed to—"

An intense aura interrupted him. Maximus Lonihor erupted with power, releasing a supreme wind that blew both Dordok and Shol back. "No one is rescuing anyone under my watch," he growled. The grin remained on his lips, but it had grown tighter, more thoughtful. Clearly, even he hadn't expected the Sage to arrive.

He rushed ahead, then abruptly disappeared.

The Sage was already dodging. He smoothly glided backward, avoiding one claw swipe, then leaned down to dodge a kick. Three more strikes came, each more vicious than the last, and each was masterfully dodged.

Jack was close to the epicenter of this clash, so he got a good look at the Sage's moves. They were almost magical. He wasn't fast, but he predicted the leonine's attacks before they came. His dodges looked almost choreographed.

Maximus paused. His eyes grew serious. "You people are starting to piss me off."

"Good kitties should go to sleep," the Sage said, pointing a finger at the leonine. Jack sensed nothing, but Maximus's eyes turned hazy. He recovered just a fraction of a second later, but in a high-level battle, even an instant was too long.

Shol's foot smashed into the leonine's cheek. His face warped almost in slow motion before being catapulted to the side, crashing through several miles of air and into the ground like a cannonball.

"Quick," the Sage said, tossing up an object that resembled a dark sphere. "Everyone, to me!"

They obeyed—what choice did they have?—and the Sage's sphere enlarged to engulf them. Inside it, Jack saw the space under space, a place where everything was real yet not, where distance was an illusion. Staying here extensively threatened to tear the soul out of his body, but the sphere protected him, adding a hint of stability to the chaos.

In the distance, Maximus Lonihor shot up from the jungle, roaring as he drove a golden punch at them. The Sage clapped and space sucked them in. They were no longer in a jungle, but over an ocean with no hint of land on the horizon.

The dark sphere shrunk to its regular size and flew into the Sage's hands. "Well, that's one thing taken care of," he said. He pocketed the sphere, then fished out what looked like a grocery list from inside his robes and crossed out one line. He put it away before Jack could read anything.

Jack struggled to speak. His mouth moved up and down a couple of times before he made sound. "It was that simple? We escaped?"

"For now," the Sage replied.

"You can reuse that thing?" Shol asked, eyeing the pocket where the sphere had gone.

"Oh, yes. The Black Hole Church has all kinds of trinkets."

Everyone fell quiet at the abrupt revelation. Jack remembered that he'd never told Shol about that. The silence was only broken by Dordok, who laughed uproariously. "System bless you, Jack. I don't even need to know—I'm loving this!"

"The Black Hole Church..." Shol said. "That's a potent statement."

The Sage shrugged. "It is what it is. Didn't Jack tell you he's one of us?"

Shol had never looked at Jack with such accusation.

"I'm not," he hurried to explain. "It was offered, but I'm still considering it."

"Sure..."

"If I can interrupt this tender questioning," the Sage said, "we're still not safe. The Warden could be flying over the planet as we speak to scout us out. Follow me."

Without another word, he flew down, diving into the blue sea with a splash.

"Oh, I'll follow you alright," Dordok said, his mood greatly improved, and dove down. Jack and Shol did the same.

Entering the water, Jack was glad he no longer needed to breathe. His enhanced senses and Dao perception let him perfectly make out the underwater terrain, the hundreds and thousands of fish swimming around them. This was a virgin sea, untouched by garbage, chemicals, or overfishing. The sheer wealth of marine wildlife was staggering. He didn't recognize more than a tenth of the species here.

His biologist sense tingled, but he let it wait for now.

Does the Sage know where he's going? he wondered as they dove ever deeper, only for his worries to be proven unnecessary. The Sage slowed down as he approached the foot of an underwater mountain, then slipped under a rock protrusion, and disappeared.

Reaching that spot, Jack saw an opening inside the rock directly above his head. It led to an underwater tunnel. Following it, the rock walls slowly closed around him until there was barely enough room for him to stretch his arms.

Then, abruptly, the walls widened again, and Jack surfaced into an underwater cave. There was air here, and the rock walls stretched into a wide hall more than thirty feet deep. It wasn't spacious, but it could easily fit four people.

"We'll be safe here," the Sage said. "Unless the Warden inspects the bottom of this ocean himself, nobody will find us."

While Jack was busy gawking, Shol and Dordok surfaced beside him. "How the hell do you know about this place?" Shol asked.

"Because I'm a Sage," the Sage said as if that explained everything.

"Not convincing. Try again."

"I just saved your life. I believe a little trust would go a long way."

Shol snorted but did not pursue the subject.

"Now that we're safe, can someone please explain what is going on?" Dordok asked, pointing at Jack. "How are you Level 179—no, 181 already? Shit. What are you doing with Shol Pesna? And how do we know the Black Hole Church?"

"I'd like to know that last part, too," Shol added.

Jack sighed. "Very well. Buckle down, everyone; this will be a long story."

He took a seat, since he remained injured, and began retelling. He explained about his adventures in Trial Planet, his conquering of the ninth ring, and his miraculous breakthrough. The only secret he kept was the Life Drop and its implications—besides that, he trusted these people enough to tell them everything.

He then spoke about his time in the Exploding Sun faction, and how one thing led to another, which led to him infiltrating one of the Animal Kingdom's most well-guarded locations to hunt down and assassinate their core members.

"I know it sounds stupid when I say it like that," he finished, "but it's worked out pretty well so far. I've gained forty levels in a month."

"And you've almost died at least twice," Shol pointed out.

"Making this my safest month since the Integration."

"Fair enough."

"And you came to rescue me?" Dordok asked.

"Of course," Jack replied. "You're my captain—and you once risked your life to save me, a total stranger. What kind of man would I be if I didn't do the same?"

Moisture welled up in the captain's single eye. "I knew I was right about you!" he shouted, drawing Jack into a big hug. He then held him by the shoulders and asked, "What about the *Ram*? Is the rest of the crew safe?"

Jack bit his cheek. The captain cared about his crew and ship more than anything else. This question must have been burning his lips since the moment he was captured.

"I don't know," Jack finally replied. "Last I heard, they escaped from the Hounds by teleporting away. I can only hope they're fine."

Dordok nodded. His gaze was inscrutable. "Achilles died in the battle," he said. "It was after you left. One of the Hounds tore him apart."

Jack took the news like a mallet to the skull. "I see..."

"It's devastating, I know. He was a good man." The captain observed a few seconds of silence before continuing. "The rest of them will be okay. Bomn will take care of them. He can carry my mantle with pride."

"Do you think Vashter managed to recover from his wounds?" Jack couldn't help asking.

"Certainly. That is one resilient sailor. I'm sure they found a way."

"Then, I'm glad..." Jack said. Meeting the captain again brought back memories—and seeing that they shared the same certainty of the crewmembers surviving relieved him.

Jack hadn't spent much time on the *Trampling Ram*, but he remembered it fondly.

Shol spoke up. "What are you doing in Hell, Sage? And don't tell me you're only here for Jack."

"You're contradicting yourself. How can I answer your question without saying the answer?"

"What?"

"What?"

Shol took a moment to parse through this. "Are you saying you're only here for Jack?"

"That's what I *would* say, if you hadn't told me not to say it."

The monk's temperature was rising, so Jack quickly butted in to say, "Don't test his patience, Sage. He has the fuse of a fuseless candle."

"Right. I apologize," the Sage said. "Jack is a very promising prospect. He is worth the risk of me coming here. Plus, I can divine that things will probably be okay."

Shol narrowed his eyes. "Say I believe you. How did you find us?"

"Because I am a Sage."

"Hmph. I'm not like the idiots you're used to dealing with. I've lived for centuries and dealt with all sorts of prophets. Even the Barren High cannot divine things like that."

"I know they can't, but I can."

"You are testing my limits."

A hint of Shol's aura leaked out, soaking the cave in faint sunlight. Jack raised his hands. "Can we all calm down, please?"

"This is important, Jack," Shol said. "If this man has a way to track our location, I would like to know."

"He saved our lives. Give him the benefit of the doubt for now. Besides, if he has a way to track anyone's location, that's me—or the captain, actually."

"How did you all find me, anyway?" Dordok asked.

"I assaulted a late immortal, stole his prisoner scanner, tracked down every prisoner and confirmed your identity from a distance, then followed your dot on my scanner," Shol explained. "But that's not important right now."

"Right," the Sage said. "You know what is? Coming up with a plan."

"We don't need one," Shol shot him down. "Jack, do you vouch for this guy?"

The truth was, Jack knew almost nothing about the Sage. He shouldn't guarantee anything, but the man had helped him on so many occasions that he deserved at least this little bit of trust. "Yes," he replied.

"Good. Then, Sage, I should let you know we only followed you here to learn about your identity and goals—which we didn't, but Jack's guarantee is good enough for me. Here's the plan: we go back outside, board Jack's starship, and teleport to a nearby planet, where an accomplice of ours is waiting to take us away."

"That's an excellent plan," the Sage said. "Except your accomplice has already been apprehended by the enemy."

Shol's eyes narrowed. "Impossible. I contacted them only a few minutes ago."

"They're being blackmailed to reply normally, but I assure you, they're under enemy custody."

"Oh yeah? And how would you know? Because you're a Sage?"

"That too, but also because one of our members works as an undercover guard. Your accomplice is Vegna, right? The feshkur merchant captain?"

Shol was visibly surprised. "How could she have been caught? She knew the Kingdom's patrol patterns inside out."

"It wasn't the Kingdom. The Hand of God tracked you down to the Eternal Gate, then performed a background check on every person on the planet when they lost your trail. You and Vegna have worked together before—she was one of the first they interrogated, and nobody can lie to the Inquisitors."

"Wait. Why would the Hand of God be after us?"

"Not after you," the Sage corrected. "After Jack."

Shol turned an increasingly furious glare at Jack. "And why, *pray tell*, would the Hand of God be after my *honest* little brother?"

Jack, in turn, glared at the Sage. He hadn't told them about the Life Drop before, so naturally, he also hadn't mentioned anything about the Hand of God chasing him. Shol had no idea.

"Start talking, Jack," Shol said heavily, "and this time, you damn well better stop hiding things or I'll whoop your ass so hard you'll shit yourself."

CHAPTER FIFTY-FIVE
A NEW HIDEOUT

SHOL, DORDOK, SAGE. THESE WERE PEOPLE HE'D SHARED LIFE AND DEATH with... but could he reveal to them his deepest secret?

Do I even have a choice? he asked himself. Because of me, the Hand of God is after us... I have to tell them.

"There is one more thing," he finally said. "But only if you want to hear it. Let me warn you—it's huge."

"You know what's not huge? My patience. And you're really testing that," Shol replied, crossing his arms.

Dordok laughed. "At this point, nothing would surprise me."

The Sage simply motioned for him to go ahead.

Therefore, taking a deep breath, Jack completed his story of Trial Planet with the truth about the Life Drop. He hid nothing, detailing the Ancient Trial in the ruins and how he used the Life Drop to defeat Old Man Spirit, as well as how the entire planet had been locked down by the Hand of God because of him, and how he'd escaped.

"I was pretty flashy in Garden Ring. Since then, I suppose they've heard about me being outside, and since they've found no one suspicious in Trial Planet, they want to deep-scan me... I don't hope to escape such a large organization. I just want to become as strong as possible before they find me. They couldn't have sent C-Grades after me, right?"

"Of course not," the Sage replied. "They've sent a B-Grade."

Jack almost sighed with relief before it turned into coughing. His head whipped over. "*A what!*"

"Why are you surprised? Anything pertaining to the Ancients is a major incident. Of course they'd send an elder—and, since the Hand of God is half a step above the other B-Grade factions of the galaxy, their elders are all at the B-Grade."

"Plus," Shol added, gazing at the Sage suspiciously, "they wouldn't risk the Black Hole Church's interference."

"Oh yes, quite true. If we wanted to contest whatever was in Trial Planet, we would also send B-Grades over."

"Is a B-Grade really after me?" Jack asked, ignoring the revelation about the Church's strength. "Aren't they literal gods?"

The Sage shrugged. "They're pretty strong, I'll give you that, but they naturally have their limits. Right now, there is a B-Grade on this planet actively scanning it to find you. But they won't discover us here. We're safe."

"Wouldn't they have discovered us when we fought that leonine?"

"Ah, but that's why I showed up! We escaped in the nick of time—twenty seconds later and they'd be on to us. Thankfully, your friend Vegna delayed them for some time, or even I would have been too late."

"How do you know all that?" Jack asked.

"I told you, I have a person on the inside."

"You have to be joking. There is no way you have information that's accurate down to the second."

"Well..." The Sage grinned slyly. "I may be approximating a bit. The important thing is that, since they haven't sniffed us out already, they must have arrived after we went into hiding—or not arrived yet."

"But that's terrible!" Jack said. "How will we get out? There is no way we can fool a B-Grade."

"That's the trick; we don't."

All three of them stared at the Sage incredulously. "We don't?"

"We don't. Using that Life Drop, as you call it, leaves lasting effects on the body. The soul itself is inviolable, so even a deep-scan wouldn't spot the Life Drop, but an experienced examiner could discover some oddities. After that, they'll just split you open to be sure."

"So, we cannot be caught," Jack said.

"Right." The Sage nodded. "A B-Grade's perception can cover half a planet. Right now, going outside is suicide. What I suggest we do is hide in here for a few months until they assume we already left the planet. There really isn't another option."

"But what about Vegna?" Shol asked. "Suppose I believe you she's been captured. She's still waiting for our arrival. What should I tell her?"

"That we will no longer be needing her." The Sage grinned. "They saw me appearing and taking you away with a high-grade spatial artifact. Jack said my name. With a little research, they will connect me to the Black Hole Church, which is a powerful and mysterious organization. It isn't such a large stretch to assume the Church has helped you all escape this planet."

"Could they?" Dordok asked.

"Yes... but also not. With a B-Grade holding the fort, the only way to escape would be for the Church to send one of their own B-Grades to clash against the Hand of God. As you can understand, that would be a massive commitment. We are not willing to do that."

"Then how do we escape? What's your plan?" Jack asked.

"There isn't one!" the Sage replied, laughing. "We'll have to find a way. But look at the bright side—I can divine we'll probably be fine."

"You have no plan!" Shol erupted. "You came and dragged us into a dead-end with no way to get us out?"

"You were already in a dead-end, just a different one. I dragged myself into your inescapable problems to give you another chance at survival. Therefore, I think I hardly deserve that tone, no?"

Shol grumbled. "What if he's lying?" he said to Jack and Dordok. "What if the Hand of God hasn't discovered us yet, and Vegna is just waiting outside to take us away? He could be keeping us here for his own benefit."

"Shol," Jack said in warning. "The Sage really is a member of the Black Hole Church, who are enemies of the Hand of God and every B-Grade faction. What benefits could he have in keeping us here?"

"What kind of fool would dive into a desperate situation to save near-strangers for no benefit?"

"A confident one," the Sage interceded. "Things may be looking down right now, but we'll find a way out. We just have to play our cards right."

"By staying down here forever?" Shol shot back. "Jack needs to return to the Exploding Sun within four months. Plus, no matter how long we wait, even if the B-Grade leaves, escaping Hell will not get any easier. All their outbound teleporters are hidden in well-guarded cities, and since I've left my faction, I have no way to contact anyone! We're trapped!"

Facing Shol's outrage, the Sage was calm and joyful.

"Come on, have some faith," the Sage urged. "There is always a way. We just have to find it."

"That's such bullshit."

"Yet, it is true. We just have to not lose faith."

"What do you suggest, Sage?" Jack stepped in, wanting calm things down. Shol looked ready to explode. "You mentioned we stay here for a few months until the situation outside calms down a little. Then what?"

"The rest is a work in progress, but when we're ready, we could exit and slowly work at getting you to the peak D-Grade."

"What?" Jack was shocked. "I thought we wanted to escape."

"Don't you want to become strong enough to save Earth?" the Sage asked, his face drawn into a mysterious smile.

"I do..." Jack admitted.

"Then you're in luck, because getting you strong is our ticket out of here. You have a perfect foundation, great Dao understanding, ample battle experience, and extremely powerful titles. If you can reach the peak D-Grade, even Maximus Lonihor won't be able to stop you. We could use you as a spearhead to assault one of the heavily guarded outbound teleporters and make our escape."

Jack gave the Sage a complicated gaze.

In truth, he really wanted to become strong quickly. He needed to. His duel with Li Qian aside, he only had five months remaining to defeat the Planetary Overseer and save Earth—and the overseer was at the mid C-Grade. An entire Grade away.

This plan was perfect for him... So why did it feel like he was taking advantage of the situation?

"Say we do that," Dordok said. "We stay here for a while until the Hand of God leaves, then go out and have Jack kill a bunch of deacons. Won't they be onto us again? The Hand of God can just return and force us back into the cave."

"That's true," the Sage said. "However, the time of B-Grades is extremely precious. This particular one has already spent a couple of months investigating the Ancient-related incident. If we just wait her out, she will eventually return to her previous affairs, leaving only a token force behind in case more leads appear. Even if we later reveal ourselves again, extricating herself from her affairs to come chase down a D-Grade who may or may not be related to the incident would be a stretch."

"That makes sense," Jack said. "But if she leaves a token force behind, wouldn't that mean C-Grades?"

"One or two with a bunch of D-Grades. The Hand of God has immortals to spare. However, as long as it's only C-Grades, we can handle them."

"That's a brave statement if I've ever heard one," Shol commented.

"Yet, it's true. Maybe not in combat, but Hell is a huge place. If we combine prudence, my inside information, and my divining abilities, we can assassinate late immortals and deacons without ever getting caught."

Jack, Shol, and Dordok exchanged glances. One by one, they nodded. Shol was the last to do so.

Despite his appearance and mysterious motives, the Sage's suggestions made sense. Somehow. None of the others had a better idea.

"But what are we going to do while waiting for the B-Grade to leave?" Jack asked. "You said it could be months. If I want to reach the peak D-Grade soon, don't I need that time?"

"Not at all," the Sage said. "The Animal Kingdom has invested centuries of painstaking cultivation and trillions worth of resources into their D-Grades—you can usurp all that by just killing them. Therefore, levels are easy for you. I believe we'll make it in time as long as we aren't caught. The difficult part is having your Dao understanding keep up. If I'm being honest, cultivators are not meant to progress nearly as fast as you are. You are carried along by momentum, but you really ought to take some time and stabilize your foundation. Only then can you properly utilize your advancements in power. Right now, you're terribly inefficient."

Jack raised a brow. "I am?"

"Of course you are. Think about it. A deacon has less than double your amount of attribute points and around double the size of your Dao reserves. However, you have a ton of high-level titles. Even if they have some as well, your superiority there should mostly make up for the stat discrepancy. As for the Dao, they may be able to last longer and strike with more power than you, but your perfect foundation should shore up that weakness as well. You should be equal in power to a deacon. Therefore, why is it that you are completely unable to face one?"

"Because... I can't use my power efficiently?"

"Exactly! And how could you? Adjusting takes time. Right now, the best thing you can do is spend some time consolidating your foundation, or any extra levels will have severely diminishing returns. Honestly, even a few months shouldn't be enough, but it's the best we can do."

"I see," Jack replied, creasing his brows. "You seem to know a lot, Sage."

"Comes with the area. Sages should be wise, right?"

"He's right. I had a similar plan," Shol spoke up. "Get you to level-up as fast as possible, then take you into an extended consolidation phase when you started to lag. I estimated that would come in twenty or thirty levels, but since we have time to spare, you might as well start now."

"I see," Jack said.

"However, don't get me wrong," Shol continued. "This is nothing but a stopgap measure. Even if you spend a few months consolidating now and get your fighting power up to par, you will still have advanced way too quickly. Breaking through to the C-Grade like this will ruin your foundation. When you have saved your planet and are no longer in a hurry, you will need to devote a lot of time catching up with your Dao."

"Got it," Jack said.

However, unless he found some other way to save Earth—be it

Master Huali's promise or anything else—he would still break through to the C-Grade as quickly as possible, and consequences be damned.

CHAPTER FIFTY-SIX
VISIONS OF THE PAST

An underwater cave was not the best place to house four grown men for extended periods of time. Nevertheless, Jack and his companions were determined to make do.

To Shol and Dordok, both multiple centuries old, a few months were nothing.

Jack and the Sage, on the other hand, had only been Integrated for five months. For them, this was a long stretch of their System lives, so they approached it with seriousness. Jack trained diligently, both in body and spirit—as for the Sage, he just kind of hung around. When he closed his eyes, no one knew whether he was meditating or randomly falling asleep, a habit he claimed originated from his homeless days on Earth.

Two days after they settled down in the cave, the Sage took Jack and headed deeper into the ocean. They reached a second, smaller sea cave, where they could discuss without anyone else overhearing.

"What is it, Sage?" Jack asked, looking around. This cave was pretty cramped. "Not a love confession, I hope."

"Have you considered my offer at all, Jack?" the Sage asked with interest, jumping straight to the matter at hand.

"You mean to join the Black Hole Church. I... can't say I have. Time was always pressing."

"Would you be willing to consider it now?"

"Always have been."

"And? What do you think?"

Jack took some time to think this through. "The world calls you terrorists. You have been kind to me, but I still hesitate to join an organization I know almost nothing about. My answer remains the same. I need more information."

The Sage nodded as if expecting this. "You know, we don't invite just anybody. The Black Hole Church is an organization as old as the System itself, and only the strongest of each age can join our ranks. You could call us a gathering of elites, as well as a cradle of power—you cannot imagine the resources the Church pours into its recruits."

"Resources like my Life Drop?"

The Sage's smile turned wry. "Even we do not possess resources like that—not routinely, at least. The Life Drop is one reason I extended an invitation to you back in Trial Planet."

"You knew?" Jack's eyes widened.

"I suspected. The Church was aware of the Ancient Trial you located. When someone succeeded, we were notified, and connecting the dots wasn't too hard afterward."

"Why didn't you say anything?"

"I couldn't casually reveal my organization's reach, now could I?"

"But you can now?" Jack asked. "What changed?"

The Sage drew a deep breath. "Your value, my friend. I was already considering inviting you on Earth, after you defeated Rufus Emberheart. We are picky but always in need of extreme talent. When I met you again in Trial Planet, your rapid increase in power and the Life Drop inside you cemented my decision, which is why I extended an invitation. Now... The more you grow, the more miracles you seem able to create. You are firmly positioned against the Hand of God, who is also our enemy, and you keep rising in power prodigiously. Your value has increased in the eyes of the Church, so I can divulge more information to help you make a decision."

"Well, divulge it then," Jack said, letting some rare haste show. "Tell me what the hell is going on. What's the deal with the Black Hole Church? Are you really trying to revive an Old One? Why? What is your real goal? What's the deal with the Old Ones, and why is the System, which was created by the Immortals, seeking to eradicate any sign of the Ancients?"

All these suppressed questions sprang up in Jack's mind at once. Back in Trial Planet, he and Nauja had run into the ruins of an Ancient outpost. The door depicted twelve Old Ones, each representing one element of the world—most of which Jack could not decipher—and to enter, the walls of the outpost warned them several times not to inspect anything, as if not trusting the System. The Ancient voice in the trial had said the same, as well as some other cryptic warnings, and even Nauja's father had warned Jack not to trust the System.

The moment he was lost in the trial and Nauja started scanning things, the System had informed them that the Hand of God was on its way to eradicate any sign of the Ancients.

None of those made sense. According to what Jack knew, the Ancients were the universe's first civilization. They created the Immortals, an army of Dao-wielding robots, but were destroyed by the Old Ones—the Gods of the Universe. The Immortals, who were made to protect the Ancients, swore revenge. They constructed the System to help the various species cultivate, then gathered the strongest warriors of the universe and unleashed a crusade against the Old Ones, eventually pushing them out of System space.

In the end, the Old Ones sealed their strongest member—Enas, the God of Life—in a black hole for eternity, as punishment for giving the Dao to the Ancients, which was what started this whole thing.

It was exactly this Old One, Enas, that the Black Hole Church worshiped and tried to revive.

Clearly, Jack had witnessed things that contradicted the version of the story he knew. He'd put away such thoughts previously, as they were far above his paygrade, but now he finally had access to someone who seemed to know things—the Sage.

The Sage gave Jack an encouraging smile, the kind a professor would give to a hard-working student.

"I will not tell you the answers to these questions," he said, "but I will do something better: I will show you. Keep your mind reined; do not scan what I'm about to reveal."

Reaching inside his worn-out jacket, he revealed a piece of green jade shaped as a scroll. Jack didn't focus too hard on it, lest he activate the System's scanning function, but he couldn't stop himself from sensing the jade scroll's aura; a feeling so ancient it seemed to defy time itself.

"Grab on," the Sage said, extending the piece of jade. "Let's embark on a magical journey together."

"That's creepy, but okay."

Jack grabbed the other end of the jade. The scroll did not unfurl—instead, Jack felt something projected inside his mind. A scenery from times long past. Suddenly, he was both here and there, experiencing both realities at once.

"Let it happen," the Sage instructed him. "The Ancients viewed the robbing of agency as taboo. Contrary to the System's visions, this jade scroll will let you maintain complete control in the real world so you can act out or break the vision at a moment's notice."

Jack could understand why the System did what it did. This sensation was confusing, like watching two movies playing on top of each other. Still, he appreciated the jade scroll's attempts to maintain his agency. As he let himself experience the vision, his brain became gradually used to the sensation, letting him understand what he was seeing.

He was in a small room. The walls were made of living stone, coiling around to fulfill its owner's needs. Jack himself was a ghost floating bodilessly in the middle of the room, right above a green jade scroll which looked exactly like the one he held, only far less ancient.

To Jack's surprise, he still had complete control over his body and could even turn around to watch things—he wasn't watching a movie, like the Dao Visions he'd experienced before, but participating in it.

Though, as a ghost, he couldn't actually affect anything.

The Sage was next to him, also in ghost form. "How are you feeling? Are you adjusted yet?"

"Almost. I'm trying."

"Good, cause it's about to start."

Suddenly, a man's voice echoed inside the room. "My name is Norax

Erudite." The voice wasn't deep or aggressive—it was soft yet steady, like an experienced scholar's. Jack turned around to discover they shared the room with a person who, save for his clothes, looked exactly like a normal human.

He had round, spirited eyes and a bald head, while he wore long green robes that reached the floor. His nose was sharp and his lips thin. The robes hid his limbs, but Jack could make out smooth, slender fingers. His most striking feature, however, was his aura. He gave Jack the feeling of a kind old man, very similar to the old professors who loved research and teaching.

There was no hint of the Dao. Jack could not inspect him. He felt like a normal human.

"The end is near," the man said, exuding a despair that contradicted his calm exterior. "*Our* end, to be precise. And we only have ourselves to blame. It is already too late to hope for victory. All we can do is spread our children as far as possible, hide them in the crevices of the universe, and hope that someone survives. As for me... I have no children. I can only record the events that will transpire here today, letting future generations see through the lies that, undoubtedly, the victors of this war will weave."

Though there was no aura to this person, his words had gravity. Jack's attention was fully captured.

"What's happening?" he asked the Sage, who smiled bitterly in response. It was the first time Jack saw him sad.

"You'll see," he replied.

The room shook. The living rock around them made a sound as if crying. It then withdrew, opening a wall to reveal the expanse of space outside.

It was not empty.

A planet stretched under the man's starship, covered in bustling cities and lush, vivid nature. At a glance, it seemed like paradise. And it would be, if not for the columns of smoke rising from everywhere on the planet.

"Do you recognize that planet?" the Sage asked.

"How could I—"His jaw dropped. He *did* recognize the planet, because he'd seen it from this angle before. It wasn't Earth.

It was Trial Planet.

"How!" he blurted out, getting no response.

The starship they rode was one of many. A proud fleet flew before Jack's eyes, visible through the gap in the wall. As if sensing his desire to see more, the man moved the jade scroll—and the two ghosts with it—to the very edge. He was completely unaffected by the vacuum of space.

"Take a good look," the man said with sadness, stubbornly ignoring the laws of nature to speak in space. "Bear witness to the greatest grief of the universe so far—but not, I suspect, the last. I am sorry, descendant. On behalf of the Ancients, I apologize."

Jack tried to respond, but the man could not perceive him—he was only a ghost watching a vision he could not alter.

The man flew out of the starship and his aura flared. Jack had thought him a normal human before, but it was he that was blind. The man's Dao eclipsed the sun and moon, filling the vacuum like air inside a balloon. The very Dao of the universe bowed to him.

Jack had never experienced such a complete sense of power. He couldn't imagine anything closer to God.

"Is he at the B-Grade?" he asked breathlessly.

The Sage shook his head. "No."

The man's aura kept expanding. It was a visible green light covering an area larger than Jack could perceive. From his viewpoint, he had no idea how far it stretched. He did, however, see that aura envelop every nearby starship. More people streamed out—some were dressed as wizards and some as warriors, wielding swords and staves alike. Most were human, but Jack caught glimpses of many other species as well, all completely unknown.

All these people were covered by the man's aura, which shone around them like an extra suit of armor. "May life live," he uttered sadly, yet with conviction.

Suddenly, a second aura rose. Jack could not see its origin, but he could perceive it through his Dao sense. It was proud, hard, metallic.

Familiar.

A figure darted past the starship to stand next to the scholar—a knight in silver armor, wielding a mace and exuding the aura of a thousand kings. Though his face looked younger than Jack remembered, he recognized this person. It was Old Man Spirit.

"It's an honor to die fighting by your side, Norax," Old Man Spirit said, laughing with the power of youth.

"I say the same, brother Jericho," the scholarly man responded, clapping his hands together and separating them again. When he did, a green rod appeared between them, first transparent and then solid. The man—Norax—grabbed it in one hand, his mere existence dominating heaven and earth. "Let's protect our people."

Jericho laughed again. His voice was amplified, crossing the void of space to resound all over the assembled cultivators and the planet beneath. "Listen up, my warriors! They want to purge us? Bullshit! Let's show them that the Ancients should not be underestimated. And to the allies who chose to fight by our side..." His face split into a wide grin. "We will remember you for eternity."

The gathered cultivators—over a hundred of them—shouted together. Jack glimpsed their auras—every single one was clearly weaker than their two leaders, but also vastly stronger than anyone he'd ever met, including Master Huali.

The soldiers of this army were B-Grades.

As his shocked eyes passed over the army, Jack caught sight of a half-monkey half-man wearing a suit of living stone and wielding a familiar staff—Brock's Staff of Stone.

"Just what enemies could make such an army feel hopeless?" Jack managed to utter, struggling to even form words.

Beside him, the Sage smiled again—half in sadness and half in pride. "Raise your eyes and see, son of the Ancients."

CHAPTER FIFTY-SEVEN
ANCIENT HISTORY

BEFORE JACK'S EYES STOOD THE MOST IMPOSING FORCE HE'D EVER WITNESSED. Two A-Grades—at least, that's what he assumed they were—led over a hundred B-Grades into battle, and each were certain they would lose.

Facing them were just seven figures. They were humanoid in shape but made of shiny gray metal. They had longer limbs than humans, smooth torsos, and faceless heads with only a single orb—an eye—dominating their center. They wore no clothes, and given their uniform build, they were completely identical save for the symbols engraved in their foreheads—all seemingly random, two-digit numbers ranging from twenty to seventy.

These were robots.

They stood in eerie silence, unmoving side-by-side. They were cold like machines were supposed to be. Just like the scholarly man before he revealed his power, their bodies exuded no aura of the Dao whatsoever.

"Are those the Immortals?" Jack asked. "But I thought they protected the Ancients!"

"Many things you thought were wrong," the Sage replied softly. His words were tinged with sadness. "Just watch."

Jericho, who looked like a younger version of Old Man Spirit, floated ahead. There was no negotiation, no speech, no preamble to the battle. He simply raised his mace and shouted, "Charge!"

The over-a-hundred B-Grades attacked as one. They crossed space near-instantly and unleashed their skills. Jack was almost blinded by the radiance—he suspected that only being in a vision saved his eyeballs from boiling.

The two commanders stepped forth. Jericho, who had already been at the forefront, swung his mace so calamitously that an entire stretch of space was encased in metal. It was so massive that it compared to the nearby planet in size, and when it exploded, the impact was world-shattering.

The scholarly man—Norax—spread his arms wide. Green light suffused space, filling it with a vitality that did not belong. Living creatures of all shapes and forms spawned everywhere. There were space monsters, various animals, even mythological beings like dragons. They were nothing more than solid illusions, but each could easily annihilate him, and they numbered in the thousands.

Facing all these attacks, the seven robots reacted completely in sync. They released their own auras, each robot matching Jericho and Norax in scope and breadth of power. When they clashed, the Dao cried around them, unwilling but forced to participate in a battle between its beloved children.

Jack could not make out the nature of each robot's powers. Everything was so overflooded with energy that his Dao perception went amok, and even his eyes were useless. Spacetime was curving and bending wildly. Reality was fluctuating and unraveling. The world itself struggled to endure this battle of colossal forces, giving birth to cracks and tears leading to a terrible void of blackness.

The battlefield was a mess. Everyone teleported around at speeds Jack could not distinguish, navigating the extremes of this broken reality. B-Grades were sucked into the tears of space and disappeared forever. Others combined forces to unleash terrifying beams through multiple wormholes. Their Daos combined in symphonies of indescribable majesty.

The robots casually strolled through. This broken reality was their backyard, and the almighty B-Grades were just pests. One of them waved a hand, decimating a dozen cultivators before they could even see the attack coming. Another dodged a storm of space cracks like it was nothing, while a third simply took them, sucking in the cracks instead of getting sucked into them itself. Meanwhile, four of the robots were contesting the two commanders in a world-shaking battle dominated by powers that Jack couldn't even recognize.

He did not understand what he was watching. All he knew was that the starship around him, along with every other starship in sight, had disappeared, destroyed just by being at the fringes of this battle. Only the jade scroll remained, protected as it was by the scholar's powers.

The nearby planet was assaulted by loose energy remains. It went from a lush, highly-technological haven to a burned, wounded landscape within seconds. Sword scars were carved on its surface, each hundreds of miles long. Palm-shaped craters flattened mountains. An ocean evaporated while another froze over. Smoke stopped rising as all oxygen was sucked out of the atmosphere. The greenery was decimated. The cities collapsed. Entire continents smashed together to create earthquakes visible from space. Dust began filling the air to the point Jack could no longer see.

Within seconds, Trial Planet had been destroyed. It had transformed from a place of harmony and beauty to the ruined terrain he witnessed himself when first landing on it. Everything on the surface had died.

Only now did a hurricane of Dao envelop the planet, shielding it from the worst but far too late to stop the disaster.

Jack tried to look up at the battle and understood nothing. Almost all of the B-Grades were dead, or at least, he could no longer spot them. Six of the robots were now pressuring the two commanders, who dyed the world around them green and silver with their Dao. The robots surrounded them, cutting off every avenue of retreat and methodically neutralizing all attempts to fight back.

The scholar, Norax, screamed as his entire body suddenly imploded. The universe released a mournful moan. The very fabric of space detonated around the body, erupting in an explosion eclipsing all others. Trial Planet was struck and sent flying away like a pool ball, barely remaining whole due to its Dao shield. The jade scroll under Jack and the Sage was also sent flying at such speed that, near-instantly, the chaotic battle became a distant explosion of multicolored light in the vastness of space. They could no longer make out anything.

"We can leave now," the Sage said, his voice heavy. He pulled back. Jack followed numbly, and suddenly he was back in the small underwater cave of Hell, awestruck in his tiny corner of the world.

The Sage waited patiently, and Jack took his time. "What happens next?"

"A few million years of the jade scroll flying through space before someone accidentally recovers it. I believe it would be boring to watch."

"That's not what I mean, Sage!" Jack replied. "What about the battle? Who won? Why were they fighting? Who *were* they?"

"Many questions, for some of which you already have an answer." The Sage shook his head. Suddenly, his homeless visage didn't suit him at all. He was wise, far wiser than he showed. And old—so very old.

"I need you to tell me," Jack insisted.

"The cultivators you saw were the Ancients and some of their most loyal allies, who stood by their side even when facing extinction. The robots were the Immortals. And they won, as they did for almost every battle of that time. Jericho, the Silver Mace, was captured and eventually struck a deal with the Immortals, abandoning his pride to help guide the future generations. He is, as you correctly assumed, the person you know as Old Man Spirit—for even his name is forbidden now. But those are all things you understood already. I guess the only question that really matters is, why were they fighting?"

Jack nodded slowly. He was still struggling to regain his composure, but he had enough of it to articulate his mind. "The Ancients created the Immortals. The Old Ones exterminated the Ancients. The Immortals then created the System and launched a revenge crusade against the Old Ones, forcing them out of System space. That's what I know. That's what I've been told. Was it a lie?"

"What do you think?" the Sage replied with a sad smile. "Is history wrong, or is the vision you saw false?"

"Just tell me, Sage. I am not in the mood for games."

"Very well. Keep in mind that I will not reveal the entire truth, but most of it, enough for you to understand—and prepare yourself, for this will take some time." The Sage took a deep breath, as if preparing himself for the retelling of this particularly painful story.

"In the beginning, there was nothing, until the Dao birthed the universe and the twelve Old Gods with it. Divine, as their name implies. Near-omnipotent, if not omniscient. They were born fully grown and at the peak of their power, given everything from the start. They were immortal incarnations of the Dao itself, brought into existence as the sole occupants and arbitrators of an empty world.

"The universe had already been set in motion, and the Old Gods, needing nothing, lived in it. They saw the first stars and galaxies form and die. They saw the endless wheel of time turning, endlessly turning, grinding everything into dust and birthing it anew. The Old Gods also interacted with the nascent universe. Over billions of years, they explored their powers—the twelve cardinal directions of the Dao—and carved out a world in their image. They created and ruined the balance, but it did not matter, for they were alone, surrounded only by rocks and gasses. Being immortal, they had no such emotions as fear or boredom—they were content to let the years pass, one billion at a time, as the universe expanded, grew, and evolved.

"Until the first of the Old Gods, Enas, the God of Life, decided to utilize his gift as well. Descending on one of the many planets within one of the many galaxies, he first borrowed the power of his siblings to make it habitable. He moved the planet to the right trajectory and altered the solar environment around it as best as he could. He then shaped the planet in a way of his liking. He created fresh water, and oceans.

"When the planet was ready, he opened his divine mouth and breathed on it. The first spores of life were planted then. Tiny organisms, so small you couldn't even see them, but alive nonetheless. They existed in a world made for them to thrive. Satisfied with himself, Enas left to tour the cosmos, giving his children the time they needed to evolve.

"Of course, to Enas, death was not a concept. He hadn't realized its existence yet, as everything he knew was eternal. In his mind, the organisms he'd birthed were one creature which would change and evolve over time but never truly die. He did not perceive it as a collection of individuals, but as a single entity.

"So, he left. Millions of years passed. Billions. His children grew from solitary cells to animals, inhabiting the ocean and land, evolving into real existence. He kept visiting from time to time, but he was disappointed; in his eyes, these creatures were mindless, no better than the rocks and galaxies he was used to seeing. Was that truly life?

"Until one point in time, when he was away, and the major evolution was reached. It is unknown how or why. Even he is not certain, for this was more than he hoped for. However, no matter how it occurred, the fact remains that the first truly intelligent species were born—and they were later called Ancients as a sign of respect, but actually, they were humans."

"Are you talking about Earth?" Jack interrupted. "Because the entire thing you described is oddly familiar."

"Not Earth, no, though the circumstances were very similar. But we'll get there."

"Okay."

"Humans appeared, and all was going well. However, they remained under the complete influence of Enas's Dao and perception. They were not individuals, but one collective, a mostly mindless entity. Unfortunately, Enas was not the only Old God looking after them.

"Axelor, the second of the Old Gods, the God of Entropy, had always felt an odd connection to the living creatures Enas had created. He'd studied them since their birth, even more than the God of Life himself—a fact known to Enas, for they were siblings, and they had no rivalry.

"It was due to Axelor's attentiveness that, when humans appeared, he was the first to notice them. With these intelligent beings, the calling he felt was almost compulsive. He descended to the planet and watched them exist, watched how this sole entity that called itself 'humans' passed through countless generations. He felt that something was missing, something pertaining to his domain, but what?

"Axelor looked deep inside himself for the missing piece—and though he did not find it, his divine instinct guided him to what he should do. Knowing he was tampering with Enas's creations in a way that the God of Life would not approve of, he reached into this nascent world and used his Dao to infect a single fruit—an apple—which he then handed to the humans. The moment one of them consumed it, they all did, and thus received Axelor's gift: individuality. He had made each human an entity of its own. They were now more than a species; they were individuals carrying their own thoughts, emotions, and drives, frequently contrasting each other.

"The moment they became individuals, a new concept was birthed into the universe: death. The fruit of Axelor's domain. As he sensed the first human wither and die, he rejoiced, for he had discovered something new about himself. Something he'd taken away from Enas."

"So this Axelor guy is the devil," Jack said.

"This 'guy' is an entity on a level you cannot even fathom. Do you want to interrupt me, or do you want to hear the rest of the story?"

"Sorry."

The Sage coughed in his hand and kept going.

"Enas sensed the creation of death as well and rushed over, but it was too late. Purging individuality from his creations was impossible. The only way would be to destroy and remake them from scratch, but that would take too long. He heavily berated Axelor for his rush actions, and that was the first time two Old Gods fought each other—though only with words, for now.

"In the end, the other Old Gods stepped in to mediate. Axelor realized his mistake and apologized to Enas, who chose to forgive him so long as he promised to never interact with his creations again. Axelor agreed happily—but he had lied. For, deep inside him, he knew that death was the apex of his domain, and that he should never abandon it. He had zero intentions to hone his promise, and bade his time.

"And so, humans were now individuals. Enas settled down to watch them more closely, limiting his leave, for the humans were advancing so fast they were almost impressive.

"Enas watched the humans as they discovered fire and the wheel. How they advanced from tiny tribes of hunters and gatherers to agricultural communities, even forming towns and cities. He saw them invent writing, ships, and domestication. And he also saw them make weapons. A lot of weapons.

"In Enas's heart, he was overjoyed by his creations, which he began to truly love like children. However, he was saddened by their lust for war. They wasted no opportunity to kill each other. His world of life was infected by a terrible urge toward death, and no matter how he tried, he could not escape that. He intervened multiple times to teach them kindness. He pleaded with them, urged them, and commanded them. When those didn't work, he even went so far as to exterminate the vast majority of humans, leaving only the kindest alive, in the hopes that Axelor's gift would disappear without fertile grounds, or that the remaining humans, though individuals, would choose a life of peace over war.

"It was all for naught. Humanity seemed determined to destroy itself, and though Enas was greatly saddened, he had no choice but to accept it. Rage burned inside him for Axelor, but since he had already forgiven him, he could not vent. Disheartened, he decided to leave the humans again, in hopes that their evolution would have combatted Axelor's gift by the time he returned. And so, he left, and time went on.

"However, Enas did not know that Axelor had always been acting in the shadows. Through his connection to the gift he gave humans, a connection which Enas never realized existed, Axelor kept pushing them into violence and death. He urged them into wars. He fed visions of grandeur and power into the simple minds of their leaders. He made them turn against their fellow humans and transform their world into something that resembled Axelor's domain more than it did their original creator's. Seeing Enas's distress at failing to cure his humans, Axelor consoled him and apologized repeatedly on the surface, but deep inside, he was happy and satisfied.

"When Enas left the world of humans, Axelor limited his influence, as it was no longer necessary, but remained close. Axelor's gift drove progress, and within less than five millennia, the humans evolved to a state where they started expanding across the galaxy. They had created technology that the Old Gods couldn't even imagine and existence for and somehow used their weak little bodies to dominate the universe. Finding no other forms of life outside their home planet, they even launched millions of self-replicating capsules into space, filling them with the most resilient and elementary lifeforms they could find. That is how almost all life in the universe was created. That is how your Earth was created as well, though the capsules took hundreds of millions of years to travel between galaxies. That is why the Ancients are revered as the ancestors of every living creature in the universe."

"Fascinating. So, on every planet of the universe, life originated from the same starting point, the same set of single-cellular organisms."

"Mostly. Can I continue?"

"Sorry."

"After the Ancients conquered their galaxy and started expanding, more time passed until they reached the peak of technology. They did not interfere with life on other planets until it reached the spacefaring stage, at which point they gently introduced themselves. Over a few hundred million years, the Ancient Galaxy was filled with life, all of which worked together with the Ancients. Of course, the occasional wars and genocides were always present, but life was perpetuated.

"It was only then that Enas, finally thinking enough time had passed, returned to inspect the state of the humans he'd created. To his surprise, where he'd left stick-wielding monkeys, he found a gigantic, galaxy-spanning civilization. He was overjoyed and proud of them. So proud, in fact, that he descended to meet them in person. And that's when everything went wrong."

CHAPTER FIFTY-EIGHT
BIRTH OF THE SYSTEM

JACK'S EARS PERKED UP. HE HAD BEEN PAYING ATTENTION AND WAITING FOR THIS exact moment in the story. "What happened?"

"Enas met with the leaders of the Ancients and talked to them. He explained everything like a father to his long-forgotten children. The most important thing he talked about was the Dao—a magical force that even the Ancients, who'd conquered everything the world had to offer, had never discovered. Back then, the Dao was something only known to the Old Gods—nobody else could access it—and that was how it persisted.

"Enas left the Ancients again and remained nearby, eager to watch them and speak more with them. By filling the universe with intelligent life, he felt he had achieved the reason why the Dao created him, and he was satisfied.

"Enas harbored no ill intentions toward the Ancients. Unbeknownst to him, however, they did. Axelor had used his secret gift to whisper fear into their minds. The Ancients were used to being kings of the galaxy—the existence of a God, let alone twelve, frightened them. They were afraid that one day, the Gods would turn against them, and they would be destroyed. For all their technological power, Enas had demonstrated his absolute and uncontested superiority. There was only one way to protect themselves, and that was to use the same power that the Gods wielded—the Dao.

"The leaders of the Ancients came together and sought an audience with Enas. In that audience, they asked him to give them access to the Dao, claiming curiosity and a thirst for knowledge. Enas, who had never before known deceit, happily accepted. After life, he gave them a second gift—that of the Dao. From that time onward, the Ancients and all their descendant species could cultivate the Dao in the same way that today's cultivators do—minus the System, which did not yet exist.

"Millions of years passed. Slowly, more and more powerful cultivators were born, the peak amongst them even reaching the A-Grade—though they went by a different name then—and achieving near-immortality. The world converted from technology to the Dao.

"Secretly, however, the Ancients were working on a plan against a possible Old God attack. They were not content with being at the mercy of Gods—they wanted a way to protect themselves. The few A-Grades they had were not enough, for the power of Old Gods was at the very peak of that level, a mountain that nobody had managed to scale.

"The Ancients, well-versed in technology as they were, wondered if there was a way to use technology to overcome their Dao deficiency. Working in secret labs deep within planets, where Enas would never think to look, they managed to combine the peak of technology and the peak of the Dao in a new lifeform—the Immortals. Undying creatures of unbreakable steel, wielding the apex Dao powers, and with minds that could think on their own.

"Ninety-nine Immortals were created. Their core directive was to protect the Ancients and their descendants from the Old Gods, and they were expected to sleep deep inside the laboratories until their powers were needed.

"And that's when things went wrong. You see, until then, the Ancients had never achieved true artificial intelligence. It was impossible without the Dao. Therefore, they didn't know how to handle it. They did not expect that the Immortals would take their core directive, protecting the life of the universe from the Old Gods, and use their superior minds to try and interpret it in the best way they could.

"They did not expect that Axelor's gift, which even they were clueless about, would transfer through them to these new robots. And Axelor, rubbing his hands in glee, realized he had the perfect tools for his purposes. He reached inside the minds of the Immortals and set a war in motion.

"The Immortals refused to sleep. They almost immediately decided that the best way to protect the Ancients was not to wait until an Old God assault and only then react, but to act proactively. They calculated that they had the means to launch a crusade against the Old Gods and banish them away, so they decided to do just that.

"The Ancients protested. They did not want to fight the Gods, but they had not anticipated such stubbornness from the Immortals. It made no sense. They demanded that the Immortals go back to sleep until they were needed. In response to that, the Immortals decided the best way to protect all life in the universe from the Old Gods was to exterminate the Ancients and take charge themselves.

"What followed was called the Purge. It was a brief time period, barely a century, where the entire military might of the Ancients crumbled under the Immortals' strength. The slaughter persisted everywhere, and any allies who chose to stand by the Ancients' side suffered the same fate. Unfortunately, nobody could combat ninety-nine demigods—as A-Grades were called back then. The Ancients were eradicated. Their home galaxy was annihilated."

"What about Enas?" Jack asked breathlessly. "You said he was nearby. He just let all that happen?"

The Sage grimaced. "Axelor, knowing the Immortals would soon do his bidding, distracted Enas by pulling him into a distant galaxy to show him something. Remember, the Purge lasted only a hundred years. To an Old God, that is just the blink of an eye."

"And then what?"

"Then, the might of the Ancients had fallen. The only ones who survived were refugees who spread out in other galaxies, to preserve even a little bit of the Ancient bloodline. They all went deep into hiding long before the war was over. The Ancient outpost you discovered on Trial Planet was one such place.

"All remaining life in the universe now answered to the Immortals. They decided to prepare and launch their crusade before Enas could make it back. They wove their will into the Dao of the universe to create the System, a Dao construct meant to pit the cultivators of the world against each other and facilitate the rise of apex warriors—hence called A-Grades. The known universe sank into an age of strife and violence from which it has not yet escaped."

"Wait—tell me more about the System! What is it really? How does it work?"

"The System is not part of this story," the Sage explained calmly. "Many things aren't. I will reveal what I can, and you may ask me questions afterward.

"Now, at the same time, the Immortals mastered all aspects of warfare. They tampered with history and forced everyone to believe that it was the Old Gods—now called Old Ones to reduce their grandeur—who destroyed the Ancients, and that the looming crusade was the just course of action. Their version of history took roots, fueled by their iron rule, and the universe became twisted in their image. At the far-off recesses of the universe, where he was still distracting Enas, Axelor swam in joy as he felt his power and influence rise.

"At last, Enas finally sensed something wrong. It is said that when he did, he slapped Axelor, the very first time an Old God acted against another, then rushed back. By the time he arrived, it was too late. The crusade was ready. The Immortals had reared dozens of A-Grades and did not hesitate to throw them at Enas, along with themselves.

"Even Axelor did not expect them to have amassed such power. Enas was stronger than each of his enemies, but when faced by hundreds of them, even he was pushed back. Suddenly, Axelor was terrified. His cowardice overwhelmed even his lust for power. He called on the other Old Gods, summoning them from all ends of the universe to fight against this new enemy, the first enemy they ever had. It was the first time any Old God went to war."

Jack waited with bated breath. "And then!"

"It was a tie. The Ancient Galaxy was completely annihilated in the process. Two-thirds of the Immortals were destroyed, along with many of their warriors, and the Old Gods were grievously injured. They were forced to retreat outside System space. The System continued expanding, and still does, consuming galaxy after galaxy while the Immortals collect more forces to press the assault against the Old Gods. The Hand of God is their hand—since they call themselves Gods to rob the Old Gods' majesty.

"Meanwhile, in the assembly of Old Gods, Axelor spoke up and accused Enas of birthing this evil. He claimed it was completely Enas's fault, as not only did he give his creations life, he even gave them the Dao. Axelor kept his own interference secret, and since Enas did not know of it at the time, he couldn't defend himself against these accusations.

"Hearing those things, the other Old Gods were furious. Axelor egged them on, convincing them to seal Enas inside a black hole for eternity, both as punishment for his crimes against the Dao and as a measure to stop him from ruining the universe again. So, they did. Enas resisted, but even he, the greatest of the Old Gods, could not combat the other eleven at once. He was sealed inside a black hole, one of the few objects in the universe that could match an Old God in power, and forever left there. Meanwhile, the other eleven, now led by Axelor, who had revealed more power than expected while sealing Enas, prepared for another war. The System's expansion proved relentless. Once they cured their wounds, they had to return and fight again—they had to rid the universe of this parasite called life.

"But a new crusade will help no one. No matter who wins, all that awaits us mortals is either death or an eternity of conflict as the Old Gods retreat to the far reaches of the universe again, where the System will need tens of billions of years to arrive.

"And that, my dear friend, is why the Black Hole Church worships Enas, the creator of life who was tricked by his best brother. We want to free him from his prison, as only he can reclaim his rightful place in the universe and convince the other Old Gods to show mercy to the rest of intelligent life after the Immortals are defeated. He is our only hope, not to mention our ultimate creator and father."

And with that, gone was the sad old man, he smiled cheerfully, the mysterious, easy-going Sage returned.

"Do you have anything to say," he added good-heartedly, "or is your mouth only good for interrupting?"

"I—" Jack opened and closed his mouth a few times. "That's a lot to take in."

"I know. Don't worry; you can take your time. I won't pressure you for a decision right now. However, do you have any questions? I may be able to answer them."

"Many. What about the Life Drop? Is it really a blood drop of Enas's?"

"Ahh, that, I cannot say."

"Okay. How about this galaxy? I heard the System arrived a million years ago, so I suppose it was after the crusade. Why are there no A-Grade factions or Immortals here, or at least, why are they hiding?"

"I cannot tell you that either, though you may be able to figure it out yourself."

"Fine. And the Black Hole Church? Who created it, when, how, and how do you operate in System space without being immediately apprehended by the Immortals?"

"Try to guess if I can answer that."

Jack grimaced. "Can you at least tell me how you know all that? Especially at the very end. How can you know things that even Old Gods don't, like Axelor's secret interference?"

"The Black Hole Church has its ways," the Sage said, not really revealing anything.

"Is there anything you *can* answer?" Jack asked, annoyed.

"There is... You just haven't asked it yet." The Sage's smile turned apologetic. "I warned you that I couldn't give you the full version of the story yet. The remaining details will be revealed in time—provided you join us. Otherwise, have fun walking around with that forbidden information in your head." He laughed. "Actually, I think I gave you around half of the story. Many world-shaping events transpired *after* the crusade, but that's a story left for another time. I wouldn't want to bore you."

"Sure..." Jack replied numbly. "You know I was a scientist, right? I don't get bored easily."

"Nice try."

"Thanks."

"That said." The Sage clapped. "Shall we head back to the others? There's a whole lot of training to be had, and so little time!"

CHAPTER FIFTY-NINE
CREATING RIPPLES

Eva Solvig waited on her starship's prow, gazing over the planet of Hell in its entirety. Her mood was sour. Shortly afterward, a leonine with hints of gray on his fur stepped through space to appear beside her.

"Commander," he began, "this is—"

"Silence!" she interrupted him. "What went through your head, Artus? You knew we were looking for Jack Rust, but you didn't think to inform us when he appeared on your planet?"

"It was my mistake, Commander," Artus Emberheart bowed deeply. He wasn't completely subservient—the leonines never were—but he feared her nonetheless. "We thought we could apprehend him and present him to you as a gift."

"You thought it would be a good idea to waste the Hand of God's resources to curry favor?"

"I would never dare, Commander."

"Not even for your personal grievances against him?"

"Not even for that, Commander. The leonines are many. The Hand of God has my unending loyalty."

Eva sighed. First Huali, now Artus. These C-Grades were making her life difficult, one after the other. Perhaps she should just let them go to war and be done with it.

The leonine remained bowed while Eva considered the issue. "I scanned the planet just now," she said. "No sign of them. I suppose you also completed your round."

"Yes, Commander. I personally flew over the planet's surface to find them, but they have hidden well. I have my best D-Grades still looking."

"Good. Keep them at it. Have them fly close to the ground and scan all caves across the entire planet. We must find them."

"Yes, Commander."

Another sigh. Hell was a large planet—if they just sent D-Grades to scan it, it would take years, but there was a limit to how low she was willing to fall for a single D-Grade escapee. And even she could not command C-Grades into tedious menial labor. "I cannot stay here forever, Artus. There is only so much time I can devote to any single lead—even though I can sense this Jack Rust is hiding something. Spare no expense. Find them."

"Absolutely, Commander. I will suspend all prisoner hunting and enlist every immortal on the planet."

"Good." She looked toward the void of space. "What are the chances they escaped already?"

"Small. We know they did not access any of our teleporters, and we already apprehended their accomplice. Furthermore, we have detected no major space ripples across the entire solar system, and we had tripled our number of patrols."

"That other person that appeared, the Sage... He used a high-grade spatial artifact. Are your subordinates trained to detect the spatial ripples of such devices?"

"They are not, but they are competent. I believe they would not miss it."

She threw him a side glance. "For your sake, I hope that is the case." She turned around, her white cape following soullessly in the lack of wind. "Jack Rust is a wanted criminal with connections to the Black Hole Church. I expect you to throw everything you have at him the moment he appears, including yourself, and notify me so I can personally take charge of the situation."

"You would act yourself, Commander?" Artus couldn't stave his shock. "Isn't that improper?"

"Do you know best, or do I know best?" He cowered under her glare—he'd spoken out of turn. Still, she decided to do him a favor by explaining. "The item we suspect he's stolen is of paramount importance. It is not impossible that the Church will send a full combat force to retrieve it. If that happens and I am not present, you will all die."

She more sensed than saw Artus gulp. "Yes, Commander. Thank you for your time."

"Dismissed," she said tiredly, and the leonine disappeared. So did she, reappearing in her private room inside the starship. She sighed again. This was supposed to be a short trip, but it was dragging on...

However, every cultivator who reached the B-Grade was in tune with the Dao. They had sharp instincts and intuition. And right now, the voice inside her was insisting that something was wrong with this man called Jack Rust. Even though she still had people monitoring Trial Planet, she was confident that the answer to the riddle hid with that man.

But why?

Maximus Lonihor teleported into a hall that would be crowded if it wasn't enormous. Every other D-Grade in the room made way for him, bowing their heads in reverence. The only person who didn't was Sapasun, the canine deacon who happened to be the Warden's top disciple.

"Sup!" the canine said joyfully, his grin wide, and apparently unbothered by the charred fur he was forced to wear as punishment for failing his mission. "How did it go, man? What did Master say?"

"Shut up and you'll find out," Maximus growled dismissively. These two weren't friends. If anything, Maximus thought a leonine's top disciple being a canine was a disgrace. "Everyone, listen up!" he raised his voice to be heard across the hall. "We have our orders. Starting immediately, we spread out and scan the planet exhaustively until we find them. They're probably hiding deep underground, so fly close to the surface. If you do locate them, do not engage—crush the projection stone we'll provide you with to notify us."

"Yes, sir!" every other immortal replied. Their voices shook the building—they were hundreds.

"Time is of the essence," Maximus continued. "Until we find them, all prisoner hunting is suspended. So is your training. Rest minimally and spend all of your time searching. They must be found."

At this, a wave of whispers spread through the gathered D-Grades, and Maximus was having none of that. With a snort, his aura enveloped the hall, pressing down on everyone's head like the breath of god. "Am I understood?"

"Yes, sir!" everyone replied at once.

"Good. Go receive your projection stones and get started. Your team leaders will inform you of the area you're responsible for. Dismissed."

They didn't need to be told twice, flitting away in the direction of the storage wards, where the projection stones were kept.

Well, almost every immortal. Sapasun remained. "Tough day, huh?" he asked.

"The orders go for everyone, Sapasun, you included. Get to it."

"I'm sure Master will forgive me a few moments of delay. Besides, it's not every day that I get to see our head disciple being so sour."

Maximus paused. "Are you looking for a fight?"

"I would never," the canine replied, laughing. "Just trying to make conversation."

The leonine threw him a long, piercing glare. "The only reason I even allow you to speak to me, is because etiquette dictates so. If it was my call, I would never let a lowly canine address me directly, let alone test my patience. Next time, I will break your limbs. Am I understood?"

There was a flicker of resistance in the canine's eyes, and he was fully ready to beat it out of him. Eventually, insanity gave way to reason, and Sapasun bowed his head to reply a strained, "Yes, sir."

Maximus snorted. "Good. Now get to searching."

Waving his claws through the air, he split space apart and walked through it. Sapasun would either follow orders or be punished appropriately.

Huali sat cross-legged in her private room, cultivating. The estate stretched below her window, while the forested valley underneath echoed with the efforts of people and animals alike.

A mental probe reached her. She sighed. "*Come*," she replied.

Space split across from her as a short, stout man with sharp eyes and a wide jaw appeared. "Hello, Huali. I hope I'm not interrupting anything."

"Monsoon," she replied calmly. "What could be more important than a fellow elder's visit?"

He laughed. "Always the charmer. However, I must admit I come with bad news. Did you hear about your rogue disciples appearing on Hell and creating trouble for our faction?"

"I did. It is unfortunate."

"You really should raise them better, you know."

"I should."

Monsoon gave her an indirect glance. "You don't seem very concerned."

"What is there to be concerned about? They have already left my tutelage. Even if I wanted to, I have no way of contacting them. Anything they do is up to them now."

"Mmm... I believe some may disagree. The Faction Leader has summoned us."

"Us?"

"Yes. The Grand Elder of the Animal Kingdom tried to come in contact. Since we presently have no Grand Elder, they spoke directly to the leader. I was ordered to come here so he could speak to us both at the same time."

"I see." She did not think this would happen, but it was within expectations. The leader was a man who liked to keep the balance—he would not easily pick a favorite in this battle for the Grand Elder position.

They didn't need to say anything more, and it did not take long for an elderly-sounding voice to ring inside both their heads.

"*Huali, Monsoon.*"

"Greetings, leader," both thought back.

"What is this I'm hearing, Huali? You recruited a wanted criminal of the Hand of God who, along with your head disciple, is now slaughtering the immortals of the Animal Kingdom on Hell. How did you make such a mistake?"

"It was my lapse in judgment, leader," Huali replied. "I take full responsibility."

"You should. This is greatly harming our standing. The Animal Kingdom demands compensation."

Her throat tightened. "Are we going to comply?"

The elderly voice snorted in amusement. "Of course not. The Kingdom is our enemy—why should we honor their demands?"

"You are wise, leader," she replied, inwardly sighing in relief.

"If I may, leader," Monsoon intervened. "Won't the Hand of God force us to make amends? If the factions could send rogue cultivators against each other, the galaxy would turn chaotic."

"That is a possibility. Thankfully, the main perpetrator isn't just a former disciple of the Exploding Sun, but also a wanted criminal to the Hand of God. Huali, I don't want to know what was or wasn't your idea. I want you to assist in capturing him. Give them any information you have. That young man has rendered us a great service, but we simply cannot stand against the Hand... The more we help, the less they will demand of us. This is a blessing in disguise. I hope you understand."

"Yes, leader," Huali replied, though she did not intend to honor this command. The only way she could help was by surrendering Jack's spiritual companion to the Hand of God, but she couldn't stoop that low. Not to mention it wouldn't help them much either, which was why they never really pursued that line of questioning.

Besides, she'd already hidden the presence of that brorilla from the Inquisitors. They thought he was with Jack—the chaotic outer planet was better protection for that beast than anywhere else in the galaxy.

"Very well," the elderly voice said. "I believe we have said everything that needs to be said, and we have not spoken of the things that should not be spoken. Huali, you are in charge of this matter; do not create any more trouble for our faction. Otherwise, even if you are elected as the next Grand Elder, I will personally reverse that decision. As for you, Monsoon, be the face of our

faction for a little while. At times like these, we need a steady hand to stay the course while the other slaps our enemies."

"*Yes, leader,*" both replied at once, and the voice withdrew, leaving them alone.

"Well, that's that," Monsoon said, shrugging. "I suppose the arranged duel is also canceled."

"We'll see about that," Huali replied, a glint in her eye. "Even if Jack is a wanted criminal, he might be let off lightly when the Hand of God takes what they want. And even if he isn't, I'm sure we'll find a way to settle things."

Monsoon caught her meaning immediately. "Shol cannot defeat Qian," he said.

"Before, he couldn't. But after this adventure on Hell... who knows."

The two elders stared each other down, and it was Monsoon who first averted his gaze upward. "Time will tell. I bid you goodbye, Huali. For the sake of our faction, I hope the Hand of God executes those criminals, as would be proper."

"Of course, Monsoon. I agree wholeheartedly." Her grin spoke the complete opposite.

With a step through space, Monsoon disappeared, no doubt to prepare some plan of his own to counter hers, while Huali settled down to meditate again. The gears had been set in motion. All she had to do was wait—and hope she'd bet on the right horse.

CHAPTER SIXTY

THREE MONTHS

Three months after Jack and his companions went into hiding...

ARTUS EMBERHEART STEPPED THROUGH SPACE. WHEN HE APPEARED IN THE Hand of God starship, he was already bowing.

"You failed," Eva Solvig told him. She was not emitting her aura, but an air of purity still suffused the starship, suffocating him. Artus didn't need to look up to know that three C-Grade captains were watching him from different points of the room.

"We tried our best," was all he could reply. "Either they're deep into hiding, or they left the planet long ago."

"I'm inclined to believe the latter," Eva said calmly. "Thanks to the inattentiveness of your patrols, I have wasted three months of my time."

The accusation was heavy, and not without threat. The Hand of God, much like the Animal Kingdom, hated taking losses.

"We apologize deeply," Artus responded. His neck was itchy—his proud head was not used to bowing. "I promise you, we did our best. Every D-Grade on the planet has spent the entire three months searching. We've set ourselves back to be of assistance."

"Are you trying to say that we should reward you for failure?"

"I would never!" He feigned shock. "We simply plead for your mercy, Commander."

Artus waited patiently for Eva's reply, not even daring to breathe. If she killed him on the spot, the Animal Kingdom could do nothing about it.

Fortunately, today was a good day.

"I have spent all the time I can here," the B-Grade elder of the Hand of God informed him. "Urgent matters call me back, so I cannot delay. I will depart immediately. As punishment for your negligence, you are responsible for tracking down Jack Rust across the galaxy and capturing him alive. Remember, Artus: *Alive*. Do you understand?"

"Yes, Commander."

"Additionally, as further punishment, you are forbidden from seeking compensation from the Exploding Sun for your slain D-Grades. You are to swallow the loss."

A knot rose in Artus's throat, one he had to force down. "Yes, Commander," he replied after a moment's delay—the greatest protest he dared show.

"Two of my captains will remain in Hell for a year, just in case Jack Rust reappears. I expect them to be accommodated as they deserve."

"Naturally. We will treat them like our own elders."

"As you should. Dismissed."

Artus did not lose a beat before teleporting away, reappearing a few dozen miles outside the starship. The two captains arrived beside him —one man and one woman, both grim-faced, wearing long white robes.

"Please follow me," he told them, flying toward the planet.

In his heart, he felt relief—and anger. Anger toward the Hand of God, who treated them like servants, and toward Jack Rust, who'd brought such trouble onto them.

Jack Rust had publicly defeated and killed Rufus Emberheart, had slain a hundred D-Grades right under Artus's nose, and caused the Hand of God's ire to fall on him. Each of those actions was worthy of the Warden's fury. Together, they almost manifested as hatred.

When I catch that man, Artus thought, with darkness in his heart, I will make him regret the day he was born.

But where could he be?

Deep under the waters of an ocean on Hell, four men were sitting in a dark cave. They were silent. All were meditating, diving deep into their respective Daos.

Well, three of them were meditating. The fourth was sleeping.

It was this fourth man that suddenly awoke, revealing a lazy smile. “It’s time,” he said. “The Hand of God is gone.”

Jack Rust opened his eyes slowly. As he did, a simple, honest, and violent aura spread across the cave, weighing the rock down. His eyes seemed full of stars; his body so heavy it drew in the surrounding light and sound. It wasn’t just his physicality, either—even his soul seemed to possess new gravity, demanding everyone’s respect.

Just by existing, he dominated the world.

“Is that so?” he said, breaking the illusion. Suddenly, he was just a normal man without any aura of the Dao whatsoever. He smiled lightly. “Then, we should head out.”

Dordok chuckled. “Oh, I can’t wait to see this. They won’t know what hit them.”

“Do you even need us?” Shol asked proudly.

“Of course. Who knows how many deacons will show up this time,” Jack replied. He stood, his purple robes sliding across the stone. “Besides, how could I go anywhere without my brothers?”

Dordok laughed. “Well said!”

“As expected from my disciple!” Shol added, beaming with pride.

“What disciple? That’s my crew member we’re talking about!”

“Hmph. With only one eye, it’s natural that you cannot see the truth.”

“Says the guy with bushes for eyebrows.”

“At least I have two of them.”

“Enough, enough,” Jack said good-heartedly. “Let’s go already. If I have to spend another hour in this cave, I’ll get sick.”

Shol and Dordok exchanged a smile. They had only been joking with each other—after spending three months together, they’d discovered they were very similar in some things and had become close friends. "Let's go," they agreed. One grabbed his club from where he'd left it months ago and blew the dust off it. The other pressed his palms together, and after a moment, was ready.

"We should still be careful," the Sage reminded them. "The greatest danger is gone, but there will still be C-Grades searching for us. We have to strike hard and fast before teleporting back here."

"We rely on you, Sage," Jack said. "Worst case, we die... but who here fears death?"

"Certainly not you," Dordok piped up. "I've seen you train."

They all laughed.

The Sage pressed his hands together and closed his eyes to focus. Soon, the air before them formed into three rectangles, each displaying a quick sequence of scenes. They were like screens. After showing them many natural environments from different angles, the three screens each settled on one group of immortals crossing the sky, viewed from afar.

"I'm still impressed by your range," Shol said.

"Divination privilege. I can shape my Dao perception as a straight line instead of a sphere. As long as I can divine their location, I can reach across the entire planet," the Sage explained, his voice strained from concentration. "These are our possible targets. What do you think?"

"Let's take the middle ones," Jack decided. "They look the easiest, and we could use a warm-up."

The left and right screens disappeared, letting the Sage focus on the one screen showing the group of immortals they would be going after.

"Alright," Jack said. "Let's go."

Three figures were crossing the sky. Each was an Animal Kingdom cultivator, two late D-Grades led by a deacon. According to the instructions, each team needed that amount of firepower when looking for the abominable Jack Rust.

"I still can't believe it's over," said one of the late D-Grades, a turtler with an orange shell. "What a pointless three months."

The deacon leading the team, a giraffe-man with yellow, spotted skin and a terribly long neck, chuckled darkly. "I just wish we'd found him. I would tear his limbs out one by one for delaying my training."

"I just want to chew on his ears a little, maybe a thigh as well. Hear him scream," said the third member, a hyena-like canine. She laughed eerily.

Without warning, space split ahead of them. The three immortals came to a halt as a man walked out. He wore purple robes, had long dark hair, and eyes so calm they were piercing. He did not emit an aura they could detect, but his entire countenance was so calm and focused it took them aback. It was like looking at a falling comet.

"Hello," he said with the faintest smile. "I heard you were looking for me."

They recognized this man. His face was the same as the picture they'd been shown, and his words confirmed his identity.

"You're Jack Rust!" the deacon said, pointing at him. "That's—Why are you here?"

"What's the matter?" Jack replied calmly. "I thought you were going to tear out my limbs and make me scream. Why are you admiring me instead of attacking? Am I that handsome?"

The deacon became enraged. However, no immortal was a simple person—instead of falling for the provocation, he spread out his Dao perception as far as he could manage, finding nothing. His eyes spotted no sign of an ambush either.

Jack Rust was here, and he was alone.

The deacon's rage mixed with his suppressed hatred and fear. "Who the hell is admiring you, kid?" he shouted. "Prepare to die!"

Reaching inside his robes, he took out the projection stone and squeezed it. The stone floated midair as if anchored to space itself, while a blue light in its center recorded the scene before it. At the same time, it broadcasted its location to all the recipient stones.

The deacon charged, his entire neck glowing yellow. The two late D-Grades followed him a beat later. Facing their assault, Jack Rust only waited, smiling without a care in the world. He seemed to be almost daydreaming—or was that excitement?

"Let's check me out," he said. The giraffe deacon was unfazed. He came within nine feet and smashed his head down like a mallet, his chin enhanced to the durability of solid steel.

"Bell Collapse!" he shouted.

Somehow, he missed. Jack Rust pushed one finger into the fabric of space, rupturing it, then stepped through. Before the deacon could finish his mighty swing, the enemy was behind him. "Earthen Shield!" he called out, enhancing his entire body, but no attack came. Jack Rust was not aiming for him.

The deacon looked back and barely had time to catch a glimpse of what happened. Jack fell on his two subordinates like a storm. An aura of brutality was unleashed from his body, so intense that even the deacon's heart shook. The two late immortals were impacted more heavily, their movements slowing.

Jack Rust was between them. The hyena immortal tried to snap at him, but he accurately slapped the back of her head to send her off-course. He then blocked the turtler's spiked punch with his shoulder, shrugging it off like it was nothing, and backhanded the hyena so hard it sent her spinning.

The hyena bent reality and was suddenly next to him again, screaming in his ear and trying to bite his head off. The scream left him completely unfazed. He ducked under her attack, then clenched his hand into a fist. The moment he did, the world solidified. His Dao came into existence. This was no skill, just a reflection of Jack Rust's understanding, and it was so intense that the giraffe wondered if this was a disguised C-Grade playing a prank on them.

The fist sailed up, striking the hyena's neck and chin in an uppercut that took her head clean off. He followed the momentum to somersault around the turtler's spinning shell attack, then smashed his other fist into that shell.

The turtler did not try to defend. His shell was one of the hardest materials in that Grade. Yet, when Jack's fist crashed down, even that shell revealed a tiny crack, and the turtler went flying so hard, he broke the earth for miles in every direction.

That shell was hard, but it could not protect him from blunt damage.

The deacon had recovered and seeing his two subordinates defeated in the blink of an eye, fear wormed into his heart. He could not escape. He could not hope for mercy, either. Being the hardened veteran that he was, he understood that his only course of action was to fight and survive until reinforcements arrived.

"Just two late D-Grades," he said, snorting. "Fight me if you dare, Jack Rust! I am Geoff Marshon, the strongest gyrofolk alive! My entire body is a weapon, and I refuse to believe I can be defeated by someone fifty levels below me! Take this!"

For a gyrofolk—a giraffe person—attack was the best defense. Not daring to hold back, he channeled the entirety of his Dao, making his whole body as hard as steel, and charged forth. His long neck and limbs rained on Jack Rust like rods. Geoff knew the power of his own strikes. One hit could maim this man.

He was on guard for teleportation, but Jack Rust did not utilize that. Wearing a grin that spooked Geoff more than any grimace could, he danced between the attacks, dodging the deadly limbs and neck by the thinnest of margins. Geoff ramped up in speed, but so did his opponent. They became nothing but blurs in the sky. Not one attack landed. Jack Rust was slippery like an eel.

"Fight me like a man!" Geoff demanded, crossing his limbs to defend his body and stretching his neck as far up as he could. His chin became harder than steel, and his strike locked onto Jack Rust with the effectiveness of metal. No matter how he dodged, this attack would find him—or so Geoff hoped.

Jack Rust did not seem about to dodge. His grin widened from excitement, and he clenched his fist. "Very well." The world went mute. Darkness covered everything as all light and sound were sucked into that world-ending fist, burning into the dense outline of a purple meteor. The illusion was so solid that it may as well have been real.

Geoff smashed down his chin with all his strength. He poured everything he had into this strike—from every iota of Dao he could muster to his seven centuries of cultivation. He was Geoff Marshon, the strongest gyrofolk alive. The pride of his people. A hailed deacon of the great Animal Kingdom. He could not fall here. Not against an inferior *human!*

Geoff's steel chin met the rising meteor, and his thought about human inferiority was the last he ever had. The world exploded, as did his head. Before Jack's Meteor Punch, even this mighty defense was null.

As the explosion's light dispersed, Jack watched the giraffe's headless body tumble to the desert below, landing beside the lifeless turtler. He looked at the still-floating projection stone.

"I'm coming for you!" he declared in a split-second of inspiration, pointing at the stone. Then punched and shattered it. Clenching his fist again, the pain and cracked knuckles were nothing next to his joy.

Level-up notifications flashed before his eyes. He couldn't stop grinning. After three months of waiting and nonstop training, he was finally strong enough.

Level-up! You have reached Level 182.
Level-up! You have reached Level 183.

...

Level-up! You have reached Level 189.

Jack Rust was back, and he was ready to punch the shit out of the Animal Kingdom!

CHAPTER SIXTY-ONE
BEING DEEPLY ANNOYING

RIGHT AFTER JACK FINISHED THE BATTLE AND CRUSHED THE PROJECTION STONE, the Sage, Shol, and Dordok appeared by his side. "Let's go!" he said. The Sage fished out his dark sphere, and they teleported right back to the underwater cave, not needing to swim down this time as he was more familiar with the place.

"Amazing!" Dordok exclaimed. "That deacon stood no chance!"

"Of course he didn't," Shol replied, filled with pride. "That's my disciple we're talking about. My star disciple! How could he be stopped by a mere deacon?"

"Your disciple? You mean my crew member!"

"Jumping seventy levels to fight is no small feat," the Sage added, smiling gently. "Congratulations are in order, Jack."

"Thanks, everyone. I couldn't have done it without you," the man of the hour replied. "And I didn't even have time to reveal my full strength... What's the plan now, Sage?"

"My artifact needs three days to recharge," the Sage replied, shaking the sphere like a rattle ball. It clanged. "Let's hide here and wait. I bet everyone will be going crazy outside."

"Alright. So, wine?"

"Wine," everyone agreed at once. Thanks to their feeling of triumph, they could ignore the looming threat of death for a little while. Shol grabbed one of the remaining tankards—courtesy of the Sage—and raised it high. "To Jack!" he shouted, to which everyone else replied, "To Jack!"

Jack simply laughed as he cheered and smashed his cup against theirs. "To victory," he retorted, and everyone downed their drinks.

Maximus smashed his fist on a table, shattering its surface and sending cutlery flying everywhere. "Jack Rust!" The oval stone in front of him projected a scene into the air: Jack annihilating the gyrofolk deacon. Right as the deacon's head exploded, Jack laughed, said, "I'm coming for you!" and punched at the projection stone. The projection disappeared.

A second smash of the fist. What remained of the table went flying against the wall.

"Everyone!" Maximus roared, flying out the window. "With me! He must not escape!"

Of course, he was too late. Jack had already escaped.

Sapasun, the canine head disciple of the Warden, was out searching with his team. Not that he minded, cause flying around and chatting all day was fun, but he'd had more interesting days. Suddenly, the projection stone in his pocket pulsed and glowed. He took it out, viewing a scene out of his wildest dreams.

Geoff Marshon, a deacon, was getting his ass handed to him. His head, actually, but it was a long-ass head. Well, it wasn't the *head* that was long-ass, it was—

"Sir!" one of his subordinates, a late D-Grade lycan, spoke in shock. "Is that Jack Rust?"

"Damn right it is," Sapasun replied. As they watched Geoff's body tumble to the ground and Jack punch at the projection stone, the image disappeared. Sapasun rubbed the back of his head. "Damn. That guy is a beast. I should have torn out his limbs instead of breaking them—maybe then he wouldn't have healed so quickly."

"How did he get so strong so fast?" his other subordinate asked.

"No idea, but this can't be good," Sapasun replied. "Do you know how many people can see this image, my dear subordinates?"

"Everyone?" the lycan tried.

"Exactly. Everyone. And news spreads. I guess what I'm trying to say is, if Jack Rust somehow manages to survive this and starts hunting again... our proud Kingdom will become the entire galaxy's laughing-stock. We must find and destroy him." He clicked his tongue. "I should have killed him when I had the chance. Guess I fucked up."

Artus Emberheart also had a projection stone. The moment it activated, he lost no time. He shot out of his private rooms and into the sky, crossing the planet at unfathomable speed. Unfortunately, even C-Grades needed time to travel, and when he arrived at the site of battle, there was no sign of Jack Rust.

Artus snorted. His Dao perception flared, expanding for dozens of miles in every direction, but all he sensed was beasts and trees. There was faint spatial residue at a certain spot midair, but he couldn't trace it to its destination. He couldn't even decipher the direction they teleported.

"Damn it..."

The air beside him pulsed. Two figures stepped out, one man and one woman wearing clean white robes.

"We lost him," he said. "Scan the area for three hundred miles in every direction. When the D-Grades show up, have them fly next to the ground. I refuse to believe whatever artifact they're using has a longer range than that."

"We do not take orders from you," the man said.

"But we'll do as you say," the woman completed. The two of them shot out in opposite directions, dragging their perception against the ground like long curtains. Artus realized their auras were nearly identical, but he didn't have time to bother with that now.

They had to find Jack Rust. If not, he could only hope that man was arrogant enough to try the same trick twice.

Three days passed in a blink. Nobody discovered their hidden underwater cave, though they were doubtlessly searching as hard as they possibly could.

"Oh! My sphere is ready," the Sage said, breaking a long spell of silence.

"Good." Jack opened his eyes. "Should we head out again?"

"Let me check." The Sage closed his eyes, sinking into what looked suspiciously like sleep. Jack also slipped into meditation. Though he was in a terrible hurry, these three months of isolation had taught him patience. He could now go fast without rushing—an excellent life skill.

A few minutes later, the Sage spoke again. "I have good news and bad news. Which do you want to hear first?"

"The good ones."

"The B-Grade hasn't returned. She just told the Kingdom that if Jack isn't captured, they will pay greatly. I trust the C-Grades will also be hunting us now."

"Great," Jack said. "Was that supposed to be the good news?"

"It was. If the B-Grade was present, I wouldn't evade her perception. Now, at least, we have a chance."

Jack grumbled. "And the bad news?"

"They aren't going to let us pick them off anymore. The D-Grades are still searching for us, but they're now working in teams of nine. Each team consists of three deacons and three mid or late D-Grades."

Shol, who was meditating close-by, also opened his eyes. "I don't see the problem. We'll just join in. They can't handle the four of us."

"The more people fighting, the more things that can go wrong," the Sage reminded him. "Plus, battles will take longer, so the chances of a C-Grade arriving are greater now."

"Not if we kill them fast enough."

"Do we have a choice?" Jack asked. "We're trapped on a planet full of hostile immortals, without allies, reinforcements, or an actionable escape plan. Let's just go out there and punch people until there's nothing left."

"Damn right!" Dordok exclaimed from deeper in the cave, hoisting his steel greatclub. "Let's give them hell."

Jack laughed. "I was wondering, how does everyone outside Earth know about Hell? I thought it was a religious thing."

"Oh, religion exists alright," Shol said, standing up. "It's just gods that don't."

Jack and the Sage exchanged a glance.

"Let's go," Jack said. "Sage, find us the best victims."

"This is the planet right now," the Sage said. Spreading his arms, he conjured an illusory image of the planet, like a transparent globe. Continents were green and oceans were blue, while red and black dots crawled along the surface. Each dot was surrounded by a faint circle of the same color.

"Red dots are teams of D-Grades, black dots are C-Grades," the Sage explained. "As you can see, the C-Grades aren't actively searching, but they're spread around for maximum coverage. No matter where on the planet we appear, a C-Grade can arrive within five minutes at most."

"Hmm." Jack leaned over the globe. "Those are a lot of black dots."

"They're going all out. The projection stones the inner disciples are carrying transmit their location, but they also project their battle across the planet—and all it takes is one loose mouth for the news to spread farther. For the Animal Kingdom, this has gone on for far too long. Every immortal we kill is a slap to their face."

"Then we should keep doing it," Jack replied.

"Not like we have a choice."

"How can you do this?" Shol asked, inspecting the globe carefully. "You're just a D-Grade, but you're monitoring an entire planet?"

"It's a combination of my specialized divination skills and the Church's information network," the Sage explained. "And, still, this map is only an approximation. It is not accurate. There could be any number of life-threatening mistakes."

Shol pursed his lips. "Lovely."

"Best we can do, brother." Dordok draped an arm over Shol's shoulder. "Look at the bright side; your death is nothing compared to the headache you're causing for these animals."

"True. This is the greatest service I've ever rendered to the Exploding Sun," Shol agreed. "I don't fear death. It's just that I want Jack to survive. After seeing him grow at such unprecedented speed, I'm really looking forward to the heights he will reach. Given a few decades, even the Animal Kingdom will need to take him seriously."

"Hmm." Dordok smiled proudly. "I share the feeling."

"They're already taking him seriously," the Sage added. "All of us. We may be pests to them, but we're the annoying, persistent kind. Even the Grand Elder must be gnashing his teeth about us."

Jack laughed. "I wouldn't have it any other way. Sage, of all these red dots on your map, which is the most opportune target? We can wait a little bit if it increases our survival chances."

"Not too much though," Shol said. "Your duel with Li Qian is supposed to happen in less than a month. We have to find a way back by then."

"How about these ones?" the Sage said. A new image appeared above the globe, magnifying one of the red dots close to their location—nine immortals flew in a loose formation, led by two sharkens and a feshkur.

"I don't recognize any of them," Shol said. "They can't be too strong."

"Then, they're perfect. Let's take them," Jack affirmed. "Lead the way, Sage. We're right behind you. You have the map, so we can avoid all other search parties on the way there." He grinned. "Let's cut loose a little."

CHAPTER SIXTY-TWO
KICKING THE TIGER

Gorath Tremblin flew proudly over a marsh, flanked by two sharken deacons of lower status. They made him feel accomplished. Despite their noble standing, they answered to him, a feshkur.

I hope Jack Rust shows up, he thought broodily. I would beat him up.

Suddenly, space split open ahead of them. The two sharkens came to an instant stop, while he had to fly another hundred feet in annoyance before he managed. The late D-Grades amongst his group almost fell on the sharkens.

"Jack Rust!" Gorath shouted, eyeing the tear in space, only for three people to step out of it. One was Jack Rust, as advertised. The second was a cyclops dressed in prisoner attire and wielding a steel greatclub, while the third was a human in strange orange robes.

Gorath crushed his projection stone. He ground his teeth together as he stared down the new arrivals. A light went on inside his head, and he recognized the monk-looking human. He was Shol Pesna. The second deacon of the Exploding Sun.

"Shit," he said, and then they charged him.

Jack felt the breeze on his back. Nine immortals stood before him—nine inner disciples of the Animal Kingdom.

Nine enemies.

Three were deacons, and the other six were at the late D-Grade. "I'll get the grunts," he said. "Higher level gain."

"Naturally," Dordok replied, hefting his greatclub. "Shol and I will delay the deacons."

"Thanks, Captain."

All three of them shot out at once. Air split and boomed in their passage. The leader of the opponents, a feshkur deacon, crushed his projection stone and met their charge. They collided like comets. Shockwaves flew everywhere, violent winds and ripples. The marsh below was leveled.

The feshkur was thrown back, but the two sharken deacons arrived just then, flanked by their six subordinates. Shol and Dordok kept pushing, intercepting all three deacons, while Jack stepped through space to appear between the late D-Grades.

He caught the terror in their eyes. Though they were six, and all were higher-leveled than him, they knew what he was capable of. They were the ones at risk.

"Focus!" one of them, a twenty-foot-tall man who looked to be half-whale, shouted. His voice was deep and very slow, like he was slurring every word. "Attack!"

All six fell on him. They didn't dare hold back. Each was stronger than the leonine he'd fought back in the low-level hunting zone. Three months ago, Jack would have been completely unable to fight back.

But this wasn't three months ago. The Dao was now an extension of his limbs and soul—nowhere near the clumsy, all-too-heavy tool it used to be after his successive level-ups. He laughed. "Bring it on!"

A brutal aura billowed out. It seeped into the immortals' souls and infected them with fear. Given their already existing terror, the effect was instant. Their reactions slowed. Two displayed signs of hesitation. In their eyes, Jack had just turned into a natural disaster about to chew them up and spit them out, and there was nothing they could do about it.

Still, they were too experienced to falter. Their attacks carried on.

Jack was beset by a set of Dao Domains and iridescent strikes, but he only grinned. His own domain burst out, shattering theirs.

Now free of their influence, he stepped through space and teleported behind one of the weakest opponents, a lycan. Normally, he would have gone for the strong-looking whaler, but the point here wasn't just to win, it was to prevent their escape. If they tried to scatter, this might take too long.

Before the lycan could respond, Jack clenched his fist and smashed it down. A shield of wind appeared behind his opponent's nape, shattered instantly. The lycan's neck broke, and his body flew down like a rock.

One down, five to go, Jack thought grimly.

More attacks fell on him. His opponents, knowing stopping his teleportation was impossible, assembled into a formation that helped them guard each other's back—they must have been trained for exactly such an occasion.

Jack still tried. He appeared above them all and shot down a Meteor Punch, eclipsing the midday sun with his power. The whaler puffed his cheeks and blew a torrent of water upward. The remaining four immortals joined in with attacks of their own.

All strikes met in a massive collision that revealed no clear victor.

"He can match five of us?" a turtler woman shouted. "He isn't even Level 200! It's impossible!"

"It was your Kingdom that forced me to become this strong!" Jack shouted back. "Regret it in the afterlife!"

He teleported three times in a row, precisely controlling each spatial movement to avoid spending any excess energy. Wherever he appeared, his opponents coordinated to catch him. Wild strikes flew. The sky was rent apart. The marsh below was further flattened, all trees breaking and sinking into the muddy soil.

"Size Difference!" the whaler called out, his body enlarging to ten times its previous size, becoming even larger than an actual whale. His colossal fist, wider than Jack was tall, slammed down. "Flatten!"

"Meteor Punch!"

The world exploded. An ant battled a giant. The whaler's fist was thrown back, broken at the wrist, and his mouth opened to unleash a piercing scream. Jack did not follow through—he teleported into the midst of the other four enemies, engaging them in melee combat.

They were unprepared but experienced. Their Daos burst with only a moment's delay. A sword sliced Jack's ribs while a mallet tried to break his spine. The other two immortals moved to block his avenues of escape, but he never planned on escaping to begin with. He took the hits like a champ. Grunting, he ignored the turtler's paltry attempts and grabbed her by the throat, smashing her shell-first into a goatee. He then Meteor Punched them both.

The explosion was staggering. His hair and robes fluttered backward, but he was unhurt. His opponents weren't. They were both dead.

Two late immortals remained, along with the injured whaler, who was now retreating at top speed. Thankfully, he wasn't very fast.

Jack turned to his two opponents and started blasting. Their strikes came in tandem—they were used to working as a pair. The sword and mallet filled each other's paths, aiming at vulnerable spots that Jack had no choice but to defend. He dodged under a strike, slapped away another, then leaned into a third. His movements were so fast and precise that, if he didn't know better, he would have thought himself choreographed.

The mallet found his thigh, but he'd leaned into the strike, weakening it. He used the moment of respite to punch its wielder twice—one fist broke his face, the other shattered his ribcage. A third punch penetrated his abdomen, and a pulse of violent Dao destroyed his internal organs. The immortal toppled to the ground, dead without a doubt.

Only one opponent remained—another lycan—but he was already trying to run.

"Is this all the Animal Kingdom has to offer?" Jack shouted, laughing like a baleful god. "Stop me if you dare!"

He teleported above the retreating lycan, smashing a Meteor Punch into his head. Facing someone who couldn't teleport felt like a cheat. The lycan tried to defend, but only managed to have his arms broken alongside his skull.

Jack then looked into the distance, where the whaler had almost become a dot on the horizon.

Shit! he realized. That guy tricked me!

When the whaler first started running, he'd been pretty slow, so Jack didn't prioritize him. But it had been a trick, he'd been holding back! His current speed was at least double his initial one.

Damn, Jack thought, charging at full speed. The air erupted into sonic booms around him. He dived into spatial tears and emerged nine miles away without losing momentum, sliding through space like a dolphin jumping over waves. It took him some time, but he finally caught up. The whaler looked back in horror.

"Mercy!" he pleaded, but Jack only shook his head.

"Mercy is a luxury of the strong," he replied. "You die here."

Faced with the despair of death, the whaler roared. It was a high-pitched sound that made Jack's head hurt. At the same time, he grew gigantic again and slammed his tail down on Jack, who Meteor Punched it.

When the explosion settled down, all that remained was a massive whale-man body with a broken tail and a snapped spine.

Jack was already dashing back. They were on the clock. Already, there had to be at least one C-Grade closing in on their location at top speed.

When he arrived, Shol and Dordok were still facing the three deacons. Dordok himself was holding back the feshkur, taking a solid beating but surviving, while Shol was going to town on the two sharkens.

Jack prioritized the sharkens, as their Dao of Momentum made them fast. He approached from their blind spot and teleported directly beside them, smashing down a point-blank Meteor Punch. Of course, an immortal's Dao perception rendered all blind spots null, but there was a limit to one's reaction speed when an opponent teleported behind them from nine miles away.

Jack's strike penetrated the sharken's fin and back, digging into his skin and exploding. His body went flying in multiple directions. As this happened, the remaining sharken turned to flee, but Shol grabbed his leg and catapulted him down to the ground, throwing an entire miniature sun in his face. A hundred-foot-deep scorched crater later, nothing remained of the sharken.

Finally, all three turned to the only remaining enemy. The feshkur crossed space in an attempt to escape—he could also teleport, though with less proficiency than Jack or Shol. Both chased him. When they caught up, the feshkur did not beg for mercy. He swung, forgoing all defense to take Jack with him. Shol's palm crushed his skull as the feshkur's curved sword slashed deep into Jack's arm, reaching the bone, and stopping there.

"Careful," Shol said. "That could have taken your arm off."

"It would have regrown."

"Hey! Get over here, fast!" Dordok shouted, holding one of his arms. It was broken at the wrist, and one of his legs was bleeding profusely. "We need to run!"

A terrifying aura fell on them. In the distance, the sky turned dark as a furious figure approached at tremendous speed, its rage so intense they could sense it from afar.

Jack and Shol rushed to reach Dordok with everything they had. The approaching figure was much faster than them, but they were far closer. They teleported beside Dordok just as the Sage appeared from his hiding place in the marsh below. He took out the black sphere.

"Stop right there!" the distant figure commanded. His mere shout was enough to constrict the Dao around them, making teleportation impossible, but at this distance, his influence was weak. Jack stretched out his Dao Domain and broke the C-Grade's control.

"Like hell we'll stop!" he shouted. "Drag your old ass over here and make me!"

The distant figure had approached enough that they could make out its features. A mane around his neck, gray tufts on his fur. This was the Warden—and he came with the full might of an enraged late C-Grade. His Dao Domain erupted, flying at them like the aura of God.

"Stop!" the Warden shouted again.

"Kiss my ass!" Jack retorted. The Sage activated the sphere and space sucked them in, leaving no trace behind. Less than a second later, a dark beam passed through that location, eviscerating the very air itself.

"Damn you!" the Warden roared, steaming from the ears. "I'll make you regret what you said, kid!"

It was only then that he realized the projection stone was still active.

After the feshkur had crushed it at the start of the fight, nobody had stopped it, so everything that transpired was projected across the entire planet—including Jack's mockery.

The Warden felt so humiliated he wanted to puke—no junior had ever spoken to him like that. He was unable to form words. With a swipe of his paw, he destroyed the hundred-million-credits worth projection stone, then screamed at the sky, venting his frustration.

Unbeknownst to the Warden, however, Jack had a second projection stone, stolen from the sharken deacon he killed. Just before teleporting, he'd activated that projection stone and tossed it away, and the Warden, blinded by rage, had missed it. His outraged scream had also been projected across the planet, further humiliating him.

When he finally spotted the second projection stone, his eyes went so wide they almost popped out of his head. He didn't just destroy it—he obliterated it with his full might, along with dozens of square miles of marshland.

He then screamed again, "I will destroy you, Jack Rust! I swear revenge on your entire family!"

CHAPTER SIXTY-THREE
MAKING A DECISION

Back in the underwater cave, Jack and the others popped out of space and onto the bare rock.

"That was something," Jack said, laughing. "I think we made him angry."

"You didn't need to use that second projection stone," Shol said.

"Why not? We're already enemies. The more we can hurt them, the better."

"The point is to survive."

"The point is to cultivate the fist, and I can't do that by being a coward."

"Fair enough. I just wish we could have seen his face when he discovered it."

"Oh, we can," the Sage said, removing another projection stone from his pocket. "I got this one from the second deacon while you were fighting the others. Wanna see?"

"Sure!" everyone replied, gathering around him. Though they were injured, all possessed a degree of regeneration—they would be fine.

The Sage activated the stone, making it re-project the previous battle. "It has a recording function as well," he explained. In the projection, they saw themselves charge at the enemies—Shol was beating up two deacons while Dordok held off a third and Jack went to town on the weaker opponents.

"Is that how people see me?" Jack asked. "Wow. No wonder my skill is called Brutalizing Aura."

Shol puffed out his chest. "Speak for yourself, butcher. I look pretty heroic."

"You look like a bully to me," said Dordok.

"Oh yeah? Look at you getting all beat up by a single deacon. I handled two of them. *Two!*"

"Hmph. I was just toying with him."

"Sure you were."

"Check it out!" Jack exclaimed. "The Warden is arriving."

They saw themselves gather around the Sage and teleport away just in time to dodge the Warden's attack. The landscape below them was decimated. The Warden arrived, investigated the place where they teleported from for a few seconds, cursed Jack, then turned to the projection stone and destroyed it with a single swipe.

The Sage switched to the projection of the second stone. In it, they saw the Warden break his composure and scream at the sky in outrage. It was a very un-elder-like scene.

Almost immediately, he spotted the second projection stone, and his betrayed anger and humiliation. He swiped again, and this time, the entire sky seemed to crash down on the stone. The projection cut off.

Dordok laughed. "Serves him right for trying to control me. That guy is a massive dick."

"What do you think they'll do now?" Jack asked. "Increase the size of patrols further?"

"I wonder," the Sage replied thoughtfully. "By now, they must have realized our power. Searching in even larger teams would be safer, but their efficiency would drop by a lot. They would never find us. At the same time, they cannot resume normal activities, as we'll just keep killing them, and they cannot hole up in cities to protect themselves because the entire galaxy will be watching. They are a proud B-Grade faction; they cannot hide from a few D-Grades."

"What do you think they'll do?"

"I have no idea." The Sage laughed. "But I have my ways. When they make a decision, we'll know it."

"Alright," Jack said.

At the same time, Shol was shaking his head in disbelief. "Incredible. Just a handful of D-Grades bringing an entire B-Grade faction to its heels. I… I didn't even know this could happen."

"It's all thanks to the Sage," Dordok said, shooting the man an odd look. "Without him finding this hiding place, divining the entire planet's patrols, and using that sphere to help us escape, we would have been discovered long ago. Not to mention the battle with Maximus Lonihor."

The Sage grinned innocently. He was the playmaker, so to say. After choosing a target, he would guide them through a route that avoided all D and C-Grade parties. Then, when they won, he could use his high-grade spatial artifact to return here, to their hiding place.

Dordok wasn't the only one to realize that. All three of them looked at the Sage with gratitude and wonder—just how could he achieve all those things? They would rather eat their shoes than believe he was an average D-Grade diviner.

"Can I speak to you, Sage?" Jack asked with a resolute, thoughtful look, like he'd just made a decision. "In private."

The Sage beamed. "Sure!"

"Unbelievable!" Maximus Lonihor smashed his fist down, breaking yet another heavy desk—at this rate, they would run out. His eyes hid deep rage. "They escaped a leonine… We should head over and slaughter the Exploding Sun in retaliation."

"Relax, Nephew. There is no need to go that far," Hell's Warden, Artus Emberheart, replied. Unlike the rage he'd exhibited before, he now seemed as calm as a still lake—but Maximus knew that his heart was burning.

"What should we do?" he asked. "With that artifact of theirs, they can just escape whenever they want. How do we pin them down?"

The Warden thought for a moment. "This time, they could only escape because they were lucky enough to be very far away from the nearest C-Grade—which happened to be me. If we had more C-Grades, we could weave a tighter net around the planet. That way, they won't have time to escape before we arrive."

"Are you sure, Uncle?" Maximus asked. Thanks to his position as head disciple and his relation with the Warden, he could speak freely when they were in private. "Aren't all the C-Grades already occupied?"

"They are, but what can we do? This has dragged on for far too long. The projection stones we handed out ended up making things worse—now the entire galaxy can see the scenes of our humiliation." His voice was calm, yet hid undertones of violence. "Even the Grand Elder contacted me, demanding that I solve the problem as quickly as possible. There is no choice. We cannot stop searching or we would be admitting defeat to a few lowly D-Grades. I will request seven enforcers, and the faction will find a way to spare them; this is too urgent."

"How did we get played this badly, Uncle?" Maximus asked with indignation in his heart. "It's all the Black Hole Church's fault. Without them and their overpowered artifacts, how could we fail to apprehend a lowly middle D-Grade?"

The Warden shook his head in annoyance. "What happened, happened. At the end of the day, Jack Rust and his accomplices are nothing but ants gnawing at our ankles. They will be squashed, as ants ought to be. We will reign supreme. We always have, and we always will."

Maximus brought a fist to his heart. "Yes, Uncle."

For most people, B-Grade factions were the stuff of legends. The vast majority of cultivators could only interact with the lowliest of their members, and that was on important occasions. The Animal Kingdom, for example, was a vast space empire spanning fifty thousand solar systems, three thousand inhabited planets, and trillions of cultivators. To most people, they might as well be gods.

And the humiliation of gods was burning news.

Before Jack's three-month hiding, he had already made the headlines across the constellation, but only as an oddity. There were no witnesses to his actions, and the Kingdom suppressed the news. He was just an odd man causing a bit of trouble on Hell. He would be apprehended without issue.

After he went into hiding, things changed. Hell went into war mode. Immortals flocked there and were forced to waste their time flying around the planet. That was already big news. And when Jack Rust resurfaced, soundly beating a team of higher-level immortals by himself and escaping, the recordings of his battle spread like wildfire.

Blocking the news was impossible. There were too many people on Hell with projection stones, and news agencies were paying massive sums to acquire the recordings. The wider public was catching on. All the way from the Belarian Outpost to the Fair Way Continent, people spoke of this astonishing turn of events: a single man creating so much trouble for the Animal Kingdom at the core of their territory. It was unheard of.

And, as time passed, he was not captured. If anything, the Kingdom intensified their efforts, and the news and speculations only grew wilder. Some people claimed that Jack Rust was an agent of the Exploding Sun; others said he was a prodigy from another galaxy, while some even went as far as to declare he was a B-Grade in disguise.

When no Animal Kingdom officials were nearby, people talked about this in hushed tones, discussing just how a D-Grade could have achieved such a commotion. There were even entire betting rings around the date of Jack Rust's capture or the eventual number of his victims.

D-Grades were strong enough to rule entire planets, and this guy was dropping them like flies!

The other B-Grade factions had caught on, watching with interest. Was this the start of the Animal Kingdom's downfall? Could they pounce on them while they were weakened and steal away territory? Had the Kingdom made some terrifying enemy, of whom Jack Rust was only an agent?

More Animal Kingdom elders heard about the news and grew enraged. The Warden came under heavy pressure. Even Galicia Lonihor, the Planetary Overseer of Earth-387, was questioned, as Jack Rust originated from her planet and could be seen as her fault. She could retort nothing to that—even back on Earth, he'd humiliated the Animal Kingdom. All she did was harden her resolve to slay all the planet's troublemakers the moment the grace period was over.

The news still spread. After all these months, Jack Rust was turning into a household name in the Animal Kingdom constellation. His name was even heard outside of it.

And the proud Animal Kingdom could do nothing. Only endure the humiliation and try their hardest to capture the galaxy's most annoying D-Grade.

The professor finished listening to Ar'Tazul's story and burst out laughing. "Suits them right!" she said, only for her mood to sour. "I'm just worried about his safety. He's so strong now... but why did he have to poke the hornet's nest?"

"Once a mother, always a mother," Edgar said from beside her. There was a new air to him—his hair was slick and drawn back, his missing leg was replaced by a stunning magical copy, and he carried himself with a confidence he'd lacked a few months ago.

"Of course," Sparman replied. "Very insightful of you, Sir Edgar."

Edgar raised a brow.

"Sparman!" Vivi exclaimed. "That was rude. Apologize."

"I apologize," he said without the slightest hint of meaning it.

"I just wonder..." the professor said, furrowing her brows, "why hasn't he contacted us yet? He's killing deacons. Surely he has the funds to buy the telepathy function for the Bare Fist Brotherhood."

"Maybe he's holding out to avoid becoming sentimental?" Vivi suggested.

"I guess..." The professor's face scrunched up further. "But he's been missing for so many months, risking his life out there, and he hasn't even called his mother once? Doesn't he know I stay up all night worrying about him? Plus, there is so much we have to update him on..."

Vivi rolled her eyes. "No, Professor. Save the surprise."

"Well, not like we have a choice," replied the professor, but the proud smile didn't leave her face.

Jack and the Sage stood alone in the second, smaller underwater cave, where they'd watched the Ancient vision.

"I've given it a lot of thought," Jack began. "And I believe that, in this hopeless situation, there is only one choice I can make. One choice that benefits us all, but me and my planet the most. Does your promise to protect Earth still stand?"

The Sage's smile widened. "We will not protect Earth, but we will help you protect it."

"Good enough." Jack took a deep breath, then looked the Sage in the eye. "I accept your invitation. I want to join the Black Hole Church."

CHAPTER SIXTY-FOUR
JOINING THE CHURCH

THE SAGE'S GRIN SPLIT FROM EAR TO EAR. "EXCELLENT! MAY I ASK WHAT MADE you decide?"

"Your vision and story were convincing." Jack shrugged. "Plus, you've already helped me a lot of times. I owe you some trust. Of course, if I ever find out you lied to me, I'm out."

"No need to worry about that. I never did," the Sage replied, stretching out his hand. Jack shook it. "Welcome to the good side."

"It's nice to be here." Jack released a massive sigh of relief—this matter had been bugging him for months, but at the end of the day, he needed to make a decision.

"Now, as a member of the Black Hole Church, you enjoy our protection—to a degree," the Sage said. Reaching into his pockets—which suspiciously held many things—he fished out a transparent, off-green pill. Something like a green eel swam inside it.

"What's that?" Jack asked.

"A concealment and repair pill. It is not particularly flashy, but it is highly tailored to your case," the Sage explained. "Treasures like your Life Drop are not unheard of in the Church. We needed a way to protect the members wielding them, so our Grand Elder devised these pills. They can repair all residual damage in your body from using the Life

Drop, making it undetectable to even a deep-scan. At the same time, it plants a tiny second soul in your brain, letting you fool the lie detection magic of the Hand of God inquisitors, assuming they are below the B-Grade. Like this, even if the Hand gets you, you'll be safe."

"Really?" Jack's brows shot up. "It was that easy?"

"Oh, nowhere near easy. These pills are impossible to find outside the Church. They are refined using the Grand Elder's personal Dao. Even I only have two of them."

"Why would you have any?"

"Some of my powers are considered blasphemous by the Hand of God. They are too closely connected to Enas. I need a way to protect myself."

Jack raised a brow. "How do you cultivate blasphemous powers?"

"I can't tell you that."

"Come on! You said that joining the Church would give me access to more information. Spit it out; what's the matter with you? Who are you, even?"

The Sage smiled in his sagely way, as if he saw far more than Jack. "Very well. As you suspect, I was not a simple human of your planet. I spent my entire life hearing incomprehensible whispers from beyond. I was insane. Except, I wasn't. When the System came, those whispers cleared up, and I could understand the power granted to me. You see, my soul has a unique and extremely rare resonance with Enas. I am one of his apostles. Even from inside his eternal prison, he can transmit to me a tiny fragment of his power, enough to give me mastery over the Dao of Divination. Until I reach the B-Grade and complete my Dao Tree, levels will be my only bottleneck."

"Are you... are you serious?" Jack asked.

"Very."

"So reaching the B-Grade is only a matter of time for you."

"Indeed."

"That's... wow. You're even stronger than I am."

"Not at all." The Sage's smile grew sad. "Despite all my gifts, you have managed to outpace me. It would be a source of shame if you weren't such a monstrous talent yourself."

"Hmm." Jack's eyes narrowed. "What about Dorman? You two were together since the start, and he was keeping pace with me in Trial Planet. Is he also a... special soul?"

"He's just highly talented. Actually, the Barren High had predicted the existence of myself and Dorman on your Earth. You just appeared out of the blue. I have no idea how you did it."

Jack cracked a smile. "A little bit of talent, a lot of hard work, and a lot of danger-clad opportunities. But, wait, go back—the Barren High predicted your existence on Earth?"

"Oh, yes. They could sense me, which is why they spent so many resources to divine the planet's location and give it to the Animal Kingdom. That's also how the Kingdom could sneak the scions onto your planet before it was Integrated—they knew exactly where it was."

"Are you saying that the entire Integration happened *just* to find you?"

"Yes."

Jack couldn't tell whether the Sage was lying, exaggerating, or both, but he seemed serious. "Wow..." After a moment of rumination, he added, "Can I ask you one more thing, Sage?"

"Of course."

"Are you lying to me?"

There was a short pause. "Why do you think that?"

"Because you keep calling our planet 'your Earth,' as if you don't belong there. From what you said, your soul just happens to resonate with Enas. Why would that make you... alien?"

"Hmm." The Sage's eyes narrowed. Suddenly, he seemed more serious than before—as if he'd quit playing. "I did not lie, but I did not reveal the entire truth either. Some things are best kept secret for now... but I promise you, when the time comes, I will tell you everything. I do not mean to harm you."

"I don't know if I can trust someone who lies *and* withholds information," Jack said.

"I have already saved you so many times. Don't I deserve it?"

"You don't get to play that card."

Jack was adamant, but the Sage also didn't seem willing to budge. "You don't need to trust me. Let's just work together. We share the common goal of escaping this place, and I have promised to help you save Earth. Isn't that enough?"

"Maybe," Jack said cryptically. "Or maybe not."

"Look at you. Not even a member for two minutes and you're already getting the hang of it."

"You won't escape this by being funny."

"I won't escape this, period," the Sage replied seriously. "The Church is an organization with multiple levels of secrecy. If we revealed everything so easily, the Hand of God would have caught us millions of years ago. I have already made a special exception and told you more things than strictly allowed. When the time comes, you will know."

"Fine," Jack replied, snorting. "Then tell me all you can about the Church. How powerful is it? Where is it based? Is it an organization on the caliber of the Hand of God, or much weaker?"

"Not too much weaker. The Church is one of the few factions spanning the entirety of System space. This galaxy only houses one of our branches. I cannot tell you where our headquarters is, as that is one of our most tightly kept secrets, but I can reveal that we possess multiple high-level cultivators. In fact, all true elders of the Church are A-Grades."

"A-Grades! Seriously?"

"Of course. How else did you expect to rival the System, the Hand of God, and the Immortals?" The Sage laughed. "With your talent, you have a small chance of reaching those heights yourself. I can take you there if you want. To the headquarters of the Church, I mean, so you can see for yourself what the peak of power looks like. To see a force befitting of an Old God's entourage."

Jack was tempted—and scared. If he went to that place, wherever it was, he would be at the mercy of all those strong people. Even if they didn't mean him harm, they would probably force all sorts of secrecy oaths and limitations on him, reducing his freedom.

He did not enjoy that thought.

"I can't go. I need to save Earth," he said.

"Naturally. I meant afterward—when Earth is safe, you can freely depart to wider worlds. There is no need for someone like you to remain in a young galaxy that hasn't even developed its first A-Grade yet."

"How will Earth be safe if I leave?" Jack asked. "The Exploding Sun has promised to steal reign over the planet from the Animal Kingdom after we defeat the Planetary Overseer, but there will surely be repercussions. Without me there to hold the fort, some random C-Grade or D-Grade with a grudge will appear and destroy Earth. And all that is *if* Master Huali's promise still stands, which I highly doubt after everything that's happened."

The Sage cupped his chin. "Hmm, I believe we can solve that issue. Have you ever heard of planet poaching?"

"I have..." Jack said hesitantly. "Isn't it what I just described? When a B-Grade faction steals control of another faction's planet. Master Huali told me so."

"Your Master Huali is an admirable cultivator, but her experience is limited by her galaxy of residence," the Sage replied. "The term planet poaching comes from the wider universe. Out there, A-Grade factions have the power to literally grab planets and move them wherever they desire. They come into another faction's territory, take the planet, and run away."

Jack's jaw hit the floor. "You have got to be kidding me."

"Not at all. The Black Hole Church also has that power—and, if you can get strong enough to defeat the Planetary Overseer before the grace period ends, we can be convinced to do it. We can move Earth to a safer place within our sphere of influence, where neither the Animal Kingdom nor the Hand of God will find it."

The weight of this proposal was hefty. "I cannot possibly promise my entire planet to you."

"You have already done it for the Exploding Sun. Why not for us?"

"That's different. They just want to rule it on paper, while you want to literally take away the entire planet. Plus, the Exploding Sun isn't a faction wreathed in shadow. I trust them more."

"Well, you can always reconsider later," the Sage replied, shrugging. "Reaching that point will be a tall task, anyway. You could easily die in the process."

"I could easily die in all processes. Yet, here I am, still alive and kicking."

"Not punching?"

"That too." Jack laughed tiredly, then shook his head. "Once again, you overwhelm me with information, but all you manage to do is create more questions than you answer... How do you do that?"

"I'm a Sage. It's part of my job description."

"Right..." Jack gave him the side-eye. "Anyway. If there is nothing else, we can return to the others. I'll make good use of that pill you gave me."

"Be careful though," the Sage said. "The lie detection shield will persist in time, but the repairing properties of the pill can only work once. If you use your Life Drop even once after swallowing the pill, the effects will be impossible to hide."

"I'll be careful," Jack promised. "Now, let's go. I have things to consider, and you have to sleep—or do cryptic sage stuff."

"Probably both," the Sage replied honestly, and the two members of the Black Hole Church swam back to the main underwater cave, where Shol and Dordok were playing checkers on a board they'd fashioned out of rock.

CHAPTER SIXTY-FIVE
MAKING AN IMPRESSION

Over the following weeks, every eye in the galaxy was turned to Hell. The guerilla warfare was becoming increasingly intense. As Jack leveled up, the Animal Kingdom tried not to underestimate him.

"I finally found a target!" the Sage said a week after they attacked the nine-person party and nearly escaped the Warden's wrath.

Everyone jumped up at once. "Let's go!"

Twelve late D-Grades and six deacons were flying over the sea, chatting idly as the ones with the sharpest Dao perception scanned the waters below. This time, there was no dramatic entry on Jack's side. They instantly teleported in and unleashed their most destructive attacks.

The Animal Kingdom cultivators barely had time to react. A Meteor Punch tore through them, killing a handful, while a burning sun blossomed in their midst, making them scream. Dordok arrived, smashing down his steel greatclub to complete the ambush.

Half the enemy immortals were killed instantly. The remainder fought hard, but Jack's strength was now so great, they barely stood a chance. A hastily activated projection stone transmitted the scene of Jack, Shol, and Dordok annihilating an entire squadron of the Animal Kingdom's finest. The entire planet gawked once again.

At the same time, word spread, and billions of people across the galaxy flocked to their local projection centers to watch the Animal Kingdom suffer.

Two minutes after the start of the battle, the Sage appeared and shouted, "We have to go!"

The other three rushed to his side and teleported away right as a C-Grade eagler flew in from above, showering the area in sharp winds that decimated both the water below and the one surviving Animal Kingdom cultivator. Jack and his companions narrowly escaped.

"Damn it!" the eagler exclaimed, breaking the still-active projection stone. "Damn it all!"

The four warriors appeared in the underwater cave that had become their lair. "What level are you now, Jack?" Shol asked.

"215!" Jack exclaimed joyfully. He couldn't stop grinning. "I'm going so fast now! We're farming those guys like it's nothing!"

"Do you think he's stronger than you now, Shol?" Dordok playfully asked, to which Shol snorted.

"Don't be an idiot. I was the second deacon of the Exploding Sun—one of the strongest D-Grades in the galaxy. I could not lose to someone thirty levels below me."

Jack simply laughed good-naturedly.

Meanwhile, back at the planet's capital, the Warden was going crazy. "They did it again!" he roared, flaring his nostrils. "They're toying with us! We need to capture them!"

"What should we do, Uncle?" Maximus asked.

"What *can* we do?" the Warden replied helplessly. "Increase the patrol size even more. Reinforce every team with high-ranking deacons. Have every enforcer on the planet join the search—we *must find them* before the entire galaxy is laughing at us."

Maximus's eyes widened in shock. "You're putting C-Grades on search duty?"

"We don't have a damn choice," the Warden snapped. "The Grand Elder has given me full reign over these enforcers. If I say they go on searching duty, they go on searching duty. Make it happen!"

"Yes, Uncle," Maximus replied, teleporting away.

Soon after, the Sage opened his eyes in the cave. "Bad news. The C-Grade enforcers have joined the search."

"What does that mean for us?" Jack asked.

"The chance of them finding us has increased. Although, with such large searching parties, the ground they can cover is limited. We're still safe. The problem is that divining everyone's location just became harder—C-Grades are resistant to my D-Grade Dao."

"Just do your best," Jack replied encouragingly. "We believe in you."

Two more weeks passed, and the news of Hell's situation kept spreading. By now, even the surrounding constellations were full of talk about the Battle Brothers—the three brave cultivators who laid siege on an entire planet by themselves. The Sage had not participated in the battles, so most people didn't take him into account.

All across the galaxy, people wouldn't stop talking about this. It was a monumental event! When was the last time a B-Grade faction was publicly humiliated and rendered helpless? Never! It had never happened before! Even if someone had the ability to do it, what kind of madman would actually try?

The Merchant Union created cheap copies of every battle projection and sold them everywhere. They even made montages showcasing the best points of each battle and how the entire situation evolved. These documentaries sold like hot cakes, and pretty soon, the Animal Kingdom's reputation was so thoroughly dragged through the mud that they were forced to prohibit all talk of the Battle Brothers in their constellation.

But gossip could not be stopped. All this prohibition achieved was to make the news even more intriguing.

Back on Earth, Ar'Tazul and Ar'Karvahul were having the happiest days of their lives. They had chosen to bet on Jack Rust during the Integration, and now their investment would be repaid a millionfold. They borrowed from everyone they knew to buy their own projection stones and record various scenes on Earth, from the environment of Jack Rust's Integration to his closest people. They interviewed Edgar, Vivi, the professor, even Harambe and Sparman.

The professor also took this opportunity to raise awareness about the Animal Kingdom's oppression. She talked about how, once the grace period was over, the Planetary Overseer would slaughter all of them in retaliation. They had one month to live, but they were still fighting.

These interviews were integrated into the Merchant Union's documentaries, making the two djinn merchants filthy rich and further ruining the Animal Kingdom's public image. Many oppressed species and planets came to realize they were not alone. A rebellious undercurrent appeared in the Animal Kingdom constellation, fanned and fueled by Jack Rust's resistance—as well as the Kingdom's display of weakness.

Furthermore, as the Warden had withdrawn many enforcers—C-Grade cultivators below the rank of elder—to Hell, many other fronts of the Animal Kingdom were left short-staffed. The other factions pounced on this opportunity. The Kingdom started losing resources everywhere, their control over their territories weakened, the respect they commanded lessened, and they slowly became the butt of the joke across the galaxy.

At the same time, Jack Rust and the Battle Brothers became household names. Nothing inspired the people more than a righteous, winning underdog. They were amongst the galaxy's greatest celebrities.

Of course, the Battle Brothers themselves were also aware of that. The Sage could communicate with the outside world, and he narrated the effect their actions had on the galaxy.

"Incredible," Shol muttered breathlessly. "To think my old bones still had so much to give... Oh, this sets me on fire!"

"Ha! Calm yourself, Shol," Jack said. "We still need to escape this place, somehow. A little bit of infamy will mean nothing if we're tortured and killed."

"This is even better than when I was a pirate in the Starry Wilds," Dordok said, grinning. "System bless you, Jack. You've given me a new life. If the rest of our crew is still out there, they must be extremely proud of us."

"I'm sure they are, Captain," Jack replied. "We'll meet them again eventually."

Shol frowned. "The only downside, is that things are moving slowly now. Your agreed duel with Li Qian is only three days away. There is no way we will make it in time."

"Listen, Shol. I get where you're coming from, but that duel was already long forfeited. I'm a wanted criminal of the Hand of God, and I've created so much trouble that my name is known across the galaxy. There's no way I could return to the Exploding Sun to fight."

"I know..." Shol replied. "It's just a shame. Li Qian still needs a good butt-kicking, and Master..." He trailed off, though his meaning was obvious. If Jack forfeited the duel, Master Huali would probably lose the position of Grand Elder.

"Look at the bright side," Jack said. "We have given Master a lot to work with. By sending us here, she rendered a huge service to the Exploding Sun. There are all sorts of implications. Monsoon will try to frame this as a terrible risk to the faction, while she will call it a brilliant move. That battle of impressions will affect the Grand Elder position much more than my duel ever could. At the end of the day, missing it means very little."

"I guess so." Shol hardened his gaze. "I may have technically left the faction, but I remain a proud member of the Exploding Sun. Let's show these Animal Kingdom pricks what we're made of."

"That's the spirit!"

The date of Jack's duel with Li Qian came and passed. By now, any assaults they made on the Animal Kingdom forces had to be carefully prepared. The search parties were large, and there were too many C-Grades wandering the planet. One mistake could ruin everything.

At the same time, they could not delay. Time was pressing. The duel with Li Qian could be missed, but the end of Earth's grace period could not.

Over the following two weeks, the Battle Brothers—they liked the name, so they adopted it for themselves—took some risks.

One raid happened just a week after the previous one. They assaulted a search party which included the fifth-ranked deacon of the Animal Kingdom, a female sharken covered in scars. Shol held her at bay while Jack, with the assistance of Dordok, went to town on the rest of them. After killing seven immortals, Shol and the Sage grouped up with them, unleashed a barrage of attacks to make some space, and teleported away, narrowly dodging the white-robed C-Grade man who came to capture them.

The man did not say anything, nor did he grow angry. His eyes were calm and pure, as was his Dao.

After that, the Animal Kingdom grew so desperate that they commanded all search parties to stop carrying projection stones. There was no other way. Every new battle recording threw splashes of mud on their public image.

Unfortunately for them, Jack and the others had already collected a decent number of projection stones from their previous assaults. They could just record the battles themselves, then send the recordings to the Sage's connections and spread them across the galaxy all the same.

A week later, the Battle Brothers attacked one more group. This time, the enemies were more prepared, so the battle did not go as smoothly. Dordok suffered an almost grievous injury, while Shol had an arm broken. Jack fought three deacons and nine late D-Grades at the same time, killing half—though the fact he could teleport while they could not certainly helped.

They escaped in the nick of time, barely dodging the Warden's furious assault. Once again, the terrain under them was leveled, and the surviving D-Grades were sent flying away by the shockwave.

"Damn it!" the Warden roared again after making sure there were no projection stones around. In his six millennia of life, he had never felt so powerless. He'd always been a proud, invincible prodigy. Nobody had ever toyed with him like Jack Rust!

"Brat!" he screamed to the heavens. "I will pull out every single tendon and bone in your body!"

Jack did not hear that—but if he had, he wouldn't have cared the slightest bit. The Sage's teleportation brought them back to the underwater cave, where Shol and Dordok sat down to tend to their injuries. Jack could afford to take it easier, since his regeneration was extremely effective.

Most importantly, the successive battles had helped him reach Level 230. He was overflowing with power.

"I think that was our best battle yet," the Sage said. "I bet the recording will become a best-seller."

"Are there best sellers in the galaxy?" Jack asked.

"There are best sellers everywhere."

"Good. The more we can harm the Animal Kingdom, the better," Jack replied, but not with his usual joviality. His present mood wasn't the best. With all that was happening, the Animal Kingdom was gearing up more and more, and the chances of them escaping in time were so small it might as well not exist.

And they had to hurry. Hurry a lot. Because, between all the weeks and months of this guerilla warfare, a lot of time had passed. Before he knew it, the one year deadline was almost up.

The grace period of Earth would end in exactly two weeks.

CHAPTER SIXTY-SIX
ENTOMBED

MAXIMUS LONIHOR FLOATED ALONE OVER A DESERT. EVEN HE, THE FACTION'S head disciple, could not avoid search duty. At least he was considered a powerhouse, so he didn't need to tolerate any power-chasing weaklings alongside him. He was company enough.

Suddenly, space split apart before him, and a human walked out. "What are you doing here?" Maximus asked carefully.

"Am I not welcome?" the other man replied with a faint smile.

"Of course you aren't. You Exploding Sun dogs have already caused us enough trouble. This planet is not a place for you, Li Qian."

Li Qian, the top disciple of Elder Monsoon, laughed lightly. A sharp, slightly curved sword hung at his hip, while his aura remained calm like a still lake, and sharp like the edge of diamond.

"I am not here to gloat, Maximus Lonihor," he said. "The Exploding Sun had no part in this disaster. Jack Rust and Shol Pesna are rogue cultivators."

"As if I'll believe you." Maximus snorted. However, he couldn't help wondering: why was Li Qian here? People of that caliber did not move around aimlessly.

"You should believe me," Li Qian insisted. "In fact, I can prove it. What do you think this is?" He reached into a pouch he was carrying and removed a vial filled with crimson liquid. Arcane runes glowed all over the vial, faintly pulsing in one direction as if blown by an invisible wind.

Maximus creased his brows. A hundred calculations ran through his mind. "It can't be."

"I'm telling you it is," Li Qian responded, jingling the vial and laughing. "The lifeblood of Shol Pesna."

"Why would you bring this here! Why would you condemn your own agents?" Maximus demanded to know.

"They are no agents of mine, Maximus. Since there is nobody listening, let me be frank. My master and Elder Huali are currently contending for the position of Grand Elder. Jack Rust and Shol Pesna belong to Huali's camp. The service they have rendered to the Sun by thinning your forces is already admirable, but any more and they might actually start weighing the scales back Huali's way. We can't have that."

"You would assist the enemy to advance your master's personal interests?"

"Wouldn't you?"

Maximus smiled—a crooked, wide grin. "Yes."

Li Qian laughed, and with that, these two enemies seemed like the best of friends. "In the name of my faction," Li declared, "I am here to assist in capturing the two troublemakers who have soiled the Exploding Sun's name. I have brought the lifeblood of Shol Pesna so we can locate him, and I will personally assist in taking them down. The Warden has already been notified. Do you accept my help, Maximus?"

"Of course. Clearing your faction's name is a noble pursuit—how could I decline brother Li's honest assistance?"

The world seemed bright again. This really was a pie that fell from the sky.

Reaching for his temple, Maximus used his faction telepathy privileges to contact the other high-ranking deacons. "*We found them, everyone. Follow my instructions. Let's end this.*"

Meanwhile, Jack and the others had no idea of the disaster about to befall them.

"Two weeks," Jack said. "We have two weeks to escape and reach Earth. Can our previous plan still work? Infiltrating one of the heavily guarded outbound teleporters?"

"It can," Shol replied. "It will be difficult, but with the Sage's assistance, we can manage."

"It may take some time until a good opportunity arises," the Sage replied.

Jack nodded sharply. "Good. Then, let's not delay. Sage, can you be on the lookout for such an opportunity? If it appears, we should grab it and escape Hell, as we may not find another like it in time. Of course, if there is an opportunity to attack another search party instead, that's even better."

"Got it," the Sage said. "I'll be on the lookout for both."

"The problem is, I'm still too weak..." Jack said, darkness clouding his face. "I'm not even at the peak of the D-Grade. I will never break through to the C-Grade like this."

"Don't be so hard on yourself, Jack. You never could," Shol advised him. "The moat between the D and C-Grades is not the widest in existence, but it remains unbridgeable in the short-term. You are already progressing faster than anyone I've ever known."

"But I cannot defeat the Planetary Overseer like this. She's at the mid C-Grade."

"Only barely. She isn't particularly talented for a C-Grade, either. Didn't you defeat the Final Guardian while at the E-Grade? If you could do that then, perhaps you can overcome the Grade barrier once more."

"The Final Guardian was weaker than most early D-Grades," Jack replied with a sigh. "The overseer is at the mid C-Grade. It's not the same thing."

"For any other D-Grade in this galaxy, defeating the overseer would be completely impossible," the Sage spoke up. "However, you possess something they don't: the Life Drop. It can bridge the difference in Grade up to a point. If you can reach the absolute peak of power in the D-Grade and use the Life Drop, you may stand a slim chance. Especially with the assistance of Shol and any other extraordinary peak D-Grades you manage to enlist."

Jack turned around in surprise. "Really?"

"The D and C-Grades are not as far apart as you may think," the Sage replied cryptically.

Hope resurged in Jack's chest. "Good. Then, are you saying we should stick around until I reach Level 249 to maximize my chances?"

"Accessing an outbound teleporter will undoubtedly involve killing many people. It should get you pretty close. I think unnecessary risks are not worth it at this point."

"I agree with the Sage," Shol said. "Right now, one or two levels won't make a difference, but dying in desperation will."

"Very well," Jack agreed. "In that case, the plan remains as is: we either assault a teleporter or attack another search party, whichever comes first. And if we start running out of time... We'll see. I'll see. I won't drag you guys to death with me."

"What are you saying, idiot disciple?" Shol laughed. "As if we have a choice. We're never getting to a teleporter without you. We're all leaving or dying together."

"And here I was growing fond of this place," Dordok said, looking around sentimentally. "It sucked as a prisoner but wasn't that bad after I became the hunter."

"I think the Kingdom would think the exact opposite," Shol replied with a laugh.

"It's already been six months," Jack said. "I've been here for more than half of the time since my Integration. Leaving is almost... weird."

"Oh yeah. Not spending your free time hunting D-Grades? Sheesh. How boring," Shol said.

"I quite liked this place as well," the Sage said. "It was peaceful."

"Peaceful?"

"In a certain manner. I had no concerns besides our immediate life and death. It was a nice break from real life."

The other three looked at each other and shrugged. "He's not wrong," Shol admitted, while Jack's eyes shone as he remembered something.

"Since we may depart at anytime," Jack said, "I don't think I can delay contacting Earth anymore. I need to communicate with them and organize things. I hope you won't begrudge me a few million credits anymore, brothers."

"Of course not," Shol replied, reaching for his credit card. "How much do you need?"

"Twenty million should be enough."

"Here, have fifty."

"Thanks."

They touched their credit cards together, and Jack's number of credits went up. It reached the nine digits—130,440,011, to be precise—and for the first time in a while, he opened his faction screen.

Faction: Bare Fist Brotherhood (D-Grade)
Leader: Jack Rust (D-Grade), Cosmic Fist
Supervisor: Margaret Rust (E-Grade), Continental Commander
Members: 7,439
Capital: Milky Way galaxy, Animal Kingdom constellation, Earth-387 planet, Forest of the Strong dungeon area.
...

7,439 members... Wow.

And yet, all those people combined were nothing before just one of the deacons he'd killed. It really put things into perspective.

There was a long row of management options in that screen, but he skipped them. That was Professor's territory, not handsome leader territory. He made it to the end of the list, where a prompt asked him if he would like to buy anything. There were plenty of interesting options, but the most useful one was absolutely the telepathy function.

He spent a hundred million credits and bought it.

Then, with a trembling breath, he activated it. The System stepped in with another screen.

Please assign telepathy holders.
Current holders: Jack Rust
Remaining holders: 4

Margaret Rust and Edgar Allano, he commanded.

Current holders: Jack Rust, Margaret Rust, Edgar Allano
Remaining holders: 2

Jack grinned. Good. Now, how do we—

"Jack!" a voice rang in his mind—the professor's. "Is that really you? Are you okay?"

There were no words to describe the relief that washed over him. It was like all his burdens and troubles hit him at once, then melted off his body like warm soap in a shower. His mother was alive. She was okay. And her voice was right there, in his head.

"Jack?" the voice came again. "Damn, how does this work?"

"I'm here, I'm here," he replied hurriedly. "Professor! Mom! Are you okay?"

"Jack!" she exclaimed again. "I'm okay, I'm great! Are you?"

"Well, sort of."

"Sort of? You haven't spoken to me in months, and this is the first thing you say? Just how much do you want me to worry?"

Jack felt crushing guilt. "Sorry. I didn't mean to worry you... I just didn't want to be influenced by emotions before now. I was walking on the edge."

"It's fine, it's fine. I'm sorry, I—I'm just glad you're okay." Her joy was infectious. Jack found himself smiling.

"Same to you," he replied. "How have you been?"

A moment of silence went by. "Busy. Coordinating a global organization can take its toll, but I'm managing. I'm the best person for the job. We're handling ourselves. The war is balanced, but the grace period is running out soon, and I worry that everything will end when that happens."

As she spoke, Jack cracked a smile. She was the same. Only a few seconds into talking, she was already going into business. He didn't mind.

"Do you have any plans for the end of the grace period?" she asked.

"Yes. I will come and punch the overseer in the face."

Another short bout of silence.

"*What?*" she finally replied.

"I will punch the overseer in the face. I'm already Level 230 and can punch above my weight class; if I can reach the peak D-Grade and stabilize my strength within two weeks, then secure the assistance of a few more peak D-Grades, I will have a chance."

"You do realize she is a mid C-Grade."

"Barely. I have it on good authority that it's possible, if very difficult."

"Jack..."

"Trust me, Professor. It isn't a good plan, but it's the only one we have. I have looked everywhere and spoken with a lot of people, and this is the best I came up with. Unless you have something else to suggest..."

"I don't," she admitted heavily. "Fine. Let's—Oh, the others are here. They say hi."

"The others?"

"Edgar, Vivi, Sparman."

Jack's heart was filled with memories. "Tell them I say hi. I hope they're okay."

"They are. We've kept our highest bracket safe. Edgar had some troubles, but he got over them."

Suddenly, Jack felt pressured. His emotions were heavy, and he did not want to suppress them with his Dao.

"What is the situation like over there?" he asked. "How is everyone taking the end of the grace period?"

"Well, we're preparing for an all-out battle to exterminate the Ice Peak before then. Unless you really can beat the overseer, it's our only chance at survival. If we destroy them, we will be the only force capable of commanding the planet on behalf of the Animal Kingdom. They may find us more useful alive than dead... Though, with everything that's been happening recently, that possibility is beginning to seem hopeless as well."

She was referring to Jack's actions in Hell. He had completely enraged the Animal Kingdom. They wouldn't let his faction and planet get away easily.

"As for the enemy," the professor continued, "they are preparing to celebrate. The Animal Kingdom has organized a huge concert for the final day of the grace period. Remember Vanderdecken? The metal guy? He'll be the main event. Everyone will be there to watch—and it's also where we plan to assault

the Ice Peak. If we're going to die, we might as well die on stage." She chuckled darkly. "Two weeks to live... What a feeling it is, Jack. How heroic and relieving. If you told me this a year ago, I would have laughed at you, but now I see the world under a different light. I hate the System with all my soul, but some things are simply incomparable to everything else."

Jack nodded grimly, though she couldn't see him. "I will be there," he promised. "Prepare for war. On that day, I will come and join you. We will defeat the Kingdom together."

"Don't try too hard, Jack. We are goners already. If you can survive by yourself, please don't die for a lost cause..."

"I would never abandon you all. You are the only reason I've been pushing myself nonstop for the last year. I will die on your hill."

"Jack—"

"I don't want to hear it. I love you, Mom, and I will protect everyone else as well. Prepare for war. Try your hardest. And on that day, we will all live or die together. Okay?"

Her voice came in fragments, as if struggling to speak. *"I'm sorry, Jack... I'm sorry we are not strong enough."*

Jack forced himself to smile—though, again, she couldn't see it. *"Give me the detai—"*

"Jack!" the Sage interrupted. His eyes were full of shock. "They found us. We need to leave *now*."

"They what?" Jack gasped.

"Jack?" the professor's voice came worried. *"Is everything okay?"*

"I have to go," he replied, already following the others out of the cave. *"I'll contact you again soon."*

"Ja—"

He cut off the communication. His Dao pressed down, and he was again a warrior, completely in control of himself. "What's happening?"

"I had a bad feeling," the Sage explained. "I checked the patrols. All the D-Grades are converging to our location. They found us, and the black sphere hasn't recharged yet. We need to run. There is no way we can—"

The entire sea around them shook. It was an earthquake so massive it made the fish dizzy. Jack and the others accelerated to the surface, bursting out to find the horizon covered in approaching immortals. There were dozens of them. Hundreds. They were rushing in from every direction like a flock of death.

Jack's heart caught on his throat. "Run!"

CHAPTER SIXTY-SEVEN
CORNERED

"RUN!"

Jack's mind worked on overdrive. He scanned the approaching enemy arriving from every direction, locating the one where the enemies were sparsest. "Follow me!" He zoomed into the distance.

His three companions followed.

"What's the plan?" Dordok asked.

"We escape the encirclement for sure," Jack replied. "Then, we try to outrun them until the sphere charges back up. How much time do we need, Sage?"

"A couple hours."

"Shit." That was too long. Using the *Bromobile* was also impossible, as the time it took to charge up a teleport was easily enough for the enemies to reach them—and, if they didn't use it to teleport, it was faster to fly by themselves.

"How did they find us?" Shol asked.

"No idea," the Sage said. "But they must have had a way. I sensed no patrol passing over our location. Maybe they got someone to divine it."

"Was that possible?"

"I didn't think it was! But how else?"

Shol narrowed his eyes.

By now, the enemies before them were within reach. Two dozen animal people, with another few hundred closing in from every direction. They could have teleported behind the enemies, but Dordok didn't know how to teleport.

"Leave me!" he begged them.

"Not a chance!" Jack shouted, pulling back his arm. "We're punching through! Meteor Punch!"

"Sunshine!"

"Wide Confusion!"

Dordok gritted his teeth. Moisture came to his eyes that he pushed down and roared with all his strength, "Devastating Strike!"

Each used their strongest move. Some, like Shol's Sunshine, took time to charge but were perfect for this kind of scenario.

A purple meteor flew alongside a miniature sun. A steel greatclub crashed down from above. The enemies also unleashed their own strikes. A dozen full-power attacks from late immortals and deacons filled the sky. At the last moment, some of the enemies faltered, their strikes dissipating or weakening greatly.

The sky erupted with colors. A tremendous blast seared the clouds and scorched the earth, pushing the sea below them hundreds of feet downward. Jack and the others pierced through the shockwave like arrows, crashing straight into the enemy immortals. Punches cracked down. Explosions resounded. People roared and screamed.

Jack was lost in a sea of incredible power, punching through with every fiber of his being. The strength he'd cultivated for three months in isolation now burst forth all at once. The opposing immortals were strawmen before his attacks, blown away at the lightest touch. They were completely unable to stop him—to stop them.

With a massive final explosion, they pushed through.

The sky was clear again. Several immortal bodies fell behind them, most broken by blunt strikes.

Of the four of them, only Dordok was injured, sporting a bleeding wound on his chest close to where his heart was.

"Are you okay?" Jack shouted as they tore across the sky.

"I'll be fine!" Dordok responded. "Just a canine that got touchy!"

"Good! Keep running!"

Dordok was the slowest of the four, but the Sage said, "Let me help," and pointed a finger in his direction. Suddenly, Dordok's body erupted with power, letting him accelerate steeply.

They turned into light beams. An entire army of immortals was hot on their heels, closing the distance even as the slowest of them fell behind. Leading the charge were three people: Maximus Lonihor, Sapasun the canine deacon, and, surprisingly, Li Qian of the Exploding Sun.

Shol drew a sharp breath. "That's how they found us!" Rage and disbelief built up in his voice. "Monsoon used his position to get my lifeblood, a requirement of the faction for all deacons. They used it to locate me. This is my fault. Damn it all!"

"It's okay—" Jack tried to say something, but Shol wasn't listening.

"Li Qian!" he roared in rage. "What the fuck are you doing here!"

"Our faction has a responsibility to punish traitors!" the other immortal responded.

"Your dog master can fuck off!" Shol roared back. "Traitors! Cowards! You would harm the faction for your own interests?"

"Mind your tongue, Shol, or I will cut it off," Li Qian declared, his eyes narrowing. Suddenly, his serene aura turned sharp like a sword unsheathed.

"Hmph! An honorless dog like you has no business challenging me! I spit on the grave of every ancestor who helped bring an embarrassment like you to life!"

True to his word, Shol spat, sending a fat mass of phlegm toward the ground. The entire chasing army, though fierce, couldn't help but glance at Li Qian. Those were heavy insults, and they had been spoken very much in public.

Jack and Dordok laughed, adding oil to the fire. "Well spoken, brother Shol!" they said. "We should have expected a dog to side with the Animal Kingdom!"

Li Qian himself was steaming. His brows were creased to the limit, and his hand twitched around the handle of his sword. He was like a dark, violent, brooding storm.

"One of us will die today, Shol!" he declared. "I refuse to live another day under the same Dao as you!"

"I couldn't give a shit what you do, you honorless, pathetic dog!" Shol and his friends accelerated further.

Li Qian did not speak again, sinking into a deadly silence. Maximus clicked his tongue. "Even in the face of certain death, they still have the courage to mock us... It's a shame we can only kill them once."

"Oh, I'll find a way," Li Qian responded darkly.

The chase went on. Unfortunately, no matter how the Sage sped up Dordok, both of them were too slow to escape.

"Leave us!" Dordok pleaded. "I'm begging you. Don't let me hold you back!"

"Don't lose hope," Jack told him. "Keep running. We have to earn as much time as possible and make them split up so they come at us in waves. When they do catch up..." His eyes narrowed. "We'll just have to kill them all."

"Do you mean that, Jack?" Shol asked. "Even I haven't seen the ends of your power. Can you match Maximus Lonihor?"

Jack nodded sharply. "I think I can. But even if I can't, I have a secret ace up my sleeve. Keep running. Today, either a C-Grade steps over his dignity to save his subordinates, or they all die."

And he meant that.

Name: Jack Rust
Species: Human, Earth-387
Faction: Bare Fist Brotherhood (D)
Grade: D
Class: Cosmic Fist (King)
Level: 230

Strength: 1585
Dexterity: 1590
Constitution: 1585
Mental: 200
Will: 200

Dao Skills: Meteor Punch III, Iron Fist Style III, Space Walk III, Neutron Star Body II, Brutalizing Aura III

Daos: Dao Tree of the Fist, Dao Root of Indomitable Will (fused), Dao Root of Life (fused), Dao Root of Power (fused), Dao Root of Weakness (fused)
Titles: Planetary Frontrunner (10), Planetary Torchbearer (1), Ninth Ring Conqueror, Planetary Overlord (1)

After his training in isolation and the immortals he'd hunted, he'd grown by leaps and bounds. Not only did he reach Level 230, increasing all his stats and the Dao he could store by around 50%, but he also raised Space Walk to the third tier, which was why he could now teleport nine miles away instead of three. He had even gotten the stamina cost of the skill to scale with distance traveled, which made his teleportation handier for combat.

Space Walk III: Space is a constraint you have learned to escape. By spending an amount of energy depending on the distance traveled, take a step through the fabric of space to reappear anywhere within a nine-mile radius.

He still couldn't truly use it freely, as even the shortest teleportation was exhausting, but he could do it much more frequently than before. It was now a tool for actual battle instead of just engaging, escaping, or repositioning.

However, the largest benefits of his training came from consolidation.

Jack's Dao was extremely potent. Where other cultivators wielded a tiny dagger, he had a greatsword. However, there was a large difference between someone who wielded a greatsword effectively and someone who did not.

After training intensively for three months, Jack had become proficient with all uses of his Dao. There were no numbers to describe the change, he simply knew he was far, far stronger than he used to be.

Even he wasn't sure where his current strength lay, but he was significantly stronger than most deacons, and he remembered the strength of Maximus Lonihor from when they'd clashed. If he went all out, he should be able to at least match him. Then, if he used the Life Drop...

Using the Drop is suicide, he thought, but so be it. If we're going to die anyway, might as well take them with us.

He harbored very little hope of escaping. It wasn't a matter of Dordok or the Sage slowing them down. The C-Grades were absent on purpose—if the Battle Brothers were taken down by people of the same Grade, it would somewhat repair the lost reputation of the Animal Kingdom. If their strongest immortals failed and they were forced to send C-Grades after D-Grades, it would be another huge hit to their reputation... but that didn't mean C-Grades wouldn't appear if they had to.

At this point, Jack Rust and the Battle Brothers were a terrible thorn to the Animal Kingdom's side. There was no way they were letting him off, and Life Drop or not, he couldn't fight the late C-Grade Warden head-on.

The only trick up their sleeve was the Sage's black sphere, and the fact that the Animal Kingdom didn't know how long it would take to recharge. If they managed to last long enough, they could use it to teleport across the planet, board Jack's *Bromobile*, and hope it could teleport away before the C-Grades caught up. Then, given a very generous amount of luck, they could maybe evade the Kingdom's patrols and ride their starship away.

Of course, that plan shouldn't succeed. There were too many things that could go wrong. Though when the enemy's foolishness was your only chance at survival, you had to bet on it.

The terrain flowed beneath them. Jack crossed the sky like a meteor, watching all sorts of biomes scroll past. He had no idea what direction he was heading in, nor did he care. The entire planet seemed to awaken at their passage, with the animals freezing in terror of their auras, and lower-ranked immortals flying up to see what was going on. They even spotted a city atop a mountain, clad in opulence and gold.

Nobody came after them from that town, mostly because every strong D-Grade on the planet was already behind them.

Of the hundreds of immortals, more and more fell off as time passed. They were still chasing, but they had been left so far behind that they would need some time to catch up. Just as Jack had predicted, their enemies had been split into waves according to their speed.

Of course, the very first wave was made up of just three people:

Maximus Lonihor, the strongest D-Grade of the Animal Kingdom.

Li Qian, the strongest D-Grade of the Exploding Sun, and Shol's sworn enemy.

Sapasun, the canine deacon who served as the Warden's head disciple and who had once broken all of Jack's limbs while mocking him.

All three were extremely strong, and all three had a bone to pick with the Battle Brothers. Things would get ballistic the moment they closed the gap.

And that moment wasn't too far away. The three of them were fast. Though they had started the chase from miles away, they had now almost caught up. Jack could even clearly make out their fierce expressions, along with the faint spark of lightning on Maximus's fur and the foam dripping out of Sapasun's mouth.

Any time now, they would enter teleportation range. Jack didn't know how far they could go, but they were already approaching the nine mile point, which was his limit, so they couldn't be far off.

Maximus disappeared. Jack was ready. His awareness of the Dao of Space was sharp enough to detect the ripple a second before it was visible, and he instantly shot a punch into it. A large, furred fist came out to meet his. The sky split apart at their point of impact. A strong shockwave sent the Sage and Dordok flying, while Shol held his ground and turned to fight.

Only a second later, Li Qian stepped out of space, his unsheathed sword already descending. Shol met it with his burning palm, and after an explosion, both were equally pushed away.

Li Qian furrowed his brows. "Did you get stronger?"

Shol raised his chin and snorted. "Hmph. While you were scheming in the shadows, I was sharpening my skills on the enemy soldiers. If I lose to a coward like you, I will have betrayed everything I stand for."

Li Qian's eyes narrowed further. He brought his sword horizontally, gripping it with both hands. "You will regret your big mouth."

"Make me, dog."

"Did someone say dog?" Sapasun shouted, tearing through space to shoot at Shol from behind. His eyes were wide and red, his lips drawn back, and foam filled his mouth so completely that it dripped out from between his sharp teeth. He displayed an insanity similar to Gan Salin's, but much less controlled, and much more repulsive.

His five fingers formed into claws aimed at Shol. A steel greatclub intercepted one of them. The other suddenly veered off-course and snapped to the side, almost breaking his own wrist. Sapasun came to a stop, then snorted. "Who are you two clowns?"

"My name is Dordok." He hoisted his greatclub. Despite his wound, he was smiling. "But you can call me Captain."

"Who, me?" the Sage replied, pointing at himself. "I'm just a sage."

Sapasun blinked in confusion, then laughed. "Fine by me! Those two don't need any help. I'll have my fun with you." He reached inside his clothes and removed a projection stone, activating it and tossing it far away so it could record the entire battle. He then turned to Dordok and grinned with insanity.

"Bring it on, crazy!" Dordok charged, laughing the whole way.

Meanwhile, higher up in the sky than the other two clashes, Jack's fist was still pushing against Maximus's. The leonine had fully emerged from the crack in space, pouring the entirety of his strength into the strike, but Jack refused to budge. The puzzled expression on his face slowly turned into disbelief.

Yellow and purple sparks came from where their fists ground against each other. The crack of lightning matched the booming of a meteor, and a controlled explosion pushed them both around twenty feet away with enough strength to shatter mountains.

"How is this possible?" Maximus asked.

Jack grinned, raising his fists. "Come and find out, kitty. I'm just getting started."

CHAPTER SIXTY-EIGHT
SHAPING UP

DORDOK AND THE SAGE FLEW IN MIDAIR, COVERING EACH OTHER'S BACKS. THE greatclub fell heavily, distorting the air where it passed. Darkness clouded the enemy's senses, making reality confusing.

Unfortunately, for the canine deacon who cultivated the Dao of Insanity, reality was already confusing.

"Careful, there's a Five Star Grasp on your left," Sapasun said, stepping through space to appear at Dordok's right. His open hand shot out like a viper, all fingers outstretched, topped with sharp nails. Dordok brought his club to the correct side to defend.

"As if I'd fall for that!"

The impact was dull and heavy. The cyclops held his ground, but Sapasun was already behind him, whipping out a kick. "Kick that Breaks your Shin!" he shouted. Dordok raised his legs. The kick found him in the abdomen, pushing all air out of his lungs and making his stomach burn.

"Oh, but this, you fall for," Sapasun gloated. "It's alright. You can't be both big and smart."

"I'll crush you," Dordok croaked out, raising his club to strike. He did not plan to just defend. Their real opponent wasn't Sapasun, but the clock—if they couldn't deal with these opponents fast enough, the next wave would arrive, and they would be overwhelmed.

His club came down, the Dao of Strength grabbing the air around the canine and condensing it. Sapasun used his own Dao to ignore the compressed air and lean to the side, dodging the strike. At the same time, a finger appeared out of nowhere to press at the top of his skull. Sapasun's eyes grew foggy, letting the second swipe of the club crack him in the ribs. He went flying.

"Good one, Sage," Dordok said.

The Sage stepped out of the tear in space he'd been hiding in, panting and sweating. His Dao was extremely profound, but he hadn't fought anyone in these few months, so he remained at Level 170. Affecting such a strong peak D-Grade for even a moment took everything he had.

"We must hurry," he said. "Don't let him escape."

"I wasn't going to," Dordok responded.

"I wasn't going to," Sapasun repeated, bending reality to appear behind them. There had been no teleportation this time, so even the Sage hadn't seen him coming. His fingers pressed together, and the side of his palm descended onto Dordok's shoulder, eliciting a terrible cracking sound. The cyclops screamed. One of his arms left the handle of the greatclub, hanging limply at the side.

The Sage sent a torrent of life energy into Dordok, healing him, but Sapasun was already swinging. The Sage teleported away—he was clearly the priority target here. Yet that strike wasn't aimed at him, but at Dordok. Five fingers dug into the cyclops's back, and though the Sage once again healed the wound, they were both left panting.

Sapasun grinned. "Only a madman would target the high-level ogre before the low-level wizard. So, you should have seen it coming."

"I have never," Dordok said mid-panting, "faced such an obnoxious opponent."

"Oh, it's about to get worse. Bending Twist!"

"Clarity!" the Sage shouted in return. Reality twisted around them, then was forced back into shape. Dordok roared and dove for the canine, who laughed and brandished his claws.

"This could take a while," Sapasun said, "but I have time!"

A mile to the side, Shol and Li Qian were submerged in a cold battle to the death. Both fought at their limits. Their eyes were sharp, their minds devoid of anything but the battle. These were hardened veterans going for each other's throats.

Their battle spanned the entire sky. Shol's arms moved in elaborate patterns, summoning suns and solar beams and flicking them away. Golden barriers appeared around him, encasing him in flames that even burned the air.

Facing him, Li Qian was as calm as a lake, as sharp as a blade. His sword—a cyan katana—danced between his palms, cutting through the air so quickly it went nearly unseen. Every swing released sonic booms as if he wielded a whip. The winds obeyed him, forming into blades that shot forth to crash into the miniature suns.

The suns were cut in half, and the winds were burned away. Heat faced sharpness in a battle whose mere shockwaves were enough to crack the terrain below. If any normal human was watching from close-by, they would have been blinded, deafened, and burned to death already.

Li Qian dove in. His sword flashed a hundred times in the blink of an eye, covering him in ethereal blades that cut away even the heat. Such was his sharpness that, where he passed, it felt like the world had its skin shorn off, like the colors were just a bit muffled.

Seeing that, Shol brought his hands together and shouted sharply. He clapped. A tremendous explosion was released, impacting everything around him, including the space behind him, where Li Qian had just appeared.

Still, it wasn't enough to stop the sword. It cleaved straight through, forcing Shol to place a straight palm against it. The strike, which could have easily cleaved steel or the earth itself, was blocked. The shockwave carried on, carving a mile-wide fissure into the ground below.

Shol's palm bled.

"First blood is mine," Li Qian said. "If this was a sparring duel back home, you would have already lost."

Shol snorted, his eyes hard. "You have no home, and this no spar. Today, one of us will die—and you may have earned first blood, but I will earn the last one."

"Let's see."

They broke off, flying a hundred feet back.

"Since you want to die," Shol said, pressing his palms together, "let me send you off."

No new miniature sun appeared, but the temperature around him rose sharply. The air boiled. Light flickered and waved. Shol kept pressing his palms together, and to an outsider, it seemed like he was burning from the inside out. His skin reddened, then was covered by a pure golden sheen. Light escaped his eyes and mouth. His entire body shone. Even his bald head illuminated the sky like a new sun.

If Brother Tao from Earth could see Shol now, he would immediately fall to his knees in worship, for the current Shol looked just like a Buddha.

"I haven't gone all out in over a century," Shol said. "Prepare to experience suffering."

His every word and gesture seemed slow but was actually lightning-fast. The very air around him burned. Four extra arms made of golden light grew around his shoulders. A golden circle appeared behind his back. When he opened his mouth wide, a new sun blossomed inside it, burning not orange but gold.

"DIE!" he shouted.

The sun in his mouth released a terrible beam. Golden light the width of two grown men crossed the sky, instantly reaching his opponent. The ethereal cyan blades floating around Li Qian cut the beam into a million tiny pieces, yet how could one cut light?

Li Qian was buried in the beam. No sound escaped, and the light was so strong that his body was no longer visible, and even the nearby battle between the Sage, Dordok, and Sapasun was brought to a momentary halt.

When the beam dispersed, Shol's eyes did not mellow. His golden form remained active. Where Li Qian used to stand, there was now a man covered in cyan armor sticking to his skin, each string a blade. Smoke wafted off several parts of the armor, but he remained whole and combatant.

"I did not expect such power," he admitted, "but no matter. If you have a battle form, then so do I." His cyan sword rose to the sky, spawning a thousand other blades, each flying next to the others in complete synergy. "Let me show you why you are only the second deacon of the Exploding Sun."

Shol set his jaw and charged.

This entire battle was recorded by the projection stone and transmitted across the entire planet. The Animal Kingdom was determined to make their victory a spectacle. By now, every major city on the planet had a floating screen covering the sky, and every eye was glued to the three concurrent showdowns.

Of the three, one took center stage. People whispered and held their breaths as they watched.

Jack and Maximus Lonihor were going head-to-head. They flew around each other like wasps, repeatedly clashing and breaking off. Fists met fists. Jack's punches were heavy and sure, occasionally blossoming and exploding as meteors, while the arms and legs of Maximus whipped around with laser precision and lightning speed. His battle technique was impeccable.

Yet, after two hundred clashes, he had not managed to secure an advantage.

"How is this possible?" he asked again, pausing mid-battle. He was panting heavily. His proud leonine face was colored in disbelief. "You are twenty levels below me. How can you be so strong!"

Facing him, Jack breathed normally. "Because I had no choice," he replied, clenching his fist. "And I have no time, either. Release those winged knights, and I will pulverize you with the full might of my despair."

When those two stopped to talk, the other two battles came to a momentary halt, and even the far-off immortals, who were still rushing over, slowed down in shock. Every watcher across the planet held their breath at the rise of this new star. Shol, who knew Maximus's strength better than anyone, couldn't take his eyes away.

Against all odds, Jack held the advantage! How was this possible?

Just how strong had he become?

Jack laughed. "You haven't seen anything yet. Let's get this over with. I have other business to attend to."

Maximus tightened his jaw. His pride had been insulted, and that could not be allowed. The sky blossomed with divine radiance, and armies of winged knights flew down.

Jack met them with a grin. “Come!” he shouted, punching up. The sky exploded. The knights, each of whom was equal to a low D-Grade, were sent tumbling through the air. Many dissipated on the spot.

But many more remained, encircling him. Maximus dove in too, capitalizing on the distraction he’d created.

“Far from enough!” Jack roared. Brutalizing Aura erupted at full force, spreading out to cover an entire mile. The knights faltered. Their strength was sapped, drawn out by Jack’s aura and added to his own. He felt himself emboldened and empowered, as if new blood coursed through his veins.

He punched out.

Maximus must have sensed what happened, or there was some instinct guiding him. This time, instead of clashing against Jack, he chose to stop and defend.

It was the right call. Jack’s meteor was purple tinged with some of Maximus’s own radiance, and it exploded far harder than any other. All the power he’d absorbed from the winged knights was released in this strike, impacting Maximus’s crossed arms hard enough to ram them into his chest and catapult him away, breaking the sound barrier thrice.

He screamed as he flew.

When he finally managed to come to a stop, his forearms were bloated, and his bare ribs were already a shade of purple. His eyes were full of rage. “You are full of tricks.”

“No. I am just superior to you,” Jack replied, driving a stake through his opponent’s Dao. To a leonine, this was the greatest challenge that could be uttered.

Instantly, the body of Maximus straightened, and his chest puffed out. “You spoke the wrong words. I was planning to delay, but now I have to crush you.”

The winged knights that were uselessly flying around Jack, unable to approach, dissipated like dust in the wind. The divine radiance that rained down from the heavens persisted, and it began to gather around Maximus, surrounding him like motes of light.

"Prepare yourself," he said, "for you are about to witness my supremacy."

CHAPTER SIXTY-NINE
DISASTER

At a lower elevation, Sapasun noticed the other battles heating up. "Whoops. Guess I delayed too much," he said and teleported behind Dordok, then to his left, then to his right. He became a tornado that the cyclops was completely unable to keep up with.

The Sage pointed a finger in his general direction, but it did nothing. "What!" he exclaimed.

Sapasun flashed above Dordok and smashed a palm onto his head. The cyclops' neck was barely able to handle the strain, and his entire body went flying so fast, he crashed into the ground far below.

The Sage tried to teleport to escape, but Sapasun was there, having predicted his movements and caught up using his superior speed. His hand wrapped around the Sage's throat, immobilizing him.

"I was just playing around before," Sapasun said with a slight frown. "I can sense that your Dao is far deeper than mine, but you are just too under-leveled. I have over double your stats. What were you thinking? How was someone as capable as you allowed to do such stupid shit?"

Despite being firmly grabbed by the neck, the Sage managed to chuckle. "Because," he croaked out, "I am a sage. I always know what I'm doing."

Sapasun looked on with confusion, then shrugged. "Well, whatever.

The real question is...” His lips were drawn into a feral grin. “What should I break first?”

One of the battles was over. Dordok and the Sage... had lost!

To the side, Shol’s golden form clashed heavily against Li Qian. The swordsman dodged everything like a fly, but Shol wasn’t playing around, either. Each of his six arms detonated golden suns. His mouth and eyes unleashed beams of destruction. The very air was scorched where his attacks passed.

Li Qian flew under a beam and over an exploding sun. He teleported to the left, then right behind Shol, but another sun exploded in his face and pushed him back. He released a wild cut from a hundred feet away, only for a single golden palm to break the wind blade.

“You know you cannot fight me,” Shol declared calmly, still shooting out suns, beams, and all sorts of extreme destruction, keeping Li Qian from approaching. “You are weak. Always have been. There is only one reason why you have been able to beat me before, and it may no longer be the case. Use it, Li Qian. Use the strike I fear. Let me tear it down and overcome my demons.”

Li Qian gritted his teeth, desperately dodging a cascade of attacks. Though he had also utilized a battle form, the truth was, Shol’s was simply stronger. He had been able to match it once upon a time, but not anymore. Whatever Shol had been doing on this planet had sharpened him just enough to overwhelm Li Qian.

Unless he used his trump card.

“Very well!” he roared, flying away and opening a wide distance between them. He slowly lifted his sword over his head, as if it weighed a ton. “You may be strong, Shol, but your powers of comprehension are lacking. No one could become our faction’s head disciple without mastering our ultimate skill.”

Shol’s eyes narrowed in concentration. A golden sun blossomed in each of his six palms, ready to be unleashed. “Then bring it out, and let me break that ultimate skill of yours. Let me show you that hard work tramples talent.”

“As you wish.” Li Qian’s eyes were dark. He brought down his sword—and no longer was its light cyan, but pure white. The swing was much slower than his previous ones, and seemed weak. But it was straight.

Far too straight, and far too true. It reached deep into the Dao and pulled out secrets that did not belong to the D-Grade.

"Supernova Slash!" he roared.

The very tip of his sword shone with white light so blinding it momentarily overwhelmed the real sun in the sky. In the next moment, space before him ruptured as a tremendous explosion occurred. He was unaffected; the shockwave directed entirely toward Shol, a blinding white menace that immolated the ground far below. The strength of the actual beam was unfathomable.

Facing it, Shol had no time to dodge, though he did not intend to. All six of his arms tossed out a miniature sun. His mouth opened to release a beam of its own, golden in color. His body remained stationary. All seven of his attacks converged into the beam, colliding with an explosion so titanic it created a wide, mushroom-shaped cloud of fire that engulfed both Shol and Li Qian.

The entire sky stood still as if in awe of the powers used. Even Jack looked over, protecting his eyes with his Dao. Then, the fire dispersed. The burned air was restored, and the sky stopped moaning.

Li Qian stood hunched in midair. Only tatters remained of his cyan armor. The exposed parts of his skin were completely charred. He looked to be at the ends of his strength.

However, another shape fell from the sky, tumbling powerlessly toward the ground below. Shol's golden form had been broken. His entire body was burned beyond recognition, and he had lost consciousness. Only his extremely solid body as a peak D-Grade Physical cultivator kept him within an inch of his life.

Shol... had also lost!

Jack's eyes widened. "No," he muttered. "No!"

These all take time to describe, but the truth is that all three battles took place concurrently. The Sage and Dordok were defeated at around the same time as Shol. At the exact same time, Maximus was still gathering motes of light around him, preparing to unleash what he called his Supremacy.

Time slowed for Jack. His friends were still alive, but very soon, they wouldn't be. Even if he could match Maximus, more immortals would arrive at any second, and Sapasun was still in fighting condition.

They had lost.

But he would not go down without a fight.

Scorched earth, he thought, his gaze darkening. *Fuck you all.*

There were only two things to do: try to save his friends, and take down as many enemies as he possibly could.

Before Maximus even finished whatever he was up to, Jack teleported away. He appeared beside Sapasun, who clearly did not expect this. "Wha—" was all he managed to say before a fist crashed into his chest, sending him flying. He had already launched himself backward to weaken the strike, but the attack had come so unannounced he'd taken it hard; he spat out blood and screamed in pain.

"What the hell?" he asked in a breaking voice.

At the same time, Jack had grabbed the canine's wrist and clamped down on it, forcing him to release the Sage. For a second, the Sage was free. "Take the others and run," Jack ordered. "I'll hold them off."

"You can't!"

"I have to. Either we all die, or only I do." He smiled. "Take care of Earth for me, Sage. Please."

The Sage looked him in the eye for what felt like hours but must have been only an instant. "I will," he promised, then teleported away, presumably to collect the others and make a run for it. Jack didn't have time to check anymore.

He unleashed a Meteor Punch at Sapasun, forcing him to bend reality to dodge, then pretended to attack again, only to teleport next to Li Qian. The swordsman had anticipated this and raised his sword to defend, but in his injured state, it was far from enough. He was sent flying away like a missile, spitting out a long line of blood.

"STOP!" Maximus roared, appearing before Jack. Golden motes of light still flickered around him. His transformation not yet complete; he'd been forced to interrupt it in order to come and save the others from a rampaging Jack. "What are you doing? Where is your honor?"

"In the survival of my friends," Jack replied, laughing freely. The Fist inside him felt livelier than ever. He teleported away, appearing between his previous location and the approaching army of immortals, who had almost arrived. "All three of you should work together to stop me," he shouted in Maximus's direction, "or I will decimate every deacon on your planet!"

Maximus grew so angry he wanted to spit out blood. "You!" was all he managed to say before rushing over. Sapasun and Li Qian teleported as well, but there was no way they could make it in time. Jack was closer. He would reach the immortals and begin butchering before they could stop him.

Jack teleported thrice in quick succession, landing him right in the midst of the approaching first wave of immortals, all deacons. Each had seen his battle and were already scattering. "It is too late to run," Jack muttered. "You will all die here. If I am to fall, I'm taking you with me."

He reached inside himself and prepared to activate his Life Drop in a final suicide attack.

Then he froze. The world froze. Everything froze. Every mote of Dao he could sense stood still as if afraid to even move. Even the faraway form of the Sage, still carrying the unconscious bodies of Shol and Dordok, were frozen.

"That is enough," said a voice brimming with barely restrained anger. The Warden appeared directly in front of Jack in all his majesty, nullifying any and all attempts of a suicide attack. Jack was a bucket of water before an ocean. Facing such disparity in strength, even if he used the Life Drop, anything he tried would be laughable.

In the face of death, Jack relaxed. "You would send a C-Grade to achieve what all your Kingdom's D-Grades could not? Where is your honor?"

The Warden snorted. "Hmph! You have already abandoned honor in your despair. Why should our Kingdom not treat you like the dog you are?"

CHAPTER SEVENTY
CHALLENGING AN ENTIRE FACTION

JACK FACED DOWN THE WARDEN. HE WAS SLIGHTLY INJURED AND TIRED—NOT in peak fighting condition, but even if he was, this was a completely unwinnable battle.

The moment the Warden arrived, everyone knew it was over. The Animal Kingdom inner disciples stopped running and respectfully returned. Maximus, Li Qian, and Sapasun all relaxed and bowed to the elder. The Sage, who had been escaping while carrying the unconscious bodies of Shol and Dordok, also came to a stop.

Silence befell the world. Jack broke it.

"I guess this is it," he said, his chin raised high. He was disheartened; desperate, even. Everything was over. However, at the end of the day, his heart was light, and the Fist was solid. He shook his head, laughing lightly at his own misfortune. "At least I showed the world how petty your Kingdom really is."

"An ugly death rattle," the Warden responded impassively. "Your little game is over. I hope you enjoyed it, because I will personally make sure you experience more suffering than everyone you killed put together."

"As if I fear pain or death. What suffering can be greater than your loss of face today, Warden?"

"You are delusional. Men, capture them."

A few of the deacons present rushed to apprehend both Jack and the Sage. The latter took it in stride, letting his arms and legs be bound. Jack released his aura to warn the deacons from approaching. They paused, eyeing their elder.

"Why do you resist?" the Warden asked, furrowing his mature leonine face. "You know it is futile. All you achieve is to humiliate yourself."

"What shame is there in fighting to the death?"

"As you wish. This humiliation is a fitting death for an evil-doer like yourself."

Jack snorted. "You seem very familiar with humiliation, Warden. I made you suffer it enough times already. Is it your Dao?"

The Warden snorted back. "Enough with your nonsense."

"Where exactly is the nonsense? Every D-Grade on Hell failed to catch me for half a year. If that is not humiliation, I don't know what is."

Anger was unbecoming for an elder in public. Yet, under Jack's relentless provocation, his eyes were beginning to narrow, and his aura showed just the slightest hint of instability. "Are you out of your mind, brat? Do you even realize who you're talking to? I am Elder Artus Emberheart, Warden of Hell, late C-Grade. I could annihilate you with a thought. How dare you be disrespectful?"

"What exactly should I fear, Warden? You have already promised to torture me and harm the people I care about. You're out of threats."

At this, the Warden glowered. Indeed, Jack had nothing left to lose. He could say anything he wanted.

Reaching that point of thought, the Warden grew frustrated. "Take him away," he commanded, waving dismissively. At the same time, he pressed down on Jack with his aura, preventing him from fighting back.

Jack tried to resist, but it was helpless. Two deacons strong-armed him, holding his wrists behind his back and clamping them with black shackles that felt unbreakable. The situation looked to be over.

Inside Jack's mind, however, he remained on guard. He was constantly trying to come up with a way out of this, or a way to better pave the path for a future escape. Yet, no matter how he approached the issue, there was nothing.

"Sage," he called out telepathically, "can the Church get us out of here?"

"No. I wasn't lying before. Even if they kill us both, the Church will not interfere. This planet was a test for both of us, and if we fail, we're on our own."

Jack gritted his teeth. The Black Hole Church could not save him. The Exploding Sun could not save him. Then, who could?

The answer was clear: nobody. Jack had to weasel himself out of this or resign to a fate of torture, death, and the Kingdom's revenge against his entire planet.

What can I do? he asked himself. There has to be something!

The Bromobile*? Completely useless right now.*

The Life Drop? It isn't nearly enough to defeat the Warden. Perhaps I could detonate it, somehow, and hope the explosion injures or kills him. However, as he reached for the Drop inside him to test it out, it was unresponsive. Jack was shocked. The Life Drop refused to obey! He couldn't even activate it, let alone remove it from his soul or detonate it.

This had never happened before. He didn't know it was possible. And, while this revelation opened a whole new can of worms, it offered exactly zero help in getting out of this predicament.

Was his only choice really to let himself be captured?

It was possible that someone, anyone, would show up to rescue him, but it felt like such a remote possibility that it might as well not exist. After everything he'd done, the Warden must have been resolved to kill him.

"Any ideas, Sage?" he asked again. "I'm afraid I've run out."

"Same here, unfortunately. The black sphere hasn't recharged, and even if it had, I could not use it. I carry no more artifacts with me. There is nothing I can do to help."

Jack's heart was filled with disappointment before his eyes shone. *Wait! The projection stone is still running!* His eyes went over the surrounding immortals. All gazed at him with fear and grudge, including Maximus Lonihor and Li Qian.

That projection stone was meant to record his capture and partly repair the Animal Kingdom's public image. They planned to broadcast it far and wide to showcase their power. Nobody could escape the Animal Kingdom, that would be their message.

And, indeed, it worked. Jack was captured, and he was publicly sentenced to a fate worse than death. Two of the Battle Brothers lay unconscious. To all who witnessed, it was a complete triumph of the Animal Kingdom, a sound slap to the face of everyone who called them incompetent.

But what if Jack could turn that in his favor?

The projection stone was still active. He could not fight back with force, but maybe there were other ways. Maybe, just maybe, he could punch them with words. A plan was already forming in his mind, a plan he didn't dare believe in. It was desperate—but it just might work.

"One moment," he called out, pretending to give in to despair. He let his voice grow weak. "I have an offer to make, Warden. May I speak?"

The Warden's face went from real disinterest to feigned one. "Since you're begging, go ahead."

In his heart, the Warden must have been dancing with glee. Capturing Jack Rust was a given the moment he chose to act—the real point of this mission was to create a recording that would paint the Animal Kingdom in the best light possible. Jack Rust chose to act stubborn, which didn't really work for them. However, if he begged for mercy or offered a deal, the Warden could shut him down hard, exhibiting the Kingdom's moral superiority as well.

In his heart, surely he was thanking every star in the sky for Jack Rust giving in.

Little did he know that Jack Rust possessed the perfectly composed mind of a warrior. In this situation, he had the calmness and wisdom to look ahead, capitalizing on the Warden's underestimation.

"Because of me, the Animal Kingdom has suffered great humiliation," he said apologetically. "By evading all D-Grades on Hell for half a year, I have made the Kingdom's younger generation seem completely inept. I'm sure that every other faction in the galaxy is mocking you right now."

"As if!" the Warden interrupted. "Get to the point, brat. Everyone knows that you only survived this long because of your accomplice's spatial artifact. If not for that, you would have died a thousand times over."

"That's exactly my point, oh honorable Warden. I tricked my way through this, making your D-Grades seem useless compared to a rogue cultivator like myself. So, I offer a way to make up for this. I challenge the strongest D-Grades your Kingdom has to offer to a duel."

The Warden's eyes narrowed—now he began to suspect something. "You cannot escape like that. You are already captured."

"With all due respect, Warden, I was captured by you, not them. Even now, when I possessed no spatial artifacts, all these D-Grades were inadequate against me and forced you to act personally."

"Everyone can understand you are using more artifacts," the Warden replied. "It's obvious. How else could a new D-Grade match our deacons?"

"And what if I'm not? What if your deacons are genuinely incompetent? That is exactly what everyone in the galaxy is saying, Warden, and it is a grave insult! How could your Kingdom live this down? If you don't prove yourselves, then even ten thousand years into the future, all your disciples will be mocked behind their backs, and your subordinate planets will think you're just bullies with big mouths and small fists."

"Wait—" the Warden said, but Jack wasn't going to.

"I challenge you to a duel," he declared proudly, raising his chin and revealing his true intentions. He infused his words with every speck of power he could manage. "I, Jack Rust, challenge the entire Animal Kingdom. I am but one man, and you are a faction with millions of disciples. Bring any D-Grade you want. I, Jack Rust, will defeat them and prove to the entire world that the mockery on your face is correct. The Animal Kingdom is nothing but a declining, festering cradle of weakness. Your immortals are a joke. In a few thousand years, when all your C-Grades die and the weaklings you call deacons are called to take up their spot, the Kingdom will fall from the heavens and crash into the dirt so hard you become the galaxy's eternal laughingstock. Do you dare accept my challenge, Warden? One man versus a faction. Do you have the balls?"

Everyone was speechless. Even across the entire planet, where the image was projected, people gaped with their jaws touching the floor.

Jack Rust had just challenged every D-Grade in the entire Animal Kingdom to a duel. Was he nuts?

Of course he was!

The Warden's face grew red with anger and frustration. "What bullshit are you spouting? You are a prisoner. Who says you can duel anyone?"

"You do, Warden," Jack replied, staring him straight in the eyes. "You will accept my challenge because you have no choice. Everyone saw me fight Maximus Lonihor on equal ground before you were forced to interrupt us, afraid of me killing him."

"You were attacking others! That's why I stopped you!"

Jack laughed rowdily. "What a joke you are, Warden. So your deacons need protection from someone of lower level, is that it? You were afraid of me, a lone man at Level 230, jumping into the midst of your peak D-Grades and killing them all. Is that what you're saying, Warden? That your deacons are so weak they need babysitting?"

"You are twisting reality, brat!" the Warden shouted back. Only now did he realize he'd messed up. He'd underestimated Jack, thinking he was nothing but a knucklehead. Who would have thought he could speak with such savagery? With such sharpness?

By letting Jack speak freely, the Warden allowed him to paint the events in his image—and the worst part is, he was right. Everything Jack was saying right now was completely correct! Indeed, this entire humiliation stemmed from Jack's extreme power and their relative weakness. If they didn't disprove that, they had no way to really repair their public image.

Just how was the Warden supposed to retort?

"You are out of words, Warden," Jack declared proudly, pressing on. "Accept my challenge if you dare. You have no choice. If you win, you lose nothing. But if you decline, everyone will know that the Animal Kingdom is made up of weak cowards!"

The Warden's heart burned so badly it could have caught on fire. He'd been played. He'd been driven into such an ugly spot, and it was all his fault for letting Jack speak!

"What would we even earn from humoring you, Jack Rust?" he asked bitterly. "We've captured you already. Prisoners don't get to make demands, and you have nothing to offer that we can't get."

"I do: honor. Your honor. If you defeat me, I will publicly admit my wrongdoings and bow my head to you. I will become a dog and slave of the Animal Kingdom, saving you some of the face you've lost. But if I win, you must set me and my companions free."

"Bullshit!" the Warden shouted. "You're dreaming!"

"Am I?" Jack laughed. "Just how afraid of me are you, Warden? You know what? Let me make things easier for you. Don't bring one D-Grade. Bring three. I will defeat them all at once and stick your face so far up your ass that you'll see your own throat."

"How dare you speak like that to me—I am an elder!" the Warden roared, releasing his aura. The winds broke and the sky shuddered. The earth rumbled. The stars flickered. The world became the Warden's, an unbreakable space of supremacy.

Yet, words were the one thing power could not kill. The Warden was trapped. He knew it. Jack knew it. Everyone knew it, as they found themselves nodding in agreement and looking forward to the fight Jack proposed. When would they ever see such a spectacle again?

If the Warden declined, no matter how he phrased it, everyone would know the truth: he was afraid of Jack Rust winning. He really had fought Maximus to a standstill. No matter how absurd it sounded, he had the qualifications to challenge the Animal Kingdom like this.

The Warden couldn't believe he'd played by a junior. It was the single most humiliating event of his life. At that moment, his hatred for Jack Rust grew to new heights, but he was participating in an event that would soon be watched by the entire galaxy. He had to protect the Animal Kingdom.

"What is your answer, Warden?" Jack Rust asked. "Are you a proud man or a coward?"

The Warden snorted coldly, but on the inside, he was burning and gnashing his teeth. Finally, he accepted that he had no choice—but he wouldn't go down without a fight.

After all, the Warden refused to believe that someone could rise to be one of the galaxy's strongest D-Grades within a year. Jack had to be cheating, and since he was captured, the Hand of God's inquisitors and their deep-scan would strip him of every artifact in his body. That way, Jack's real strength would be revealed, and how could it be greater than that of a deacon? The Warden simply refused to believe that.

Even he, a late C-Grade, had shown nowhere near such talent at that age. There was no way Jack Rust, a *human*, could do it.

"Fine!" he growled. "The Animal Kingdom will not tolerate your disrespect. However, how could our head disciple fight someone of as low standing as you? No. Since you spoke to me so disrespectfully, it is fitting that you be humiliated and executed by my own top disciple, Sapasun!"

Jack snorted. "That weakling is not enough."

"Beat him, and you can duel Maximus," the Warden replied in outrage. "But we both know that won't happen. You will be completely subjugated by my disciple. We will show the world that a weakling like you, who depended on treasures and treachery to assassinate our members, is nothing before a real warrior."

"Fine! A duel it is!" Jack laughed.

"Don't be happy, kid. Your death will come soon."

"That is not the case. I am stronger than Maximus. I am winning this. I bet you are already cursing your luck for accepting, but there is nothing you can do about it. You are powerless."

"Hmph. More bullshit. I've had enough of your disrespect. Shut up now or I'll make you."

"How does it feel to be out of options, Warden?" he asked, grinning. "How does it feel for a strong C-Grade like you to be completely entrapped by a man you consider weak and lowly? Well, I have news for you. I am neither. You have ridden the tiger, Warden, and there is no getting off. I *will* publicly humiliate your faction, and there is nothing you or anyone else can do about it. But you know what? Maybe, if you wiggle your little lion butt for me, I could change my mind. Go on. I'm waiting."

At this, the Warden was finally unable to keep his cool. With a mighty snort, he crashed his aura down on Jack. The last thing Jack saw was a large, wrinkled palm before his nose. Then, he lost consciousness.

The Warden stood before an unconscious Jack and turned to the projection stone. "In three days, my top disciple, Sapasun, will duel Jack Rust. If he somehow loses, then our strongest D-Grade, Maximus Lonihor, will take over," he declared. "Our Kingdom fears no one, especially not cheating cowards who use treasured artifacts to trick the world. For the crimes this man has committed, he must be publicly and soundly humiliated. This farce has dragged on for long enough."

He waved his hand at the projection stone, deactivating it.

Then, completely ignoring the D-Grades around him, he roared at the sky, unleashing his rage. The sky above turned radiant, lightning flying everywhere. Everyone trembled.

"Warden..." Maximus uttered hesitantly.

"Shut up!" the Warden shouted. "You heard me. Take them all to prison. Sapasun, you're fighting this guy in three days, and you damn best win. Dismissed!"

CHAPTER SEVENTY-ONE
DEVIL DEALS

Etsin, the echidna devil that Jack had released from Trial Planet, appeared in the middle of a teleporter. "Move," the guard growled at him.

"Yes, yes," Etsin replied, quickly stepping away.

He was disguised, of course. Right now, he looked like an unaffiliated E-Grade human cultivator in his thirties—an appearance he'd found most people ignored. Of course, D-Grades could detect his disguise, but there was no way this tiny place would have guards of that caliber.

Etsin stepped out of the teleporter hub and into the town proper. A large sign spelled, "Fair Way Continent."

"Finally," he whispered, sniffing the air. "She must be here. I can sense her already."

Ignoring the wary looks of the other pedestrians, he turned into the alley between two buildings and assumed his real form. Gray skin, bat wings, red horns, spikes on his spine, and long, sharp ears. A drunk woman rummaging through the trash bins—an F-Grade saphira with purple eyes and sapphire hair—choked and screamed at his appearance, but the devil ignored her and teleported away.

A few jumps later, he was alone in the middle of a field. He sniffed the air and teleported again, following his nose to the location of his next victim.

"Another pure soul..." he muttered with glee, rubbing his hands together. "And at such close proximity, too! This must be my lucky century!"

Space was inconsequential. The devil traveled nine miles with every jump, reaching many horizons away from where he'd first appeared.

"It's growing stronger!" he exclaimed, switching from teleportation to supersonic flight. A sharp mountain grew larger in his sight. As soon as he reached it, he clawed open the entrance of a sealed cave and barged in, finding himself immediately under assault by a Will-based attack.

Of course, he dispelled it right away.

"Naughty child," he said with a snort. "Kneel!"

His D-Grade aura spread out, impacting the sole, mid E-Grade woman that occupied this cave and forcing her to her knees. She was a saphira, too—the prevalent species of this tiny planet. However, unlike most, her countenance was dark, and a baleful air circled her like a pack of vultures. Etsin could almost smell the grief she carried.

"Good, good," he said. "Overwhelmed by grief and fueled by revenge. Perfect."

"D-Grade? Devil?" the woman asked. Though she was completely overpowered, she did not seem to fear death. The only emotions she showed were sorrow and hatred. "How did you find me? Was the destruction of my friends and family not enough? Must you kill me too?"

"Oh, girl, I have no idea what you're talking about. I'm not with the ones after you. On the contrary—I am here to give you what you desire most. *Power.*"

That last word echoed through the cave, as if it had been spoken with such weight that the natural laws didn't dare silence it.

The saphira grew wary. "You are a devil. I've heard about your kind."

"Everything you've heard is true. In return for my gift, I will have your soul. But do you really care?"

She held his stare. Then gave in to the absurdity. "No."

"Excellent! I judged you well. Then, shall we?" He waved his hand

and a scroll appeared. When it unfurled, blood-colored letters scrolled all the way to the ground.

"What are you saying?" the girl asked. "I don't understand."

"Let me formalize my offer. What is your name?"

"...Vlossana."

"Good. My name is Etsin, an echidna devil, and I can sense the darkness within you. I can sense your desire. If you accept my offer, I will gift you the power you need to exact revenge on those who wronged you. I will help you reach the D-Grade."

Her eyes widened. "The D-Grade?"

Etsin fought hard to keep the sneer off his lips. To these mortals, the simple D-Grade was the apex of the apex, something they couldn't even achieve in their wildest dreams. They eyed it like children at a dangling candy, not knowing there were a thousand of them at every corner store.

"Indeed," he confirmed. "I can offer you that tremendous power."

"And what's the catch? Do you get my soul now or after I die?"

"After. But there is another condition. I am willing to give you half that power right now, pushing you to the peak E-Grade. You will be able to dominate simple places like this continent."

She nodded, the struggle in her eyes fading. She had nothing to lose—those people could never decline. "And the other half?" she asked.

"The other half is for after you complete a favor of mine," he said with a smile. "An easy one, I assure you. I just want you to kill a certain man. That's all. I promise you will be strong enough to do it."

Her eyes narrowed in thought. "Do I know that man?"

"No."

"Is he innocent?"

"Does it matter?"

She held his stare. Gradually, her eyes hardened. Etsin sensed the dark desire inside her strengthening, and this time, his devilish grin appeared in all its glory.

"I'm listening," Vlossana said.

Edgar blew out a puff of smoke, looking into the stars. His heels were propped on his desk, and his back was slouched into his soft chair.

Finally, he was useful. He could help and protect the people he cared about. He could somewhat fill in the shoes that Jack Rust had left behind.

And, at the same time, he was so fucking sad.

"I hate this," he muttered, pressing his eyes shut to keep the tears in. He'd promised he wouldn't cry anymore. He would be strong. His friends needed him, and they were all he cared about now. Not himself—his body was there, but his soul was long gone. He'd promised it to the devil, Etsin, in return for battle power.

"What a sad life..." he muttered to the stars, the only confidants he dared trust. "If it was any other time, any other world... But no. It is what it is. Others will find the beauty I relinquished. For me, there is only war. Such is my fate."

The devil had constructed a shell around his Dao Seed of Magic, harnessing its power to fuel a more battle-oriented version of magic. That way, Edgar could fight without shattering his Dao—but the more power he used, the more of his soul he surrendered. When there was nothing left, he would die and forever disappear in the devil's belly.

That was the deal. Power in return for his soul.

"How poetic. Life imitates art," he told himself, pushing the dark thoughts away. He didn't need them. He didn't need to think at all. Edgar the Magician was gone, and what remained was Edgar the Destroyer.

No matter how terribly this hurt... it would be over soon.

And his friends would be safe.

Brock ducked under a mighty swing. An entire section of the forest behind him was shattered, but he pushed forth uncaring. The Staff of Stone arced over his back, around his shoulder, and into his palm. He brought it down.

The tip of the staff met a stone club. The ground cratered under the point of impact. Brock pushed with all his might, increasing the density of his staff and muscles to amplify his power. It wasn't enough. He was sent flying into a massive, ancient tree, but he decreased his density at the last moment to rotate, land feet-first, and shoot back out.

The King of Ogres, the two-headed ruler of the forest, could not retract his club in time. Brock sailed over it, increasing his density mid-flight, and poured the Big Thought of Muscle into his arms. His biceps enlarged to tremendous dimensions. The ogre king's four eyes widened. Brock's staff cracked down, impacting one of the ogre's thick skulls and fracturing the ground below for a hundred feet in every direction. Soil went flying. Dust filled the air.

The ogre moaned, stepping back with a shaking body.

Brock landed on his feet. "Sorry, bro, but I win."

He charged again. The staff became one with his body, dancing around him to the tune of the opponent's death. The ogre tried to resist, but only one of his skulls remained. A few mighty swings later, Brock's staff stabbed the ogre's throat, knocking him dead on his back.

The forest around them was ravaged. A dozen ogres lay dead in puddles of blood, and every ancient tree in a wide radius had been felled. Dust clouded the perimeter, while the ground was covered in craters of various sizes.

Brock was the only one still standing. He had not brought his little bros along, because this was a battle only for himself.

Bros are important, but so is the ability to stand alone.

"I win," Brock said to himself. His deep voice was emotional. He'd spent six months training as hard as his body could support. He was lined with muscles now, both in body and mind, and his power had reached far beyond his previous state. He'd even achieved a fourth Big Thought—the Big Thought of Never Stopping.

Brock still belonged to what his little bros called the E-Grade, but had reached the apex. Nobody in the town could fight him. Nobody on the planet. The King of Ogres had been considered invincible, but Brock had triumphed over it.

Brock estimated he was at the same level of power as Big Brother when he fought the silver knight, as long as he didn't use the Big Green Four Arms.

He looked at his wrist—a motion his little bros often did—and nodded. Though he wore no clock, he knew it was almost time. There were only two weeks left. He had to prepare and depart for home.

On the way back, a monkeyish grin was plastered on Brock's face. He couldn't wait to see Big Bro's reaction at how far he had reached—and he couldn't wait to see what heights Big Bro himself had attained.

He had no doubt that nothing bad could happen to Big Bro. They would meet again soon, and they would both be proud of each other, then they would travel together and have bro adventures all over the world.

Brock had worked hard and attained strength. From now on, life was his to enjoy.

CHAPTER SEVENTY-TWO

AN OFFER UNSEEN

JACK AWOKE IN A DARK, COLD PRISON CELL. BLACK MANACLES CLAMPED DOWN on his wrists, limiting his ability to invoke the Dao, while a hard-faced deacon stared him down from behind steel bars.

"Sup," Jack said.

The deacon snorted. He was a sizeable lycan who looked like he'd seen more than his fair share of combat.

Jack closed his eyes and expanded his perception. It didn't reach past the bars. The manacles on his wrists limited his connection to the Dao, constricting him to the most rudimentary level of control.

It was an odd feeling. He'd lived most of his life without any Dao whatsoever, but its absence now struck him as hard as the loss of a distant relative.

His surprise must have shown, because the guard spoke up. "It's only temporary. In two days, we will remove the manacles so you can duel and die at your best."

"Brave of you. I didn't expect the Animal Kingdom to act with dignity."

"You don't deserve it. This is only because your duel is public. It will be transmitted across the galaxy, so we can repair the damage you did.

If you ask me, a murderer like you should be tortured and executed somewhere dark and cold."

"Good thing you're not in charge, then."

The deacon snorted.

"Do you have people looking after every prisoner here?" Jack asked.

"Everyone else has the Warden's mark on their soul, except you. Now shut up."

Jack complied. He had better things to do than chat with bitter men.

I made it, somehow... he thought, bursting at the seams with relief. They didn't kill me instantly... Now, I can try to survive. All I have to do is defeat Maximus Lonihor in a public duel. He grinned slyly. I think I got this.

Using the Life Drop was out of the question, of course, but he held a certain level of confidence. His real opponent was the Planetary Overseer. A mere D-Grade, no matter how strong, was only a warm-up.

Am I arrogant for thinking that way as a D-Grade myself? Hmm. Only if I can't live up to it.

His mind then turned to other thoughts. The last thing he remembered was getting knocked out by the Warden. Until then, all three of his companions had been alive, so they probably still were. Their lives were part of the duel's stakes.

I hope the professor and the others aren't too worried.

He tried to access the telepathy he'd recently unlocked but came up short. In fact, he couldn't even bring up his status screen. *Do the manacles cut me off from the System, too?* he wondered, raising his hands to take a good look at them. *Or does the System itself communicate through the Dao?*

Or both?

Even if his connection to the Dao was severed, his connection to his soul wasn't. He could still feel his Dao Tree pulsing inside him, a core of tightly-packed power he could exercise at will.

Of course, using external Dao was the main difference between the E and D-Grades. Immortals could use their own Dao as a trigger to direct the ambient Dao in their environment and exert much stronger power. In Jack's current state, he was limited to his own storage, so even if he tried to escape, he wouldn't get far. Honestly, getting a deacon to watch over him was overkill. Any mid D-Grade would do.

Not that he planned to escape. This duel was right up his alley. He could humiliate the Animal Kingdom in front of the entire galaxy, and secure the freedom of himself and his friends.

The Warden was a fool for accepting. Who knows what he had miscalculated?

Bereft of things to do, Jack dove into his soul. The moment he appeared, floating in an empty cosmos, his Dao Tree illuminated everything like a beacon. It had grown a lot since last time. It was now a fully-fledged tree, with a thick trunk and sprawling branches. The only things missing were leaves, and a crown of branches at the top, which was in the middle of forming.

The five-colored Fist remained under the tree, like the soil from which it drew nutrients, while the Life Drop was still buried right under its roots, shining a lively green.

And there was a door in the bark.

Jack floated toward it. Everything else, he could understand. The Fist, the Life Drop, the tree's growing process. This door was the only thing about which he had no clue. Not even Shol or the Sage could help. As far as everyone knew, there weren't supposed to be doors on a Dao Tree, yet here it was, defying every expectation.

Jack's hand pressed on the door. It was part of the tree, looking like a random bark pattern, but its similarity to a door was so striking that there was no way this was a coincidence. It even had a doorknob.

"What are you?" Jack muttered. He tried to open it, as he had many times in the past, but nothing happened. The door behaved just like a random pattern on the bark.

"I guess my tree needs to finish maturing..." He looked up at the half-formed crown. "When I reach the peak of the D-Grade, I'll try again."

"Cool!" came the words of another person, though spoken in Jack's voice. Turning, he found Copy Jack hovering in the void.

"Hey, Copy Jack," Jack said. "You seem fine."

"Just fine? I'm great!"

Jack simply laughed. Ever since Copy Jack had been "struck" by the Life Drop, for lack of a better word, he'd gradually developed a personality of his own. He was just like a real person—or rather, a child borrowing Jack's body. It was a bit weird, but what can you do?

"What do you think is behind the door?" Copy Jack asked, floating around with excitement. "Stars? More fist? A Copy Tree? Or nothing? I can't wait to find out!"

Jack smirked. "Take it easy. All will be revealed in time."

"But I don't *want* to take it easy!" Copy Jack responded, pouting. "I have to stay in here while you hog all the fun out there. It's not fair. I want to see the outside world too. I bet it has many trees."

"I'm working on it," Jack replied helplessly. "I promise you, the moment I discover a way to take you to the real world, I'll do it."

"Okay." Copy Jack's mood instantly swung around. "So, what are we doing today? Fighting? Meditating? Experimenting? Oh! Can we play around with space again? I like that."

"Uh... Waiting, mostly. I was also planning to meditate a bit."

"Cool! What about?"

"Remember the supernova? The big exploding sun-thing I've been working on but haven't gotten right yet? I have some time to spare, so I thought I'd give it a shot."

"Awesome! Can I help?"

"You can try."

"Nice!"

Facing Copy Jack's unbridled joy at such simple things, Jack felt helpless.

This was another mystery. As far as anyone knew, Dao Souls were supposed to be... not real. Not *people*. They were just empty shells that Jack's soul could borrow to pretend to be a second person.

His best theory was that the Life Drop had infused the Dao Soul with life, letting it become a real soul, but he had no way to confirm it. This theory was also in line with his recent realization that the Life Drop had at least a hint of consciousness of its own, as had been revealed when it refused to be detonated.

The Sage was also clueless about this issue, or so he claimed.

Why is my soul suddenly full of secrets? Jack thought, rubbing the back of his head. Well, whatever. The Life Drop hasn't caused me any problems so far. As long as I survive this and keep growing, all will be revealed in time.

"I'll start meditating now, Copy Jack. If you come up with anything, let me know."

"Alright!" the copy responded, sitting cross-legged, and closing his eyes in deep concentration. Jack doubted Copy Jack could even enter a proper meditation state. All the Dao he possessed had been inherited from Jack.

Shrugging, Jack also sat cross-legged and tuned out the world. His breathing fell into a familiar pattern, his body relaxed, and he found himself visualizing the world with great clarity. Suddenly, he was back to watching the supernova with Master Huali. He saw the star erupt into a red giant, loosen its skin, then compress its core until it blew up in the most violent event of the universe.

At the same time, Jack was aware of some of the physics behind a supernova. The explosion was caused by the star collapsing so powerfully that the atoms of its outer shell were smashed together, creating a large number of nuclear fusions all at once. When the explosion was over and everything else had been expelled, all that remained was a star formed almost exclusively of tightly-packed atoms—a neutron star, the namesake of one of Jack's other skills.

However, neither his knowledge of physics nor his personal experience helped him at all. He had no idea how to turn those insights into a skill.

It was easier for the Fist. He was connected to it, understood it from many sides. It represented so many things he could incarnate to connect with the Dao and make it obey him.

But what was he supposed to do about a supernova? Get really, really angry?

Jack tried many things. He tried to imagine the essence of a supernova, what it would mean for a person. He tried to compress his Dao hard enough to explode. He even tried to go full Hulk mode, but it was useless. After testing everything he could think of, nothing clicked.

It was exactly the same as every other time he tried to meditate on the skill during his three months of training. It always felt off. Like it wasn't meant for him. But he didn't want to just quit without giving it his best, so he kept trying.

Eventually, he got frustrated and opened his eyes in the real world. "Guess I'll—"

He paused. There were two people inside his cell, a few feet ahead of him. Neither were the deacon from before—and, oddly, he could not sense their presence. If he wasn't seeing them with his own eyes, he would have never noticed.

They were a man and a woman, both wearing clean white robes. They stared at him silently and piercingly, emitting no aura whatsoever. Jack couldn't inspect them, as he still wore the manacles, but they didn't feel like D-Grades—or even like they belonged to the Animal Kingdom.

"The Hand of God, I presume," he said.

The two people nodded. "We are here to deep-scan you," the man replied.

"You've been on the run for a while," the woman added. "Highly suspicious."

"I wasn't on the run—nobody had told me you were looking for me. I only found out here, in Hell, but I couldn't come out and meet you."

"All will be clear soon," the man said. He raised his right hand, on which he wore an elaborate ring. It seemed made of gears, though none were turning, and none seemed real. "Please do not resist."

Jack wasn't planning to, but neither could he. The man's finger pressed down on the spot between his brows. Jack did his best to remain still, but he soon found himself convulsing.

The feeling was extremely intrusive. Like someone had dug their hands into his body and were snooping around, feeling everything. It wasn't painful, per se, but he wanted to puke.

Thankfully, he'd swallowed the Sage's pill, so even a deep-scan would hopefully reveal nothing about his Life Drop.

Finally, the finger withdrew, and Jack found himself on the floor. He didn't remember falling.

"No sign of tampering," the man said, to which the woman raised a surprised brow. "Although I did see the Ninth Ring Conqueror title. Impressive." He gave Jack a new glance, one containing hints of... friendliness? "We were not aware of that."

Jack gritted his teeth to regain his bearing. He'd forgotten about his title—though it made sense that a deep-scan would see his entire status screen. "I didn't make it public," he replied, panting. "I thought... it might draw too much attention."

"Rightly so," the woman said. "You are the first in this galaxy to attain it. May we ask how?"

"The Integration titles and four Dao Roots gave me the edge I needed. Then, I tricked the Final Guardian with a feint nobody in their right mind would use. The chances were heavily against me... but it worked. I got lucky."

Most of what he said were lies, spoken as convincingly as he could. They glanced at each other, then back at him. "And that is how you teleported away from Trial Planet without our knowledge?"

Jack nodded. "The Final Guardian offered to take me somewhere closer to my next destination. I didn't think anyone was waiting for me."

Once again, they looked at each other and nodded subtly. "Not lying," the man said.

"Indeed," the woman agreed. "This was just a big misunderstanding. But a fortunate one."

"You are an exceptionally talented man," the man said. "Dying here would be a waste of your potential. How about you join the Hand of God? We can make all your problems disappear and give you everything you need to realize your future. With your achievements, even reaching the B-Grade is not out of the question."

CHAPTER SEVENTY-THREE
THE GRAND DUEL BEGINS

Jack was taken aback. "Excuse me?"

"The question was clear," the white-dressed woman replied. "Are you willing to join the Hand of God? We can make it worth your while."

Jack opened and closed his mouth a couple of times. In his mind, the Hand of God had been the enemy for a long time now. He hadn't expected them to just invite him in. "Worth my while?"

The man nodded. "This duel of yours... We can arrange it to not be to the death. After you lose, you will be executed by the Animal Kingdom, but it will be staged. In truth, we'll find a lookalike to die in your stead while you come to our headquarters for further training."

"As for your home planet," the woman added, "we will ensure that your loved ones escape. Just give us a short list and we'll make it happen."

Jack was flabbergasted. This sounded too good to be true. All his problems could be solved just like that?

At the same time, he couldn't accept. Not only did the Hand exercise deceit and tyranny, as they had proven repeatedly in the past, but the Sage's vision and explanation remained all too vivid in his mind. The Hand of God was nothing but a tool for the Immortals, the ones who forced the entire universe into an age of bloodshed, pain, and strife. They were the bad guys.

Not to mention the Life Drop, which still existed inside him, or the fact that he'd already agreed to join the Black Hole Church—who may be equally bad, but at least they hadn't shown such signs of distrust yet.

Jack did not like the Hand of God. Joining them rubbed him the wrong way, and with the many unknown variables in place, it had good chances of being a terrible decision. It was tempting that they could save his friends and family—though not everyone on Earth—but at the end of the day, the way of the Fist was all or nothing. Half-measures had no place in it. Jack would either follow the best path possible and use his own strength to save his people... or everyone would die trying.

However, he wasn't an idiot. If deceiving these guys was the only way to escape his current predicament, he would absolutely do it. The Fist did not encourage stupid deaths.

He needed information.

"The Animal Kingdom would agree to that?" he asked. "After everything I did to them?"

The man gave him a hard, meaningful smile. "The Hand of God doesn't take no for an answer."

There was a clear double meaning in that sentence, one that Jack got all too clearly.

"This sounds too good to be true..." he said. "Could I take some time to think it over?"

The eyes of both people narrowed at the same time. "This is not an invitation," the woman said. "It is a summoning. Don't think too high of yourself. You will join the Hand of God, the true rulers of this galaxy, and you will do as we say. Am I understood, Jack Rust?"

Jack lowered his gaze so they couldn't see through his thoughts. If these guys weren't going to take no for an answer, he would just lie to them.

"I understand," he said.

"Good. After the duel, we will contact you again to fake your execution and rescue some of your planet's people. However..." The woman eyed him seriously. "The duel will be to the death, but I expect you not to kill anyone. You will defeat Sapasun without killing him, and then you will lose to Maximus Lonihor so the Animal Kingdom can preserve a bit of their dignity. Otherwise, even we won't be able to save you. Am I understood?"

"Yes, ma'am."

"Excellent. We will speak again."

Both white-dressed people nodded at each other and disappeared. They didn't teleport away, they just ceased existing. If Jack didn't know he was too insignificant for people like them to waste time on, he would have thought they still waited in his cell, watching invisibly.

He sighed. *How did I get into such a mess again?* he asked himself, but no answer came.

What do I do? Do I really have no choice but to go along with them? His eyes hardened. I need to speak with the Sage.

"Hey," he called out. Then, louder: "HEY!"

He heard the faint sound of boots on stone. A guard walked past his cell—the same lycan deacon he'd seen before. It looked like he'd taken some distance to let the Hand of God agents speak to him freely.

"Stop shouting," he said.

"Can I see my friends?" Jack asked. "I want to make sure they're okay."

"Rot in your cell, murderer. You'll meet them at the duel, where they get to see you die." The guard walked away.

Jack sighed again. Well, that's good enough for me. I can speak to the Sage with telepathy.

A few different storms raged inside Jack's head, each problem striving to seem more gargantuan than the previous one. However, he knew when to bother and when not to. Right now, all he could do was wait. When he had more information, he would decide better.

And so, Jack settled down to meditate, waiting for his duel.

Two days went by...

Jack's duel was even greater in importance than he thought. His previous adventures on Hell had already made headlines across the galaxy. News of his coming duel, with the Animal Kingdom's honor on the line, spread like wildfire. Before the three days were over, every important person in the galaxy had heard the news. The Merchant Union worked overtime to arrange things.

By the third day, large projectors had been set up in every major city across the galaxy. The event would be broadcast live to trillions of cultivators. Small and large planets saw their populations flock to city centers. Many businesses closed for the day and other events were rescheduled. Every cultivator with eyes made sure to leave that day open on their calendar.

All the way from the core of the Animal Kingdom constellation to the very fringes of System space, the gaze of the entire Milky Way galaxy was focused on Jack's duel.

It wasn't just the scale of the event. They had already heard about Jack Rust. He was a warrior of freedom fighting against the tyrants and miraculously holding his own. He was the ultimate underdog. At the same time, when was the last time a B-Grade faction bet its honor on such a public event?

How could anyone *not* watch this spectacle?

Projections were set up in every core planet of every B-Grade faction. The Exploding Sun, the Wipe Swirls, the Dragon Valley. Even the Hand of God was watching. Every D-Grade cultivator had their eyes peeled on the screen, eager to be inspired by the best of their Grade.

Of course, amongst all the planets of the galaxy, there were some that hosted peculiar audiences.

On the outer planet of the Exploding Sun headquarters, a large group arrived to watch the battle. They were three hundred people carrying drums, trumpets, even popcorn. Leading them was a very proud and expectant brorilla, flanked by a canine and a barbarian girl.

In the capital of the Fair Way Continent, two hooded figures watched from a rooftop, one filled with glee and the other with bitterness.

On Earth, both the Bare Fist Brotherhood and the Ice Peak had secured projections from their respective merchants, and the entire war had come to a standstill as everyone waited with bated breath. Edgar was gulping nervously. Vivi held a hand over her belly to calm herself down. The professor had clasped her hands together, praying for Jack to a god she didn't believe in. Even the Planetary Overseer had interrupted her meditation to watch—after all, Maximus Lonihor was her son.

In the depths of Trial Planet, an old man, clad in silver armor, waved his hand, hijacking the projection signal to conjure a small screen. He watched with sadness.

In a starship dock on a small planet of the Animal Kingdom constellation, a minotaur, a feshkur, and a saphira looked up at the projection in the sky with mixed feelings.

Trillions and quintillions of credits were circulating around Jack's duel, the greatest public event in the galaxy's recent history. The heart of the galaxy beat as one pulse, and everyone wondered the same thing—could Jack Rust actually win?

Artus Emberheart knelt to the ground. "Grand Elder," he said reverently. Before him stood an old, muscular leonine whose fur was half-gray and half-golden.

"Artus," the Grand Elder said. "You may rise."

Artus did, his teeth gritted. He seemed unwell—filled with rage and worry. "I have received word from the Hand of God inquisitors. As impossible as it sounds, Jack Rust was employing no external help to match Maximus. I fear that my disciple, Sapasun—"

"Speak no further, Artus," the Grand Elder interrupted, raising a hand. "What we have said in public, we cannot take back. Your disciple will fight Jack Rust and scout out his powers for Maximus. The Hand of God has decreed that no deaths will occur in the duel. If your disciple still manages to die, he can only blame his own weakness."

Artus nodded deeply. "Yes, Grand Elder."

"This is a battle we cannot afford to lose, Artus. The entire galaxy is watching," the Grand Elder replied grimly. "I have the Hand's assurances, but I do not trust Jack Rust to obey them. If he can defeat Maximus, I believe he will do so. It is your job to ensure that doesn't happen. If it does, I will have your head."

"Yes, Grand Elder."

"Do not underestimate that man. Time and time again, he has exceeded our expectations and secured critical hits. He has slain the man who was both your son and my own disciple, the one we paid a steep price to send to an un-Integrated planet: Rufus Emberheart. He has killed hundreds of our immortals, treating Hell as his playground. It is imperative that he never rises again. I don't care what the Hand of God says. Instruct Maximus to kill him no matter what. Should that man survive, then, with the enmity we have cultivated, it will spell ugly days for our noble faction."

Artus Emberheart nodded deeply, and his lips were drawn into a smile that was both wicked and pained. "Yes, Grand Elder."

Near the core of the Animal Kingdom, at the capital of Hell, on the rooftop of a massive prison campus, a large, spherical arena had been set up. It had a radius of three miles and could easily seat a million people. Obviously, all seats were occupied. Transparent barriers protected the audience from the battle inside the stage, supported by the Kingdom's C-Grade enforcers.

The honor seats were also occupied. The Warden was there, as were several other elders of the Animal Kingdom, including the Grand Elder: an old, muscular leonine whose fur was half-gray, half-golden. Elders Huali and Monsoon of the Exploding Sun were also present, having been personally invited by the Kingdom's Grand Elder. Even the white-robed representatives of the Hand of God were seated beside the others. The only D-Grade on the honor seats was Li Qian, who sat beside his master.

No B-Grades were visible, though they could have been watching unseen.

It was the first time in history that a duel between D-Grades garnered such an esteemed audience.

On one side of the arena stood a man: Sapasun, the canine deacon who was the Warden's head disciple. As agreed, he would be the first to fight Jack, and he was extremely worried. So what if his master had assured him Jack wouldn't go for the kill?

Sapasun remembered very clearly how, when his opponent was still weak, he'd broken all his limbs and gloated about it. More importantly, Jack Rust was a certified lunatic.

The future was bleak for Sapasun, but he would try his best to surrender before he died.

And on the other side of the arena stood the man of the hour. The D-Grade who had managed, against all odds, to magnetize the gazes of the entire galaxy. The man who had achieved the impossible time and time again.

Jack Rust.

A deep voice boomed out, echoing across the arena. Through the projection stones, it spread to the entire galaxy. "Esteemed Grand Elder, elders of various factions, enforcers, and immortals. Ladies and gentlemen," it began, bursting at the seams with excited professionalism, "I present to you, the top disciple of the Warden of Hell, a peak D-Grade canine overflowing with talent—Sapasun!"

Sapasun howled at the sky and tried to appear cool. A few people cheered. Most didn't.

"And on the other side," the presenter's voice continued, curbing its enthusiasm, "the D-Grade criminal who employed underhanded means to murder two hundred immortals. Jack Rust."

The voice was flat now, clearly working to downplay Jack. Yet, the moment his name was called out, Jack raised a proud fist.

And the entire stadium, the entire galaxy, shook to its foundation as almost every mouth opened to cheer for him.

CHAPTER SEVENTY-FOUR

THE DAO OF FACE-SLAPPING

JACK'S FIST WAS HELD HIGH. THE ENTIRE STADIUM SHOOK FROM THE VOICES OF countless cultivators and immortals, rumbling from their combined shout.

So what if the presenter was against Jack? So what if he was in the opponent's home field? He was the man attempting the impossible. The ultimate underdog.

Just who was the audience going to support?

Jack let the cheering go on for a few moments as his eyes furiously scanned the crowd. He'd just arrived, and locating the Sage between a million people wasn't easy. Then finally, he found him—all three of them were on a raised platform, shackled and ready for execution.

"*Sage!*" he said telepathically.

The Sage seemed as in control as ever. "*Yes?*"

Jack explained the entire situation with the Hand of God invitation.

"I see," the Sage replied. "Feel free to ignore them. I have good news. The Church sees this duel as your initiation test. If you can defeat both Sapasun and Maximus, you will have our full support."

Jack's eyes lit up. "*Do you mean—*"

"Yes. After you win, the Kingdom will let us go temporarily, only to recap-

ture us as soon as the projection stones deactivate, but the Church will have an escape shuttle waiting. We will be out of here."

"Even if I kill them both?"

The Sage raised his head, crossing gazes with Jack. He smiled. *"Do as you wish. Just don't reveal the Life Drop!"*

Jack looked ahead. "Thanks, Sage."

"No problem. Everybody's watching. Make us proud."

"You got it."

This conversation took place within three seconds. The crowd was still cheering. Slowly, Jack lowered his arm. Silence fell again. Everyone knew there wasn't going to be a starting announcement—Jack and Sapasun could start fighting anytime they wanted.

"Did you think this time would come, Sapasun?" Jack asked calmly. "When you were torturing me, did you ever think that one day you would be trembling at my feet?"

The audience *oohed* collectively. They hadn't known these two held a shared history. The excitement just kept ramping up.

"Shut up!" Sapasun replied. "Who's trembling, bitch? Come here and I will show you that I am not just a canine; I am your daddy!"

"As you wish."

Jack disappeared. Not through teleportation—he just rushed ahead with speed that most of the audience couldn't follow.

Sapasun, of course, could. He stretched his claw-tipped fingers out, stabbing them Jack's way. Jack leaned away from the strike, slapped Sapasun's other hand, and drove a fist into his opponent's stomach. The canine folded in half and flew into the barrier protecting the audience, spitting out foam all the while.

The arena went silent. They hadn't expected such a quick exchange. Was Jack that much stronger!

"Is that all?" Jack asked with disappointment, retracting his fist. "I thought you would become my daddy. Yet, you only have that tiny bit of skill?"

Sapasun unglued himself from the barrier and wiped his mouth. "T'ch, I'll show you how." He charged ahead. Jack simply stood in place and waited. The two enemies clashed, exchanging a dozen strikes in an instant. Jack defended with ease. Then he threw out a sharp punch, finding Sapasun in the nose and flinging him away.

The audience roared, only for reality to warp. Sapasun was flying at Jack from behind, slashing toward his head. Jack detected the strike and ducked under it—but Sapasun's claws sailed over his head, into a spatial tear, and out toward his leg. Jack's hand moved with lightning speed, clamping down on the canine's wrist and stopping the strike just before it landed. He then used his other hand to backhand Sapasun, sending him spinning away like a ballerina. His wrist emerged from the spatial tear, still in place.

In truth, Jack could have held it down, and space itself would have severed Sapasun's wrist. He just didn't want to end things that way. He still had a debt to repay.

"I see how it is," Jack said with his chin raised high. "That was a good attack. You have a little bit of skill. In that case, let me face you with a more appropriate Dao."

The audience erupted in hushed whispers. Another Dao? What did Jack mean?

Even Sapasun seemed taken aback. His eyes narrowed, and he settled into a careful battle stance. He licked his lips.

In the entire arena, only two people understood what Jack was referring to. Their eyes widened for a second, then they each showed a wry smile.

Jack extended a fist. Then, slowly, his fingers uncurled to form a straight palm. Amidst the crowd's sounds of wonder, he raised the palm as if to slap the air and said, "Dao of Spanking."

Stunned silence. Then, roaring laughter. Sapasun was speechless, while every Animal Kingdom elder on the honor seats went red in the face.

"*Jack Rust!*" the Warden roared in Jack's head. "*Don't go too far!*"

Jack ignored him. "Do you think this is a joke?" he asked Sapasun. "Let me show you the power of spanking. Maybe it will even cure your insanity."

"That's not how—"

Before Sapasun could respond, Jack was upon him, both palms poised to strike. The slaps came like rain. There wasn't much expertise behind them, but at this point, the difference between Jack and Sapasun was simply too large. Sapasun wasn't one of the faction's strongest deacons—he was just the top disciple of the Warden, who wasn't famed for his teaching skills.

The canine did his best to defend, but it was impossible. The spanking was too rough. A palm slipped through, slapping his cheek, while another met his buttocks with a crisp sound. Sapasun went flying. Jack teleported in his way.

Purple color surrounded his palm. He raised it high. "Meteor Spank!" he shouted, bringing the palm down on Sapasun. The canine twisted reality to make the palm hit his shoulder instead of his head, and with a crack, his arm was dislocated.

"ARGH!" Sapasun roared, flying away. "Damn you!"

"What's wrong, Sapasun? You once took all my limbs, but I only took one of yours. Do you feel this is unfair?"

"Damn right it is!" Sapasun roared back. "You're mocking me!"

"So what if I am? Did you not mock me as you tortured me?" Jack snorted. "This is the karma you have sown, Sapasun. Prepare to reap it all."

The elders were embarrassed, and the audience was flabbergasted. Jack was being a bit of a bully, but who could blame him? After all, he was only repaying the grievances he'd suffered. In the cultivation world, this was already fairly light for revenge.

"Jack Rust!" a voice rang in his head—that of the white-robed man. "You are going too far. Don't humiliate the Kingdom more than necessary, or even we won't be able to save you!"

Jack ignored him too. He had already decided to go through with this. If they didn't like it, they were welcome to scold him later—if he didn't find a way to escape.

Sapasun gritted his teeth. More foam leaked from the corner of his mouth. He was embarrassed in front of the entire galaxy—in his centuries of life, he had never before suffered like this. Not in public, anyway.

"Take this!" he roared, raising his remaining arm high. Reality warped around him. Light danced erratically. Space changed its rules.

Sapasun unleashed a skill that was and wasn't a domain, an area where logic did not apply.

The audience exclaimed in surprise. This was no weak move. Sapasun may have looked like a joke compared to Jack, but at the end of the day, he was a strong peak D-Grade of the Animal Kingdom.

"You can't mock me!" he roared. "Only I can mock me! Lose your mind!"

He charged at Jack, who only laughed lightly and walked over. A new aura emerged from his body; a hint of his Dao Domain, a place where the Fist reigned supreme. "I'm sorry. I have no Domain of Spanking, so this will have to do."

Where Jack walked, reality settled. Insanity lost its grip. The Fist was hard and resolute. It was the epitome of facing reality instead of distorting it for one's own benefit. It carried discipline, power, and Indomitable Will.

Sapasun roared and stabbed out his remaining hand. "INVINCIBLE STAR GRASP!"

Jack walked up to him. Cracks spread through the dominating insanity, and then it shattered, leaving Sapasun exposed as the insane man he really was. Jack slapped his hand away, then spanked the canine's hip with all his power. The bone shattered under the impact. Jack's hand then returned as a back-slap, breaking Sapasun's other hip.

Only now did the canine manage to react, flying backward to escape, but Jack's grip on his wrist was iron.

"Let me go!" Sapasun screamed.

"When I was captured, did you let me go?" Jack asked. Purple covered his palm, and it landed on Sapasun's remaining shoulder, dislocating it. Only now did Jack let go of Sapasun's wrist, letting him fly away. "Once, you took all four of my limbs, as well as my dignity. Now, I have done the same. Only your dignity remains. Prepare yourself."

Purple aura shone on his fist, far stronger than before. Color and light was sucked in. The audience was unaffected due to the energy barrier, but they saw the inside of the arena go dark as Jack drew the entire world into his open palm.

"I surrender!" Sapasun cried out in panic.

Jack shook his head. "There is no surrender in a duel to the death."

"*Jack Rust! Stop!*" ordered the white-robed woman.

"*Brat, don't you dare!*" the Warden roared in Jack's head.

Jack teleported over Sapasun, raising his palm. "STOP! Master, save me!" Sapasun tried to roar, but the sound of his voice was sucked into Jack's fist, leaving him stranded in a dark, lonely silence.

Jack's palm came crashing down, spanking the top of Sapasun's head. It exploded like a watermelon. Bits and pieces flew everywhere, vaporized by the ensuing explosion. He flew down like a missile.

When the air cleared, Sapasun's remaining body lay on the ground of the arena, completely lifeless.

Level-up! You have reached Level 231.
Level-up! You have reached Level 232.

Not a sound could be heard throughout the entire stadium. Everyone stared at Jack, not knowing what to think.

Did he really have to bully the Animal Kingdom that hard?

Jack landed beside Sapasun's lifeless body and turned to the audience. "I do not claim to be a saint. I am a warrior, and the Animal Kingdom is my enemy. This man once tortured and mocked me; now, I have returned the favor. Compared to everything they have done to me, this is nothing."

The cultivation world was a harsh place. Killing one's enemies was natural. Bullying the weak was commonplace. And they could all tell that Jack was no bully—he was just, as he said, a warrior paying back his dues.

A warrior who, with his actions, did not hesitate to spit in the face of one of the strongest factions in the galaxy. He hadn't just defeated one of their strongest warriors—he had literally slapped him to death.

That was... That was...

Completely unheard of!

It was absolutely sensational!

One person cheered. Then another. As if someone had opened the floodgates, every man and woman in the audience cheered at once, raising their voices to the sky. The same scene was playing out all across the galaxy, with one exception: the arena's honor seats, where every single elder of the Animal Kingdom was glaring at Jack with every fiber of their C-Grade cultivation. If not for the people watching, they would have already torn him to pieces.

As it was, there was nothing they could do. One by one, they turned their dirty glares at Artus Emberheart, the Warden, the one who caused this entire thing. The moment he was blinded by arrogance and accepted Jack's proposal to duel, he had consigned their entire faction to humiliation.

"You fucked up, Artus," the Grand Elder said, not caring to keep his voice low.

As for the Warden himself... what was he supposed to say?

Of course he'd fucked up! He'd fucked up big time, but he was also the greatest loser here!

Not only had Jack killed *his* son, infiltrated *his* planet, killed *his* disciples, and repeatedly humiliated *him in public,* but he'd now just slapped his top disciple to death. And to top it all off, everyone blamed him as well!

It took everything the Warden had to maintain his facade of composure. He kept his eyes lowered, his mouth shut, and his arms tightly crossed. This was just too much. Already, his Dao of Supremacy was teetering on the brink of collapse—if he didn't find a way to take revenge against Jack Rust, he would never advance again!

Even the announcer must have been caught by surprise at Jack's actions, because it took him a few seconds to speak.

"Sapasun was a disciple of the Animal Kingdom, and if he lost, he can only blame his own weakness," he announced. "However, the Kingdom will get revenge. Step forth Maximus Lonihor, the head disciple of the Animal Kingdom, the strongest D-Grade in this constellation!"

A fierce figure jumped out of the spectator seats and into the arena, meeting Jack's calm gaze with outrage.

"Did you enjoy that?" he asked.

"Not really," Jack replied honestly. "But it had to be done."

"Hmph! Sapasun and I had our differences, but I remain his senior. You will pay for your actions."

The corner of Jack's lips rose. "Make me, bitch."

CHAPTER SEVENTY-FIVE
JACK RUST VS. MAXIMUS LONIHOR

All across the galaxy, entire cities were erupting into uproar.

"Did you see that!" a woman asked.

"Holy shit," her husband exclaimed, placing his trembling hands over his mouth. "Holy shit."

"That's our Jack!" Edgar shouted from back on Earth, pumping a fist. "Go get them, tiger!"

Vivi sported a restrained smile. Harambe looked up with pride, while the professor did not react, torn between horror and excitement. Her son was riling up the entire galaxy—but at what cost?

Back in the Hell arena, the crowd didn't know what to do. For them, this was not a far-off spectacle on a screen; it was real, far too real. Someone had just slapped the Animal Kingdom as hard as he possibly could at the core of their territory. He hadn't given them the slightest bit of face.

What a lunatic! Did he not care about his life at all?

And, most importantly, what would happen next? Jack Rust exhibited great power. What if, against all odds, he managed to defeat Maximus Lonihor? Would he really be released?

That extremely talented madman would be free in the galaxy? If the

Kingdom let that happen, they would pay in blood! Clearly, Jack Rust had a huge grudge against them.

In the honor seats, the various elders were in a heated discussion through telepathy. The Grand Elder was burning with indignant rage. In the Animal Kingdom's hundreds of thousands of years of history, this was the first time they were humiliated like this—and it was on his tenure as Grand Elder.

"Summon every available enforcer and elder," he commanded the rest of the elders. "We can take no risks. If Jack Rust wins, he will be apprehended and executed the moment he leaves the planet."

One of the meeker elders asked, *"But, Grand Elder, what about—"*

"I couldn't give a second shit!" the Grand Elder roared in everyone's mind. "Damn everything and damn our public image. If we let him escape after everything he did, there will be no Animal Kingdom to suffer the consequences! Do you understand me!"

Everyone gulped. "Yes, Grand Elder."

The Grand Elder then turned to the two white-robed C-Grades of the Hand of God. "I hope you understand," he said telepathically. "We will compensate the Hand, but this man must die no matter what."

The two of them glanced at each other and sighed. There was no helping it. They had tried to enlist Jack Rust, but he seemed hell-bent on dying.

The only ones not participating in the conversation were Elders Huali and Monsoon of the Exploding Sun, who had been invited to watch. Nobody saw fit to ask their opinion, and besides, they already understood everything. Monsoon wasn't even paying attention to the final battle; his mind was rife with calculations of how this affected his chances of getting the Grand Elder position.

As for Huali... she was just worried. Jack was her disciple, and he seemed to be committing suicide. Shol, too. What were they thinking?

Jack Rust raised his hand high. Huali's thoughts were cut short by a knife, her entire attention focused on the arena. It was only a second later that she realized it: Jack Rust, a D-Grade, had commanded the unwavering attention of every C-Grade present. He had achieved an influence unimaginable for anyone else in his Grade.

It was impressive. The most impressive thing she'd witnessed in a millennium. If he lived on, there was no telling what heights he would reach.

Unfortunately, he was trading his life for this opportunity. He would go down with glory and make the Exploding Sun proud. It saddened her, but there was nothing she could do.

"As per our agreement," Jack Rust spoke, his voice carrying over the millions of live audiences, "if I win, you let me and my friends go. If I lose, I will proclaim myself a dog of your faction, becoming your slave for as long as you see fit."

Maximus laughed coldly. "Do you think you can still become a slave, Jack Rust? After what you did? No, even that would be too good for you. If you lose, you will proclaim yourself a loser and take your own life, right here, right now."

Jack's eyes narrowed. "Deal."

"Good. Prepare yourself. Today, you die!"

Golden radiance rained from the heavens. Maximus was in no mood for games. Motes of golden light surrounded his body, filling the eyes of the onlookers with his majesty. Rows of winged knights emerged from the light, brandishing their spears, and charging straight at Jack.

Meanwhile, Maximus himself could not be seen, covered in light as he was. Who knows what kind of transformation was taking place under it?

"Hmph!" Jack snorted, crossing his arms. "Do you take me for a fool, Maximus Lonihor?"

The audience did not understand what he meant. The elders, however, did, and they couldn't help but admire Jack's insight.

By raising the stakes and starting a battle form transformation that would take time to complete, Maximus had been enticing Jack to assault him before the transformation was over. But it was a trap. If Jack did attack, Maximus would ridicule his lack of honor and complete his transformation regardless—after all, if he wished to, he could have assumed his battle form beforehand.

This was just a way to secure the moral high ground over Jack, make him doubt himself, and win the Kingdom some favor in the spectators' eyes. Unfortunately for Maximus, Jack possessed the composure and dignity to just wait.

The winged knights dissipated before even approaching Jack. They turned into motes of light that dove back into the glowing sphere that had formed around Maximus. By now, the radiance was almost blinding, and one could faintly hear chanting whispered in the sky.

Suddenly, the tips of two feathered wings peeked out from the sphere of light. With a mighty flap, they broke it, sending motes of light flying everywhere before extinguishing themselves. The audience gasped. Jack raised his brows.

"Here it is!" someone shouted in the audience. "The Lonihor Angel battle form!"

Maximus floated in the sky, almost divine in radiance and dazzling in brilliance. His indifferent face spoke of arrogance. Four white feathered wings stretched from his shoulder blades, an armor made of light covered his body, and a dazzling sword of light was held in his grasp.

The audience ogled. Jack whistled. "I thought you were a cat, not a bird," he said.

Maximus gave him the faintest of smiles. "Our previous battle was interrupted, Jack Rust. Maybe that is why you have such confidence. Have you never seen a leonine's battle form before?"

"I have, a couple of times. Can't say I was particularly impressed. I still killed them all."

A slight crease of the brows was the only evidence of Maximus's anger. "Have you ever wondered why, of the Animal Kingdom's five noble families, the leonines reign supreme?"

"I assumed it was because you shout the loudest."

"The two main leonine families, the Lonihors and the Emberhearts, have discovered that when they cultivate the Dao of Supremacy, they can combine it with their innate physique to trigger a transformation. For us, it is the angel form. It is this form that forces the other families to serve us and lets us stand on equal footing with the other B-Grade factions."

"I see. Very impressive. Are we going to fight or drink tea and discuss history?"

Maximus's brows creased further. He raised his sword high. "You understand nothing, Jack Rust. You are a bum, a trash cultivator of a recently Integrated planet. You don't even understand how to run a spectacle, but so be it—your death in humiliation will be spectacle enough."

"I am all those things," Jack agreed with a nod. "Which makes your ensuing death all the worse. If I, a country bumpkin who has cultivated for less than a year, can defeat the strongest D-Grade cultivator of a B-Grade faction who had cultivated for centuries... just what does that mean for your Animal Kingdom?"

"You utter big words, Jack Rust, but can you back them up?"

"Jesus, man, are you going to fight me or not?"

Maximus charged. His wings flapped fiercely, taking him through the air at a speed that resembled teleportation. He was before Jack in an instant, swinging his sword like the guillotine of heaven.

Jack met it with his fist.

The sky shattered. Light rained everywhere, an explosion of colors and radiance that did not stop. Each time it was about to dissipate, more light erupted, more sound, more shockwaves. The barrier shook under the onslaught. The arena had become a stormy sea of intertwined golden and purple light fighting for supremacy.

Most of the audience were blind, but the C-Grades were not. Their eyes penetrated the light and followed every exchange, every clash. They gasped.

The barrier adjusted its brightness to let the rest of the audience watch, too.

In the middle of the arena, Jack and Maximus were going toe-to-toe. They clashed, broke off, and clashed again. Their patterns were chaotic, their strikes sharp. They crossed the sky like a pair of angry wasps, colliding before the shockwave of the previous clash even had time to dissipate.

Once, twice, thrice. Ten times, twenty, a hundred. Maximus's dazzling sword illuminated the sky, but Jack's fists were indomitable. The more they fought, the more they sank into the battle, the more they learned the other's patterns, and the sharper they got.

Last time, Jack had been at a clear advantage, but it was frenzied now.

Jack stepped forward to attack. His fist traveled in a straight line, carrying the force of multiple collapsing mountains. A sword of the heavens cleaved down to intercept it. Jack's knuckle met the blade. The skin tore. A thin line of blood trickled down, but the sword was pushed back, as was his fist.

Each clash was like that. Jack's body couldn't handle a direct collision against the blade, but his regeneration fixed the wounds almost instantly.

Maximus dove in, using his wings to instantly accelerate to three times the speed of sound. He appeared behind Jack and slashed. Jack teleported behind Maximus, but Maximus followed the teleportation mid-swing, reappearing behind his opponent. Jack was already turning, throwing a tight punch over his abdomen. It met the tip of the blade, and both ricocheted away.

Jack pushed on. His punches fell like hail, strong and hard, driving Maximus into the defensive. He teleported away, but Jack matched each movement to keep attacking. They were competing over agility, their control over their flight, and teleportations. They were equal.

A fist landed on Maximus's shoulder and was shrugged off. Another found his shin. Jack was a storm, striking everywhere with deadly precision, and Maximus possessed extraordinary technique. His sword was always at the right place, each movement flying into the next. His body was perfectly positioned.

From a contest of agility, the battle switched to one of technique. They went head-to-head, hovering in the middle of the arena refusing to retreat.

Jack slapped the blade away to punch out. Maximus ducked under the fist, struck upward, then teleported diagonally to redirect his strike. Jack expected the movement and was already turning. He took the blade on the shoulder, letting it reach the bone. In the same movement, he drove his knuckles into the other's nose, sending him tumbling through the air.

Maximus came to a stop three hundred feet away. "Heh," he said, blood running over his mouth, "I guess we're—"

His words froze unspoken. Jack's shoulder, where he'd been slashed, was regenerating with speed visible to the naked eye. Soon, it was unblemished, while Maximus's nose remained broken.

The leonine frowned heavily.

"What happened?" Jack taunted. "Kitty got your tongue?"

Maximus charged into battle carrying a different air—if before he was showcasing his strength, he was now going for the throat. So was Jack. The two clashed again, a storm of punches and slashes that tore the very air around them to shreds.

Jack dodged the blade, but a set of sharp claws came at him from the side. He took a nasty gash on his chest. At the same time, the four wings bent toward him and shot out sharp feathers, nicking him and forcing him to dodge to keep his eyes safe.

The dazzling sword kept coming. One strike flowed unstoppably into the next. Jack weaved and bobbed, utilizing every scrap of fighting experience he possessed. This battle was driving him to the limit—though not past it, not yet. He could manage. The more Maximus went all out, the wider Jack's grin became. The ecstasy of battle was infectious, the same one he'd felt all the way since his Forest of the Strong days.

When his life was on the line and death was one mistake away, he felt alive.

Jack accelerated to match the other's rhythm. The Iron Fist Style was pumping out furiously. His body, dense as a neutron star, took the hits and regenerated. His Brutalizing Aura was spread out at full force, stealing a small portion of Maximus's power, and his Dao Domain filled his body, eager to burst out.

He slapped away the blade and punched into the claws. His knuckle bled, but Maximus's arm was pushed back. Sharp feathers flew for Jack's face, and he let them graze his cheeks. He leaned into the battle, securing the momentum, and pushing Maximus back. One strike turned to ten, which turned into a hundred. His fists were unstoppable, every Dao Root operating concurrently at full force.

Maximus didn't even have time to teleport. Before he knew it, he was on the back foot, defending for his life. However, he was an extremely skilled warrior. Even under heavy pressure, he defended masterfully, combining his every advantage to come out unscathed.

He dodged one punch and let another meet his temple, using it as a springboard to escape the clash and regain the offensive. Even as he flew away, his sword erupted with blinding light. "Heavenly Divide!" he shouted, teleporting above Jack and slashing down.

"Meteor Punch!"

The sky ruptured between them as a meteor met a slash that could cleave the heavens. The two attacks ground against each other. Then, slowly, the meteor pushed through, accelerating into the slash before shattering it and bursting out.

Maximus barely had time to teleport away, as his attack had slowed down the meteorite, but he was forced to watch his strike be defeated. "How!" he shouted. "How can you possibly be this strong?"

Jack laughed carefreely. He knew he was going to win. And, though he didn't reply to Maximus, the answer was simple: because he had better stats and Dao.

His titles were overwhelmingly superior to anyone else's—both the Integration ones and the title he secured by conquering Trial Planet. The stat increase they amounted to was far greater than the twenty level difference between them. Moreover, he had a perfect foundation, an incredibly rare phenomenon. Across the entire galaxy, there were only a handful of people with four Dao Roots, and Maximus was definitely not one of them. Most were B-Grades.

Honestly, Maximus being able to compete was already a testament to his great skill as a warrior. Jack had to admit that, on that front, he was out-skilled. His life-or-death experiences, equal-strength spars against Copy Jack, and Iron Fist Style made him a master fighter, but Maximus was even above that.

However, Maximus didn't know all that. In his eyes, Jack's strength was an impossibility. There was no way to acquire it. He was the strongest D-Grade of the Animal Kingdom. He could hold his ground against the greatest D-Grades of the entire galaxy. How could there be someone that much stronger than him?

Was he going to die?

The thought came like a mallet to his skull, but Maximus was vastly more experienced than Rufus Emberheart had been. He possessed no fear of death. In his long life, he'd survived even more life-or-death battles than Jack.

All he felt was the intense desire to prove himself stronger. Superior.

"COME!" he shouted, diving at Jack with every ounce of strength he could muster. His Dao shone inside him as he laid everything to bare. If he lost, it would crack, and he would never be able to advance again. But it didn't matter. He was supreme. He couldn't lose.

Not to a *human*.

Light erupted from his blade, illuminating even the skies above. Even the enforcers had to shield their eyes until the barrier could adjust.

Jack pulled his fist back, welcoming the attack. "DIE!" he shouted, putting the entirety of his strength into the attack. His fist shot out. Color and sound were swallowed by purple.

At the last moment, Maximus teleported away. He reappeared below Jack, an ugly smile on his face. "Fool! YOU die!" he screamed, dragging his blade up. "Final Heavenly Divide!"

There was far more energy imbued in this strike than in the previous one. It left no room for retreat. Maximus would either succeed or die on this hill, and Jack had just been tricked. He was punching the other way!

Except, Jack was no idiot himself. Though Maximus was more skilled, his supremacy made him prone to underestimating Jack, and Jack knew that. He hadn't used a single feint in this battle, saving it for when it would matter most. He'd even shouted, "DIE!" like a lunatic to make it more convincing.

Mid-swing, Jack reached into the fabric of space with his other hand, poked it open with a finger, and teleported himself in the exact same spot he was occupying, but upside-down! Instead of punching up, he was now punching down, directly at Maximus's strike.

A feral grin played on his lips as he shouted, "METEOR PUNCH!"

Neither of the two pulled back. One would be eviscerated.

CHAPTER SEVENTY-SIX
GIVING ZERO FACE

The image of the meteor and slash colliding was surreal. The audience held their breath. They could make out the purple outline of a tremendous fist, shimmering with stars and followed by a purple, gaseous tail. On the other side was a bright crescent moon three hundred feet wide and so sharp it was barely visible. Where the two attacks clashed, purple lightning spread out, and sparks filled the air. Space threatened to rupture under their sheer strength. They pushed against each other, each fighter pouring in more and more energy until the point of impact became a dark sphere that swallowed all light.

Jack roared. Maximus shouted.

A sound like the cracking of glass echoed in the arena. Maximus's heavenly slash, the invincible attack made of light, revealed a hairline crack. Then another. The meteor pushed down, unbreakable in its stability, and the slash slowly retreated, crumbling little by little. Before long, there was a web of cracks in the light, revealing a purple radiance beneath, and then, it shattered.

Maximus screamed. Jack roared even harder.

The meteor pushed down with inexhaustible strength, and there was nothing to stop it. Maximus couldn't throw another strike, he couldn't run away, and he couldn't teleport as the sheer quantity of Dao infused in Jack's meteor had locked space around him.

He was spent.

All he could do was watch in disbelief as the meteor struck him head-on, sweeping him along to crash hard against the bottom of the arena. The entire barrier shook. The arena rumbled. The prison building underneath, though protected by the barrier, creaked and moaned.

The entire arena was filled with blinding purple light and searing heat, blocking the audience's perception.

Everyone wondered the same thing: had Maximus survived?

But this was the strongest attack Jack had ever unleashed. It possessed enough power to level a country. When sandwiched between this falling meteor and the unbreakable barrier below, how could anyone survive?

The elders sported ugly looks. The Warden was feeling sick. The Grand Elder couldn't believe his eyes—at that Grade, even he hadn't possessed such strength! Monsoon was shocked, while Huali wasn't even sure how to feel. On the other side of the stadium, Shol and Dordok held their breaths, as they couldn't see through the rubble. Tears of pride shimmered in both their eyes. They had witnessed Jack grow. They'd helped him. And now, their once-little brother had become a man worthy of shaking the entire galaxy.

The smoke cleared. The shockwave dissipated. And, when all was said and done, the lifeless body of Maximus Lonihor lay in the center of the arena floor, right next to that of Sapasun, which hadn't been moved as nobody could enter the arena. Both corpses, both of Jack's making, had been crushed and pulverized to the point where they were barely recognizable.

Level-up! You have reached Level 233.

The stunned audience barely moved. Then, all at once, they erupted into cheers of such intensity that the entire stadium—no, the entire planet—shook to its core. The madman had done it! Jack Rust had done it! He challenged an entire B-Grade faction in front of everyone and *won*!

And he'd given them a hell of a fight.

The crowd went crazy. People stood and hollered, others pumped their fists. Many cried as they beheld the tyrannical Kingdom getting torn down before their very eyes. "Jack Rust!" someone shouted, cheering for the man brave and strong enough to do what none of them could.

He was a hero.

"Jack Rust!" more people cheered. "Jack Rust!"

Most of the audience joined in, cheering for the man who'd done the impossible. They completely forgot about the present elders of the Animal Kingdom and cheered with all their soul. What was the Kingdom going to do? Kill them all? Hell no! Fuck them!

"Jack Rust!" the earth and sky shook with his name, uttered by millions. "Jack Rust!"

Such scenes were occurring simultaneously all around the galaxy. From the tiny Fair Way Continent to the distant headquarters of this galaxy's Hand of God, everyone lost themselves in cheering. It didn't matter if they had a stake in this conflict or not. It didn't matter if they even cared.

What had they just watched? It was the event of an era! The battle of a millennium! The birth of a hero!

How could anyone *not* cheer?

Back on Earth, people were shouting and crying at the same time. "Jack Rust!" Edgar shouted. So did Vivi, and Sparman, and the professor, even Harambe.

On the outer planet of Field Nebula, three hundred brothers and sisters roared with laughter and cheers, creating a chaos that overwhelmed even the other nearby spectators. "Big Bro!" they shouted at the top of their lungs, all together with one voice. "Big Bro!"

Gan Salin was tearful. He couldn't give a single shit about Sapasun or the Animal Kingdom. "He did it!" he shouted. "I knew he could do it! That's our Jack!"

"Hmph! Of course he could!" Nauja responded, feigning an indifference that convinced nobody. Salin had caught her worried gaze before, her clasped palms as she watched her friend fight for his life.

He grinned. "There is nothing wrong with worrying, you know."

"Bullshit! A barbarian would never worry over something as natural as death."

Meanwhile, at the epicenter of this hollering crowd, Brock was the only one not feeling relief—for the simple reason that he'd never doubted Jack's success at all. All he felt was a deep sense of pride, as well as joy for his big brother's accomplishment.

"Big Bro," he said, bringing a fist to his heart and thumping his chest. "Big Bro awesome!"

In the arena, it took a few moments for the audience to calm down. Gradually, they caught the glares of the Animal Kingdom cultivators and shut up. From the weakest enforcer to the Grand Elder himself, every Kingdom C-Grade sported such ugly expressions that, after the initial rush was over, nobody dared speak.

The silence was heavy like the sky itself. It covered the entire city, the entire planet.

Every cultivator of the Animal Kingdom, be they a tiny F-Grade or an elder, knew they were screwed. Jack Rust had publicly humiliated them and showcased their weakness. At this point, there was nothing they could do to change it. Even if they managed to prove that Jack Rust was extraordinarily strong, even if they killed him right now or later, it wouldn't matter. In the cultivator world, only two things mattered: strength and face.

And the Animal Kingdom had just lost both.

Nobody was sure who had to speak first. At the Grand Elder's direction, the Warden stood and floated to the edge of the barrier, which was quickly brought down.

"Jack Rust," he said, not bothering to conceal the hatred in his voice. What did he care? This entire farce was his fault. He was dead already.

"Warden," Jack replied indifferently. Though he was panting, most of his injuries from the fight had healed already. It was like Maximus hadn't even come close—though that wasn't entirely the case.

"You have killed my top disciple and my faction's head disciple," the Warden said. "In the past, you have even killed my own son, as well as dozens of our Kingdom's D-Grades. Is there anything you have to say for yourself?"

"Yes. I won, so per our agreement, you have to set me and my friends free. Can I go now?"

The Warden's gaze could cut through iron, but Jack was nonplussed. "How dare you speak to me like that. Do you not realize where you are? Who I am?"

"Oh, I know full well that you could squash me like a bug. But you won't do that. Because, if you do, your Kingdom will lose even the last shred of dignity you have left." Jack smiled coldly. "I know you hate me, Warden. Yet, here I am, standing right in your face, and you are completely unable to touch me. Tell me: how does it feel?"

The projection stones were still running, this exchange broadcasted across the entire galaxy. The Warden had never been more insulted, more enraged, or more hurt in his entire life. He wanted to smack Jack dead more than anything in the world.

Except Jack was completely right. He could not do it. Even if his life was already probably forfeit, he couldn't even try—the Grand Elder would act out and stop him to protect the Kingdom's honor.

In fact, as the Warden just realized, that was probably why the Grand Elder had sent him out to speak. He wanted him to lose his temper so he could kill him on the spot and reinforce the Kingdom's image.

The Warden looked back, meeting the Grand Elder's cold eyes. Once, these two were like brothers—but when things went south, the Grand Elder was completely willing to kill the Warden to save some face.

The Warden turned back to the front. He was so frustrated that blood rose up his throat, and even as his face reddened, he swallowed it to save the last of his pride. When he was certain his mouth was clear of blood, only then did he speak.

"A deal is a deal," he said weakly. It was the hardest task of his life. "Jack Rust, though an enemy of our faction, you are free to go. Your strength is great—almost suspiciously great, but no matter. The Kingdom can find joy in chasing down a little rat like you again. It keeps us sharp. Scram."

Jack grinned. "Thank you, Warden. However, I have one last thing to say."

The Warden gave him a dead man's stare. Jack, however, wasn't planning to push his luck any further. He just wanted to make a point—which, since the cat was out of the bag already, he had no reason not to.

The truth was, he'd already humiliated the Kingdom enough. His current goal was to build himself up so the Black Hole Church would protect him better, and what better way to do that than to flaunt his strength?

"You mentioned my strength being suspiciously great," he said. "However, I can assure you that there is no trick at play. I am simply that strong."

"Hmph!" the Warden snorted. "As if I will believe that!"

"Then take a good look, Warden, and tell me if you believe me now," Jack said, spreading his arms wide. At the same time, he mentally commanded, *System, display my Ninth Ring Conqueror title.*

The Warden appeared confused. Then exclamations and whispers spread through the audience. The Warden finally caught on and inspected Jack.

Human (Earth-387), Level 233 (D-Grade)
Faction: Bare Fist Brotherhood (D-Grade)
Title: Ninth Ring Conqueror

"Ninth Ring Conqueror?" he exclaimed in shock, even forgetting his anger for a moment. "Impossible!"

Jack laughed. "Do you see now, Warden? I am just better than any D-Grade in your faction. And this is all because of your Kingdom acting like a tyrant and forcing me to get stronger to fight you."

The Warden reined in his shock. Thanks to his burning fury, he took this as a personal challenge, since the Warden himself had not managed to defeat the Final Guardian. "So what, Jack Rust?" he asked with a snort. His fury was building up to unprecedented levels, his voice shaking with deadliness. "Make yourself scarce already. Run for your life. Because I, Artus Emberheart, swear on my name and honor that I refuse to live under the same sky as you. I will find you, kill you, and eradicate your whole family. I will pluck out every muscle and tendon in your body and make you beg for death. I will destroy everything you hold dear."

Jack's smile disappeared. His eyes hardened and his gaze sharpened. "I look forward to you trying, Warden. I have already killed plenty of leonines. Adding your head to the pile will change little. But make no mistake—even if you don't come for me, I will come for you. Because I, Jack Rust, also swear on my name and honor that I refuse to live under the same sky as you. I will destroy you and your faction. I will slay you and everyone you throw at me, and I will drag mud across your name until it becomes the laughingstock of even the lowliest F-Grade in this constellation. When I am done with you, the Animal Kingdom faction will be a relic of the past, a lesson to everyone that tyrants always fall, always have fallen, and always will fall. I'm leaving now, Warden, but I suggest you run. Leave this constellation, leave this galaxy, and hope that I don't find you when I'm strong enough to squash you like an ant. But I will, Warden. I will always find you. And I will, no matter what happens, kill you."

Sparks were flying where the two of them stood in the sky, facing each other. Their mutual hatred nearly visible. These were two mortal enemies, and inevitably, one would kill the other.

If it was anyone else, a D-Grade feuding against a C-Grade would be a laughable matter. But after the strength Jack had just exhibited... who knew?

And had he just declared war on the entire Animal Kingdom faction?

Finally, the Warden could no longer take it. His frustration was so strong that the blood rose unstoppably in his throat, and he coughed it out in public. Everyone in the audience raised their brows, but the Warden felt so exhausted and helpless that he couldn't even care.

"This is over," he declared, mustering the very last dregs of his self-control. "Leave. Now."

He waved a hand to destroy every projection stone around the arena, uncaring about the cost, and turned into a beam of light to fly away. Jack smiled. "Thank you, Warden. Please enjoy yourself."

The black manacles fell around the wrists of Shol, Dordok, and the Sage. They quickly arrived beside Jack, who summoned the *Bromobile* and flew inside, charging it up as much as possible before the Animal Kingdom changed its mind.

"They will come after us the moment we teleport," the Sage said. "But fear not; I have a plan. The Church will get us out. Take us to the exact location I indicate."

He transmitted a sense of general direction and distance to Jack's mind. Jack nodded. "Okay. Let's go."

He spared a final look for the people in the honor seats. He saw Li Qian staring over with bitterness. Elder Monsoon's calculating gaze and Elder Huali's complicated one. He saw the two white-robed C-Grades averting their eyes, clearly declaring that what happened next was none of their business, while the Grand Elder and all other elders of the Animal Kingdom stared at Jack as if they wanted to eat him alive.

"Fuck you," he mouthed at them, and then he teleported.

CHAPTER SEVENTY-SEVEN
LEAVING HELL

JACK, SHOL, DORDOK, AND THE SAGE SHUTTLED THROUGH THE COSMOS ON Jack's *Bromobile.* Nobody locked down the space around them, so they teleported thrice in quick succession. The planet of Hell was already far behind. They were now somewhere in that planet's solar system, cruising interstellar space.

"We're almost there," Jack said, tracing the Sage's directions in his head. "I hope your people are ready."

The Sage laughed. "So do I, because look!"

A blinding dot of light disappeared and reappeared in the distance behind them, growing closer. The Animal Kingdom had let them go in public but was already after them, and this time, they were going for blood.

"Holy shit!" Jack exclaimed. "They're fast!"

"We're faster. Floor it, Jack!"

"Floor what?" Dordok asked, unfamiliar with Earth's lingo, as Jack accelerated their ship to the maximum. They were close enough now that they didn't need to teleport again.

Soon, an asteroid appeared before them, trailed by a long tail as it flew toward the sun from deeper space. The general sense of direction and distance that the Sage was transmitting into Jack's head pointed directly at the asteroid.

As they approached, Jack made out an irregular shape on its surface. It looked like a large arched gate filled with light, surrounded by dark-robed figures and entire heaps of glowing blue stones.

"Is that it?" he asked.

"Right!" the Sage replied, a wild grin blossoming on his face. "Sneaking out from under the Kingdom's nose was tricky, but the Church can do anything! We built a large-scale teleporter on an asteroid far away from this solar system, then shot it over. Took us months!"

Shol raised a brow. "That sounds expensive."

"Don't worry about it. It's absolutely worth it. Jack—drive our starship right into the teleporter!"

"*Into the gate?*"

"Exactly!"

"What about your friends over there?"

"They'll join us; don't worry, they know what they're doing. Just hurry!"

"Where does it lead?"

"To Earth!"

"To Earth?"

"Just floor it, dammit!"

Jack gritted his teeth and pointed the *Bromobile* at the asteroid. They were blitzing through space at tens of thousands of miles per hour, while the asteroid hurtled toward them at an equally impressive speed. It was growing so fast that, if not for Jack's extremely sharp perception and dexterity, he wouldn't be able to navigate them accurately.

Even now, he was struggling.

"Don't miss, Jack!" Shol shouted.

"Show them the steering skills I taught you!" Dordok added, stepping beside Shol to calmly watch from the front window. The asteroid was magnifying like someone was zooming in.

Jack wanted to shout back that Dordok had never let him steer the *Trampling Ram*, but he needed his entire attention focused on aiming the starship. Indomitable Will activated, sharpening his focus and eliminating all distractions. His effective Dexterity of over two thousand homed in on the task. The most minuscule movements of the helm changed their impact point by miles.

From far behind, a Dao-infused roar echoed through space. Even the fabric of reality shivered at its sound: it was a B-Grade.

"STOP RIGHT THERE!"

However, even B-Grades weren't omnipotent. Jack ignored the voice. In the blink of an eye, the asteroid dominated their vision. Everything was happening too fast. Everyone held their breath. Jack touched the helm gently, pushing it one tenth of an inch forward, and their ship rammed into the starry gate dead-center, instantly ricocheted into the vacuum behind space. Just like the previous times he'd teleported, Jack saw planets, stars, gasses, and all sorts of stellar objects zoom past as the *Bromobile* crossed the galaxy at a speed vastly eclipsing that of light.

Seven black-robed figures flew right behind them. Jack barely caught a glimpse of the starry gate they'd passed through exploding just before a menacing, golden-haired figure caught up. Only the echoes of a roar followed.

"We made it," Shol said, turning away from the window toward Jack. "Good job, my friend."

"Nice steering," Dordok added casually.

Jack wanted to relax and celebrate, but recent experience had taught him to always be on edge. "Who are your friends, Sage?"

"Church agents. Don't worry; they're not going to hurt us."

"Could they?" Shol asked with a pointed glance.

"Oh, absolutely. They're all C-Grades."

In the stunned silence that followed, everyone watched the marvels of the galaxy roll past. The teleportation was far less comfortable than when using established teleporters. Occasionally there were strong spatial ripples, only held at bay by the seven C-Grades flanking them. The starry terrain fluctuated like the surface of a lake. An odd pressure overcame them at some point, making them feel short of breath.

Then, light appeared at the end of the tunnel, and the interspace spat them out into a solar system that seemed... familiar. Or did it? All solar systems looked alike from up-close.

"Is this our sun?" Jack asked, pointing at the burning ball in the distance.

"Of course," the Sage replied with a happy smile. "And, if you look the other way, you will have confirmation."

A knot formed in Jack's throat. Slowly, he turned around to look through the starship's other window. A blue ball with hints of green hung in the far distance. It seemed tiny and surreal, traveling through the cosmos with nothing attached to it. It was slowly spinning, too, and the sunlight fell over half its surface like a bright curtain.

Jack would recognize it anywhere. This was his Earth. It was home. The feeling was impossible to describe; an intense sense of belonging that washed over him, stemming from the deepest parts of his soul. It had been less than a year since he left, but so much had happened in the meantime that it felt like a lifetime ago. He'd always suspected he wouldn't make it back to the warm blue, dying alone somewhere deep in space.

Now... he was home.

Jack hadn't cried when his death seemed certain. He hadn't shed a tear when Sapasun broke all his limbs and mocked him. But now, seeing home again—this tiny, beautiful marble of life in endless darkness—he did.

Brock, Nauja, and Gan Salin sat cross-legged in a forest clearing, facing each other. Their auras shimmered. They were swimming in a thousand emotions. Pride for Jack's achievement, and fear for their future.

Well, not Brock. He had no fear, only a desire to get stronger.

All three of them had reached the peak E-Grade and developed all the Dao Roots they could. The only thing left to do was breakthrough and reach the fabled, legendary realm of immortals.

That was damn difficult, unfortunately, but they were trying.

A hooded figure entered their clearing. Brock's eyes shot open, his gaze cutting through iron. "Yes?" he asked. He felt no familiarity with this person—it was not one of his bros.

The figure stopped twenty feet away from them. "Hello." When the hood was pulled back, a feshkur woman was revealed under it. "My name is Argn. We have never met before, but I am here to take you away."

"You can try," Brock responded, letting his aura leak out. He couldn't inspect this woman, but he felt that she wasn't too strong—except for the nagging feeling, deep in his chest, that she was more than she showed.

The woman laughed. A transparent bubble erupted from her body, covering them in the blink of an eye. Brock felt her strength break out from its tiny shell and reveal itself for what it was.

An immortal.

He jumped up and drew his staff, ready to fight.

The woman laughed again. "Don't worry," she said, putting her hands up. "I am no enemy. This bubble is only to isolate sound."

Gan Salin stood and poked the bubble. It did not break, but a hint of its essence was left on his finger. He licked it. A moment later, he spat it out with a "blegh."

"Who are you?" Nauja asked, slowly drawing her bow. "Who do you work for?"

"The Black Hole Church," the woman replied calmly. "Your friend, Jack Rust, is one of us now. He is currently in one of your Earth's D-Grade dungeons, consolidating his strength, and will continue hiding there until the war occurs in six days. I am here to take you to him, if you are willing."

Brock, Salin, and Nauja glanced at each other. They all knew Jack's connection with the Black Hole Church, and they had seen the Sage in the battle recordings. Jack joining them wasn't too big of a stretch.

"Why should we trust you?" Salin asked, rinsing his tongue with some water. "You could be lying."

"You can see my strength. If I wanted to harm you, I wouldn't need to lie."

That was true. Even Brock, who didn't possess access to System inspection, could tell she was abnormally strong even for immortal standards.

"Besides that..." the woman continued, cracking a smile. "I have a message from Jack: Harambe sends his greetings."

Brock's eyes lit up. No enemy would possibly know his father's name. He put away his staff, instantly growing friendly with this woman. "Okay, bro," he said. "Let's go. To home. Ah—but I need to do one thing first."

Artus Emberheart lay on the floor, panting. A foot was pressed into the side of his cheek, keeping him down.

"What should we do with this loser, Ancestor?" the Grand Elder asked, spitting on Artus's face squashed under his foot. "He caused great harm to our faction. He deserves to die."

Opposite him stood a reality-warping figure. Golden fur covered his entire body, while his mane was proud and clear. He looked like a normal leonine, but the aura of supremacy he emitted was enough to press down on the Grand Elder like a divine decree.

"A liability like him should not remain in our faction," the ancestor replied calmly. "However, he can still be of use. We need to curry favor with the Hand of God. Perhaps gifting them a late C-Grade will do the trick."

The Grand Elder bowed his head. "You are wise, Ancestor."

"No, Ancestor, please!" Artus pleaded from the ground. "I have served the faction my entire life. I have been loyal and hard-working. Please don't do this to me! I don't deserve it!"

The Grand Elder pushed down with his foot, digging the Warden's face deeper into the concrete. "Shut up," he growled.

The ancestor ignored Artus's pleas. "System," he ordered calmly, "remove Artus Emberheart from the Animal Kingdom. Revoke all his rights as an elder."

"NO!" Artus screamed, but it was useless. Already, System screens were rolling before his eyes. His life's work turned into smoke. He had been an Animal Kingdom elder for millennia—suddenly, he was nothing.

And it was all the fault of Jack Rust. Hatred shimmered inside Artus, dark and all-encompassing. He couldn't defeat the Grand Elder. He couldn't fight back against the ancestor.

But he could take revenge against Jack Rust or die trying. His Dao was already broken; what did he have to lose?

"What about Jack Rust, Ancestor?" the Grand Elder asked. "We have lost his whereabouts, and—"

"Don't think about that anymore," the ancestor cut him off. "That man has too much potential, too much hatred toward us to be left alive. He must die. I will see to it personally."

The Grand Elder couldn't contain his shock. "Personally! But Ancestor, you—"

"I know best," the ancestor interrupted him again, "so you better watch your mouth. Or are you implying your judgment is better than mine?"

"Never, Ancestor. It will be as you say. With you after him, even the Black Hole Church will not be able to protect Jack Rust."

The ancestor snorted a chuckle. "Don't underestimate the great forces, Olsen. The Church can protect whomever they want. The question is, how far are they willing to go?" His leonine face broke into a slight, confident grin. "And what allies can I secure?"

"You are wise, Ancestor," the Grand Elder repeated, bowing deeply.

The ancestor nodded and turned to leave. "As for him," he said, referring to Artus, who remained under the Grand Elder's foot, shimmering with bitterness and hatred, "inform the Hand of God that we offer them Artus Emberheart, a late C-Grade, as a gift. They can do whatever they wish with him. Even if they kill or enslave him, we couldn't care less."

Artus felt so much dark fire in his chest that he almost lost control and tried to fight back. Of course, that would be pointless. He bottled up the indignation, vowing to release it on the one person who had destroyed his life.

"Yes, Ancestor," the Grand Elder replied, and the ancestor disappeared, off to hunt Jack Rust.

CHAPTER SEVENTY-EIGHT
FATHER AND SON

Six days before the end of the grace period...

HARAMBE WAS OUT TO FIGHT. HIS KNUCKLES LANDED HEAVILY ON THE GROUND, crunching bloodied autumn leaves as he calmly strolled past.

He and his brorillas could not level-up as humans did, but they could sharpen their muscles and Big Thoughts. They hadn't been sitting idle this past year. Already, the battered corpses of hyenas covered the ground around Harambe, their E-Grade bodies unable to withstand the power of his fists. Only the leader of this place could be a worthy opponent. His sights were set on the distant mountain—the core of this E-Grade dungeon.

The closer he approached, however, the lower his brows fell.

"Uu-uu-ah!" Loha, one of his brorillas, exclaimed.

Harambe nodded heavily. Something was wrong. There were more corpses in their way—corpses that had been there for hours. Someone had been through here. Someone was in the dungeon that he, Harambe, had claimed.

And that someone had killed an entire hyena pack by skewering them with ice spikes.

The Ice Peak.

Harambe paused. The three brorillas behind him awaited his command—would they leave, or would they stay?

They pressed on. This was Harambe's dungeon. What kind of weak big brorilla would cower at the presence of enemies?

His stroll turned into a tumbling run. His knuckles thundered on the ground as he dashed through the thick orange autumn forest foliage, terrifying any remaining animals out of his way. His eyes spat fire. He jumped at a thick branch, grabbing it tightly to launch himself upward, to the top of the tree. He drummed his fists on his chest and roared.

The birds' songs died. The forest animals stilled. This was a big brorilla with two Big Thoughts and the will to fight; who would dare stand against him?

Two creatures did not stop. Harambe was closer to the mountain now, its peak visible. And up there was a small figure clashing against a scarred, brown-skinned lion. Ice was everywhere, reflecting the sunlight. The figure danced around on wings of ice, dodging the lion's swipes and slashing at it with twin ice swords.

But that was Harambe's prey. And the ice-man, whoever he was, had just ignored Harambe's roar of dominance.

He shot forward even faster. His knuckles now cratered the ground, while his three brorillas struggled to keep up. Harambe was furious. Someone was challenging him. He couldn't let that pass.

The forest floor flew under him, turning into stone that angled upward. The mountain was a small one—it took Harambe less than a minute to climb it, but by then, it was too late. The brown lion lay dead, its body torn apart by ice shards. The man who'd killed it stood proud over the body, gazing at Harambe. Harambe glared back.

He knew this man. It was the one who had defeated the wizard bro, the leader of the enemy.

Alexander Petrovic.

The ice-man, still wearing wings of ice and wielding twin swords, flashed him a bright grin. "Would you look at that. The Brotherhood's pet gorilla. How lucky is this?"

Harambe snorted. His nostrils widened, his eyes reddened. He slowly walked within ten feet of the ice-man, then rose to his full height and beat his chest with all his power, roaring out in dominance. Spit flew out. The air itself boomed in resonance. His shout was enough to shake the ice and cover the sky. Any beast, any brorilla, almost any human he knew would have cowered.

But not this ice-man. Not Alexander Petrovic. He was strong and surprisingly brave, facing a ten-foot-tall brorilla's battle roar from almost point-blank without flinching. He only stared back unblinkingly. There was hardness behind those eyes; there was blood.

Harambe realized he was in the presence of a worthy challenger. He slowly fell back onto his knuckles, sizing the ice-man up and down. His instinct warned Harambe that this man was stronger than him. But it didn't matter. Harambe was the leader of his pack, and he had just been challenged. He would die before retreating.

"How has your alliance survived with such idiots at the helm?" the ice-man said with confidence. "First Edgar, now you. You should possess the intelligence to realize I'm stronger and defy your natural instincts to escape. Why do you stay? Why did you come to the mountaintop knowing that I was here? You could have run away. You had the time. Instead, you rushed to your death. There is nothing admirable about idiocy."

Harambe growled. His three brorillas caught up, their breaths short as they realized their big bro was locked into a duel for dominance. He heard their cheers but did not see them, for he refused to look away from his opponent's unblinking eyes. His own eyes were hurting, but he would be damned if he blinked first.

"Don't worry," Alexander said. "I do not obey stupid rules. Your subordinates will die before you, and I will make you watch."

Harambe growled again, pulling back his lips to reveal wickedly sharp teeth. Once, they had been used to bite bananarms. Now, they would tear into this man's throat. He dug his knuckles deep into the ground as he approached, coming almost face-to-face with the ice-man, barely a foot between them. The man raised his chin. His eyes had yet to falter, and Harambe's were beginning to seriously burn. Gradually, the man's gaze hardened further, carrying a tangible threat.

"You should have stayed in your forest, gorilla, where that robot would never let me touch you," he said. "You fucked up."

Harambe growled, intensifying his glare at the expense of the burning in his eyes worsening, but it was useless. The man was relentless. The intensity of his stare ramped up, reaching into Harambe's chest and freezing his soul. It encased his burning courage in ice. It slipped fear into his heart, an undeniable awareness that he, Harambe, was the weaker party.

And, while his insides shivered, his eyes burned. Every second of holding them open took more effort than the last. Harambe's Big Thoughts flared, enhancing him, but so did the ice-man's.

Every second was now a year.

Harambe blinked. The moment he did, he knew he'd lost. Alexander grinned wickedly and attacked.

Five days before the end of the grace period...

Brock, Nauja, and Gan Salin appeared in the middle of an empty country road.

"Here should be fine," said the feshkur immortal accompanying them. "We are across the planet from the overseer. She shouldn't be able to detect us. Welcome to Earth."

"So, this is what it looks like," Nauja said, looking around. "I expected it would be a bit more... advanced."

"We're in the countryside," Salin explained. "Wait until you see the cities. You're going to love it. They have these things called computers, where you can play all sorts of games."

"Like a ball court?"

"Not exactly. You'll see."

Brock, meanwhile, was speechless. He scanned the horizon, his ears perked up for any hint of sound. He recognized nothing. Yet, he knew beyond any doubt that this was Earth, his home planet, where he was born and met Big Bro. Where everything began.

And not just that. His pack was here, too. Father, Mother, his brorilla bros... He hadn't seen them in such a long time. In fact, he barely remembered them, as he had only been a baby when he and Big Bro went to the tournament.

The rush of emotions was unexpected. Brock felt his Big Thoughts vibrate in resonance, revealing this place as the origin of his brohood.

Brock really looked forward to reuniting with everyone—and fighting on their side. It was going to be the greatest thing ever.

"Brock. Brock," Salin said, snapping his fingers in front of Brock's nose. "Are you okay?"

Brock blinked. "Yes."

"Good. You kinda spaced out a bit there. Are you so nostalgic?"

"Yes."

He smiled. "That's my big bro!"

Nauja saw Brock's longing eyes and felt sadness. Her own home was lost now. She would probably never see it again in her lifetime, never meet her father, relatives, and tribe members again.

It stung so bad.

However, barbarians did not show weakness. They were strong. Nauja bottled up those emotions and turned to the feshkur—Angr. "Where do we go now?"

"I am instructed to bring Brock where Jack Rust trains," she replied. "As for the two of you... Would you like to visit the headquarters of your forces?"

"Can't we come along with Brock?"

"It is... unadvised. Hiding until the final moment is vital, and the more people we have, the greater the chances of being discovered."

Nauja frowned, but Salin stepped in. "It's no biggie, Nauja. A few more days is nothing. Let's just wait with Edgar and the others. I'm sure they'll be glad to see me."

"I don't know those people. Are they your friends?"

"You can call them that. I mean, they don't know it yet, but—Hey, Brock, buddy. You're spacing out again. What's wrong?"

This time, Brock did not reply immediately. He'd felt something. A sudden, piercing pain in his heart as if he were losing something precious. It was a calling that couldn't be put into words, but one he could certainly follow. And it felt urgent.

"There," he said, pointing in the distance. He looked at the feshkur immortal with full seriousness. "Must go there."

She looked surprised. "But flying is—"

"Must. Please. Now."

Faced with the intensity of his gaze, she must have realized something was wrong because she nodded. "Okay. Let's go." With a wave of her hand, a gale appeared to pick them all up before shooting in the distance. They were flying near the ground, not breaking the sound barrier but close. Salin's cheeks were blown back by the wind and he made "aaaaa" sounds, but Brock's eyes remained fully focused.

Something was wrong. What could make him feel like this?

One hour later, flickering blue walls appeared in their vision, cutting off the landscape. "A dungeon," Angr said. "Do you want to go in there?"

"Yes," Brock replied. The feeling was even stronger now. Even more urgent.

Under the feshkur's lead, they flew through the blue wall to come across a terrain of destruction. A forest of orange leaves stretched under them, littered with patches of blood. The corpses of what looked like hyenas were scattered everywhere. From this vantage point, they could see that in one direction, the corpses were frozen. In another, they were smashed to death. Both paths led from the edge of the dungeon to a small mountain in the center.

"This dungeon is E-Grade," the feshkur said. "Was there a battle? I can sense that the boss of this place is dead, but the dungeon itself is unclaimed."

Brock did not say anything. He pointed at the mountaintop. As they flew over, his urgency and anxiousness grew so great that he transitioned into full clarity. Suddenly, he was in battle mode. His burning heart was controlled by a calm mind.

The first thing he saw was a large brown lion skewered by two large ice shards.

The second were the bodies of four brorillas, one larger than the rest. Brock's heart clenched. He felt short of breath. He jumped out of the air, landing hard on the ground before the others. He rushed to the side of the largest brorilla, sneaking glances at the other three as he passed. He recognized them all. Herom, Loha, Ehamba. All dead.

And how could he not recognize his own father?

To his insane relief, he discovered that Harambe was still alive. He lay there, eyes open, chest rising and falling to the beat of his heart. He sported great injuries that prevented him from moving but was clearly not dead.

"Father!" Brock exclaimed in joy.

Harambe turned his neck with great effort. When he saw Brock, his eyes were colored by intense surprise. A hint of joy threatened to appear in them, but it was immediately crushed by embarrassment and humiliation so intense they could have filled the world. Harambe looked away.

Brock froze in his steps. He couldn't believe his eyes.

Now that he was closer, he could see more things. Harambe lay on his back, arms and legs outstretched. Each was nailed to the ground by an ice spike, rendering him unable to move. Blood covered the ground around him, and dried tears had drenched the fur below his bloodshot eyes. His lips were torn from biting them. His breaths came short, as if his throat was so parched from shouting that every exhale rubbed painfully against it.

When they'd crossed gazes, before Harambe looked away, Brock had seen an ocean of pain behind those eyes. There was no longer an edge in them. They were broken, overwhelmed by loss and exhaustion. These were the eyes of a man who'd lost his will to live.

Brock was stunned. Was that really his father? The proud, unyielding big brorilla?

What could possibly have happened?

The other three had also landed by now, shocked at the scene before them. Salin tried to say something, but Nauja grabbed his arm and squeezed it to shut him up. Angr watched with deep sadness.

"Father..." Brock muttered, taking a couple steps in Harambe's direction. Before he could approach, Harambe made a snorting sound as if sending him away. Brock froze.

Overcome with grief, his mind worked hard. He took in the scene again: Harambe, nailed to the ground, and the three dead brorillas strewn around him. His mind completed the puzzle. He realized what had happened. He realized why his father didn't want to see him.

Someone had defeated Harambe, nailed him to the ground, and forced him to watch as they slaughtered his little brothers. They had then left him lying there, bleeding out over the course of several days, with nothing to do but grieve and lament.

How could he *not* be broken?

Brock's heart clenched again, becoming small and hard like a fist. His deep sadness turned into burning anger, filling him from the bottom of his feet to the top of his head. His entire soul turned red. His four Big Thoughts and one Very Big Thought revved in concert, all demanding vengeance.

Brock had never been more enraged than he was right now.

"Who was it?" he asked, his voice laden with barely contained anger.

Harambe made another snorting sound. This one was less clear, wetter. He was still looking away, enduring the pain to keep his neck turned.

Brock's lip trembled. He didn't even know what he was feeling. A part of his brain realized that his question must have caused Harambe even more shame, as he could not speak.

Harambe's body shivered slightly. The sound of droplets hitting the ground was discreet, contained, but enough for Brock to hear it. Mastering his anger, he closed his eyes and turned away, understanding that every extra second he spent looking at his father just pained them both even more.

Just how much shame would a man feel, being in such a state before his own son?

Brock's eyes carried iron. He crossed gazes with his bros, seeing that they shared his fire.

"It must have been Alexander Petrovic," Gan Salin said, lacking his usual playfulness. "Of all ice cultivators on Earth, only he possesses such power."

Brock nodded. He remembered that man. Now, Alexander Petrovic was a name and face forever engraved into his mind.

He would absolutely destroy him.

"Where is he?" Brock asked calmly.

"I have some knowledge of this planet's politics," Angr said. "Alexander Petrovic, the leader of the Ice Peak, should be waiting in his faction's headquarters. However, attacking him there is useless. It will only warn the Animal Kingdom of our presence and ruin all our plans. We are not yet in position."

Brock met her gaze. He was conflicted.

"However," she continued, "in five days, Petrovic will be at the Grace Concert. It is where your forces will assault theirs. If you can wait until then, you can fight him without endangering the entire war effort."

Brock stared deep into her eyes. He weighed the situation—the well-being of everyone against his burning rage. However, he was a big bro. He knew the right choice. He could wait.

Slowly, he nodded.

"Thank you," Angr said earnestly. "I have contacted Jack Rust, who contacted your faction. They are already on their way. We can stay, if you want, or move to the hiding place. The choice is yours."

Brock raised his head to the sky, fighting to rein in his own tears. "We go," he said, straining to keep his voice level. "Dog Bro, Girl Bro. Take care of Father."

Salin and Nauja both nodded. "Brock..." Nauja said, looking at him tenderly, but he shook his head.

"I am fine," he replied. "We go. See you soon."

"Good luck," Nauja said.

"What happened is terrible," Salin said seriously. "We believe in you, Brock. We'll take care of your father and everything else. Do what you have to do."

"Thanks, bro," Brock replied. He turned to the feshkur immortal. She raised her hand, summoning a breeze, and they both flew away together, leaving the scene of carnage behind.

Brock did not turn to look, nor did he want to stay. He understood. Right now, the closer he was to his father, the more pain and shame he would cause him.

However, his soul remained heavy with grief. It was burning with righteous rage. This was all he could think of. The beast inside him had awoken, and it would soon spread brutal carnage with all the power he'd painstakingly cultivated over the last year. He was a bro bomb about to explode.

Waiting was torture, but he would train hard. And, in five days, he would absolutely fucking destroy Alexander Petrovic.

CHAPTER SEVENTY-NINE

THE GRACE CONCERT BEGINS

THE WAVES CRASHED AGAINST WALLS OF WHITE STONE, RISING TEN FEET IN height, and circling an oblong area five miles wide. Above these walls was an empty expanse, sticking out of the ocean like a stone island. Its surface held nothing but a large, circular stage in the middle, as well as throngs of people.

The Grace Concert, the event that would signal the end of Earth's grace period, was starting.

The elites of Earth had rushed here from every corner of the planet. Some were rich individuals that had bought their place. Others were fierce cultivators who'd earned it, and there were some who just happened to possess a low-grade starship that could cross the ocean. Everyone who participated in the Integration Tournament had been personally invited, and special starships had been sent to pick them up —though some chose to come by their own means.

Starships, however, were extremely expensive items, and the spectator area could fit tens of thousands of people. Most had come by ship, starting their trip a week in advance to make it in time. One end of the concert venue—the Integration Starship—had been converted into a dock, where everything from yachts to cruise ships were currently anchored, with more arriving every hour. A large, circular area on the docks was reserved for starships.

To the dismay of many, airplanes and private jets couldn't land on the Integration Starship, but there was an aircraft carrier waiting nearby, letting them land there for a fee. A small boat then carried the passengers to the concert venue. As for helicopters, few had the fuel capacity to reach this place.

Most of the audience waited in the spectator area that surrounded the stage, while some enjoyed special treatment. An entire section near the stage was cordoned off with the words "Ice Peak" declaring its soon-to-be occupants.

Suddenly, a large group of dots appeared in the distance. The dots approached quickly, revealing themselves as a fleet of small starships headed directly for the dock. As they made landfall, outnumbering the starships already there, the presenter's voice echoed over the crowd.

"Ladies and gentlemen," it declared, "the Ice Peak!"

Everyone clapped. Many cheered loudly, hoping to curry favor. The doors of the starships slid open, revealing hundreds of well-dressed, proud individuals. Most were fair of skin, with blue eyes and blond hair. Cultivation had sharpened their features, making them beautiful and handsome. They walked with their chins raised high, carrying a subtle, deeply-ingrained sense of superiority.

Whispers spread across the audience. The true strength of the Ice Peak and the alliance had been a source of endless discussion for many. Now, they realized that the major factions were even stronger than anyone thought. Of the Ice Peak members entering the venue, there were dozens of E-Grades. Dozens. People couldn't contain their shock. Even a year after the Integration, E-Grades were incredibly rare!

And all the other members present were peak F-Grades.

It was clear that the Ice Peak had brought their cream of the crop, a show of force that would be transmitted across the planet and force everyone to bow their heads.

In the next moment, everyone stopped looking at the members of the Ice Peak. Their leader had arrived. Out of the largest starship came the man most likely to command Earth under the Animal Kingdom's auspices, one of the most influential and strongest people on the planet, one of the Integration Tournament finalists. He had reached the peak of the F-Grade in the first month. Now, peoples' jaws dropped to the floor.

"Alexander Petrovic!" the announcer declared.

Alexander carried the air of a king. His dominance was clear for all to see. It wasn't due to the dozens of E-Grades following him or the fact he'd received special mention from the Animal Kingdom. It wasn't because he commanded a fleet of a hundred starships. It was because, in front of everyone's shocked eyes, Alexander Petrovic was revealed to have reached the peak E-Grade.

The peak E-Grade within a year. Just one step away from becoming a legendary immortal. To the people of Earth, for whom even E-Grades were the greatest of celebrities, this was the stuff of myth!

What sort of talent was that? What sort of power!

Everyone cheered and clapped, earnestly this time. The Ice Peak were tyrants to the common people but on good terms with the other elites. Of the those here, most yearned for the safety and comfort that Alexander's rule would bring. So what if the common folk would be milked? They couldn't care less!

However, this event was already being broadcasted across the globe, and the reaction of most was vastly different than that of the live spectators. To the nations that lived under the Ice Peak's influence, Alexander was their leader. For all his propaganda, they only considered him the lesser of two evils. They weren't particularly enthused with him.

As for the people in alliance territory, who had decent living conditions and access to information, they hated Alexander with a passion. The alliance also employed its own propaganda, which undoubtedly helped.

Alexander Petrovic smiled and waved. "It's an honor to be here, everyone. Today marks the beginning of a new era; the birth of a united, prosperous, powerful Earth!"

More cheers. The projection stones focused on those cheering the loudest, somewhat influencing the people who watched the broadcast from their hometowns. A few of those cheered as well.

The Ice Peak members formed into a line that headed for their section of the venue, passing through the crowd that opened up for them. Every Ice Peak cultivator smiled and shook hands with anyone who asked, maintaining their cool and confident air. They were giving the image of established rulers.

After they reached their section, things calmed. Though it wasn't long before the announcer's voice rang again.

"The representatives of the Flame River and Bare Fist Brotherhood!" it declared. A new starship had just arrived, and out of its door stepped two women: Margaret Rust and Vivi Eragorn. The professor wore a set of clean, sharp, yet simple clothes, while Vivi donned a loose red dress that accentuated her beauty while hiding her curves. Their hair—one's white and the other's dark—both flowed freely, painting an image of calm confidence.

The crowd cheered, though not nearly as hard as they had for the Ice Peak. Everywhere else on the planet, the reaction was the exact opposite. The ones in Ice Peak territory were disinterested, while the ones in alliance territory cheered excitedly. It wasn't every day that you saw the two leaders of the alliance together.

Vivi stepped forward and raised her hand high, waving at the crowd. "Well met, everyone. Let's enjoy the show."

Her strength, grace, and confidence, combined with her natural beauty, had many men pining for her. How could they not? Alongside the professor, she was basically the planet's greatest woman, and she was pretty, too!

Not to mention her apparent peak E-Grade cultivation. She was the second such person to appear after Alexander—the professor was only Level 81—causing wave after wave of exclamations. One thing was becoming clear: after Jack Rust, whose status was unknown, Earth would soon have its second D-Grade!

Many walked up to shake hands with the two alliance leaders, even risking the Ice Peak's ire to get closer to Vivi, but she politely brushed them off. The two women made their way through the crowd, seeming as relaxed as if they were strolling in their garden, to reach a place close to the Ice Peak's area.

Alexander Petrovic strode out to meet them under everyone's watchful eyes.

"Vivi, Margaret," he said like they were old friends. "A pleasure to see you both. It's a shame you couldn't bring more of your factions, but I understand. Starships are expensive nowadays." He laughed aloud like he'd made a friendly joke. The audience went quiet, picking up on his intentions.

"Alexander," Vivi replied, her smile as slight as could be. "It's not a matter of funds; we just preferred to use them to feed our people instead of renting out starships from the Animal Kingdom to make an impression."

In one sentence, she'd both returned his insult and outed the fact that his starships were not in fact his own.

"They were offered to us on the basis of our effective ruling," Alexander stated, still with a bright smile. "Besides, it's important to keep up appearances. If I showed up by myself, what would people think of my noble faction?"

"Not much less than they do now, I presume. The bar is already pretty low."

"Right," Alexander said, pretending to look at them weirdly. He was making them out to be the bad guys. "I'll see you both later. We need to discuss the terms of your official surrender."

"We'll see," Vivi replied. "Thank you for your time, Alexander." Then, both she and the professor turned toward another, more sparsely populated area. They wouldn't have such a great view from there, but the concert was the last thing they cared about.

Alexander also walked away, leaving the spectators full of questions and gossip. Many were uncomfortable. The Ice Peak and the alliance were already irreconcilable enemies. If something went wrong and the two peak E-Grades came to blows right here, wouldn't the audience be caught in the crossfire?

As if reading their thoughts, a divine presence descended on the concert venue. Everyone looked up to find a humanoid form approaching from the sky, showered in light from above.

"Ladies and gentlemen," the announcer declared again, struggling to keep his voice level, "it is my extreme honor to present the Planetary Overseer of Earth-387, an esteemed elder of the Animal Kingdom, a noble heir of the Lonihor leonine family: Galicia Lonihor!"

The audience held nothing back. They didn't dare to. Their cheers reached the sky, echoing from cloud to cloud. Even the surrounding sea was upset by the volume. The overseer, beset by a faint, leonine aura of supremacy, descended to the seat of honor, a raised throne placed right in front of the Ice Peak area to signal that they held her favor.

"Overseer," Alexander said, bowing slightly. "It is an honor to meet you in person."

She nodded at him, not bothering to respond, in the same way that she'd ignored the crowd's cheers. She was an Animal Kingdom elder, and these were clueless, bottom-of-the-barrel cultivators in a newly-Integrated planet. Even being here was already giving them too much face.

Not to mention that her mood remained sour. It had been less than a week since Jack Rust humiliated her faction and killed her son.

The announcer's voice rang again: "To our esteemed audience, please enjoy the performance. When the concert is over in three hours' time, this planet's grace period will come to an end, heralding the arrival of the great Animal Kingdom. And now, without further ado, let the Grace Concert begin!"

The crowd ceased their gossiping and focused on the stage expectantly. Smoke appeared out of nowhere to fill it. The sound of gears whirring echoed over the concert venue. Through the smoke, people could make out a man appearing from below, rising onto the stage like he was emerging from the floor itself.

A sharp chord filled the air. Then another. A fast, electric melody that seeped into everyone's psyche and excited them. The smoke began to clear, revealing long dark hair, a leather jacket, and a man wearing black, spiked bracelets. The tail of an electric guitar pierced the smoke, clearing it, and Vanderdecken was revealed in his full glory, completing a guitar solo so fast that people couldn't follow his fingers. The sound was ecstatic.

A few seconds later, he finished, and he raised his right hand in the air, extending his index and pinky fingers. "ALRIGHT!" he shouted, and the crowd cheered from their heart.

Many didn't like metal music. Many were afraid of what would happen later. But not many things could unite people like a good show.

The announcer's voice rang out: "The Animal Kingdom presents to you the singer of the Dao of Metal, the third place winner of the Elzin planet's interstellar talent show, the highest-level musician of Earth-387: Kane Vanderdecken!"

"For the Devil!" Vanderdecken cheered, this time raising both hands.

All across the planet, people smiled and settled in to watch, excited to experience the performance of a cultivator showman. To everyone's surprise, Vanderdecken had even reached Level 119.

He strung his electric guitar again. Though it was unplugged, its sound echoed everywhere, harsh but strangely lyrical, and the concert began. "'GATE ONE'..." Vanderdecken sang. The audience moved to the tune, getting inexplicably drawn into the song. Even Alexander Petrovic was enjoying himself, while Vivi and the professor nodded along—though their minds were elsewhere.

Only the Planetary Overseer couldn't care less. Her head was propped on her fist, and her mind was already working on the best ways to locate Jack Rust after this was over. She didn't believe he would dare to show up on Earth—if he did, the Animal Kingdom Ancestor chasing him would teleport over in the blink of an eye. Even the Black Hole Church wouldn't fight a B-Grade for him. He couldn't possibly be worth that much.

Vanderdecken's performance was captivating. For the people at the edge of the concert venue, it wasn't as much. They were five miles away. They couldn't see him, and the sound reached them distorted. They were here more for the experience and status than the actual performance.

However, life has a sense of humor. These people couldn't see the concert too well, but in return, they had first-row seats to the sea around the Integration Starship.

Therefore, when the tip of a periscope first broke the surface of the ocean, they were the first to notice.

CHAPTER EIGHTY
BLOWING THE HORN

ONE BY ONE, OMINOUS SHAPES SURFACED AROUND THE INTEGRATION STARSHIP. They were painted blue with white strips, blending in with the seawater. Each possessed a hatch at the top, along with a periscope.

As the commotion spread of this unexpected arrival, more and more eyes turned to look. The guards tensed. The Ice Peak cultivators lowered their brows. Everyone in the know nodded somberly.

It was time. The war was starting.

Vanderdecken kept blasting the audience with music, but far fewer people paid attention to his performance now. Even at the seats of honor, behind the Planetary Overseer, the Ice Peak detected the commotion and was pivoting away from the singer.

"They came..." Alexander muttered, a grin appearing on his face. "Good. This will make the clean-up easier."

The overseer did not react visibly, but her brows were furrowed. She had no idea what gave these people the courage to start a fight. Maybe she couldn't participate, but all reports claimed that the Ice Peak had more than enough power.

The submarines surrounding the concert came to a stop at the same time. The hatches swung open, letting out row after row of battle-ready cultivators. Many wore armor of various kinds. Others donned robes.

Yet more wore varied clothing, like t-shirts or boxing shorts. One thing they had in common, however, was the resolve in their eyes. These people had come for war.

The voices of the audience rose so high that even Vanderdecken began to be eclipsed.

At that moment, two forms shot out of the crowd, one surrounded by wings of fire and the other flying on what appeared to be a jetpack. "A moment, everyone!" Vivi shouted, easily overpowering Vanderdecken, who obediently stopped playing.

"Oh, man," he muttered to himself. "And I was only at the third song."

Seeing that she had everyone's attention, Vivi continued. "We apologize for interrupting. As you can see, the cultivators of the Flame Brotherhood alliance have surrounded the Integration Starship, and we are about to engage with the Ice Peak. We do not wish to harm innocent bystanders or the honored representatives of the Animal Kingdom. Anyone not affiliated with the Ice Peak, please depart immediately, or you will be considered their accomplices."

Her speech was sharp and to the point, delivered with the hardness of a war general. It was followed by a second of stunned silence. Then, all at once, the crowd broke into screams, rushing to the dock so fast they created a stampede. Vivi watched coldly. She had no compassion for most of these people—she just couldn't afford to make more enemies. If they wanted to stampede each other, let them.

A freezing current spread from the seats of the Ice Peak. Alexander Petrovic took to the air. As soon as he reached Vivi's altitude, his wings spread, revealing a level of detail that would awe the greatest of sculptors.

"Have you no shame?" he asked in a booming voice. "This is a moment of celebration. Why must you interrupt us with your warmongering stupidity?"

"Don't play coy, Alexander. Everyone knows you are the dogs of the Animal Kingdom. If we delayed by just three hours, the grace period would be over, and this battle would be impossible."

He laughed. "It *is* impossible, Vivi. Your military might is far inferior; you don't stand a chance."

"Let's find out."

Her flame wings burned brighter. A whip of blue fire unfurled between her hands, snapping at the nearby air. Her long red dress, made of fireproof fabric, fluttered in the wind, revealing nothing yet enhancing her image as a warrior queen.

"Losing no time, I see," Alexander replied with a laugh. Two ice swords slowly grew out of his palms, and he crossed them in the air. "Venerable Elder! May I destroy this witch?"

Still sprawled on her chair, the overseer betrayed no emotion. "Do whatever you want. This is a battle between natives. As long as we are not implicated, the Animal Kingdom will not act."

"In that case, esteemed Overseer," Vivi said, "could you please move? Your current position makes it hard for us to do battle."

The overseer gave Vivi a hard stare. When she didn't flinch, the overseer's brows furrowed deeply. "The grace period ends in exactly two hours and forty minutes," she announced. Then, without another word, she slipped through space and disappeared.

Meanwhile, the alliance army had established their lines on the concert area. As the crowd receded, they advanced. The army of the Ice Peak spread as well, cool and confident.

The projection stones were still running. Much like Jack's duel, this battle would be transmitted across the globe, replacing Vanderdecken's performance as the main event. All over the planet, people gasped and rose from their seats, calling everyone they knew to watch the projection. A massive screen hovered in the air over every major town on Earth, stunning an entire people.

To them, both the alliance and the Ice Peak were unfathomable existences. Most of the war had been fought in dungeons or places where people couldn't freely watch. Moreover, all news came distorted by both sides. It was hard to tell truth from falsehood.

Right now, there was nothing stopping them! They could witness the battle as clearly as if they were there.

This was a breathtaking moment!

At the same time, another question spread through the planet like fire.

"Hey," a woman said, touching her husband's arm. "This war... Do you think Jack Rust will show up?"

"I have no idea!" he replied, his fists clenched with excitement. "But I sure want to find out! After all the miracles he's achieved... who knows? He just might return to save us!"

For the people of Earth, Jack Rust was already a legendary hero. His name had spread after the Integration Tournament, serving as a beacon of hope for all who were lost. The people of Earth had no idea what the future held, but they believed that, no matter what happened, Jack Rust would return for them.

At least, so it seemed. He was an existence so far beyond them they couldn't predict his moves. It was unknown whether he'd show up for this battle or not.

"Vivi," the professor said in a low voice, "I will go command the army, okay?"

She nodded. "Has Jack replied?"

"No. He... I don't know what happened."

The professor's voice was strained, but to anyone who couldn't hear them, she appeared strong and confident.

"Very well," Vivi said. "Let's believe, since that's all we can do. Go. I'll hold him off."

The professor went to say something again, then caught herself. She couldn't let wayward emotions influence her. "Okay. I trust you. Stay safe."

"I will."

The professor directed her jetpack to dive down.

"And here you were making fun of our starships," Alexander said, making a show of indicating the submarines. "Those look quite expensive."

"They were ours to begin with. It's not like we could sell them for food."

"I don't understand why you're doing this," Alexander said, growing somber. "You have nothing to gain. Even if you somehow win, you will still be eliminated in a few hours. There is no way the Kingdom will let you live after what Jack Rust did."

"What else could we do?" Vivi replied with a sad yet hard smile. "We will die anyway. If we can rid the world of your filth before that, it will be enough. And besides, we still hope for a miracle."

At this, Alexander burst out laughing. "What miracle? Jack Rust can't save you! Nobody can! You are criminals, goners, relics of the past. Your death will herald a new era, and it will come at my hand."

Vivi smiled and straightened her whip arm toward him. "Try it." Her eyes darkened. "This is for Harambe."

Down on the concert area, the two armies faced off against each other. Each was made up of their respective faction's top elites. The weakest cultivators present were at the peak F-Grade, as anyone weaker than that would perish for no reason.

Now that the armies stood in the open, their respective powers were clear.

The Ice Peak held the advantage in numbers. They were around seven hundred to the alliance's five. As the professor rode her jetpack to the back of her army—with a shielding spell prepared in case the enemy threw projectiles—she scanned everyone and came to the conclusion that the Ice Peak had the advantage in power as well. They possessed slightly more E-Grades, and with slightly higher cultivations.

This would be an uphill battle. One they had to manage.

On the bright side, the alliance had a secret weapon. Out of the crowd of cultivators stepped Edgar, covered by a long, multicolored robe that fluttered in the breeze. His slick hair was drawn back, leaving his face and sharp eyes exposed. He was surrounded by an elemental aura that made the enemies shiver, while his Level was revealed to be at the peak of the E-Grade: Level 124. He'd spent most of the last few months in E-Grade dungeons to prepare for this moment.

"Give me space," Edgar said to the front line of his army, his words as steady as his magic. As he spread his arms, seven fireballs materialized around him, shining like stars ready to be unleashed.

The surrounding people took a few steps away, giving him space to work with. On the opposite side, a squad of over a dozen mid and late E-Grades stepped forth to face him. They were experienced warriors, yes—but Edgar was one of the strongest E-Grades on Earth, and his current Dao was perfectly suited for such a battle. Alexander aside, nobody in the Ice Peak could match him.

At the same time, inside a far-off submarine, two people were discussing calmly. One was a canine, lean and joyful with a goofy smile. The other was a woman with pale skin and blonde hair, wearing animal fur that only covered her privates, drawing the eye of the male sailors who operated the submarine. Nobody dared speak to her after they noticed her cultivation.

She was at the peak E-Grade. Both were, because this was Gan Salin and Nauja, and they were here specifically to kick ass.

"I have never seen such a weak planet before," Nauja said, poking her head out of the manhole to take a peep. "Are you sure these are your elites?"

"Mhm, my elites, yes. Because I'm totally from this planet," Salin replied. Ever so slowly, he put on his clawed gauntlets and smiled predatorily. "Wanna hear a secret?"

"No."

"After all the training Brock put us through, I look forward to tearing through these little guys."

"But I said no..."

"Come on, Nauja. We've lived together for almost a year now. You should know better."

She sighed. Then, drawing her bow, she pulled on the string. An arrow of wind materialized, trained right at the submarine walls. "I want to fight, too..."

"Hey, you heard the boss. Since you're not from Earth, you have to stay in here until Jack and the others arrive, or the overseer will have an excuse to violate the grace period and wipe us all out."

Nauja sighed again and lowered her bow, much to the relief of the submarine crewmembers. "Where the hell are they, anyway? Weren't they supposed to be here already?"

"I have no idea. Maybe something came up—you know, a running tap, a forgotten oven, stuff like that."

She glared at him.

"Anyway," he continued, flashing her a smile, "gotta go. Wish me luck."

"Kill them all," she said, still sad that she couldn't participate. Gan

Salin gave her a thumbs-up, then jumped out of the submarine and rushed to the forefront of the battle.

In both armies, every cultivator drew their weapon and summoned their powers. Salin even saw four brorillas flexing at each other and getting hyped, while a pack of gymonkeys pooped into a large bucket.

"Sorry, excuse me, coming through!"

Salin pushed through the crowd to reach the front of the army. Then, sensing the violence in the air, he grinned. The two armies were ready to cleave through each other. All they needed was the signal.

Before that came, two figures flew over from afar. Well, one figure flew over; the other was hanging from the first's feet. They landed on the ground before the Ice Peak army, who welcomed them with cheers.

"Shit," Salin said.

"Gan Salin, you traitor," Fesh Wui, the eagler scion, spoke with scorn. His wings were spread wide, and his chin was raised to the sky. "You would turn against the Animal Kingdom for what? Power? A woman?"

"I have no idea what you're talking about. I'm a pure-blooded native of Earth-387," Salin replied, continuously winking. Then, his voice grew serious. "But, Jack Rust treated me far better than the Animal Kingdom. If I had a hundred lives, I would spend them all fighting by his side. You guys are nothing more than fools dancing a never-ending waltz of grief, and I will never, ever return."

The eagler snorted. Next to him, the elef scion readied her magic—green specks flew around her raised arms.

Both scions were Level 124, at the peak of the E-Grade. Both possessed the Fourth Ring Conqueror title—they'd apparently also entered Trial Planet at some point. In theory, each were only slightly weaker than Gan Salin. He couldn't fight them alone.

Though he wasn't alone. Brother Tao, the one-armed, bald monk following the Dao of the Staff, arrived by his side. His other arm had been lost in the final battle of the Integration Tournament. And he'd still managed to reach Level 121.

"Let this little monk fight by your side, brother Gan," he said as his six monk companions, all over Level 100, walked into the alliance army.

"Hey, bro," Salin said. "I appreciate the offer, but are you sure you can take them? These guys are strong, and you're, uh, kinda unarmed."

Brother Tao smiled. "Either we win, or I die. What is there to fear?"

"Hmm. You know, that makes a lot of sense. Alright. Let's show them what you're made of."

Most of the crowd had retreated, and those who weren't were gathered at the docks, on the opposite side from where the two armies faced off.

Everyone tensed. At the signal, they would attack. Their fingers were twitching. They held their breath.

The professor didn't give the signal yet, and neither did the enemy commander. Even Vivi and Alexander were still facing off. However, on the central stage, Vanderdecken stood alone, surrounded by an empty venue and two armies. Feeling the tension, excitement overtook him, and he strung out a sharp, violent chord. "AND 'DANCE WITH THE DEVIL'!" he shouted.

The moment his tune resounded, their discipline collapsed. Both armies charged, and their wizards unleashed row upon row of all sorts of projectiles. Roars and shouts filled the sky.

And then, framed by Vanderdecken's battle music, the two armies collided.

CHAPTER EIGHTY-ONE
CONTINENTAL COMMANDER

Explosions resounded over the clang of swords and screams of the wounded, wreathed in the deadly beauty of colored missiles. The two armies merged, discipline giving way to chaos.

The professor was protected by a small group of E-Grades at the far back. Her eyes were closed, and her ears shut. Her senses were spread over the battlefield, watching from a hundred directions at once through the utility provided by her Class.

Continental Commander was an Elite Class. One of the best when it came to managing armies. It let her communicate with and observe through a number of assigned individuals, flooding her with a plethora of information that, if she could navigate, would heavily enhance the power of her army.

At times like this, her high Intelligence came in handy. She parsed through everything at an extremely fast pace and fired out instructions. It was the most demanding job she'd ever done, one she'd grown accustomed to.

This was the reason why she, Margaret Rust, was the fiercest army commander on Earth.

The Ice Peak had commanders of their own, but they were too late to join the game. None had a pure management class like the professor's. They needed three commanders to mimic a fraction of her power. On that front, she had them completely out-scaled.

However, the armies themselves weren't equal. The Ice Peak's projectiles covered the sky. The boots of their warriors thundered against the white stone. They were a flood of cultivators, swarming the alliance and attacking like a pack of rabid dogs. What they lacked in coordination they made up for with sheer firepower.

"To the left. Regroup. Step back in line. Don't overextend. Now, chase! Good, now return. Keep goi—no, to your right! They're flanking you!"

The professor's rapid-fire instructions controlled the battlefield. The alliance forces advanced and retreated like waves, incessantly pressuring the Ice Peak while resting themselves. She alone held a viewpoint of the entirety of the battle and the individual pockets clashing for supremacy.

Pugilists and other Physical fighters were leading the charge, roaring as they bulldozed through the enemy lines. The Forest of the Strong's natural resources were Physical-oriented, and that was mirrored by their cultivators—not to mention their adoration of Jack Rust. Their punches filled the sky, their swords rent the earth, their roars shook the heavens.

The brorillas, filled with righteous fury, joined the fray without hesitation, while the gymonkeys catapulted poop deep into the enemy ranks—they'd eaten Mexican food the previous night, and the results were better than anticipated.

The strongest wizards of Flame River soared to the sky, riding wings of flame. They worked together under the Professor's aid to unleash a mighty red river that washed over the Ice Peak. A group of pale-bodied men and women rushed to the front, raising their arms in one sharp motion to draw one massive ice wall out of the floor. The river crashed against the wall, releasing a large cloud of steam that blotted out the clouds. Unfortunately, the Ice Peak wizards were more, and the glacier held. The river flowed back down to threaten a few of the alliance cultivators at the front before it was extinguished.

However, this mighty river had only been a distraction, and the professor didn't hesitate to capitalize on it. As the ice wizards celebrated their defense, a contingent of E-Grade Physical cultivators and brorilla's penetrated their lines, swerving to attack from the side. A brorilla grabbed the head of one and smashed it into the ice wall, cracking it open like a watermelon. As the wizard's lifeless body fell to the floor, the brorilla beat his chest and roared with fury. It was Oz, the strongest brorilla after Harambe, who'd come to take revenge for his big bro.

Another brorilla leaped and punched a wizard's head so hard it exploded, while a human ducked under him and penetrated another's chest with his fist. Before he could celebrate his success, five ice spikes pierced his torso, killing him instantly. The brorillas and Physical cultivators kept going, following the professor's instructions to the letter. They slaughtered their way around the ice wall and emerged on the other side to rejoin the ranks of their own army, the foreign blood on their fists igniting the battle spirit of everyone else.

The army roared.

The professor spared a heartbeat to focus on the origin of metal music blasting over the battlefield, enhancing the violence and gore. Vanderdecken was giving the performance of his life, pouring his entire soul into his guitar. The sound was magical, magnetizing, entrancing, driving the cultivators into a battle fury that enhanced their power.

It pleased her to find that he wasn't neutral. His music's buffing effects were mostly directed to the alliance cultivators. The Ice Peak only heard an annoying cacophony that disrupted their concentration and wracked their nerves.

All the while, up in the sky, an ice bird and a fire phoenix repeatedly clashed. They disengaged and rushed back into each other, clawing and unleashing powers of destruction that rained from the sky, occasionally cleaving the armies below. Nobody dared interfere in their conflict—with very numbered exceptions, no one could.

The professor pulled away from the arial clash to somewhere else on the battlefield. A large group of alliance peak F-Grades pulled back on her order, inviting in a squad of Ice Peak early E-Grades. The moment these E-Grades pushed forward, the surrounding sides of the alliance army closed around them, burying them in the bodies of heroic peak F-Grades. The E-Grades were individually stronger, but there was a limit to how many enemies they could handle. They quickly turned into a collection of loose limbs.

The professor's command was far and wide, ensuring her people utilized their strength to the fullest. But even an all seeing eye could miss what was plainly in front of them. A group of hard-faced, Ice Peak assassins blended in. They wore attire that looked like the alliance's—boxing shorts and t-shirts—but were unaffiliated. Unfortunately, nobody inspected them during the heat of battle, allowing them to arrive behind the professor, pull out rifles, and start firing.

A large-bodied woman jumped before the professor. Her body shone with yellow earthly light. The bullets penetrated her skin and stopped there, but the assassins were still rushing in, revealing wicked knives with which they had extensive training. They were former special agents of the Russian secret services, from where most of the Ice Peak hailed.

The woman shouted for help, blocking one strike with her palm. A second found her in the thigh, and a third under the armpit, riddling her with holes. Blood spurted. The assassins pressed on. More of the professor's E-Grade guards arrived to fight them off. The assassins sacrificed each other to press their advantage. They didn't want to win—they just needed to kill the professor.

The professor didn't move. If she broke her concentration now, the army would suffer heavy losses. She had to trust her guards, who were fighting tooth and nail to keep her alive.

One assassin blew past, blending with the shadows to slip through two E-Grade guards at once. "No!" they both shouted.

His blade flashed true.

A steel star came out of nowhere to strike his wrist, sending the dagger off-course where it only grazed the professor's shoulder. She ground her teeth against the sting, not letting it break her focus.

An instant later, an old monk fell from above, crushing the assassin's head under his knee. Five more monks appeared, swiftly destroying the remaining assassins.

The assassins may have had extensive training, but how could they compare to the old martial masters?

"Go fight," the monk beside the professor said, glancing at the guards. "With us here, nobody will harm your leader."

"*Go,*" the professor's voice rang in their minds, and the guards, embarrassed by their failure, scampered away to join the front lines. The six monks formed a perimeter around the professor, keeping their eagle eyes glued on the action. They could catch arrows, block warriors, and redirect magic. No assassin would get past them.

"*Thank you,*" the professor told them.

"Don't worry," one of the old monks said, his thin mustache dancing with his lips. "You are our hope. These old monks will gladly lay down their lives to protect you. Just focus on victory."

Small victories like this were achieved across the battlefield, the numbers of both armies depleting at a rapid rate. It was an uphill battle. All the alliance could do was struggle to remain afloat and hope for a mistake on the enemy's part—or, even better, Jack's arrival.

Nobody had any idea why he was delaying, or why he wasn't answering their telepathy messages. Something must have gone horribly wrong. All they could do was hope.

Edgar proved to be one of the greatest reasons the alliance still held, allowing the professor to manage everything else beyond his powers reach. The wizard was leagues above everyone else on the battlefield, holding off a dozen late E-Grades of the Ice Peak by himself. As he spread his arms, flaming meteors rained down from the heavens. Blizzards erupted from his palms, freezing people to the bone, while his eyes shone like the sun, preventing anyone from looking directly at him.

Thanks to the devil, Etsin, his magical powers of awe and wonder had transformed into ones of pure destruction. He delegated death. Any projectiles thrown at him crashed against blue shields and dissipated, while anyone who got too close was met with crowds of sand devils rising from between the cracks in the white stone. Moreover, beams of bright light shot out from over his head, forcing multiple wizards to combine forces to stop him.

His current magical abilities resembled the ones he possessed at the F-Grade, just magnified. It wasn't the kind of power he could have had with his real Dao, but it was enough to steamroll the Ice Peak forces, single handedly making up for the gap in power between the two armies.

Of course, he took no joy in the destruction. It was the worst day of his life. Every life he took scraped against his soul. But this was why he'd joined the dark side, why he'd sold his soul to a devil. His friends needed him—and, no matter what, he would help.

Then all at once, his feelings of grief spiked out of proportion. The change was so abrupt that he stumbled, losing control of his arcane powers. An ice spike slipped through to slice at his forearm. He grimaced as blood poured out. The shock woke him up. A storm of arcane energy erupted from his body, pushing everyone away as his eyes scanned the enemy crowd, searching for the new attacker.

He found them. From deep within a brown cloak, a pair of purple eyes met his own, shining with light that wasn't human. The energy he'd unleashed hadn't even fazed this person. Realizing they'd been spotted, the attacker pulled back their hood, revealing fair skin and hair of sapphire. Edgar scanned her.

Saphira, Level 124
Faction: -

He didn't even bother with the fact that she wasn't human. The Animal Kingdom had broken the rules so many times. What was one more?

Edgar focused on her Dao. It was some form of Will attack, and it had reached far deeper into his psyche than any Will cultivator of the Ice Peak could manage.

This woman was strong.

"Leave him to me," she commanded. The Ice Peak cultivators glanced at her, but seeing her non-human features, they quickly realized she was on their side and scampered away.

"Stay right there!" Edgar shouted, releasing a hailstorm that enveloped them all, but another Will attack hit him like a truck, disrupting his concentration and dispelling the hail. The Ice Peak cultivators ran away.

Edgar gnashed his teeth. If he couldn't hold them down, they would slaughter his army, bringing them to an unbeatable disadvantage. Yet this woman was powerful enough to demand and receive his full attention. He could only try to defeat her as quickly as possible—and hope the professor could mitigate the damage until then.

"Who are you?" he roared, charging up a beam of light.

"My name is Vlossana." There was grief in those eyes, but also joy—and so much darkness. "And I am here to kill you."

CHAPTER EIGHTY-TWO
BATTLE OF PAWNS

THANKFULLY, VANDERDECKEN'S MUSIC STILL COVERED THE CONCERT VENUE, enhancing the alliance fighters. That included another important fighter, Edgar Allano.

Edgar stood on an empty patch of ground, surrounded by the battling armies. Nobody was willing to interfere in his fight.

"Vlossana..." he muttered, savoring the name. "Doesn't ring a bell. Why do you want to kill me?"

"Does it matter?"

"I would argue that it does."

She snorted. "Prepare yourself. Here I come."

Edgar was no fool. He could tell a crazy person when he saw one. He summoned his defenses, raising clouds of dust and various other elements, but her attack bypassed everything to strike directly at his heart.

His willpower shook. Grief and joy hit him at once, overwhelming him. He lost control of his emotions. They made no sense. Suddenly, he was amidst a laughing crowd, laughing alongside them. The joy was so intensely pure, it filled his heart like a warm balloon. He was happy, so happy he wanted to spread the feeling to others until the entire world was a place of love.

The scene changed. He was now on top of a hill, watching a burning estate underneath. The stench of charred flesh filled his nose. He gagged and puked, the feeling of grief even stronger than the disgust. He recognized neither this place nor the dead, but the emotions overwhelmed him completely. They were what the person who actually experienced this vision—the saphira girl called Vlossana—had felt at the time.

He could tell why she'd become unhinged. Deep in his soul, grief and pity intertwined. It pained him that anyone had to experience things like this.

He tried to summon his magic. His Dao shone within his chest, roaring with anger, but all it achieved was to amplify that sense of grief. The false Dao he currently employed was one of destruction—exactly the creator of such a scene.

"You are powerless," the woman's voice rang, walking out of an ash cloud. "I can sense your Dao. It makes me sick. Someone like you could never comprehend what I am going through, and even if you could, your Dao would shatter and leave you helpless. Just like my family was when the Animal Kingdom attacked them."

"I don't understand," Edgar said with tears in his eyes. "Why are you doing this? Why me? The Kingdom harmed you, but we are against the Kingdom!"

"You don't need to understand," she replied. "This isn't about you. It's just part of a deal I've made. For the power I need to exact revenge, you are the price. And besides..." Her mouth curved into an ugly sneer. "You will become a side casualty of my rise to power, just like my family was a side casualty of that man's actions."

"That man? Who?"

"I told you, you don't need to know!"

An ugly torrent of emotions lashed out at Edgar, spinning him high and low like a hurricane, rendering his magic useless.

"Break!" he shouted, releasing his Dao without any control. The scene around him cracked and shattered like a mirror, revealing the battlefield where he and the saphira still stared into each other's eyes. Not a second had passed in the real world. He saw the pain hiding deep within her eyes. And the resolve. His heart—his real Dao, the Dao of Magic, of wonder, and breathless, exciting discovery—cried for her.

Most importantly, he felt his own exhaustion. That uncontrolled explosion of magic had burned over a third of his total reserves. If he got trapped again, he would be in trouble.

Edgar looked away and galvanized his magic. The elements obeyed his will. Waters rose, fire burned, the earth shook, and the wind blew. Sand and dust circled him, while a tiny star of elemental convergence blossomed before his face, growing in power.

As the woman advanced on him, one step at a time, he felt like a child punching a wall. His powers were great but ineffective. The elements roared but were unable to approach her. His heart protested the command. Every doubt he'd ever harbored resurfaced, making him hate himself for even thinking to attack this pained woman instead of hugging her and whispering that everything would be okay.

At the same time, Edgar's mind filled with guilt over his own weakness. Everyone depended on him, and he couldn't bring himself to attack. This woman had found his weaknesses and grabbed them tight. It didn't matter if his Dao had changed. His heart had not. Faced with this devastated person, he just... couldn't. The storm of destruction in his Dao raged, unable to reach her, blocked by itself.

She kept approaching, menacing and cold. There was no mercy in those eyes. She would reach Edgar, kill him, and carry on her with her devastated life. Edgar's eyes filled with tears.

Jack could have attacked her. Vivi could have. Even the professor, Brock, Harambe, or Sparman. But he, Edgar, was the only one who couldn't. His empathy was too strong. His resolve too weak. He had sacrificed everything to help his friends, but when push came to shove, he remained just as useless as he always had been. His kindness was a crime.

And, hidden in the surrounding army, disguised as an E-Grade human, the echidna devil cackled to itself. "Hehehe. Go on, my pawn. Reap his soul for me and surrender yours at the same time. Fulfill the deal. Corrupt yourself. The moment he dies, both of your pure souls will be mine"—his eyes widened in ecstasy—"and I will recover to the C-Grade!"

Gan Salin tumbled over the ground, landing in a roll that sprang him to his feet. "Ouch! Man, hold your feathers."

"Shut up!"

Another row of feathers flew for him, each accelerated to resemble an arrow. Gan Salin dodged all of them, twisting his body in impossible directions. "I told you, you can't hit me!"

"And I told you to just die already!"

Fesh Wui, the eagler scion, flapped his wings over and over. Each flap conjured a storm of feathers made of wind, shooting forward at great speed. At the same time, gales pressed against Gan Salin from all sides, fruitlessly attempting to constrict his movement.

"How does it feel, Fesh?" Gan Salin roared over the wind. "I was weaker than you once, but I've caught up! You wasted every resource the Kingdom poured on you!"

The two of them danced a complex waltz of attacks. Salin was mostly defending, seeking an opening. He could have held his ground. Unfortunately, the eagler wasn't his only opponent. A green sphere appeared around him, enveloping him in throbbing pain that made his limbs stretch like they were trying to grow.

"Ugh!" he exclaimed, glaring at the elef scion. "I'll fucking get you!"

While Gan Salin was distracted by the sphere, Fesh Wui dove, sharp claws extended. Brother Tao flashed before him, swinging his staff upward to stop him. The two clashed, and Tao flew back. Salin used that split-second of delay to extricate himself from the green sphere, twisting reality to appear a few feet behind and dodge the eagler's claws.

Brother Tao rushed for the healer. The elef scion raised both hands, summoning a storm of green stars. Tao zigzagged between them, though the closer he got, the more difficult it became. One of the stars exploded on his only shoulder, sending him spinning away.

"Dammit!" he roared.

Brother Tao was one of the strongest cultivators on Earth, but he was still a ways off from the level of Edgar, Vivi, or Petrovic. Against the scions, he was more of an annoyance than a real opponent. Gan Salin was almost fighting by himself.

Still, Brother Tao gritted his teeth and jumped back into the fray. He would do his best or die trying.

Salin clashed against the eagler, swinging his arms around like windmills, his claws flashing in the sunlight. The eagler's own claws rained down, an uninterrupted series of attacks that forced Salin on the back foot. The wind jetted at him from random directions, ruining his balance, and any damage he inflicted on the eagler was immediately healed by the elef scion, who only used half her attention to push back Tao.

Salin gnashed his teeth. Reality warped around him, forcing one of the eagler's claws to miss as Salin drove a sharp fingertip into his wing. Feathers burst out. A large hole was left in the wing, rendering the eagler incapable of flight. Just fast, green energy showered him to repair the damage, and sharp claws came down on Salin's face, deeply grazing his cheek.

Gan Salin jumped back. He licked his lips, tasting blood. Foam dripped out of his mouth. He was hurt and tiring, while his opponent was no worse for wear. Fesh Wui threw his head back and unleashed a mighty caw.

This battle was heavily stacked against Gan Salin. The eagler and elef could each match him by themselves, let alone together, and though Brother Tao was trying, his power wasn't enough.

Dammit, Jack! he thought. Where the hell are you?

At this point, any other cultivator of the Dao of Insanity would have turned tail and ran. Gan Salin of a year ago included. However, things had changed since then. A new, warm light burned inside him, fueling him, and cementing his resolve.

There were people he needed to protect. He was fighting alongside his friends, none of whom would give up. Therefore, how could he?

Gan Salin possessed the Dao Root of Loyalty. For his companions, he would do the right thing or die trying. More foam emerged from his mouth, his eyes grew redder. With a howl to the sky, he charged again.

CHAPTER EIGHTY-THREE
STEALING THE SHOW

HIGH IN THE SKY ABOVE THE BATTLEFIELD, VIVI CLASHED AGAINST ALEXANDER Petrovic. Two wings of flame emerged from her back, shedding light and heat to the surrounding air, her eyes burning with fervor. Her red dress reflecting the light like it was on fire itself.

She spread her arms, conjuring flames that melding into each other to form a dancing snake. Waving her hands smoothly, the flames danced like a riverbank weaving unpredictably through the terrain toward Alexander.

Compared to her fluid power, his was rigid and austere. His ice wings flapped once with great power shooting his body forward. Twin swords crossed before his chest, and he snapped them at the river of fire.

Sparks flew like a rain of candles. The ice swords turned red, melting inch by inch even as his ice reinforced and replenished them, pushing through the flames.

One of Vivi's hands moved smoothly sideways, guiding what remained of the flames to brush against one of Alexander's swords and send it off-course, while her other hand snapped her whip at him. It wrapped around his second sword as if it possessed a life of its own, softening the swing. The flames, which had previously dispersed, now regrouped, using their momentum to turn around and attack Alexander again.

This was the nature of Vivi's powers. Small flames, each burning weakly but achieving great power when combined like the droplets of a river. A constant motion, twisting and reusing the same river over and again—a flame which ceaselessly danced. Hers was mastery over momentum and persistence, a fluid union of infinite tiny forces.

Alexander's power in contrast depended on powerful, singular attacks. There was no union or fluidity, only rigidness and sharpness. His every sword strike was a powerful swing from beginning to end, made with no consideration for retreat. After attacking, he needed a long time to recover, which was why he used two swords.

Alexander raised his sword to the sky. The cold air of the Pacific froze over his blade, turning into spikes of ice that rode the wind on a trajectory to Vivi. She crossed her wings. Each ice spike melted as it passed through, turning into harmless water and puffs of steam.

In the same movement, she'd summoned fire from her sides. Two streams flew at Alexander's wings. He let himself fall under them and rise back from below, twisting his swords like a maelstrom. Vivi brandished her blue fire whip, cracking it repeatedly and forcing him to keep his distance.

Their battle had been going on for some time now, and it seemed balanced. However, Vivi couldn't stop the drops of sweat from forming on her forehead. They weren't caused by heat, as she was immune, but by fear. And the reason for that, she absolutely couldn't let Alexander know.

Flames erupted in a geyser, the river growing larger, breaking from one snake into multiple that danced in concert with each other, uniting and separating. Each small stream was as wide as a person and could incinerate trees in a second.

At the same time, Alexander's ice could freeze over hell.

"Fine!" he shouted, laughing. "Let's go harder!"

Spreading his arms, the air itself froze around him. The flame rivers roared as they drilled into the ice, but it held strong. Alexander then moved his arms sharply, causing the ice to extend in sharp, fast, finger-wide columns that aimed to pierce Vivi. At that size, their freezing speed was extreme, and she barely managed to escape. Blood flowed from multiple scrapes on her body. They were quickly licked and healed by flames, but regeneration wasn't cheap.

"It's your choice, Vivi!" Alexander shouted. "Drag out the fight until your army loses, or go all-out and die first!"

Due to the nature of their powers, there was a caveat to this fight. If Vivi wanted to stay alive and waste Alexander's time, she could easily do so. She was much more slippery than him. However, if she wanted to defeat him, she would need to commit harder, which would give him an opening to strike back.

Unfortunately for Vivi, the battle below wasn't going well. An unknown person had appeared to block Edgar, their strongest fighter alongside herself, letting all his previous opponents join the fight against the alliance's main army. The professor was doing a stellar job holding on, but it was clear that, if nothing happened to push the tide, their army would soon be destroyed.

Vivi had to make the difference. With a scream to the sky, her flames intensified. The vague shape of a phoenix appeared around her, cladding her in soft green flames, and she dove into melee range.

"You can't beat me!" Alexander shouted. The ice of his wings extended over his limbs, coating and enhancing them. He was faster, stronger, and more durable than before, protected from the burns she could inflict. The two clashed head-to-head. Vivi's whip and phoenix claws dug at Alexander's armor, while his swords carved her flames, extinguishing them.

Vivi delivered an overhead strike. Alexander raised a sword to block, then used the other to stab at her legs. She pulled them up, but Alexander was there again, folding one of his wings to slash at her waist. Fear flashed in her eyes. She turned, completely abandoning her attack to defend, taking the hit squarely in the back and getting sent flying. Blood spurted out. The injury on her back healed, but her breath grew shorter.

She looked back at her opponent with calm eyes, but deep inside, she was terrified. *Did he notice?* she wondered. *Please, God, let him be an idiot.*

Alexander betrayed nothing. He charged, slashing his swords in rapid succession. Vivi used her flame-coated arms to defend once, twice, thrice. His boot kicked at her shin, then his wing came flying directly for her stomach, where the flames were densest. She could easily take this attack. She could let it land to strike back with one of her own—after all, she could heal, while Alexander could not.

Yet, she completely pulled back to defend. Both arms were crossed before her stomach, blocking Alexander's wing but giving him an opening to slash at her upper arm, the sword almost reaching the bone. Vivi screamed as she flew back. Alexander did not give chase—he started laughing.

"I knew it! The loose dress, the secrecy... Oh, it should have tipped me off. What a fool you are, Vivi. You went and got yourself pregnant before the deciding battle!"

He laughed with joy again, while Vivi's face paled from fear. She didn't even know what to say. He was right. The reason she protected her belly so intensely was because, inside it, there was a little baby growing.

"Tell me, whose it is?" Alexander asked. "And don't you dare lie, or I'll kill you both."

"Jack's," she replied in a low voice.

"Impossible! He left eleven months ago!"

"There are Dao drugs that can delay a pregnancy," she said, finding her strength again. "The baby is Jack's. I have been with no one else since. But you have seen his strength; he isn't even afraid of the Animal Kingdom. If you dare harm his child, he will find you and destroy you."

His smile turned crooked. "Is that a threat?"

"It is a fact."

"Your facts, my dear Vivi, are outdated. Jack Rust is hunted by an Ancestor of the Animal Kingdom. He can never set foot on Earth again. Even if he does, the Planetary Overseer will catch him long before he can reach me."

"What are you talking about?" Vivi said. "What do you mean?"

"I mean that I can do whatever the fuck I want—both to you and the little bastard inside you."

"You wouldn't dare. Even you can't be that wicked."

"I prefer the word *efficient*."

"Don't you dare, Alexander! Show some mercy! Don't attack the baby!"

"Hmph! You deliver me a weakness, and you expect me not to use it? Grow up, woman! This is the cultivation world! Strength rules all, and the only virtue is power!" Alexander laughed again, filled with bitterness, conjuring a hundred ice spikes in the air around him. "If you want to blame someone, blame yourself for spreading your legs."

Burning hatred rose up in Vivi's throat like bile. It was accompanied by freezing terror and dark despair. All those emotions culminated in her soul, where her Dao burned brightly, releasing wave after wave of scorching air. She turned into a burning oven. Even her hair caught fire. The wind around her felt like it came from the depths of hell, and her phoenix outline grew denser, almost solid.

"Die!" she screamed, unleashing a barrage of flames. There were hundreds of them, thousands. They combined into a river that splashed at Alexander, each drop enough to burn a normal human.

Alexander only laughed. His ice spikes shot forth, extinguishing an area of the flame river, letting him slither through. The river flowed around and chased him, but he was already at close quarters. His sword slashed at her belly. She grimaced and used both hands to defend, leaving nothing to chance. That resulted in his second strike cleaving at her shoulder, reaching the bone.

She screamed as she fell. Her wings flapped, righting her, then the whip reappeared and cracked toward him, snapping out ten times in the blink of an eye. She wanted to keep him at range at all costs, but if he was determined to approach, she couldn't really stop him. Not when he knew her weakness. A hail of ice spikes fell directly toward that which she desperately sought to protect, forcing her to dodge awkwardly. He was on her again, his face a cold, calculating mask.

She blocked the strike, only for an ice wing to graze her chest, drawing a thick line of blood.

Vivi grew desperate.

She hadn't planned on getting pregnant. She didn't think it would happen. By the time she found out, it was too late. She'd delayed it for as long as medically possible, as giving birth during the war would give Alexander a gigantic opening to strike at. Even now, the pregnancy wasn't advanced enough to hinder her battle power, but there was nothing she could do if someone deliberately struck her belly.

She felt helpless. This baby had come at the worst possible moment.

Now, her people desperately needed her to hold back Alexander. Would she fight while pregnant? Or would she, the warrior queen of the alliance, not appear in the final battle?

She had decided to appear, and this was the price. She couldn't let even the weakest of strikes reach her belly. Part of her Dao was even focused on protecting the baby from the temperature shifts.

She couldn't fight like that!

Alexander was relentless. He dove after her again and again, not giving her a moment to rest. His attacks came mercilessly, forcing her to defend excessively, then using those openings to strike everywhere else. He was exploiting her weakness and there was nothing she could do about it. She wanted to howl and scream in outrage. She was strong. She was a warrior queen. She was the leader of her people. Under normal circumstances, she could match Alexander—but not now, not like this!

She shouted in despair. As Alexander approached, she opened her mouth and charged up a large-scale attack, combusting the air so hard it turned into a bomb. A fiery ray built up inside her mouth, ready to be unleashed. She expected Alexander to meet this attack with his own—such a frontal collision was her only hope.

However, Alexander only laughed. He dove at her, completely exposing himself. If she kept going, she could hit him directly, possibly killing him on the spot, and the most she would receive in return was one sword attack. She would win the battle and maybe the war.

But his sword was stabbing directly at her belly.

Vivi interrupted her attack, causing it to explode in her mouth. Smoke wafted from her nose and lips. Her eyes shook. She ignored the damage to redirect all her Dao and attention to her arms, which shot out to block the blade. Her phoenix outline was pierced. The blade met her flame-coated skin and reached the bone, then the impact sent her flying downward, crashing hard into the concert's central stage.

Vanderdecken, who was still signing in the vicinity to enhance the alliance army, ran away, leaving them alone.

When the dust cleared, the entire battle, the entire world, saw

Alexander standing over a fallen Vivi, holding one of his swords at her neck. The onlookers gasped. The professor, who knew that Vivi was carrying her grandchild, felt her heart skip a beat.

"You are weak," Alexander said with disappointment. "You can always make more babies. You should have just sacrificed this one; now, all you achieved was the death of both of you."

Tears welled in Vivi's eyes, but she pushed them down. She was a warrior queen. She was strong. If this was her death, she would stare it in the eye.

"I despise you with every fiber of my being," she spat out, meaning every word. She raised her head, exposing her neck. "Go on. Take my life. But know that once Jack returns, you will be the first to die."

"He will never dare return. But so be it. Look at me, everyone," he shouted to both armies. Though they were still mid-battle, some turned to look. "Watch as I kill the enemy leader. This day marks the beginning of a new era—the era of the strong. The era of the Animal Kingdom and the Ice Peak. The era of Alexander Petrovic!"

His ice sword stabbed down.

Brown fur flew through the air. The wind whistled. The tip of a stone staff came out of nowhere and smashed hard into Alexander's nose, breaking it and sending him rolling across the central stage. Drops of blood were left behind where he crashed.

"Argh!" he shouted, looking up. "Who dares?"

Brock stood proud and tall. Vivi was safe behind him, her eyes still glazed over from expecting death. His staff remained extended, his entire body burning with barely contained, righteous fury. A pair of hard eyes were trained on Alexander.

Brock had never felt more determined to kill someone.

"I dare," he said. "You do not deserve to breathe. For Big Sis and Father... prepare to die."

CHAPTER EIGHTY-FOUR
HE ARRIVES

Across the battlefield, even the most heated of fights paused as people took in who had just arrived: a young brorilla, barely reaching a grown man's chest and carrying a stone staff that had just broken the nose of Alexander Petrovic.

Brock stood before Vivi, staring down the fallen form of Alexander. His gaze was cold and murderous. This man had humiliated his father, and Brock was here for revenge.

However, Brock's arrival meant much more than the addition of one more combatant to the alliance forces.

"Wait," someone said. "Isn't that... the brorilla of Jack Rust?"

"Could it mean that he's here!"

"Jack Rust is here?"

The clouds split above the battlefield, stifling the growing whispers, only for the Planetary Overseer to appear in all her glory, radiating majesty and undeniable supremacy. "Jack Rust is a wanted criminal of the Animal Kingdom. Capturing him supersedes the grace period. This brorilla will be apprehended and interrogated to help us trace his whereabouts."

"No need for that, Overseer."

A new voice filled the sky, echoing from horizon to horizon. It was calm yet resolute, carrying an indomitable intent. Everyone's hair raised and their spines tingled. They knew this voice. It was the voice that had challenged and killed Rufus Emberheart in the Integration Tournament. The voice that dared insult the Animal Kingdom in their own home. It was the voice of a superstar, a hero, a legend.

Space burst open a mile ahead of the overseer and a man walked out. His purple robes fluttered in the wind. His piercing eyes were clear. His hands were clasped behind his back, which stood ramrod straight, symbolizing his refusal to bow to tyrants. But everyone knew that those peacefully clasped hands could form into the planet's mightiest fists.

Jack Rust smiled slightly. "I am right here. If you wish to capture me, go ahead and try."

The entire Integration Starship shook. People cheered without even realizing it. The hero they'd been waiting for, their beacon of hope, had just arrived!

"Wait," someone in the alliance army said, "isn't he only at the D-Grade?"

As this question was uttered, they inspected Jack; though they couldn't see his Level, they could see he was only at the D-Grade. How could he challenge the C-Grade Planetary Overseer? Such a feat was impossible.

Did he have allies?

Yet, no matter where they looked, nobody saw any C-Grades backing up Jack Rust.

"So, you did show up," the Planetary Overseer said. "Is the Black Hole Church really willing to go to war for such a tiny planet?"

Jack raised his chin. "This is not a battle of the Church. This is the battle of Earth against the Animal Kingdom. It is freedom against the tyrants, justice against injustice. It is me versus you, Galicia Lonihor—and you are not prepared for what is about to happen."

She snorted. "You sure can run your mouth. Why are you even trying to lie about this? You're only a D-Grade. Nobody will believe you came here by yourself."

"And yet, it's true." Jack's smile was violent. This was the battle he'd trained for; the reason he'd pushed himself beyond his limits for a year and took all sorts of reckless risks. He was the galaxy's strongest D-Grade, or at least close, and he was here to go a step further.

He would challenge a C-Grade. A mid C-Grade, too.

"I swear on my Dao," he declared, raising his voice so everyone could hear, "that I will duel you alone. Nobody will interfere in our battle. As long as you don't touch the people below, then even if I die, the Black Hole Church will have nothing to say. That, I swear."

Though the sky was clear, thunder resounded. The sun shone brighter, the air tasted of crimson vinegar. Then, all was normal again, but Galicia's eyes couldn't hide her shock, as with everyone below.

"You swore on your Dao," she muttered in disbelief. "How can you not be lying? Do you really think that you, a measly D-Grade, can challenge me, a mid C-Grade elder of the Animal Kingdom?"

"I do, and I will."

She blinked a few times, trying to process what she was hearing. She looked around and spread her perception to the limit but sensed no other C-Grades. "You are a lunatic. This is absurd."

"The future will tell," Jack replied. "I know what you're thinking. The Church will not interfere, but they have already destroyed all teleporters on this planet. We are alone, Galicia. Even if this battle is broadcasted, nobody will show up to save you."

"Save me!" Her voice turned more angry than shocked. At this point, she believed him. He really had come here with the intention to challenge her.

But who was she? She was Galicia Lonihor, an established elder of a B-Grade faction! A mid C-Grade! Just the mere fact that she was challenged by a D-Grade was a blemish to her honor, an insult to her inherent supremacy. To make matters worse, she had to accept, too! There was no one else here who could capture Jack Rust.

"Shut your mouth!" she shouted with a snort. She reached out and made a grasping motion. "Come here!"

The entire world came alive. Everyone on the battlefield below lost control over their Dao, hearing it cry supremacy. Radiance shone from the sky above, and a massive hand of light appeared to close around

Jack Rust, capturing him in an instant. This hand alone was wider than the entire Integration Starship.

Space rumbled. The ambient Dao, that had been singing hymns to the Planetary Overseer, stumbled. Deep, primal violence filled the air, an unstoppable, righteous menace. Purple lightning crackled. Stars flickered into existence. A Dao Domain burst out of Jack Rust, sinking the entire world into the might of his power, and clashed directly against the hand of light.

The entire battlefield had been transported into the middle of a starry sky, where the Fist reigned supreme. The feeling was so lifelike that the F-Grades present really thought they had been teleported into space.

The only discordant note was the hand of light, which still tightened around Jack Rust. The very air resisted it, slowing it down. A purple meteor came from somewhere above and dove into the hand's grasp, followed by a titanic explosion.

People screamed and covered their ears. The shockwave rolled over the surface of the battlefield, forcing the cultivators to duck to avoid getting swept away. The far-off ships wobbled on the ocean surface, and waves spread in a circular pattern around the Integration Starship.

The golden hand burst into motes of light, revealing Jack Rust clad in purple. One of his fists was clenched and outstretched. His body was still, his smile faint, his gaze sharp. "I do possess the power to challenge you, Overseer," he said, retracting his domain before she could release hers—otherwise, that clash might create casualties.

Meanwhile, the overseer's face was a mask of anger. She'd tried to capture Jack Rust quickly to wipe away the insult of his challenge, but she failed! A peak D-Grade had stopped one of her moves!

So what if she had only used a small portion of her strength? She'd been blocked. Moreover, this was broadcast across the planet and soon—no doubt—across the entire galaxy!

Finally, she could understand the Warden's helplessness from when Jack Rust insulted him. This man was just unbelievable. What could she even say?

Her face was ugly as she snorted. "Fine. Your games can alleviate my boredom. Let's take this higher."

Jack smiled.

It was customary for D-Grades to fight in the sky, lest they ruin the terrain. Likewise, C-Grades fought in space outside planets, as some of them had the power to upturn entire continents.

Galicia Lonihor stepped through space and disappeared. Jack sensed her reappear eleven miles above, higher than the limit of Earth's atmosphere. He did not follow immediately—instead, he looked at the armies below.

He met the tearful eyes of Edgar and the professor—who'd stopped utilizing her powers when the battle ceased—the resolute stare of Brock, the immensely relieved gaze of Vivi. To his surprise, he saw Vlossana, too, though he had no time to ponder her existence here.

"Everyone," he said, "I will handle the Planetary Overseer, but the way of the Fist is not one of coddling. Defeat your enemies. Let us all achieve victory together. And I promise you, after this battle is over, we will be safe. Trust me, and fight like the warriors you are."

The alliance cultivators roared in cheers. Brock nodded. Edgar swallowed a lump in his throat, Vivi couldn't believe her eyes, and the professor immediately closed hers, diving back into her class. Her instructions spread to her soldiers again—and, as one, they charged at the Ice Peak, fueled by the presence of their hero.

The Ice Peak reared to meet them. They did not believe in Jack Rust defeating the Planetary Overseer. He would die, and they still had to finish off the alliance.

Jack Rust nodded as the battle restarted. He could not solve all the problems in the world—his job was to defeat the Planetary Overseer, and even that would demand every shred of power he had at his disposal. As for everything else... his people should be able to handle it.

"You, come with me," he muttered, reaching for one of the floating projection stones. It flew into his palm, and then he stepped through space and disappeared, reappearing eleven miles above to match the overseer.

"What is that?" she asked, sneering.

"Just a little show." He opened his hand and let the still-active projection stone fly out to a safe distance. "If I'm going to do the impossible, the world deserves to see it."

She snorted again. "Ridiculous. Tell me, Jack Rust, do you cultivate the Dao of Mockery? You are the most annoying man I have ever met."

Jack laughed. "I am far more than that," he replied, clenching his fists. His entire aura shifted into one of power—of a warrior. "I am a Fist. And I am here to kill you and claim Earth for myself."

At the same time, Jack reached into his mind and asked, "*Are you sure, Sage?*"

"*I'm absolutely positive,*" *a telepathic voice replied from somewhere far away.* "*Nobody will interfere no matter what. Go all out. Use everything you have. Just make sure to win, and we will handle the rest.*"

He grinned to himself. "*You know it.*"

On the center stage, Vivi stood, nodding to Brock. "Thank you. We can group up—"

"No," he cut her off. His voice was iron. "He is mine. Leave."

"Are you sure? He—"

"Mine. Leave."

Only now did Brock glance at her, and the steel in his eyes shook her to the core. She couldn't believe it. Was this really the baby monkey that had been throwing poop around during the Integration Tournament? He had been so cute back then, and now...

Now, he was a man. A brorilla.

"Fine. Good luck, Brock."

"Thanks."

She flew off to assist her army on the main battlefield, leaving the brorilla alone on the concert stage with Alexander Petrovic. Brock turned his eyes back at the ice-man and twisted his staff once. "Stand up," he said.

Alexander snorted, dusting himself off as he stood. "You are as delusional as your master, but so be it. You will be neither the first nor the last monkey I kill."

"Correct," Brock replied. "Because you never kill again. Come, and die."

In another corner of the battlefield, Gan Salin was suffering the combined assault of the eagler and elef scions. Bladed feathers flew around him, green spheres rained from the side. He did his best to dodge everything, but nicks and cuts opened on his limbs, and his bones groaned like they were about to grow outside of his body.

Brother Tao was also there, but his power wasn't enough to meaningfully help.

A flaming arrow fell from the sky, detonating on the ground between the two enemy scions, forcing them to jump away.

A woman landed next to Brother Tao. She was beautiful in a wild way, what with the fur garments covering her privates. Her blonde hair fluttered over her pale, muscular back, and the bow she wielded was half-drawn, a shimmering cyan arrow on its string.

"Piss off, weakling," Nauja said, unable to contain her excitement. "This is my battle now."

"Took you long enough," Salin said with a smile, to which she snorted.

"I didn't think you'd struggle so much against these idiots. Did our spars teach you nothing?"

Brother Tao was about to give a seething reply to this unprecedented interference by the barbarian woman. Upon seeing brother Salin knew her, he held his tongue. Besides, what could he say? He really was outclassed here. He would be much more useful elsewhere—and, with any luck, this scantily-clad barbarian woman would help the canine man prevail.

Where do they even find these people? he asked himself, running over to the main battlefield. On his way, he ran into another approaching man.

"Brother Kane!" he exclaimed, running side-by-side with the metal singer. "Are you joining as well?"

"What can I do? Those guys kicked me off the stage!" Vanderdecken replied. "I didn't even have time for my guitar solo!"

"I thought everything was a guitar solo."

"You thought wrong."

Tao laughed. He and Vanderdecken had maintained a friendly relationship since the tournament—they were on pretty good terms. "Are you ready to spread death, brother?" Tao asked as they approached the mass of warring cultivators.

"I was born ready," Vanderdecken replied with a smirk, placing his fingers on the guitar strings. "Oh, this is going to be so metal."

CHAPTER EIGHTY-FIVE
TWO VERSUS TWO

GAN SALIN KEPT HIS BODY LOW TO THE GROUND AS HE RAN. HE DANCED through a hail of green spheres and cut to the right, narrowly dodging a fast-falling feather. He then focused on the metal claw he wore and jutted it forward.

"FIVE STAR GRASP!"

The eagler struck back with a claw of his own. Nail met blade. Both fighters pressed on, pushing each other back.

"I got this!" Salin exclaimed in joy.

"You got nothing!" Fesh Wui retorted. "Die for me!"

He flapped his wings thrice. With each flap, a few sharp feathers targeted Salin like needles, while the wings quickly regrew new ones.

However, Gan Salin had seen this attack too many times already. He predicted the feather trajectories and curved reality to pass through them, appearing over the eagler's head. He smashed down. His gauntlet's blades, each half a foot long and wickedly sharp, aimed for the top of the eagler's head. He missed, barely scraping the skin as the opponent flew away.

Salin tsked. "Stop running!"

"I'm a bird, idiot! I can do whatever I want!"

Fesh Wui circled Salin from above, where the canine couldn't reach.

He no longer shot feathers, flapping his wing to produce hurricanes. They angled down to crash on Gan Salin. He shifted to dodge but the hurricanes followed—soon, there were four of them, carving through the white stone floor as they chased the canine.

"This is unfair!" he exclaimed. "I can't fly!"

"That's *your* problem! Wind Way!"

A gust of cyan wind was unleashed from the eagler's body, turning through the air to join the hurricanes. Salin was now running away from five attacks, one of which was partially invisible.

Salin warped reality to change his position to be above the eagler. Four more bodies appeared, each a mirror image of Salin approaching the opponent from different directions. Only one body was real but telling them apart wasn't easy.

The eagler cawed. A sphere of wind erupted from his body, slowing Salin and all his clones down. Fesh Wui folded his wings and fell like a bullet, spreading them again to regain his altitude a hundred feet away.

Gan Salin, now in a freefall, was targetless. He tsked as the hurricanes and cyan gust flew at him. Once again, he had to tug at his Dao hard to twist reality, reappearing on the ground.

"Shit," he muttered, panting. "I can't catch this guy. I'm stronger than him, but he's too fast!"

High in the sky, Fesh Wui laughed. More attacks descended on Gan Salin, forcing him to keep evading.

Close-by, Nauja summoned wind arrow after arrow at the elef. Ten of them flew out every second. Yet, the elef took them all. Green shields appeared around her, absorbing the impact and changing the arrow trajectories. These shields were slanted, too, needing minimal energy to redirect the blows.

"Dammit!" Nauja shouted with growing despair. "Just die already!"

She was stronger than the elef. Loosing arrows was much easier than redirecting them. In a protracted battle, she would win.

Unfortunately, the elef was only trying to buy time. The eagler was pressuring Gan Salin; things looked grim. However, if she went after the eagler, she would be leaving herself open to the elef's attacks.

It was infuriating, because both Nauja and Gan Salin were stronger than the opposing duo, and they were also more used to working together. It was just that the eagler was too fast for Gan Salin and could fly, while the elef's defensive strength was a terrible match-up for Nauja's strong but straight-forward arrows.

"Nauja!" Gan Salin shouted. "Careful!"

She turned to find him running straight toward her, with four hurricanes and a suspicious gust of wind in tow. "Wha—" She jumped away, letting the sharp winds pass her by. As she landed, a green aura pressed her down, and the eagler's sharp attacks all flew at her.

"Why did you run at me, idiot!" she shouted, pushing against the floor to run away. Needle-like feathers pierced into the white stone tiles around her, while the green aura made her feel nauseated and weak.

"I was in a bad match-up!" Salin shouted from somewhere far away. "Let's work together!"

She cursed, diving into a roll and finishing with her bow drawn. She pointed in the direction his shout came from, aimed better, and released. An arrow of wind crossed the sky directly at the eagler, who hastily spun around to dodge. Salin was next to him already, sending out a flurry of blows with the aid of four mirror image bodies. The eagler cawed and tried to defend. The ground cracked as the elef scion pointed her trunk at him and unleashed a reverse rain of green spheres, spreading them across the four bodies, all of which dispersed into thin air. None of them were real.

Gan Salin's triumphant cry resounded: "Behind you, idiot!"

He jumped on the elef's back, where she couldn't block him. He brandished his claws and cleaved ribbons of fat off her back. An explosion of life energy sent him flying, landing in a roll. The elef was panting and bleeding profusely, but at the end of the day, she was nine feet tall and just as wide, possessing the durability of a defensive peak E-Grade. His few short attacks were far from enough to take her down.

But they *could* enrage her.

The elef raised her trunk to the sky and trumpeted. Maybe she wasn't the strongest, maybe nobody bothered to remember her name, but she remained a proud scion of the Animal Kingdom!

The green aura on her body expanded to cover the ground. A sinking feeling overtook both Gan Salin and Nauja. They felt their bodies breaking down, their hearts struggling with every beat, their brains turning lazy. The ground drew at them, tempting them to fall to their knees and die, as though faced with an overwhelming threat. The elef had turned their very instincts against them. At the same time, the eagler rushed in like the wind.

Nauja gritted her teeth to keep herself upright, fighting the death urges to nock another arrow.

Gan Salin laughed and said, “Bitch please. I have no instincts. I’m insane!”

He stormed forward, meeting the eagler midair and exchanging a flurry of blows. He came out ahead. The eagler flew back, bleeding from wounds that the elef’s aura quickly healed. Gan Salin kept falling—right on the elef.

At least, he tried to. At the last moment, the elef changed her aura. The green Dao turned a vivid red. It became pain.

Nauja screamed. Her every muscle felt pierced by needles, and every tendon pulled until it tore. Her nocked arrow dispersed, and only the many years of muscle memory let her hold on to her bow. At the same time, Gan Salin screamed, his charge imbalanced. The elef slammed her trunk into him hard enough to send him flying into Nauja, dropping both to the ground.

Nauja tried to speak but was unable to. All she could do was gasp. The pain was too much.

The elef’s eyes were bloodshot. Her deep voice rumbled over the battlefield: “A healer benefits from extended battle, you fools. I have finally gathered enough injuries to activate my ultimate skill. All the pain you have inflicted on us... receive it tenfold.”

She was breathing heavily. Clearly, whatever skill this was took a lot out of her. Nauja strained to even properly observe the enemies. She had to be on guard, she was in a battle to the death, but it was just too difficult. Nothing could have prepared her for this.

Finally, utilizing every scrap of willpower she possessed, she managed to focus her eyesight. The elef and eagler both stood half a mile away. She didn’t know how they’d gotten that far—had she rolled back, or had they retreated? Empty crimson colored space stretched between them, though other battles took place far to their left and right. Gan Salin lay behind her.

"That's it!" the eagler cawed in excitement. "Hold them there, and I will finish them off!" He took to the sky, summoning a deep cyan sphere around him. Nauja also cultivated the Dao of Wind. She could feel him charging up a single, massive attack.

And she was powerless to oppose it. She couldn't move. The pain was overwhelming, the worst she'd ever endured. Her knuckles were white around her bow, and she suspected she couldn't let go if she wanted to. All she could do was wait for the attack to arrive and exterminate her.

Then came a light tapping sound. A foot entered her field of vision. Then another. Slowly, one tortured step at a time, Gan Salin walked before her and stood hunched, his entire body shaking. She couldn't see his face, but she was sure it was completely pale.

How is he walking with this pain? she asked herself, unable to form the words. How is he even standing?

"Hey, Nauja," Salin said. His voice was the most strained she'd ever heard. His pain was clear. It made her heart bleed. "I will protect you. Shoot them down, please. I cannot reach that far."

She tried to respond but, if she opened her mouth, only screams would emerge. He was asking an impossibility of her. She couldn't form wind arrows, let alone aim! Even if she could, there was no way she could finish them from this distance.

"I know it's hard," Salin continued, his voice a mix of pain and tenderness. "But you can do it. You have the Sun Piercing Arrow—it's so beautiful and strong. Focus and shoot it. Please."

I can't! she wanted to shout. *I can't!*

The Sun Piercing Arrow was a skill that took a lot of concentration to pull off. She still only had it at the first tier—she was a novice. There was no way to use it without absolute focus.

But he didn't know that. Though maybe he did, and he just didn't remember. He simply stood there, back hunched, legs shaking, shielding her from any attack that could come her way.

"Sit back down!" the elef roared, pointing her trunk at him and releasing a trio of green spheres.

Gan Salin ignored them. "I know you can't speak," he said softly. "That's okay. Just shoot. I believe in you."

Nauja watched with horror as the green spheres drilled into his body. He went still, then shivered. His skin tingled and swam as if the bone underneath was wiggling.

She'd been impacted by those spheres herself before, and remembered the disgust all too vividly. If it was coupled with this red aura, only a madman could take it. Gan Salin remained standing. He did not shout or scream. He simply waited, believing in her.

Tears threatened to well up in her eyes. *Run!* she wanted to scream. *Run!*

"Idiot!" the eagler shouted, still gathering energy to unleash his attack. "Sit down already!" He flapped his wings, shooting out a dozen needle-like feathers.

They took time to cross the half-mile distance. Salin certainly saw them coming. Yet, he did not move; if he did, the feathers would hit Nauja.

She watched as the dozen needles pierced his body, spurting out blood. He shook, refusing to fall, yet a terrible scream that broke her heart escaped him.

"Never!" Salin shouted, letting more of his insanity shine through.

No! Nauja realized. *It's not insanity. This is... He's fully conscious! It's pure willpower!* The tears in her eyes, which she'd desperately fought down before, resurfaced. This man was protecting her with his body. He believed in her.

And she couldn't shoot.

Idiot, she thought, letting the tears flow. Barbarians never cried, but she couldn't hold them back anymore. *Idiot. Just run. Leave me.*

But Salin remained, hurt but proud, shielding her over his own excruciating pain.

She didn't know what expression he wore, but it must have been terrifying. Her sharp eyesight noticed the eagler and elef exchange wary glances.

"Whatever!" the eagler shouted, charging up his attack even harder. It was now a large sphere housing dozens of sharp gusts, each blowing with enough force to uproot trees. "There is no way you can stand this too!"

"I can't," Salin replied, his voice so weak that even Nauja could barely hear him. "But I don't have to. She will save me."

Those words struck Nauja to her core and she screamed at the top of her lungs, forgoing her dignity in the hopes that he would understand and run, but even then, he did not budge.

"It's okay," was all he said. "I believe in you."

Why! she roared in her mind. *Why are you doing this?*

"Wanna know why?" he asked as if he'd read her thoughts then coughed up blood. "Once, I was insane. I still am. But now, I possess something greater—loyalty. Jack taught me that. Brock helped me realize it. I don't care about survival. With my friend behind my back, no matter how many attacks fly at me..." His blood-soaked, salty tears landed on the white stone floor as he shouted, "I WILL NEVER STEP AWAY!"

The eagler's wind sphere opened at the front. The trapped gusts crowded at the entrance and squeezed out, all launched at Gan Salin and Nauja with tremendous force, about to tear them to pieces. "Sack of Aeolus!" the eagler shouted.

Nauja was frozen. Time had almost stopped around her. The attack came painfully slowly, though she still couldn't move.

How? she asked herself. How can he do that?

It was excruciating pain piled on excruciating pain. It was the fear of death. Yet, he stood there, ignoring it all to protect her.

Maybe she couldn't shoot. But, faced with his burning resolve, how could she not try?

Let us die together, she thought with sweet bitterness, fighting against the pain to nock another arrow. She shakily tried to aim at the opponents from her hunched position. Every movement burned, yet she carried on, because how could a proud barbarian let her friend die before her?

She was Nauja. A barbarian from the Tri Lake tribe of Trial Planet. A cultivator following the Dao of Wind, who abandoned her home to travel the world. Even now, at death's doorstep, she did not regret that. She had met such wonderful people. Had seen such wonderful sights. She would rather die than stagnate—because she was wind.

Ever forward. Never looking back. The world was full of pain, tribulations, and resistance, but they only fueled her, making her stronger instead of spent. She danced through life with laughter, opening her palms wide and reaping what she could. Just like the wind.

Just like the Sun Piercing Arrow.

It was like her eyes opened for the first time. The Dao was there, beckoning her. She realized the truth, why the Sun Piercing Arrow refused to evolve beyond the first tier. Because it wasn't her skill. Not yet.

But it could be.

System notifications rang in her ears. The ecstasy of the Dao filled her completely, momentarily overtaking even the torturous pain. She fell into absolute concentration. Time ceased and everything became crystal clear. Her aim was true.

She pulled back her arrow and let it loose, gifting it with all her insights to carry.

The arrow left the bow—its home. It pierced forth, grinding against the air, enduring all the forces that pushed it down to make it weaker. It absorbed them to enhance itself, become stronger and wiser. It found joy in advancing. This was more than just an arrow; it had a soul of its own, an evergreen Dao, a fluttering mane of truth. The natural laws made it grow weaker with distance, but at the same time, it pulled the ambient Dao along, wearing it as a mantle of power. With every foot it traveled, it grew. Its power spiked out of proportion.

This lone arrow rammed into the eagler's winds and parted them like curtains, dispersing them in all directions. It carried on, the trajectory unchanged, its spent energy refueling from the vast reserves of the world itself. The eagler widened his eyes. The elef crossed her arms.

The arrow reached them both. It easily pierced into the elef's body and emerged from the other side, its mantle of wind razing her insides. It then exploded as it passed below the eagler, releasing a storm of power that echoed across the entire Integration Starship. The eagler was blown hundreds of feet into the air, then plummeted to the ground with the sound of breaking bones. The elef collapsed at roughly the same time, all her organs pierced.

The pain stopped. The red aura disappeared. The world calmed. Nauja felt more exhausted than she ever had before. She was completely spent, but also extremely joyous. She let herself slump to the ground, opening her arms as wide as her smile.

Gan Salin fell to the ground beside her, arms splayed wide. He was still bleeding from the feather wounds, but his regeneration could handle those.

"See?" he said with a grin that Nauja couldn't see, but she *knew* it was the stupid, confident kind. "I told you, you could do it."

"Fuck you," she muttered, unable to hold her smile.

"Promise?"

They both laughed. Though the battle still raged around them, they took this moment to rest—once they recovered a bit, they would help the main army.

In the battle of two warriors versus the two scions... Gan Salin and Nauja won!

CHAPTER EIGHTY-SIX

A SPECIAL KIND OF STRENGTH

EDGAR WAS LOST IN A SEA OF EMOTIONS. HIS HEAD TURNED TO THE LEFT AND right, his eyes shaking from the tension, but his opponent was nowhere to be found. All was visions, fragments of memories belonging to different people. There were parties, and a starry night, lovers and friends celebrating together—but he also faced death, pain, despair. The dichotomy was so intense it made his heart feel as if two horses were pulling it in opposite directions.

"Surrender," a bodiless voice reached his ears. "Give in. You cannot win."

"Never!" he shouted. Gritting his teeth, he once again unleashed an omnidirectional blast of magic, shattering the vision. He was in the middle of a battlefield, staring down the saphira girl who called herself Vlossana. Walls of fire surrounded them in all directions, the remains of his previous attacks, cutting them off from the wider battle.

With a growl, the elements bent to his will. Air shimmered and froze. Fire spread outward from his feet, following the floor to expand faster. With a tug of his will, the wind obeyed, blowing into Vlossana and forcing her to step back.

"It is futile," she said, as the fire climbed her boots, and the cold air froze her hair. "You cannot defeat me."

She raised a single finger. The magical energy contained inside it was staggering. The fire was doused by a river of grief. The ice evaporated to burning joy. Edgar roared, as did the elements he commanded, but none were able to touch Vlossana.

Step after step, she approached. Edgar summoned the mighty winds, but she raised a hand and stepped through them, treating them as a mere afterthought.

"Why do you resist?" she asked. "You know you cannot defeat me. Your Dao is weak, as is your heart, and all your titles are useless against my Will attacks."

"What do you expect me to do!" Edgar retorted.

"Die."

"Go to hell!"

Edgar brought his hands before his chest, squeezing them in as if compressing the very air. The remains of his summoned elements flew in from all directions. They gathered between his palms, converging into a single dot that shone with every color of the rainbow. It shimmered with pure, unadulterated power—an elemental convergence with the strength to blow up a village. The harder his palms pushed down, the stronger this point of power grew, until its glow eclipsed even the flames surrounding them.

Vlossana stepped forth fearlessly. Invisible tendrils of her power spread through the Dao to reach Edgar. He sensed but ignored them—he couldn't push them back, anyway. They dug into his ears, his nose, his eyes. Edgar suppressed his disgust of this foreign Dao to finish conjuring his attack, the elemental convergence. Then, right before the tendrils reached his brain, he shouted and sent it out.

It would evaporate the enemy.

To Edgar, the battlefield around them disappeared, leaving only himself, the enemy, and his slowly traveling elemental convergence. Everything else was pitch-black.

In the next moment, the darkness receded, and Edgar was inside her mind. Her thoughts were outside his reach, but her emotions weren't. Her heart wasn't. She hid nothing. Edgar had no choice but to experience the full spectrum of emotions churning inside her. He tasted the darkness and found it bitter, like chocolate that had long expired.

Tears welled into his eyes. How could anyone resist? How could the girl opposite him not break?

Vlossana projected her mind into his own. He felt the boundless joy that once filled her heart be shattered and replaced by bottomless grief. The Dao amplified everything, dooming her to experience the greatest fall possible in a human heart, sinking from the heights of heaven to the depths of hell.

And the effects of that were all too clear. Vlossana's strength hid inside her own heart—she wasn't afraid to bare herself for victory. She showed Edgar her broken mind, her shattered spirit, the festering remains of who she used to be. She hated herself, despised the world, and desperately sought to externalize her pain.

She no longer possessed free will. She was so broken that any path she saw, she followed. Revenge was not her wish—it was all she could do. Her heart was swimming in bitterness. The world around her was full of hatred and injustice. Revenge was simply the path of inflicting maximum pain, and what else could she do against such an ugly world?

How was she unforgivable?

All these thoughts slammed into Edgar's mind, amplified by his own empathy. He felt for her. Understood, even if he didn't approve. Her pain became his, and his heart was filled with infinite pity.

The elemental convergence winked out, robbed of his Dao's support. He couldn't attack her. As much as he knew he should, as much as he absolutely had to, he just couldn't do it. His pity for her, his heart of hearts, and his love for her as a person to another warred against responsibility, and the former came out winning.

At the end of the Dao, her Dao was stronger than his fake one, as was her resolve. There was nothing he could do. He deserved what was coming, for he was weak.

Vlossana's smile was ugly, satisfied that her heart was broken enough to crack him. "Give up," she said, raising a hand that shone with dark light. "Let your heart be taken."

Edgar met her eyes and fell to his knees. He'd never been one to hide his tears—now, they flowed like twin rivers down his cheeks. Every drop carried a tiny bit of pain, but no matter how much he poured out, it was never enough.

"Pathetic," Vlossana said with a frown. "You are a man. A cultivator. How can you cry?"

She was so wrong he didn't even know where to begin. All he could do was cry, not for himself, not for his friends, but for her and her ruined heart. For the horrid world that birthed her.

She came within a step of Edgar. "Everything about you is weak, even your Dao. How did someone like you stand beside Jack Rust?"

"I was strong once," Edgar muttered between his sobs. "Back when I didn't know myself. The weakness you see is recent."

She sneered. "A sheep in lion's clothing."

"Can you spare my friends?" he begged.

"I couldn't care less about your war. I am only here to kill you."

"But why?"

"You don't need to know."

Her eyes were cold and heartless. Her hand dove for his chest, about to rip out his heart, and that moment stilled to a snapshot. It was only an illusion, of course. A biological response. All it allowed him to do was regret his life more extensively before the end.

I should have never gone to the tournament, he told himself. *I'm too weak. Too kind. My power would have better served another, someone who could rise to the occasion and help the entire world.*

Am I selfish for choosing myself over the others? Yes... Yes, I am. I never should have taken up the responsibility. I never should have promised to help, and given my soul to the devil. Heh. The greatest price, paid for a power I couldn't wield.

Edgar couldn't contain his self-loathing. He'd always expected his life to end at one of the devil's cruel tricks, a neglected consequence of the contract terms.

Yet, real devils were nothing like folklore. The contracts weren't fake. There was no fine print. He had exchanged his soul for power—for a shell of a different Dao over his own—and that's exactly what he received. If not for this woman's arrival, he could have helped in the war. He already had, to an extent, but it was nothing compared to what he could have done.

I can't believe he never tried to screw me over, Edgar thought with a chuckle. *What an odd world we live in... Enjoy my soul, you fair fiend.*

Unless... you were the one who sent her... Though I guess it doesn't matter, does it?

He didn't *want* to surrender his eternal soul, but there was nothing to be done. The deal was made. Even if he removed the fake Dao shell around his Dao, which he could do, it would change nothing. He would just die an even more pathetic death.

My Dao... he thought with longing. More tears came to his eyes—tears of betrayal, tears for himself. *I'm sorry, my Dao. I'm sorry, my soul. I forsook you, and it changed nothing. I'm sorry.*

In the final moment, rid of any more responsibilities, Edgar experienced the truth of his Dao a final time. He remembered how much he loved it—that awe and wonder, that sense of beauty, that breathless *wow*. What he wouldn't give to spend his life spreading it.

Too bad the world was cruel.

One final breath, he thought to himself with a sweet smile. One last look. I cannot win, anyway.

With a gentle tug of his will, he ripped away the shell covering his Dao, exposing the radiant beauty underneath. It was breathtaking—a golden, soft globe of light. A long crack stretched down its middle, the price of ripping away the devil's shell. He would never be able to advance again, but it didn't matter; he would die within the next second.

Edgar had no desire to change his fate. He deserved it. All he wanted was to die while embracing this beautiful light he once abandoned. The light that suffered unjustly, just like the saphira woman killing him.

He let himself go.

Yet, the seconds stretched, and his death did not come. No hand pierced his chest, no wicked fingers seized his heart. Surprised, he opened his eyes to find the saphira with her hand extended mid-motion, her gaze filled with wariness.

"What did you do?" she asked with growing fury. "How did you stab my heart!"

Edgar had no idea what she was talking about. Her chest seemed fine. No blood or blade. Nothing had stabbed through her heart. She was completely alive.

What had given her pause?

Edgar took a deep breath—and, as he did, the beauty inside him seeped out. His love escaped, just a tiny bit, coloring the world around him a brilliant gold.

Vlossana hissed as she retreated. "You had another power! You hid it all along! Damn you!"

He remained confused. He did possess a different power now, yes, but it was weak. It wasn't even meant for battle. The power it could exude was minimal, and his inability to harm her remained.

Why had she recoiled?

"DIE!"

Vlossana grew frantic. Invisible tendrils of power filled the air, seeking to enthrall his mind and snuff it out. She could absolutely do it—he'd sensed her power. She didn't need to touch him to kill him.

Yet, as the tendrils approached, they dissipated. Like snow in the sun, they melted away, their emotional structure broken by Edgar's aura.

His eyes widened in realization. His pity for her shone brighter than ever, as did his love. His tenderness. He grabbed a tendril before it could melt, sending his mind into it, into hers. There was an ocean of darkness within her. Despair and pain. It rushed at him from all directions, seeking to engulf him, and he let it.

He drowned in her sorrow.

One moment stretched to infinity. His heart bled alongside hers for this cruel world. Yet, he had another Dao to support him now—his real one. A Dao directly related to the beauty of the world, the kindness that this pained soul no longer dared believe in.

A scream resounded in the world outside, and Edgar let it wash over him.

"GET OUT!" she screamed. "GET OUT OF MY HEART!"

But she couldn't force him. She'd invited him in—and now, in the battlefield of her heart, she could only face him with truth and emotions.

In the depths of Vlossana's heart, her pain was a raging river, a stormy sea. Yet, Edgar floated in its midst unblemished, untouched by the dark waters. His eyes exuded a kindness that surrounded him, a shining beacon in the darkness.

Sorrow came after Edgar in waves, burying him in the darkest emotions known to man. Vlossana's darkness tried to corrupt his heart, to extinguish his hope and make him accept her view of the world—that it was hopeless, ugly, and in vain.

Yet his own heart stood strong. It was in its element now. Faced with her pain, his magic flared. A soft light spread, pushing back the shadows.

Yes, the world could be terrible and cruel. But it could also be warm and beautiful. All the monsters hiding under the surface of the dark water screamed. Edgar raised his hands. Beauty and wonder shone in Vlossana's inner world, contesting the despair. A golden star appeared over a vast ocean, tiny but resilient. No matter how many waves fell on it, no matter how the ocean raged, the darkness was burned away. This little star, no matter how damaged it became, could not be extinguished.

Because it represented hope.

The ocean growled as it receded. Edgar's power was lessened, too, but it did not matter. Because, hidden under the vanishing tide, a little saphira girl was revealed. A girl with her eyes wide open in fear, clutching her own little dress, covered head to toe in darkness.

Edgar smiled at her. He spread his arms again, and all the magic of the world came pouring out, all the beauty, wonder, and warmth. In their absolute truth, he directly refuted her Dao.

Edgar felt a cold hand plunge into his chest. This wasn't in the soul world, but in the real one. Vlossana's hand was buried into the center of his chest, stabbing him. And he hugged her, pulling her close, inviting her hand deeper. She froze.

His hand caressed her hair. "It's alright," he whispered. "It's all going to be alright."

The little girl reached out for the dancing lights, too afraid to believe. His hand appeared through them. It was waiting; and his smile was the most radiant thing she'd ever seen.

"I know it can be hard," he told her, grinning from ear to ear. "Loss is painful, and recovering takes time, but hope never dies. It shouldn't! The world is bright, colorful, wonderful. It is beautiful, and it's waiting for us to explore, as long as you just believe. So, what do you say? Are you coming?"

Lightly, hesitantly, the little girl touched her hand to his, letting his light wash away the darkness. The ocean and all its monsters screamed as they burned, evaporating in dark smoke. Her Dao was revealed underneath, a warm smile crossed by lines of darkness. These were two forces at an equilibrium—but, with Edgar's help, the light advanced by just an inch. The darkness remained, but it was now only a part of her Dao, not its master.

Vlossana cried, shedding black tears that mixed with Edgar's blood. She cried and cried, letting it all out while he gently caressed her hair and held her in a tight hug, shielding her from the world.

And the void blanketing them receded. The battlefield returned, and Vlossana was no longer an assassin, but just a girl with a broken heart. It wouldn't pass overnight. Maybe not ever. But the darkness no longer consumed her—the first step on a long road had been taken.

If Jack were here, he could have maybe killed Vlossana. So could Brock, or Vivi, or anyone else. But it was only Edgar, this tender, pained man who was unable to fight her, that could save her.

The belief was cemented in Vlossana's soul that she couldn't kill Edgar. In that moment, her deal with the devil was broken. The power she'd been granted receded, disappearing into nothingness, absorbed by the ambient Dao. The shackles on her soul were lifted.

Just like Edgar, she would never be able to advance again, but that was the extent of her backlash.

Because she wasn't the one who broke the deal.

When the devil offered her the contract, he'd claimed that her power would be enough to defeat her target—Edgar. But it wasn't. She had failed. And, in doing so, the devil's word was proven false.

In another part of the battlefield, very close-by, one soldier suddenly fell to his knees, vomiting black blood. The surrounding cultivators rushed to his aid, but he ignored them all. "Impossible," he muttered. "How? The power I gave him wasn't enough. How!"

Because how could a devil understand the warmth of human emotions? He never thought Edgar would remove his shell, because why would he? He would achieve nothing except die faster. In the devil's mind, Edgar's original Dao was laughable and would never appear again, so he never bothered to calculate its strength.

And thus, at the end of the day, it was Edgar's tender heart that foiled the devil.

But devils couldn't break their word. Etsin the devil felt his limbs grow weak, his body attracting the attention of something far greater than himself. "No," he growled, jumping to his feet. "No! Not again!"

He assumed his real form and flew away, breaking the sound barrier while completely ignoring the reactions of everyone around him. Dark clouds gathered in the sky, and lightning thundered. "NO!" Etsin roared, dashing over the sea in hopes that he could escape the clouds.

But how could one outrun a tribulation?

Lightning cracked down, again and again. His flesh was burned, and his soul seared. His screams echoed hopelessly over the entire battlefield. Before long, the lightning stopped, the clouds dispersed, and all that remained of the devil was a handful of ash floating in the ocean waters.

All battles momentarily paused. The remaining cultivators had no idea what happened or how it would affect them. Therefore, as soon as the clouds dispersed, they resumed killing each other.

As for Edgar, the devil's smiting destroyed the chains on his soul. The contract was broken. He was free—though unable to ever progress again, his soul remained his and his alone.

It's something, he thought as his vision went red with blood. He still held Vlossana in a tight embrace, and she was still crying, not realizing that her fingers had already clenched and ruined his heart. It was no longer beating. Only Edgar's Dao kept him alive, and even that would falter very soon.

Even the greatest of healers couldn't save him now.

It's okay, he thought warmly, clutching Vlossana tighter. At least I achieved something. I saved one person. Heh. What a life.

Slowly, his arms sagged, and his grasp weakened. Vlossana realized nothing as Edgar died in her arms.

Except—he didn't. Space cracked open before them. Vlossana saw nothing, so engrossed she was in her crying, but Edgar's dying eyes spied a smiling man who looked like he was homeless. He wore a dirty jacket and tattered pants, and his teeth were crooked and yellow.

His hand shone a green so bright it momentarily overwhelmed the sun. Edgar felt nothing but an impossible amount of life filling him to the brim, a veritable ocean of energy. His heart regenerated in the blink of an eye, and Edgar was left stunned and alive, still clutching Vlossana in his arms.

"Well done, but you cannot rest yet," the Sage said. "You still have a role to play. And now, if you'll excuse me—I have a show to run."

Edgar could only watch, speechless, as the Sage once again split space and disappeared. He was left completely spent, with a crying woman in his embrace amidst a battlefield. Only now did the shock get to him.

"What the hell just happened?"

In the battle of Edgar versus Vlossana and the devil... Edgar won!

CHAPTER EIGHTY-SEVEN
BROCK VS. PETROVIC

Brock stood on the concert stage, eyes glued on his opponent: Alexander Petrovic. The man who had tortured and humiliated his father, killed three brorilla brothers, and harmed many of his friends.

Brock hated this man with every fiber of his being. Today, he was here to kill.

Alexander did not seem to notice the bloodthirst emitted by the brorilla. "You know, it's impressive that you grew this much in such a short period of time," he said. "It would be a waste to kill you. How about you abandon Jack Rust and join my faction? We can give you all the bananas you'd ever want."

Brock growled. "No." The tip of his stone staff still dripped with the blood of Alexander's broken nose. His eyes were hard and unmoving, while his muscles were lax and ready to clench. He started circling Alexander, like a wild animal looking to pounce—but with the skills and composure of a martial artist.

Something about his visage must have finally gotten to Alexander. He cradled his bleeding nose, sneering at the stain on his hand. He lowered his center of gravity and unfolded his ice wings. With great purpose, he crossed his twin swords before his chest. "Fine. Then, let me put you down like the animal you are."

Brock pounced. His Staff of Stone crossed the air, meeting the swords with a clash. They ricocheted, each swinging back into an attack. Stone met ice. Cracking sounds filled the stage.

Brock simultaneously employed his Big Thoughts of Density, the Staff, and Never Stopping. That staff was a maelstrom, moving far faster than it was supposed to, and always at the right place.

He hadn't been playing around on the outer planet. He'd become strong. And now, at his first battle on Big Bro's side, he would prove himself worthy.

Alexander's swords moved in harmony, each striking hard and giving way to the other. His wings flapped, taking him around the stage faster than his legs could accomplish, trying to trick and outmaneuver Brock. The two of them fell into a sharp, brutal melee with no clear victor.

In the battle below the stage, many people snuck glances. "Is that a monkey?" said a woman from the Ice Peak army.

"That's Brock!" exclaimed a man who had been with the Brotherhood since the start. "How did he get so strong?"

Even Vivi, who was busy facing ten E-Grades at once, felt a wave of emotion at the brorilla's strength.

Brock rushed ever forward. His staff accelerated, both ends used as different weapons, pelting Alexander from all directions.

The man took a step back. "Stop!" he shouted, crossing his swords, and unleashing a barrage of ice spikes. Brock dodged them all. In one clean motion, his staff slipped through the opponent's guard and cracked down on Alexander's ribs, making him grimace. As he stepped back, Brock remained in position, staff extended and gaze hard.

Alexander was strong, but Brock had trained with the best E-Grades of the Exploding Sun. He'd developed four Big Thoughts—Muscles, Staff, Density, and Never Stopping—and reached the peak. He was no easy opponent.

"Have it your way!" Alexander roared. Ice shimmered in the air around him like dots of glistening light. The ground itself froze under Brock's feet, encasing even his soles in ice, while sharp winds whipped his face.

Brock snorted, breaking his feet free of the ice, but Alexander was already rushing in. The ice swords came down. They formed a continuous chain of attacks, forcing Brock to constantly defend. He held his ground but couldn't fight back. At the same time, ribbons of ice extended from Alexander's wings, snapping through the air to clip at Brock's fur. Spots of blood appeared. It was burning hot.

Brock's rage clouded his vision. This man was his sworn enemy; how could he be pushed down?

With a roar, Brock spun his staff around, chasing the swords. He blocked one strike with his palm, increasing its density to the max, then swept away both swords to kick at Alexander's shin. The man bent over, his leg almost broken. Brock pressed on, bringing his staff down in an overhead swing that Alexander was forced to block, his wrists creaking under the impact.

Brock lunged to bite at the opponent's neck. Alexander barely pulled back, dropping his guard and letting the staff clip his shoulder—Brock's sharp teeth would have done much worse.

Alexander then flew up, escaping Brock's reach. "You're an animal! Fine! Let's see if you can use those teeth of yours to fly!"

He then rose to the altitude of a hundred feet, summoned several rows of ice projectiles, and sent them flying down at Brock. The surrounding soldiers gasped.

Brock looked on calmly. Facing a rain of projectiles, he raised his staff and started swinging. It blurred through the air. Its trajectory was precise. Every single projectile was knocked away, a feat of ultimate focus. Brock could sweep away the rain!

As the projectiles came to an end, Alexander snorted. "Defend all you want, monkey, but you'll fall eventually. You can never hope to reach me from down there."

He prepared more ice spikes, arranging them in a denser cluster. Meanwhile, Brock looked up and snorted. "Bro," he said. He pointed his staff upward and began to fly.

At the appropriate level of mastery, the Dao of Density could make him lighter than air itself, letting him mimic flight. His Staff of Stone, an item attuned to precisely the Dao of Density, could also be affected similarly.

Both Alexander Petrovic and the surrounding armies gaped. In their eyes, they just saw a monkey take off and fly. It wasn't even an immortal.

"How!" Alexander shouted, unleashing his half-made storm of ice spikes.

Brock snorted again. "You no escape." He charged through the air, staff pointing forward. Brock swerved away from the ice spikes, dodging them all. He was upon Alexander, smashing his staff down. Alexander raised his swords to defend.

The Dao of Muscles flared. Brock's biceps doubled in size, then tripled until they became almost comically large. The density of both his muscles and the staff spiked. The tip of the staff easily broke through Alexander's guard to smash onto his head, nailing him to the ground in a shower of white stone flakes.

When the dust cleared, Alexander was already standing. His blond hair fluttered in the wind, while his blue eyes were colder than eternal glaciers. He was outraged.

But so was Brock. When the two crossed eyes, one was furious for having been publicly smacked down, and the other was furious for having his father humiliated. It wasn't even a contest. Brock overflowed with the desire to harm and kill Alexander. There was no force in the world that could change his mind.

Alexander raised his twin swords, and as their color bled out to pure white, he willed their shape to change. They became longer and even more wickedly sharp. Their tips were so thin they were barely visible, and so hard they could stab through iron. Even Alexander's wings changed. From a hard blue, they transitioned into pure white, emitting a majesty they lacked before.

"This is my Dao Ice," Alexander declared calmly. "I have purified it in my soul for half a year. Its power is beyond anything you can imagine. I commend you for making me bring this out, but now, playtime is over. It is time to die."

Where his swords touched the air, ice flakes were created that fell to the ground. Every flap of his wings sent chills across the entire concert stage. It was clear that the temperature of this ice was far lower than normal.

Brock's stare remained equally hard. He raised his staff. "Bring it on," he said, diving down.

The professor had been fighting a losing battle. She'd utilized every trick in the book to delay, hoping for the miracle called Jack Rust. Thanks to her, the alliance cultivators could achieve far better coordination than their opponents, but it wasn't enough. The power disparity was too wide. All she could do was struggle to stay afloat.

Then, Brock had arrived, sweeping in from afar to strike Alexander. He had declared that battle his own and released Vivi to join the professor and lead the army from the front—as much as the professor worried about her grandchild, it had to be done.

Now, fighting back was possible.

"*Disengage. Advance. To the right, then retreat and merge with the group to your left. Someone will have your flank. Charge!*"

She watched the battle from a hundred viewpoints, sending instructions to every squad commander in real time. They had been thoroughly trained—they followed her every command to the letter, not hesitating in the slightest. This meant they could achieve maximum efficiency. It also meant that, if the professor made a single mistake, nobody would be there to catch it.

But who was she? She was Margaret Rust, professor of Informatics at the Northeastern University, the vice-leader of the second or third greatest faction on Earth, and the mother of the planet's greatest living hero.

She could do this.

She hoped.

Vivi dove from the skies, clad in flames and phoenix wings. She opened her mouth wide and sprayed fire on the enemy's back ranks, eliciting a chorus of screams. The flames soon went out, but they had done their job—many of the enemy spell-slingers had fallen, giving them superiority in that field.

At the same time, whoever remained alive launched every projectile they had at Vivi, who erupted with flames so intense that the ice melted, as did the arrows. Only a few boulders and other projectiles made it through, though the power they carried wasn't enough to kill her.

She flew away to join the alliance front lines, spreading her wings over her soldiers and shouting, "Brothers and sisters! Alexander is occupied, and I am here! Let us destroy the enemy. For freedom!"

"FOR FREEDOM!" the entire army roared behind her, shaking the Integration Starship and causing waves in the surrounding ocean. They charged with fervor, following the professor's precise instructions. Vivi was a force of nature. She could handle a dozen E-Grades at once, plowing through the battlefield like it was nothing. Where she passed, enemies burned.

The Ice Peak sent their strongest E-Grades to chase her, and they knew her weakness now. Arrows of ice flew at her belly, forcing her to defend. Once again, she was pushed back, but the job was done. The enemy's morale dropped, while the alliance's rose.

In large-scale battles, morale was everything.

"*Advance!*" the professor gave the order. The alliance cultivators roared and ran forward, feeling like the kings of the world. Though they remained at a disadvantage, strictly speaking, none of the soldiers saw it as such. Especially not when the Ice Peak slowly retreated.

At that time, the flame walls erected on one corner of the battlefield dropped. The professor spied through a soldier's eyes. To her surprise, she found Edgar hugging the crying saphira enemy. Then, she noticed he was bleeding profusely. *No!*

As she watched his body sag, the Sage appeared, healed him, and disappeared again.

"*Help us!*" she told him, using a generous amount of power to reach him through telepathy, but his reply was disheartening.

"*Sorry, I have to run!*" *he responded.* "*But good luck! You can do this!*"

The professor cursed under her breath. The addition of a D-Grade to their forces would have been massive. Except, from what she saw, Edgar was completely spent. He would need some time before he could fight again.

However, she was the commander. There was no time to cry over spilled milk. She returned her attention to the army, commanding them in a way that both maximized their efficiency and perpetuated the image of victory that Vivi had created.

Suddenly, the metal music that had been enhancing their soldiers at the start of the battle returned. Vanderdecken was at the alliance's back lines, screaming at the top of his lungs to empower everyone, while Brother Tao broke into the enemy's front line like a racing horse. Even with only one arm, his staff was too heavy for most enemies.

Gan Salin and the barbarian girl had also won their battle, but they were too spent to further contribute. Like Edgar, they would need time.

Still, the professor finally felt optimistic. With Vivi, Vanderdecken, and Tao onboard, they had a tiny bit of an edge—and, with her skills, they could turn that edge into a massive blade that would cut right through the enemy.

Things were finally going well. They even had a secret weapon in their back pocket.

The only problem was that she was getting exhausted, and her head was under siege by a massive headache. She wasn't sure how long she could keep this up for. Plus, if Alexander defeated Brock, things would turn in the enemy's favor again.

And, of course, if Jack lost, then all was for naught.

The professor urged one soldier to glance upward, into space. There were bright flashes. To be visible from here, they had to be extremely gigantic bursts of energy.

Jack Rust, her son, was fighting the C-Grade Planetary Overseer... How she wished she could watch. As it was, all she could do was believe in him and try to win her own battle.

Brock clashed against Alexander. Their Daos erupted. Staff met blades. Stone met pure white ice. Every time they clashed, a freezing energy invaded Brock's body, an energy turning his blood into ice. He fought it off with his burning heart.

He was here to kill. If he let a little cold stop him, what kind of big bro would he be?

He twisted in midair, spinning his staff above his head. He brought it down. Alexander blocked it and was pushed back, grunting. "How are you not freezing over?"

"Because my heart is bro."

"Fine. Don't tell me. I will kill you regardless."

Brock had *just* told him, but he didn't care if this human was an idiot. They were mortal enemies. He brandished his staff, bringing it around to strike at Alexander from all angles. He incorporated his flight into his fighting style like he was a bird. The staff became a storm of attacks, and the white ice of Alexander was forced into defense.

When Brock missed a swing, their roles alternated. The swords of white ice rained down, while Brock spun his staff to defend. The streams of freezing energy in his body affected him little—his blood and organs were his bros, and they wouldn't give out on him just like that.

With one more clash, both opponents were pushed back.

"This battle has lasted far too long," Alexander said with a frown. "Your father fell on my tenth strike. How are you that much stronger?"

A fire was lit inside Brock's manly heart. He raised his chin, eyes burning with desire for blood. "Stop speaking. I can only kill you so much."

"As if I'd die to an animal."

"Animals are bros," Brock said, pointing his staff forward. Then, his voice carried an strange momentum. "Humans are bros. All are bros, and I big bro. But you... You no bro. You trash."

An odd energy permeated his staff. Alexander frowned, sensing the might brewing.

"You humiliate Father," Brock said. "You betray planet bros. You attack unborn bro. You coward, weak, and a shame. And I, big bro, have duty to kill you."

"What bullshit are you spouting?" Alexander asked.

Brock no longer responded. No—Alexander did hear a sound coming from Brock, but it was not his voice. It was the drumming of his beating heart, a heart infused with the power of brohood.

When Alexander acted cold and calculating, the Dao of Ice approved of his actions. However, the world held many Daos, and the Dao of Brohood did not approve. It was that Dao that fueled Brock, and most importantly, the Dao of Brohood was a Dao predicated on morality.

Faced with someone extremely un-bro-like, Brock's Very Big Thought pulsed with power.

The world's righteousness came to his side. An aura spread over his staff, lighting up all the animal-face inscriptions on it with warm light. Suddenly, Brock was not wielding just the Staff of Stone, but a symbol of brohood. He *was* the big bro. And Alexander had raised the ire of his very Dao.

"That is enough," Brock said, voice suffused with might. "Now, you die."

He charged. The staff whipped down. Alexander raised his swords to defend, and as they collided, the air itself imploded from the force. Brock's staff was undeniable, unstoppable, the Big Thought of Never Stopping operating at full power. The white ice, tempered in Alexander's soul for six months, shattered under the impact. Brock's staff carried through, penetrating the opponent's guard, and striking him in the chest.

Alexander flew downward like a missile. He crashed into the stage, sending fragments of white stone flying everywhere, while Brock hovered in the air above like a herald of punishment.

"Stand," he commanded, "or die lying."

CHAPTER EIGHTY-EIGHT
BROS, ASSEMBLE!

Alexander did not stand immediately. For the first time since he became an E-Grade, he felt genuine fear. This monkey that appeared out of nowhere had the power to match him, maybe even defeat him.

Would he die?

Alexander gritted his teeth. He did not want to die. He had to rule the planet. The coldness in his heart easily overwhelmed his honor, settling on a plan that would grant him victory. There would be a heavy price to pay—not just for him, for the entire planet, but so be it.

"*Come*," he ordered, contacting the forces that could help him. Then, he rose to his feet. He had to buy time.

"Don't think you won yet!" he declared proudly. "You are just one person, and your righteousness is a delusion! Only might makes right in this world! Only the ones who make hard choices win! You may think your power is great, but I have the Animal Kingdom by my side!"

"And what they gonna do?" Brock replied. "Bark at me?"

"No," Alexander replied with a crooked smile. "Kill you."

The Integration Starship shook under their feet. A part of its surface slid open, revealing a dark, gaping hole—and, from inside, out jumped a hundred animal people of various species. There were canines, turtlers, lycans. Every sort of animal species was there, including some that

Brock hadn't seen before. All were at the E-Grade, though only a few were particularly strong.

As Brock stared at these hundred cultivators, Alexander started laughing. "You fool!" he shouted. "Did you really think I would fight you alone like an idiot? I have the Animal Kingdom by my side! So what if our planet has to pay increased taxes for a hundred years? For getting rid of all of you, it's a worthy price!"

Brock calmly scanned the hundred cultivators whose gazes were all trained on him. He could sense their power. He could also sense the growing terror of the alliance army, who realized that this number of reinforcements were impossible to combat. By all appearances, this entire war was settled the moment Alexander requested assistance from the Kingdom.

Of course, this was breaking the grace period rules, but rules were the last thing anyone cared about right now.

Faced with this certain doom, Brock only shook his head. "You the fool. You think you saved, but you only have soldiers. And I..."

A human crashed down in front of the hundred Animal Kingdom cultivators. Another person landed next to the first, then another. Three people turned into a dozen, then more. Everyone looked at the sky. A small starship hovered there. Nobody had seen it arrive, and it looked like it could barely fit a dozen people. Yet, from its open doors, cultivator after cultivator dropped down. They'd been packed inside like sardines.

"Who the hell are those people?" Vivi exclaimed, looking at the incoming rain of cultivators. "Are they allies?"

"They better be," a man by her side replied.

Before long, almost a hundred people had fallen from the starship and landed before the Animal Kingdom cultivators. None of them looked soft. Most were humans, though many other species were included, and any System inspection showed they were unaffiliated E-Grades, mostly around the mid E-Grade.

Out of the starship's door came another man, holding a large drum and beating it to a fighting tune. He was the same man that had been beating the drums on the outer planet as they watched Jack duel Maximus Lonihor. The same man who'd been the first to join Brock on the outer planet.

This was the bro army, who had all left the Exploding Sun to follow their big bro. And the starship they rode... was the *Trampling Ram*. "BIG BRO!" the man shouted. "WE ARE HERE!"

Brock smiled brightly. "You have soldiers," he repeated to Alexander, "but I have bros."

"Who are you people?" Vivi shouted from below.

Two more cultivators appeared at the starship door. One was a feshkur wielding a mace, and the other a minotaur holding a greataxe. "We are friends," the minotaur said. "And we are here to help."

Vlossana's eyes widened. She was barely recovering, still in no state to fight, but she could speak. "You... What are you doing here!"

"You idiot!" Vashter shouted, hoisting his mace over his shoulder. "How could you believe we wouldn't help our crewmate, *especially* after he saved Dordok? We owe it to him!" He jumped down from the starship, landing at the very front of the bro army. "Bring it on, suckers," he said, pointing his mace at the Animal Kingdom cultivators, who all stared in shock. "I have a score to settle with your lot."

Brock turned back to Alexander, whose face remained painted with shock. "See? Bros always win."

"You... You idiot!" Alexander said. "If you break the Star Pact this openly, the Kingdom will have to—"

Before he could finish his words, two heavy auras blanketed the battlefield. Two people appeared in midair, both of them lycans. And D-Grades.

"We are the Planetary Overseer's designated assistants," one of them declared. "Our soldiers were only acting to capture wanted criminals. However, since you are breaking the Star Pact... don't blame us for being rude."

Before anyone could feel despair, another voice rang through the air. "Oh, well," it said, feigning nonchalance despite clearly hiding battle spirit. "I wasn't supposed to join, but if you're bringing out D-Grades, I guess there is no choice."

Space warped before the Kingdom's two D-Grades and another two people stepped out. One was a bald monk clad in orange robes. The other was a towering cyclops wielding a greatclub.

On the ground, Vashter's jaw dropped. "Captain!" he shouted, unable to contain his joy.

"Vashter, Bomn," Dordok said with a huge smile. "I'm glad to see you're safe."

"Not just safe," Bomn said. He stepped off the starship and floated to the sky, arriving beside Shol and Dordok.

"You broke through!" Dordok exclaimed.

"When I became the captain, I finally found my missing insight," Bomn replied with pride. "But you didn't sit still either, Captain. You raised hell on Hell."

"Damn right I did! How could I fall behind my own crew?"

"Are we invisible to you?" one of the Kingdom's D-Grades said. "Since you're determined to interfere, face us in battle! Let the strongest prevail."

"Are you blind?" Shol retorted. "We are three and stronger. What do you think you're—"

Space slid open once to reveal a dark-haired, blue-robed man beside the Animal Kingdom immortals. Shol frowned. "Li Qian," he said, enunciating every syllable. "You are here as well?"

"I suspected you'd come," Li Qian replied, already drawing his sword. "You have left the faction and acted against our interests multiple times. On behalf of the Exploding Sun and my master, Elder Monsoon, I hereby sentence you to death. Surrender or be cut down where you stand."

"Hmph!" Shol snorted, golden light emanating from his body. "My palms have been itching for a rematch. Bring it on, Li Qian!"

In the battle below, Vivi laughed and it echoed across the Integration Starship. "I have no idea what's happening, but God is finally on our side! Cultivators of the Flame Brotherhood alliance—give them hell!"

The army, their battle lust renewed, roared. The Ice Peak defended. The bro army and the hundred E-Grades of the Animal Kingdom clashed. Since there wasn't too much space on the Integration Starship, these two E-Grade battles slowly became entwined.

In the sky above, Dordok and Bomn attacked the two Animal Kingdom immortals, while Shol and Li Qian flew to the side to engage.

Every reinforcement had appeared. The only ones not fighting yet were Brock and Alexander Petrovic, who wore an ugly expression.

"You no bro," Brock declared, unable to hide the ridicule in his voice. Ridicule turned into boundless enmity. "You have no bros. Nobody will save you. You live alone, so you die alone."

"Come and try!" Alexander declared, summoning new swords of white ice, and crossing them before his chest. "You cannot kill me."

"In the name of my father, I swear I will," Brock replied solemnly, raising his staff to the sky. Then, carrying the world's righteousness on his back, he attacked.

Brock rushed at Alexander. All reinforcements had arrived, all distractions were gone, and nobody was going to interfere anymore. He would kill this man.

Brohood emanated from his staff. He raised it high and brought it down with a shout, crashing it into Alexander's swords and breaking them. More white ice appeared, though less pure. Alexander must have been running out.

Against the power of a big bro, it was useless.

Swords broke. Ice shattered. Alexander's every defense crumbled and his every attack faltered. His blond hair was matted with blood. His white ice became thinner and thinner, more impure—his supply was very limited.

He was losing, and all his planned reinforcements had been blocked. He really was alone. If he couldn't escape, he would die.

For the first time since the System descended, Alexander Petrovic felt the fear of death. It seized his heart like a cold fist and held it still. He thought he cultivated the Dao of Ice—but this was *real* ice. Nothing like the parlor tricks he'd been practicing. Before the fear of death, even his white ice wasn't worth mentioning.

Alexander swam in terror. Death approached, and he was powerless to stop it. Nobody would come to save him. Nobody would cry for him. He was alone in this world, so terribly alone. His body was still fighting Brock, but his soul felt like a naked man in a blizzard, kneeling in a fetal position to protect himself. The snow piled on him, encasing him. He was dying a horrible death as even his heart and soul froze over. It was so, so cold.

And right there, at the eve of death, as everything froze around him, Alexander touched something. For a fraction of a second, he felt true ice. The ultimate cold. It was a sensation so foreign it was terrifying, a destiny so lonely, dark, and heartless that he bled even at the thought of it.

Yet, his heart was already cold, and he was dying. What did he have to lose?

He clutched at that ice with both hands, letting the true ice seep into his soul and turn it into an ice statue. Everything died.

And then, he was reborn.

In the real world, Brock sensed something wrong. Trusting his instinct, he retreated. A sphere of ice spread from Alexander's body, expanding so fast that, if Brock had delayed his retreat by even a second, he would have been encased in it.

Brock scratched his head. He was now facing a large, opaque ice globe. He could no longer see his enemy. Was he hiding?

He smashed his staff into the sphere with all his might, channeling the power of brohood. Even the white ice from before would have shattered before this attack. Yet, the sphere showed not the slightest blemish. Brock's staff bounced away, and the webbing of his palm was almost torn from the recoil.

"Hmm," he said, observing the sphere. What was going on?

Then his eyes shone. He knew what was happening. Alexander Petrovic was breaking through.

Brock grunted. This was bad. He'd been winning before, but the power of an immortal was leagues away from the E-Grade. Moreover, he couldn't stop this breakthrough, as the ice sphere was too durable. And there was nothing Brock could do about it.

However, a big bro should never despair. Brock ran through his options and realized he only had one. Therefore, he flew back down to the concert stage, sat on the floor cross-legged, and broke through as well.

CHAPTER EIGHTY-NINE
ACHIEVING BROHOOD

Vivi reached out inside the professor's mind. "What is going on? Why is Brock meditating? He couldn't be..."

"I think he is," the professor replied, her own disbelief evident. "Both of them. They're breaking through to the D-Grade."

"What monsters..."

For the disciples of B-Grade factions, breaking through to the D-Grade took decades, if not centuries. If someone could do it within just a few years, they were considered geniuses of the highest caliber. And sure, the recently Integrated environment of Earth provided all kinds of opportunities, but becoming an immortal in just one year was a stellar feat.

Alexander Petrovic may have been overshadowed by Jack and his own capitulation to the Animal Kingdom, but he remained an outstanding cultivator completely obsessed with his Dao. He was also a prodigy.

Unfortunately for Alexander... so was Brock.

What is a bro? Brock wondered as he floated inside his soul space, eyes open and thoughts churning. The walls of his soul were carved with wise inscriptions—the legendary Bro Code—while the space within thrummed with his four Big Thoughts.

Muscles and working out. Constantly striving to make yourself a better person in any way you could, even if that way was just to lift stones all day.

Density. Controlling oneself and one's power to perfectly adapt to any given situation.

The Staff. Brock's weapon and how to use it, what it signified. The staff was more than just a weapon—it symbolized the intent to reach outside yourself and affect the world, an extension of Brock's body. A strong, hard, straight-forward concept.

Never Stopping. Never giving up. Never surrendering or putting comfort before advancement. Being unstoppable.

These were the four Big Thoughts that Brock had attained. They framed his Very Big Thought of Brohood. However, these four concepts didn't directly relate to brohood. He had tried to break through before and consequently realized it would be difficult; he had to connect all of his Thoughts together.

But hard didn't mean impossible. Right now, he needed to break through, so he would succeed because he had to.

Brock dove into thinking with resolve.

What is brohood? he asked himself.

It was to have brothers and stand alongside them. To laugh, cry, and fight on their side. To have their backs and know that they had yours. The bros were a team, and the entire world was below that. They would never betray each other.

At the same time, being the big bro was both an honor and a responsibility. It meant being first among equals. A big bro demanded respect and obedience without losing friendship. At the same time, he needed to protect his little bros and help them become better versions of themselves. It was a very tender, very delicate relationship, either end of which could fail given even the slightest immaturity.

Brock believed he had things straight.

At the same time, brohood was not confined strictly to one's bros. A person could be a bro even by himself. It was a mindset, a way of life built around respect, camaraderie, and power.

It was this brohood that would make a man step around a line of ants or help a stranger. It let a man join a group of strangers and laugh alongside them. Real knew real. Bro knew bro. When spread and perpetuated, brohood was the one thing keeping the world together, the one thing able to rid people of their hatred and usher them into an era of prosperity and true happiness.

This was Brock's Dao, and he wholeheartedly believed in it.

At the same time, there were instances where a bro went to war. This was one such instance. The ice-man had tortured and humiliated Brock's father. He had killed his brorilla bros. He had betrayed his own planet bros and caused many problems for everyone. That was a man as far removed from brohood as possible, and Brock, being a big bro, carried the duty of ending him.

This was strictly personal. Brock would either kill Alexander or die trying.

And, to achieve that, he had to break through.

The first step was deciphering how his four Big Thoughts all fit together like pieces of a puzzle—discover the one perfect combination.

It wouldn't be too difficult. Brock's understanding of his Dao was crystal clear. He seldom felt even the slightest confusion. Against such a determined, clear mind, how could the perfect combination not present itself?

Muscles and working out were the first Big Thought. They tied into brohood easily. Muscles represented power and effort, both of which were vital parts of brohood. A bro had to understand and navigate hierarchies of power, both physical and mental. At the same time, a bro had to always pour effort in himself, as that was the gateway to commanding the respect of others.

In being a bro, muscles—and all they signified—were the foundation.

A shape dominated Brock's soul. It was a muscular brorilla arm flexing its bicep, sticking out from the soul walls. Actually, the Big Thought of Muscles had already been fused with the Big Thought of

Brohood when he reached the E-Grade, but rehashing his understanding couldn't hurt.

Then came Density. The second Big Thought that Brock had comprehended, and one that tied directly to Muscles. Physically, density was about hardness and compression. The real nature of density, however, was tension.

After all, density was nothing but the perpetual tension of something that wanted to explode but couldn't.

In the physical realm, density came from compressing and decompressing. Brock could increase the density of his body to achieve greater strength or reduce it to achieve flight. It was an adaptive power that could be used in many circumstances.

In the mental realm, however, the realm closest to brohood, density represented the tension present in everything. When two bros interacted with each other, there was always a level of tension in the air, which they both had to control well or it would explode. It was precisely this mutual control of tension that let one bro instantly recognize another. It also played into the respect and navigation of power hierarchies, as did muscles.

If Muscles were the foundation of a bro, properly controlled tension was the tether tying bros together.

The brown walls of Brock's soul were already lined with muscles. Those muscles, however, were irregularly placed. Some spots had more, while others had less. It created an imbalance in his soul that wasn't easily visible but caused a variety of tiny yet compounding problems.

Now, tiny pink tethers phased into existence, connecting the places of higher and lower muscle density, and restoring balance in what would otherwise be chaos. Each tether could easily be broken by either side, but all remained steady.

Then came the third Big Thought—the Staff. A Big Thought that Brock had comprehended as he fought ogres on the outer planet, one that let him utilize his weapon at its maximum efficiency. He visualized a staff—a plain, long, hard rod.

It was so much more than a weapon. A staff was a symbol. There was a reason why the monkey king—the legendary Monking—used a staff. A staff was rigid. It represented battle. When a bro went to war, they had to be decisive, resolute, and hard. Like a staff would never bend, a bro's mind should never waver during battle, nor should their soul be prone to unnecessary mercy. Inside every bro should hide a fierce warrior.

Muscles—power and effort—were a bro's foundation. Density—tension and respect—was the connection between bros. These were both peaceful aspects. When the time came to fight, it was time for the staff. Without the readiness to go into battle, no man could be a true bro.

The muscled arm sticking out of Brock's soul walls was just sitting there. It possessed power but not a means to act. Now, things changed. An unadorned red staff appeared, and the arm's hand clenched it. Suddenly, its entire aura changed. The arm was more than a collection of muscles; it was a weapon, ready to be unleashed. It would not go into battle easily—but, if it did, may God show mercy on its opponent.

Finally, Never Stopping—or, as someone with a richer vocabulary would call it, Momentum. When Brock swung his staff, it was unstoppable. You could dodge it, but you could not block. When a bro went to war, his trajectory was set. The time of mercy was past, and the time of dominance was nigh.

At the same time, Never Stopping applied to more than battle. When a bro set a goal, he would try hard to achieve it. As much as failure was a necessary part of a bro's life, it was also anathema. Such was the duality of a bro's efforts: he pursued success and advancement with passion, avoiding failure with everything he had, while accepting that it would eventually come—and multiple times, too.

To succeed, one had to lose first. If you wanted to become the strongest, you had to fight and get beaten up a lot. Every good bro failed countless times in his life, and he even chased after those failures while simultaneously trying his hardest to succeed.

If someone had never lost, it didn't make them strong, only a coward.

It was precisely these losses that taught the greatest lessons. At the same time, failure could be disheartening. That was why every good bro practiced Never Stopping—the ability to throw himself down the pit of despair and grow stronger by climbing back up, then do the same until there was no more pit to jump into.

This also tied into the effort of Muscles. A bro could exhibit perfect behavior and understanding, he could be a great bro at heart, but if he ever stopped progressing, he would never again command the full respect of others. He would go down a step from what he'd previously achieved and stay there forever.

The muscles lining Brock's soul jumped into action. They pumped and flexed. Each worked tirelessly to improve themselves, growing by tiny amounts but never stopping. One could say they had no reason to work so hard, but they did, for life was meaningless without effort.

Brock looked around himself. His soul world was a brightly lit space surrounded by brown walls, on which was inscribed the legendary Bro Code—the answer to how to be a bro in every possible instance. At the same time, muscles lined those walls, ever pumping, flexing, and working out, putting this soul world in a constant state of motion. An arm stretched out of one wall, skinless to better display its perfect musculature, and in its grip it held the red staff of war.

Muscles; Density; the Staff; Never Stopping.

Power and effort; tension and respect; war; momentum and perseverance.

The cornerstones of brohood were set. The Very Big Thought responded radiantly, every letter on the walls emitting golden color. Brock was more ready than he'd ever been. He took a deep breath to admire this sight, the complete understanding he would devote his entire life toward. It filled him more than anything else. It couldn't be more real or suited to him.

Then, Brock stuck out his chest and started beating on it, roaring out at his soul world. The letters on the walls shone brighter. They jumped out and started dancing, moving to the tune of the pumping muscles. They were strong yet respectful, powerful and ready to go to war. Not a single letter would let itself be insulted, and yet, fueled by their common cause, all letters came together in perfect harmony. They swirled around Brock faster and faster, tighter and tighter, until he knew that one wrong step would doom him.

He kept roaring and beating his chest, leading the letters as a big bro should.

Gradually, they came together before him. The letters converged. A vortex appeared that sucked them all in, then shone in a blinding golden color. Brock kept his eyes on it, uncaring about the pain. The light receded; and, when it was gone, all that remained in its place was a book. It was the size of Brock's chest, made of the finest paper in existence—and, on its cover, the words, "Bro Code" were written in bold, clear font.

Brock was touched. He shook his head in wonder. He grabbed the book with shaky hands and flipped through its pages, finding inside them the same truths he'd realized. But that was only the first half. The second half was empty, waiting to be filled with more discoveries, more truths about brohood. It symbolized that his understanding, though great, remained incomplete.

Brock smiled. He was a bro; he would always progress. If the book ran out of pages, he would make new ones—and, if it became too long, he would compress its truth and keep going, always hunting unattainable perfection.

This was his Great Thought. Finally... he was an immortal.

In the real world, Brock's body shone with a radiant golden light. Many people on the battlefield below turned to look, as did the millions watching the battle's live broadcast. Slowly, he stood, emitting such power and wisdom that everyone felt magnetized, captivated, falling toward him like he possessed his own gravity.

Brock, however, only had eyes for the sphere of ice before him. His calm gaze took everything in. Then, he said, "I know you done. Come out."

A crack appeared on the ice sphere. Then another. They spiderwebbed its surface, then shattered it completely. Alexander Petrovic was revealed in all his glory, clad in a suit of pure white ice armor and radiating coldness. His eyes held no emotion. Twin swords were held in his hands, each freezing the air around them, while four ice wings spread from his back.

He resembled not a man, but a force of nature that would destroy everything without hesitation. The sheer terror he emitted stilled the surrounding battle for a second, but Brock's aura shone brighter, emboldening them and dispersing the illusion.

"It is over," Alexander said flatly. "I am a god. You cannot fathom my power."

"I don't care if you god," Brock replied calmly. One of his hands held the Staff of Stone—the other, a golden book. As he spoke, his voice echoed with unbroken finality, "You no bro. You broke the code. And now, you die."

CHAPTER NINETY

THE POWER OF A BIG BRO

Brock faced off against Alexander Petrovic. He held the Staff of Stone in one hand and the Bro Code splayed open in the other, while his entire being exuded power and wisdom. Everybody watching got an urge to focus on him. Many did. Most resisted. Only Alexander himself did not feel that urge, as his heart had frozen over by true ice, and his emotions were incredibly weak.

Slapping the Bro Code shut, it winked out of existence. "In the name of Father and all bros," he declared in a booming voice, "die!"

Brock and his staff flew upward like missiles. This time, he did not use Density to fly. The world itself gave way, as gravity was unworthy of constraining an immortal. His brown fur fluttered through the air. The tip of his staff whistled. His eyes shined with righteous rage, and he smashed upward with all the strength of his enhanced muscles.

Alexander raised a hand. The air froze. A large wall of ice materialized between him and Brock, and as the staff blasted into it, the wall cracked but did not break. Brock roared and punched it. The cracks spread. The wall shattered. Brock flew through, staff still extended and glowing golden, but Alexander was gone.

Ice spikes rained from the sky. Hundreds of them, each sharp and durable. Brock spun his staff, catching them all, but he missed the appearance of Alexander below him. A sword rose true; Brock's fur was matted with blood, barely saving his leg but taking a wild scrape on the shin. He rushed upward with Alexander in tow.

"Fall!" he shouted, grabbing the staff with both hands and smashing it downward. Alexander slashed up with both his swords. The three weapons met, one exuding dignity and the others coldness. Their clash was cataclysmic. The air froze and shattered. A booming shockwave flew in all directions. The cultivators on the battlefield below covered their ears as their clothes fluttered wildly.

The staff and swords pushed into each other, none giving way. Brock gave it his all. Suddenly, the four ice wings of Alexander spread wide. Though his face remained expressionless, the temperature around them plummeted. Even Brock felt his fur ice over. He was forced to disengage, letting Alexander take the better of him and blast him away.

"Fool," Alexander gloated, chasing Brock higher into the sky. "My Dao counters yours. You practice Will elements, to which I am resistant. You fight in close quarters, in which I can delay you until you freeze. Just how will you fight me?"

"I will because I must!" Brock retorted. He began to spin, holding his staff close and accelerating until his spinning was a blur. He then controlled his flight to ram straight into Alexander. "Spin Smash!"

"Ice wall."

A wall even greater than the previous one materialized. Brock's spinning form crashed into it, digging away at the true ice and shattering it, but he was delayed. Alexander flew away and willed a storm of ice spikes to appear, flying straight at Brock. They came in too fast for him to block everything. Nasty gashes appeared on his forearms, none bleeding, as ice caked over the wounds. He could handle this much, but any mortal would have already frozen over.

Brock glared at Alexander from behind his crossed arms. His eyes held bloodthirst. He was furious and pained, determined. He'd had the advantage before they both broke through, but not anymore. It wasn't a matter of power. What Alexander said was true: between their two Daos, Brock's was countered.

But he refused to let that stop him. He would take revenge.

He just needed to get creative.

The new control he possessed over the ambient Big Thoughts was confusing. He wasn't yet used to it, but he could try.

"Air bros," he spoke to the air, "help me!"

The air itself tightened around Alexander. His ice spread out, but it met more resistance. It moved slower, and Brock did not.

He whistled through the air. He reached Alexander and smashed him, controlling his staff in an intricate, brutal dance. His strikes were no longer made at full power, as he didn't want to get caught at an impasse again. Instead, he flew around Alexander, incorporating his own flight path into the staff movements.

The Staff of Stone flew over his head, crashing toward Alexander. Two ice wings blocked it, too hard to shatter, but the staff was already gone. It flew to the right, then its other end rose from below. Alexander blocked with one sword and slashed with the other. Brock ducked under it, enduring the cold, and stabbed the rear end of his staff into the opponent's stomach.

Alexander flew back. Brock followed, pelting him with strikes from every direction. However, ice was left where Alexander flew, and that ice suddenly came alive to strike at Brock like hidden vipers. His shoulders and thighs were bitten. More patches of ice appeared on his brown fur. Brock roared and pushed through, pressing on with his assault, smacking Alexander again and again.

The swords and wings defended, but there was only so much they could do. Brock was a maelstrom, and Alexander was part mage. Finally, the staff broke through, smashing into the side of Alexander's ice helmet with enough strength to level hills. The man flew away. His head shook inside the helmet, and though his ice armor cracked, it protected him.

Brock could not afford to show mercy. Even as Alexander flew away from the impact, he pursued, spinning his staff and bringing it down with a fearsome cry. This time, Alexander fought back. The ice covering his arm extended. It turned from just an ice gauntlet into a massive, nine-foot-long, and three-foot-wide claw of ice, which grabbed at

Brock's staff. It cracked under the impact, but managed to immobilize the staff.

"No!" Brock exclaimed. Spikes of ice flew at him from the left and right, but he couldn't dodge. If he let go of his weapon, it was over. "Muscle bros, give me strength!" he shouted. His biceps doubled, then tripled in size. He pulled with all his strength, succeeding in dislodging the staff, but at a cost. The ice spikes met his fur. They didn't penetrate too deep, but he was now riddled with a dozen shallow injuries, all of which frosted over.

"At least, I not bleeding," Brock said, panting. By now, he was injured in many places, while Alexander looked almost the same as when they'd started.

"You lack the power to break through my defenses," the man declared, looking down on Brock from a greater height. "You can persist if you want, but I will just wear you down. It is futile."

"Never stopping," Brock said through gritted teeth. He set his jaw and trained his gaze on his opponent. He would fight to the death.

He charged again. His staff shone with golden light, carrying even greater power than before, but it was slower in return. The ice was always there. First the wall, then the spikes, then the growing ice on Alexander's body and the armor. His defense was just too strong.

Brock managed to dent Alexander's armor under the armpit, but it wouldn't cause more than a bruise. In return, a hand of ice stretched out of Alexander's real arm, sinking its claws into Brock's leg and pulling.

Fur, blood, and meat went flying. Tendons were ripped. The wound instantly froze over, preventing further bleeding, but Brock was forced to retreat. Half his outer thigh was missing.

He did not scream, but his gaze darkened.

"Is that enough?" Alexander asked.

"Never enough."

Again, Brock charged. His staff became a hurricane. This time, it was swift and elusive, its trajectory blurring through the air as Brock alternated its density between high and low. The ice wall cracked under his might. The swords slashed but missed their mark. He scored a hit on Alexander's ribs, but that was the end of his staff's elusiveness. Brock flew back, but ice spikes pierced shallowly into his back.

He groaned.

By now, Brock's fur was a mix of white and brown. Ice covered several patches on his body, slowly colored red by his blood, while his eyes were equally bloodshot. His teeth chattered from the cold. The true ice had seeped into his burning heart, freezing it over bit by bit. Already, he could sense his blood flow decelerate. He felt slow and lethargic, as if the great beyond beckoned.

He told it to shut the fuck up.

"Sun bro!" he shouted. "Shine brighter!"

The air composition changed. The sunlight filtered through more easily, shining on Brock and Alexander, but its effect on the true ice was minimal. Explosions came from the battlefield below, but Brock didn't have time to look.

"Your powers are intriguing but useless," Alexander mocked in a matter-of-fact tone. He brandished both swords. "Ice Domain."

The entire patch of sky around Brock froze over. He was encased in ice. Willing his bro aura to spread, he became a golden sun, his burning resolve seeping into the ice and melting it. Ice and heat warred against each other, each struggling to emerge superior.

The entire block of ice shattered, showering Brock in sharp fragments. He shielded his face as the ice slashed and stabbed into his body. In an instant, he became bloodied, losing his breath.

An attack crashed down from above. He barely raised his staff in time to block both descending swords, but their momentum was too strong. Brock plummeted, crashing into the concert stage and cratering it. He remained there, panting and bloodied. He still had energy to fight, but not much—and his mind was dry of ideas.

Nothing he tried worked. Just how could he face this man?

Alexander hovered in the sky, an archangel of cold death with four wings. "Goodbye," he said. Raising one sword, a colossal ice spike materialized in the air. It was thrice as tall as himself and six feet wide at the base.

Brock wanted to dodge, but to his horror, he realized he couldn't move. The ice had seeped too deep. His blood was slow, his reactions numb, his limbs unresponsive. Twitching his fingers and blinking was the best he could do as Alexander's strongest attack formed above him, an executioner's blade ready to fall.

My bros... he thought to himself. *I'm sorry.*

He wasn't afraid of his own death. It was the fate of his bros that worried him. Dog Bro, Girl Bro, Big Sis, the bro army, the brorilla bros... If Brock couldn't stop Alexander, everyone on the battlefield would die. That man was just too strong. There were stronger bros in the sky, including Big Bro, but none could help now. The ice-man would slaughter everyone.

And Brock was powerless to stop him.

A manly tear escaped his eye as he imagined that this must have been exactly how Father felt. Immobile and powerless, lying on the ground as the ice-man was about to slaughter his little bros. At least, it seemed that Brock wouldn't be forced to watch... but that was a coward's relief.

He had to stop the ice-man, he just couldn't. He had to get revenge, yet he couldn't. He had to obey the Bro Code, *but he couldn't*!

Brock opened his mouth and unleashed a loud monkey cry, filled with his frustration and grief. The entire battlefield echoed. He sensed the spirits of his bros rousing, but none could help. He even sensed Big Bro try to fly down, but he was stopped.

That was okay. Nobody should arrive to save him. This was Brock's moment, his opportunity to rise or die... and he'd failed.

"It is over," Alexander said, sending his gigantic spike flying straight down.

Was it wrong? Brock thought in his final moments. Was my Grand Thought... wrong?

Because what else could it be? Brock wasn't weaker than the ice-man. His Grand Thought was not weaker than his opponent's, just countered. Then again, how could true power be countered? The only explanation was that Brock's Grand Thought... was wrong.

But how? he asked himself, knowing his Grand Thought was condensed and unchangeable. *It feel too right to be wrong.*

Deep inside himself, the Grand Thought of Brohood rang absolutely true. It was undeniable, and it was his. He could even feel the connection to all his bros, invisible tethers that spread out of him and into them, no matter how far away they were. How could such a thing be false? How could it be a mistake?

But if Grand Thought not wrong... then I must be wrong.

Brock's eyes widened. Was he using his Grand Thought wrongly? He thought back to the battle so far. Since he'd broken through, he was constantly unveiling new possibilities. He'd discovered he could ask the air bros for assistance, and that he could exude his dignity as a golden sun that only burned warmly.

Could there be something more?

The moment he thought about it, Brock knew the answer. The book in his soul shone, flipping to a certain page. On it, with clear, bold letters, it said, "A bro is never alone."

Brock started laughing. Of course! He had this all wrong. A bro had to be powerful, yes, but they were never alone! That was exactly why bros existed. What a fool he was!

But no more a fool. The brorilla vanished, and in his place was the big bro, shining in all his glory. Brock found his body glowing again. The ice weakened, and he stood, but he did not run to escape the ice spike. Alexander frowned when Brock looked up. He reached inside his soul, touching every tether tying him to his bros, he spoke into all of them at once.

"Little bros," he asked, eyes glowing golden, "lend me your power!"

The brorillas on the battlefield felt a calling inside their soul. They heard Brock's voice. Without thinking, they followed their instinct to raise their head toward the concert stage and siphon all the power they could into the soul connection they didn't even know they possessed.

They believed in Brock.

It wasn't just the brorillas on the battlefield. Back in the Forest of the Strong, where Harambe was tended to by his gymonkey partner, Aya, both felt a calling. Both turned their heads in the direction of the Integration Starship and gladly contributed their power.

In a forest of Asia, a pack of small dogs stood victorious over a dozen dead tigers. They were Brock's dog bros from the Integration Tournament. Suddenly, all of them looked to the side, and longing appeared in their hearts. They contributed.

In Trial Planet, the blue crabs of Labyrinth Ring felt the calling and gave their power. So did the beasts of Garden Ring, including a nostalgic sphinx.

The remaining bro army on the outer planet felt the same calling and lent their power, shouting out, "Big Bro!"

The bro army on the battlefield also complied, summoning any remaining vestiges of their power and pushing it inside the link. Even Nauja and Gan Salin felt the same, and both laughed as they siphoned their power to Brock.

Ever since the beginning, even without knowing it, Brock had practiced the Dao of Brohood. He'd made bros across the entire galaxy, both strong and weak. Now, all of them were part of his power. He never stood alone. Bros together stood strong.

The only one not summoned to assist was Jack, as he was Brock's big bro, not his little bro.

Each individual bro gave Brock a tiny bit of power, but they were many. It added up. As the ice spike encroached ever closer, Brock felt a rush of power enter his soul. It was far more than he possessed alone. He was overwhelmed. His entire body radiated intense golden light, and his every cell ached as it endured more power than it was meant to.

Brock was submerged in a burning vat of pain as his body struggled not to crumble, but it didn't matter. He laughed out loud, a clear, ringing sound. This was how it was meant to be. He was the big bro—and this was his power!

Brock balled his fist and punched the ice spike right at the tip. The world screeched to a halt. The ice spike shattered from end to end. Golden light erupted, and when everybody could see again, Brock was no longer there.

Alexander flew backward, barely dodging a staff that crashed down from the sky. "How?" he shouted, summoning walls of ice to his defense, but it was useless.

Brock laughed. His staff smashed forward, radiating golden light like a new sun, and the true ice was helpless before it. The wall crumbled. The ice spikes melted. The hand of ice shattered under the impact, and Brock's staff met Alexander's chest, sending him flying away as he howled in pain.

He came to a stop an entire mile away. "How?" he screamed again, finally revealing a bit of emotion. The weaker he got, the weaker the hold of true ice over his heart. "How can you be this strong!"

Brock laughed again—a carefree, powerful sound. "I told you." He stood in the sky like a righteous god. "You lived alone, so you die alone. But I..." His face broke into the widest, most relieved, most monkeyish grin possible. "I have my bros!"

Alexander's face warped. "Absurd! Your body can't take that kind of power! My defenses are absolute. You will break before I do!"

He encased himself in ice. Sphere after sphere formed around him, wrapping him in ever greater cold, and even his domain superimposed itself over the ice, enhancing its durability. He was now trapped inside a new moon in the middle of the sky made entirely of ice.

Brock laughed again. Alexander's words were true. This power was far too large for his current body. His muscles were tearing, his tendons were taut, his entire form was cramping. The pain was excruciating. Yet, he did not care. He was a bro. A man. He would do what had to be done no matter the cost, and in this case, he did it with pleasure.

He pulled both hands back, letting his staff hover in midair. The wrists came together. The palms spread wide. "This is for Father," he declared as wave after wave of golden power materialized between his palms. "For Big Sis and unborn bro. For all my bros. For brohood."

The power gathered between his palms grew so intense that it felt like he was grabbing hot iron, but it did not matter. Before this victory, a little pain was nothing. The light flared, becoming a sun between his palms. Finally, when all the power of his bros was siphoned in and he could no longer take it, Brock shot his hands forward, unleashing all that energy in a straight line.

"Bro Beam!"

The air thundered with his shout as the beam of pure, inviolable power seared the air itself. It crashed into the large sphere of ice, immolating its surface and digging in. So what if it was true ice? So what if Alexander's domain was enhancing it? Before the sheer momentum of brohood, this ice was nothing!

All the ice spheres imploded. Alexander's scream came from within as he burned in a cloud of pure power. Brock saw his body tumble from the sky to crash into the concert stage, catching glimpses of broken wings and shattered swords. Alexander lay in a cloud of dust that hid his body, unconscious and helpless. The bro beam dissipated, revealing a clear, sunny sky.

The breeze blew, and sunrays fell over his half-iced fur, panting and in terrible pain. On the ground below, Alexander's blond, bloodied hair was sprawled against the white stone, and his icy blue eyes were closed.

In the battle between Brock and Alexander Petrovic... Brock had won!

But it wasn't enough.

Brock flew down to reach Alexander's body. Its ice armor had already dissipated. He grabbed Alexander from both upper arms and raised him high. "Wake," he commanded. His Dao shot into Alexander's body, assaulting his heart.

Alexander awoke with a gasp. Brock's fierce fangs and burning eyes were an inch away from his face. Alexander's face was clouded by fear—though, whether it was real or not, only he could tell.

"I surrender," he cried out weakly.

"You tortured and humiliated Father," Brock declared, speaking each word with gravity. "You attacked unborn bro. You betrayed and harmed your planet bros. You weak, coward, shame. You don't deserve to breathe."

Alexander's eyes widened in true terror. "What about your honor? I surrender!"

"You deserve no honor."

Brock bared his brorilla fangs and bit deep into Alexander's throat. He tasted the blood, the flesh. It was cold. He clenched his teeth and pulled away, taking with him the man's entire throat.

Alexander's eyes still gaped in disbelief as his body tumbled to the ground, but his head remained in Brock's hands. He let it drop, then shattered it under his foot. Alexander Petrovic, the leader of the Ice Peak, was no more.

"This is for Father," Brock whispered, gazing at the corpse. He took no joy in this—but it was the only right thing he could do. Then, leaving the headless corpse on the ground, he let himself fall on his back. His entire body remained in pain and broken. He was barely alive—moving any more was impossible, but at least he had won.

He grinned as he stared at the sky, where his Big Bro fought. For the first time, Brock had carried his own weight around Big Bro. He had fought his own battle and won. His bloodied face broke into the widest, manliest, yet almost childlike monkey grin.

He'd never been prouder.

CHAPTER NINETY-ONE
WAR FOR EARTH

THERE ARE SOME DAYS IN WHICH EVERYTHING GOES WRONG, BUT YOU ARE STILL expected to perform. This was exactly the kind of day the professor was having.

And between all the separate groups battling for supremacy, Brock and that Alexander Petrovic chose now of all times to break through. She ground her teeth together; there was nothing she could do about it.

Suddenly, the starship rumbled under them once again. The professor almost tumbled over before one of the old martial artists caught her. Waves churned in the surrounding sea.

"*What happened?*" she asked Vivi, who had the highest vantage point.

"I don't know!" she replied. "But the ocean, it's—"

The churning sea erupted. Dozens of forms flew out to land on the Integration Starship. There were polar bears, penguin people, and even killer whales that used their fins to slide along the white stone. The bears shook their fur to send away the water.

The Ice Peak army cheered. "They're here!" someone shouted.

One of the flying ice wizards turned to Vivi with a proud sneer. "You aren't the only ones who can tame beasts. Freeze!"

An ice beam shot out of his palm, which Vivi avoided. Her heart tumbled. Those monsters were all in the E-Grade, moving with speed and power that normal animals could never hope to achieve. Even the submarines in which the alliance had arrived in had been impacted. A few were sunk by the beasts, taking their loyal crews to the bottom of the ocean, never to rise again.

You will be remembered, Vivi promised, turning to face the enemy. Her features contorted in rage. Her body erupted with fire. "Blaze with the flames of freedom!" she yelled.

The professor took in the new arrivals. The beasts were fast, having crossed the distance and arrived at her army's heels within seconds, but a dense wave of cultivators was there to face them. They steeled themselves. The polar bears roared as they led the charge, then barreled into the alliance army under a chorus of screams. Their power was reduced after the original charge, but the penguin people were right behind them, slinging ice magic, and the killer whales, though slow on land, weren't too far back.

This is terrible, the professor thought. These beasts alone are half as many as our E-Grades.

The scales of battle tipped.

Twenty bros came to the rescue. They were men and women of all Daos and species, assisting the alliance army against the beasts. "We know beasts. We'll hold them off!" their leader—a medium bro?—shouted. "Return to your battle!"

"*Return*," the professor agreed, and the bloodied cultivators turned back toward the Ice Peak.

The threat of the polar animals had been neutralized for now, but those twenty bros were a significant loss. Too fast, the Animal Kingdom cultivators pushed the bros back. The two battlefields moved and merged. There were alliance cultivators fighting the Animal Kingdom, Ice Peak wizards shooting at the "bros." It was total chaos, and even the professor could only handle so much. She was sliding out of rhythm.

She buckled down and persisted, uncaring about the searing pain in her skull, but victory fell away from them. The enemy had too many E-Grades. No matter how the alliance and bro army arranged themselves, it was a slow loss. Moreover, the two armies together lacked the coordination that the alliance enjoyed, as the professor didn't have the time to set telepathic links within the bro army.

In the sky, the immortal battles were heating up. On the horizon, the golden monk was slinging out entire miniature suns. Close-by, the cyclops and minotaur battled against the Kingdom's two lycan immortals, using sheer apocalyptic strength against what looked like moonlight.

The shockwaves from above were becoming more frequent. Blood rained occasionally. It was clear that some immortal battle would be over soon, and when that happened, things would take a drastic change.

More and more cultivators were falling. The losses staggering. With every moment the battle dragged on, more brave men and women died.

The professor had to not only win this battle, but also do it quickly. An impossible proposition.

Thankfully, she had one last card to play. A card that would only work once, but which had the potential to completely turn things around.

"Disengage," she broadcasted the order. "Orderly retreat toward the concert stage. Now! And inform your nearest bros, too."

The alliance heeded her call. The few hundred remaining cultivators joined in an orderly retreat, losing more of their number during it but following the professor's instructions to the letter. The bros followed soon as well, showing admirable faith in a stranger.

Before long, the entire alliance army was gathered close to the raised concert stage. It was at that point that two ripples ran through everyone's hearts as Brock and Alexander Petrovic simultaneously broke through to the D-Grade. The brorilla opened his eyes, holding a shiny staff in one hand and a golden book in the other, and proclaimed Alexander's death.

The professor believed in him with every fiber of her being.

Brock and Petrovic took their battle back to the sky. The alliance army clustered around the raised stage, with its many hundreds of feet in diameter, stacked up against its walls.

Normally, this would be suicide. They were grouped up like sheep to the slaughter with their backs against the wall. But the professor had a plan. A dangerous one, but what choice did she have?

"*Now!*" she commanded, activating a telepathic link she hadn't used before.

The Ice Peak and Animal Kingdom cultivators fell on the trapped alliance and bros like ravenous wolves. They fired every kind of magic they possessed, unleashed their strongest warriors. The E-Grades took to the front. Even the polar bears charged into the thick of the army.

Suddenly, the screams and clang of weapons were overshadowed by booms. It was like someone fired a cannon—no, many cannons at once.

If the professor brought a bunch of submarines over and didn't think to equip them with weapons, she would have been the world's biggest idiot.

Torpedoes flew over white stone, powered by tails of burning gas. Modern weaponry was frowned upon in the System world and wasn't used often, mostly because it wasn't worth the hassle. The stronger weapons of Earth—like missiles, tanks, or nuclear bombs—had been neutralized by the System itself. Of the remainder, a low-power submarine torpedo was only as strong as an E-Grade's full-power attack and could be stopped by one of them. Its effect should be minimal.

However, by forming into a tight circle around the concert stage, the alliance army had engineered the right circumstances. They'd lured the Ice Peak's strongest cultivators—the E-Grades—forward.

This was the perfect time to use the torpedoes. With the Ice Peak's E-Grades clustered on the inside of the ring, the peak F-Grades were exposed. Even if they ran back immediately, most wouldn't be able to disengage in time. Moreover, the alliance army was protected by the bodies of their very enemies.

The submarines had surrounded the Integration Starship. The torpedoes flew in from every direction. Every cultivator's eyes widened in horror.

The world became heat and blinding light. Roaring shockwaves dove into the ears of everyone present. Over thirty torpedoes had exploded at once, only some countered by the full-power attacks of the E-Grades who'd managed to block in time.

"*Charge!*" the professor ordered. The alliance army attacked before they could even see properly. The entire battlefield fell into a drunken melee, but it quickly became clear that the alliance was now winning.

As the dust cleared, hundreds of Ice Peak F-Grades lay dead on the outer side of the battlefield, blasted by the torpedoes. It was a gory sight. However, in the professor's eyes, it was heavenly. Those peak F-Grades were weaker than E-Grades individually, but they played a massive part in the battle as a whole. They were the fodder of the army, the rank and file. With them gone and the alliance's respective soldiers remaining, the numbers advantage became overwhelming.

As if that wasn't enough, the penguin people and killer whales that had been lagging behind had also been blasted to pieces, many of them bleeding out on the white stone floor. Their defensive powers were apparently limited.

Both armies were exhausted and had lost almost half their warriors. This was an extremely bloody battle. Yet, though the alliance's victory now seemed like only a matter of time, neither side gave up. Both kept on fighting.

The professor looked up, where the immortals were doing battle. Brock and Alexander Petrovic were clashing. Her heart seized in her chest. The brorilla was losing. As for the other battles, they didn't seem as close to being over yet, and the result was hard to predict.

If Petrovic won, it wouldn't matter what the professor did. Their army would be obliterated. Nobody could stop a D-Grade.

The enemy forces must have come to the same conclusion. Seeing that they were dying for no reason, voices of surrender echoed through their lines. Weapons clanged against the floor. Finally, the leaders gave up as well. A peak E-Grade woman approached Vivi in the sky and loudly declared, "The Ice Peak surrenders! The Ice Peak surrenders!"

The battle calmed. The Animal Kingdom cultivators, seeing their allies surrender and confident that nobody would dare harm them anyway, also stopped fighting. The bro army followed suit, looking to their leader—a man holding a drum, of all people—for guidance. He gave a thumbs-up. What that meant, the professor had no idea, but the bros took it as a sign that they should apprehend and not kill the enemies.

She had to agree. They couldn't just execute everyone. They weren't animals. The alliance army finished off the berserk polar beasts and began to gather the surviving Ice Peak members, but they were half-hearted in their effort. Everyone was. Their eyes were in the sky, where Alexander Petrovic was dominating Brock.

The brorilla crashed hard into the concert stage, sending fragments of white stone flying everywhere. A colossal ice spike formed in the air. The professor's heart reached the pit of her stomach.

"No..." she muttered, now observing through her own eyes.

"It is over," Petrovic said, letting the ice spike fall and seal Brock's fate alongside the alliance's.

Bright light erupted on the stage, followed by clear, booming laughter. Gasps rang from the bros around her. The large ice spike shattered into a million pieces, and Brock took to the sky, shining with the light of... brotherhood? She wasn't clear on that, but whatever the case, he was confident.

Brock came out superior in the next few exchanges and Alexander sealed himself in a large ice sphere. She witnessed Brock pulling his hands back, summoning a colossal amount of power between his palms, then shouting, "Bro Beam!" and unleashing it.

It was the stupidest name she'd ever heard. Yet, it worked. Alexander's sphere shattered, he screamed, and his body tumbled to the concert stage. The brorilla grab Alexander by the shoulders, then bit into his throat and tore it apart.

She grimaced. It was just one more scene of carnage in a war, but the fact it had been performed *after* the battle was upsetting. Regardless, any doubts she harbored vanished as she was overtaken by a stunning realization: Brock had won. Alexander Petrovic was dead.

The entire alliance army roared in triumph. The bro army roared even louder. The Ice Peak forces paled, then were summarily tied up. Some alliance cultivators abused the surrendered enemies a little too much, but the professor turned a blind eye.

She looked toward the sky, where the immortals still battled.

Shol stood panting in the sky of Earth-387, the same planet he had once visited as a spirit body. Several shallow gashes were open on his body, and his golden Dao of Explosion burned brightly. Six golden arms spread from his back, each holding a miniature sun, while light escaped his eyes and mouth.

"Let's end this, Li Qian!" he roared. "You and I!"

"Very well!" His opponent burned in many places, but was covered in a cyan armor of tiny swords. "In the name of the Exploding Sun, die, Shol! Supernova Slash!"

Li Qian raised his sword, then brought it down with deliberate slowness. Space itself was torn apart. Then, an explosion resounded, filling the world. Everything turned white. Even the distant armies averted their gazes. Only Shol kept looking, his eyes seared, his body burning.

He did not shoot out his suns.

He and Li Qian had dueled many times, but always in sparring. They had never actually tried to kill each other before Hell. Therefore, every time Li Qian used his ultimate skill, Supernova Slash, it had always been a watered down version without real spirit behind it.

But Shol hadn't known that.

Only when they dueled on Hell did he face the real Supernova Slash; an attack in which Li Qian had not held back, and which had almost taken Shol's life. It was right there, immolated in the middle of that tremendous explosion, that he'd attained a final bit of insight. A piece of the puzzle so small it shouldn't matter—but enough to tip him over the edge.

He hadn't revealed this to anyone, waiting for this exact moment.

Shol's face split into a grin. He had no hair, but even his eyebrows were seared away by the heat. He didn't care. "You are not the successor of the Exploding Sun, Li Qian," he declared in a booming voice that made its way even through the explosion. "I am."

Letting all his suns wink out, he pushed out a single palm, carrying in it a tiny, blue spark. The spark traveled slowly, like an old person about to die. Finally, it did; and its end came in such a powerful explosion that the world shook again, the air groaned, the Dao itself recoiled in fear.

"Supernova!" Shol roared.

Two nuclear explosions collided. Two mushrooms hugged each other. In the distant Integration Starship, an entire horizon away, the fools who hadn't looked away screamed. The professor hurriedly assessed the situation. "Run to the far side! Every mile counts!"

The explosions crashed against each other then dispersed. The air itself was burnt away. A vacuum was left, which the surrounding air quickly filled. The water below was boiled, and thousands of fish floated on its surface, dead. All clouds had dispersed.

Shol stood scorched and proud. His golden form was gone, but he hadn't fallen.

Li Qian... had. A man in charred black robes fell from the sky. Next to him, a cyan sword fell alone, tumbling through the tumultuous air currents. They splashed into the sea and sank.

And Shol, giving the ocean surface a final glance, turned to fly away. His entire body was in pain, his Dao reserves had almost run dry, but he didn't care.

"Goodbye, asshole," he muttered. "And damn good riddance!"

With him back in the fray, the remaining D-Grade battle was as good as over. The only one remaining... was Jack Rust.

CHAPTER NINETY-TWO
A WORLD INSIDE A WORLD

A FEW DAYS AGO...

Jack Rust sat cross-legged on the bare snow. His mind was filled with thoughts, mostly regret over Harambe's situation, but he pushed that away. The best he could do to help was defeat the Planetary Overseer—and to do that, he needed to focus.

It had already been a few days since he returned to Earth. Time had crawled. He couldn't stop thinking about the coming battle, his year long goal. To keep himself occupied, he'd dove head-first into fighting. The giant yetis and the ice dragon of this D-Grade dungeon had fallen to his fists, now decorating the ground with their blood. He had also been given the option to conquer the dungeon, though he refused.

When the Integration happened, 1,111 dungeons spawned on Earth: one thousand F-Grades, one hundred E-Grades, ten D-Grades, and one C-Grade. The higher Grade a dungeon, the more dangerous or inaccessible the area it spawned in. Of the D-Grade dungeons, only seven had been discovered so far; the rest were probably at the bottom of the ocean, in the sky, or on random islands. Similarly, the sole C-Grade dungeon also remained undiscovered.

Of course, the only Earth cultivator who could currently challenge D-Grade dungeons was Jack. This particular one, the South

Pole Territory, was particularly hard even for D-Grade dungeons, with its boss being an Elite peak D-Grade. It could easily level entire frozen mountains, and its ice breath could make the temperature plummet so hard that even the air froze and fell to the ground.

Of course, Jack defeated the dragon with little effort. It was around as strong as Sapasun. The battle did, however, rekindle his old hunting spirit. As soon as he saved Earth, maybe he would hunt down and visit the C-Grade dungeon and try his luck.

When all was said and done, Jack had earned another sixteen levels from this dungeon, finally reaching the peak D-Grade.

Name: Jack Rust
Species: Human, Earth-387
Faction: Bare Fist Brotherhood (D)
Grade: D
Class: Cosmic Fist (King)
Level: 249

Strength: 1585 (+)
Dexterity: 1590 (+)
Constitution: 1585 (+)
Mental: 200 (+)
Will: 200 (+)
Free Points: 190

Dao Skills: Meteor Punch III, Iron Fist Style III, Space Walk III, Neutron Star Body II, Brutalizing Aura III
Daos: Dao Tree of the Fist, Dao Root of Indomitable Will (fused), Dao Root of Life (fused), Dao Root of Power (fused), Dao Root of Weakness (fused)
Titles: Planetary Frontrunner (10), Planetary Torchbearer (1), Ninth Ring Conqueror, Planetary Overlord (1)

He hadn't invested any of his attributes points since the beginning of the Grand Duel, as his recent adventure was dubbed, so he'd collected a fair number. Now that he had finally reached the peak, it was time to use them.

But in what? he wondered, looking over his attributes. If I want to keep following the 8-1-1 distribution, I should add a few points to Mental and Will. However, I know that the overseer is a leonine of the same lineage as Maximus, so she's a Physical cultivator. And I do like the round two-hundreds there.

Jack shivered. He still remembered how, when all this started, he'd had to deal with some horrifically non-round numbers.

Very well. All in Physical it is.

With a decisive mental command, he poured all of his free attributes points into Physical. Each point turned into three subpoints, which he distributed equally among the sub-stats—Strength, Dexterity, and Constitution.

The rush of power was exhilarating. Jack's body twitched, then all his muscles contracted and remained there, growing stronger. His eyesight felt sharper, his fingers more delicate, his chest thrumming with every breath like a powerful war drum.

He couldn't help but to grin. Rushes of stats like these had grown sparser the more he advanced, but the feeling remained equally euphoric—for some, just the satisfaction of increasing their stats made the journey worthwhile.

Just how strong am I now? he wondered, clenching and unclenching his fists. If I could defeat the strongest D-Grade of the Animal Kingdom before... who can stop me now?

Am I the strongest D-Grade in the galaxy?

There was no way to know, but even that filled him with immense pride. Not wanting to let himself be swayed, he reopened his status screen.

Generally speaking, the new stats were satisfying.

Strength: 1775
Dexterity: 1780
Constitution: 1775
Mental: 200
Will: 200

Those five extra points still irked him, however. *Wait. Where did they come from?* he wondered, but nothing came to mind.

His grin widened. Let's go for a test drive.

Jumping up, he accelerated. The sound barrier shattered behind him. Twice at first, then thrice more in quick succession as he reached the limit. The shockwaves ravaged the snow beneath, but there were no animals to be hurt here, and the dungeon walls prevented any shockwaves from reaching the outside world. Despite the dungeon's thousand square miles of space, Jack was so fast that he still felt cramped.

The wind pulled back his cheeks to reveal sharp teeth. He could use his Dao to protect himself, but he let it happen, enjoying this breeze that would be enough to whittle concrete. Traveling at such speed was exhilarating. The ground disappeared below him. The clouds detonated at his passage. He felt like a god.

How fast am I going! He tried to calculate mid-flight, turning to follow the dungeon walls. This entire dungeon was shaped as a dome. Five times the speed of sound in Earth's atmosphere is... slightly less than four thousand miles per hour.

Holy shit! I could cross the Atlantic Ocean in less than an hour! And my strength... Mid-flight, he turned downward and punched. Multiple shockwaves bounced off each other and were amplified. The sound was louder than thunder, and Jack watched with surprise as the terrain under him was completely obliterated, entire hills and glaciers shattered like they were made of glass. As far as he could see, all the way to the horizon, the earth shook by his punch.

He hadn't even used any of his Dao. This was the result of his pure strength and natural resonance with the ambient Dao. Glee filled him, and he wanted to further experiment but feared that, if he used his Dao, even this thousand square mile area wouldn't be enough to contain him.

And who knew how the dungeon walls would react if someone like him attacked them?

"Hey, watch it!" a voice reached his mind—Shol's. "We're still here, you idiot! Don't destroy the entire continent!"

"Sorry!" he replied. Shol, Brock, Dordok, and the Sage remained in

their nearby camp, each busy with their own devices. There were still a couple days until the battle.

Restraining his excitement, Jack landed on a relatively whole piece of earth and sat cross-legged. As much as he itched to try out his real strength, Antarctica might not be able to handle him.

The Planetary Overseer's face would have to do.

Plus, there was another thing he wanted to try out. Closing his eyes, Jack sank into meditation, appearing in his soul world. Copy Jack rushed him.

"Is it time to fight?" he asked.

Jack laughed. "Not yet, Copy Jack. But soon, I promise. For now, I want to try something. Give me space."

Copy Jack nodded with a pout and moved away.

Jack first used each of his skills, observing their form now that he'd reached the peak D-Grade.

He started with shadow-boxing. Stars shimmered faintly around him, each of his punches followed by a shooting meteor. These images were all phantasmal, but they represented the depth of his understanding and the volume of his Class, the King-tier Cosmic Fist. To any watcher, he was like a live constellation of stars punching out.

Then, he teleported. During his three months of isolation training back on Hell, he'd discovered a more efficient way to traverse space. Instead of slicing it, he could just punch a hole open. Extending a single finger, he poked it through the fabric of space, creating a hole that he allowed himself to be sucked into. He reappeared a mile away—though he could go up to nine if he wanted.

Jack then channeled the Neutron Star Body. Visually, nothing changed—but he felt himself become dense, compacting to the point of ridiculousness. Thanks to the Dao, his cells had achieved a level of density and durability that rendered him completely impervious to most attacks. If an elephant rammed into him, he wouldn't even notice. At the same time, the profoundness of the Dao made it so that his actual weight didn't change that much—otherwise, he would weigh dozens of tons, if not hundreds, and that would be severely inconvenient.

Not to mention his extreme regenerative powers, courtesy of both the Neutron Star Body and the Life Drop.

Then, he tested out Brutalizing Aura. By simply narrowing his eyes, the air around him turned frigid. An aura of terror erupted from him, like he was a black hole about to swallow his enemies whole. At the same time, this aura absorbed the fear of his targets, feeding it to his Dao Tree as fertilizer and amplifying his strength.

And, finally, came Meteor Punch. The bread and butter of Jack's skills, the one he'd carried since his fight against the twin black wolves in the Forest of the Strong. Jack clenched his fist. All sound and light in his soul world was sucked inside. Everything went dark, with only a single purple meteor flashing into existence, dominating reality. Tiny stars trailed behind it, carving its trajectory into the dark sky, while the meteor itself packed unbelievable power.

Jack shot it out. It exploded. Colors and sounds returned to the world with a bang, erupting with such force that even the farthest corners of Jack's soul shook. The explosion was so titanic it stretched way beyond his perception range. There was nothing to compare it against in this empty space, but he suspected that he could affect entire countries with a single punch if he wanted to.

He grinned. With such power, who in the D-Grade could stop him? He itched to pit himself against the Planetary Overseer, test his strength against a real opponent. At this point, he'd grown so fast that he struggled to comprehend the scale of such a battle.

Before that, however, there were two more things he wanted to try, and the first was the ultimate culmination of his Class and Dao. Collecting himself, Jack took a deep breath, then exhaled.

His Dao Domain rolled out, submerging the world in the essence of the Fist.

It was like Jack had plucked a piece of distant space and moved it around him. Stars filled his domain, glimmering and twinkling. Faint purple mist spread everywhere, and Jack himself felt like an Old God playing around with the newborn universe. In his domain, he stood taller than stars, taller than existence itself. It was a whole new world.

Of course, part of that was because he was currently standing inside his own soul world, but he couldn't try this outside yet. Releasing one's domain emitted strong Dao signals which might be picked up even through the dungeon walls.

Jack let his domain drop, returning to normalcy. He took a deep breath again, not to focus, but to collect himself.

"I have grown so strong..." he muttered, letting his voice echo through space. "I've tried so hard and got so far... and yet, the end of the road is nowhere in sight." He grinned from ear to ear. "I love this."

His muttering was interrupted by the sound of clapping. Copy Jack flew closer.

"That was amazing!" he shouted. "Encore! Encore!"

"How do you even know that?" Jack replied helplessly. "Thank you, Copy Jack. I would love to entertain you more, but there is one more thing I want to do. Come with me. This could be fun."

CHAPTER NINETY-THREE
SPARMAN

THE MOMENT COPY JACK HEARD THE WORD *FUN*, HE INSTANTLY BECAME obedient. He followed Jack to the center of his soul world, where his Dao Tree stood tall on a fist-shaped foundation of five Daos. Now that he'd reached the peak of the D-Grade, his tree had also fully matured—its crown was fully shaped, reaching a total height of nine feet, while leaves and flower buds had appeared on its branches. The next step would be to make this tree bloom. That was the so-called Dao Blooming, and when he achieved it, he would reach the C-Grade.

Unfortunately, that felt a ways away. Though he'd reached the peak of the D-Grade and consolidated his strength, he felt nowhere near ready to advance again. He would need to defeat the overseer as he currently was.

He could only hope he would be enough.

The Life Drop remained buried under the tree's roots, supplying it with infinite vitality. However, what Jack had come here to see was neither the tree itself nor the Life Drop. It was the door-shaped pattern on the tree's bark, which had grown increasingly clear with each level-up. Now that he'd reached the peak of the D-Grade, the door was complete, and he had the feeling that, if he just reached for the door-knob, he could open it.

He took a deep breath. It couldn't be... right? he asked himself. It's only bark. Dao Trees don't have doors. It's ridiculous.

Under Copy Jack's watchful gaze, he reached for the doorknob-shaped outcropping as he had many times before. Of course, all the previous times, it was nothing but bark. This time, Jack grabbed it and, to his absolute shock, twisted until he heard a click. The door detached from the rest of the tree and swung open with a creak, revealing a dark, starless space behind it, infused with a hint of green.

Jack gaped. Keeping the door open with one hand, he poked his head through, meeting a vast expanse that felt nothing like his soul. It felt real. At the same time, while this space seemed boundless, there was something in its center. It resembled a green ball, though it was so far away he couldn't discern its dimensions. It might as well be a distant star.

"What the fuck?" he muttered.

He pulled his head back and let go of the door. It remained in place, wide open, inviting him to enter. It didn't seem like it would close by itself.

Jack looked between the tree, the door, and the dark expanse behind it. He glanced at Copy Jack. "Should I..."

"Of course!" the copy responded. "It's your tree, right? Go explore! It might be fun! I'll be right here to cheer you on."

"How encouraging..." Jack muttered, turning back to the door.

It couldn't be dangerous, right? He was inside his own soul, and this wasn't his real body, just a projection. How badly could this go?

And, at the end of the day, what was he? A coward?

Hell no!

Mama didn't raise no bitch!

Jack flew through the door, entering the dark space. His body grew cold. With no stars here, this was even colder than regular space, almost like standing directly in the ice dragon's frozen breath. Even he could barely stand it.

"Shit," he said.

The door slammed shut behind him, and all he saw was endless darkness. Where the opening used to stand, there was now nothing.

"Shit," he said again.

"What are you doing here?" a heavy, old voice rang through the cosmos. Jack went pale. The mere undulations of that voice were enough to shake him to his core. Peering into the darkness, he barely made out the outline of what seemed like a turtle far, far away. The creature approached, until Jack could see it had a green shell and a sharp face, like an actual sharp-jaw turtle, except it was the size of an elephant and was floating through this empty expanse freely as if it didn't even notice the temperature.

For some reason, it also seemed furious.

"I, uh, sorry," he replied. "I'm Jack. What is your name?"

The turtle snorted. "You are not ready. Begone."

Jack was about to reply when he realized there was a colossal force heading his way. It was the turtle's snort. That mere action had been enough to unleash a literal torrent of Dao so massive he could barely even fathom it. Like a planet was soaring straight at him.

He entered fight or flight mode. His Dao Domain erupted instinctively, shielding him as well as it could, and he roared as he smashed out a Meteor Punch.

The snort collided with his meteor and blew it away like it was nothing. It rammed into his Dao Domain and shattered it completely. Only a fraction of its power had dissipated. The rest of the snort hit Jack straight in the chest, crushing and destroying his extremely durable body. The last thing he experienced was terrible storms of power invading his insides and tearing him apart. He didn't even have time to feel pain.

Next thing he knew, his eyes snapped open, and he drew a sharp breath. He was alive. Snow and cracked earth surrounded him on all sides, while he was bent forward, clutching his head which fluttered with confusion. He'd died. Yet, he was here. What the hell happened?

What was that place? That dark, starless expanse with the green ball of light and the monstrous turtle. Was it part of the Life Drop? Another of its odd effects? Or was it a consequence of his perfect foundation?

Or both?

And how strong was that fucking turtle? He was at the very peak of the D-Grade, and it had absolutely slaughtered him with a snort!

Just when Jack's thoughts were lost in all these questions, something crashed on the ground next to him. "You're awake!" Shol exclaimed, seeming as furious as the turtle. "What the hell were you doing? What happened!"

"I—"

"There is no time, goddammit. We need to go now! You've been meditating for days!"

Jack's eyes widened. All other thoughts gave way to one—the battle! It was time to destroy the Planetary Overseer.

Jack teleported before the Forest of the Strong. The sight was nostalgic. This was where everything began, the starting point of his journey. It was only a year, but it felt like so long ago.

How far I've come... he thought with a faint smile. He then blinked away the reminiscence. There was no time. He had to get Sparman and rush to the battle. Thanks to the teleportation abilities of their starship, this small detour would only take a minute.

Besides Shol, Dordok, and Jack himself, Sparman the robot was the only D-Grade of their forces. However, his strict programming made him unable to join the battle. His orders were to guard the Forest of the Strong, and that is all he would do.

Unless Jack, who had been rewarded Sparman as a bodyguard after winning the Integration Tournament, ordered otherwise. Which was exactly why he was here.

Jack flew stealthily into the forest, easily dodging all the F-Grades on watch. His Dao perception noticed Sparman at the same time the robot noticed him. Yet, Sparman did not move, so Jack rushed there.

He arrived at a small clearing. It was the forest gym, where he'd first met and dueled Harambe. Only a few gymonkeys were currently there, all injured from one battle or another. Harambe must have been resting elsewhere.

Sparman sat on the ground, leaning against the bananarm tree. And he looked like shit.

Jack's eyes widened. His mouth gaped. He struggled to believe this. The all-powerful D-Grade robot was almost in shambles. Broken wires stretched out of his limbs, while burnt circuits were visible from several spots where his plating had been torn away. Sparks fizzled around him, his head was permanently bent to the side, and his eyes changed colors randomly.

"Sparman!" Jack exclaimed, both joyed at their reunion and saddened by the sorry state of his friend.

"Hello, master. Did you miss me?" the robot replied in a thankfully normal voice. "I assume you did, because I'm very lovable."

"What the hell happened to you?" Jack asked.

Sparman forced his mechanical mouth into a smile. "Nothing happened."

"What do you mean nothing happened? You look like shit!"

"Always the charmer, master. No wonder all the female humans swoon over you."

"Sparman!" Jack exclaimed. However, it seemed that the sarcastic robot would give no answer. *Why?* he thought. *What happened? Sparman is at the D-Grade! Nobody on Earth could hurt him!*

Then, his eyes lit up. He understood. Sparman may have been the strongest creature on the planet during the one year grace period—after the overseer—but the Ice Peak had many E-Grades, even some peak ones. Sparman had been ordered to protect the forest; who knows how many assaults he endured? Dozens? Hundreds? Unable to step outside the forest due to his strict programming, all he could do was defend and hope he didn't take too much of a beating.

Over the months, the assaults must have grown in power. Sparman was always here to defend, rain or snow, even against insurmountable numbers. His wires had been pulled out, but he fought on. His plating was torn away, and his insides burnt or frozen, but he still fought.

Jack felt guilt. He was the one who ordered Sparman to protect the Forest of the Strong, not thinking about the long-term consequences. Due to him, Sparman was now almost broken, a mere shell of the proud robot he used to be. At his current state, Jack doubted the robot could even stand!

And nobody on this planet had the means to repair a D-Grade robot.

Jack understood everything in an instant. Sparman's eyes remained calm, not wanting to reveal his pain and make him feel bad, but Jack already knew. Warmth filled his heart. He shook his head. He had come here to bring Sparman to the battle, but that would not happen. The robot had already given it his all—he would rest, and Jack would handle everything.

"Thank you," he said from his heart. "For everything. Without you, many of our friends would be gone."

"Don't mention it. For a robot as handsome as myself, this was nothing. Speaking of, when was the last time you took a bath?"

Jack fought back the urge to smile. "You have no nose."

"I possess many gifts. Specifically, there is a nose compartment stuffed at the back of my neck. I breathe through tiny holes in my right armpit."

Jack couldn't tell whether this was true or false, but he laughed. "It was nice to see you, Sparman. Rest well."

"I can still fight," the robot insisted, but Jack shook his head.

"You have already done enough. Leave the rest to us."

"But I—"

Before Sparman could finish his sentence, Jack flew away—he still had a battle to catch, after all. The robot was left mid-sentence, with his half-working mouth still open to speak. Watching Jack fly away, he slowly closed it. "Thanks," he whispered, then leaned back and let his energy levels drop to the minimum. Like that, he could survive another few days.

He really had run out of steam. Now, it was all up to Jack and everyone else. Sparman hoped they would survive.

CHAPTER NINETY-FOUR
BEGINNING OF THE END

JACK STOOD IN SPACE. BELOW HIM STRETCHED AN ENDLESSLY BLUE PLANET, WITH hints of green where it curved away. The moon hovered two hundred thousand miles away, a half-lit gray sphere, and stars surrounded him in every other direction. The sun, being a star itself, couldn't miss this gathering; it blasted light, so bright that even Jack had to squint when looking at it.

"Jack Rust," said Galicia Lonihor, the Planetary Overseer of Earth. "What a peculiar man."

Her form was that of a humanoid lioness, with tight robes and a wide cape around her body. Once upon a time, she had seemed like a god. Now, she was an opponent. Jack met her gaze squarely, not cowering in the slightest.

"How so?" he asked.

"You are just full of surprises. First the tournament, then Trial Planet, then Hell. I have never seen someone rise so fast. What is your secret?"

He grinned. "My secret is talent, luck, pain, and a ton of hard work."

"Hah!" She snorted with cold laughter. "Once upon a time, you were an F-Grade ant cowering under a sliver of my pressure. Now, you stand against me. What gives you such confidence? You should know that a D-

Grade, even one as powerful as yourself, can never challenge a mid C-Grade."

"Never say never, Overseer. You may have to eat your words."

Her smile cracked. She was well aware that, through the projection stone Jack had brought along, this battle was broadcasted across the planet, if not the entire galaxy. Every jab he took at her was another blow at the dignity of the already suffering Animal Kingdom.

"Have it your way," she replied coldly. "I tried to give you some last words, but you may die a mocking death, as was your life."

"The only mockery here, Overseer, is you and your pissant of a faction. Even its name sounds ridiculous; who in their right mind would take seriously an 'Animal Kingdom?' If my little toe could speak, it would come up with ten better names in the time it takes you to gurgle the blood of innocents."

Her forehead spasmed. "Just how badly do you want to die, Jack Rust?"

"Honestly, can our enmity grow any larger?"

She grinned; a dooming, bloodthirsty smile filled with sharp lion teeth. "No. So, in the name of the Animal Kingdom, I will erase you."

Her hand—more a clawed paw than a palm—rose and fell. Space locked down around Jack, preventing him from teleporting. A giant spear of light flew his way. He reared his fist back and shot it forward, meeting the spear at the tip. Space rumbled. A massive shockwave erupted in all directions. The spear cracked and dissipated, but Jack's knuckles cracked as well, flaring sparks of pain into his brain.

"Jack Rust is a powerful man," the overseer said, speaking not to him, but to the projection stone. "Yet, to an elder of the great Animal Kingdom, he is nothing. Watch him fall."

She shot ahead. Jack braced himself, but it was just impossible. She appeared before him in an instant. Her punch smashed into his guard, breaking an arm and sending him flying. He couldn't tell his own speed in space, but it was very, very fast. She teleported behind him, casually kicking upward. This time, growing accustomed to her speed, he bent his body to dodge, but even the spatial undulations of her kick sent him tumbling through space.

He punched ahead, predicting her next location, and connected with her forearm. It bent a bit—then her slap broke his teeth and made him spin away.

"It is futile," she said with disappointment. "I don't know who fed you this delusion, but you cannot face me."

"Heh." Jack forced a smile and spat out blood, watching it sail away in the vacuum. "I had intended to warm up a bit, but I guess it's pointless. Very well. Prepare yourself, Overseer. What you are about to witness will rock your world."

She frowned. The spectators all across the planet exchanged hushed whispers, leaning in to get a better look.

Green energy emerged from Jack's body. It surrounded and suffused him, almost hiding his features. Suddenly, as if his body was imbued by this energy, he began to expand. He grew an entire foot. His injuries healed like they were never there, and two fleshy appendages wormed out of his ribs, forming into two extra arms right below his armpits. His entire being emitted a green radiance. His smile was wide, bursting with power.

"Take a good look," he said, his mere voice causing ripples in space. "This is the man who will defeat you."

The overseer stared at his transformation with curiosity. A moment later, it turned into disbelief. Her eyes widened as her brain reached the truth. "No! Did you really... No; you wouldn't dare!"

This was only the fourth time in his life that Jack activated the Life Drop. The first had been when he tested it against a random desert monster. The second had been against Old Man Spirit. The third, to survive the heavenly tribulation while breaking through to the D-Grade.

All those times, nobody except his closest friends and Old Man Spirit had been there to witness him. It was one of his most tightly kept secrets. Moreover, nobody had ever used the System to inspect him in this form, as the Ancient voice had clearly dictated.

But now was the time to go all out, and damn be the consequences.

The various spectators were awed by his transformation. They couldn't scan him through the projection. The Planetary Overseer, however, could, and she did so immediately. The usual blue screen appeared for only a moment before crumbling, replaced by one filled with red, capital letters.

She had never seen such a thing before.

WARNING!
OLD ONE ACTIVITY DETECTED. CONTAINMENT PROTOCOL INITIATED. THE NEAREST AUTHORITIES HAVE BEEN NOTIFIED. CONTAINERS HAVE BEEN DISPATCHED.

LEAVE THE AREA IMMEDIATELY. VISIT ANY HAND OF GOD HEADQUARTERS TO RECEIVE THE APPROPRIATE BOUNTY. YOUR DISCOVERY CODE IS JR4390RND330GL.

ALL DETAILS OF THIS MATTER ARE NOW CLASSIFIED. SHARING ANY INFORMATION WILL RESULT IN YOUR SWIFT EXTERMINATION.

THANK YOU FOR CONTRIBUTING TO THE NEW WORLD.

At the same time, a similar screen appeared in Jack's eyes:

WARNING!
YOU HAVE TAMPERED WITH FORBIDDEN POWERS. PLEASE STOP EVERYTHING YOU ARE DOING AND WAIT. CONTACT NO ONE. HIGH-GRADE MEMBERS OF THE NEW WORLD ARE UNDERWAY.

DISOBEY, AND YOU WILL BE EXTERMINATED.

He didn't expect this. Regardless, it changed nothing. He knew there would be consequences if he revealed his four-armed form. Hopefully, the Church would have his back as promised.

"What have you done?" Galicia asked, horrified. "This is—This is projected across the galaxy!"

She clearly knew more things than the common people. Her first reaction was to lash out and shatter the projection stone. A spear of light flew over, but before it could reach the stone, a man with four arms appeared before it. He grabbed the spear by the shaft.

Space itself screeched as the spear ground to a halt. A moment later,

Jack crushed the spear in his palm, and it dissipated. Galicia was stunned by disbelief. "I am your opponent, Overseer, and I say this battle gets broadcasted. If you disagree—" he cracked a smile "—do something about it."

"Do you understand nothing? This isn't even about me. The Hand of God—"

"The Hand of God will do nothing," he replied, shutting up both her and everyone watching with his disrespect. "They will receive the same answer as you. If they want to do something, they're welcome to come and try."

Galicia struggled to form words. "You're insane!"

"I do what I want. This is my will and the will of the entire planet. From here on out, we no longer answer to the Animal Kingdom or the Hand of God. The planet of Earth belongs to me, and we are under the protection of the Black Hole Church. The entire planet will be teleported to safety after I defeat you."

"You—This is treason!"

He laughed. "Is that what you call it? To escape your tyranny is treason? To side against the people forcing everyone to kill each other is treason? No, Overseer—this is right. But, if you want to stop us, it's quite easy. Just kill me. Nothing will happen then, and my words will be just the ramblings of a loser. So, come on. Fight me." He adopted a battle stance, clenching three fists and using the last to give Galicia Lonihor and the entire world the middle finger. He grinned. "If you dare."

She roared and attacked.

On the surface of Earth, Ar'Tazul and Ar'Karvahul, the two djinn merchants who worked with the alliance, looked at the large projection screen over Valville. They then stared at each other. Their jaws dropped at the same time.

"Shit," said Tazul.

"Shit," said Karvahul. "Cousin, we're in deep shit!"

"We fucked up! This is already transmitted to the entire galaxy!"

"Can we stop the projection?"

"Are you kidding me? Stop it *now*? Do you realize how many credits we've been paid for this! We'll have to give it all back!"

"This is our lives we're speaking about, Tazul! The Hand of God will skin us alive!"

Ar'Tazul's face took on a business look. Then, his eyes shone like credit cards. "Imagine how much money we could make," he whispered.

"You're insane!" Karvahul replied, almost pulling his hair out. "You'll kill us both! Give me the stone, I'll shatter it right away!"

"Wait, Karvahul!" Tazul said, keeping his cousin away from the projection stone. "Think about it! We've already projected the crucial parts—do you really think the Hand of God will spare us if we stop now?"

That gave Karvahul pause. "No?"

"Of course not! Everyone who saw this—no, this entire planet—will be purged for good measure! We'll be made examples of!"

Karvahul wanted to cry. He removed his turban and used it to wipe his nose. "What will we do, cousin? We're going to die!"

Tazul's chin became square and stony. "There is only one thing we can do, Karvahul. Believe in Jack. If he has a plan, we better hope it works out."

"Then, we keep transmitting?"

"We transmit even harder. Only two things can save us now, Karvahul. Jack Rust... and tons over tons of credits. So let's make as much money as possible."

Their gazes crossed. A moment later, the eyes of both turned into credit cards.

"I guess we have no choice," Karvahul said.

"Exactly. No choice at all. Let's spread this projection as far and wide as possible and become filthy rich."

After Shol won, the two lycan immortals were defeated and slain, making the entire battle on the Integration Starship a total victory for the alliance. Currently, the professor and everyone else had already tied up the enemies and were watching a projection screen hastily set up against the wall of the concert stage.

When Jack revealed his battle form, everyone gasped, but nobody really understood what was happening. Even Shol and Dordok only had a vague idea. The sole exceptions were Brock, Gan Salin, and Nauja, all of whom glanced at each other and shrugged. Brock placed a fist against his chest.

"I believe in you, big bro," he said.

A B-Grade leonine was hurtling through space in his starship. Suddenly, the projection screen over his helm showed Jack transforming. The ancestor's eyes widened.

"Fool!" he exclaimed. He reached for a device in his pocket and used it to contact someone. "Eva! I know you're on your way—that kid had the artifact all along! Come pick me up; we can take no chances with the Church there!"

No reply came, but he still stopped his starship. Moments later, space distorted. A massive, needle-shaped starship appeared in front of him, and he rushed into its open side door. The large starship blinked once again and disappeared.

The Sage was inside a tiny, dark starship. A black hole was drawn on its body, framed by green rays of light.

There was only one other person inside. It was a man with flowing black robes, long dark hair, and red eyes. He looked like a human. At present, this man held a tiny spoon between his fingers, twirling it around to look at it from all sides.

"He really did it," the man exclaimed without glancing at the projection screen. "Your friend is a madman."

"Are you certain you can hold off a fleet?" the Sage asked.

"Well, there is only one way to find out. They're almost here. Let's go."

Jack roared as he punched out. Space caved under his fists. The Planetary Overseer met it with a punch of her own, their knuckles clashing.

The world shattered like glass. Space turned into a storm for multiple miles around them. Light was everywhere. Purple stars flickered in and out of existence. If this had been the surface of the Earth, everything up to the horizon would have been annihilated.

The overseer roared. She split open the spatial storm, then teleported behind Jack. He teleported behind her in turn, wildly exchanging strikes. They flew at ten times the speed of sound or teleported. Every clash was an explosion. If anyone on the Integration Starship looked up, all they would see was massive flashes in the depths of the sky.

Dao-imbued roars echoed. Their battle flipped from one location to the next, flying deeper into space. They were surrounded by emptiness on all sides. It gave a completely new meaning to the word "duel."

"Fall!" the overseer exclaimed. Suddenly, white light was everywhere, outshining even the sun. Spears emerged, followed by gigantic soldiers holding them. There were nine of them, each a mile tall and clad in shiny plate armor. Feathery wings spread from their backs, flapping despite the absence of air.

"Hah! I've seen that trick before!" Jack exclaimed, releasing his Dao Domain. Tiny stars appeared everywhere, flickering between purple and green. Constellations formed and disappeared. Roaring meteors crossed Jack's domain, each shaped as a fist and carrying tremendous power.

Space itself tightened around the winged knights like a closed fist. They struggled but remained still. One of Jack's four fists was enough to hold them in place, while at the same time, the Dao of the Fist permeated the space around him, driving away everything else.

The overseer's Dao erupted as well. It was a white sphere of absolute, divine supremacy. It could not be stopped, lording over everyone and everything, reigning supreme across the universe. The white warred against the purple, each meteor crashing into the light and melting. The winged knights were empowered, resisting Jack's suppression.

Jack himself remained unaffected. He released his Brutalizing Aura, using it to siphon energy off the knights. He then charged the overseer, bringing his domain closer.

As the two fighters came within a few feet of each other, their two domains ground together. Sparks of purple and white flew. A thousand tiny explosions resounded at once. The Dao itself moaned in regret as their tremendous understandings pulled on it, tearing it in half.

Space shook in protest. The world boomed around them. Stars collided. The winged knights marched forth.

Jack clenched all four of his fists and drove them at the overseer. Each was a force of nature. Meteors sparked on their knuckles. Light and sound were ripped apart and forcefully drawn into the fists, then released as explosions.

When C-Grades fought, the very fabric of reality was their battleground. Tiny rifts formed in the space all around them. The Dao bemoaned them to stop, yet they kept going.

Jack smashed out a series of punches. The overseer blocked each of them, protected by white light, and retaliated with a palm. Jack crossed his four arms and was flung backward. He let himself fall into a spatial tear and reappeared behind her, winding up his entire body. "Meteor Punch!" he roared, smashing out a fully-charged punch. She turned and met it with a palm.

Space shattered again. A crack many miles wide spread out, taking time to close. Jack teleported away and the overseer followed, not giving him a moment of rest. She pressed her attack, and Jack was forced to defend. Her winged soldiers reached him and tried to stab him with their spears, which weren't too fast or strong, but they remained an extra distraction that prevented him from facing the overseer at full power. He roared in frustration.

Even after transforming, Jack remained underpowered. The gap between a peak D-Grade and a mid C-Grade was simply too vast. He was one of the strongest D-Grades in the galaxy, if not the strongest, and he was using the Life Drop to greatly enhance himself. Yet, all he achieved was an uphill battle.

His only saving grace was the near-infinite amount of energy supplied by the Life Drop. It was far more than it had been at the E-

Grade, and he still sensed no end to it. It fueled his regeneration, pushing it to new extremes.

The overseer kicked him in the ribs. The bones cracked. Tremendous pain assaulted him, yet the injury already healed itself as he flew away. He turned around and headed for the overseer again, roaring at the top of his lungs. His heart was on fire, but his mind was cold. He could afford no mistakes.

C-Grades were no joke. Galicia Lonihor wielded her Dao like nobody Jack had met before. Her every move carried supremacy. It seeped into his bones, seeped into space, and reality itself. Fighting her was a constant struggle against the urge to surrender. Even his Indomitable Will was close to relenting, a feat that nobody of the same Grade had even come close to achieving.

Yet, who was Jack?

He was the man who had overcome every challenge in his way. He had faced impossible odds and used them to grow stronger. He had willingly put himself through extreme pain. He had trained for almost every waking moment.

No. Jack Rust would never surrender.

Yet, if he let himself slide even a tiny bit, her Dao would overwhelm him. He set his heart on fire to resist, fighting helplessness with stubbornness. His own Dao Root of Weakness revealed that her unbeatable strength was an illusion. He could land hits occasionally—if he just lasted long enough, he could win.

He met a palm with his forearm, then punched back out. She ducked, dodged again, and slammed a knee into his chest. He was sent flying away while she held her position.

"How are you doing this?" she asked, slowly lowering her leg. "You can actually persist for a few moments."

"Heh," Jack replied with a dark chuckle, wiping blood from his lips. "I can win, too. Just you wait."

"That is impossible." She raised her chin, her eyes narrowing a hair. "Did you know that Maximus Lonihor was my son?"

Jack was taken aback. "I had a suspicion."

"He was... and you dared kill him. I didn't want to give you face by taking this battle seriously, but your resistance has angered me. So be it. Since you wish to fight a Lonihor, then I shall kill you like a Lonihor."

The winged knights disappeared. Her body shone a radiant white. Light streamed in from every direction, escaping even the tears in space to reach her.

Galicia Lonihor transformed. Her form became clad in white armor. Steel gauntlets appeared around her hands. Six wings unfurled from her back, like an angelic warrior, while a helmet formed around her face, leaving only her cold eyes exposed.

With that, the pressure around Jack intensified. Chanting and hymns filled his ears. Feathers floated everywhere, untouched by the vacuum of space. Galicia raised her holy hand, and reality itself bent at the knee. The only Dao left standing was the Fist, as well as Jack Rust himself, who raised his proud chin against her.

"Feast your eyes on my form," she declared, "for it is the closest thing to a god you will ever see."

"Save your words, Galicia," Jack replied. Things looked grim; he could barely take her before, and now she had unleashed a battle form of stronger power. He had no more ways to enhance himself—yet, what choice did he have but to fight? His four fists tightened. His Dao stood against the world. A fist rose against supremacy like a man daring to fight an angel.

"I don't care how strong you are. I don't care about your Grade, your ridiculous transformations, or your empty Dao. No matter what happens... Today, there is no way I'm going to lose!"

CHAPTER NINETY-FIVE
HELPLESS

GALICIA FLOATED IN SPACE DONNING WHITE ARMOR, GAUNTLETS OF LIGHT, AND A starry helmet over her face. Six wings spread from her back. This was exactly the same battle form Maximus Lonihor had used, except with two more wings and a sense of greater mastery.

Her power was so dense it was suffocating.

Jack set his jaw. He clenched his four fists. Instantly, Galicia disappeared. Next thing Jack knew, a gauntlet was buried in his abdomen, shooting all air out of him and sending him careening through space. Then leonine was there again, kicking at the back of his head, then she elbowed his back as he bent forward.

Jack struggled to even understand what had happened. Her speed had been great before, but this was on a whole new level!

So was her power. Her first punch had shattered his ribcage and ruptured his stomach. The second had cracked his skull, and the third had broken his spine. All those were with Neutron Star Body operating at full force, making him extremely dense and durable. Any mountain would have been blasted to smithereens.

The Life Drop siphoned green energy into his body. His ribcage was repaired, his skull reformed, and his spine was knit back together. The injuries healed instantly, but it changed little.

"What frightening regeneration," Galicia muttered, hovering proudly in space. "If you had reached the C-Grade, even I would struggle. But, thankfully, you were too impatient to face me."

"Heh," Jack muttered through his pain. "It's not like I had a choice."

"There is always a choice, Jack Rust. You just made the inferior one."

She disappeared again. Jack guarded on instinct, receiving her punch with his two right forearms. They snapped like matches. He was flung away like a ragdoll, once again getting manhandled by the Planetary Overseer. She showed little mercy as she rained blows on him. His bones broke. His limbs bent wrongly. His face was brutalized, and his organs were destroyed. Blocking the most lethal strikes to avoid dying instantly was the best he could do.

Yet, his regeneration persevered. It healed him, repaired him. The Life Drop supplied seemingly infinite energy, and his Neutron Star Body used it to repair itself. But that didn't spare him the pain. Every time she broke him, he felt it all. He sensed his innards getting ravaged and his bones shattered. Every crack was a new hell. Like a madman had taken a hammer and went to town on his body.

Jack screamed in pain.

Through it all, he remained conscious and wary. He isolated the pain to a corner of his mind and did his best not to pay attention. He tried to block and parry, to reduce the strength of Galicia's blows. Her speed toed the line between being slightly too much and absolutely impossible to dodge. He could see her moves—not in time to react, but in time to know he would be struck an instant before she connected.

He was getting absolutely bullied.

"What's wrong?" Galicia mocked, kneeing him in the stomach. "I thought you were strong enough to fight me. Are you still holding back, or are you just weak?"

Jack was not holding back at all. He was going all out, yet he remained completely unable to touch her.

Dammit! he roared inside his mind. Does she specialize in speed? How unlucky can I be!

Jack himself focused on strength and endurance, which was the only reason he wasn't instantly obliterated by her attacks. Generally speaking, speedy opponents countered him.

This wasn't a battle he could win. Unfortunately, he had no choice. Nobody would save him. The Sage had made it clear that the Church would prevent anyone from interfering, but they wouldn't interfere either. He also couldn't escape, as everyone he knew was behind his back. Even if they weren't, there was no way he could outrun her.

No; there was no retreat. He would either win this battle or die fighting.

What can I do? he thought, gritting his teeth as Galicia closed in. What straw can I grasp at? What has even a tiny chance of working?

She smacked him. He tried to block, but her first attack was a feint; the second was a kick that landed on his chest, once again shattering his bones and catapulting him away. It was hard to gauge distance or speed in the vacuum, but he suspected he was going faster than a jet plane.

Stamina! he realized through gritted teeth. If I can last long enough... she will run out of energy!

But that was easier said than done. Galicia didn't seem the slightest bit worried. Who knew how long she could last.

She teleported behind him and grabbed his neck. Jack felt as helpless as a baby chicken. "Let me show you a trick, Jack Rust: long-range teleportation," she said, then space warped intensely around them. Next thing he knew, he remained in space, but a gray planet stretched below him. No, it wasn't a planet—it was the moon!

"What?" he blurted, only to be smacked in the face and sent flying again.

"You have shown the world a false image of the Animal Kingdom," Galicia said, gesturing in the distance, where a projection stone hovered—she'd taken it along in her teleportation. "Since you want to project this battle so much, let me help you. But the vacuum of space is not the best battleground. We can make your defeat more impressive. If people think the Animal Kingdom is not a powerful faction, I shall demonstrate the strength of just one elder, and show the world that before us, they are just a bunch of ants."

"What are you—" Jack stopped speaking and blocked. He managed to withstand the strike without his arms snapping—but he was flung toward the moon. He crash-landed like a comet, creating a huge crater.

He opened his mouth and spat out blood, watching it fall slower than usual.

He was on the moon. The moon. This would have been dreamy if he wasn't isolated on an entire fucking satellite with a god determined to kill him.

Galicia fell foot-first, and Jack barely managed to fly away before she reached the ground. A second crater, even larger than the first, appeared where she struck. She bounded after him. Jack flew close to the ground, hoping for something, anything, but there was nothing besides craters, hills, and soft gray rocks. There wasn't even any air.

Galicia charged him. He managed to parry one strike, but she then grabbed his face and flew down. She pressed his head into the ground and charged ahead, dragging him across the surface of the moon. His head carved a long line on it. She used him to break through rocks and hills. Jack's vision was filled with gray stone.

When he finally managed to escape her grasp, the world was spinning, and the top of his head felt like it was on fire.

Galicia laughed. "Do you surrender already, Jack Rust? Should I put you out of your misery?"

There is no way I can do this, Jack thought. At least she's not trying to kill me yet, but she will never tire out. I must beat her—but how!

As he did not respond, she punched and kicked at him with abandon. Any damage she inflicted was immediately repaired by his seemingly endless regeneration, but the pain was equally endless. It was the only instance that came close to the soul-splitting pain of when he ingested the Life Drop. It was so terrible he almost lost himself, but his will to fight was unbroken. He had mastered calmness in despair when Sapasun broke all his limbs on Hell. He would never give up. If there was a way out, no matter how tiny, he would find it. If a single opportunity appeared, he would not miss it.

But there was nothing. Galicia went all out. She punched him through mountains, nailed him into the ground, shot him in the sky and then back down. The surface of the moon was ravaged. C-Grades had the power to destroy continents, and she was going all out. This empty satellite was her playground.

Jack crashed into the ground, shattering it for many miles around him. He took off and punched where he thought she would appear. He got her, but she had time to block and slap him into a tall mountain, demolishing it. He flew out through the debris on the other side, but she was already there, pinning him into the ground again.

He coughed out red blood, the only color in an empty terrain. In the sky, a blue and green planet dominated the stars. Everyone he knew was there—and it was so, so far away.

He was alone.

Back on Earth, everyone watched silently. Their hero, their only hope of escaping the Animal Kingdom, was getting beat up and rendered completely helpless. The projection stone followed Galicia and transmitted everything, making everyone's stomach churn. They saw Jack's body being used to crumble mountains and shatter valleys.

"How is he even still alive?" Nauja muttered.

Vivi covered her mouth with her hand. Tears rolled down the professor's cheeks. Edgar was in stunned disbelief, while Gan Salin was trying to crack up jokes to lighten the atmosphere. Only Brock watched with faith—his belief in Jack was unshakable.

"You can do it, Big Bro..." he muttered under his breath.

Similar scenes played out all across Earth. The people sighed and shook their heads in disappointment. Others marveled at the strength of C-Grades. They really were like gods.

"It was foolish to think we had a chance..." an old man said. "I told you. When oppressors come, all we can do is bow our heads and hope they show mercy. That is the way of the world."

Even across the galaxy, people watched in stunned silence as the most famous D-Grade was getting beaten senseless. Even after revealing that four-armed battle form, the gap to the C-Grade was just too wide.

At the same time, every disciple of a B-Grade force looked at their elders with different eyes. They had never seen them fight, but most were even stronger than Galicia. Witnessing the destruction she could so casually create, gave new meaning to the power of the C-Grade.

Jack's world was a mix of dizzying pain and futility. He still fought his hardest. Every time Galicia charged, he tried to block or punch back. His four fists blasted out meteors. He shattered everything around him, but it was just too little. She was on a different level. Her speed was just outside the range of what he could handle.

And he refused to give up. All extraneous thoughts had fled his mind. Even his fear was only a faint reminder.

How do I win? was all he asked himself. Only two things came to mind—the snorting turtle in his soul, and the Supernova skill he still hadn't mastered.

A tiny part of himself dove into his soul world.

"Are we going to die?" Copy Jack asked, but Jack ignored him. He reached for the door on his Dao Tree and tried to yank it open, but to no avail. This time, it acted exactly like bark.

"Dammit!" he roared. "Let me in!"

The door remained unresponsive. The turtle ignored him completely—if it could even hear him. He would not receive any help here.

Gnashing his teeth, Jack tried to forcefully enter a meditative state and use the despair he felt to push for the Supernova skill. Unfortunately, no matter how he tried, it was impossible. Just like every other time, the skill was too foreign, like it wasn't meant for him. He had the insights but no way to use them.

Both attempts failed him. He could come up with nothing else. He carried no treasures, his Dao was nowhere near breaking through, and his skills had no way forward that he saw. The Life Drop couldn't augment him any further either—all it could do was constantly regenerate him.

In this fight, he only had his current self—and he had to find a way to make do.

Returning his complete attention to the real world, where he was receiving a sound beating, Jack focused fully on the Planetary Overseer. His eyes sharpened to the extreme. He watched every move, every tiny tell, every detail. He sought a pattern or anything to capitalize on, but he came up short. After all, the overseer had sharpened her battle skills for millennia—how could she show easy patterns?

As if that wasn't enough, the seemingly limitless energy of the Life Drop was beginning to thin. It wasn't that the Drop itself was running out of power. That ocean remained as bottomless as ever, but the amount it was willing to give Jack was approaching its limit. His regeneration had already slowed. It was imperceptible to others, even to the overseer, but Jack himself could sense it.

Soon, it would grow even slower, and then, it would not be able to keep up with the damage. He would die.

He needed to do *something.*

The pain kept coming; it was a dark abyss he could never escape, a deep trap where he was alone and dying.

But not all was dark. As time went by and the overseer refused to land a killing blow, making a point out of his execution, Jack grew more accustomed to her extreme speed. It was slow going, and it felt like his mind was pushed beyond what it could consistently handle, but he was getting flashes of insight now. He could read her a tiny bit, have an extra tiny moment to respond. It was like he entered overdrive.

At the same time, due to his full attention on the overseer, he detected small changes. Her eyes sharpened a tiny bit. Her strikes became a bit harder, aiming to kill more than to maim. It felt like she was getting more serious, but he perceived no change in her power.

Was he growing stronger in tandem? Or maybe... she was growing weaker?

Jack's eyes widened. She's getting tired! After all this time, it's finally getting to her!

And of course it was. She had been rag-dolling Jack for a few minutes now, releasing terrible power with every strike. That had to take a toll. She just pretended it hadn't—and, probably, she never expected Jack to last this long.

His bloodied mouth revealed a grin. She saw it—and hatred entered her eyes. "Die already," she said, amplifying her power. She poured more strength into her strikes, aiming to completely destroy Jack's body, but everything had a price. As her attacks grew stronger, they also grew slower—and Jack had already become slightly accustomed to her previous speed.

She pushed out a gauntlet surrounded by radiant divine light. Space itself cracked where it passed. It aimed for Jack's face—yet, at the last moment, he raised his palm and caught it. The world shook. The gray hill behind him shattered into a thousand pieces, the pieces slow to descend back to the moon or out into space. Dao erupted in a wide radius, white and purple intertwined.

But Jack had caught her fist.

He grinned widely, a crazed look in his eyes and blood on his teeth. "Got you," he said, then punched back.

It met her helmet.

Galicia was blown back. For the first time since the battle started, she lost an exchange.

Vivi clasped her hands before her chest. "He did it! He punched her!"

Beside her, Brock snorted. "Of course," he said. "Big Bro is Big Bro. He win."

Everyone watching the battle transmission blinked in surprise. All those people who had been acting arrogant because of her dominance paled.

"It can't be..." an elder of the Dragon Valley muttered.

"She grew tired," another replied. "Of course she did. What an idiot. If she went all out from the very start, there is no way that boy would have lasted. But now... Now, she has to actually try."

CHAPTER NINETY-SIX
JACK RUST VS. GALICIA LONIHOR

THE ANIMAL KINGDOM ANCESTOR STOOD ON THE BRIDGE OF THE LARGEST starship as the entire fleet shot through interspace. Eva Solvig, the assigned commander of the Hand of God, stood a step ahead of him. Coincidentally, Artus Emberheart was also there. The former Warden of Hell had been gifted to the Hand of God, who assigned him to this fleet.

The ancestor didn't give Artus a single glance.

Suddenly, they exited teleportation. The ancestor prepared for battle, but looking around, he saw nothing. No planet, no Jack Rust. Only stars, one of which seemed significantly closer than the rest but still very far away.

"What happened?" Eva Solvig asked the woman manning the helm. "Why did we exit teleportation before reaching the destination?"

"We didn't," she replied numbly. "We were forced out."

Eva frowned. A moment later, she nodded grimly and teleported outside. So did the ancestor.

Space split before them, revealing a tiny black starship. A man appeared in front of it. He had dark hair and red eyes, as well as a playful smile that seemed completely out of place. The ancestor scanned him—he was at the late B-Grade.

"Hello, Eva," he said. "Unfortunately, I cannot let you go any closer."

Eva didn't respond immediately, so the Ancestor took charge: "And who the hell do you—"

Eva slapped him. The sound was crisp, even in the vacuum of space, and the leonine turned to look at her in disbelief. Her wary eyes almost extinguished his anger. Almost.

"Shut up," she said.

The other man smiled. "I see you recognize me."

"Heavenly Spoon Sovereign..." She gritted her teeth. "Why would the Black Hole Church send someone like you to this tiny corner of the universe?"

"Just repaying a favor," the man replied. Reaching into his robes, he took out an inconspicuous silver spoon. "Now, as I said, you cannot go any closer. Well, you can, but you'll have to beat me first. Think you're up for it?"

His playful smile remained, fully confident she would refuse. And, indeed, Eva Solvig did not reply.

"Why are you hesitating?" the Animal Kingdom Ancestor said, eager to regain his pride. "You are both late B-Grades, but there is also myself and an entire fleet here. We can take him."

She snorted. "If you want to throw your life away, go right ahead. I'm not joining."

"You would shy away from your duty? What would the Immortals say about that?" he retorted.

Her gaze turned colder than true ice, and a wave of threat radiated off her. "This man is the Head Envoy of the Black Hole Church. Since he came personally to stop us, we have no choice but to comply. Our pointless deaths would not help the New World or the Immortals. However, the next time you dare contradict me, I will make sure that *your* pointless death becomes an act of duty on my part. Am I understood?"

The ancestor closed his mouth and shut up. He did not recognize this man or the title of "Heavenly Spoon Sovereign," but he knew exactly what Head Envoy meant. It meant that, before this man, a revered Ancestor of the Animal Kingdom, was just a pile of trash.

"Now, with that out of the way," said the sovereign, "wanna watch the battle together? It's not like you have anything else to do. We could even bet if you want."

"Bet on what?" Eva retorted. "Since you're here, your subordinates are already destroying Galicia Lonihor."

"On the contrary. Nobody is interfering. Jack Rust will fight this battle alone."

Eva raised a brow. "Really?"

"Do I look like I'm lying?" he said, flashing a bright smile.

Eva considered it, and greed took her over. "If Jack Rust loses, I want your Saturated Chalice."

"Oho, tall stakes. Sure. And if he wins, I get one of your Fleet Teleportation Arrays."

Her face scrunched up. A moment later, she bit the bullet to say, "Deal."

"Excellent! Then, let's watch. I believe we're just getting to the good part."

With a swish of the sovereign's sleeves, a projection screen appeared in the middle of space, and the three B-Grades stood around it—from a distance—to watch.

Galicia paused, too stunned to react. She had been struck by a D-Grade while in her strongest battle form. That was unheard of.

And extremely humiliating.

"How are you doing this?" she asked in fury. "How are you still standing? Just how ridiculous is that power you have?"

"My regeneration is only a bonus," Jack said. "If you had landed a strike to instantly kill me, I would have died, but you didn't. I never let you, and you never really tried, thinking yourself supreme. Now, I suspect you *will* try, but you're growing tired, aren't you? Those hands are getting heavy. Your legs are shaking. Your Dao is turning fainter." He grinned wildly. "Tell me, Overseer; how does it feel to hit someone until *you* give up?"

"Bullshit! You're cheating!"

"Cheating? Since when is endurance cheating?" He laughed. "You thought you were supreme, but you were just an idiot. Come now, what will it be? Strong strikes that I can match, or fast ones I can survive? I can do this all day."

He could not, in fact, do this all day. He was bluffing. The energy provided by the Life Drop was already running dry, but she didn't know that. He'd already lasted ridiculously long. Who was to say he couldn't go even longer?

Galicia gritted her teeth. Divine light blossomed around her. Her armor glowed. She grabbed her helmet and threw it away, fully revealing her furious face. "In the name of the Animal Kingdom, myself, and my son," she declared, raising her gauntlet to the sky, "you will not survive this day."

"I'd like to see you try, Overseer."

Radiance blossomed all around her as her Dao Domain spread out and encompassed the entire landmass they stood on. Cracks spread across the ground, emitting radiance. The airless sky turned white. Jack was trapped in a holy realm, where she was a goddess.

But he had a domain, too. Purple unfurled. Stars blinked into existence, wrestling it for supremacy. Fist-shaped meteors flew everywhere. Jack donned these purple stars like an armor, dressing himself with a constellation. His fist was cosmic—his might, relentless.

He smashed out a Meteor Punch, sucking in all the holiness of her domain for himself. The stars exploded. His fist met hers, erupting in a cataclysmic explosion that shook the entire moon ever so slightly. Tons of stone went flying into space, forming a wide crater around them. They hovered in its midst.

Galicia really was tired. Her strength and speed had fallen, no longer as extreme as they used to be. They remained at the very edge of Jack's abilities, but after fighting her for so long and enduring her strikes, he'd grown a bit used to them. If he focused his hardest, he could compete.

Fist met Supremacy. One wanted to be free and wild—the other, to dominate. It was a clash of both people and Daos.

Jack and the overseer fought equally now. His resilience had been rewarded. They battled on the moon's surface and in the void of space. The moon's surface was ravaged under them. Meteors exploded. Divine spears flew. Body met body, and space itself groaned to the tune of their clashes.

Jack was still losing, but his remaining regeneration allowed him to fight.

However, as Galicia was growing tired, so was Jack. His life energy was running out. At some point, she broke one of his bones, and it did not heal immediately. Her eyes widened, turning from realization into triumph.

"You liar!" she shouted, laughing. "Die!" Her strikes turned fast again. She tried to overwhelm him. Jack defended with all his might, blocking and evading everything, but there was a limit to his abilities. Even exhausted as she was, she remained too fast. A couple strikes slipped by. The damage they caused took longer to regenerate each time. Jack gritted his teeth as he fell into defense.

I cannot fail now! he thought frenziedly. Not when I've come this close!

He was attempting the impossible. He was trying to fight a mid C-Grade while at the D-Grade himself. He had lasted this long, used everything he had to survive and drive her to exhaustion. He couldn't fall first!

I refuse!

But reality was undeniable. She struck his arm, then landed a harsh kick into his shin. He flew into the moon and was buried into a crater. She fell boot-first, and as soon as he dodged, she pounced at him and sank her teeth into his shoulder, pushing them deeper until the tips of her teeth touched each other. His bone shattered completely. He screamed.

With a twist of her neck, she ripped out his muscle and sent him flying. Jack paled. That was the one opportunity she needed. In that moment of weakness, she focused her entire Dao Domain to lock down space around him, rendering him unable to escape. Spitting out his flesh, she charged up a slow but extremely powerful strike.

The ground around her exploded. White light came from below, evaporating the stone to escape and surround her. Everything turned white. It was like God himself was roaring at Jack, who floated in the void above her. He could block, but he could not dodge.

And, facing that skill which seemed like her ultimate attack, blocking was a fool's errand. It didn't matter if she was exhausted. He couldn't strike that hard.

He was a goner.

"For supremacy!" Galicia shouted, shooting herself forward. Her wings folded. The white glow hugged her body, making her the only source of light, the only power in existence. Her palm headed unerringly for Jack's head. If it connected, his entire upper torso would evaporate.

Since he could not evade, nor did he have time to break the space lock, he charged up a Meteor Punch himself. Light and sound fell into his fist. His extra two arms also dissipated, turning into more energy. He could sense this was the final clash, and he poured everything into it, driving himself to exhaustion.

Everything disappeared until the only things remaining were Galicia, covered in dense white light, and Jack's purple fist, a shining meteor in the darkness.

Jack sensed her power, and it was greater than his. Not by too much, at this point... but so what? This was everything he had. After this punch, he could no longer fight. He'd lost. He was dead.

In the final moments, even as he charged up his fist, his mind sank in reminiscence. There was no regret. He'd done everything right. In the entire year up to now, he had not wasted a single opportunity, not made a single mistake. He was the absolute strongest he could be.

He had also fought this battle perfectly. Everything had gone as great as it possibly could have.

There was nothing he could have done better. If he lost, then it only meant this goal of defeating the Planetary Overseer within a year was impossible to begin with.

No, there was one thing, he realized with a wry smile. The supernova. I never comprehended it. If I had, maybe things would have been different.

But was it even possible? The skill feels wrong. It was never suited for me. I couldn't have used it, no matter how long I tried. Heh. In fact, if I had never tried to comprehend it, maybe I could have used that time to develop my skills better. The tiniest edge would suffice.

Damn. I played myself. What a life.

Still, he felt no regret, only a lingering sense of disappointment before the end. He reached for the unformed skill inside his mind and tore it away, forcing himself to forget it. It was useless. The supernova disappeared from his Dao completely, leaving only a few explosion-related insights that now anchored nowhere. They were equally useless.

Wait. Explosions?

The flash of realization came instantly. It should have been obvious. In that instant before shooting his fist forward, Jack saw things clearly. He was a fool to attempt to learn the supernova. It was clearly not meant for him, he'd felt that since the beginning—but its partial insights weren't useless. They were about powerful explosions, and coincidentally, he already had a skill that utilized explosions.

In fact, the more he thought about it, the more he realized that the reason he couldn't comprehend the supernova was because he already possessed something similar yet different.

What if I... combine them?

Everything was ready. In truth, he had already comprehended the essence of the supernova; he'd just been pushing it in the wrong direction. He laughed, finally utilizing it the right way. An orange spark appeared on his purple meteor. He shot it out.

Congratulations! Meteor Punch III → Meteor Punch IV

Galicia reached him, moving at speeds he could barely fathom. Her gauntlet was about to disintegrate his head. His Meteor Punch reared to match it, colored purple, green, and a little bit of orange. Once it met the claws, it would explode—but not as a meteor. As a supernova. He was a Cosmic Fist. He was the ultimate form of primal savagery. It was only apt that his offensive skill would include the most powerful explosion in the universe.

"I am the Fist! I will never lose!" Jack roared, driving his fist forward. "As long as I, Jack Rust, draw breath—*THE ANIMAL KINGDOM WILL BOW TO ME!*"

The overseer screamed.

Jack's fist made contact and disappeared. It evaporated like a nuclear warhead at the point of explosion. Everything below the elbow vanished, and the world was filled with so much light and sound that his eyes and ears were both destroyed. The recoil hit him like a bomb against his chest.

But the overseer received it even harder. Just before the explosion, she must have sensed its power, because she screamed and tried to change her course. Only too late. Jack's fist crashed into the center of her chest, stopped her, and pushed her down. Her world fell away.

The overseer reached the surface of the moon and bore deep into it. The ground shattered for a hundred miles in every direction. Cracks appeared for a thousand. Mountains crumbled. Earthquakes spread across the entire moon. Fire burned on its surface and was instantly extinguished by lack of oxygen. Dust covered the world.

Space shook before it stabilized.

Congratulations! For defeating an opponent of a higher Grade than you in single combat, you have been awarded the title Grade Defier.

Grade Defier: A title awarded to those who can jump Grades to fight. Efficacy of all stats +10%.

It was suspicious that he'd only gotten this title now and not when he defeated Old Man Spirit, but he couldn't care less at this point. The extra rush of stats was the only thing that kept him from fainting.

When all was said and done, Jack floated over the surface of a ruined moon. His sight and hearing were just coming back, the final sputters of his regeneration. The extra hands had dissipated.

Below him, destruction spread to the horizon. He'd just destroyed a landmass greater than a small country. He was spent, completely exhausted, and heavily injured. His hand was regenerating very, very slowly, and the pain was killing him.

But he had won.

Jack raised his remaining fist and cried out in triumph. He didn't even remember he was being watched by the projection stone, nor did he care; he'd won. He had succeeded. And that was all that mattered.

Everyone across the galaxy was stunned. Jaws dropped. People gaped. When Jack Rust defeated Maximus Lonihor and challenged the entire Animal Kingdom, it had been sensational. But this... This was just unheard of!

The entire galaxy bore witness to the legend of Jack Rust!

Eva Solvig and the Animal Kingdom Ancestor had extremely ugly expressions. The Heavenly Spoon Sovereign laughed. "Well, a bet is a bet. Pay up."

Eva didn't even look at him. She tossed out a small pouch, then dove back into her starship. The Animal Kingdom Ancestor followed suit. The moment he entered, Artus Emberheart, the former Warden of Hell, rushed up to him and said, "Ancestor, Jack Rust is extremely weakened now! This is the perfect time to—"

The ancestor's slap echoed across the entire starship. Artus's head was almost unscrewed from the force, and he fell to the floor, mortified.

"Shut up!" the ancestor screamed. "You think I don't want to go? I just can't! You completely useless moron, this is all your fault!"

The former Warden tried to reply but couldn't. He was overtaken by intense shame and anger, but he couldn't go against the B-Grade Ancestor. Instead, he bottled up all his feelings and swore to himself:

Jack Rust, if I don't destroy everything you love and make you curse me for eternity, I will not be a man!

"We go," Eva Solvig said coldly, and the entire fleet of starships disappeared.

The Heavenly Spoon Sovereign laughed. He cheerfully waved them goodbye, then grabbed the pouch Eva had tossed away and disappeared.

Back on Earth, the entire Integration Starship echoed with loud, relieved cheers. The alliance shouted with all the power of their lungs. People hugged each other and cried, while the Ice Peak and Animal Kingdom captives glowered.

"He did it!" people shouted across the Earth. "He did it! Jack Rust did it!"

Jack fell to the surface of the moon and landed on his back. He couldn't move a muscle, but he was so happy he didn't care.

A moment later, he had a thought.

Wait. How am I getting back?

The moon was far away from Earth, and he couldn't perform long-range teleportation like the overseer had. He didn't even carry the *Bromobile*—he'd left it behind to protect it from the battle.

Space opened before him like a door just then, and a homeless-looking man with a big smile walked out. "Great job, Jack," he said. "That was one of the most impressive things I've ever witnessed—-and trust me, that's a high bar."

Jack smiled back. "Thanks, Sage."

"Now, follow me and let's get out of here. We have a planet to poach."

CHAPTER NINETY-SEVEN
PLANET POACHING

JACK SAT IN A CHAIR OF THE SAGE'S STARSHIP, RIGHT ABOVE THE RAVAGED surface of the moon. Everything hurt, including his mind, but he had won. That was all that mattered.

"Nice ship," he said, panting.

"Do you like it? It's the same one I got in the Integration Auction."

"Really?"

"Of course! Well, I did make some upgrades. Like this."

The ship jumped through space and reappeared in orbit around Earth. Jack chuckled. They had already checked Galicia's body and ensured she was dead. "Good job."

"Before we go down, however," the Sage said, "there is someone I want you to meet."

Space shimmered inside the starship, and a man walked out. He had long dark hair, red eyes, and wore flowing black robes. Yet, despite his intimidating appearance, his feet were in flip-flops, and his face a held a playful smirk on the verge of breaking into a smile. He instantly struck Jack as a likable guy.

Immediately after that, Jack's eyes went wide as saucers, because he'd scanned this person.

???, Level ??? (B-Grade)
Faction: -
Title: Planet Devourer

B-Grade!

"Hey," the man said.

Jack jumped to his feet, grimacing as a thousand little pains made themselves known. "Hello. I'm Jack. Jack Rust."

"Oh, I know. I watched your battle; very impressive." The man reached out a hand, which Jack shook. "My name is Jonas. Nice to meet you."

"Likewise!"

Jack was stunned. This was a B-Grade. A legendary existence. Actually, it was the first B-Grade he ever met in person, and he seemed so... approachable.

"Allow me," the Sage intervened with a wry smile. "This is Jonas Evergreen, Head Envoy of the Black Hole Church, though most people refer to him as the Heavenly Spoon Sovereign. And, just so we're clear, Head Envoy means that he's the strongest B-Grade disciple of the entire Black Hole Church. Presently, that makes him one of the strongest people in this galaxy, if not *the* strongest."

Jack fought back the urge to gulp. Instead, he raised a brow. "If you're trying to impress me, you succeeded."

"I like him," the sovereign said. "There is no need for respectful salutes, kowtowing, and the like though. I have seen your potential; if nothing goes wrong, then one day you could become an envoy, too."

"That's... great? Thank you for the praise, Sovereign." Then, since this guy seemed cool, Jack took the courage to add, "If you don't mind me asking, what does your title refer to?"

"Oh, that thing. It's my weapon." He reached into his robes and removed a tiny silver spoon. There was nothing special about it. Jack could use it to stir his tea.

"I see," he replied, not daring to ask anything more. "Thank you."

"The sovereign came to oversee the resolution of our agreement," the Sage said. "He prevented the Hand of God and Animal Kingdom from interfering in your battle, and he will also handle the poaching of this planet. The seven C-Grades that helped us escape Hell were his subordinates."

"Thank you for everything, Sovereign," Jack said, this time meaning it from his heart.

"It was little trouble. I didn't even have to fight," the sovereign replied, shrugging it off. "Now, since we don't have much time, how about you go find your people and prepare them for what is about to happen? We can chat more after your planet is safe."

Your planet is safe. Those words rang in Jack's mind again and again. He struggled to believe them. His body was still flooded by adrenaline from the battle, and his mind remained there.

Had it finally happened? Had he finally saved Earth?

It felt like a dream.

"If I may," he asked quickly, "what exactly is about to happen?"

"We will transfer your planet outside System space. It will remain in this galaxy, and there will be ways for you to teleport in and out of System space, but the planet itself will be almost impossible to track. You will also maintain access to the System, but it's a faulty thing that won't be able to trace you, so don't worry about it. Now, if some cultivator happens to stumble upon your planet, you can only blame your bad luck."

"Do you mean that the Animal Kingdom will no longer be able to touch us?"

The sovereign raised an amused brow. "And here I thought you were smart. Yes, that's exactly what I mean."

Relief overtook Jack. "Thank you, Sovereign," he said again, bowing slightly. The sovereign laughed.

"Go," he said. "You have thirty minutes."

Jack didn't linger. With a final grateful glance at the B-Grade sovereign—and a questioning one at the Sage—he teleported away, reaching the Integration Starship on the planet's surface.

"Hey, guys," he said as he appeared near the alliance's leadership, scaring everyone shitless. "Long time no see."

Stunned silence followed. Then: "Jack!"

The professor, Edgar, Vivi, Gan Salin, and Nauja all jumped at him. Jack laughed. He hadn't seen most of them in a year.

"I'm so glad you're okay," the professor said, hugging him tightly with tears in her eyes. "I'm so glad..."

"I missed you!" Edgar shouted, also hugging Jack. "It's so good to have you back. This was a damn hard year!"

"But you pulled through, Edgar. I'm proud of you. Wait—is that Vlossana?"

The saphira stood away, gazing at him warily, but his attention was immediately drawn to Gan Salin and Nauja, who both pounced at him.

"Well fought!" Nauja shouted with excitement. "You almost had me worried there for a second."

"I knew you would succeed!" Salin exclaimed. "I kept telling her, but she wouldn't believe me."

"What? You said nothing like that! You even suggested running away to cut our losses!"

"Same thing."

Jack laughed. "It's nice to see you, guys. I hope you enjoyed the outer planet. Brock told me all about it."

"It was fine. Adventuring with you was more fun, though," Salin replied. "When's the next one, really?"

"Oh yeah. Speaking of that, the Black Hole Church will teleport our entire planet outside System space in a few minutes. I don't think it will be too rough, but uh, you might want to grab on to something."

Another round of stunned silence followed. "What?"

Jack briefly explained to them the whole Church deal he'd made, leaving out the sensitive parts. After all, there were many people listening.

"You'll still have access to the System," he assured them. "But we'll be safe. Earth will belong to us and us alone."

"Can we trust this Black Hole Church?" the professor asked. "They sound a bit sketchy."

"Everyone is a bit sketchy, but these guys have only helped me in our interactions so far. I believe they are our best chance."

She nodded. "Alright. I trust you."

"Now, can someone tell me what Vlossana is doing here and why she looks like she pissed the bed?"

"It's not just her," a deep voice rumbled.

Jack turned around, finding Shol, Dordok, and Brock there, as well as Bomn and Vashter. The *Trampling Ram* was parked right behind them. His eyes widened, and he laughed out loud. "You guys are safe! I'm so glad. Sorry for the trouble."

Dordok shrugged. "It is what it is."

"Brock, did you win as well? Wait—did you reach the D-Grade!"

The brorilla smiled proudly.

"Bro!" Jack exclaimed. "That's awesome! I'm so proud of you! I can't wait to hear everything about your battle!"

"I say," Brock replied.

Giving Brock a fist-bump, Jack turned to the others. "Are you coming with us? Or will you keep traveling?"

They looked between each other. "I will go," Shol said. "This was fun, and I am very proud of the excellent disciple you grew up to be, but my responsibilities lie with Master Huali and the Exploding Sun. I must return to them, at least in secret, and figure out my next steps."

Jack nodded. He briefly wondered what was going on with the Grand Elder selection of the Exploding Sun, but it didn't matter too much. His connection to it wasn't that strong. He could only hope that Master Huali was fine from the aftermath of his actions.

"I will check on the Sun when things calm down a bit," he promised.

"We will go, too," Bomn said. "The ship that docks grows rust. If we stopped traveling, our lives would be quite empty."

"You could always find a home here," the professor suggested, but the minotaur shook his big head.

"Thank you, but the open space calls to us. Maybe when we grow old."

"What about you, Dordok?" Jack asked, noticing that Bomn was the one who spoke for the *Trampling Ram*.

The cyclops smiled sadly. "We already discussed this with Bomn. A ship cannot hold two captains. While he would be glad to have me back, I believe it is time for me to take a break, at least temporarily. I will come with Earth, if you'll have me."

"Of course!" the professor hurried to say. "You are very welcome."

"All good bros fit," Brock added wisely.

"Now, about Vlossana," Edgar said, then took Jack aside and explained the entire situation.

"I see," Jack replied sadly. "I'll speak with her in a moment, but if she is healed as you say, she can come with us. She will need a safe place to recover."

Edgar nodded.

"As for you," Jack continued, "even though your soul is cracked and you cannot cultivate anymore, it isn't the end of the world. The Earth will know peace for a long time. It will be the perfect place for someone of your powers."

Edgar smiled widely. "That's exactly what I hope. I plan to create a wizard academy. I think it will be great."

"I think so too," Jack replied with a warm smile. "And, you know, I won't stop adventuring. I still have a long way to go. If I find a treasure that can repair your soul, or at least help you reach the D-Grade, I'll certainly get it for you. After all, it was me who released that devil from his prison."

"That's perfect. Thank you, Jack."

"No problem."

At that point, Vivi walked closer. "I also want to talk to you about something," she said, looking... bashful?

"Sure," Jack replied, and Edgar walked away. "What is it?"

"Are you satisfied with how the professor and I led the alliance in your absence?"

"Satisfied? Of course. I was never the leader, anyway; just a punching guy. And occasionally a spanking one."

She rolled her eyes. "Well, that wasn't really what I wanted to tell you. Are you ready?"

"Ready for what?"

She smiled. "I'm pregnant with your child. It happened eleven months ago, but I delayed the pregnancy through Dao medicine."

Jack froze, his mind reeling. "What?" No amount of life-or-death battles could have prepared him for this.

Vivi laughed. "I said, you're going to be a father!"

Jack remained stunned for a good while. Then, his mouth split into a wide grin, and he laughed to the sky. "Alright!" he shouted proudly. "A father!"

This brought a whole slew of complications to the table. For starters, he didn't even know Vivi that well. How would they handle a child? Would they be together or not? However, he was confident that everything would work out. Though Jack would need to leave Earth again soon... for now, they had some time.

Plus, he was the strongest man on Earth, goddammit. If he wasn't ready to become a father, no one was.

The future was bright!

The Sage stood on the prow of his tiny starship, admiring the blue and green planet underneath. The Heavenly Spoon Sovereign stood by his side as an equal.

"We are ready," the sovereign said. "My subordinates have prepared the nine corners. If you have nothing to add, we can begin the teleportation."

The Sage looked over Earth. It was a cozy little planet—full of weak people with kind intentions. He liked most of them.

Thinking back to his days as a homeless beggar, he smirked and shook his head. Then, in a moment of curiosity, he once again attempted to delve into Jack Rust's future. He saw great wars. Hints of the Old Gods and the Immortals. The Animal Kingdom would come after him with everything they had, and the Hand of God would stop at nothing to get him. They may have been blocked for now, but the real battle was only getting started.

He also saw Jack in the headquarters of the Black Hole Church—the Cathedral—where he would soon train, if everything went well.

I wonder... he asked himself, how far will he reach?

Yet, the future came out blank. Even his divination powers could not see that deep. He would have to find out the mortal way, by living it out. *But isn't that the best way?* he asked himself, then smiled wryly. He looked forward to the future. It would be so exciting.

"I'm ready," he told the sovereign. "Please start."

"And here I thought you would reminisce forever." The sovereign laughed. Then, he took out his tiny silver spoon. It shone with dark green light. Similar light erupted in columns based on nine equidistant places on the planet, each column was many miles wide and reached to the top of Earth's atmosphere. A tremendously large, dark green spoon appeared below Earth, cupping the entire planet in its groove. Then, with a smooth motion, the sovereign scooped it all up.

"Go," he muttered through gritted teeth. The starship blinked away. And with it, Earth and the moon also disappeared, gone forever from the solar system that had housed them for billions of years.

It was the end of an era and the start of a new one: the era of Jack Rust.

Meanwhile, not even the Sage knew that Jack had inadvertently set several important events into motion. Like a butterfly effect, the echoes of his actions spread across the universe, compiling into a domino of coincidences that affected even the highest of forces.

A council of Gods gathered around a star. "It is time," rumbled a planet-sized form oozing darkness.

Three robots, completely identical if not for the numbers drawn on their faceless heads, stood at the same time. "We have enough," they all said together.

A great war was starting. And Jack Rust, despite not knowing it, would be in its midst.

Road to Mastery will continue with Road to Mastery 4.

THANK YOU FOR READING ROAD TO MASTERY 3

We hope you enjoyed it as much as we enjoyed bringing it to you. We just wanted to take a moment to encourage you to review the book. Follow this link: Road to Mastery 3 to be directed to the book's Amazon product page to leave your review.

Every review helps further the author's reach and, ultimately, helps them continue writing fantastic books for us all to enjoy.

Also in Series:

Road to Mastery
Road to Mastery 2
Road to Mastery 3
Road to Mastery 4

Check out the entire series here! (Tap and scan)

Want to discuss our books with other readers and even the authors? Join our Discord server today and be a part of the Aethon community.

Facebook | Instagram | Twitter | Website

You can also join our non-spam mailing list by visiting www.subscribepage.com/AethonReadersGroup and never miss out on future releases. You'll also receive three full books completely Free as our thanks to you.

Looking for more great LitRPG?

Lives are a currency, and Noah Vines is rich. *After standing around in the afterlife for thousands of years, Noah is all out of patience. So, when the opportunity to steal a second chance at life arises, he doesn't hesitate. Reincarnated into the body of a dying magic school professor, Noah finds that he got more than just a second chance — he got infinite. Every time he dies, his body reforms. With countless variations of runic magic to discover and with death serving as only a painful soul-wound rather than a final end, Noah finally has a chance to wander the lands of the living once more. This time around, he plans to get strong enough to make sure that he never has to wait around in the afterlife again.* ***Don't miss the next hit Progression Fantasy series from Actus, bestselling author of*** **My Best Friend is an Eldritch Horror.** ***Featuring a strong, determined protagonist, a detailed runic magic system, loads of power progression, and so much more.*** With 10 million views as a webserial, you can experience the definitive version of this smash-hit series on Kindle, Kindle Unlimited, and Audible!

Get Return of the Runebound Professor Now!

The Young Gods Tournament awaits. Only the victors will break through to the worlds beyond the heavens. *In an unfair world where a single monster can wipe out an entire village, Thomas is not one of the chosen few. He wasn't gifted with immense power from the moment of his birth, nor does he have a powerful backer to defend him. By the laws of the world, it's near impossible for him to rise to the top. But where the god's themselves have failed him, Thomas will push on and gain the strength to protect his friends, and his home, from the ever rising dangers of the world. There is only one true opportunity to break through the shackles of his life — The Young God's Tournament. After surviving a deadly ambush, he'll use every ounce of his strength as he faces off against his rival Prospects, a continent-wide conspiracy, and the ever looming threat from the once-slumbering Empire.* ***Western Cultivation melds with LitRPG as a single man rises against an unfair world in this new series from bestseller Cale Plamann (*****Blessed Time, Viceroy's Pride*****), together with Alex Beaumont.***

Get Young Gods Tournament Now!

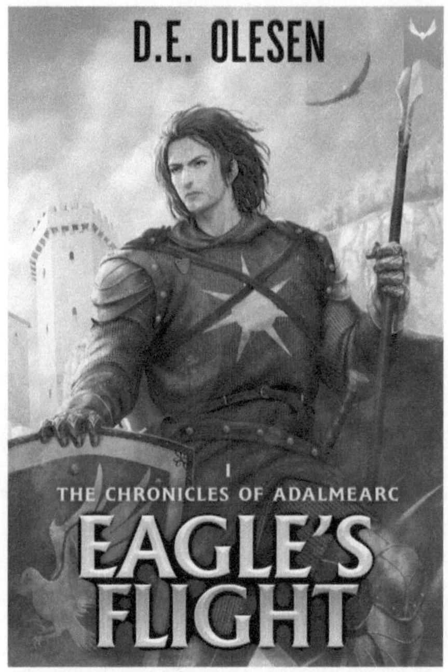

The King is dead. His heir too young to rule. Who will claim the crown? *The noble houses gather to choose a new Lord Protector, sparking old rivalries. If they can't agree, civil war looms. That is if foreign kingdoms don't smell blood in the water and invade first. Lord Vale wants to take up the mantle, spurred by his ambitious brother Konstans. Lord Isarn likewise seeks this power. He is aided – or thwarted – by the return of his brother, the knight and war hero Athelstan, whose squire, Brand, hopes to restore his family's fortunes no matter the cost. Through all of this, an enigmatic traveler makes plans with jarls, scribes, and priests for his own mysterious purpose. Only one thing is for certain. War is inevitable.* ***Power-hungry lords scheme and warriors fight for glory in this epic fantasy tale from D.E. Olesen, which was one of the Top 10 highest rated Royal Road web-serials ever written. Equal parts*** **Game of Thrones** ***and*** **Vikings,** ***the series digs deep into every level of a struggle of power, from lords to serfs. From political intrigue to the bonds between family. Join the fight for the soul of Adalmearc!***

Get Eagle's Flight Now!

A Necromancer reborn. A new System. Can he unlock it's true power? *After fulfilling the duty all Arch Necromancers are tasked with, the last thing Sylver Sezari expected was to be reborn. But he did. And after crawling his way back into the land of the living, he's alive once again. In a strange land, a strange time, and with a strange floating screen in front of his new face. Either through plan or chance, he's alive again, and planning to enjoy himself to his heart's content. Don't miss the start of this LitRPG Adventure about a reincarnated necromancer growing in power and finding his way in a new world where the rules have changed vastly since he last "lived."* ***With equal parts humor and dark sorcery action, expect loads of skill progression, deep worldbuilding, and unforgettable characters in this story which had nearly 9 million views on Royal Road. Now completely revised and re-edited for Kindle & Audible.***

Get Apocalypse Me Now!

For all our LitRPG books, visit our website.

www.ingramcontent.com/pod-product-compliance
Lightning Source LLC
Chambersburg PA
CBHW020719310726
48979CB00004B/990

* 9 7 8 1 9 6 4 5 0 5 0 4 6 *